Jane of Battery Park

Jane of Battery Park

a novel

JAYE VINER

RED HEN PRESS | PASADENA, CA

Book design by Mark E. Cull

Library of Congress Cataloging-in-Publication Data

TBA

ISBN: 978-1-59709-117-6

The National Endowment for the Arts, the Los Angeles County Arts Commission, the Ahmanson Foundation, the Dwight Stuart Youth Fund, the Max Factor Family Foundation, the Pasadena Tournament of Roses Foundation, the Pasadena Arts & Culture Commission and the City of Pasadena Cultural Affairs Division, the City of Los Angeles Department of Cultural Affairs, the Audrey & Sydney Irmas Charitable Foundation, the Meta & George Rosenberg Foundation, the Albert and Elaine Borchard Foundation, the Adams Family Foundation, Amazon Literary Partnership, the Sam Francis Foundation, and the Mara W. Breech Foundation partially support Red Hen Press.

First Edition
Published by Red Hen Press
www.redhen.org

For Christopher, who helped
me build a new home

and

James Horner

1953 – 2015

Jane of Battery Park

CHAPTER 1

Jane saw her husband, Seth, walk across the restaurant's foyer. She sat at a table all the way across the restaurant. He had his back to her, but she was sure it was him. The self-conscious hunch in his shoulders from always being the tall one in the room. The too casual, mismatched clothes because he did not believe appearances mattered. The stiff wariness of his body, alert for movement coming at him from any direction, a holdover from his army days, and also his current occupation as leader of the Vanguard, a grassroots organization that put celebrities on trial for sins against family values.

As the hostess guided her husband into the restaurant, Jane twisted the silky cloth napkin in her lap. In a few moments, he would see her, would come tell her date she belonged with him, in the world of mismatched clothes and higher callings. She had lost track of the conversation at her table. Beneath the table, she moved her feet to one side of her chair, prepared to spring up and run.

Seth looked right at her as he took his seat. It wasn't him.

Because he has no reason to be here, thought Jane. *He doesn't know where I am.*

"Everything alright?" asked her date.

Jane turned her attention to the man across from her.

Online, he was the perfect man for the woman she hoped to become.

Three of their four interest areas—travel, food, and the arts—had been perfect matches. The outlier had been fly fishing. Jane didn't have any interest in fly fishing. But if it was something he really cared about she could learn. She was willing to learn about anything.

Her perfect man poured the wine and studied her over the tops of his horn-rimmed glasses. Sophistication oozed from his fingertips. Jane imagined how he might transform her into a chic column of a woman, magically taller and slimmer, without bowling balls for breasts, who went to gallery openings and opera galas. A woman who could hold a conversation with his coworkers in the art world, and knowingly critique auctions at Tiffany's.

"You don't look anything like your profile picture," he said, not quite joking.

"Audrey Hepburn is my alter ego."

"Is there a reason she didn't come on this date?"

"Profiles are so public. You never know who's watching. I like to be mysterious." Jane wiggled her eyebrows in a way she imagined was sexy and mysterious.

"Visibility is kind of the point."

"So . . . I went to that exhibit you did, *The Impressionists*? So beautiful. It was like being in a dream."

He cringed, tastefully. "You're one of ten people who saw that disaster, thank God."

"I didn't think it was that bad."

Jane took a deep breath. *Calm. You're in a safe place.* She had prepared these thoughts on art and his exhibit to impress him. Now, all the words felt jumbled. She found herself saying something a little too close to her truth. "We all want to create our version of reality, but those artists—Monet, Renoir—actually achieved it."

The more enthusiasm she forced into her voice, the more distressed her date appeared.

The waiter brought their food. Both Jane and her date took advantage of the interruption to withdraw into their wine glasses and regroup.

They surveyed the two identical orders of California rolls and some kind of cooked meat wrapped in rice covered in a sweet sauce that had been delivered to their table. Neither item was quite what Jane had imagined sushi to be, but she trusted his judgement. When she went on dates, she always deferred to her potential partner's expertise.

"So, how do you eat this?"

He looked at her with that mild amusement that made her feel small. "However you like."

"But Japan is such a ritualized culture. Aren't there like . . . rules?"

Her date poured soy sauce over his entire plate and stabbed the first roll with his fork.

Jane considered the shiny silver chopsticks tucked beside her plate. She'd been looking forward to using them, had assumed her date would know how. Instead, she also picked up her fork, followed his example of the soy sauce deluge.

"I appreciate how invested you are in your work," he said. "Nursing is such an important profession."

"Actually, I'm looking to get out of nursing. Maybe go into something with the arts." Jane took a bite of her first California roll and nearly choked. The saltiness was on par with swallowing a gallon of ocean.

"There's nothing for you in the arts. It's just trust fund sycophants arguing over things that don't matter."

"Is that how you got into it?" Too late, Jane snapped her mouth shut. A familiar sinking feeling followed the California roll down her gullet. Another failure. To punish herself, she watched the impatient expression flicker across her date's gaze, saw it linger too long before he was able to smooth it back into polite solicitation.

"I think I'd be good at art," said Jane. "I know what I want when I see it." This time her eyebrows arched with immaculately clear suggestion. He was not the one she wanted. Perhaps she should've been more subtle, but her disappointment was rising disproportionately to her self-control. The man who looked like Seth sitting three tables away wasn't helping.

Her date stood to leave. "You could've cancelled and saved me a drive."

Jane smiled her goodbye. She held it even after he'd turned the corner to the restaurant's foyer. She held it even as she felt the inevitable burn pricking the corners of her eyes. The man who looked like Seth glanced in her direction. She wondered what the real Seth was doing that night. Maybe he was sitting in his recliner watching a game. Or he was out at the farm with Tommy, her youngest brother, hunched in a deer blind. No, it was the wrong season for that.

Or he's out on a mission, she thought. The Vanguard had just finished a trial, but sometimes, to throw the FBI off their trail, they did two close together. A sharp pain twisted in Jane's stomach. *What they do doesn't matter. I don't belong to that world anymore.*

She picked up her chopsticks. With discrete glances to the nearby tables, she tried to imitate the motions of her fellow diners' hands with their chopsticks. She could make her hand look like theirs, but every time she pinched a roll her grip fell apart, the chopsticks slid. The roll fell and splattered soy sauce on her best dress.

"I've made an executive decision." Jane pinched her phone against her shoulder so she could unzip the cardboard carton of her frozen dinner. Her best friend Alma, sci-fi geek extraordinaire, was on the other end of the line. "I'm going to date my lava lamp."

"It couldn't have been that bad."

"Like soggy bread bad."

"Maybe it's not realistic to think people are going to pour out their passions on a first date?"

"If they don't, it's not passion." Jane stood over her dinner *Psycho* style with a knife. She couldn't remember which sections she was supposed to ventilate.

"You mean, it's not Daniel."

"No one is ever going to be Daniel." Jane let the knife fall. She stared into space with a desperate hunger the TV dinner wouldn't come close to satisfying.

"I saw online that he's in Italy. You could take all those vacation days you never use and go find him."

"I can't go to Italy. I know nothing about Italy."

"Even Italians don't know enough about Italy to satisfy you."

Jane's gaze turned dreamy. But only for a moment before she shook herself back into reality. "He won't remember me."

"And yet here we are."

"You can't understand what it was like to have someone open up a world you had no idea existed and then never see them again."

"Sure I do. You just don't want to believe I have those skills. For example, last night Ben Browder came through his wormhole trying to find his lost love Claudia Black. He found me instead and decided to stay."

"Is that the guy from the show with the big circle that takes people to other planets or the one where Earth is destroyed, and humanity is homeless and being chased around the galaxy by robots?"

"Neither. Seriously, I'm offended. You're all about learning everything there is to know about everything else but it's fine that sci-fi for you stops at Star Wars."

"What I had with Daniel is not what you think you have with Ben Bower."

"Browder."

"Maybe Daniel knows him."

"We could both go to Italy and find ourselves some B-list movie stars."

"He's probably become some self-entitled jerk who seduces a new woman every night just because he can."

"Why would he stop at one?"

Jane hated this suggestion so much, she couldn't think of a reply.

"Alright, forget Daniel, and forget soggy bread guy," said Alma. "Speed dating has always been our density."

"You still want to go? I thought things were going well with that guy you met online. The one who's always asking personal questions?"

"I'm keeping my options open. Pick you up at eight?"

"For your sake, I will go. But I go under protest." Jane accidentally on purpose stabbed her TV dinner so hard it flew off the counter.

CHAPTER 2

Morning encroached on one of the most exclusive seaside villas of the southern Italian coast like an unwelcome neighbor poking its nose into the villa's business. And what a business it had been. A party that had run for three days, the who's who of fashion, music, and cinema, representing over a dozen countries, had flooded the little road from the village and snaked their way to the villa where all manner of pleasurable indulgences had been on offer.

The Fletchers had hosted the party of the year and now, having exhausted itself and the restaurant staff of the entire village, the stars had gone home, the blockbuster god had finally gone to bed, and the villa had settled into its foundations, bruised, cracked, but satisfied.

The master bedroom had been the scene of a series of nightly climaxes where the most damage had been done. The room was a ruin of extravagant debauchery. The potted hibiscus shrubs, previously lining the driveway, had been brought inside. Shredded leaves and wilting beheaded flowers littered the floor. The chairs lay on their sides or upside down. One had lost a leg. The bed had been upended, its headboard wedged against the ceiling, the sheets draped so they hung like curtains around the golden bodies of the god and his consorts as they lay blissfully entwined in a sea of tangled bedding on the cool tile floor.

Though Jane imagined Daniel in such a scene, it was in fact his older brother Steve who lived the life of a prince in a pleasure palace. Daniel had made appearances at various stages of the party, mostly to check on supplies. But at ten o'clock every night, he'd taken an Ambien, secured his noise-cancelling headphones, and gone to bed.

As the sun rose on his brother's final day in Italy, Daniel sipped espresso at an al fresco café overlooking a white pebbled beach. He sat with his back to the water, pretending to read *Cloud Atlas*, a book both too complicated and too depressing to be approached so early in the morning.

Even though he could not see the ocean, Daniel heard her. The white pebbles chattered as her breath washed them up the beach and then gently drew them back into her body. She called to him, whispered of her warm depths, of weightlessness, of being taken into something bigger than himself. An old promise, and an empty one at that.

Daniel ordered another espresso and resolutely turned the page of his book.

"Buon Giorno," said the woman at the adjacent table.

Daniel continued to pretend to read, but he couldn't help adjusting his posture. He straightened his legs beneath his chair, brought his hand down from the table to rest on his knee as though to shelter it. He could feel her watching him. The longer he remained passive, the more she would see, so he hazarded a glance up.

The woman gazed at him over the top of her sunglasses. Her translucent coverall slipped suggestively down her shoulder. Not Italian, a tourist.

"You look very familiar," she said. "We didn't meet at the bar last night, did we?"

"No, we did not." Daniel checked his corners for an escape route. The villa was down the beach path at the end of the piazza, but he'd have to walk past the woman to pay his tab at the café stand, and then she would be watching him walk away for at least half a mile. He could leave money on the table and walk around the back of the café and hope he didn't get lost on the crooked medieval streets when he tried to circle back around to the beach path once he was out of sight of the café. Or he could just talk to her. Sign an autograph, then make an excuse about time.

Daniel leaned across his little table and extended his hand. "Steve Fletcher."

"*The* Steve Fletcher?" The false arch in her tone revealed she'd already known.

Daniel was mistaken for Steve so often that he'd become practiced imitating Steve's smile, his sly pauses. Harder to replicate was the buoyant invincibility of his voice, the carefree carnival of a man who always got what he wanted with very little effort. But such nuance was usually lost on his fans.

"I've never thought of you as a reader."

"Many actors are readers," said Daniel. "It feeds the craft." This was generally true, but Steve was not an actor who read.

"So, what are you doing here? I thought *Poseidon* was filming further north."

"Production ended last week."

"You must be keeping a very low profile." Her bottom lip protruded in a pout.

Daniel thought of the traffic backed up for miles on the one road that ran along the coast, the special fee Daniel had paid so Steve could play music so loud its pulse became a second nervous system for the villa, feeding guests an all-encompassing sensory experience enhanced by drugs, alcohol, and a general lack of attire. No one for fifteen miles could plausibly claim not to know the Fletchers were in town.

"I'm a very private person." Daniel pushed back his irritation at the woman for interrupting his morning, laying her trail of hints like breadcrumbs for Steve to follow like an idiot. Most irritating of all was the fact that Steve, had he been in Daniel's place, would've devoured whatever she offered.

"Do you think maybe you could . . ." She pretended embarrassment.

"Of course." Daniel pulled yesterday's café receipt out of *Cloud Atlas* and scribbled an illegible signature on the back. He stood up and handed it to her on his way off the patio.

"Maybe I'll see you around?"

He blew her a kiss. "I know I'll be seeing you in my dreams."

Steve rarely used such lines in real life, but they were so prominent in his movies, and he carried them off so well that fans expected them. For Steve, art imitated life much more than life imitated art.

At the villa, Daniel picked his way through apocalyptic carnage to reach the kitchen where he cleared enough space on the stove for the coffee boiler. Shot glasses, lighters, and glowsticks littered the terracotta floor. The kitchen opened onto the living room where, among bottles and discarded clothes, Daniel found Steve's unconscious high school best friend, Kai Yukiyama, a scrawny bone sack of a man who smoked too much and drank too much, who always supported even Steve's stupidest ideas.

Daniel collected coffee mugs from the mess. He took them back to the kitchen and washed all but the one that had been used as an ashtray.

The coffee had just started to boil when the alarm sounded on Daniel's phone. He bunched an empty food carton into a ball and lobbed it across the kitchen bar into the living room at Kai's head.

"Morning sunshine."

"Fuck you."

Daniel handed Kai a mug of coffee. He went from room to room with his wake up greeting and coffee as a peace offering. There were three guys Steve kept around him to help make his life in the limelight more bearable. Two had been friends with Steve in high school before he'd had his big break and moved from Oahu to Los Angeles. Ziek, last name long ago jettisoned, was a bodybuilder. He'd been Daniel's school friend, requisitioned as Steve's friend because Steve could afford to employ full time friends. On his taxes, Ziek called himself a professional bodyguard.

Daniel found Steve's wife, Riley, a fierce stuntwoman adrenaline junky, in bed with an Italian who had come to the villa as a catering staff member two days before and never left. She inhaled the steam of her coffee with deep satisfaction. "Make sure he checks messages," she said to Daniel. "Garrett ditched our movie."

"It will be fine," said Daniel. If Steve's life had been a movie, this would've been Daniel's one memorable line. It was a lie. And his job was to make it true.

A body-shaped dent marred the varnished sheen of the master bedroom's door. Daniel paused before it. As he listened to the grumbling stirrings in the rest of the house, he considered leaving it to someone else to wake Steve. If the entourage was late for their connection in Munich, oh well. Daniel wouldn't be around to deal with the consequences this time. He could assert himself now, stretch his freedom just a little early. But if Rome didn't work out, he'd have to come back to Steve, and Steve would make him pay. And then there was the worn-out sense of obligation. Steve was the brother he had, even if he wasn't quite the brother he wanted. If this was his last day as Steve's manager, he would finish the job well.

Daniel could only open the door part way. He had to shove it to fit through. Once he was inside, he took in the scene of conquest piece by piece, the desiccated hibiscuses, the open patio doors with a gecko sunning itself, the precariously balanced bedframe. He parted the hanging sheets and gazed down on the three perfect bodies gilded in dappled sunlight.

A small bubble of nausea bloomed in Daniel's stomach as his eyes traveled over them. Steve lay with his face buried in the generous breasts of the woman to his right, his legs drawn up, his arms tucked against his chest while her arms encircled him. Her face was pressed into his hair. The woman on Steve's left wrapped him from behind with her face in the valley between his shoulder blades. Her legs and arms enveloped him as they reached towards the other woman. Together, they enclosed him like a child in a womb.

Daniel again considered walking away and letting Steve try to manage his own life for the day. Daniel had tried to leave before. But without a concrete something else to leave for, it was too easy for Steve to tempt Daniel back. In Rome, there was the promise of something Steve wouldn't be able to deny him. It would give Daniel back his career, make him independent. *This is the last day,* thought Daniel as he roused energy into his voice. "Time to get up."

There was a slight stirring. One of the women smiled.

"You can't be late this time, Steve."

He saw Steve's toes stretch and expand outward. The god was conscious but pretending not to be. Daniel moved towards the door. He knew how to play this game.

"You got a message from Garrett. He's pulling out of the Hawaii project."

"I got you," murmured Steve.

Daniel slipped out the door and walked quickly down the hall to the kitchen. He heard a thump followed by Steve swearing. "Where's my fucking phone? There's no fucking way he—"

More swearing followed bruising blows to the villa as Steve yanked open the broken door, threw himself down the hallway, and lurched into the kitchen. "You're a fucking bastard. Tell me you made that up."

Daniel held out Steve's phone and a steaming mug.

At the breakfast bar Kai cradled his head. "Would you please shut the fuck up?"

Steve squinted at his phone. "No, no no no. He can't do this to me." He scrolled through his contacts for Garrett's number.

"It's the middle of the night stateside," said Daniel, the voice of reason.

"Then he'll be home." Steve gulped down his coffee while the phone rang. "If that coward is fucking screening his calls, I—Rett-o, what's up brah?"

Daniel and Kai exchanged knowing glances as Steve, all cheerful friendliness drifted out to the deck to ply his charm. Riley shuffled down the hallway with her Italian caterer in tow. "How much time we got?"

"Car should be here in half an hour," said Daniel.

"And you've got a guy for me in Munich so this whole thing doesn't get fucked up?"

Daniel flipped open *Cloud Atlas* to the envelope of documents he kept in the back jacket. He pulled out a business card and handed it to her. "He'll find you when you land and get you through customs. Anything you need, ask him." Daniel handed Riley another card. "This is Steve's salon appointment, don't let him miss it. He's got that interview on Thursday."

She leaned into him and whispered so Kai couldn't hear. "It's really going to suck breaking in a new manager."

"We'll worry about that when we have to."

"You'll get the job. I hope you don't of course. He's worse when you're not around."

Daniel shrugged. Riley had her own mechanisms for manipulation. He hated even having to trust her with his secret errand in Rome. But someone had to take responsibility for the group and she was the only one capable of withholding information from Steve; she liked wielding bits of knowledge like weapons revealed at just the right moment. She would probably find a reason to tell his secret before the plane touched down at LAX. But that would be enough. By then Daniel would know if he had the part.

Steve spent the entire ride to the airstrip on the phone, but nothing he said could change the fact that Garrett's TV show had been renewed, thanks to fan petition, and the filming dates conflicted with Steve's movie. Garrett couldn't break his contract.

As the conversation went on Steve became more desperate. His voice lost its friendliness. The limo became a metal box of blustering reverberating sound waves. Riley huddled in a corner behind her sunglasses. Kai had headphones on, his hoodie up. He pressed against the limo's wall and gazed out at the passing landscape in desperation. Kyle, Steve's other high school friend, played a game on his phone.

"A *niche* movie? Are you serious? Garrett, think about who's telling you this bullshit, man. You've been in Hollywood too long. You know they've got a name for that disease now—when you start buying in and can't tell what's real? Is *Point Break* niche? James Bond?"

"Steve, could you just—" Ziek thought better of what he'd planned to say as Steve swiveled to glare at him.

While he was distracted, Daniel plucked Steve's phone from his hand and hung it up.

"What the fuck?"

"He got the point."

"I wasn't finished."

"Rowan probably has a list of guys to replace him already."

"This late in the game, they'll all be shit. Garrett was the one for a reason. I can't have some small wave mainlander costarring in a movie about our life."

From within the cave of his hoodie Kai snorted with laughter. "I don't remember training to sabotage Soviet spies when we were skipping seventh period."

"I mean our *culture* you fucking idiot." Steve punched Kai in the shoulder.

"I could do it," said Daniel.

The limo fell silent. Riley peeled her sunglasses down the front of her face. Her bright eyes darted between the two brothers. Neither looked at each other. Zeik studied the floor. Kai looked to Steve for a clue on how to react. Kyle played his game.

"Interesting idea," said Riley.

"I thought you were done with acting," said Steve.

Daniel shrugged.

"You don't surf anymore. This movie is about surfing."

"I've been thinking of getting back into it."

Something particular to the cruelty of brothers flickered behind Steve's eyes, but whatever he'd thought to say he decided against it. Instead, he broke into his trademark grin. "That'd be fucking awesome! The Fletcher brothers starring in a movie together."

"People used to talk about it," said Daniel. "Remember that martial arts movie Universal pitched us?"

Steve's grin faded. "Maybe you should start smaller. Like figure out how to get yourself a girl first. No one's gonna believe you're worth anything on screen if they know you live like a monk."

Daniel deflected this truth disguised as a joke with a jocular smile. "I'll get right on that."

"Bet that's what he's being so secretive about," said Kai. "Dan's got a girl in Rome. He's afraid one of us will filch her."

"Right on, brah," Kyle murmured to his screen.

Steve latched onto this idea. "That's exactly what I'm saying! Because no woman is gonna pass up this," he pointed at the pectorals straining his T shirt, "for that," he pointed at Daniel. "Unless she's got something wrong with her."

CHAPTER 3

The traffic in LA was reason enough for the most even-keeled person to lose their mind, but Jane liked the traffic. It made her feel like she was part of something. She had plenty of other ways to lose her mind. Phantom husbands in restaurants was one. Eating fast food every day, a habit that made her life in LA feel impermanent was another. She wiped at the fallen shredded cheese and lettuce in her lap as she drove to work and resolved to do more cooking.

Sleep deprivation was another way the darkness crept in. Coming home from a hectic night shift at the hospital, a spider had found Jane. Fuzzy and black, its body the size and perfect roundness of a quarter, it had dodged her flying shoe and made for the bed where it hid itself in the clutter, and Jane hadn't been able to work up the courage to go in after it. Six hours on the Goodwill couch in the living room without light-blocking curtains did not a happy Jane make. The ticking of the AC unit felt menacing. The sounds of neighbors' footsteps outside were portents of doom.

The spider added to what had already been a surreal night. At work, a patient recovering from a procedure that put twenty screws in her shattered femur had started bleeding internally. Jane had discovered it while helping her to the bathroom. She kept saying it was just bruising from the jet ski accident and then she'd flat-lined. When Jane had finally left at eight thirty that morning the patient was still in surgery, and the outcome hadn't looked good. It took hours for the combined adrenaline of the patient's emergency and the spider's invasion to wear off so Jane could sleep.

When her alarm sounded, Jane was already half-conscious, trying to ignore a lump in the couch cushion that bit into her thigh. Her daily inspirational quote appeared with pink and purple hearts on her phone screen: *When you say, "It's hard," it means "I'm not strong enough to fight for it." Stop saying it's hard. Think positive!!!* Because one exclamation point wasn't enough. Jane gave her phone a good shake and asked how positively it would be thinking if she only recharged it for two minutes instead of thirty. She dragged herself into a sitting position and kicked at the bottom of the couch. Time to start the day.

Taco Bell was the savior of bad planners and the ill-prepared. Jane piloted her Jeep through the asteroid field of the LA freeway system while eating a taco and singing along with Elton John. Her singing poured out the windows into a smoggy afternoon dusk, almost carefree. Still, she felt a nudge at the back of her head that something was wrong. She pushed it away with rational justifications, the spider invasion, the patient who might now be dead.

But this was more than that. An entire chorus of *Rocket Man* passed while Jane filtered through all the possible 'things wrong' that might be bothering her until she found the right one.

I didn't arm the alarm.

Jane stomped the brake and swerved onto the upcoming exit ramp. Two lanes of drivers laid on their horns in righteous fury. Elton carried on his merry singing, oblivious, while Jane calculated the time it would take to turn around, drive home, arm the alarm, and start off again. In the past, she'd forgotten, and it had been okay. But with the spider, and the patient last night, Jane felt the universe conspiring against her more than usual.

She pulled into the condo parking lot as Elton announced her arrival to the kids showing off their surfboards at the adjacent In-N-Out as she pulled into her condo parking lot. This was home, a two-tower high rise not quite in Santa Monica. There was no ocean view and no security guard in the parking lot to watch the gate that rolled open for anyone and their dog. Literally. Jane once saw it open for a man walking a Saint Bernard. The ocean was out there somewhere because families in swimsuits stopped off from Highway 1 to grab snacks and cheap towels from the neighborhood CVS, but it was part of another world. Here, there was no salt spray in the air, just fast food grease and exhaust. The condo stairwell smelled like a swamp.

Jogging up five stories in flip flops, not recommended, but Jane's sneakers were in her locker at the hospital. Elton's voice crooned in her head as she clapped her way up to her unit. Outside her door, Jane paused to investigate for any sign of forced entry. Silly, but she couldn't help it.

Shayla across the way had a dachshund, and a mother who owned the unit Jane subleased so her name didn't show up on any online housing directories. They were just stepping out for a walk. Such a nice thing— mothers and daughters who took walks together, shared common interests, pets. Jane's mother had withheld cookies when she couldn't recite Bible verses without mistakes. She ducked inside to avoid them.

On the alarm panel, Jane punched in her code, hit ARM, and started off again. Jogging down the stairs, she ditched the flip flops and offered the soles of her feet to whatever bacteria were feeding on the damp cement.

Off to work for real this time. Jane skipped the CD back to *I Guess That's Why They Call It the Blues*, unwrapped her second taco, and spewed some half-masticated shell onto her steering wheel when she tried to resume singing. Everything was fine.

The east nurse's station and the west nurse's station of the seventh floor of the hospital were divided by the elevator. Each desk was staffed by two nurses per shift. Doraceli, the East 7 dayshift nurse, wasn't snarky enough to look at the wall clock when Jane walked in, but she checked the computer clock. Usually it was her shift partner, Grace, at the desk waiting to go through the reports with Jane. Jane preferred Grace. Doraceli knew nursing, but her bedside manners, her table manners; all of her manners oozed sticky condescension that Jane could do without, especially today.

Alma, best shift partner ever, had already arrived. She looked the way Jane felt, like they'd been inflated into a blueberry by Willy Wonka and it was easier to roll than walk. She spilled an impressive number of antihistamines, antacids, anti-nauseas, Dayquil, and Advil onto her half of the station's desk. She pitched forward and let her head crash into Jane's shoulder. "I think I'm dying."

"Did the jet ski lady make it out alive?" Jane asked Doraceli.

"More than alive." Doraceli lowered her voice and leaned forward in a way that made it feel like they were almost friends. "She might be Steve Fletcher's mom."

"Really."

"But she said she didn't know him."

"Who doesn't know Steve Fletcher?" Alma sounded like she was wearing a clothespin on her nose. "Doesn't she watch movies? Even Jane knows Steve Fletcher. No offence, buddy."

"I called her listed emergency contact twice last night, no answer." Jane spoke slowly while in her head she rushed to put some impossible pieces of information together. She couldn't remember looking at the patient's name the night before. The orderly had done that part of the job.

Alma opened Fletcher's patient file. "There's no name on either of the contact numbers."

"Call now and see who answers. God, I'd die to meet Steve or his gorgeous brother—what's his name, who was in *SLUT* way back when?"

"Daniel," Alma and Jane said at the same time.

Doraceli handed Jane the shift report. Jane pretended to read it until Doraceli's attention was on her phone, then she shot bug eyes at Alma.

"Call," mouthed Alma.

"It's a really common name," she hedged as she stared at the pair of ten-digit numbers that might summon Daniel to the hospital. It seemed impossible that she'd called him the night before. After all this time he was suddenly so close. Jane wished Doraceli would finish checking her phone and leave.

"I'm not starting my day until you call." Alma held her Diet Coke with her free hand suspended over it, waiting to pop the tab and pour it into her water bottle. Along with various other delusions that came from a reality co-created with science fiction, Alma believed climbing the stairs once a week and drinking her Coke from a Pink Ribbon Bottle would magically get her in shape for Race for the Cure. It was an endearing and beautiful self-delusion that suddenly made Jane want to cry.

Alma glared at Doraceli. "I'll text you if they show up."

"You better." Doraceli grabbed her purse and whisked down the corridor. They heard her excited whispers with the West 7 nurses as she waited for the elevator.

"You have to call," said Alma.

"And say what?"

"That his mom's in the hospital and had to be rushed into surgery last night."

Jane still didn't reach for the phone.

Alma took her hand. "You've been thinking about this guy as long as I've known you. If he's even half as perfect as you think, you have to try this."

"He probably doesn't remember me."

"You'll help him remember."

"Or he's turned into an arrogant prick."

"Then you'll be able to cry about it and move on."

Jane pushed away a giddy rush of hope as she reached for the phone. She dialed the first number. It immediately went to voicemail; an automated message repeated the number and told her to leave a message after the tone.

"Well?" asked Alma.

"The phone is off."

"Try the other one."

Jane hung up and dialed the second number. The phone rang almost six times before it picked up. A rich baritone slurred into Jane's ear, "Who is this and how'd you get this fucking number?"

Anyone who watched movies knew that voice. Not Daniel, but his older brother, Steve.

"Hello? Start fucking talking or I'm hanging up."

"Yes . . . this is Jane at the—"

"This about my mother? She's not getting out any earlier than the doctor says. I'm not pulling any fucking strings for her this time."

"There was a complication. She had to have heart surgery last night."

"Is this a fucking joke? My mother's heart is fine. Who is this?"

"I'm the night nurse. Her accident caused more trauma than we initially thought. She's stable for the moment. We have visiting hours tomorrow afternoon." Jane added this last piece of information because she was a professional, even though what she wanted more than anything was for Steve, and hopefully Daniel, to visit during her shift.

"You're serious." Steve now sounded bewildered instead of angry. "Fuck." The line went quiet. Jane heard a woman's voice murmuring in the background. Steve's voice returned to the line. "My brother usually handles these things."

Jane's breath caught in her throat. She nearly choked as she said, "Do you want me to call him?"

"No, he's . . . out of town—I feel like you're saying she might not make it. Is that what you're saying?"

"I'm just a nurse."

"Right. Thanks for that."

The line went dead. Alma was staring, waiting, but Jane couldn't think of anything to say. It'd been so long since she'd considered the possibility of seeing Daniel again. Real flesh and blood Daniel, not the dream of him that she'd constructed in her head.

"And?" asked Alma.

"It was Steve."

"Oh frack."

"I'm going to do rounds."

"Are you kidding me?"

"If he comes, he comes."

"Fine, be that way. But I know you. You're not as calm as you look."

Jane was never as calm as she appeared, but she'd learned to survive by pretending. Alma wasn't the only one who ran her life with a carefully curated collection of self-delusion. She worked her way around the West 7 with steely single-minded focus. The hip replacement grandmother of sixteen perfect children told Jane her water jug was empty. Maybe she'd repeated herself a couple of times while Jane stood with her back to the bed, pink dry erase marker poised in the air while Jane tried to remember how to spell her name. The patient in the next room wanted ice chips instead of ice cubes. And could Jane bring her a heated blanket?

On break, she went down to the ICU and checked on Rhea Fletcher. She was asleep, listed as stable. Jane stood for a few moments at the end of her bed trying to see Daniel in her face. She wondered if Daniel had ever told his mother about the girl he'd once met in Battery Park.

CHAPTER 4

NEW YORK CITY, EIGHT YEARS AGO

Jane Dalton's boy meets girl story could be titled, *Girl Meets Daniel Fletcher and Totally Blows It.* It spanned five hours on a perfect spring day during her sophomore year of nursing school when she fled campus for Battery Park, bought a bag of popcorn, and threw most of it at the pigeons.

College in New York was Jane's first significant attempt to escape family. She'd been allowed to go to college halfway across the country only because she was the first one in her family to do well enough in school to qualify for scholarships that made such a thing affordable. That she'd been allowed to attend a secular school instead of a faith-based institution was due to the fact that she was dangerously close to being considered a lost cause after dumping her high school boyfriend, Seth, the man who would later become her husband, the man half the world now thought was a terrorist and the other half thought was a hero. In a world where even teenagers dated with the intention of marriage, Jane was a social and moral disaster of the kind only Puritans could appreciate.

The transition from her home bubble to a secular college dorm had been troubled. She'd become Jane, her middle name, instead of Rachel, in a naïve belief that changing her name would somehow help her belong. Most students lived day to day without any clear direction. They went to parties where they had sex with strangers and drank so much alcohol they had to be taken to the ER. They complained about bad grades on papers that they'd written for two hours in the middle of the night before they were due. They wanted all the good things in life, but they didn't want to work for them. They left Jane bewildered and just as isolated as she had been at home.

That fall, Jane had applied to transfer to a music academy in Boston. Most of her life, music had been the one thing she'd felt truly belonged to her. It also had the added rebellious benefit of being a degree her family had been stringently against. A week earlier, she'd called home to announce her acceptance into the academy. She'd been determined to assert her right to this decision, had believed there was no way anyone could talk her out of it. Now, Aaron, her oldest brother, and the man who had raised her after her father died, was flying to New York to do just that.

While she waited to meet him, Jane aimed her popcorn at pigeon tail feathers. She aimed at heads. She flung a handful up into the air and watched the pigeons kill each other for the stale kernels. Her next projection was released with such blind rage, Jane accidently hit a skateboarder gliding into the line of fire.

At this point Daniel Fletcher was not the suave young movie star who would be vaulted from an unknown indie talent into teen idol stardom about five months down the road. He'd filmed three movies, two small budget productions and one high school drama, *SLUT, a Love Story,* slated for wide release that summer. It would be a surprise breakout hit. He still thought of himself as more of a professional surfer than an actor. He wore board shorts and a Billabong cap and T-shirt, not usual garb for Manhattan. But anyone who bothered to take a second look would've recognized the same features that made his blockbuster star brother *People's* Sexiest Man—dark eyebrows framing recessed eyes, oversized lips, a slight cleft in the chin. Each feature a perfect cut waiting for a stylist's polishing touch.

"Did you just throw something at me?" he asked.

"No."

"Liar."

"I didn't."

"I can prove it." Quick as a cat, he bent down and scooped popcorn off the cement. Jane preemptively let fly the remainder of her bag into his face.

"See? You did it again," he said.

"That's a cheap trick."

"Serves you right."

Her laughter was short lived as Daniel sat down on her concrete bench and she was suddenly fighting to keep her attention on his words rather than his unexpected nearness.

"Why are you throwing popcorn instead of eating it?" he asked.

"I'm feeding the birds. What're you doing here?"

"Had some time to kill while the older bro was at work, so I came to see what east coast waves looked like."

"There aren't any waves." Jane laughed. "There's no beach."

He shook his head. "There are always waves. The ocean is the most powerful force on Earth."

"*God* is the most powerful force on Earth."

"Unless he doesn't live on Earth."

She was ready to argue until she saw his eyes laughing at her, then she wanted something else to throw at him. As the second youngest of four children, all the rest boys, Jane was most comfortable with violence. She knew the importance of being able to aim and throw because a brother's strength and size could not be stopped once it got going. If Daniel had been one of Jane's brothers, she'd have had her fist in his kidney, but something told her that wasn't the way to go.

"You're from California?" she asked.

"Originally from Hawaii, but now California. What gave me away?"

"You look like you live on a beach."

"You don't look like you're from anywhere."

He was still playing, but Jane had become somber, remembering how

Aaron was on his way. Being from California pretty much guaranteed that Daniel's family didn't have a moral imperative against music school. Where Jane came from, her decision to transfer was probably being discussed at church and the grocery store, while well-meaning friends brought her mother sympathetic hot dishes, and told her that one way-ward child out of five was forgivable in God's eyes.

Interventions were supposed to be for addicts and bad dating deci-sions. The New York natives in Jane's dorm staged interventions almost every week. *Dawson's Creek* interventions, and chocolate interventions, and study interventions during finals. None of them had an older broth-er who flew halfway across the country to prevent them from changing schools.

"Do you get along with your brother?" Jane asked.

Daniel's laugh came out like a cough. He stood and tested his foot against the end of the skateboard like he was about to leave. The ocean suddenly seemed more interesting to him than she did.

Somewhere in these silent moments, while Daniel toyed with his board and looked out at the bay, Jane fell in love with him. Maybe not Daniel exactly, she barely knew him. Rather, she fell in love with the pos-sibility of someone like him. Someone who cared about things she knew nothing about, but who was also not driven by the hedonistic pursuit of pleasure like her roommates were.

This was the realization of eight years of meditation. At the time, all that Jane could articulate was an awareness of the exotic and of a life gov-erned by rules entirely different than those that governed her commu-nity. Scruffy and slouching, with the air of an unemployed beach dude proud of his poverty, Daniel oozed an intimate connection to the salty grime of the ocean. He felt as foreign as visiting India. He was exactly what she'd come to New York to find, someone who didn't follow the rules of her world, but still lived with respect and reverence. He valued beautiful things, but he didn't have to justify his interest in them by ascribing then with a higher purpose.

Daniel's silence lasted so long that Jane worried she'd ruined their grand beginning. It was the first conversation she'd enjoyed in months. Unlike her roommates, Daniel didn't seem full of inflated ideas about his importance in the universe. He was thoughtful when he spoke. He seemed to care about what he said when he finally made up his mind to answer her question.

"My brother mostly gives me advice. He got married last year, so now all he can do is give advice." A sly grin slid around one side of Daniel's mouth, part rogue, part boy. "You've probably heard of him. Steve Fletcher. He's an actor, likes to play hero types."

"I don't watch many movies."

A thick ungroomed eyebrow arched in surprise. He turned and faced her. She'd presented a challenge, but in a good way. He wasn't going to make fun of her like her roommates. He was interested. "Steve's breakout role was *Poseidon: The God Rises.*"

"Haven't seen it."

"*The Last Centurion?*"

Jane suppressed a giggle.

Daniel's eyes slanted like he suspected she was lying. "*Lord of the Rings.*"

"People I know have read the books."

"*Die Hard.*"

"Sounds familiar."

"*Star Wars.*"

"Your brother was in *Star Wars?*"

"He hasn't been in the last three."

"Oh." Jane tried to laugh, but the noise that came from her throat sounded like she was imitating the pigeons. So often since starting college she'd been embarrassed to have the gaps in her pop culture acumen pointed out, but with Daniel, ignorance felt okay. Maybe a bit sexy, not that she had any idea what was sexy.

He leaned forward and scratched the scruff on his chin. "I don't understand. You look like a normal person. Do you just watch girl movies? What about *The Devil Wears Prada* or *You've Got Mail?*"

"I saw *Juno*," she offered. "The one about the teenager who chooses life rather than an abortion. My church youth group went to see it."

"*Ah-ha?*"

Jane watched Daniel revise his initial impression. She couldn't tell if this revision worked in her favor or not. She certainly wasn't going to say that her youth group consisted of fifty kids who doubled as homeschooled classmates. They'd gone to *Juno* on a field trip. Afterwards everyone wrote a rhetorical essay on the pro-life argument of the movie.

It took Daniel longer than Jane liked to figure out what to say next. He rode his skateboard back and forth in front of her, only an extra push away from zipping down the sidewalk. Each time Daniel flipped his board around and came back for another pass by the bench, her heart beat a little faster, small hopes multiplied and piled on top of each other.

Finally, he dropped down and sat on the board, braced his feet on either side of hers and rolled back and forth. He looked up at her and asked with a grin, "So . . . if no movies, what *do* you like?"

Jane floated among the clouds. She believed anything she said, no matter how out of context, would make sense because Daniel hadn't gone running at the mention of church, or burst out a bunch of expletives and said something like 'oh you're one of those'. She imagined this was what doing drugs felt like. What being drunk felt like. "A perfect fifth," she said.

"I don't know what that is."

Earth to Jane, please return to Earth. "Oh, right. Sorry. It's a music interval. Sometimes called the patriotic interval. If your brother had a theme, it would involve perfect fifths because he's the hero."

"Are you a musician?"

"I'm a nursing student."

"Oh."

"Actually, I'm hoping to move to Boston next semester. There's a piano performance program that wants me."

"I always thought piano would be fun." Daniel drifted back into thoughtful mode, studying Jane as she basked in the glow of his miraculous attention. "If you ever start watching movies, you could choose them by score composer. I'm really into James Horner. He does a lot of movies that sound like water."

Jane nodded as though she understood, but she was thinking, *movie music that sounds like water . . . right.*

"I suppose you haven't heard of *Titanic*. Horner won an Oscar for the music. Or the *Perfect Storm*? There's this awesome guitar—"

"Hang on, you need to write these down." Jane dug in her backpack. There were too many formulae and definitions and the names of all the bones in the human skeleton running around in her brain to add anything extra.

On the back of a library check-out slip, Daniel wrote 'James Horner'. He added another name below it, and then another, until most of the slip was covered with his cramped manuscript scrawl.

"Now, when you go to Boston, you'll have some new tunes for your new life."

He said it like the move had been decided. He'd taken her at her word about Boston. No argument, no having to state her case, no feeling guilty for wanting something that was forbidden. This gift of acceptance had never been granted by anyone else. It made whatever would come next more significant. The stakes felt higher. They both sensed there was something there. Unsure of what to do about it, they watched the tourists board the ferry to see the Statue of Liberty. They each waited for the other to speak first.

The ferry returned from its tour and disembarked bucket hats, walking shoes, and cameras with lenses the size of Jane's arm. And those were just the white people, a minority in the load of mostly sleek Asians with their top-of-the-line cell phones with talismans hanging from the ends.

Jane was about to say something about New York being every tourist's dream of a hometown, when she thought she saw her youngest brother, Tommy, in her peripheral vision, standing beside the ice cream vendor. She turned her head. Whoever it was had gone. She wanted to dismiss it as her imagination, but she knew better than to underestimate her brothers. They were part of the Vanguard. Surveillance was a family hobby.

She was searching for him in the clusters of people swarming the park when a sharp wail pierced the air. Jane's attention swiveled back to the ferry just in time to see a girl's inflated souvenir ball fall into the water below. She was instantly inconsolable, stopping the line of passengers with heaving wet sobs punctuated by wailing pleas in Mandarin. Her thoroughly embarrassed parents could not convince her to move.

"Five bucks says you can't get that kid to stop crying," said Daniel.

Jane was already shaking her head. "I don't do kids. You get her to stop crying and I'll give you the five bucks or . . ."

"Or what?" He handed her his phone and wallet. He took off his shirt.

An embarrassed heat crept up Jane's cheeks. She looked away. "Or you'll have to buy me ice cream."

"Deal."

Leaving her to sit with his sandals, Daniel jogged barefoot across the cement onto the wharf, unaware of the stares, the swiveling heads, the Japanese *obaachans* talking behind their hands. And then he was gone, over the railing into the water. Several of the twenty-odd people trapped on the ferry simultaneously cried out in surprise.

Jane couldn't see into the water. She tried standing on the bench, but the added height wasn't enough. She considered picking up his sandals and walking down to the water. Her brothers' shoes were always gross. But these were not her brothers' sandals. The thought of touching them thrilled her. She was just about to cross this physical barrier when the runaway ball suddenly flew straight up into the air and landed on the wharf just past the gangway entrance. The waiting passengers cheered as the girl rushed forward and claimed her souvenir. A pair of bucket hatters helped Daniel up over the railing. Not that he needed it. He made quick work of receiving the broken-English thanks from the child's parents, then he came at Jane with arms outstretched.

"Want a hug?" He chased her around the bench, bouncing, laughing, so full of energy she imagined he could swim the length of the bay and not be tired.

"You have any idea how gross that water is?" Jane gasped between bursts of laughter that she liked to remember as less high-pitched than they probably were. She hoped her disgust hid her disquiet as he stood before her, dripping and half-naked, his shorts clinging to his thighs like a second skin.

They bought ice cream sandwiches and found an unoccupied square of half-dead grass in the sunshine. He waited until she finished eating to vigorously shake the water from his hair into her face. She mashed her creamy wrapper into his arm. He was ready to get her back with his own wrapper but stopped short. In his gaze, Jane saw that she was as much of a revelation to him as he was to her. She sensed he wanted to know her as much as she wanted to know him. No one, especially not her high school boyfriend, had ever seen her as someone worth exploring as an individual.

"Last year, I had what I think is a perfect day," said Daniel. "Family vacation in Bali. Usually we surf together. But this day I went out alone. The water looked like greasy sea glass. There was a breeze just strong enough to lift the waves up and hold them for a few extra seconds before they peeled over into white water.

"I didn't just ride those waves. They carried me through a tunnel to another place."

His fingers traced her face as he spoke. A small voice at the back of Jane's head reminded her about the girls she'd known in high school, the ones who'd ended up with broken hearts, and in one case, a baby. Their mistakes had begun like this, allowing some boy to squander away the treasures reserved for a future husband. What that small voice didn't understand was how much Jane liked Daniel's gentle hand and his steady gaze absorbing her every move, every facial twitch, the blades of grass she'd been plucking and how her hands had become still. She imagined he read her the same way he read a wave, tracking its ever-shifting power beneath his feet as it rose around him and over his head. His hands explored her forearm, grazed the fine hairs along her neck. He maneuvered with confidence, his right pointer finger moving from forehead to nose to lips, like a surfer dropping from the lip of a wave into the barrel to glide through a magical, ever-shifting, tunnel of water.

She felt his heat rising. He moved to kiss her.

Jane drew back and made up an excuse—studying; and then another, promises to roommates—to sound her retreat. Her sudden rejection banished the magic from the fading afternoon. They became what they were, two almost-adults who had nothing in common. Daniel was slower to give up than Jane, saying, "After Steve gets done with his shoot tomorrow, we're driving up to Montauk Beach to check out the waves. Why don't you come with us?"

A tempting offer. But what then? Jane imagined the arrival of the moment when she had to admit she was saving herself for marriage, that dating in her world was a chaste gauntlet of do's and don'ts, how she'd promised the grave of her father that her first kiss would be on her wedding day. It all felt silly and insubstantial compared to the very solid presence of a boy who came from that other world called California, a place where people followed their feelings rather than some impersonal set of rules.

Still, Daniel didn't give up. "We'll only be there a few days. I could meet you here, at this exact bench on Monday."

On the Metro riding uptown, Jane thought she might return to Battery Park that Monday to meet Daniel. She'd explain where she was coming from, and if Daniel still wasn't scared, maybe there was a possibility they could try it for a while as long as she didn't tell her family. She imagined if they could make it work, she might never have to go home again.

After her shift, Jane drove home and made herself a TV dinner. She played the album of movie soundtrack highlights that she had compiled from the music recommendations Daniel had given her at Battery Park. The soundtracks were the foundation of what had, over the years, become an immense collection, a guiding compass, the place she went when there was nowhere else to go. As she ate her Salisbury steak and half-frozen mashed potatoes she was transported, not just to those hours in Battery Park, but to other worlds, and times, and places. She listened to James Horner and heard the ocean. At the very least, she hoped Daniel came to the hospital so she'd have the chance to tell him what a gift he'd given her.

That next night, when Jane did her rounds, Rhea was back in her room on East 7.

Usually morphine made people sleepy, but when she saw Jane, she cried out, "My savior! Come, sit. There's nothing on TV. It's all who's been having sex with who, and Congress fighting over the value of our lives." Rhea waved her hand with exasperation towards the wall-mounted television. "And then there's this poor woman . . ."

A former Vanguard trial defendant was being interviewed because she'd written a self-help book called, *Living with the Brand*. She wasn't talking about the about the Vanguard's mission to help people make better choices, but Jane was used to people missing the point. She propped pillows under Rhea's full leg cast and tried to act natural.

"That necklace. It suits on you." Rhea reached forward like she was in a trance and stroked the obsidian pendant that sat in the gully of Jane's breastbone, strands of blue, and purple, and green glass beads extended out on either side.

"It was a gift."

"Someone you loved?"

"It wasn't a good kind of love."

"No shame in that. My husband and I used to fight all the time. Now he's never home, and we have the best marriage I know." Rhea laughed. The laugh turned into a grimace. She braced her chest with her hand.

"Mrs. Fletcher, you need to talk less . . . vigorously. You've just had a very serious procedure."

"You don't know what this body can do." She matched Jane's serious tone. "I have more scars than a Florida manatee. Do you have any?"

Jane was working hard to concentrate. Her fight or flight instinct had kicked into high alert and she wasn't sure why. Goosebumps rose along Jane's arms. It felt like something was watching her. *Do I have any . . .* "What?"

"Scars."

"Excuse me, I need to check other patients."

Rhea leaned towards Jane as far as she could with her leg propped up, her eyes comically wide as she tried to focus on Jane's face. "When I get out of here, you'll have to come visit me at home and tell me about your scars. Don't say no."

The watcher was behind her, real not imagined. Jane felt the shift of a body in the doorway. With it came a light waft of lavender. Jane knew him before she heard his voice.

"Come on, Mom. Don't tell me you're that desperate."

Rhea grabbed Jane's hand as she tried to run. "You must meet my youngest."

In long sleeves, long pants, and sunglasses, Daniel looked like he'd been transported from some other place instead of walking off the streets of LA's October heatwave. The sunglasses stayed on even as Rhea introduced him. There was no way for Jane to tell if he recognized her.

"Daniel, this is Jane, the best nurse in the whole fucking world."

"Nice to meet you." He didn't smile. "I'd like some privacy with my mother if you're finished."

Jane ran from the room.

Alma had left a trail of tin foil pill tabs at the desk. Jane picked them up and shredded them to bits with her nails. She rearranged the charts. She picked up all the stray pens. She wiped the dust behind the computer tower. The AC switched on and rustled a wall of construction plastic at the end of the hall with its invisible breath. Jane watched its restless twitching. She imagined the shadow of a man behind it. After all this time, it was impossible Daniel remembered her. She needed to calm down, be professional. She wanted to stop feeling like the world was about to betray her at the exact moment it was offering her the fulfillment of her dreams.

When Alma returned to the desk, Jane retreated to the rec room. Each in-patient floor had a lounge with board games and a piano keyboard. Jane had been carrying her new Elton John piano book in her purse hoping for a chance to come and play. She went through a ritual bending and creasing of the spine to make the book stand up. The city glow through the rec room windows provided just enough light to read the notes, no need for the harsh intrusion of florescent overheads.

She tested the opening chords. Their isolation drew sadness from the night. It reached into the seamless eastern void beyond the city to where Jane's family lived, and beyond, to New York, where she'd buried the cloying loss that concluded her childhood rebellion under the cement of a city that absorbed all the hurts of the world and turned them into something new.

Bede Benjamin's Breakdown Proves *Libertines* Lives up to Mission Statement

By Krystal Fraier

Fans of the better-off-forgotten Sci-Fi show, *Singularity: AΩ*, were treated to an up close and personal Q & A with Bede Benjamin at ComicCon this weekend.

The clearly emotional thirty-two-year-old actor belched loudly into the mic, swaying from side to side as he addressed the crowd. "I just want to take this opportunity to say I'm sorry to you guys. You guys—the fans—you've been so great—so forgiving."

During his time on *Singularity*, Benjamin was a junior spokesperson for the National Science Council. He recorded evolution propaganda films for school children and an album of songs to help memorize information about the solar system.

He left the show two weeks after his *Libertines* trial during which he broke down in tears and admitted that he deserved to be punished for his lifestyle and his advocacy.

At the Con, Benjamin responded to on-going questions about his trial. "Love 'em or hate 'em, the Vanguard saved my life, like seriously. I was raised in the church, but I got in this way of thinking that I could make it on my own. They reminded me that life is sacred, and that I can make mine count for something."

See Also:

- Tancredo Allen donates money to foundation for single mothers
- Sixteen DUI's and counting: Bede Benjamin's slide into addiction
- The Vanguard's Slow Road to Moral Reformation

Though others have come close, Benjamin's confession marks him as the first *Libertines* target to come out in full support of his trial. His remarks act as a rebuttal to the growing number of voices judging the Vanguard without pausing to weigh the good they have accomplished. Hopefully, this first step is one of many Benjamin intends to take to repair the damage he has done to so many young minds by promoting the doctrine of infallible science and atheism.

CHAPTER 5

ROME

Daniel felt her watching him as soon as he walked in the door. A pair of dark expressive eyes framed by long lashes radiated their potent gaze from a recessed alcove at the back of the restaurant. She peered out from behind the dividing curtain like an ingenue in the harem of some old film where white actors played Arabs and young girls paraded in veils for a hero's pleasure. Except Claudia was fully clothed in an elegant shawl and leggings. She wore no makeup either to accent her features or to conceal the fine wrinkles around her eyes and mouth. The long luscious hair that had been her trademark as a sex icon in another era was pulled back and arranged with pins, an old-fashioned style that highlighted her long neck.

He drew his spine up, forced some swagger into his shoulders and walked through the restaurant at a snail's pace. He pretended he hadn't seen her so he did not have to maintain eye contact. This allowed him to focus on walking as confidently and normally as he could.

"Ciao Daniel." She extended her hand, not to shake, but for him to kiss, which he did almost without thinking. Claudia and the Italian New Wave had been his first exposure to the craft of conveying character in image; he'd been too enraptured to keep track of the subtitles and thus, had experienced the films without language. He'd seen the open souls of people he felt he knew in those films. He'd agonized over their decisions with them, Claudia most of all.

He'd planned a summation of these thoughts in a brief opening monologue. But her eyes, peeling back his armor like it was so much tissue paper, banished the prepared speech from his head. Taking his seat at the intimate table beside a window overlooking the Villa Borghese where he'd spent the morning walking and reading, Daniel tried to stay calm. A waiter brought espresso and biscotti. Claudia gazed at him with an expression of marvel, the way a student of sculpture might gaze at a Bernini marble.

She continued to gaze at him, seemingly unaware of the lengthening silence. Finally, he said, "I'm glad you liked my tape," and immediately cringed. He felt like such an uncouth provincial. "I think I can bring a lot to Thomas and his frustration over always being second to Carraldo."

"I have no doubt you could do anything," said Claudia. "I'm so glad you decided to come out of retirement. Our little film is the perfect way to reintroduce you to the world." She reached across the table and set her hand on his just as he was returning his cup to its saucer. He swallowed the instinct to pull away. He adjusted his feet under the table to make sure both appeared squarely resting on the floor even though she couldn't see them.

"Daniel, I think we should be honest with each other. It's very clear to me that you chose to audition for Thomas because you weren't confident that you could get a lead part after being away from work for so long."

"Thomas resonated with me. I think—"

"You're a Carraldo."

Daniel coughed out a laugh. "Thank you, but—"

"I've seen over a hundred auditions. But no one had the look the way you do. You're the swaggering cowboy, the superhero, the victorious soldier. The prototypical hero. That aura radiates from within you."

Daniel looked out the window at the green canopy of the villa's park. A light rain had begun to fall, one of those distinctly Italian rain showers that came out of nowhere and lasted just long enough to ruin the day of the man caught without an umbrella. Shrouded in mist, the park, with the roof of the Temple of Asclepius just visible in the gray-green dusk, looked like the scene of a fairy tale. If he could just walk into the trees he could return to childhood where the paths to one's dreams were always clearly marked and easy to follow.

For a moment Daniel thought he would cry.

"Claudia, I'm thrilled by your faith in me. It's a lot more than I have a right to expect. But I can't play Carraldo."

She looked ready to argue, so he pressed forward, his voice low and defensive.

"You claim to be a progressive, but here you are saying I'm too attractive to play the serious role. You just want me to take my clothes off." Daniel channeled Steve's growling sarcasm as his words gained speed. "You've invited me here never intending to offer me the part I want. Assuming I would be desperate enough to do anything you wanted. I'm not going to play a character that amounts to the male version of window dressing."

As he continued, Daniel tapped into his trove of American stereotypes, raising his voice and swearing, so that people in the restaurant began to look in their direction. Claudia held up her hand in surrender. She apologized for taking up his time. She left the restaurant like a crane who'd had its feathers ruffled by a tornado.

It was a kind of career suicide. Claudia had enough pull with other European directors to make sure no one would hire him. American productions were still possible, but with their stricter safety regulations, and the practice of executive ass covering by insuring every actor against injury, any job Daniel accepted would also mean submitting to a medical examination.

He remained at the table. He could see his hand jittering with tremors, but couldn't feel it because everything had gone numb. He briefly wondered if maybe he would die at that little table looking out at the dreamscape of the Villa Borghese. He wondered if perhaps that would be a mercy.

At airport security, Daniel waved a guard over and handed her his TSA disability card. Airports were one of his least favorite places, but at least the Italians knew how to use discretion. He still had to walk through the body scanner, but the alarms were muted. He was shown into a private screening room with the guard and her manager.

"May I please see it?" asked the guard.

Daniel took a seat in the nearest folding chair and slowly rolled up the right leg of his pants, careful not to go so far that she would see the end of the brand on his thigh. He removed the suction cup of his prosthetic from the nub of his knee and handed it to her. She laid it on the counter and waved a wand over it. The manager looked apologetic that his guard was being so thorough.

Normally, Daniel tried to make these situations more comfortable, tried to convey that he knew they were just doing their job. But he didn't have any energy left to make other people feel better about themselves. He leaned back in the chair, closed his eyes, and tried not to feel.

He had what Steve considered a very bad habit of zoning-out during points of high stress. Daniel called them his *Nude Descending the Stairs* moments. He could completely disengage from whatever was going on and enter a timeless, motionless space in which he ceased to become the fractured, earth-toned approximation of a body descending through darkness, and became instead weightless, effortless, polychromatic energy ascending to light. In this space, there was no disabled body, only consciousness, and even that, Daniel had discovered, he could turn off and simply float without a name, or relationships, or purpose.

His ringing cell phone summoned Daniel's consciousness back to the airport lounge where he sat waiting for his boarding call with no memory of how he'd arrived there or how long he had been waiting.

Steve was calling. The last person Daniel wanted to talk to. He watched the call go to voicemail only to have the screen immediately light up with another call, and then another. The fifth time Steve called, Daniel answered.

"Where are you?"

"Riley has my itinerary."

"You could just answer my question instead of fucking criminalizing me."

"What's the problem, Steve?"

"The problem? I'll tell you what, your fucking mother is fucking dying, apparently. I thought you should know."

The line went dead.

Daniel felt the pull back to his void so strongly that the room spun. Someday, if there was justice in the world, Steve would know what it was like to—

He was calling again.

"Yes?"

"All the guys Rowan thinks could replace Garrett are crap but he's breathing down my neck to pick one, like it's no big deal. Like it's just a fill in the blank. This is what I get for working with a suit from New York."

"What happened to Mom?"

"Jet ski. But Riley went to see her and she was fine. And then she kept calling and saying I had to come sign her out because she didn't want to sit like a cripple—"

"Which I did last time."

"Right, which was a fucking terrible decision. So, I stopped answering her calls because I've got enough to deal with right now. And then I get a call from this nurse saying like, there was a complication, and another surgery, and maybe Mom wouldn't make it."

"When was this?"

"I dunno, a couple hours ago."

The receiver filled with the static of Steve exhaling into his phone. In the hazy background of the airport din, Daniel heard his flight called for boarding.

"You have to go to the hospital. Figure out what's going on and send me an email. My flight's leaving, you won't be able to call me."

More heavy breathing.

"Or I'll call Riley. Is that what you want? Send your wife over to take care of Mom?"

"Riley's in Mexico."

"Then you'll have to do it yourself."

More heavy breathing.

"Steve, I'm serious."

"Yeah, I'm on it."

"Send me an email."

"I said I got it."

Daniel turned on his Bluetooth so he could put his phone in his pocket while he carried his bags. He listened to Steve breathing. Each interval that passed without Steve speaking increased Daniel's dread. Steve saying their mother was dead could be dismissed as dramatic. But Steve rendered nonverbal was an unusually genuine expression that lent weight to the dramatics.

He took his place in the first-class priority line. He'd just set down his carry on when he felt someone touch his arm. Alarms sounded in Daniel's head. The floor tilted. His legs tensed to run though he knew he couldn't run. This time they'd have him for good.

But it was only a small boy wearing a T-shirt covered in the cracked and faded applique of the Avengers, and holding out his ticket envelope for an autograph.

"Poseidon, could you please . . ." Too bashful to finish, the boy turned and ran into the legs of his father.

Daniel's eyes swept his fellow passengers for signs of danger even though he knew there were none. He walked back to the boy. "Hey buddy, let me see that." Sometimes it was so easy to pretend. The threatening black expanse of panic could be pushed back, life could be performed as though everything was *fine*. Daniel signed the ticket in Steve's name, and politely refused to take a picture. It was time to board the plane. People moved forward. The steady beep of the ticket scanner began. Everything as it should be, except for him.

"How do people think I'm Poseidon?" Daniel asked Steve. "I get them mistaking me for you, but I don't have the Poseidon hair. There's no way to mistake me as your character."

"My Poseidon transcends the hair," said Steve. "He is me as you are me and we are all together."

"Are you high?"

"It's been a fucking stressful day."

Daniel laughed despite himself. His breathing had begun to return to normal. "I'm on the plane now. When are you going to the hospital?"

"Soonish, just have to grab a bite."

"Send me an email."

"Yep."

"Steve?"

"What?"

"She's not dead. Drive over there. You'll see it was all blown out of proportion."

"Just get here, okay?"

Daniel stayed on the phone until the cabin doors closed. As soon as he hung up, he felt distinctly untethered, an unnerving feeling since he was almost always surrounded by people and wishing to be alone. He chose to believe Steve would go to the hospital, discover that their mother was fine, and send the email. He decided he would wait an hour before unpacking his laptop. He passed that hour reading. He had a glass of wine even though alcohol interacted with his meds. The interaction ended up being stronger than he remembered from his last break with sobriety. He passed out. When he woke up five hours later and checked messages there was no email from Steve.

It was easy to jump to conclusions.

Nearly every other passenger was asleep. The rest were zoned into in-flight entertainment. Daniel paced the dimly lit aisles. If she was dead, his first call would be to their father. He was out on a research project studying microbial life in the South Pacific. Communication was difficult. He would be able to speak to funeral requests and burial preferences, but probably Daniel would have to make the arrangements.

He was so tired of being the one everyone looked to for miracles. Daniel recognized this as a self-defeating line of thinking. He knew what was down that road. But he also knew that since there was now no movie with Claudia and no chance of Steve giving him Garett's role in the Hawaii project, he wasn't likely to have anything better to do than work miracles anytime soon.

With the iron pragmatism of a man who had once been told he'd never walk again, Daniel sifted through his mother's life and organized her relationships into categories of notification. He made lists of names for the calls that would have to be made. By the time the final descent was announced he had a short list of family and friends to call as soon as he could confirm what had happened. He had a longer second list of people who could wait a few days. He had a script memorized of what he would say. It conveyed the necessary information without inviting emotional sharing. He'd also spent some time organizing a cutting diatribe against Steve for failing to send the email.

The first thing Daniel noticed when he climbed into the '74 Dodge Challenger idling in the airport loading zone was that Steve had managed to make it to his salon appointment. His hair was shorter and Poseidon's dirty blonde highlights had been rinsed out and lightened to match Steve's natural color.

"Well?"

"I think they're uneven. He took too much off the end of this one, see?" Steve punched the dome light and shoved his forehead into Daniel's face while jabbing at his left eyebrow.

"What about Mom?"

"Haven't seen her. Waited for you."

Daniel took a deep breath in and very slowly released it. Someday, he vowed, Steve would get what he deserved. Someone would figure out how to make Steve feel consequences.

"She wants something with meatballs. But I figured we wouldn't because you're not supposed to eat right after surgery, right?"

It had been a long time since his mother should've gotten out of surgery, but Daniel chose not to ask for clarification. Steve wasn't likely to know. And Daniel didn't want to dig further into a subject that was uncomfortable for both of them. When Daniel had been in the hospital recovering from hip replacement surgery, Steve had brought him a plate lunch like they'd eaten in Hawaii as kids. Five minutes after Daniel had eaten it, the food plus some stomach acid had made like Vesuvius all over the bed.

At the hospital, Steve only went in as far as the lobby where he glad-handed the security guard and signed an autograph while Daniel snuck into the stairwell. They'd planned a twenty-minute visit. The time-limit was Steve's insistence because he, who avoided hospitals as though they could make him impotent, would be waiting in the car. And because he believed hospitals were second only to surfing competitions in their potential to trigger one of Daniel's panic attacks, which sometimes led to seizures, and a great deal of embarrassment for the family. If Steve had known the kid at the airport in Rome had startled Daniel so badly he was already predisposed to an attack, he probably wouldn't have let Daniel visit the hospital at all. For his part, Daniel was feeling optimistic. He still had no hope for reviving his career, but his mother was not dead, which was an improvement on the last thirteen hours.

He felt out of place being a visitor instead of a patient. Nights spent hooked up to machines had never been as peaceful as the hospital felt now, walking the empty hallways lined with clean, well ordered rooms full of healing patients. The steady hum of state-of-the-art climate control kept the furnace outside at bay.

Slipping into her room, Daniel sensed the distinct disturbance of cosmic energy that was his mother. He took a moment, concealed behind the privacy curtain, to appreciate knowing she was in fact alive. She was talking to her nurse, already making plans for her post-hospital convalescence, insisting the nurse come visit. The nurse was trying to be professional. Daniel knew how hard his mother was to dissuade when she was sober. High on whatever post-op painkillers they had her on was like trying to deny a hurricane. He drew aside the curtain to intervene.

"Come on, Mom, don't tell me you're that desperate."

The nurse tried to excuse herself, but his mother grabbed her hand and insisted on making introductions.

Daniel felt a shock wave ten times more potent than the boy at the airport when the nurse looked at him. Just one quick glance and he knew her, the girl from Battery Park. A twitch of dysphoria began in his spine and traveled down every nerve, like the Matrix making adjustments. With it spread a sudden uncomfortable heat. In a few minutes the back of Daniel's head would go numb. The tremors would begin after that. He had maybe ten minutes before he lost total control of his body.

It was clear she also knew him, not as Steve, not even as Daniel Fletcher the one-hit teen idol. No, to her he was Daniel the college drop-out surfer who lived in pursuit of the next wave. This was a revelation he didn't have time to enjoy. The numbness came in a tidal wave that made the room tilt. He hadn't had an attack this severe in years. He swayed as Jane rushed by, embarrassed or shy, or something else, he couldn't tell in the midst of his brain rushing through disorganized signals. What was most important in that moment was that he leave the hospital before he became a seizing mass of tissue unable to control his bowels. He did not want to end up as her patient.

"Didn't you get my message about the meatballs?" His mother's voice arched with frustration. "I knew Steve wasn't listening when I told him—"

"Mom, I need to go. Meatballs tomorrow, promise." Daniel rushed to give her a hug. Then, seeing the bandages peeking out from the collar of her gown, he stopped short, gave her a salute instead, turned on his heel and walked as quickly as he could to the elevator.

Blood swelled Daniel's pulse to a pounding throb. His tongue had turned to sandpaper. It scratched against the roof of his mouth. He made the first milestone of the elevator. He accidentally pushed three other buttons along with the lobby button. He counted breaths.

He tried to scare his system into calming down. "You do not want to do this in front of her," he said as the elevator chimed and opened for no one on the fifth floor.

He tried calming his nerves with hope. "What are the chances? Here in LA, Mom's nurse after all these years." It was a sign of something, but he wasn't sure what. It wasn't like he could have a relationship with a woman who thought he was still that man.

Or could he?

Daniel's good leg thumped spastically against the floor of the elevator as it stopped on the second floor.

"She was really into me, like really. We had a connection. She didn't seem like the type who cared about being tough. So maybe . . ." His jaw clenched. It became too difficult to continue talking to himself. Silently, he continued to interrogate the possibility that maybe the Battery Park girl . . .

Jane.

That maybe she was one of the few women—maybe the only woman—in the world who could be okay with him being a partial instead of a whole.

The security guard gave Daniel a look as he staggered across the atrium and out the front door with his arms clenched across his chest and his good leg nearly flaccid with the shakes.

The Challenger idled in the circular drive. Daniel stumbled across acres of cement like a wounded bank robber trying to reach the getaway car. It would've been nice if Steve had thought to open the car door so Daniel wouldn't have had to try and grasp the handle and pull, an impossible series of muscular interactions he only managed on the fourth attempt.

"What the fuck happened?"

"Water," gasped Daniel.

Steve gave him the 'here we go again' look, as though he was somehow impositioned by Daniel's tired song and dance of dysfunction. But he reached into the back and produced an over-heated bottle of water from the case behind the passenger seat.

"The girl from New York."

"Which girl from New York?"

"*My* . . . girl. Mom's nurse."

"Well, fuck."

Daniel braced one arm against his car door and the other against the center console. He repeated the jumbled mantras of five different psychiatrists in his head. *This is a safe place. No one can hurt me here.* But the one thought that brought a modicum of clarity through the cacophony of psychological and physiological alarms was Jane.

She knew him as he used to be, which was still the man he wanted to be. There were just some very fundamental barriers to realizing it. She could help him.

"She-re-mem-ber-erzzzz-me." Daniel shook so hard his seatbelt rattled.

Steve arched a doubtful eyebrow. The shorter one. "Forget it, she's obviously a trigger." He drove toward the parking lot exit at a crawl, stalling to see if this was going to turn into an emergency room visit. "She's probably more my type, anyway."

"You-think-ev-rrr-eee-one . . . is your type." Daniel finished off his water and focused on the empty bottle. Empty was not a trap, he told himself. Every Fletcher family car, except Steve's Maserati, had a case of bottled water specifically for this purpose. Knowing there was more water was an important part of Daniel believing he was safe.

"My type likes a guy with two legs, so yeah, they're all my type."

"As far as she knows, I have two legs." The tremors decreased in intensity by a few degrees. Breathing began to come more easily. "It would be like a vacation."

"You want a vacation where you pretend you have two legs?" Steve wore a small, almost bitter smile, as he put on his blinker and pulled the Challenger into traffic. "Bet you fifty bucks she dumps you when she finds out."

"If I tell her and she still wants to go out, you give me Garrett's job."

"No way."

"In Italy, you said, start small, get a girl."

"That's not what I fucking meant." Steve careened up the interstate onramp like he was preparing to launch into the air. "Even if I said bets on, you couldn't make it happen that fast. You'd have to go from monk to Casanova in like a week, less than that. We're fucking leaving for Hawaii in . . ." he searched for an answer he'd never had to know because Daniel managed his schedule.

"Eleven days."

"Exactly. You can't do it. Besides, I put my movie in danger waiting on you."

"Did you screen any of Rowan's new options?"

Steve made a face.

"You don't have to stop looking. But if you don't find anyone, it's me."

"She'll dump you."

"Bets off if you interfere."

"You have to bring her around, so I see that it's legit."

"Fine."

"But she's going to dump you."

"She's probably married with three kids. Or she's hung up on the fact I never met her at the park when I said I would. We won't even make it to our first date."

"Sure you will," said Steve. "You're my brother. She'll at least let you take her out so she can tell her friends she was that close to greatness."

Daniel tossed his empty water bottle at Steve. It ricocheted off his head and clattered onto the dashboard. "If you sweep in and be all movie star, I'm going to break your face." He was only half-joking.

GLAMOUR
Subscribe and Get 2 free gifts!

Dating

Do you know this Butt? Five Questions Reveal how Vanguard Fandom affects your Dating Life

By Tae Loveless // *Yesterday*

It's that time of year again. Time for us to pause and remember what our lives were like before the October 24th, 2008 trial of Kristine Bariens. She confirmed what we had been imagining was true: there was a living breathing man under that Vanguard mask and damn it, he had a hot ass.

During the last of her three escape attempts, Bariens, the founder of Independent Women for America, got a hold of two solid fistfuls of pants and bared a Vanguard soldier's cheeks to the world. Beneath those monotonous black uniforms, we glimpsed a hint of the sexy bad boys we dreamed would find a reason to kidnap us.

Since 2008, much has been made of the three seconds of butt screenshots widely believed to belong to Bones, a hefty giant most prominent during the sentencing portion of a trial broadcast.

In honor of the anniversary of Bariens' liberation of Bones' luscious backside, and partially inspired by @MrBonesLove who provides the world with daily mashups of Bones screenshots with known celebrities, I have made a list of five questions every woman must ask herself when trying to accommodate real life dating around her infatuation with the mysterious soldiers of the Vanguard.

1. When do I tell Mr. Right about my collection of *Libertines* screenshots? If he shows you his porn collection or asks you to watch porn with him, it's safe to test him with your own naughty secret. Always keep the scales balanced.

2. How do I schedule a date when I'm waiting for a new trial to be posted? There's a trial at least once, sometimes twice, a month. Usually we only have a day or less notice. The certainty of this uncertainty makes things like dating complicated. It's best to find someone who likes to be spontaneous. Or plan dates that can be rescheduled without a lot of hassle. For example, IHOP is open 24 hours a day, so if you can't make dinner, you can have a midnight snack.

3. Is it a deal breaker if Mr. Right's butt doesn't quite look like Bones' butt? People come in all shapes and sizes. Lacking in one area usually means others are even better. Just make sure Mr. Right doesn't have an inferiority complex.

4. Is sending naked pictures to the Vanguard PO box in South Dakota taking fandom too far? If you want a real shot at getting the attention of Bones, Mirt, Gnosh, or Enoch, consider writing a letter. These guys aren't quite the full-blooded males we're used to. They live more in their heads and enjoy intellectual conversations. Prove you know something smart before you send a picture.

5. At what point should I feel guilty about my interest? In celebrity worship, ideologies rarely come into play. If you're concerned about this, it's probably a sign you've watched too many trials and now you're starting to read moral arguments into every thought you have. People in the past have gotten turned on by pirates, and political traitors, and Charles Manson. This didn't make them bad people.

CHAPTER 6

"Is this it?" Alma was barely understandable through the tissue she had pinched around her nose. She turned her computer screen so Jane, sitting at the other end of their station, could see the spider Google had found.

Jane glanced at it and quickly turned away. "That's him."

"Did it bite you?"

"No."

"Good."

"You're supposed to be making me feel better."

"There's no info on how to kill it. Maybe hire an exterminator?"

"So he can charge me a hundred bucks to move the crap around under my bed and tell me there's nothing there?"

"At least you'd know."

Jane glared at her. "I can take care of it myself."

"Those 'day three of sleeping on the couch' bags under your eyes say otherwise."

"I'm working up to it."

"Uh huh. I think—" Alma doubled over and sneezed.

"You should go home and rest."

"It's allergies. I'll be like this the whole month unless I can find an antihistamine that doesn't hate me."

Jane pushed back from the desk in preparation to do the last round of the shift. "Maybe one of our patients will have a way to solve my spider problem."

"You're making this too complicated," Alma called after her.

Jane started with room six. The lone survivor of a three-car wreck had plowed through an intersection while texting. He was on a ventilator, in a chemically induced coma. A patient who belonged in the ICU, but there hadn't been space. A kidney was on its way even though he only had a fifty percent chance of survival from the other injuries. He had money, or his parents had money. Someone was paying a lot to save his life.

She kept the lights dim as she worked, checking his vital signs, preparing to change the dressings on his burned legs. She talked to him while she worked, asked him if he liked spiders. She thought someone like him must like spiders. The humming machines that kept him alive seemed to answer in the affirmative.

When Jane had worked in the Cardiac ICU, death had been so near, the sounds of machines so omnipresent, that she and the other nurses had made up dances to the beats of the ventilators. Now, she did a tense, jig-step as she walked down the hall, leaving the machine sounds behind.

The other patients were all asleep except for Rhea. Jane found her greedily devouring a meatball sub sandwich.

"The food here is godawful. Don't judge me."

Jane held up her hands in surrender. "That's two nights in a row you've had visitors after hours. Our security guards must be lazy."

"The rules don't apply to my son. Everyone loves him. They want to make him happy. He does the schmoozing to get Daniel in the door with my contraband so he doesn't have to come up himself, which is fine. I wouldn't voluntarily visit a hospital unless last rites were needed."

"Daniel was here?" Jane tried to sound casual.

"You just missed him. He's on Italian time, makes it hard to visit during the day, or I'm sure he'd be following the rules. He's my little stickler."

Jane had been listening for Daniel's arrival the whole night. No one had come up in the elevator. She would've heard the West 7 nurses greet him. But she also hadn't heard the latch on the stairwell door. She'd thought maybe Daniel would stop by the nurse's station to say hello, maybe marvel at the coincidence of her again. Knowing he'd already come and gone felt like a much bigger disappointment than reasonable. Maybe he hadn't remembered her. Or worse, he'd remembered her and wanted to avoid further interaction. Maybe he hated her for not coming to meet him at the park like they'd planned.

Her mother's voice echoed in Jane's head. *Hate is a strong word, Jane. It will ruin you.* As she finished her shift and made her way downstairs to the parking garage, Jane chastised herself for judging Daniel's avoidance. She had no reason to expect anything from him.

She'd almost reached her Jeep when she saw him, her dream of Daniel turned flesh, leaning not quite casually against the side of a black Prius. He still wore long sleeves and long pants even though the temperature at sunrise had been ninety-degrees.

"Do you have a minute?"

She stopped just before the front bumper on the opposite side of the car from where he stood. She waited. He didn't speak. The radio was on inside the Prius. Classical music. Jane smiled. She expected nothing less from him. The piece that had been playing ended. The announcer gave a brief introduction of the next one, a Sibelius symphony. Still, Daniel didn't speak.

It occurred to Jane that perhaps Daniel couldn't figure out what to say to a woman he'd once spent one afternoon with almost a decade ago. She decided to take the lead.

"I never thought I'd see you again."

"Me neither. But I've thought a lot about that day and what would've happened if . . ."

There it was. The not quite spoke question of: *Why didn't you meet me?* Jane carefully stepped around it. "Considering you had hordes of screaming girls chasing you around just a few months after that, I don't think we would've made it very far."

"Because you would've been jealous?" A tentative teasing smile.

Jane had been trained not to evaluate people by their looks, but it was impossible not to notice how beautiful he was, especially when he smiled.

"Maybe you wouldn't have had time for me once you were a serious music student. Didn't you have to practice like ten hours a day?"

"I didn't end up going to Boston." She watched Daniel's face as he adjusted his expectations. She imagined there was a shade of disappointment he was quickly pushing away.

"Obviously, I'm glad you didn't transfer," he said. "Who knows if another nurse could've saved Mom the way you did."

"My life didn't turn out quite the way I expected."

"Mine neither." He laughed.

Jane moved closer, allowed her hip to slide forward and rest on the hood of the Prius. "I always thought I'd see you in the surfing world with one of those jobs where you travel all over the world and don't have to wear shoes. For a while I followed all these surf news sites and the WSL so if you were ever doing something here I could 'run into you' on the beach—Wow it sounds creepy saying that out loud."

"Steve has like a dozen serious stalkers. I've always felt a little left out."

"I meant to go to one of the competitions, even if you weren't going to be there. You made it sound so romantic—the ocean. That's how I chose California."

"I'm flattered."

"Actually, I haven't quite made it to the beach yet."

"You've lived here how many years?'

"Almost five."

"We should go."

Jane could barely believe the words as she dared to say, "There's a surf event this week in Santa Monica. Maybe you could initiate me." She wasn't usually so obvious in her desire. Everything she had been taught about relations between men and women reflected a reserved, desire-less feminine role. Surely Daniel had something better to do. She didn't want to scare him away by being so demanding.

His expression seemed to confirm she'd overstepped. His lips pressed together in what appeared to her as disapproval. His posture stiffened. An eternity seemed to pass before he said, "Why don't we start with breakfast? Or whatever meal comes next for you."

"What, like now?"

"Or tomorrow, if you're busy . . ."

"Now is good."

He blew out what must have been a full lung of withheld air and laughed. "Where would you like to go?"

"Know any good sushi places?"

"None that are open this early. But I do know a twenty-four-hour *kaiten-zushi* that's passable."

A small thrill bubbled up through Jane's chest. It hardly seemed possible after so many years of fantasies that Daniel in real life had somehow remained as interesting and as sophisticated as she had dreamed. Most impossible of all, he was interested in her.

Kaiten-zushi was Japanese for conveyor belt sushi. Customers sat at a bar around a conveyor belt filled with little plates of sushi color-coded by price. Customers selected what they wanted to eat and then paid at the end based on the number and color of empty plates.

"You can also order special items like noodles or soup and extra rice," said Daniel.

"What do you usually get?"

"Soup and rice go with the manners I was taught."

"Let's do that. But you have to teach me," said Jane.

Daniel had spent almost a month in Tokyo when Steve had been filming his cyber terrorism thriller *Wireless*. Jane had never met anyone who'd been to Japan. She had so many questions. The fact that Daniel seemed to enjoy talking about it, that maybe no one had ever asked him what it had been like or what he'd learned, encouraged her to ask more questions. He had a smooth, articulate voice. He knew how to tell stories without frustrating divergences or distracting details. When he described his difficulties being six-foot-four navigating a world where the average person was five-three, his laughter trickled out of him in a warm inviting stream.

He showed her how to hold her rice bowl with her four long fingers on the bottom lip and her thumb tucked around the rim. He demonstrated how to hold the cheap wood chopsticks. But when she failed miserably at scooping rice out of her bowl, he stood up from his stool, came around behind her, put his hand around her hand, and guided it through the motions. Even after she'd managed it successfully, he lingered behind her, so near she could feel the heat of his breath on the crown of her head. When he returned to his seat she felt his absence like the loss of a fortune.

They let an entire cycle of sushi roll by so Daniel could describe each kind. He wasn't afraid to admit there were some he didn't recognize. He recommended the tekka maki as a starter so Jane could decide if she liked raw fish. He separated a small slice of pickled ginger from the pile of it in a little dish beside the soy sauce and set it on her rice.

"You eat this first to cleanse your palate."

"It looks like skin."

"You'll be fine."

And she was. She loved the ginger, the tekka. She loved everything she tried, even the fish eggs wrapped in seaweed.

"You can't imagine how many Japanese restaurants I've been to with men who had no idea what they were doing. This is fantastic."

"Thank you."

"When you were in Japan, did you go to any of their traditional theatre? What's it called, Ka—something."

"Jane?"

"Hm?"

"I've been doing all the talking."

"Have you?"

"You're a professional interrogator."

"I like learning new things."

"I think you also like to hide."

It thrilled her that he'd noticed. So many men were oblivious. They were flattered by her questions. They fell into pontificating, never noticing that they learned nothing about her while she learned everything she needed to know about them. Not Daniel. Of course not Daniel.

"Alright, what do you want to know?"

He turned sideways so he faced her, and thoughtfully tapped his chopsticks to his chin. "What happened to music school? It seemed like such a sure thing."

Jane broke eye contact. She stared down at her second bowl of miso soup. It looked like mud, but it tasted like heaven. After only an hour together he had once again transformed her world. She had nothing of comparable value to offer him.

"My family really wanted me to be a nurse. That day we met, I was waiting for my older brother. He flew halfway across the country to pressure me into giving up the music school idea."

"Wow."

"Actually, he also had to be in New York for work, but I didn't know that until later, so it felt like this big thing. It was stupid. I should've stood up to him."

"I don't think it's stupid. Trying to be the right person to the people we care about is a thing."

"But it's so uncool. Like, you never see people in the movies being fulfilled and happy doing what their families want. It isn't a legit thing to do. After graduation, I had job offers in New York, but I moved home because that's what they wanted. I got married because that's what they wanted, which of course was a disaster because I had no idea what *I* wanted, and it's not possible to be in a relationship with someone long term where you only do what they—" Jane stopped.

Married. How had that popped out? Jane snuck a sidelong glance at

Daniel. He was very studiously picking one kernel of rice out of his bowl at a time and eating them.

"I suppose it didn't end well?"

"I left him six years ago." Jane paused. She knew if she had a prayer of making it with Daniel she needed to be as honest as possible. "It was . . . abusive, not physically, but maybe that would've happened if I'd dared challenge him. We're still legally married because I can't—if he finds me. I mean, I don't even know if he's looking. We haven't had any contact. I take a self-defense class once a week to try and be ready just in case. I changed my legal name, but I've heard that kind of thing doesn't matter with technology the way it is now. So, I've got a duffle bag under my bed with a fake passport, a train ticket, and two grand in cash in case I need to leave fast. Hopefully, I don't need it soon because there's this giant spider hiding under my bed right now."

Daniel had run out of rice kernels. He meditatively turned the bowl in circles by extending his fingers and lowering his hand like a claw around the rim of the bowl, rotating it, releasing, then retracting his hand.

"I suppose you've never gone on a date with a girl who has a fake passport."

"Not that I know of."

He had lovely hands. Large and powerful, but also graceful. She was sure he could reach over an octave on the piano without trying. It was all she could do not to reach over and grab his hand, and beg him not to be disappointed.

"I think I can help you with the spider," he said.

Jane nodded. She couldn't speak.

"The husband thing . . . I can't imagine what that'd be like. You'd never feel safe. On the other hand, it must give you a lot of appreciation. You don't take your life for granted."

Jane laughed. "Sometimes I do. But yes, it's hard to relax."

"And you haven't been to the beach." He finally stopped adjusting his rice bowl and looked at her. "As the one responsible for instilling this idea of the romantic ocean in your head it should also be my responsibility to show you that the Los Angeles beaches are some of the ugliest, dirtiest, most commercialized beaches in the world."

Daniel drove his Prius like an octogenarian going blind, his hands clenched at ten and two on the steering wheel, maintaining the exact speed limit. It was a strange contrast to his free-floating surfer lifestyle. Though on reflection, Jane realized his driving was more Daniel of now than of her memory. He still had that deeply thoughtful gaze that made her knees week. He still looked the same physically. But his energy had diminished or been contained somehow. Like his brain had tamed what before had been the wild power of an animal.

It made sense that he'd changed. They were almost ten years older. Knowing he probably had also detected changes in her that he might not have expected, Jane was determined not be disappointed. It was enough to be sitting beside him, in his car, staring but not staring at him because she was afraid that he would vanish at any moment and she would wake up on her couch in her spider-infested apartment.

There were too many cars to park anywhere near the beach. When he finally found a spot, Daniel braked a little too hard and lurched the Prius into a parking stall. He picked up his keys from the cupholder and began to twist them around his finger. "In the interest of full disclosure, you should know that I don't surf anymore. I haven't been anywhere near a comp since before I met you."

Jane laughed, then stopped. "You're serious." She clapped her hand over her mouth. "I'm sorry. I had no idea. Let's not do this today. We can come back another time."

"We're here now. We might as well."

"Clearly you don't want to."

"I do, it's just not that simple. You should be aware I might . . . wig out a bit. But you can probably handle that." He tried to smile.

Jane wanted to tell him no, she couldn't handle him wigging out. He was Daniel, the man who had jumped into the bay to save a girl's toy, the surfer, the invincible one. Instead she nodded and tried to look encouraging.

There were people everywhere. Most of them were young and tan and half-dressed. Jane and Daniel walked past a fleet of tents set up outside a skate park. Kids on roller blades and skateboards milled around checking out displays of gear and a virtual reality machine that imitated the feel of a half pipe.

The beach was full of spectators camped out with lawn chairs, and towels, and rented umbrellas stamped with the Hurley logo. From the boardwalk where Jane and Daniel paused to get their bearings, the two surfers out in the water were specks of color on glistening waves rushing towards the beach. Gobs of foam flew into the air and drifted like cotton on the breeze. A giant screen at the edge of the beach projected close-up footage of the surfers.

Daniel walked her through the rules of the event with stiff abrupt sentences that made Jane feel like she'd coerced him into talking. She had to fight her instinct not to take it personally. To assuage her discomfort, she tried looping her arm through his and drawing closer so that her left side brushed up against his right side. He flinched away.

The heat was almost over. Red was in the lead. Blue needed an eight-point ride to win. A wave came into the contest zone that seemed impossibly small to Jane, something a child would ride for practice. She knew eight points was a very good score and that, to get a good score most surfers needed a pretty good wave as a starting point.

As they watched, Blue coursed down the length of the wave, bobbing and weaving along its face until, just before it collapsed into foam, he shifted his weight and pointed the nose of his board upward. He flew straight into the air, rotating a full circle with his board clutched against his chest before coming back down and landing in the whitewash just ahead of the wave. The crowd went wild.

"I used to be better than that guy." Daniel's eyes searched the horizon as though he might find the answer to the riddle of how Blue was living the life he had wanted. "In my family, we—they—act like they can do anything." Daniel's voice was soft and husky. Jane had to lean in to hear him over the beach announcer. "You've seen what happens when my mother thinks she can do anything." His attempt at a small wry smile was so sad it made her want to cry. "It's been hard for me to recognize my limits aren't the same as faults." He drew a deep staggered breath. "It's completely useless that my first thought when I see that guy is that I could be doing the same thing if I'd just tried harder. Like . . . I'm not allowed to feel sorry for myself because it's my own fault for giving up."

"I feel like that sometimes."

He gave her a hard look, like she couldn't possibly know what he was talking about.

"I gave up music. I mean, I play Elton John on a crappy keyboard at work, but I don't have any discipline. My posture is crap. I don't run scales. The Beethoven Sonata that got me accepted into that school in Boston? I can only play half of it now; it's too difficult. But I know all that work wasn't a waste. It taught me how to listen to music, which is like the only highbrow thing I know anything about. It counts. Just because it didn't become my career doesn't mean it isn't valuable. Besides, you're much less likely to end up as my patient if you don't surf." She tried to lighten her smile with a teasing twist, but her surprise at his confession made it difficult to perform.

"You're disappointed."

Yes. "I'm just wondering what you found to replace it."

Daniel made a face. "I'm Steve's manager."

"Besides that."

He shrugged. "I read a lot."

"What are you reading right now?"

"While Steve was filming his new Poseidon, I read all of David Mitchell's books. I'm just finishing."

"What do you like about him?"

"It's just a pastime. You don't have to pretend to be interested. Reading is nothing compared to this."

"I don't know anything about books. You could give me another list." She reached into her purse and withdrew the old library checkout slip where Daniel had written his list of movie composers. "This list gave me the courage to leave my husband."

"How do you still have this?" Daniel gingerly fingered the thin paper.

"You never know what's going to make a difference."

He looked at her, his face a mixture of marvel and disbelief. "Thank you."

"Thank you for what?"

"For having breakfast with me, and coming out here."

"Likewise. We should do it again sometime."

"I could bring you dinner. You have a break sometime tonight, right?"

"Tonight would be great."

On the drive back to her car, Jane curled up in the passenger seat of the Prius, and texted Alma: *The dream of Daniel is real.* Mere moments later Alma texted back a series of exclamation points and emoji kisses. Jane looked at Daniel, his driving more relaxed than it had been before, his expression full of cautious hope when he snatched glances at her. It seemed impossible that the universe had conspired to bring them together again. And yet here he was, a man who had walked out of the past almost exactly as she had imagined him. *If only I'd gone back to meet him at the park that day,* she thought bitterly. Jane pushed the thought away. They were together now; nothing that had come before mattered.

CHAPTER 7

The *Libertines* trial was announced at 8 a.m. Eastern. By the time Jane's alarm went off at 4 p.m. Pacific, the media was consumed with it. Drivers stranded with Jane on the freeway killed the time by calling in to 'Share Your Five O'clock Drive with Clive' and speculating. Who was the defendant? Would the FBI catch the Vanguard in the act this time? As always, what people seemed most interested in was if it would be the last one, the one where the terrorists were finally unmasked, the great mystery of their identities solved. No one ever described the end of the Vanguard as an end to crime or terror. By this point, most of the people doing the talking tacitly agreed that the celebrities put on trial deserved it. If they disagreed with the Vanguard's methods, they kept it to themselves.

A new billboard had gone up at the hospital exit. A lonely woman watched over her sleeping angelic child. From the distance of Jane's perspective in the car, that woman could've been her; straight brown hair, white skin, late twenties or early thirties, except the woman had the body of a model, cardboard flat and rail thin, while Jane had baby bearing hips accentuating her double-wide ass, a troublesome double-wide chest, and less-troubling, but equally conspicuous, over-sized lips and eyes.

Traffic suddenly sped up and Jane reached her exit. She gave the billboard the finger as she took the ramp. The last thing she needed was a daily dose of motherhood guilt on her way to work. She narrowed her gaze as she narrowed her thoughts. She didn't care about the billboard. She didn't care about the trial. She focused on Daniel. He was bringing her dinner. It was going to be a good night.

Jane floated up to the nurse's station and wrapped her arms around the back of Alma's chair. "The dream of Daniel is real," she whispered.

"I'm happy for you," said Alma like she was the queen bitch in *Mean Girls.*

"What's wrong?"

"Nothing."

Jane wheeled her desk chair up beside Alma's and fixed her with a look until Alma finally broke her gaze from the computer screen.

"I have to tell you something really crazy."

"Go for it." Jane didn't pause to imagine what kind of secret could make Alma so tense. It didn't matter just as long as they got it out in the open and declawed it, then they'd be able to talk about Daniel.

"Remember that guy I met online last month? He liked asking me questions?"

"Too many questions, I thought."

Alma lowered her voice, glanced down the hall towards the East 7 nurse's station like she'd been zapped into a spy thriller. "He's in the Vanguard."

Jane scrambled through several expressions before she managed to find words. "That's not possible." She gained control of her face enough to laugh. "If he is, why would he tell you that? You could report him."

"We've been very honest with each other." Alma paused. "I think he loves me."

"But we went speed dating last week. Why didn't you say anything?"

"I knew you'd do what you're doing right now: looking at me like I've made another mistake. But I haven't. I did what you said I should. I gave him a test. He had to prove he was telling the truth before I told him my address. Yesterday, he told me there would be a trial."

A damp chill slid down Jane's shoulders. "So you gave him your address?"

"He's coming to visit."

Don't panic. It's just some weird guy. Alma's always finding the weird ones.

"What else have you told him?" asked Jane.

"Just regular stuff. What everyone talks about. We're watching *Far-scape* together."

"You've told him about me?"

"Kind of. I mean, he knows I have friends. We haven't really gotten that far—"

"You can't tell him about me."

Alma drew back. "Sure, okay. But you're my best friend. It will be hard not to at least mention your existence."

She's already told him about me.

"I'm sure he's great. I just . . ." Jane searched for words that sounded reasonable. "You know how I feel about the Internet."

"Yeah, I get it. But promise you'll meet him when he comes if he's not totally bonkers."

Jane stared at Alma's computer screen where she'd been scanning news coverage about the Vanguard trial. The words blurred and swirled together. It was impossible that this could have happened. And yet Jane had an overwhelming sense that yes, of course this had happened. It had only been a matter of time before they'd find her.

Alarms sounded from room six.

"Don't freak out, okay? I'll be right back."

Jane barely noticed as Alma rushed away. She sat like a statue. The world rotated around her. If she moved it would fracture into a million pieces and she would be left in darkness. She could feel the Vanguard lurking beyond her vision, the darkness of home and its accompanying duties—her husband, the Family, the Church.

The computer pinged a summons to Rhea's room. Jane took a deep breath. She seized a dry erase marker from the pen cup and determinedly set off to do her job.

The anticipation of Daniel's arrival carried Jane through her rounds. She smiled her biggest, warmest smile as she entered each patient's room. She ignored the televisions narrating unending gossip about the trial. She focused on best-case scenarios. Alma claimed she hadn't told her boyfriend about Jane. If the boyfriend was really in the Vanguard, he'd soon give up, move to a different nurse. Alma would be left heartbroken, but at least Jane would be there to comfort her. Probably he was just a weird dude of the kind that used and abused the hopes of innocent people online. Jane would make sure and ask Grace if she would keep an eye on Alma during the first meeting.

But if it is really the Vanguard, and she did talk about me . . .

By the time Jane had finished rounds, she'd funneled her shock into a more productive fury at her family for pretending to date nurses in order to find her. They had no shame, only rules. Those rules said she belonged to them, no matter what. When she returned to the station desk, Alma held out a jittery hand. "Look at me. I'm so nervous. I guess this is love, huh? It makes a hot mess of us all."

The idea that Alma believed herself in love with a member of the Vanguard disturbed Jane even more than the possibility that they had found her. She couldn't tell Alma that whoever had contacted her had ulterior motives, because revealing Jane's connection to the Vanguard meant not only revealing she was an accessory to criminal behavior, it meant the person she told would become an accomplice.

"Will you watch it with me?"

Jane looked at her friend, the woman she had watched struggle through three terrible relationships, a woman whose desire to be loved never failed to override any sense of self-preservation or obvious warning signs. Of course the Vanguard had found her. The world was a cruel, godless place that sought out and destroyed its most vulnerable people.

"We'll watch it," said Jane. "But if security comes by I'm totally throwing you under the bus."

Jane loaded the streaming window on her computer because the angle of the screen made it harder to see than Alma's screen if anyone happened to come around the corner from the west side of the floor. The *Libertines'* title credits played against a flag of red, white, and blue vertical bands emblazoned with the insignia of a sandal with a sword through it like a cross. Jane felt a small flutter of nostalgia seeing it. She could smell the canvas of the flag mingle with sterilizer and floor wax. She remembered her mother sewing that flag the summer before Jane started eighth grade. It had been left unfinished when her father had died, and her mother had sequestered herself in her room. Later, Jane had finished the flag herself, a fact she kept carefully inert in the back of her brain.

The camera shifted from the flag to the defendant sitting in a bare cinderblock room with two masked Vanguard soldiers standing on either side of her. Her feathered hair was caught up in a headband, so it rose up out of her skull and spilled over the crown like a fountain. The thick lines of black makeup around her eyes had smeared. She wore a glittery tube top that barely kept her breasts in. She'd lost one of her huge hoop earrings.

In every trial there were four soldiers on camera, plus one running the camera, and one managing the livestream, and a couple standing watch for intruders. Two of the soldiers on camera were white, one was black, and one was Asian. Two had blue eyes, two had brown. Three of them were in relatively good shape. The tallest one weighed the most. These were the personal details America knew. But Jane knew more.

Alma leaned toward the computer and pointed to the masked man standing to the left of the defendant. "That's him, Mirt."

"He seems nice." Jane couldn't think of anything less ridiculous to say. If the man Alma was dating was the real Mirt, then Alma was in love with Jane's youngest brother, Tommy and he was most certainly dating Alma in order to find Jane.

Jane's husband Seth, aka Bones, was the tall masked man on the defendant's right. Both Seth and Tommy looked nervous. Tommy tapped his fingers on the defendant's bare shoulder. Seth made fists along the seams of his pants. Someone out of frame bumped the camera so hard it fell over. For five full seconds the stream was steel-toed boots on dusty concrete. Jane exchanged looks with Alma. Something had the Vanguard spooked.

"They'll be fine," said Alma with determination. "Who are they doing this time?"

Jane opened the defendant's profile from a little box below the streaming window. "Annie Sunderland?" She was barely aware of speaking as she noticed Tommy's eyes skittering around. Seth began to read out the charges in a voice so wired with tension even the digital alteration used to disguise his identity couldn't conceal it. Their nervousness made Jane nervous. For a moment, she forgot they might be manipulating Alma to find her. She prayed that they would be safe.

Alma worried the black metallic orb of her tongue ring. Minutes ticked by like they were hours. Finally, she removed the ring and tucked it away in the cloth satchel where she'd already stored the rest of her contraband jewelry. "What's wrong, do you think?"

The pop-up window for audience voting appeared as Seth explained that a guilty verdict would only be pronounced if at least ten percent more of the audience voted guilty instead of innocent. A guilty vote meant there would be a branding. All guilty defendants were branded with the Vanguard sword and sandal insignia as a reminder that their fans had found them guilty of living a lifestyle that devalued life, a kind of modern Scarlet Letter.

"Do you want to vote?" asked Jane.

"You can if you want. I won't look."

Along the bottom of the window the votes tallied.

"Why is it taking so long? They need to get out. The FBI could be coming." Alma stood at Jane's shoulder, her fingers picking at the plastic netting of the chair. Out of three and a half million voters watching the trial, 2,740,325 voted the defendant guilty.

The trial moved to the disciplinary phase.

"I can't watch this part," said Alma. "You text me when it's over. Promise?"

Jane nodded. She didn't like the disciplinary phase either, but she always watched it. She'd been taught it was important. There had to be permanent consequences, or the trial would not fulfill its purpose, the news cycle would sweep the celebrity's shame away, they could continue their lives as usual. The brand forced them to remember.

Tommy held Sunderland by the shoulders so Seth could set the brand into the flesh of her chest just above the exposed tops of her breasts.

During the disciplinary part of a trial Jane always had to remind herself that Seth was a solider who lived his life by strict discipline and rigorous principles. It wasn't that he liked branding people. He'd trained himself to think of it as a necessary means to his end of helping America become a better place for families. She wondered if Alma had trouble justifying Tommy's participation in the branding. She wished they could talk about it.

Jane muted the stream so she wouldn't have to hear Sunderland scream when the brand seared her skin. With punishment, complete, the trial ended quickly. Annie Sunderland, the blood-red sword and sandal followed by GUILTY emblazoned across her chest, sobbed into the camera as she told her fans she would do better. The FBI did not rush in guns blazing. Jane texted Alma that everything was fine.

But Jane was not fine. She felt like a tightly wound spring ready to burst apart. Trials were the most tangible reminder of where she'd come from. Each one sliced small cuts into her carefully reconstructed life, tearing holes in her belief that she could pretend her connection to them didn't exist.

Jane texted Daniel to say she would meet him in the rec room. She had less than an hour before he would arrive. She hoped it would be enough time to re-center. She played the piano in the dark with her eyes closed. The uncurtained windows of the rec room looked east over the city into the inky blackness of the continent. Somewhere out there, Seth and Tommy and the rest of the Vanguard were packing up their gear and preparing to return home, hoping that they had done their work well and that Annie Sunderland had been set on her way to a better, more upright life. In all Jane's years living in LA, they had never felt so close.

CHAPTER 8

Daniel ducked down along the plane of his board. A sheet of frothing water hurtled over his head, enclosing him in a churning tunnel. He dug his hand into the face of the wave to slow down so he could stay in the barrel longer. He didn't need to worry about slowing down. The tunnel went on and on. He couldn't see the end. It was a perfect ride stretching to infinity, but there was something wrong. Someone was with him in the barrel. And there was this noise, not the rushing of a wave, but indistinct voices, advertising jingles. Something poked him in the ribs.

The wave disappeared. As Daniel returned to consciousness his sensations of the wave around him, of his muscles poised in a perfect coordination of balance and awareness, vanished. Instead, he felt the enclosure of his duvet, his extra-firm mattress tilting down on one side under Steve's weight. He had pulled Daniel's pillow out from under his head to use as a prop to cushion the headboard while he sat flipping between sports channels.

"What are you doing here?"

"Came to say hi."

"I'm sleeping."

"Not anymore." Steve grinned. "Do you always sleep fully dressed? Because seriously, the monk thing isn't going to make it with your nurse."

"What time is it?"

"Five. Or maybe it's six by now, I'm not sure."

"You're supposed to be at—"

"Finished early. Thought we could do dinner. The guys all went to some video game expo."

"I'm eating with Jane."

"You were with her all morning."

"You should be happy I'm moving fast."

"I get that you must be feeling it since you took her to a fucking surf comp and somehow survived without losing your shit, but there's a very compelling line of philosophy that says it's good to make a girl wait. If you're too available, you set yourself up for failure."

"Have you found a replacement for Garrett?"

"You and me are due for some bro time. I was thinking pizza, a couple movies. Or there's a Warriors game."

Something was very off. Daniel shook off the last dregs of sleep. He reached for his phone on the nightstand. It wasn't there. "Where's my phone?"

"You're fucking impossible sometimes, you know that? I'm trying to help you out, but no, you just have to know everything."

"You're right. I do. So tell me."

"There's a trial tonight."

Daniel leaned over and snatched the remote from Steve before he had time to react. Steve had been carefully skipping over the news channels and now, as Daniel punched the number, the screen was flooded with information about the Vanguard. A list of known facts was on the sidebar. The ticker ran with the headline: *Vanguard announces trial for 10 PM ET. Target unknown. FBI says they're pursuing several leads.*

"So your plan was for me to sit and eat pizza while someone was being tortured?"

"It's a better plan than you watching it. I'm sick and tired of you falling to fucking shit every time these bastards run their little show. Their power over you is fucking sick."

"You mean if I was you, I'd be over it, right? Steve and his kahunas don't take shit from anyone. It's just too bad the Vanguard grabbed the wrong Fletcher."

Steve flinched. His voice diminished as he said, almost pleading, "You don't have to watch it."

"This one will be different." Daniel leaned over the side of the bed and pulled on his prosthetic. "Jane's already helped me. I feel good. If I can make it through the whole trial, I might remember something useful."

"You're not going to figure anything out that the FBI doesn't already know."

"They haven't spent four days with the Vanguard like I have."

Daniel felt Steve rolling his eyes. They'd played out this conversation more times than either cared to admit. No matter how confident Daniel felt going into a trial, he'd never watched an entire *Libertines* episode without a seizure. He felt a warning twinge travel down his back. His water bottle was not on the nightstand.

"You took my water, too?"

Steve reluctantly handed over Daniel's phone, keys, and water bottle from where he'd stashed them behind the pillow. Daniel walked across the room and opened his closet door.

"What time is your date tonight?"

Daniel opened the water and took three gulping swallows while he surveyed his wardrobe. "Eight. She doesn't have a lot of time. I said I'd pick something up and bring it in."

"Is she . . . adventurous?"

"Come on, don't be like that. What's a good place?"

"I was thinking about food. You're the one who read into it."

"What about tacos? Those are easy. I could just—" Daniel lost the end of his thought as his vision went blurry. His head began to swim. "What the—" Steve jumped up and gently leaned him into the bed.

"You're okay buddy. Don't fight it."

"You dosed me. You—Jane."

"I'll take care of her. Don't worry. You'll thank me for this later."

Steve reached across the bed and snatched Daniel's pillow back from the headboard just in time to rest Daniel's head beneath it. He gingerly removed the prosthetic and set it beside the bed where it would be easy to reach. He removed Daniel's bottle of Klonopin—the drug he took at night to sleep—from his pocket and set it on the nightstand beside Daniel's phone.

"Don't go near her, you promised—Steve." Daniel couldn't fight off sleep any longer. The last he saw, Steve was walking out the door.

CHAPTER 9

Jane was just starting the last song in her Elton John book when there was a knock on the rec room door. She raked a hurried hand through her hair. She considered rushing to turn on the lights and open the door, but she had cried a little as she'd been playing and she thought maybe the darkness would be better, so she wouldn't have to explain. Besides, she thought maybe the dark would be romantic. They could sit and eat dinner while looking out on the city.

"Come in," she called.

The door swung open. He stood as a silhouette in the doorway. His shoulder to hip ratio formed a primordial triangle of perfection, with muscles straining against his T-shirt in all the right places, board shorts hanging from a lithe waist as securely as a towel after a shower. Steve appeared every bit the heroic god-figure Daniel described once upon a time in that other life when he and Jane had said goodbye in Battery Park and never seen each other again. In the dark, anyone could mistake one Fletcher for the other. She hurried to flip on the lights before her mind started playing tricks and conjuring the wrong brother.

Even illuminated, the resemblance unnerved her. The posture and aura were completely different, but any fleeting sidelong glance could easily draw confusion. Jane mapped her memories of Daniel from that morning and set them against Steve's features—the face shape, the strong jaw, eyes set back beneath dominant eyebrows—all eerily familiar and all the more potent because she wanted him to be Daniel.

"You're Steve Fletcher."

He grinned. "Why yes I am."

"You look so much like your brother."

This stopped him short of delivering his next line, a moment of surprise, then redirection, adjustment, finally a renewed grin. "You're Jane. You saved my mother's life." He closed the space between them, took her hand as though to shake it but instead closed his other hand around the top of hers. "She really likes you. I can see why." His eyes traveled over Jane's conspicuous body parts, skipping what she considered the better ones—her graceful neck and flat belly—in favor of her disproportionate curves.

"You're not supposed to visit after hours."

"That's one of my little secrets. I'll tell you more if you have dinner with me."

For a moment, Jane wondered how many women he had taken in this way, the double-handed handshake, a mechanism for moving closer, the warm smile still hinting at playfulness, drawing her into a secret joke, the facade of ready-made intimacy.

"I'm eating with Daniel."

"Yeah, about that, something came up and he couldn't make it. He sent me instead."

"I find that unlikely." Jane gathered her phone and her music book and walked towards the door, backing Steve into the hallway.

"Okay, he didn't exactly send me. But I was with him and he was having some issues, and I knew you guys had these plans, and I hate to see a pretty girl stood up, so I thought I'd fill in."

Jane edged past Steve and walked down the hallway, past the stares of the West 7 nurses who had heard that distinct baritone of Poseidon, god of the sea, and were waiting to confirm the impossible presence of a movie star on their floor. Jane turned the corner to the East side of the floor. At the East 7 desk Alma struggled to open a bottle of Advil while watching post-trial news coverage. As Jane approached, she looked up from her screen and saw Steve. "Oh frack."

Jane took refuge behind the desk. She texted Daniel. *Your brother is here. Where are you?*

Steve leaned on the desk. He tilted his head so his hair fell extravagantly forward bringing with it a waft of potent aftershave. "This is a great opportunity for us to get to know each other. Dan and I share everything."

"Mr. Fletcher, you can't be here right now."

Jane dialed Daniel's number. It rang through to voicemail.

"I could tell you all his secrets."

"I'd rather hear from him."

"He's missing half his leg. Did he tell you that?"

Jane trained her gaze on her phone. She knew Steve was trying to get a reaction. No matter how surprised she was she wouldn't satisfy him by showing it.

"Alma, call security."

"Security?" Steve laughed. "You mean Gary downstairs? He knows I'm here." His eyes dared her to play her next card and watch him beat it.

Alma leaned over and whispered in Jane's ear. "Just do whatever he wants. Daniel will forgive you."

"I'm only asking for your dinner break." Steve held his hands up, feigning innocence.

"I have twenty minutes."

"Then we should get going."

Jane shook her head. This was a bad idea, but acquiescence seemed the best way to get rid of him.

They walked down the hall side by side. Steve kept moving closer, Jane kept stepping away until she was nearly rubbing against the handrailing on the wall. She ignored the giddy waves of the West 7 nurses as she and Steve waited for the elevator. "Why isn't Daniel answering his phone?"

"He's asleep."

"Is that your fault?"

"Whatever he's said about me it's only half true." Steve looked down at her and grinned.

They boarded the elevator. Jane retreated to the far corner. This didn't feel far enough. Steve seemed to take up the space of three men, with every inch of the great big mass of him homed in on her, trying reveal what she was. Jane didn't know where to put her hands. Every posture she chose seemed to convey unease, which seemed to feed his ego.

Steve gave Gary the security guard a salute as they walked across the lobby. A wine-red Maserati was parked illegally in the circular drive. It was the nicest car Jane had ever been in. Even in the dark, she sensed its luxury. The way the seat gently hugged her body. The wood varnished dashboard, the electronic displays that looked like something out of science fiction. The Maserati had no center console. There was nothing between her and Steve except a slim middle seat. Jane took her keys with their mace cannister out of her purse and discreetly tucked them between her legs.

The engine roared when Steve turned the ignition, sending vibrations of life through the body of the car. The stereo also roared to life in the middle of a pop song that seemed to be stuck on a loop, the male voice, with augmentation making it sound like many voices, singing about being knocked down and getting up again over and over.

"You don't like Chumbawamba?" asked Steve with disbelief.

Chumbawamba is something you say to a child when trying to feed them, thought Jane.

"Dan said you were particular." Steve flicked the forward button on the CD player. "There's a lot of good stuff on here. This is my 90's throwback list. What do you like?" Another pop song started, which seemed to Jane just as repetitive and inane as the first. Next came the opening strings of the *Beauty and the Beast* love song, which reminded Jane of college.

"I know this one," she said, not quite sure why she felt the need to prove cultural acumen to Steve. "One of my college roommates was in this play for drama club."

"Don't think anyone would call it a play, but sure, I guess I could see that." Steve turned the stereo off. He seemed confused, like he was debating something. He gave her several sidelong glances before he said, "So, you're the Battery Park girl." He offered this knowledge with a sly grin that looked like it belonged to a more salacious statement opening a different kind of conversation. "I remember him talking about meeting you." Steve's grin became a conspiracy between them. "Honestly, I thought he was exaggerating, but now, I can totally see it. You're pretty hot for a nurse—in a natural way, I mean. You'd definitely get my vote for most beautiful woman without makeup."

He paused, probably waiting for Jane to appreciate his compliment. He frowned when he didn't get it. "How was the surfing in Montauk?" she asked.

"That's your question? Any other girl hears their boyfriend is missing half his leg, she jumps on that."

"He already told me."

"Bullshit."

"We were very open with each other this morning."

"How open?"

"You can't even imagine."

Steve swallowed. "Good, because I wouldn't want him to get hurt. There've been a lot of girls who've tried to get to me through him. We have a very strict screening process."

"And have I passed?"

Steve frowned. "For now."

"I'm so glad I meet with your approval."

He glanced at her like he couldn't tell if she was flirting, which was exactly the point. Jane would've enjoyed toying with him more if their meeting hadn't been as a result of Daniel's absence. Steve's arrival implied Daniel's interest was genuine. She drew confidence from this. But that still didn't explain why he hadn't contacted her, warned her at least.

He didn't seem like the type to spring his brother on her as some kind of test. She could explain the hinting of a prosthetic—most likely a surfing accident, maybe a shark attack, which also explained why he now avoided surf competitions—but his complete lack of communication made her the worst kind of insecure.

**Sunderland Trial Marks Terrorists'
Anniversary**
By Tate Matthews

The trial of beauty queen, Annie Sunderland, marks the 100th episode of *Libertines on Trial*, the web series in which a group of masked vigilantes put celebrities on trial for their 'sins.' The identities of these men remain as mysterious as they did ten years ago when their first broadcast invited us to see our pop culture in a different, if disturbed, light.

Despite being declared terrorists by the Department of Homeland Security, the popularity of the Vanguard's show trials continues to rise without any clear division along ideological or political lines. The staunch Christian conservative may donate funds through an anonymous website to support the Vanguard's mission. But the atheist liberal is just as likely to tune in live and vote a celebrity guilty or innocent as they would text their vote to American Idol. Christopher VanDenning, a sociologist at Berkley College attributes the enduring popularity of *Libertines on Trial* to its audience participation.

"Allowing people to vote as if they were a judge and jury in a real trial is an invitation even for those opposed to the idea that these celebrities have committed crimes. For example, we used to follow Miley Cyrus on Twitter and tweet at her, but now we have the possibility of actually changing her life. It takes away the question of should or shouldn't. There is some bias because the Vanguard doesn't target people they consider innocent, but when an audience sees their favorite star genuinely contrite about having an affair or promoting a product that isn't healthy, it also gives us the chance to forgive them."

More on this . . .

- Christopher VanDenning and the Vanguard effect.
- Ten years of *Libertines* in Screenshots
- Location, Location, Location: How the Vanguard choose their trial sites

This week, I will be posting a series of retrospectives looking back at some of the iconic Vanguard trials and how the vigilantes have changed America.

CHAPTER 10

Water; it was such a simple thing, most people never thought about it. But in its absence, water became everything. A few hours without it and every discomfort became a sideshow to the scratch at the back of Daniel's throat. It crawled up into his skull. The question of when he'd get his next drink became a demand, then a shout, and when enough time had slogged by with no answer, it became a plea, aided and abetted by one of the most commonly known medical absolutes: the human body could only survive a finite amount of time without water. Daniel had gone four days and six hours when the Vanguard held him.

Doctors believed he would've died if not for the drink he'd been given the first night of his captivity. The touch of the solider who had brought him water had been full of compassion, a hand pressed against his heart, assuring him everything would be fine. This one act robbed him of the pure unadulterated hatred that would've allowed him to objectify them as terrorists or religious wackos as other victims often did.

When he woke up from the nap Steve had imposed upon him, it was morning and he felt like he hadn't had water for days. He watched the news even though this was the worst possible activity. He had to know how the trial had gone. He took his regular meds plus half a Klonopin and an Ativan and limited himself to one bottle of water an hour so he wouldn't wash the drugs out of his system. He turned on his emergency monitoring system and slung the little monitor around his neck. His grandmother had had one, an eye in the sky monitoring her vitals, ready to call an ambulance if she fell, or had a heart attack, or if her pulse dipped too low. He was probably the only twenty-eight-year-old on the entire planet who owned such a device.

When it was announced that the victim, Annie Sunderland, would be making a statement later that morning he felt a rush of anticipation. Not all victims chose to speak publicly about their experience, but when they did, he devoured every detail and compared it to his own experience. He was the only Vanguard victim ever held more than twenty-four hours, the only one punished without a trial. While he waited for the press conference to start, he called Jane.

He decided to call even though he didn't have a good excuse for why he hadn't kept their date. He considered several possible explanations, but they all sounded like the lies they were. And yet, telling the truth, especially over the phone, unable to read her reactions, seemed impossible. The truth itself defied articulation. He had thought they'd have more time together before it came to this.

"Jane—hi."

"Good morning." She sounded cheerful, not at all upset that he'd stood her up.

"How was work?"

"Mostly good, we have one patient who may not make it. Machines are keeping him alive. I'm not sure how I feel about dragging it out, you know?"

Daniel wondered if she was hinting at something.

"Are you okay?" she asked. "Steve said you weren't feeling well."

"Did he." Daniel had thought his memory of Steve saying he'd take care of Jane and then walking out the door had been a particularly visceral nightmare produced by the Klonopin. He'd thought Steve's phobia of hospitals would keep him away from Jane.

Daniel paced the length of his apartment, unsteady on his feet but still unable to keep still. Jane was talking but Daniel couldn't listen. He reached for his car keys, quietly switched to his Bluetooth so he could put on his shoes. "So, the two of you got along?"

"He's a poor replacement for you." She laughed. "You can't say two words to the guy before bumping into his gigantic ego."

"It's a socially-conditioned ego. Most women like confident men so Steve acts confident."

"Is that an excuse to be a jerk?" She paused. "Sorry."

"Don't be."

"He seems very protective of you."

"What makes you think that?" Daniel muted the phone's speaker so he could get into his Prius and close the door without her hearing.

"I think he was testing me. Like he kept talking about your health and implying maybe you were hiding things that would scare me off."

Daniel pounded his fist into the steering wheel.

"You're right about your family only seeing life from a place of invincibility. The idea that someone could have a problem outside of their control terrifies them."

The Prius squealed out of the parking garage.

"Daniel? You still there?"

Daniel pried his right hand off the steering wheel and felt for his phone. He swerved up the freeway onramp going fifty, cut off two drivers, and bulleted down the 10 toward Malibu.

"I'm here," he said.

"It was fine. I mean, I was going to meet him eventually, right?"

Daniel swerved into the adjacent lane to pass a slow semi. He swerved back into his lane right in front of the semi. The driver laid on the horn.

"I'm off tonight. I'm having dinner with my neighbors but after that . . . if you're feeling better. Maybe we could do something? It doesn't have to be a big deal."

Daniel careened off the freeway and slammed on the brakes at a stoplight he couldn't ignore. He said, "Yeah, that would be great." But then he thought about it. The Vanguard was all over the news. The Ativan wasn't working as well as he needed. Half his mind was sending him bad signals, wondering when he'd get another drink, listening for approaching footsteps, trying to brace himself for the next blow. He wasn't supposed to be driving, but that didn't seem to matter. He punched the code at the gate to Steve's neighborhood and drummed his fingers on the steering wheel while he waited for it to roll open. There was silence on the other end of the line. She was waiting for him to say something. He struggled to remember what.

"Why don't I call you after dinner and we'll see how things are?"

"Yeah, that works."

There was space for him to say more, to explain, to express interest in seeing her. They were all beyond his reach, lost in the wandering darkness that lapped at the edge of his mind. There was only one clear thought, and it was about Steve.

"Okay, well I guess I should go to bed now."

"I'll talk to you later." Daniel ripped the Bluetooth off his ear and tossed it onto the passenger seat.

Steve and Riley's primary residence was a three-bedroom bungalow off a private beach. They'd recently begun teaching their daughter, Poppy, to surf despite Rhea's admonition that no child can learn to surf 'well' anywhere except Hawaii.

Daniel opened the front door without a sound, not that he had to be quiet in Steve's house, there was always someone yelling at someone else, or the television was on, or the stereo was on. He found them in the kitchen, a deceptively tranquil family scene. They'd just come in from the beach. Riley was making breakfast. Steve was on his phone, sitting like a gorilla on a breakfast bar stool beside Poppy. She saw him first.

"Uncle Dan, come see the dead fish we found at the beach!" She jumped off her stool and ran to her collection of buckets beside the patio door.

Riley sucked her cheeks in between her teeth when she saw him. Her eyes were two solid turquoise rocks. Steve often jokingly described her as the most dangerous woman he'd ever met. "Do me a favor and take your asshole brother down to the beach and drown him, will you? He forgot about the nanny's day off."

"I said I'd fix it," muttered Steve.

"What would you have done if I was still in Todos Santos? Left her here—Poppy don't make that face. Every growing girl loves Nutella."

"Nanny Mara makes my toast with peanut butter."

"Well, we're out of peanut butter." She turned to Daniel. "I hear you have a girlfriend who is very . . . what was the word you used?" She glared at Steve. "*Naturally* attractive."

"Like I give a fuck what she looks like. I was just trying to prove to you that he wasn't going for the bottom of the barrel."

"What'd you tell her, Steve?" Daniel edged in from the periphery of the kitchen. He spoke in a low tone that should've been a warning, but Steve still believed Riley with a steak knife covered in Nutella was his most threatening opponent. He gave Daniel an exasperated look.

"I just wanted to see if she'd cut and run. She didn't believe me anyway. Really, you should thank me. Now you know you're safe telling her. She's so into you I could've told her you were a serial killer and she wouldn't have blinked."

"Is someone in trouble?" asked Poppy. She had her bucket with her dead fish in hand, but Daniel wasn't paying attention.

"You said you'd leave her alone." His bad signals drew together and morphed into a living beast that ate fear and turned it into rage. Telling Jane about Daniel's problems was so typical, so god-complex Steve. He couldn't leave Daniel to his own life just this once.

Steve threw up his hands. "For fuck's sake, Dan, I'm saying you might've found the only woman who would go for a cripple even if he wasn't my brother. We should be fucking celebrating."

The beast swelled. It filled Daniel's abdominal core with energy he had no right to have given the drugs he was on. It coiled his muscles into coiled springs.

"You had no right."

The springs released. Daniel pushed off his good leg, used his prosthetic to pivot as he drove his fist forward and landed a right hook in Steve's cheek. He deserved more, but the sudden expulsion of energy left nothing in reserve. Daniel stumbled into the breakfast bar as Steve dodged a second, half-winded punch.

Daniel drew himself up, breathing heavily from the exertion. Poppy stood wide-eyed, with Nutella on the corners of her mouth. Riley looked concerned and then impressed and then concerned again. Steve retreated to one of the columns that divided the open space between the kitchen and the living room. "Feel better?" He smirked.

"You stay away from her."

Steve shrugged. "Whatever you say, brah. You're the man."

Daniel didn't remember driving home. The energy build-up and then its release, the surge in blood-flow, the drugs—everything was a haze. At his apartment, he cracked open a new water bottle and sat down to watch Annie Sunderland's press conference. It was like all the others. She'd been a captive for less than twelve hours. Except for the branding, she hadn't been hurt. Of course, she claimed all kinds of physical and psychological damage, but her wounds felt like part of a performance. *She doesn't know what real trauma is*, he thought.

Still, Daniel made notes of the details. Like him, she'd been picked up and drugged during a moment of public isolation. Her bodyguard had just gone to get her a protein shake while she'd waited in the car. Someone else had returned in his place. She'd woken up in a cement basement. Sunderland said she'd known immediately it was the Vanguard and not one of the many other groups that sent her hate mail. They were polite, controlled by duty like any other officers in a public proceeding. She said the only thing that had kept her from panic was knowing they wouldn't kill her. Daniel hadn't had that knowledge.

As always, he sifted through her words to decide what it had really been like for her. He wanted to answer the unanswerable question: why had he been different? He hadn't been famous. Even if the Vanguard believed they'd kidnapped Steve, they hadn't followed the standard protocol. What they'd done to Daniel had been personal.

He remembered only fractions of his kidnapping, the result of a head injury, doctors thought. Every time there was a trial, new fractures of memory seemed to reveal themselves, though his current counselor said it was more likely he was creating memories to explain the gaps than actually remembering. Today, Daniel remembered an indistinct voice yelling at him about a woman. Brutal, furious hands had held him down, while someone else had . . .

The foot he no longer had began to pulse. Numbness spread at the back of his head. Daniel knew he needed to quiet his thoughts, focus on something else so his nervous system could return to equilibrium, but the memory felt so close, so important. If he could just concentrate enough it would become clear. Fat fleshy hands had burned into him an incomprehensible hatred. It had been intimate, private, nothing like the sterile procedure of a typical Vanguard trial.

Daniel felt his nervous system shift into high alert. Two waves of Matrix-like glitches coursed through him. Daniel flipped back to his notes from the previous trial. Most trial targets were like Sunderland, shaken, ashamed, trying to regain lost dignity. With the Vanguard victims there was a hyper awareness of the public nature of the trial, dirty laundry aired, sins exposed. Their nightmares centered around embarrassment. Daniel's nightmares were the horror plays of grisly blood and splintered bone, of a madman's hands.

The madman had yelled about a woman. The only woman Daniel had known in New York was his *SLUT* costar. Not a likely connection to the Vanguard. But hadn't the voice had called him by Steve's name? Part of Daniel knew his mind could be projecting, but the memory was so clear, it had to be real.

It would make sense the Vanguard would yell at Steve about his women, the way his marriage failed to follow the conventions of conservative morality. This new memory seemed to confirm what Daniel had always believed: that he'd been mistaken as Steve. But that didn't explain why his experience felt like personal revenge rather than a trial.

The tremors came. Daniel barely noticed them. His attention was back on the television. Sunderland's tone had shifted. She had stopped playing the victim. She was describing a confrontation right before her trial started. She'd managed to get her hands free. She'd pulled off one of their masks.

This was what he'd been waiting for. Finally, a mistake had been made. Sunderland could identify a member of the Vanguard. When they were found, a tape of his trial would be found also. He'd finally know why they'd done what they'd done.

Such news should've brought relief, but Daniel was too far gone. The last thing he saw before his vision went black was the bobbing blonde mass of Annie Sunderland's hair as she gave the crowd of reporters a little beauty queen wave and retreated up the steps of her South Carolina plantation house.

AP BREAKING NEWS Bulletin:
Sunderland claims she can identify
Vanguard Terrorist

Friday October, 26th 7:45 P.M. EST.
Chapel Hill, North Carolina

At a press conference outside her
home in South Carolina, former Miss
America, Annie Sunderland, the most
recent victim of the Vanguard terrorists,
announced she had been able to remove
one of her captor's masks and see his face
prior to the beginning of her trial.

She described him as, "just a little
taller than me, Asian with a round nose
and a patch of acne on his right cheek."

Please report anyone matching this
description to the FBI's Los Angeles
bureau.

CHAPTER 11

CNN streamed on Jane's computer. Any minute she expected the breaking headline of her family's arrest. Maybe the FBI would come for her first, before there was any leak to the press. She'd be forced to confess she knew the Vanguard. She'd allowed crimes to be committed. Even if her lack of Internet presence and credit cards was enough to hide her from the Vanguard, she doubted it could hide her from the FBI.

She tried to decide which was worse, the possibility that Tommy, and probably Seth, were going to find her through Alma, or being arrested by the FBI. Both would push a future with Daniel back into an impossible dream world.

Alma called Jane just after Annie Sunderland's press conference. "Mirt was supposed to call me this morning and he didn't."

"That doesn't mean anything."

"What if they've gone into hiding and he's never able to talk to me again?"

"Then at least he'll be safe."

Jane sat in the corner of her living room beside the couch where the lamp usually stood. Wedged in between the couch and the wall, she could see her front door. She would also be able to see the shadow of anyone on her balcony.

"Is there any chance you haven't heard from him because he's on his way here?" Jane held her breath.

"So soon after a trial? No. I mean, maybe. That would mean he's prioritizing me, wouldn't it? Or wait, does it mean that maybe he's the one that messed up and let that woman get a look at one of his friends because he was distracted thinking about me?"

"You should go to bed."

"If he is caught, I would visit him in prison."

"I believe you. You should go to bed."

A huff of Alma's exhaling breath crackled over the phoneline. "I'm sorry I'm such a mess. Do you still have another date with Daniel tonight? Am I keeping you up?"

"I wasn't sleeping anyway."

Jane waited for Alma to ask why she hadn't been sleeping. A few moments of silence ticked by, the two of them in their respective homes watching the news, thinking private thoughts. "Hey Alma?"

"Hm?"

"You'd visit me in prison, right?"

"Of course I would. I love you more than any guy I've never met. Obviously."

"More than Ben Browder?" asked Jane.

"Maybe even more than Ben." Alma sighed. "Okay. I'm going to try and sleep. I'll call you before work."

Jane let her phone fall between her knees. Her body felt like it was being crushed beneath a ten-ton weight, but her mind was alert. The Vanguard had protocols for this kind of thing. It had never happened, but that didn't mean they weren't ready. Even if one solider was revealed, that didn't necessarily mean all of them could be discovered. It depended who was revealed. Every solider took special precautions with their public life. They didn't go out together. They didn't attend the same church. But if Seth or Tommy were identified they could be connected to each other through Jane. Fortunately, it was only Adam Sun that Sunderland had unmasked, a boy Jane remembered being jealous of when they were in high school because he'd been so good at the guitar. She wondered how long he'd been part of the Vanguard and who had recruited him; he didn't seem like a single-minded moral reformer type.

She fell asleep trying to imagine how Daniel would feel if he saw her face on the news that night. At five, she leapt from her restless slumber mistaking her phone chime for sirens. Shayla was texting to remind Jane about dinner. She combed her hair back in a half-hearted ponytail and changed from her scrubs to jeans and an oversized Henley that pulled tight across her chest but was baggy everywhere else.

In the hallway, a flickering light bulb in the stairwell had finally burned out, abandoning to darkness the six yards from Jane's door to Shayla's. For a moment, she was seized by the completely irrational belief that Seth had found her and was lurking ahead. Jane ducked back into the apartment and grabbed her keys with the mace. She darted down the hallway on her toes like a tourist on a strip of hot coals, dodging the burning edges and groping tendrils of flame until she slid up against Shayla's door.

Shayla and her mother, Colleen, had been Jane's neighbors for just over a year. Walking into the condo, Jane was immediately greeted by a crucifix and a painting of Jesus. On the adjacent wall hung a quilt, opposite which were shelves with miniature tea sets. Life burst off every surface as though the array of Colleen's interests, hobbies, and pleasures waited for the moment they could escape out the door and spill into the world. Jane's mother would've called Colleen 'worldly,' and meant it in the worst possible way.

Tonight, Colleen was not her usual vibrant self. She offered Jane only a thin smile. "I thought adolescence was the worst. No one said she'd be like this in her twenties." Over Colleen's shoulder Jane saw Shayla come down the hall from her bedroom and slouch into her chair at the table. "It's that boy," Colleen whispered. "He's dating someone new and not making a secret of it. Can you say something to her?"

Jane thought she was the last person to give advice to anyone, especially about love. But Colleen kept giving her looks. After dinner, she nudged Jane out of the kitchen while she turned on the news and set to work on the dishes. Jane watched Shayla slink down the hallway to her bedroom. The door remained open like she expected Jane to follow.

Members of a boyband smiled their white-toothed adolescence from posters on walls washed in the purple light of two naked black-lights. Shayla sat on her twin bed. She didn't even wait for Jane to close the door before she said, "I wish I'd done it with him. At least now I'd have that." Her purple glowing face blinked black-socket eyes with neon white eyeballs. The ceiling had glow-in-the-dark stars on it. Jane pictured her having sex in that bed, under those stars, in this room that looked like it belonged to a high school student. She wanted to cry without knowing why.

"If you had don't you think you'd regret it when you met someone new?"

"Someone new would be a completely different relationship. Separate."

"But you might compare them."

"Yeah, so?"

Jane wished she'd been as confident when she'd been Shayla's age. *I would've stayed with Daniel that day. We would've gone to Montauk. Everything would've been different.*

The idea that love didn't have to be constrained to one marriage or even one relationship would've been an incredibly dangerous suggestion where Jane came from, the beginning of an unraveling of the tightly knit fabric of belief. Following the rules hadn't worked out for Jane. She couldn't advocate Shayla follow the same system. But she couldn't argue for an alternative either. Threads of those old rules still bound her to her marriage and condemned the way she'd abandoned it.

If they're arrested, maybe I'll be free of it.

"I don't think I know what's right anymore," said Jane. After a moment, because Jane had Shayla's rapt attention, and because she looked more alive than she'd been all evening, Jane continued. "But I do know that humans are complex and messy, capable of tremendous beauty as well as tremendous horror . . . and that God didn't give us these hearts and these desires without cause."

Breathe, breathe, breathe.

"I don't know anything about the right kind of love. If it's what we've been taught, or if it's something else. But I hope—"

Colleen screamed from the kitchen. Jane jumped up from the bed, hands reaching for her mace.

Shayla yawned. "She does that when something on the news surprises her. Just wait, she'll come tell us."

A moment later, Colleen was at the door. "There's been a shootout in South Carolina. The Vanguard attacked that beauty pageant woman."

Shayla rolled her eyes and fell back onto her bed.

Jane pretended to pick food out of her teeth to hide the contortions skewing her face. "How many dead?"

"Two state troopers and Sunderland's security team. They're still counting the terrorists. They were hiding out in the woods around her estate. It's taking time to find all the bodies."

"I should get going," said Jane.

"Oh no, are you sick? Don't tell me the food was bad." Colleen looked pained, fragile.

"No, I'm just tired." She fought off Colleen insisting she walk Jane to her condo. She had to be alone. She had to think. Her insides churned like she was on the deck of a ship in a storm, her brain crashing around on waves of over-heated blood.

The Vanguard wouldn't kill someone, even a former defendant. They didn't carry guns. They wouldn't take life. They couldn't.

But what if . . .

I could call them. Just to see. If they answer . . .

It was protocol for all civilian cell phones to be off during a mission. This attack on Annie Sunderland wasn't their mission, therefore the phones would be on. Calling was a risk. But how long would she have to wait before the news reported what had really happened? By then

Jane would probably have torn herself out of her skin. She looked at her phone. No message from Alma.

Charging out of Colleen's condo into the dark hallway, Jane didn't register the shadow of a man sitting in the stairwell until he stood. Her arms flew up, elbows out, mace in hand. "Who's there?"

"Whoa, chill out, it's just me."

Steve was lucky he had such a distinct voice. Anyone else, Jane probably wouldn't have recognized before giving them a face full of phenacyl chloride.

"What are you doing here?" Jane bypassed him to reach her door, only to realize she couldn't get her key in the lock. The door seemed to be moving or her hand was moving. She couldn't tell which was to blame for them not lining up.

"I didn't mean to scare you."

"No, sitting in dark deserted hallways staking-out a woman's front door isn't scary at all."

He held out his hand for her keys. She wanted to shove him, push him down the stairs. But she also needed him. The darkness was coming up behind her. Somehow, she managed to loosen her fingers so Steve could commandeer her keys and unlock the door.

Jane punched her alarm code and gingerly stepped into the central kitchen/living room to check for signs of intrusion.

"What are you doing?"

"Checking for spiders."

"Oh-kay." He held up a six pack with two empty bottles. "Beer?"

She vaguely noticed that Steve had cleaned up since the previous night, washed his hair, exchanged the beach clothes for a slinky button down and extremely fitted slacks, a date night look.

"How did you find out where I live?"

"Dan puts everything important in his phone."

"And I suppose you're here to tell me he's not feeling well tonight."

"He's just running behind." Steve surveyed Jane's living room. "Did you just move in or something?"

She leaned her full weight against the door, deadbolt digging into her shoulder blade, phone in hand scrolling the headlines. Nothing had changed since she'd left Colleen and Shayla. "I need to make a phone call."

"That's cool."

Jane waited by the door, a hint. But Steve didn't give any indication of leaving. He flipped through her CD tower. She saw her living room as he saw it, the Goodwill couch, a single stool at the breakfast bar, a plastic storage crate as the coffee table. The Ikea lamp in the middle of the floor where she'd left it after taking over its corner by the couch. Nothing on the walls, no clutter to reveal her interests. Everything spare and cheap and functional. And then there was Steve, a glossy walking luxury item making everything around him appear monochrome. Either his broad shoulders or his massive ego seemed to fill the room, Jane couldn't tell which.

She went into the bedroom. Four years of covering her trail and her family was about to have her area code, which could give them a narrow enough population to search for active nursing licenses and find her address. *If they don't already have it.* Jane decided she'd call Aaron first. He was less likely to investigate a wrong number in the middle of the night.

The phone rang five times. Jane hung up. Was this her answer? The phone was on. Aaron wasn't on a mission. She dialed Tommy. Two rings, the line opened, silence.

Jane couldn't help herself. "Hello?"

Something crashed in the bathroom and made her drop the phone. She heard Steve swearing.

When Jane got the phone back up to her ear someone was breathing into the other end.

"Tommy?"

The line clicked off.

With buttery fingers Jane struggled to unclip the phone's battery pack. She punched out the SIM card and snapped it in half.

Breathe, breathe, breathe.

She found Steve in her bathroom examining the roots of his hair. Her PMS Advil, Q-tips, and the sampler vials of makeup Jane once picked up at a department store before determining makeup wasn't her thing, had fallen out of the vanity cabinet and lay in the sink. In the overexposed light of the vanity she noticed one side of his face was a different color. Makeup concealed a bruise he hadn't had the previous night.

"Two gray hairs." He sounded exasperated. "Can you believe that?"

"Someone your age usually has more."

"I couldn't find your tweezers."

"I don't have any."

"No way. How do you live without tweezers?" He wrapped the offending hairs around his finger and tugged them out. "Ready for beer?"

"When is Daniel coming?"

"Mom wants to make sure you come to her party."

"I'm working that night."

"Can't you skip?"

"It doesn't work like that."

He peered out at her from under the hoods of his eyebrows like she was some hellish creature sent to confound him. Jane smelled sex on him like a second aftershave. It wasn't so much the act of sex as his awareness of her as a woman, not attraction per se, just the possibility of someone.

"Well, we can still drink beer, right?"

"Fine, one beer." She thought maybe agreement would speed him on his way out the door. They moved into the living room. Steve was so big and Jane's condo's so small, mere inches of light showed between him and the walls and ceiling. He took a seat on the couch with his feet propped up on the rung of a stool dragged over from the breakfast bar. Jane powered up her laptop and turned on a CNN livestream. She settled herself sideways on the opposite end of the couch.

"Crazy what happened, huh?" Steve waved at the laptop.

Jane nodded. She wrapped and re-wrapped her pointer finger around the neck of her beer. The phone call had been stupid. She'd risked too much for nothing. Now, they knew she was in LA. She needed to start thinking about running. It was easier to focus on Steve's presence and Daniel's absence.

"Can I use your phone?"

Steve tossed his cell across the couch towards her. "He's not going to answer."

"Why isn't he going to answer?"

She saw Steve's last call to Daniel had been within the hour. It had gone unanswered. She dialed. Steve sipped his beer and watched the news.

Daniel's phone rang through to voicemail. Jane tossed Steve's cell back across the couch.

"So last night, I was a little aggressive. I said some things I shouldn't have. It's been a very stressful twenty-four hours for me."

Steve had no idea about stress.

"Dan's a really great—normal—he's a totally normal guy. I don't want you to get the wrong idea. This is just a bad time for him."

"You got in trouble, huh? He's the one who hit you."

Steve's hand went to his face. "You can see it? Fuck, I worked so hard to blend."

"It's fine."

"You should know that's the hardest he's ever hit me. He could've broken my jaw. That's how much he's into this."

"I'd have punched you too."

"Why? Don't you think I'm attractive?"

The way he said it, laboring to naturally slip this question into their conversation, Jane got the impression he'd been waiting for an opportunity to determine the source of her resistance to his charms. He looked so concerned that she started to laugh, and then choke, on her beer. It felt good to laugh, a little out of control. If it went a step further, she'd be crying instead.

"Oh, come on. Eighty-nine percent of women like you put me in their top three American actors."

"Women like me?"

"Single, thirty to forty-something's who aren't mothers."

"What is that, some target market demographic?"

"Exactly." He looked proud.

"I'm only twenty-nine."

"But you'll be thirty soon, won't you?" A sly grin slid across his face inviting her to just give in and admit he was right.

"November nineteenth." As soon as she said it Jane hated herself. It felt like ammunition he'd use against her later.

He sat up straighter. His chest puffed out. "So why do you look at me like I'm some Toby Maguire knock off?"

Jane went to the kitchen for another beer. Steve rushed ahead of her and blocked the fridge. She glared up at him. "Please move."

"You're avoiding."

A hitch was forming in Jane's neck as she tried to maintain eye contact. *You've picked the wrong night to mess with me.* She said this forcefully to herself because she needed some fortifying gumption, because standing this close to a man so imbued with awareness of his reproductive organs had her a little . . . ungrounded.

"Move."

"Let's go out. I'll show you what I'm talking about. Get dressed."

"This is me dressed."

Jane's unshaven legs in gym shorts that reduced the visibility of her butt, and the oversized Henley so worn out the bulges of her breasts remained in the fabric when she took it off, gave Steve pause.

"You don't need to do your, you know, face or hair or anything?"

"Nope."

"Huh." He tugged down one of the Henley's sleeves to expose her shoulder, adjusted her necklace so the pendant was centered. Jane determinedly ignored the riot of small explosions in her chest and pulled the Henley back up. She should be reminding him there was only one Fletcher she was interested in going out with. Instead, she fed off Steve's hesitation. She wanted to punish him for judging her appearance as inadequate. She wanted to punish him for Daniel's absence, for her family, for everything.

"Still want to go?" She was so sure he'd back off, she barely heard him when he asked if they should drive or walk.

The nearest bar was one of those semi-dives trying to cater to any possible patronage. There was a beach vibe in the front and a mahogany city vibe in the back. It was too far away from the beach to attract tourists; most of the patrons were neighborhood people—some Jane even recognized as fellow night dwellers who trudged off to bed when the sun came up.

The back room was crammed with twenty-somethings—a stag party on a bar crawl, a nervous first date couple, college students who'd come for happy hour specials and never left. A dance beat competed with shouted conversations and two television screens. Steve's frown over her appearance became much less a personal critique and more a wise foresight as she found herself jostled by guys in preppy layers and breezy synthetics and women in boob shirts, their hair ironed, faces painted beyond recognition. Jane had been raised by a man who had Sunday clothes, huntin' clothes, and jeans and T-shirts. And Alma, with her rotation of *Star Wars* graphic T's, wasn't the kind of friend likely to point out Jane's lack of fashion sense. She'd been waiting for her Henry Higgins to remold her.

What am I doing here?

"Drink?" Steve's eyes seemed to laugh at her discomfort.

Jane shrugged, then immediately regretted her ambivalence as Steve left her in the middle of the swirling crowd. She edged out of the flow of traffic, found a wall and kept her back against it. Commercials played on both televisions, a conspiracy to feed her anxiety. She found it amazing that all these people could go about their night like nothing had happened. Maybe they'd even seen the headlines and assumed murder was inevitable for a group of men willing to kidnap people. There were so many mass shootings at schools, maybe any kind of shooting had lost its shock value.

Turning her attention from the televisions, she focused on Steve working his way across the room. A distinct moment passed as Steve maneuvered up to the bar. It was the last moment Steve, and by association Jane, were anonymous. The bartender did a double take. He exchanged drinks for an autograph. Recognition spread outward from the epicenter that was Steve, first to the people sitting at the bar, then those nearest the bar, then the level of conversation vaulted whole decibels above the music and it seemed like every pair of eyes in the room followed him as he made his way back to Jane. "They all watching?"

Jane pointedly leaned sideways to see past the wall of his bicep. "Nope, not a soul."

"We'll give it another minute."

"What happens in another minute?"

"We meet people." His eyebrows arched into the wave of sun-streaked hair that fell to one side of his forehead.

"You do this often?"

"My wife and I used to do it all the time."

"She likes this kind of thing, huh?"

"What's not to like? As soon as I walk away you'll have every guy here offering to buy you a drink. All you'll have to do is pick. Ready?"

"I'd rather not."

"Three, two, one . . . have fun." And he was off, gliding into the cluster of waiting coeds, hips swaying, the orbs of his butt in those sculpted slacks clenching as he danced, moving from one girl to the next like he was trying them on for size.

Jane's drink went down fast. She had no idea what it was. Something too sweet. It had barely registered. Hormones, overstimulated perhaps for the first time in their mostly-dormant lives, buzzed through her bloodstream. One clear thought reached up out of the haze. She realized that as much as she had suppressed her sexuality, Steve had practiced bringing his out. *This is his job,* she thought.

What a thing it must be to have his career and his family's future dependent on whether women wanted to pretend he was seducing them. This thought somehow made Steve's behavior sympathetic. Jane shook herself. She wanted to think about Daniel. But thinking of Daniel only brought up troubling questions about where he was and why he hadn't called.

Two guys looked Jane over and started their approach. For a moment, their progress cleared a space through the bodies and Jane could see the televisions. One showed college football highlights, the other showed the news. An expert in a three-piece suit and academic glasses was being interviewed by the anchor.

"I'm Ryan." The first guy blocked her view of the television. "Are you an actress?"

Jane moved to the left but the second guy and a cocktail table blocked her in. She was too far away to read the headlines scrolling along the bottom of the TV screen.

"But you're here with Steve Fletcher, right?" asked Ryan.

The other guy didn't bother using words. He came in from behind and snaked his arms around Jane's waist. He shoved his junk at the seat of her shorts. Halfway across the room Steve did the same thing to a girl who didn't look old enough to be in a bar. Jane wished there was a way to draw his attention so he would witness what she did to men who did what he was doing.

The reflexes she'd trained in her self-defense class came to life and worked their magic with very little effort. Jane waited for the guy to get good and cozy and then she pounced. Elbow to his solar plexus, heel hard to his toes, elbow to his groin. He dropped to the floor clutching his parts. His bovine eyes rolled back in his head. For the briefest moment, Jane felt she had restored order to her universe at the expense of this half-drunk idiot.

Ryan, the only apparent witness to her fit of violence, vamoosed to the bar for some liquid courage, or to hide from her. Hiding seemed a wise course of action. Jane slunk along the wall down the hallway and into the more casual beachy front half of the bar where four guys in trucker hats watched ESPN and nursed draft domestics.

The western wall of the beach bar was inset with a garage door pulled up to give access to the smokers' patio. Oversized ceiling fans struggled to stir the sultry evening heat. Sitting on the picnic table with only a string of patchy party lanterns for company, Jane had a perfect view of the news broadcast and no one interested in bothering her.

The headline scroll ran through its cycle three times before her breathing returned to normal. Eight dead gunmen but no familiar faces. Jane sat up straight, suddenly lighter. The Vanguard hadn't killed anyone. The talking heads continued blaming them, but they'd changed their tune. They claimed the terrorists were inspiring grass roots movements, paramilitary copycats. Like everything else, the heads spoke as though no one was safe. *Arm yourselves*, they said with their eyes. The crazies were out there.

Their fear-mongering abruptly ended when they received notice of a new Vanguard video posted online.

"No," breathed Jane.

"Ladies and gentlemen," the male talking head groped for breath, "we are bringing this to you at the same time we are seeing it. Please be aware it may not be appropriate for children."

Jane was vaguely aware of Steve drifting in from the back half of the bar followed by an under-aged woman doing a drunken jig step while trying to update her lip gloss. Jane hoped he was leaving. If she was lucky, he wouldn't even stop to say goodbye.

On the TV, two blue eyes gazed into the camera as though they could see her. *Seth.* Those sad sack eyes, they looked tired, uncertain. In an instant, despite everything, Jane's heart went out to him.

"The Vanguard of the Lord's army wish to thank their supporters in Chapel Hill for the sacrifice they made tonight in response to the perceived threat to our mission. However, we do not support their actions. Murder works against the very principles that we seek to defend. All life is valuable and a gift from God. We would gladly be arrested rather than facilitate the loss of a life . . ."

Steve plopped down on the picnic table beside Jane. "You escaped."

"Shush."

". . . this act illustrates how desperately the people of this country believe a change must be made. Those who do not wish their country to be swallowed up by the false idols of the liberal left—"

"A bunch of sadist wackos I could knock out in five seconds," muttered Steve.

"Shut up."

". . . they have taken away our choice to define beauty in the eye of the beholder. They have deprived us of the right to one true faith, and one true marriage, and given us instead a morality fit for inebriate animals who live by instinct, rolling in the dirt, eating refuse, and copulating without regard for consequences—"

"That's just gross," said Steve.

Seth's voice rose; his clenched fist entered the shot, but those sad eyes prevented him from looking fierce. For a minute Jane imagined he even looked scared. "Tonight, those who doubted now know there is a war in America. They must also recognize that there are consequences for our sin. The Vanguard of the Lord's Army are not the only ones who want to see justice done."

"I'd like to get my hands on one of them," said Steve. "See how tough they are then."

Jane wondered who had written the script. Aaron maybe. Seth would not have been able to organize his thoughts after such a disaster. Seeing him, knowing how his mind must be a mess as he tried to understand what had happened, Jane felt the old temptation towards the familiar, to play her role as helpmate, an unquestioning column support.

She caught Steve watching her out of the corner of his eye, sly like a high school boy waiting to make a move. "In case you care, I fixed things with Craig," he said.

"Who?"

"That guy you attacked. I want you to know I respect tough women."

Jane nodded towards the girl waiting for him by the door. "You should go."

"You sure?"

"Yep."

"What about Dan?"

Jane blinked back hot threatening tears. "What about him? He's clearly not going to call. I can take a hint."

For a moment, the softening of Steve's expression made him seem almost human, like he knew how she felt. "Come on," he said, "let's go."

"I'll walk back alone, thanks."

"I mean, let's go for a drive."

"I'm not interested."

"I'll take you to him. Come on."

"Steve, I'm too tired to play your games. Please just leave."

"No games. Promise." He offered her a hand down from the picnic table.

She glared at it. But then she imagined the rest of the night ahead, alone in her condo unable to shake the feeling that someone or something was about to invade. If Steve could take her to Daniel at least she'd have an answer. She could look him in the face and see he didn't want her.

On the way out of the bar, Steve stopped to give the waiting girl a kiss. He promised to call her. She gave Jane the finger.

Steve's Maserati smelled like lemongrass and stale semen. Jane pulled her knees up to her chest, rested her chin on them and stared out the windshield only half aware of where they were going. When Steve stopped at a gas station to buy a bottle of whisky, she thought about getting out and walking away but even that small task felt like it would take too much energy.

They drove to a private clinic in Beverly Hills, a pristine white building with manicured grounds and a gated entrance with a security guard.

"Evening Mr. Fletcher," said the guard. "I'll phone up to the desk and let them know you're back." Steve pulled through the gate and crawled the Maserati up the drive.

"I almost applied to work at one of these places when I moved here," murmured Jane. "But I decided I didn't want to deal with entitled rich people."

"We're not all bad, you know."

"I'm sure."

"This place is pretty safe, but we still have to be careful. If anyone asks, you're our cousin."

"Why?"

"Because you never know who's going to talk. Believe me, you don't want to wake up tomorrow with paparazzi staking out your stairwell demanding to know how long you've been dating Dan."

"My address isn't listed, they can't—"

"Just trust me, will you?"

"Fine. Whatever you say. I don't even know what we're doing here."

"We're visiting Dan."

Visiting. Like he's a patient.

Steve tucked his brown paper bag with the whisky under his arm. "Showtime."

Inside, Steve guided her past the front desk, up to the second floor, past another desk where he saluted a nurse who gave him a look of melting adoration. They stopped outside the closed door of room 210.

"This is not on me, you understand? You wanted to do this, I'm just helping you out."

"What am I going to find here?"

"You're smart. You'll get it. I'm uh, gonna go find some cups. It's not quite a 'drink from the bottle' night."

Jane remained at the door as Steve walked down the hall. He stopped to chat with the nurse. Jane saw him lean on the station counter exactly the same way he'd leaned on hers. *Yesterday. That was just yesterday he came to the hospital.* She reached out and touched the door handle. She told herself that what Steve thought was such a big deal probably wouldn't be so big to her. She told herself that whatever was behind the door, it would be okay. She could make it work. She was an expert at making the impossible work.

The starched white plain of the bed somehow gave the impression of Daniel shrinking, not taking up the space in the bed Jane's memory said he should. Maybe it was the way he laid, like a corpse, one stiff line from head to foot held by a tension that defied the sedative ID drip. Most people spread to fill the bed, let their hips fall open, their knees separate. The Daniel Jane remembered wouldn't be asleep in the first place. He'd be sitting up, alert, more fully alive than any person she'd ever met.

She made her way through the features she recognized. Long eyelashes that made him look like a boy as he slept, wavy brown hair blending well with a summer tan, those lips. He was beautiful, and elegant, and healthy and had no reason to be in a hospital bed.

His hand lay rigid on the bedding just inches from where she stood. She slowly crept her hand forward. It closed over the white tributaries of the thin blanket. Her fingers bumped into his and cupped the ridge of his knuckles in her palm. She allowed herself these few minutes of feeling him as a person before he became a patient.

Slowly, mechanically, Jane went through her intake checklist. She checked his pulse. She noted the limited number of monitors, the IV. She began to check for injuries, starting at his shoulders and working her way down, lightly feeling his form but keeping the sheet between them like a protective sheath that would somehow prevent him from feeling her inspection.

The closer she got to his legs the slower she worked. She knew she wasn't looking for a new injury. Steve often came to this clinic. Whatever had happened, it was routine. She moved to the foot of the bed where Daniel's heels hung over the edge. She set one of her hands on the shape of each of his feet. The left one was flesh. The right one was just the shape of a foot.

She told herself it was okay. She'd already known, hadn't she, that there had to be some truth in what Steve said? She'd already decided there must've been a surfing accident. It all made sense, nothing to worry about. Daniel had wanted to know her a little better before he told her, which was fine.

But none of what she'd decided to be true explained why he was in the hospital now, sedated. Whatever had happened he either hadn't wanted to tell her ahead of time or it had happened too quickly for him to give an excuse.

Jane pulled back the corner of the sheet and traced the prosthetic up to its top. It had come loose from the stub of Daniel's knee. She wondered why the staff hadn't set it aside. Surely, he would be more comfortable in bed without it. The stub was a neat surgical amputation. And there, on the inner thigh, was something Jane had never seen in person: lines of puckered skin in the faded outline of the Vanguard sword and sandal and the letters Y and T. Daniel's boxers obscured the rest of the word.

Jane dropped the blanket, but the falling white curtain couldn't erase what she'd seen. Her knees buckled. She collapsed beside the bed heaving silent breathless sobs at the marble tiled floor.

Steve found her sometime later, kneeling, with her hands clinging to the bedrail, her forehead pressed against it. "You're not helping anyone down there. Come on. I found food." He entered the room in two fast strides, pulled her up and guided her out as quickly as he'd come in.

They sat on the floor behind an empty nurses' station where Steve had set up an impromptu camp. His phone and wallet lay on the floor beside the half empty bottle of whisky. He gently guided her to the floor and then he sat, his legs splayed in a wide V for balance. He dug into a greasy take out bag and produced a taco.

"I didn't know what kind . . . I think this one's black bean and this is chicken and this—fuck, they didn't give me the queso I wanted."

"How did it happen?" Jane felt her voice rise up out of her like it belonged to someone else. It cracked along her dry throat and moved her aching jaw against her will.

Steve stared at the back of a desk chair draped with a cardigan sweater littered with black hairs. "I hate when Dan does this. These attacks, they're just fucking ridiculous. He should be over it by now."

Jane knitted her fingers together as fortification against the impulse to strangle the words out of him. Perhaps he sensed this. He became serious, narrowed his eyes like was going to try very hard to focus.

"That day you met in New York didn't end up being a great day. I found his phone on his skateboard two blocks from the set. The police found him four days later in the exact same spot. A bunch of thugs had dragged him off, some kind of overblown mugging. They almost—"

"I saw the brand."

Steve reached for his bottle. "So maybe it wasn't quite a mugging. But that's what we decided to tell the family."

Jane clutched at the beads around her throat, pressed them into her collarbone.

"Want a drink? No? Fine." Steve took a long pull of the bottle. His arm fell to his side as though exhausted. "I went exclusive with my wife after it happened, no more open marriage thing. Fuck. I wanted to make it work. I owed that to Dan. But it's like this . . . it's like a disease. Every new movie, every show, photo shoot, the red light at an intersection, there are women, and they want me. It's the only thing I've ever been good at."

Jane had no idea what he was talking about. She wanted to scream at him, but she couldn't. He had this look on his face, complete bewilderment, as though encountering something he couldn't conquer wiped him blank.

"I'm just a face, you know. No one will ever give me a real dramatic role. Gio Corito is never gonna call me up and say, come be in my movie. Wanna know how I got my first gig? I worked the gas station off Sunset Beach. Filled a jet ski for an exec on vacation. His next project was a kind of teen romantic *Lord of the Flies* on a tropical island. *LOST* was a big deal then, so everyone wanted a tropical island project. He asks if I'd mind taking off my shirt. Then he asks if I'd like to be in a movie. BAM! Just like that I became the Tab Hunter of the Millennials. Hey, you keep pulling on that necklace you're gonna break it."

The necklace felt like it was burning through her skin, but she couldn't get it off. The clasp had rusted shut years ago. Wire cutters would be needed.

"How can there be a brand?" Jane spoke more to herself than to Steve. "There wasn't a trial. Taking Daniel was a mistake."

"I think it was some jerkoffs imitating the terrorists. You know, like sabotaging them?"

"They wanted you."

Steve reached for his bottle. "There's no proof of that."

"I need to go home."

"You're going to leave me here, alone?"

"You can call a ride for yourself the same as I can." Jane struggled to get to her feet.

"You don't want a taco first?" Steve looked plaintive, almost childlike.

Jane used the desk to steady herself the first few steps as she walked down the hall. She tried to smile at the nurse. "I need a taxi but I don't have my phone with me."

"We have a service for that. Is your destination within fifteen miles?"

Jane nodded.

"Someone will be waiting for you at the front entrance."

"Thanks."

Jane followed the trickling sound of the fountain in the main floor lobby and found the stairs. She was just about to start down them when Steve caught up to her.

"You're going to see him again, right?"

She edged her foot down the first stair and shifted her weight.

"I need to know if this is like a dealbreaker or whatever."

"Why would you need to know that?"

"I want him to be happy, obviously. And you're great together. I mean, you can't judge him on this. It doesn't happen very often. It's just with all the terrorist stuff going on right now . . . He *is* really normal. Not at all like me. You obviously hate me, so . . ."

"Daniel and I will talk when he's ready."

"That's not an answer."

They'd reached the bottom of the stairs. The fountain warbled in a circle of potted mums, all white, all perfect, like they were fed by the fountain of youth. Jane swallowed back tears. It was a beautiful fountain; probably done by a local artist whose work she'd have recognized if she'd ever found a way to learn about art in the city. Now it was too late.

"You need to put a number in your phone for him." She held out her hand. "Or I'll do it. You're too drunk."

He handed it to her.

"My phone is broken. He'll need to call me at this number."

"Come on, work with me. He'll think I sabotaged him."

"Goodnight, Steve."

She dragged herself across the lobby and out the sliding doors to the waiting sedan. A uniformed driver opened the back door for her. For the twenty-minute drive she managed to hold herself together. She climbed the five flights of stairs up to her condo. She unlocked her door and didn't bother checking for spiders.

In her bedroom, she pulled her emergency duffle bag out from under her bed and found her burner phone. She plugged it into its charger and cradled it in her palm. She wanted to call Seth. She wanted to tell him she knew what he'd done and that she'd never forgive him. Instead, she went to her computer in the kitchen and started the album of soundtrack highlights she'd compiled from Daniel's list.

Tears came with the music, the kind of crying that came before conscious thought, as though her body already knew and was responding to something her brain hadn't accepted yet: the brand on Daniel's leg made any future with him impossible. Her family had ruined his life. She could not go forward with their relationship lying to him, and she could not expect him to forgive the truth.

Mr. Fuzzy Black, the spider Daniel had promised to help her evict, slid his legs under the bedroom door, probably to investigate the noise. Next came his black as black fuzzy body. He skittered a few feet into the living room. Normally Jane would've leapt to high ground looking for the nearest Raid can. Instead she dug her butt into the carpet, pitched her broken phone at him and screamed.

"Leave me alone!"

Magically he took the hint and made a beeline for the front door, pushing past the rubber guard strip like it wasn't even there and sliding outside into freedom.

CHAPTER 12

NEW YORK CITY, EIGHT YEARS AGO

Dinner with Aaron began quietly. There were no opening pleasantries, no put-on expressions of familial sentiment. It was not the Schaben way to say the obvious. Aaron, as the eldest, particularly adhered to their parents' stern reservation when it came to affection. Actions expressed love, words did not. The fact that he had flown from Nebraska to New York to discuss Jane's decision to switch from nursing to music was his love in action. It probably never occurred to him that Jane might find a few words comforting.

Seeing Aaron brought her back to the good parts of home, the safety of a community of people who had the same values, who genuinely cared and listened to each other's problems. People who would've been saddened by the sight of a dorm bathroom covered in puke on Sunday mornings. People who knew they were created for more. The tricky part was Aaron had a strong belief that Jane was created to be a nurse. She couldn't let her guard down and talk about things she cared about: rock and roll, whether Joey would end up with Dawson, her blossoming addiction to crossword puzzles.

"I'm glad you came. It makes it feel like it's really happening." Jane put on a bit of extra excitement, selling music school to him the way she'd learned to sell a certain degree of enthusiasm to her roommates when trying on clothes, talking about TV, shoes, and the trendy young adult novel they were all reading.

"Tell me again, why music?" Aaron checked his watch.

"I'm good at it."

"That's vanity, Jane." He stopped eating to fix her with his instructive face. Unlike the other Schaben kids who tended to be big-boned and rounded like their mother, Aaron had inherited Pastor Schaben's gaunt chain-smoker's body minus the nicotine addiction. His wrists were smaller than Jane's. The restaurant's mood lighting accentuated the recesses under his cheeks. They were eating at a Korean place. Aaron didn't know how to use chopsticks. Jane didn't either, but she was making an attempt because it felt inappropriate not to.

Aaron instructed her with his fork. "You could be even better at nursing if you set your mind to it."

"I could play for churches," said Jane even though she didn't want to play for churches.

"You can do that now and still become a nurse." He checked his watch again.

Jane fought to mask her irritation. "Are you doing something else tonight?"

"We're picking someone up."

Aaron hadn't come to New York because he was worried about her career plans. He'd probably bought his plane ticket months before Jane had had the courage tell him about school. Unable to eat, she stared at him while he carried on, looking ridiculous trying to fork noodles, the slippery strings sliding off the tines as he tried to wind them like spaghetti.

Something about his eating, the insistence on using a lesser utensil while being surrounded by diners all using chopsticks, made Jane want to shout at him, *Don't you care that you don't know how to be like everyone else?* Instead she channeled that same tone, minus the shouting, and said, "This is important to me."

The fork wearily came to rest on the table. "Jane . . ." He said it the way their father had said it when Jane had been in trouble as a child. "God wants to use what He's given you for His glory."

"I don't want to be a nurse."

A text message beeped on Aaron's phone. "Hurry up and finish," he said as he signaled for the waiter to bring the check. Jane rushed to cram bulgogi into her mouth, but Aaron was already rising, impatient. He handed the waiter three twenties on his way to the door. Jane scrambled to catch up and then struggled to keep pace as he walked with urgent strides to the subway. The clattering chaos of Manhattan revving up for the night was an asteroid field through which Aaron impatiently maneuvered, sidestepping the little lives that impeded his holy mission. Even having to wait thirty seconds on the subway platform seemed to be a terrible inconvenience to his plans.

"I *am* moving to Boston at the end of the semester," said Jane.

"God knows your heart. He'll guide you in His time." Aaron put his arm around her shoulders and kissed the top of her head. "You'll always have a home to come to when you realize you've lost your way."

She was about to insist that music school was where she belonged when she realized Aaron was going through the motions. If their conversation had been about Jane joining a prostitution ring he still would have kissed her and reminded her of home. His mind was on his men pulling their target off the street, sedating them, and driving to the site where the trial would be held.

The subway made its way uptown. Jane stared out the window and fought back tears. She knew what she wanted but she hated feeling like what she wanted was wrong, or worse, insignificant.

For a moment Aaron drew himself out of his thoughts enough to remember her. "Seth is here. He says he'll be home for good by the end of the summer."

Jane tried to laugh but she felt a twinge of betrayal, as though Aaron unconsciously threatened a choice: nursing or Seth. *He chose the army over me. We're done.* The voice in her head was vehement, but when she spoke Jane sounded anxious.

"How is Seth?" Jane held her breath as she waited for Aaron's reply. *Seth doesn't matter*, she told herself. On Monday, she was going to meet Daniel in Battery Park. He would teach her a different way to live. She would finally leave home, and Seth, behind.

"He's worried about you. Everyone is."

Jane wanted to tell Aaron there was no need to worry. But every reason she had to justify this claim involved pursuits he didn't believe in, so she stayed quiet.

They exited the subway in a residential neighborhood lined with trees trimmed by iron fencing and doormen in sharp black suits. Aaron jogged up a few steps to a grey brick house and unlocked the door as though he lived there.

Vanguard trials were usually filmed in the basements or soundproof attics of longtime supporters' private homes. This house belonged to a newspaper editor. His wife had left a gift basket in the entryway while they vacationed in the Hamptons. Jane pictured them sitting on a patio looking out at the ocean pretending not to worry that they'd see their home on the evening news setting the stage for a police standoff.

Inside, unholy shadows lurked in the corners of dark echoing rooms. Heavy curtains had been drawn, all lights off except the dome over the oven in the kitchen. Phil, the tech specialist sat at the table, the fingers of his right hand posed over his laptop keyboard while he spoke into a radio in his left, keeping in touch with the two guys stationed outside on lookout. Tommy and Jamal, one of Aaron's army buddies, sat tossing their masks back and forth, feeding coffee to their jittery nervous systems.

During their weekly phone calls since Jane had been away at school, Tommy had talked about his new role as Vanguard soldier-in-training. Jane knew he'd been on a few missions but it was jarring to see him sitting with these men who had always seemed like adults to Jane, who had been trained as soldiers or police officers, while Tommy had always been with Jane, children on the outside looking in.

"Hey look, it's Rachel," said Tommy. He kept his nonchalant slouch in his chair even though it was clear he wanted to bound over to her like an overjoyed puppy. "Tired of your fancy school yet?"

Yes.

Jane was surprised by how powerful her relief was at seeing him, remembering how good it had felt to belong. It was easy to forget what had driven her away. Here, among the sleek black marble and stainless steel, with a china cabinet lit up by its own spotlight prominent through the dining room doorway, Jane saw these familiar men differently than she did at home. They knew nothing about the cultural values that curated the house, the price tag of the china collection, the framed art on the walls, and yet they occupied the kitchen with confidence, unimpressed by its display of wealth. They had a higher purpose. They believed it was more than right for the editor to grant them his home. Their daring filled Jane's chest with pride.

Seth came in behind her and tried to be casual as he stationed himself beside Phil, looking over his shoulder at the laptop. Jane hadn't spoken to him since Christmas break when he'd been on leave from his first deployment and had brought her the necklace she now wanted to saw off her neck. She'd expected him to apologize for enlisting. Instead their conversation had devolved into a yelling match with mostly Jane yelling.

"Were there any problems?" Aaron joined Seth and Phil at the laptop. An inset window showed the feed from the camera monitoring the defendant in the basement, blindfolded, gagged, and bound at his hands and feet according to procedure. Except this man's hands were tied in front rather than back with two extra zip ties binding the ankles to the wrists, which bent his knees against his chest making it impossible for him to stand.

"He didn't see it coming," reported Tommy, smug with accomplishment.

Seth began, "He woke up early but we—"

Tommy jumped in, "He got Bones pinned to the wall. Three seconds flat."

Seth glared at Tommy. "Won't happen again." He glanced toward Jane, appeared to consider saying something, didn't.

"Who are you doing tonight?" Jane moved for a better view of the screen and had to work quickly to keep her face neutral. The trial target wore board shorts, Manhattan's most unlikely fashion item. His sandals lay discarded in the upper corner of the screen.

"Steve Fletcher," Phil read from a Word document, "adultery, outright disregard for the sanctity of marriage. He thinks all women should love him while he leaves his wife and daughter alone at home. Two DUI's, three citations for reckless driving."

Tommy followed Jane's line of sight to the computer. His eyes flicked up to hers, watching too closely. They were all watching, like they could read her thoughts. Jane's hands flailed, trying to find the back of Phil's chair for support. "Did you check his wallet?"

"We know what we're doing," said Jamal.

"I know it's just . . . my roommate was talking about the—those guys—there's two brothers. I guess they look a lot alike."

Seth looked to Aaron. Silent communication Jane couldn't interpret passed between them. "Go get the wallet," said Aaron.

Seth jogged out of the room. A door slammed. She heard the rumble of feet on the stairs. Seth appeared on the video feed, muscling the target onto his side and checking his pockets. Tommy made space for Jane as she sank into his chair, her face burning. She felt embarrassed in a complicated junior high way. She loved her family, but did they really have to show their colors like this to her potential boyfriend? How would she explain this to him on Monday?

Seth stomped up the basement steps, came down the hall to the kitchen and slapped the wallet open on the table. "*Daniel* Fletcher." He jabbed his finger at Tommy. "You said it was him."

"It looks like him."

"Both of you, quiet!" Phil got up and peeked behind the curtain out the kitchen window.

"He didn't see your faces, right? We're good." Jamal was the only one still smiling, thinking this was an easy fix.

"We could still do it." Tommy looked guilty. "A proxy trial. We say the real criminal was too much of a wimp to stand up under the weight of his sins."

Jane prayed no one heard the sharp intake of her breath as she bit back an instinctual protest. Seth ignored Tommy in favor of more silent communication with Aaron. They deliberated. And deliberated. Phil paced. Jamal tossed his mask between his hands.

Jane couldn't sit still. It was as though the walls of the house were spying on her, a trespasser. She wondered how long Daniel had been sitting in the basement with no idea what was going on, feeling the groping darkness latch its snaking fingers around his limbs. Jane wanted to make him feel safe, even if it was just for a few minutes, while Aaron decided how best to release him.

"I'd like to take him some water."

In slow motion they each turned her way, Aaron bemused, Phil worried, and Tommy incredulous as only a teenager trying to stake his claim among men could be. Maybe it was the creepy house that made Jane imagine Seth's blue irises turned black, seeing betrayal in her simple request.

"He doesn't deserve anything more than other targets." Tommy crossed his arms, crushing the excess blubber of his chest into breasts that folded over his wrists.

Jane focused on Aaron because he was the one who would make the ultimate decision. She knew he would remain caul when Jane admitted, "I met this man at the park today. I'd like to help him."

For a moment no one said anything. It wasn't quite what she'd expected, this silence. If Jane had been less nervous, she might've realized they already knew about the park. Later, she would remember Tommy had been there watching her.

Phil cleared his throat. "Does he know your name?"

"We just talked . . ."

Seth spoke to Aaron as though they were the only ones in the room. "She should go home."

Under the table, Tommy grabbed Jane's hand and held onto it. Sweat ran down his arm and slicked their fingers. "Don't go down there," he whispered.

Aaron studied the video feed. "Be careful, Rachel. No names." He said Jane's name with emphasis as though to impress upon her the need for secrecy. It felt like a line being drawn in the sand, as though she had to choose between Jane the civilian and Rachel, sister of the Vanguard.

Jane found a glass and ran the tap. She felt them waiting for her to leave so they could talk freely. Whatever would be said in her absence was only a vague worry compared with the pressure of Daniel alone downstairs, blindfolded, unable to move. She couldn't imagine anything worse for him than an outside force impinging on his physical freedom. The image of him leaping like a jungle cat off the ferry dock urged her through clumsy actions, steps she couldn't help but take even as the guilt tore through her. There would be consequences for this, but they didn't feel real compared with reaching Daniel. She would accept whatever came.

The basement was one of those old foundations no one had bothered to replace when the modern house was built on top of it. Modern grey cinder block gave way to red brick with crumbling mortar, a layer of plaster peeling away. Shards of it littered the floor where the carpet had been pulled back from moist moldy walls. A perfect place for spiders, but this was before Jane had learned to fear them.

Daniel heard her coming. He planted his bound feet against the floor, tensing as though ready to spring. Jane put a hand on his shoulder, gentle, unthreatening. She knelt beside him. His breathing dialed up a notch. She felt anticipation radiating off him, a wild scavenging fear that left no vulnerability concealed.

In this moment, the secret of her identity and, through her, the Vanguard identities, meant nothing compared to the possibility of relieving Daniel from the hours of waiting for some undefined evil to find him in the darkness. She felt his heart rocketing against the barrier of his rib cage. She counted his pulse, not because it was important, but because it was what she'd been trained to do. She untied the rope of old socks used as a gag and held the cup to his lips.

He drank at the same rate as his heart, which throbbed beneath her hand. "What do you want?" he asked.

Jane wanted to promise nothing worse would happen. She wanted to apologize for Tommy and his failure to check the driver's license. But if she spoke, she would reveal herself as the girl from Battery Park. She couldn't betray her family while they watched from the video screen on the floor above. A sinking sensation in her gut said she would never truly be without them.

"You're going to kill me, aren't you?" Daniel's chest began heaving. The heaving gained speed until the motion took over his whole body.

Jane closed her eyes and prayed for Daniel to feel calm. Soon he'd go back to his life. She would go back to hers. They'd remember each other sometimes, enjoy imagining what could have been without the trouble of what really was. For the first time Jane felt what would later become a commonplace sting of bitterness towards her family and the culture that set her apart from other people. As her last goodbye, she pressed her palm into Daniel's chest and willed some kind of cosmic peace to pass into him.

The Vanguard had formed a line of confrontation to meet her as Jane came up from the basement. Only Seth remained behind them sitting at the kitchen table.

Tommy took the lead. "What were you doing in the park with that guy?" A lightning flash of fury glinted in the semi-darkness and marked shadows across Tommy's face. Jane had never seen him so angry.

"We were just—"

"He knows who we are, doesn't he?" Jamal shouldered past Phil to get up in Jane's face.

"He doesn't know anything. We're just friends." This admission was also a mistake. Jane wasn't supposed to be friends with people like Daniel. Aaron looked mournful over this new evidence of Jane's floundering.

"He's one of them," said Tommy.

"He's not anything like his brother." Jane scrambled for explanations that wouldn't make her look even more guilty. "We just talked." And then, desperate to remove their accusing expressions, she burst out, "I'm sorry. I know it was wrong."

Seth rose from the table and stepped through the line of his fellow soldiers as though making a theatrical entrance on cue. He positioned himself between Jane and Aaron. "It's okay, Rachel. Everyone makes mistakes. You had us surprised, is all." Seth put his arm around Jane's shoulder. "Mirt and I will drop him off at the park tonight and that will be that, okay? Just don't talk to him again."

Jane fell into him as hot tears of relief coursed down her cheeks. He put his arms around her, a completely enveloping full frontal hug, not the one-armed side hugs they'd always used. She smelled the Irish Spring soap he showered with, and for a moment, all she wanted to do was go home.

She thanked each one of the other soldiers for being understanding of her trespass and promised she wouldn't do it again, even though the 'it' of what she'd done remained indistinct. The potential consequences if she hadn't admitted a wrongdoing were equally unclear. Jane knew only the sweet haze of relief. Daniel would be fine. She'd lost a future with him, but she'd been delusional to want it in the first place. When she didn't show up at the park on Monday, he would forget her, and forget this night.

Seth escorted her downtown all the way to the door of her dorm suite. Before he said goodbye, he went down on one knee and apologized for leaving her to join the army. It was an embarrassing display. He cried, said he'd been miserable without her, asked if she'd give him another chance. He talked about how worried he'd been for her at NYU, how she must be so lonely. For the first time in their relationship, it felt like he really knew her. He even used some of the same phrases Jane had been using to express her frustration to Tommy during the semester. Without Daniel as her hope for a life in the secular world, and with Seth so real and present drawing her back to the safe and familiar, Jane didn't have the energy to say no.

They wrote emails through the rest of the semester. In May, Jane moved home for the summer, planning to move to Boston in August. In June, Seth asked her to marry him. He allowed her time to think about it. In that time both he and Tommy embarked on a campaign to convince her not to leave again. Seth reminded her of how miserable she'd been in New York, how Boston wouldn't be any better. He picked away at her ambitions. Why did she need a degree in music? What would she do with it when she was done? Did she really want to take steps that would lead her further away from home? From him? But it was Tommy with his nagging, his pouting about how he couldn't stand to have her living across the country again, that pushed Jane into accepting Seth's proposal.

Once she'd made the concession, she stood by it like a martyr. She chastised herself for the way she'd sometimes thought of Seth as a loser completely out of touch with reality. She convinced herself that another breakup would leave her wallowing in even more guilt than she'd felt the first time. She convinced herself that holding out for some Prince Charming like Daniel was a fantasy that hurt her chances of happiness. She knew how to work with Seth. If she held onto a dream of someone outside of her community, how did she know it would even work? She forced herself to believe Seth would make a good partner. It was exhausting work but eventually Jane settled with her choice. They married two weeks before her twenty-first birthday. Three years later she left for Colorado driving their minivan, 18 weeks pregnant.

CHAPTER 13

It took all of Jane's energy to drag herself to work. She'd barely slept. She hadn't eaten. Steve had sent her several texts pestering her for an answer she couldn't give him, but there had been no contact from Daniel. She tried to appreciate this for the fact that it gave her time to plan what she would say to him. The more time that passed the more time her brain had to convince her that she could still have Daniel if only she became a very good liar and keep her secret from him forever. It wasn't a very good plan, but it was all she had.

"What's wrong with your phone?" Alma's face was puffy and splotched, her voice void of energy, her big black mass of hair even wilder than usual.

"Died on me." Jane handed her the burner. "I couldn't download the numbers."

Alma entered her phone number into the burner. "I needed you last night."

"I know. I'm sorry. Have you heard from him?"

"Yeah, I—We talked this morning."

Jane was staring blankly at the charge board. She missed the significance of Alma's hesitation, her expression pleading with Jane to ask more, to show that she was listening.

"What were you doing last night? I came by, you weren't home."

"I was out with Steve."

"Steve . . . Fletcher?"

"It was nothing. He and Daniel have this competitive—I don't know what exactly. It's weird. I'm not sure Daniel and I are going to work out." Jane drew a deep breath. "I'm going to do rounds, okay?"

"Hang on. You were out with Steve Fletcher while I was freaking out thinking my boyfriend was dead?"

"The Vanguard don't kill people, Alma. I'm sorry I wasn't there for you, but if you were really a fan you would know that."

Jane didn't hear Alma say, "You're wrong about them," as she walked away, the ground not quite solid beneath her feet, vaguely aware she was being a bitch.

There were not enough patients to keep Jane away from the desk for as long as she needed, so she worked as slowly as possible. The car accident victim in bed six slept off the anesthesia from his kidney transplant. His face looked like it had finally begun to heal. There was less bruising. Jane set up a fresh bag of IV meds and paused to listen to the humming of the machines. They sang a little chorus of life-giving harmony, all operating at different frequencies, almost like they were singing to her.

From the caddy at the foot of the bed Jane filled her hands with gauze and swabs and pump bottles to clean his burned feet. Confronting the festering red blisters, all she could think about was Daniel and the trauma that must have been inflicted on his right leg to make saving it impossible. She wished the Vanguard had been the ones killed while attacking Annie Sunderland instead of those other people. And then she was glad they hadn't been killed because that kind of death was too easy for them.

They all lied to me that night. They were lying to me every day after that.

The machines soothed her. She remembered that she was a good nurse. Even if it wasn't what she wanted, she would always have that. She whispered quiet words of reassurance to her patient's brutalized body. She asked him if he wondered how he had come to this place, this less than pristine condition of himself, and if he had a plan for recovery. The machines answered her. There was always a way.

She saved Rhea's room for last knowing it would be the most difficult. Pausing behind the privacy curtain, she listened for visitors. Rhea was on the phone with her husband, the conversation a playful flirtation full of innuendo, and what sounded like a debate about the best kinds of boats.

"Have to go, my savior is here," said Rhea when Jane revealed herself. "Catch some good ones for me."

Jane frowned her disapproval when she saw Rhea sitting in the recliner beside the bed. "You need to elevate that leg."

"So I've been told." Rhea pushed herself up and hobbled over to the bed. "But one can only sit in this bed for so many hours a day. Once I'm home, I promise I will do everything I'm supposed to, scout's honor." Her smirk looked remarkably like Steve's. "I'll even eat my vegetables."

"You better." Jane tried to sound playful, but it seemed like everything she said came out sounding like a threat.

"I'm expecting you at my welcome home bash tomorrow night. I want to show you off."

"I'll be here tomorrow."

"Shame."

"I guess this is goodbye then."

"Is it?" Rhea frowned. "Did I miss something?"

"Goodbye for now, I mean."

"Don't let my son scare you off. He's an expert at self-sabotage. We know you're right for him. Don't forget that."

Jane turned the words over in her head as she made a hasty retreat so Rhea wouldn't see her cry. *We know you're right for him.* Her confidence made Jane feel even worse.

After her shift, Jane drove home and went straight to bed. She slept through both alarms, three texts from Steve, and a phone call from Alma saying they had to talk. Something—a nightmare or imagined movement outside her bedroom door—startled Jane awake twenty minutes before her shift started. She didn't rush.

First, she stopped at Taco Bell for lunch, then she drove through Starbucks for what turned out to be a poorly blended Frappuccino. She jabbed at the ice chunks as she drove. Drivers honked their horns and passed her, furious for no apparent reason. There was that billboard again, the woman who looked like Jane, gazing at her perfect, sleeping child. She made Jane want to throw things. She cultivated fantasies of objects flying end over end through the air, splatting, thudding, crashing.

At the gas station off the hospital exit, she stopped and bought three fistfuls of little bottles of Wild Turkey whisky. The gas station guy asked if she wouldn't rather just buy a pint. Jane laughed in his face. "A pint? A pint! I'm going to work, you moron."

He gave her a look; she felt the need to clarify.

"I'm not going to drink at work, but I *need* these . . . for later."

The gas station attendant's right hand moved beneath the counter like he was reaching for the alarm.

"Don't you hate that billboard? Someone should complain. That's not how it is you know, being a parent."

The guy pretended he didn't know what she was talking about.

Jane drove the rest of the way to the hospital with the bottles in her lap, one hand keeping them in place, one hand steering. One or two accidentally found their way into her purse as she parked. Jane patted the knobs of their bottoms poking against the canvas as she walked across the parking garage. One never knew when some low-life or the gas station guy could break into your car and Jane didn't want all her little bottles to disappear without her.

Alma waited at the elevator. "Where the frack have you been?" Her hair was a tangled mass amplifying every movement of her head. "I've been calling you." A rush of tears flooded her eyes. She choked on a sob.

"I'm here now, relax." Jane sensed a nervous anticipation in the air, a conspiring of the universe. It occurred to her that only men had the power to make Alma this upset.

"I've done something terrible. You have to help me make it right."

"That's what I'm here for. But, like, I think we're late for work; Doraceli's going to be pissed." Jane sipped her frappe of sweet processed sugar goodness and wondered what made a Frappuccino a Frappuccino. Which was better, almond or soy lattes? Was the buzz around this flat white thing really deserving? These were questions her family never asked. *Daniel probably knows about coffee,* she thought.

"The morning after South Carolina, I talked to him."

"Yesterday."

"Yes, yesterday. He told me . . ." Another sob disrupted the end of Alma's sentence. "When we talk, he's really vocal about how the Vanguard needs to change because people aren't getting the message . . . the culture isn't reforming fast enough. And I've been agreeing with him. It seemed harmless, just venting. But Jane—he had them killed."

Jane's frappe drinking picked up speed. "I bet your guy is just pretending to be one of them."

"I talked to him again this morning and I don't think . . . I think he was dating me because he was interested in me."

Jane sucked down so much frappe she gave herself a brain freeze. The fact that the sun had risen bright and beautiful was beginning to feel like a cruel joke.

"He's interested in you. Jane—I'm so sorry. I know you have problems with your ex, and you want to stay under the radar, but I had no idea who Mirt was when I told him about you. I can't tell you how stupid I feel. Don't hate me, okay? I have a plan. I was awake all day thinking about it, and I'm sure it will work. You and I can go to the FBI."

Jane's frappie straw jabbed into the roof of her mouth as she misjudged its position relative to her lips. The residual momentum bent the straw so forcefully it crunched through the flimsy plastic lid.

"We'll set a trap so when your husband comes to find you, he'll be arrested. If the Vanguard are really going the way Mirt says they are, we, have a responsibility to make sure something like South Carolina can't happen again."

Jane turned her back on Alma and scanned the parking garage. In movies and TV shows, bad things happened in parking garages. Seth could be there, right now, watching them, waiting for the opportune moment.

Jane wanted to argue with Alma about Tommy having something to do with South Carolina. It felt easier than confronting the fact that the secret was out; her life was about to change. And she was so tired of defending what she thought she knew about her family.

When Jane turned back to Alma, she was holding up her phone. On the screen was a family picture from Jane's wedding. She almost didn't recognize herself as the smiling young woman in a veil enveloped by the arms of a grizzly bear of a man in a tux. They looked so happy together. Tommy stood at Jane's other side, edging into the frame with an anxious expression like he worried he'd be left behind.

"The FBI can catch them if you give them the names of the guys they're looking for. You know them." An iron determination filled Alma's voice. "Help me stop them."

Jane shook her head. "That isn't me." She brushed past Alma and punched the elevator button.

"He told me about your daughter," said Alma. "Leah."

The name sent pinpricks up Jane's spine.

"Your husband wants to see her. Unless you've got a kid stashed away somewhere that I don't know about, I think that means you're in trouble."

A sharp pain spasmed across Jane's gut. She sensed Alma edging closer. "I know you're good at secrets, Jane. You've obviously got reasons for some of them, but this one you should've shared. No woman can bear the loss of a child alone."

It would've been so easy for Jane to turn and bury her head in Alma's shoulder, wait for the tears to seed her confession. But she couldn't allow that much of a concession to the truth. The elevator chimed its arrival. "I'll see you upstairs."

Jane pushed the button for every floor between the Ground and the 7th. She needed to think. Alma had told Tommy she knew Jane. Tommy knew where to find Jane. He would tell Seth. Seth would come. Maybe he was already on his way. She pulled her brain back to her filmy first days in LA and found the Amtrak schedule she had memorized. A train left for Vancouver at ten the next morning. That was option one. Option two, wait and see what happened; maybe going back to Seth wasn't such a bad idea. Part of her thought maybe it'd be easier to just give up and be his wife. Option three, go with Alma to the FBI and pray they'd allow her to be an anonymous witness. She'd get her family arrested so they could never find her again. She'd live out her life as a good nurse.

None of these options got her what she wanted.

Doraceli's usual sour expression devolved into a smirk when she saw Jane, who had been riding the elevator and drinking wild turkey for almost ten minutes before she arrived on her floor. Her feet felt like lead. Alma had not come up from the garage.

"Not on your A game today, huh?"

"I'm here, aren't I?"

"So you are." Doraceli handed over the shift log. "Bed six is still alive. Order came down from the doctor to speed up the drip on IV. His vitals weren't so great today. And Rhea Fletcher was released."

Alma came down the corridor from the elevator with a put-on smile. She'd dried her eyes and fixed her makeup.

"You two have fun," Doraceli signed off. "I'll make sure and be super late tomorrow morning, so you know how it feels."

And then they were alone.

Alma's hair was a tent hiding her neck and shoulders like an ancient Egyptian headdress. Her eyes beamed into Jane with supernatural power. They were the eyes of Isis, goddess of downtrodden women, slaves, and the poor. Jane's idea of Isis had come from a date with a grad student in archeology who had not wanted to go into archeology, so maybe she was some other kind of goddess. For a moment, this question was a blissful distraction Jane could hide in.

"Jane, listen to me. I know they're your family," whispered Alma, "but people are getting hurt. We need to stop them."

"If that's how you feel, go for it."

"Jane, please."

"You want to punish Mirt for not being interested in you. That's your thing not mine."

"He's your brother."

Jane glared at her. And then, as she felt the glaze of her anger splintering into something more dangerous, Jane escaped from the desk to mix the new IV bag for bed six. Doraceli had written the proportions in big letters in the log. Jane had read them. But now she couldn't remember, and she didn't want to go back to the desk to check. It was two parts to one, Jane was pretty sure.

Bed six and his humming machines were the same as she'd left them the night before. She replaced the IV bag and allowed herself a moment to absorb the stillness. She wanted to enjoy it while it lasted. Once her patient was awake and knew the long road to recovery that lay before him, peace would be a distant memory for both of them. Maybe she wouldn't be around for his recovery. None of the options Jane had considered in the elevator involved remaining in LA as a practicing nurse who worked alongside her best friend.

She needed to say something to Alma. The poor woman's heart was broken and Jane had cut herself off from any expression of support. She'd suspected Tommy had ulterior motives and said nothing. There wasn't anything she could say now that would fix any of the three hundred million new cracks in their relationship.

Maybe there was one thing.

Jane set aside the gauze she was about to use on her patient's burns and walked back to the desk. She walked slowly. Time seemed slower than usual. Nothing and everything felt important. She saw Alma running toward her.

"I was thinking about your idea—"

"What are you doing?" Alma called as she ran by. "Don't you hear the alarms in six?"

It took more energy than it should have for Jane to turn herself around and follow Alma. "Caution, this woman makes wide turns," whispered Jane. She found this incredibly funny.

"He's going into shock," cried Alma to the West 7 nurses as they rushed into room six just ahead of Jane.

The machines' chorus no longer hummed in harmony. They'd erupted in staccato screams. Alma rushed from one display to another, from machine to patient, and back. Jane stood against the wall out of the way. She wondered if maybe she could help. But there seemed more than enough people already involved. And here came the doctor, also not in a rush, coffee in hand. Jane's brain had turned into a soggy gray mush that might or might not be leaking out her ears. She couldn't feel them.

"He's dead," said the doctor.

Alma's Isis eyes turned on Jane, no sympathy, only accusation. Jane felt the need to throw something. She marked a target in the middle of Alma's forehead only to find her hands empty.

"Was this fatality expected?" asked the doctor.

"Yes," said Jane. "No," said Alma. The West 7 nurses looked at each other and silently edged past Jane and out of the room. Jane rushed to clarify. "Not exactly expected, but he was barely hanging on."

"He was fine," said Alma.

"That's not what Doraceli said."

"I'll get his chart and we'll see." Alma brushed past Jane.

Jane followed her. "You think this is my fault, don't you?"

"You're the expert."

"Stop walking and look at me." Jane grabbed at Alma's arm and missed.

"What did you put in that IV when you changed it?"

"Exactly what it should have been."

"What was it?"

This was a test, Jane could tell. "Don't you know?"

"I'm asking you."

Jane guessed. "Three parts to one part."

"You killed him."

"Did I say three parts to one? I meant one and one."

They'd arrived at the desk. Alma pulled out her tablet and synched it with the computer records.

"It was an accident."

Alma ignored her.

Jane looked around for some way to get Alma's attention. Her phone sat beside the computer. The phone with Jane's wedding picture on it.

The weight of it felt solid in her hands, a little unwieldy. She wound up and pitched it in Alma's direction a little harder than she should have. It covered the four feet between them in slow motion, graceful, not as dangerous as Jane felt. The corner of the phone connected with the side of Alma's head. She fell back, startled. She tripped over the wheels of her chair, tried to grab the back and stop her momentum but grabbed her track jacket instead. It slipped. Her head connected with the edge of the desk on its way to the floor.

For a moment Jane felt an alarming, almost blinding sense of triumph. She'd won. She would survive another day. She picked up Alma's phone and slid it into her pocket. Aaron had taught her to always put away her tools after she used them. The triumphant feeling faded. Jane fell to her knees and cradled Alma's head in her lap.

"I'm sorry. I'm sorry. Alma? Can you hear me?"

Alma's head shifted from side to side. Her eyes fluttered open then closed. "You can't let them control you," she whispered.

Jane sensed movement at her back and jerked her head around. The doctor had followed them from room six. *How long has she been there?* The doctor was staring at Jane like she was some sort of demon who threw cell phones. "What happened?"

"She slipped." Jane moved her hands like she was helping Alma up.

"Stay here," the doctor said, but nervously, which meant if Jane could summon the willpower, she could escape. It was easier to sit. While waiting for security Jane considered the irony bound up with the fact that Tommy had been the one who had taught her to throw. If Alma had been more conscious, maybe Jane would've admitted this, the closest thing to a confession she could muster.

Ten minutes later Gary, the night watchman, gave Jane orders to clean out her locker and leave the campus pending what would likely be a two-week suspension leading up to at least one review board interview. The on-call doctor had tried to convince Alma to file assault charges with the city police as well, and for Gary to arrest her so she couldn't escape in the meantime, but neither of them had been up to a fight with teeth in it. There was irony here also, in the doctor's dramatic insistence, which neither Alma nor Gary took seriously, and the fact that Jane was in fact plotting escape.

Because no one had searched her, Jane still had her remaining bottles of Wild Turkey. She also still had Alma's phone. She carried them out to the garage with the rest of her belongings and sat in her Jeep scrolling through Alma's pictures. Alma and her cat. Alma and her cat. Alma at ComicCon dressed in a *Star Trek* jumpsuit. Jane and Alma at a church retreat the previous summer. Jane and Alma, Jane and Alma. And then there was Jane and Seth in their wedding costumes. Alma had several more than she'd showed Jane—which really begged the question of what Tommy had been thinking. Almost ten pictures of Jane and he was only in two. In one they stood together dressed for homeschool prom looking more like a couple than siblings—not something a guy normally sent his out of town girlfriend. The other was a family photo—Jane's brother Amos and his wife and their kids, her mother flanked by Aaron and Tommy, with Jane and Seth beside them. Jane hated how she looked like she belonged, how she had pretended so well and for so long that sometimes she'd forgotten it was pretend. She deleted every picture.

Nine hours until the train left for Toronto. She needed to say goodbye to Daniel. Even if he wasn't ready to talk to her yet, he was surely out of the clinic by now. She needed closure. She texted Steve. *Finished work early. Party still on?*

Steve replied in less than three seconds. *Waiting on you.*

Jane started up the Jeep and stomped on the gas. A party would be just the thing to distract her from the magnificent train wreck that had become her life. Her last hurrah in Los Angeles. It was fitting that it would end with Daniel and his family since he was the one she had come to Los Angeles to find. While she was thinking this, Jane was supposed to be backing up. Imagine her surprise when stomping on the gas propelled her forward instead of backward and she plowed into a cement support column. The engine sputtered, smoked and then died a slow ticking death. Unfazed, she texted Steve again. *Off work, need a ride, hosp parking garage, SAVE ME.*

Jane waited five minutes, ten, twenty. No reply. She considered trying Daniel. *Maybe he needs me to initiate?* Instead, she cracked open a whisky and wondered how many bottles it would take before she felt something she wanted to feel.

Forty minutes and three Wild Turkeys later, Steve's Maserati roared into the garage. Jane offered him his own bottle of Wild Turkey and slid into the passenger seat. He didn't need to say anything. The smile Jane gave him let him think he'd won her over and that this drive was a prelude to the final stage of his conquest. He seemed a little nervous that she would be so open, that Daniel could be dismissed so easily.

The whisky burned through her nerves. Leather seats had never felt so warm. The new lemon and pine air freshener was a little too strong, so Jane rolled down the window. The wind in her hair was like ten expert hands at a top-of-the-line salon massaging her scalp.

She decided there was nothing, absolutely nothing, more romantic than driving out of the city along the coast at night. This was why people lived in California. It wasn't the beaches or the movie stars or Silicon Valley or endless days of uninterrupted smoggy sunshine. It was the way the night felt as it came across the continent, bringing an entire country's worth of daily lives to conclusion before it drove off with the sunset. Night saved the best for last, tucking them in like a favorite youngest child.

CHAPTER 14

The ocean remembered him.

It used to be, on clear nights like this one Daniel would be out there, a silhouette of negative space bobbing among the wave-washed stars, the moon keeping watch as he flew through the darkness. Now Daniel also watched. Together he and the moon marked the passing of the tides.

Steve had bought their mother this house on the coast the year he was named *People's* Sexiest for the first time. It was one of the last old beach houses on the cliffs of Palos Verdes, half a hexagon cut into the sides of the rocks with the flat side facing the road and the three planes of the half-hex looking out on the ocean. Great view, but erosion estimates weren't positive for long-term stability. Daniel sat on the third-floor deck. If he looked straight down, he could see the second-floor deck and the stairs set in the cliffs leading down to a strip of sand that got smaller every year.

Tonight, the bonfire on the beach illuminated an impromptu game of football. It hemorrhaged couples as they slunk away into the darkness for a few intimate moments, their perfect bodies meeting in what was for them the most ordinary of acts before brushing off the sand and returning to the light. At his worst moments—and tonight was close to his worst—Daniel wished he was capable of showing them what it was to be less whole. He hated that Jane had called Steve instead of him. That he'd expected it didn't make him feel any better.

When Daniel had woken up at the clinic and heard from his nurse that Steve had brought a woman to visit, it had felt impossible to call Jane. He could no longer lie. But he had no idea what version of the truth Steve had given her. Certain that any conversation would end in rejection, Daniel couldn't bring himself to confront the end. There was also this nagging thought that, since she seemed to have moved on so quickly to Steve, Jane might never have been interested in him.

Rhea roasted marshmallows at the fire. She wore her surgical bandage like it concealed a third breast in the middle of her favorite bikini. She hobbled among her guests with the endurance of a marathon runner. Whenever she wanted to climb the stairs from the beach to the house, she had Zeik carry her up to the first deck. She was there, two floors below Daniel, about to go into the kitchen, when Steve returned with Jane.

Daniel listened to them exchange greetings. Jane sounded different than he expected. Her voice had a higher pitch, loose, with her words running over each other. He wondered if she might be drunk.

The reverberation of Steve jogging down the stairs to the beach thrummed up to Daniel's deck. Leaning over the railing he watched the top of Jane's head as she followed Zeik with Rhea out of the kitchen and back to the beach. Wearing her nursing scrubs, Jane was easy to keep track of as Steve and Rhea took her around to make introductions. She didn't cling to him the way Steve's girls usually clung. She seemed distracted. She kept looking around. Daniel dared to hope she was looking for him.

When Jane returned to the house she returned alone. Daniel grabbed the deck rail and pulled himself up out of his chair. Almost two days of sleeping, but his body was exhausted. He began to work his way down to the main floor. They would probably only have a few minutes. As soon as Steve noticed Daniel had left the deck, he'd known to come looking for her. He only wanted Jane because Daniel wanted her. He believed he deserved more than his brother who had failed to be invincible. He'd never said it aloud, but Daniel knew Steve frequently bolstered his confidence by telling himself that he would have done better than Daniel had their situations been reversed.

The bathroom was empty. Jane was also not in the living room or on the sunporch. Daniel found her in the room that had become his when he'd moved from Oahu to California to film *SLUT*. Originally a transitional place between his transient surfing life and his acting career, the room became the place he'd spent hours in semi darkness looking for patterns in the plaster ceiling, knowing he needed to get out of bed and do physical therapy but unable to summon the will to move.

Jane stood very still just past the doorway. Her hand rested in a clenched fist on the salt shingle dresser. She drew deep breaths through her nose in a motion that consumed her entire upper body. It rose and fell with increasing speed, like she was getting ready to take off and fly away. Daniel imagined she was bothered by the smell, a slight mildew in the carpet grown from too many wet boardies left on the floor, the sand tracked in and never completely vacuumed, the remnants of a life lived in the water.

With a reverence usually reserved for graveyards, her eyes traveled over the two double beds overshadowed by Daniel's surfboard mounted on the wall, the dumbbells lined up on the floor, Grandpa Fletcher's scratched-up desk shoved into the corner. With each step into the room she seemed smaller, as though the room was swallowing her head, which sat so tenuously on her braced shoulders. Everything below them spoke of hard angles rounded by the substance of maturity, curves Daniel could sink into and become lost. She seemed to have absorbed blows and withstood tides. She could've given him the strength to get out of bed each day.

She paused at the Pablo Neruda quote framed in four bits of driftwood that Daniel had nailed together for an eighth-grade shop class. "I need the sea because it teaches me." The words lisped over her lips. Daniel heard his loss in the way her voice reached out, as if she searched for a place to land that would not shift under her weight. She wasn't quite the same girl he'd met in the park eight years ago. Like him, she had been damaged, a woman with an open wound. Seeing her like this stirred in him an obscene hope that maybe his leg didn't matter. What he'd liked about her in New York—her vulnerability, her openness to new things, and willingness to admit she didn't know something—was even more attractive. And now, even though they'd traveled so far alone, it felt like they matched. Even their fears of being overexposed aligned. She could accept him because she knew what it was to lose one's self.

Jane turned. For a moment, she appeared frightened. A uniquely naked expression. But then her face softened into a bashful smile, crooked on the left side. Daniel couldn't quite believe she was smiling, looking at him as though nothing had changed.

"I thought you had work tonight," he said.

"I did. But I got in this fight and my boss wanted me to take some time off."

"It's difficult to imagine you fighting with anyone."

"Yeah, well, I get crabby when I haven't had enough sleep. And I talk too much." She laughed, more to herself than Daniel, as though this was a conversation she'd been having in her mind: the perils of sleeplessness. The laugh became a hiccup. She swayed backwards, caught herself. Daniel offered her a hand and guided her to the nearest bed. He sat with his good hip beside hers and tried to stay calm.

"My mother had this rule: no boys were allowed in my room. And I wasn't allowed to go into theirs. Bedrooms were private places, she said. I never really believed it until now. There's so much of you in this room."

Daniel almost said, 'Mom's the one who keeps it like this,' but tears filled Jane's eyes. He didn't need to explain. She already understood the room was a memorial.

"I'm so sorry."

"For what?" His words fell dully, placeholders in a script they were reciting, a scene that didn't end well. She pitied him, he thought, the poor invalid, the victim.

"Your leg," another hiccup, "I think it's my fault." She began to cry in earnest.

Daniel ventured his arm around her back and enclosed her even though it was hard to stay near her. His mother had spent months acting the same way after the full truth of Daniel's condition set in. She'd wandered around the house looking at Daniel's belongings and bursting into tears as though he'd died.

"Steve told you about my . . . situation."

Jane stared up at his old surfboard, now two different colors of blue from the dust fading the top ridge, the rough waxed plane with little hatch marks of grey. Daniel wondered if she'd heard him. "It isn't as bad as it sounds," he said. "I lead a really normal—"

"I know." She sucked in air. "I know, I just . . . I can't do this right now."

"Do what, exactly?" asked Daniel even though he knew.

"There's a lot going on and I—I think there are a lot of women who would be so lucky to be with you."

"Jane."

"I wish it could be me."

Daniel spoke through his clenched jaw. "I'd like to know why it can't be you."

Her eyes rose to the ceiling as though she would find answers. "I can't."

He reached over for her hand thinking maybe his touch would elicit an answer. She drew away, which was enough for him to give up. She wasn't in any condition to be packed off into a taxi, so he said, "How about I drive you home?"

Her head jerked toward him, startled. "Why?"

"Obviously I make you uncomfortable."

"You don't. I just—"

"It's no problem."

"I came with Steve."

"He's probably forgotten you're here." Daniel waited for her to argue. But Jane only sat with her little fists in her lap and stared at the floor.

It seemed clear that she would rather be anywhere but there with him, which was fine because Daniel didn't need her pity. Didn't need her lies about all the women who supposedly wanted him when what he wanted had been her.

Steve would have a surprise when he found her gone. Or maybe he wouldn't notice. Or he'd laugh it off. But by driving Jane home at least Daniel would know he took something from him. Depriving Steve of something he wanted every day for the rest of his life might equal what he'd taken. If only he lived a very long time.

CHAPTER 15

They were going to Jane's condo. She couldn't remember how they'd gotten through the steps of deciding to take her home. She had a vague impression that before her crying fit, Daniel had seemed friendlier. Maybe she could still bring him back to the friendly stage. If she could stay with him a little longer, maybe . . .

Maybe what?

Maybe they could talk.

Maybe if they spent a few minutes alone in the same room talking about something normal they'd be able to get past this awkward place. But all Daniel seemed to care about was convincing her that Steve was a terrible excuse for a boyfriend and that the only women who were happy with him were the ones who liked to cut and run. Daniel seemed to think this was what Jane wanted. When she tried to shift the conversation back to him (and her) he wouldn't talk at all.

He turned onto Jane's street. Her condo tower loomed. She was running out of time. "Would you like to come up for a drink?"

Daniel wore this little the-joke's-on-me smile as he said, with a touch of bitterness, "Maybe some other time." (Never.)

She wanted to stay in the car and force Daniel to talk to her until she felt they'd reached an understanding and she could leave without feeling like she was taking his heart with her. Since she couldn't explain why she was no longer interested in him, and he clearly was upset that she wouldn't explain, it was unclear what understanding was possible. If only she could describe how, though Daniel gave every impression of wanting to boot her out the door, she felt less of an alien than she had the three years she'd lived with Seth and they'd called themselves 'happy.' But if she said that it would only further beg the question of why she didn't want to be with him.

Strobes of streaky lights from two cop cars made the condo parking lot look like an eighties disco gone wrong. Jane wasn't worried. The police often busted up parties. But the commotion kept Daniel from pulling into the parking lot. He stopped in the street, gripping the steering wheel like he was preparing to drag race down the main as soon as she got out of the Prius. The tower gate rolled open.

"Once, that gate opened for a St. Bernard," Jane tried to joke. "Like it thought the dog was a car."

"Huh."

"You sure you don't want to . . . "

"Yep."

"Thanks for the ride."

She paused to give him the chance for any last thoughts. He looked straight ahead.

"I'm really sorry about falling apart like that back at your mom's house . . . I'd like to—"

"Have a nice night, Jane Dalton."

It was the way he said her name that put Jane's hand on the door handle and pulled the latch. It sounded unfamiliar on his tongue, the way people who'd just met tried new names on. If he thought of her as a stranger there was no point in staying in the car. Jane was going to cry again, and she didn't want him to see. "I guess this is goodbye."

"If you know what's good for you, you'll stay away from Steve."

She wanted to yell at him that she could care less about Steve. But the spasms in her throat made talking impossible. Jane had barely closed the passenger door before he zoomed away. She watched the taillights flare down the road, shrink, and disappear around the corner. She waited on the sidewalk to see if the Prius would return. It didn't. The only car that passed was a Camry with airport rental stickers, probably tourists checking in late to a cheap hotel.

She told herself it was better that he'd cut her off. There was no negotiating with the facts. It was almost a relief to know she would never have to tell him about her family. She'd said goodbye, found as much closure as she could hope for. Now she only had to kill five hours before her train left. She sucked in her belly, thrust out her breasts, clenched her butt and, when she felt everything properly tensed and fortified, she turned and approached the caution tape barricade.

"I live here," she told the first officer who tried to stop her.

"Name?"

"I'm the sublease for Colleen McNamara."

"Unit?"

"5C."

"We've been trying to reach you. Someone forced entry into your home this evening."

Jane froze her face so the officer couldn't see the effect of her words. She scanned the parking lot for a familiar silhouette. The shadows between strobe lights grew eyes that stared at her without blinking. Every car window became a lair in which intruders lurked. Her skin crawled with the scales of their gaze.

"Did you catch anyone?"

"Not yet. You'll need to go up and confirm if anything's been stolen."

Jane backed away. "That's okay. I'm sure it's all there."

"Miss, you need to come upstairs with me."

"I'll be back in a minute."

"Miss!"

Jane sprinted out of the parking lot and down the sidewalk. Her brain scrambled for a plan. Should she surround herself with people, or look for an isolated place to hide? Her getaway bag was in the condo. She couldn't leave town without it. But Seth was surely there watching for her. The tower would be a trap.

Jane caught her breath beside the door of the In-N-Out. There were only a few customers: a trucker and some teenagers pushing curfew. The street in both directions was desolate and still. If Jane could make it three blocks there was a Super Eight. She could come back to the condo in daylight. Or she could call Colleen and maybe . . .

A car swerved into the parking lot. Jane braced herself.

The car was a Prius. Daniel leaned over and opened the passenger door. Jane rolled her ankle on a water bottle as she collapsed into the seat. The Prius squealed out of the parking lot and sped towards the 405 onramp.

"What happened?" Daniel's left hand gripped the top of the steering wheel as his right side opened toward her, alert and powerful and ready to act.

"Someone broke into my apartment."

"So you ran from the police?"

"Were you spying on me the whole time?"

"In this part of town, I like to make sure a woman makes it inside."

His hand rested on the plastic center console so close Jane could feel the heat of his skin. She wanted to touch him, to take his fingers in hers and thank him over and over.

"Why did you run?" he asked again.

Deep breath. "I think my husband is here."

"How long have you known about this?"

It wasn't the question she'd expected, but it immediately became the right one.

"I've felt someone watching me for a couple days. That's why I decided to go out with Steve when you didn't call because I didn't want to be alone. And then today, my husband came to the hospital asking about me. I was planning to leave town, but I didn't want to tell you because . . . I don't know. It seemed simpler to just leave. There's a ten o'clock train to Vancouver." Jane glanced at Daniel out of the corner of her eye to see if the bullshit she'd just thrown together was convincing. His face betrayed nothing of his thoughts, but she felt the tension drain out of him little by little as the lies took hold and he chose to believe everything she had done over the past forty-eight hours had been about Seth, not about Daniel's leg.

"Let's go back. The police are there. I'll be there. Nothing will happen. It will be better to settle this so you won't have to leave." Daniel was so absolute in his confidence, so willing to step ahead of her and lead, that she almost believed him.

He flipped on his turn signal.

"Don't!" Jane grabbed the steering wheel and jerked the Prius out of the lane. "You can't reason with him like that. He's dangerous."

"If he demonstrates he's dangerous, the police will be on your side."

"No, it—he was in the military. He's got PTSD. He won't accept anything the police tell him. Do you have any idea how ineffective restraining orders are?"

Daniel absorbed this without comment. He continued driving south, back to Rhea's house.

Jane tried to stabilize her breathing as she watched a Buick in her mirror as it changed lanes at the same time the Prius changed lanes. Seth was in that car. She felt sure of it. Even when Daniel took the turn to Palos Verdes and the Buick sped past Jane couldn't relax. Five years of living as though he'd never existed and now Seth had come. It didn't seem possible.

Daniel passed Rhea's driveway and turned down an access road with bushes so overgrown they scratched at the sides of the car. Here there were no streetlights, no sounds except the murmuring roll of the ocean and the haze of insects. It felt like they were about to drive off the cliff into oblivion. But then they rounded the bend and the bushes thinned into brush and they were on a ledge on the side of the cliff, the thrum of a bass beat and the dancing light of the bonfire on the beach below them, steps up to the house ahead and above. Daniel pushed a button in the ceiling console and a sliver of light appeared in what Jane had thought was solid cliff as a garage door began to grind open.

Rhea's garage had space for four cars, a jet ski trailer, and racks of surfboards. Tools were everywhere, some neatly lined up on pegboards, others scattered on the floor. In the stall beside the Prius, the raised hood of a retro muscle car exposed a hole where its engine used to be. Daniel pulled in. Jane listened to the garage door roll shut.

Daniel came around and opened her door. "Can you walk?"

"Do you mind if I just sit here for a little while?" Jane pulled her door shut and locked it. Two layers of locked doors between her and outside was better. She was going to stay in the Prius forever. No one could stop her.

Tears began to slip out of her eyes. They came faster and faster until she was crying so loudly the sobs echoed off the garage walls. She cried for self-pity, for lack of sleep, for Daniel's measured consideration as he sat near her door in a lawn chair. He looked worried. Whether he worried for her or about what he would do with her, she'd rather not guess.

She thought about calling Alma to see if Tommy had made contact. Maybe it was only Tommy and not Seth who had broken in. Maybe the distinction didn't matter. She'd been found. If she stayed in the city, sooner or later they would catch her, and Seth would make her tell him about Leah.

Jane's crying took her through several false endings in which she believed she'd pulled herself together only to have a fresh thought set her off again. When her tears subsided for the final time and she was a dried-out rubbery mess, she rolled down the window and Daniel handed her a prescription bottle and a glass of water.

"Swallow two of those, then I'm taking you up to bed. It's late."

Jane stared dumbly at the bottle. Ativan. Two of these and Jane would be unconscious in ten minutes flat. If she was unconscious, she wouldn't see Seth coming. She could wake up in Nebraska instead of Canada.

"You're safe here." Daniel's eyes locked on hers, slate grey, a little cold, but understanding. Those eyes said he knew panic in all its shape-shifting cracks and crannies. She could trust him.

Jane swallowed the pills.

Half a flight of stairs and then a landing and then another flight of stairs brought them from the garage up into the main floor of Rhea's house with its odd mix of beach villa and handmade kitsch. Daniel had Jane walk in front of him, probably thinking she might collapse. His steps behind her were confident and even, a solid presence that half tempted her to play the damsel and let herself fall.

The windows rattled with reverberations from the music on the beach. Jane set her hand against a pane to steady herself and felt the pulse in her fingers. Two drunk guys banged through the kitchen screen and began a clumsy job of refilling a cooler. They spilled half a bag of ice. Jane jumped at the rattle of cubes scattering across the kitchen tile.

On the deck, bodies crowded the hot tub. Laughter filtered in through the screen door. Steve was out there somewhere, probably with some girl, his sunset drive with Jane long forgotten. Daniel took her arm and gently led her down the hall into his bedroom with its two empty beds and the surfboard turned wall decoration. There was that smell again: New York Daniel. The smell that would still be Daniel if not for her family.

If not for me.

He removed her shoes and her earrings. The pads of his fingers were soft and warm on the back of her neck as he tried to remove her necklace. Jane closed her eyes and tuned every one of her nerve endings to his touch. She hoped he'd somehow have more success removing it than she had, but he quickly gave up. He pulled back the sheets on the second double bed and waited for Jane to lie down.

She grabbed his arm. "Stay with me."

"I'll be here all night." He pointed to the first bed, the one between Jane and the door.

"I'm sorry about this."

"It's fine." The corner of his jaw tightened, "I just wish you'd told me earlier."

He began to walk away. Jane rushed to find something that would keep him. Even the other bed was too far. Tonight couldn't end with him going through all the right motions of a heroic rescuer but refusing to look her in the eye.

"I went back to Battery Park like we planned."

He stopped.

Yes, it was a lie. But it was also what should have happened. She'd imagined it so many times: Daniel waiting, hoping she would come but not allowing himself to believe. And then Jane did come, and he kissed her for the first time and there was no doubt they were supposed to be together.

The way Daniel looked at Jane, it was clear he'd also nurtured a version of this fantasy. For eight years he'd wondered if that single afternoon had been powerful enough for her to return. Her lie gave him hope. It wasn't quite fair to encourage him, but Jane couldn't help herself.

He sat on the side of her bed. A bit of warmth returned to his expression. He was ready to talk. It would be a happy conversation. They'd both exercise their pretending skills to ignore the barriers that had risen between them. They'd talk through the rest of the night, like teenagers in love for the first time.

But Jane had forgotten the pills. She felt the swell of chemicals hitting her system and fought to keep her eyes open.

"You should sleep," he said.

Jane pushed herself up in bed. "The marriage was a mistake. I—" She knew the words, but before she could gather them, they faded. She dropped down to the pillow. She couldn't be sure Daniel heard her when she said, "I never loved him."

CHAPTER 16

When Jane woke up it took a few beats to remember she was in Daniel's old bedroom in Rhea's house. There was a slight indentation on the other bed where Daniel had slept. It was ten-thirty; Jane had missed her train. But it was okay. Seth had no idea she was with the Fletchers. His break-in had inadvertently bought her one more day with Daniel.

An exhausted quiet stilled the house as Jane ventured out of the bedroom. Sleeping bodies in various stages of undress littered the living room. Someone had fallen asleep at the piano. Jane stepped over a woman wrapped up in the sailor's quilt that had hung on the entryway wall.

Spilled potato chips crunched under her feet in the kitchen, the apparent scene of an early morning feeding frenzy. Every surface was crammed with half-eaten snacks and beer bottles. A pan of boxed mac-n-cheese turned crusty on the stove. Wind whipped the screen door against its frame. Jane stepped out onto the deck. One corner of the hot tub cover snapped in the breeze that blew a thin cold mist in from the ocean. It stretched in a grey seam as far as she could see. The heat wave had finally broken.

"Jane dearie, we're up here," called Rhea.

Jane used her hand to shield her eyes from the rain and saw three pairs of feet through the slats of another deck on the floor above—heavy duty men's sneakers, Rhea's sandal beside the clubbed bottom of her cast, and two ovals of pink foam—a child's shoes. Goosebumps surged and covered Jane's arms and legs. Little girl shoes like those Jane might have purchased on sale at Target or received as hand-me-downs when Leah had reached the right age.

Rhea's head and shoulders appeared over the edge of the railing, a faded version of the vibrant hostess from the previous night. Her hair hung in greasy clumps. The surgical bandage on her chest was smudged and peeling at the edges. She waved at Jane to join them.

The top deck wasn't much more than a front porch for the single room on the third floor that rose above the rest of the house like a stunted bell tower. Two lawn chairs took up most of the space.

Daniel stood at the railing looking up the beach through binoculars, a water bottle pinched under one arm. The child, a little girl with blue eyes and sun streaked hair, leaned against his good leg. "Those waves get any higher he's not going to be able to paddle them," said Daniel.

"Riley will get him out in time," said Rhea.

"They drank too much to be pulling shit like this."

Jane's eyes followed the line of the binoculars. Half a mile away, a cluster of surfers bobbed in the choppy water.

"I wanna see." The girl squeezed between Daniel and the railing and climbed up to balance on the rung.

Daniel held the binoculars over her eyes. "Tell me who's wearing blue and who's wearing orange."

Rhea pulled Jane in for a hug. "Nothing like an early surf to cap off a good night." She waited for Jane's professional disapproval. When Jane smiled as if surfing on no sleep with alcohol for energy was just fine, Rhea motioned towards the water. "They went out at dawn with perfect conditions. But the storm's getting the wind up now."

"Mom's in blue and Dad's in orange," said the girl.

"Good job. Now, down you go before you fall." Daniel lifted the girl with one arm around her belly. She crouched and swung until he shook her and she dropped her feet for a landing. "Will you run down and grab me a sweatshirt?" he asked.

Jane did a jump-step-shuffle toward the wall to avoid touching the girl as she ran by, a life-sized doll with a jacket over her Tinkerbell nightie. A living ghost.

Daniel passed Rhea the binoculars. "Those waves are draining the water right out of the break. If he falls we can forget Hawaii."

"Hawaii?" Jane made her voice bright and extra interested, but Daniel didn't bite.

"He's in position for a big one." Rhea sounded awed. "He's up—beautiful—he's caught a lump . . . headfirst wipeout."

Daniel took back the binoculars. "Fucking—" He cut himself off as the door below them opened and the girl's little feet sounded on the stairs.

"Give it to your dad's friend." Daniel kept his eyes on the water. Jane didn't realize he was talking about her until the girl turned and shyly held out the sweatshirt. "My name's Poppy, what's yours?"

"Jane." She made sure their fingers didn't accidently touch as Jane took the sweatshirt. The girl looked up at Jane for only a moment before she bounced over to the opposite side of the deck and climbed up on a chair. But it was a moment Jane stopped breathing.

"Riley's swimming out," said Daniel. "Looks like she's got him."

"I wanna see!"

"Let Grandma see first." Reaching over Poppy's arms, Rhea took the binoculars from Daniel.

"I'm going to drive down and pick them up. I'll call if we have to go to the ER."

"If he lets you take him to the ER," muttered Rhea.

Daniel passed Jane on the way to the stairs without notice. He descended the stairs two at a time, as easily as anyone with two legs.

"I'm going with Uncle Dan."

"Let Uncle Dan go by himself, sweetie," said Rhea. "You need to get dressed so you can go home."

"Why can't I stay here?"

"Get dressed."

Jane did more awkward dance steps to get out of the way as Rhea opened the door to the third-floor room, a bedroom that looked like it belonged to a fairy tale princess. Dolls, stuffed animals, and brightly-colored pillows covered with bows and glitter filled window seats along three walls. Gauzy curtains hung from the canopy bed. Jane couldn't help but lean forward and reach out to test the barrier of the doorframe, the gateway into a dreamscape of childhood, a world filled with frivolous pastimes and colorful decorations and toys intended only for play. When Jane had been a child, any belongings she had considered toys had also been tools of instruction.

When Jane had been four, the neighbor girl showed up uninvited to her birthday party and gave Jane Beach Party Barbie, the only gift Jane ever received that looked like it came from this girl's room. Jane's mother had used Beach Party Barbie to teach Jane that bikinis were underwear and the women who wore them didn't respect themselves or men, and then she'd thrown it away.

Rhea's hand on Jane's arm made her jump. "I know you're supposed to be my guest, but I think Steve will need your help. He had a bad wipeout." She handed Jane her phone. "Dan will call if they head to the ER. Otherwise the first aid kit is in the cabinet under the kitchen sink. Would you mind?"

Jane started to tell her that it was illegal for her to act as a nurse outside a clinical setting, then she realized it didn't matter. Jane was suspended for attacking Alma. She was going to Canada. No reason not to help Steve out. Maybe she could stab his overinflated ego in the process.

Jane wriggled herself around in Daniel's sweatshirt as she navigated the wet stairs. The sweatshirt had been a genius idea. It was warm and soft and so huge it managed to subsume the giant lumps of Jane's breasts. The events of the previous night had become a fast-fading nightmare. She was with the Fletchers wearing Daniel's sweatshirt. It hung halfway to her knees like a baggy dress, like armor. As long as she wore it no one could touch her, not even little girl ghosts. Before she left for Canada,

Jane was going to find a way to prove to Daniel she was only interested in him. It would be her parting gift to him.

This was what she was thinking as she opened the cabinet under the sink and failed to notice the spider sitting just inside until it flew out. It ricocheted off her knee and came to rest on the kitchen floor. Jane leapt up onto the counter. Chips crunched. Granola rattled into the sink. The spider lurched sideways.

Jane grabbed the long silver neck of the sink faucet; she was shaking so badly she almost shook herself right back onto the floor, which was now killer spider territory. The spider that had just touched her knee could swallow Mr. Fuzzy Black from her condo whole. It was grey brown with a body shaped like a butterfly's thorax, but twice as thick, and a leg circumference bigger than her hand.

It touched me, it touched me. IT TOUCHED ME. Her skin crawled a mile a minute. Jane closed her eyes so she didn't have to see it. But she couldn't not look. She'd be seeing it the rest of her life.

Footsteps began stomping up the steps from the garage. The surfers burst into the living room whooping and laughing, drawing the hungover groans of those trying to sleep. Steve called out, "I need a nurse. Nurse Jane! I'm in need of fucking medical assistance," just before Zeik, the Arnold of Austria guy Jane had met the night before, stepped into the kitchen, his bulging muscles bursting out of his wetsuit.

"Don't come in!" she shouted.

He jumped back. "Fucking Christ, that's a spider!"

"Step aside, step aside, I'm bleeding here." Steve pushed into the doorway. Blood pulsed from a gash in his forehead. He pinched his nose closed to stop more bleeding. When he saw the spider, he drew back. His heel came down hard on the toes of a woman with striking turquoise eyes and black hair. Jane had seen Steve's wife at the party the night before, but they hadn't been introduced.

"Excuse me, my foot?" She looked at the spider then at Jane on the counter. "*That's* the Battery Park girl?"

Despite his grisly appearance, Steve sounded like he was flirting when he told Jane, "You can run faster than that spider."

"I'm not moving."

"But I need you. See my face?"

She glared at him.

Daniel's head appeared over Steve' shoulder. He quickly assessed the situation. "Everyone, stand back. I've got it." He circled the kitchen, making a wide arc around the spider. Steve's wife stood at the door, tapping her front teeth together. She kept shooting Jane looks like the situation was her fault. "Can't you just reach down and get the kit?" she asked. "If you throw it to me, I'll take care of him."

Steve reappeared behind her still pinching his nose and now holding a bathroom towel against his forehead. "Don't. She'll make me look like Frankenstein."

Daniel opened a cabinet and pulled out a Tupperware lid and bowl. His eyes never left the spider. He crouched, one, two, three, Tupperware down, spider trapped.

"Careful when you step down," he said as he offered her his hand.

Jane was afraid of pushing him off balance and setting the spider free, so she got herself down along with a cascade of crushed snacks. The spider thumped against the Tupperware. Jane grabbed the first aid kit and ran into the sun porch adjacent to the kitchen. She shoved herself into a corner and sucked in the ocean's endless horizon darkening with storm rain. She counted three seconds for every inhale and exhale.

Steve followed her. His wife followed him. Jane felt them at her back shooting silences at each other. The surfers and some of the no-longer-sleeping party guests ventured into the kitchen to get a look at the spider.

"Give it a kiss Zeik," said one.

"No way, brah," said Zeik.

"Way cool bug, man."

"You gonna keep it?"

"I think we should call it Godzilla," said Zeik.

"Hey Steve-O, come look at this thing."

Steve didn't answer. Jane felt the shift of energy at her back, a new tension. She turned. Steve sat on the dining table in a silent discussion with his wife. Intimations rocketed between them so thickly they were like the vortex of a black hole. The surfers, dripping and sandy, clustered at the half wall arch dividing the kitchen and the sun porch, watching.

The wife was clearly winning the silent debate, giving Steve a silent dressing-down as only a wife knew how. Jane imagined the unspoken words rushing out of her completely reasonable anger. *The next time you want to surf drunk, I'll let you drown.* Jane found herself momentarily mesmerized by this new source of power in the family. Jane had assumed Steve was always on top.

Daniel cleared his throat to draw attention away from Steve and his wife. "I'm taking the spider outside. Want to see it run?"

The screen door slammed as the surfers and the party guests herded outside with Daniel. For the first few moments, the stillness of their absence felt more dangerous than their watching eyes. Jane was the only one left as a witness.

Steve wilted into a chair, hands flopping down at his sides in exasperation. "Okay! Fine! It was stupid. But you'd have done the same thing if you'd been in the right position."

"I'd have been smart about it. You acted like some idiot big wave kahuna."

"Why is it always me, huh? Why can't Dan be the idiot? Or Mom? Did you see her lifting the cooler last night?"

"*She* doesn't have a dependent child. Don't think I won't leave you."

"Go ahead and try."

Steve's wife turned on her heel. She came at Jane. "You're Jane? I'm Riley. Don't feel obligated to help him. He deserves that scar."

Jane clutched the first aid kit and prayed Riley didn't come any closer. She looked angry enough to drop kick Jane just for being alive. "It's fine."

"Lucky for you then." She shot a pointed look at Steve, "While she's sticking needles in you, maybe you could try and get the two shits you have for a brain to remember you have a daughter." She turned back to Jane, slightly less frosty. "I'm going to make coffee. You do coffee?"

Jane nodded.

With Riley removed to the kitchen, Steve perked up. "Okay runaway nurse, I'm ready for you to glue me back together." He beamed on Jane the full force of his movie star grin. He stripped off the top of his wet-suit to display his perfectly chiseled, hairless chest glistening with water droplets. "Just be careful. This face is worth a lot."

Jane peeled off Daniel's sweatshirt so the sleeves wouldn't get in her way, and took a deep breath. She stood before Steve's chair, their knees al-most touching. "Follow my finger with your eyes. Don't move your head."

"Seriously? I'm bleeding here."

"Follow my finger, please. Any blank spots in your vision?"

"Nope."

"Nausea?"

"I don't think I'm a fan of you doing your nurse thing on me. It's kinda . . ."

"Illuminating?"

"Impersonal. It's supposed to be like, sexy."

Little did he know how difficult it was to concentrate with him shirt-less and those muscles dominating Jane's peripheral vision. Or maybe he did know. But Jane wasn't going to give him the satisfaction of showing she was affected. She did a cursory check for other injuries and counted Steve's pulse. "What's the last thing you remember before hitting your head?"

"I was setting up for this great ride, but I hit a lump going down the face and wiped out." He shifted the bloody towel from his hand to the table. *Those biceps.*

"Looks like your nose is broken."

"No way. I've got a photoshoot in like five days, or six days—what day is today?"

Riley returned with coffee for Jane but not for Steve. Jane expected her presence would curb his flirting, but he only puffed out his chest and dared Jane to blush with his eyes. They looked a lot like Daniel's used to, animated from the inside with playful energy, but darker.

"Hold still," she whispered.

Jane's shaken nerves ran haywire. *Do the nose first,* she thought, *it'll be easier.* But she couldn't figure out how to position her hands on Steve's face. She blamed the spider. Fight or flight chemicals took time to wear off. And the weird twilight zone feeling she'd had meeting Steve's kid was also a valid explanation. But this was more than that. It was like standing too close to a fire or trying not to look at the sun.

Jane felt the cartilage for the correct position. She set her thumbs on either side of the bridge, the right hand a little higher than the left and spread her fingers around Steve's cheeks and jaw for support. He had the softest skin she'd ever touched on an adult male, perfectly hairless, perfectly smooth, and *warm.*

His eyes were level with her breasts.

"Don't jerk back when I push."

"I'm ready." He winked.

One, two, three—Jane pushed with her thumbs.

"Fucking hell." His eyes ran. "Did it work?" He looked to Riley. "Is it straight?"

She rolled her eyes and picked up her phone. She pretended disinterest but Jane felt her attention.

The screen door slapped against the frame announcing the arrival of Poppy followed by Zeik carrying Rhea down from the third floor. Poppy ran into the sun porch and threw herself at Steve. "Does it hurt?"

"Nurse Jane is fixing me up. You wanna watch?" He lifted her onto his lap. It was a position she'd outgrown but with some adjustment they made it work. Poppy watched wide-eyed as Jane unpacked the first aid kit—gauze and alcohol wipes, a sterilized needle, and surgical thread— to stitch the gash in Steve's forehead.

"She's going to sew you like clothes?"

"No sewing. It's like last time when your mom used the glue to stick my skin together, remember?" Steve hadn't stopped looking at Jane's breasts. He was staring at them like he was *trying* to see nothing but Jane's breasts.

"This cut's too deep for gluing," said Jane. "You need stitches."

"Let's skip the stitches," said Steve, like there were options.

"Can't, sorry." Jane noticed Steve swallow with difficulty as his jaw tightened, the same unconscious reflex Daniel used, except Steve used it when he was scared; for Daniel it was a reflex of frustration.

Jane detached wet hair from the gash and tilted Steve's head up to get the best light. His eyes stayed on her breasts, hooded. Jane pressed an alcohol wipe along the gash. Steve bounced his heels against the floor, bobbing Poppy up and down. He dropped his free hand down beside his chair and made a fist, bracing himself. Jane unwrapped the needle. Steve's eyes followed her movement. The needle was more compelling than her breasts, apparently. For the first time since they'd met, Jane felt she had the upper hand.

"There's some sand in the wound." She looked to Poppy and did her best not to sound like one of those adults who didn't know how to talk to kids. "Could you please bring me a glass of water?"

"Warm or cold?"

"Just a little warm."

Poppy hopped to the floor and ran into the kitchen.

Jane looked to Riley, but she was typing on her phone, not paying attention. Rhea was in the kitchen dropping paper towels on the wet spots on the floor left by the surfers. It was just Jane and Steve and Steve looked nervous. "You know the thing about nursing?" asked Jane.

"What's that?"

"Even the most practiced patient never manages a believable performance in an exam room."

"That's what I meant by not sexy."

Jane threaded the needle.

She brought the needle forward, bending over him.

Steve grabbed her hand. "You said there was sand."

"I lied."

His eyes flicked up to her face. In that one brief moment, she saw that he was so terrified, he could not hide behind even a single layer of his usual camouflage. The screen door snapped open and Daniel and the surfers trooped in and caught them like this, Steve holding Jane back as she leaned over him with her threatening needle. Jane was doing her job, but she knew from the now familiar stiffening of Daniel's posture that what he saw confirmed his belief that she was interested in Steve.

"Whoop, looks like Steve's putting the moves on his nurse," said one of the surfers. They crowded into the sun porch, bringing with them a wave of stale sweat and beer breath. Riley glanced up, smiled a little maniacal smile, and returned to her phone.

Steve's grin reappeared for his audience but he continued to hold Jane's arm so tightly he was beginning to cut off circulation. He focused all his rays of playboy sunshine up at her. The performance had resumed. "I heard you spent the night in Dan's room."

Someone let out a low whistle of appreciation.

"You know, it's been years," continued Steve. "Was he a little . . . rusty?"

In her peripheral vision Jane sensed Daniel become a statue at the far end of the table. Steve's friends smiled with slack jaws and malicious hunger. Nothing would better conclude their night of revelry than to hear how the weakest among them failed where they surely would have succeeded. They were the boys she had known in college, cocky, invincible, living only in the pleasure of a moment.

"Some of my guys aren't even sure Dan can get it up."

She saw Daniel train his eyes out the window. In his mother's house, surrounded by the people who should've supported him, he looked trapped. Jane knew that feeling. This was her chance to prove he was wrong about her.

She offered Steve's audience the secretive smile she used on the old men in the Cardiac ICU to help them feel like they were still men. "Rusty isn't what I'd call it." Jane shifted the needle to her other hand. Steve's eyes followed it, hypnotized. "More like, well-oiled. After the third round I just couldn't take any more."

The surfers exchanged grins. Jane looked to Daniel for some sign of encouragement, but his back was a solid wall dividing him from the rest of the room. Jane returned her attention to Steve. He was working hard to find some smart retort that called her out as a liar without making him sound like a sore loser. He was too aware of how it looked, her over him with all the power, him unable to affect an exit because he needed her to fix his head. Even as he kept up his jocular posture for his friends, there was venom in his eyes just for her.

Jane moved the needle back to her right hand. The color drained out of his face as she pinched the edges of the gash together.

"Wait." His voice came out breathless.

"Waiting increases the chance of a scar."

His hand came up, feebly trying to fend her off, but then his eyes rolled back in his head. He tilted sideways, crashing onto the plank floor in a dead faint that just missed the cushion of the faded rag rug. Jane could've caught him.

"Daddy!" Poppy ran forward, spilling water.

Jane shoved out an arm to stop her. "Don't wake him. It's okay."

"Way harsh," said Zeik. "Death by nurse."

"Three rounds," someone let out a low appreciative whistle, "his dick just couldn't imagine lasting that long."

"He'll need something strong when he wakes up."

"Too bad we drank all the booze," muttered Riley. She looked at Jane with new respect.

They all gathered around to watch Jane kneel on the floor and stitch the gash closed. When she'd finished, the surfers carried Steve out to the living room couch. Rhea headed to bed. Riley took Poppy home to her nanny. The other guests found their own reasons to leave Jane alone in the sunroom with Daniel.

The mist had become a rain of surprising substance for California. Jane didn't notice it until the absence of people drew attention to Daniel's silence. The steady patter on the tin roof enclosed the sun porch in a cocoon of white noise.

She decided not to push him, even though he looked so lonely over by the window that she wanted to go to him and put her arms around him and tell him she was never going to choose Steve instead. But she couldn't do that. She couldn't lead him on knowing there was no chance of a future together.

She slowly packed up the first aid kit.

As he turned to face her, he drew a deep breath that came out like a sigh. "Would you be interested in having breakfast with me?" His voice was so soft and vulnerable, like he still somehow expected her to say no, that she thought her heart would explode.

CHAPTER 17

Daniel had never seen anyone stand up to Steve the way Jane had that morning. Riley of course fought with him all the time, but she always stopped short of using her knowledge of Steve's weaknesses against him. She, like their parents and like most people in Steve's life, had bought into the idea that he needed to be the way he was and challenging it wasn't a good idea. Humbling a god was, after all, an unpredictable enterprise. But Jane had dared to do it. For him.

He took her to Delco's in Malibu even though he knew it would be crowded so late on a Saturday morning. The family often went there because it was close to Steve's house and because it was one of those places celebrities went. For some reason, Daniel thought Jane would like to go to such a place, be one step closer to the stars. But when they arrived, and he saw the paparazzi prowling around the patio railing, he wondered what he'd been thinking to rationalize such a choice.

"It just occurred to me that maybe you're not the kind of person who is impressed by something like this," he said. "We could go somewhere else."

"How's the food?"

"It's good. I mean, some people do come for the food." He laughed. "I'd just imagined something quieter."

"I think this will work." She led the way to the host station and pointed to a table in the far corner that was just being vacated by a couple and their toddler. "We'd like that table, whenever it's ready," she told the host.

While they waited, Daniel leaned up against the wall so the paparazzi couldn't see him through the big round windows that dominated Delco's front entrance. A television hung from the corner of the waiting area. The news channels were still parsing through details from the South Carolina massacre. The shooters had been identified as members of a white supremacist group. No one who'd known them could explain why they'd done what they'd done, so the talking heads were calling on experts to fill in the narrative. The experts were mostly psychiatrists and other mental health professionals telling America that white people only committed senseless killings when they were mentally ill.

Daniel noticed Jane was also listening. He remembered that he still didn't know which version of the story about his leg Steve had told her. The mugging narrative was what the family knew; even their mother had no knowledge of the Vanguard brand on his thigh. For the sake of Steve's career, Daniel had not gone to the police. But it seemed possible maybe Steve had told Jane the truth, which was why she was so interested in the news. Daniel wondered if she followed the Vanguard closely enough to know that what had happened to him had been an aberration.

The host showed them to their table. It was far enough away they could no longer hear the TV. Instead, they heard the clatter of dishes in the kitchen, the radio tuned to classic rock. They ordered coffee. Jane briefly looked over the menu then set it at the edge of the table.

"You know what you want?" he asked.

"I'm having what you're having. You're the expert."

"I usually get the number five omelet."

"Fine with me."

He placed the order. The menus gone, their coffee steaming in two ceramic mugs before them, there was nothing left to do but talk. He realized he had no idea where to start. He hated the idea of her leaving. But it didn't quite seem fair to argue about the situation with her husband since Daniel was just coming into it and didn't want to assume he understood. He poured cream into his coffee. After a moment of consideration, Jane also took up the little silver pitcher and added cream to her mug. In the kitchen the radio played *I Guess That's Why They Call it the Blues*.

"I can never decide if this song is a love story or a tragedy," said Jane. "Is it the blues when you're in love and you want to be with someone all the time? Or is it the blues because you know another person can never fully know you?"

"I've never thought of Elton as a love ballad kind of guy."

"Me neither." Jane's smile was quiet, an expression for herself. She looked so sad.

"Jane, there's got to be a way to fix this. Even if you don't like me and you want to end this—whatever we've been doing—you can't let this guy control your life."

"You're not the problem."

"Then let me try and solve the problem. Steve's got great lawyers. They can find a way to make you safe here."

Jane sipped her coffee. "Coffee's a lot better with cream. The texture changes." She took another sip before she returned the mug to the table. "There is something you can do."

"Anything."

"I need to go to my condo and pick up my bag. And then I need a ride to the train station." Her voice was firm, determined.

He let out a laugh. "I'm just supposed to send you off to Canada? Do you have any idea how maddening that is?"

"Why can't you trust me when I say there's nothing that can be done?"

"Because I solve problems. Everything Steve wants, no matter how impossible, I find a way. I've gotten him out of two lawsuits for property damage, one for sexual harassment. I get him into sold out concerts. I find him flights where there were no flights. I've opened restaurants that were closed. I have bribed police, reporters, and elected city officials. It's very difficult for me to believe your husband is harder to manage than my brother."

"I don't want your help."

"Because of my condition?"

"Yes. Because of your condition."

"I don't believe you."

She lifted her eyes from her coffee and looked at him with a fierce ugly glare. "I get paid to take care of people. I don't want to bring that kind of work home with me. There, you happy?"

He still didn't believe her, but the words stung. He felt them rush in and take up residence in his brain. "I don't need someone to take care of me," he said.

Jane shrugged.

"You can't trust what Steve said while I was in the clinic. You know that, right? He was out to sabotage us from the start, so I wouldn't win our bet."

Jane arched a surprised eyebrow, but her glare didn't waver.

"Steve and I had a bet. He probably didn't tell you that. If I could get a girlfriend, tell her about my leg, and not break up with me, he'd give me a role in his movie."

"I'm sorry you've lost your bet."

"I haven't yet. After this morning, everyone thinks we're more together than we've ever been."

"I'm leaving."

"I just need two more days."

"You're not listening to me. I *need* to leave."

"We could do it in less than two days. I promise you will be on a train tomorrow night."

"You want me to pretend I'm in love with you so you can be in Steve's movie?"

He recognized that she was still trying to hurt him. But he also knew, despite what she claimed, she wasn't ambivalent. Instead of saying that he doubted there would be much pretending involved, he simply said, "I would make it worth your time."

"You have no idea what you're asking."

"I would if you told me."

Their food arrived. Jane stared down at her omelet. She picked up her fork. It hovered sideways in the air. She set it back on the table. A concession. "I'm on a train tomorrow night."

"I will keep you safe."

"We'll see."

"I promise." He didn't usually make such emphatic claims when he knew so little about a situation, but it seemed impossible that he couldn't protect Jane from one man for the rest of the weekend. It wasn't like anyone knew where to find her.

For a second, Daniel thought of the paparazzo who had most likely taken their picture when they'd walked into Delco's. It wasn't likely Daniel was important enough to warrant someone buying that photo. But even if someone did, and the husband saw that picture, there was no way for him to find out where Daniel lived. Every Fletcher address was unlisted. And even if all these impossibilities became possible, and Daniel somehow found himself face to face with this mysterious husband, Daniel felt he would be able to keep him away from Jane. Worse case, Daniel would hire a bodyguard.

Jane slowly picked her way through the omelet. She cut little squares off the edges and ate them one by one without seeming to taste them. She looked like she might cry. When she finished, she carefully set her fork across her plate and looked up at him. "So, what should we do to convince Steve you've won?"

"He'll be asleep until at least four. We'll probably hang out at Mom's tonight, have dinner."

"So we have time now to go get my bag."

"I guess we do."

In the parking lot of her condo tower, Jane sat in the Prius watching the mirrors for a full ten minutes before she decided it was safe to get out. Daniel couldn't help but be impressed with the authority with which she moved once she'd decided no one was watching. She took the stairs up to the fifth floor two at a time; he had trouble keeping up. She pulled back the caution tape and entered her condo as though the "WARNING: Crime Scene do not enter" did not apply to her.

He stood in the entryway while she went to get her bag. The condo wasn't what he'd expected. Or maybe he hadn't considered what kind of home Jane would set up. The bare functionality only made him want to help her more. There had to be a way for her to feel safe enough to make a home for herself.

Jane emerged from the bedroom with a grey duffle bag smaller than his gym bag.

"That's all you need?"

"I travel light."

He nodded. "I noticed there's no damage to the door. How do you think he got in?"

Jane walked into the living room and examined the balcony door. She came back to the entryway and examined the front door. "He picked the lock." She checked the panel of her security system. "Good thing the alarm went off or he'd probably have been sitting here waiting for me when I came home." A visible shudder ran through her.

"You could still go to the police. Maybe it won't be how you think."

She appeared to push off her fear with a shrug. "Let's go to the beach. Maybe the surf comp's still on. This is the end of my life in California. I'd like you to teach me about surfing." Her eyes dared him to say no. Those eyes, so full of a loss he couldn't understand, made him want to enclose her in his arms and hold her forever.

CHAPTER 18

Maybe it was cruel to ask Daniel to spend the afternoon at the beach, like she was punishing him for refusing to believe her when she'd said she needed to leave. Maybe the only way to keep herself from falling into his arms and daring to believe he could solve all her problems was to be cruel even if she couldn't keep it up for very long.

At the beach, it was difficult to find a spot with a good view of the competition zone. Daniel explained that it was finals day. Each winner of the quarter finals would advance to the semis, each winner of the semifinals would advance to the final, and then a champion would be crowned.

The crowd was alive with anticipation. After a few tense minutes, Jane forgot Daniel was supposed to be uncomfortable. His explanations came effortlessly, his break-down of the scoring system transformed what had seemed to her an arbitrary and subjective guessing game into a quantifiable rubric where even she, after a bit of practice, could estimate how a ride would be scored.

As the heats passed and surfers were either eliminated or advanced toward the final, Jane and Daniel exchanged bets on who would win the comp. They decided the loser had to buy the other ice cream. Jane forgot about Seth, forgot about Daniel's brand. The world beyond the beach became irrelevant.

Jane's surfer won the competition on a buzzer-beater ride. She jumped up and threw her hands into the air as the audience rushed towards the water. The surfer, a rookie who had never been expected to make it to the quarters, let alone win, was chaired up the beach on the shoulders of his friends. His victory felt personal, as though Jane's belief in him had somehow made the win possible, the same way Daniel's belief in her music career had once made it seem possible.

They moved up to the boardwalk and sat together on a bench outside the ice cream store while the awards ceremony closed out the competition on the beach. Daniel still seemed happy, no hint of trauma. It felt safe to ask a dangerous question.

"Are you angry at the people who took your leg?"

"The doctors?"

"The uh—the Vanguard."

"Sometimes, I guess. But it's hard to be angry at a faceless organization. I don't remember a lot of what happened so it's not like I can point to a voice or an impression of them and have an object to focus on. Instead I've been angry at the doctors, at my shrink, at Steve."

"He makes that easy."

"That he does. But I think when the Vanguard—whoever they are— are finally caught, then I'll be angry. It scares me sometimes, what I might do once I know who they are. They've taken everything from me and I have no idea why."

"Maybe it's good you don't remember."

"It's like walking around with a jigsaw puzzle in your head. Five thousand pieces and you've lost the picture. Some of the pieces just don't match any others. My two clearest memories are of these really fat hands grabbing and hitting me. That person was so angry I thought he was going to tear me to pieces just with his hands. But then I remember someone else coming to bring me a drink of water. That person put their hand on my chest, like this," he reached over and pressed the heel of his palm over Jane's heart, "like they were trying to help me be calm. It worked actually. I thought I was going to be okay. And then other people came in and dragged me out. Everything gets dark and scattered after that."

The ice cream turned sour in Jane's stomach.

Tell him.

He'll hate me.

You're being selfish. It will give him peace.

Daniel's voice broke through her thoughts. "It bothers you, doesn't it?"

"It doesn't make sense that they'd attack you. They're not violent."

Except maybe Tommy.

"There could be others like me. Private trials."

"Or it could've been personal." Jane's voice came out in a whisper. She held her breath as Daniel shrugged, making an effort to push the conversation away.

"We should be getting back." When he stood up, he did not offer her his hand. Jane told herself it was her imagination, but it felt like he knew what she couldn't tell him.

During the day, a cleaning service had erased all signs of the party from Rhea's house. When Daniel and Jane arrived, Rhea was supervising Riley at the grill on the main level deck. Steve sprawled on the couch in the living room frowning at a script. He wore glasses that were probably real, but Jane couldn't help but feel they were a prop for a role he was preparing. Poppy was in the front room at the piano feeling her way through London Bridge.

Steve set down his script. Looked at them over the rims of his glasses. "Where have you two been?"

"Finals day," said Daniel. Jane thought he sounded proud. "Jane is now an expert judge of surfing."

"Of *watching* surfing." She laughed. "The next step is actually doing it."

This piqued Steve's interest. "You're going to teach her to surf?"

"We thought we'd go out to Oahu early, get her going before the big winter swells start showing up."

Jane put on a mock terror. "I only want baby waves."

Steve didn't look convinced. "Since Dan hasn't been on a board in almost a decade, you'd better start in a pond."

"Is that possible? To surf in a pond? I'd rather do that." Jane grabbed at Daniel's arm and looked desperate.

"Don't listen to him. He's just being an ass."

Riley poked her head through the kitchen archway. "You're here, good. Dan, come look at the chicken and tell me if it's done. Your mother says yes, but she eats everything half raw."

Daniel leaned over and kissed the side of Jane's head. "Back in a minute. Play nice."

Steve's eyes narrowed. He waited until they heard the screen door bang shut before he said, "I'm glad you've decided you can live with a cripple."

"He's more than that."

"Uh huh. Tell me, what's he like in bed? Does he hold himself up with that stub or does he lay on his back and make you do all the work?"

"Wouldn't you like to know."

"Seems like just yesterday you were in the clinic losing your mind."

"Why is it so impossible for you to believe someone might like him?"

"You mean besides being a cripple with chronic mental health issues? Let's see—"

"I think the idea that someone might want him is threatening to the idea that you can have any woman you want."

"Who said I wanted you?" Steve's eyes glittered with the same dark look she'd seen that morning.

Jane backed into the hallway and blew him a kiss as she turned the corner and walked into the kitchen. Her pulse pounded in her ears. Her cheeks felt flushed. When she walked out onto the deck, Rhea looked her over and said, "Jane, I believe you're glowing. Or are those my meds?"

Riley also took notice. Jane saw her catch Daniel's eye and wink at him.

At dinner, Poppy dominated the conversation. She complained that the mushrooms had touched her pineapple. When Rhea started talking about their upcoming trip to Hawaii, and Daniel questioned whether or not she could travel with her leg in a cast, Poppy interrupted with a story about a dead fish she'd found and how she needed to take it back to Hawaii where it had been born.

Jane tried to listen like Poppy was just one of the adults, but whenever she looked at the girl it was hard not to imagine her as Leah. They would've been about the same age, though of course Seth's strict discipline would've never allowed a child to challenge what she ate for dinner or stand up on her chair to reach across the table for the honey to add more sweetness to the huli huli chicken. Riley and Steve mostly ignored her, which made it harder for Jane to ignore her. She imagined what a family dinner would look like now if she'd stayed with Seth. The three of them around the small square of the kitchen table, or perhaps at a more formal setting in the dining room. Everything Leah would say Seth would find some way to turn it into instruction. Everything about Poppy's exuberance, her energy, her enthusiasm for describing the world as she saw it, seemed ripe for stern correction, which of course was one of many reasons why there was no Leah.

"Jane, you okay?" Riley waved her fork across Jane's field of vision.

"Sorry. Just tired." Jane drew herself up, put on a smile. "The food is excellent."

Riley beamed.

Jane focused her attention on Rhea who sat at the opposite end of the table from Poppy. "So I've only heard pieces of the story from Steve and Daniel. You started out in Hawaii but now you're here? Is that just because of Steve's career?"

"It's because she knows if she moved home, I wouldn't pay for her life anymore," said Steve.

"I grew up here actually," said Rhea. "But then my husband finished his PhD and he took a post doc fellowship on Oahu at the Oceanic Institute. And then he got a job, so we stayed."

"I like the ocean," said Poppy. "Grandpa says there's so, so many things in it, like *this* many things," Poppy spread her hands so wide she almost smacked Daniel in the face, "and some of them we can't even see."

Jane kept her attention on Rhea.

"Steve started acting so young, we didn't really know where it would go. I moved here with him and Daniel stayed in Hawaii with his father. And then, when Daniel got that fluke role—what was it, you were visiting for spring break?"

"I was waiting for him to finish an audition and the PA saw me and asked me to read. He said younger was always better."

"Go fuck yourself."

"Dad, you're not supposed to say that." Poppy shook her spoon at him. There was mashed potato on the spoon. Small white clumps flew into the air and landed on Steve's plate and in his water glass.

"Would you just calm the fuck down?" Steve snatched up his water and stormed into the kitchen.

Poppy crossed her arms over her chest and stuck out her lower lip. Two big tears formed at the corners of her eyes.

Daniel gently pulled her over onto his lap. "It's okay. It was an accident. Let's see what we can do about these mushrooms, huh? I don't think they're so bad. You know fish eat mushrooms?"

Jane watched him for only a moment before she knew she wouldn't be able to hold herself together. She excused herself and went out onto the deck, but she could still hear Daniel talking to Poppy. She climbed the stairs to the third floor, sank into one of the lawn chairs, and drew her legs up against her chest. She pulled Daniel's sweatshirt over them to keep warm.

Her mind swam with impossible alternative histories. What if she'd gone to Battery Park to meet Daniel? What if they'd run away together? He could've toured as a professional surfer. She would've always been on the beach cheering him on. They would've explored the world, tried new food, met interesting people, learned about anything and everything. If there'd been children, she wouldn't have been afraid of leaving Daniel alone with them. She wouldn't have had to watch their innocence be exploited for an indoctrination that would make them an alien to the rest of the world, a system that would leave them with nothing to hang onto if they someday didn't want to be part of that system.

She wasn't sure how long she'd been sitting there before Daniel joined her. He had her purse with him. "Your phone has been ringing."

"Thanks."

It was Alma's phone that had been ringing. There were two missed calls from their boss.

"Everything okay?" Daniel sat down beside her.

"Not really."

"My family is an acquired taste."

Jane laughed. "I'm not used to being around kids."

"We don't have to be here. We could go to my place."

"Will Steve stay here tonight?"

"Probably. The forecast is good for the cove tomorrow. He'll probably stay and surf."

"Then we should stay. He needs to think we're sleeping together. That's what's going to do it for him, I think."

"Sounds about right. We'll be up in Mom's room since she's stuck on the first floor."

"Good."

He hesitated. She sensed him debating something. Finally, he said, "Since we're never going to see each other again after tomorrow night if there's anything you want to say, you know, just to say it, I'm a pretty low stakes audience."

Jane wanted to laugh, but she was afraid she'd cry. She hated how easily he read her, how he seemed to know what she needed even when she couldn't admit what she needed to herself.

The setting sun was breaking through the clouds to cast hazy orange and pink beams of light out across the grey water. She considered that perhaps there was one secret she could tell Daniel. Maybe it would help her to have someone pass judgement who could be impartial.

Five years and sixty-three days ago Jane had stood under the swaying palm trees outside the Los Angeles Amtrak station facing the distended Eduard Munch heads of graffiti figures on the side of a Mexican restaurant. It was her first clear memory of California. Staring at those empty screaming heads, she thought her nightmares had followed her. She was heavy-headed after failing to sleep on an overnight from Denver and still wearing the thick maxi pads the nurse had given her for the spotting she'd said was normal after the procedure.

While Jane stood trying to decide what she would do now that she'd arrived in the city she thought would be the most difficult place for Seth to find her, it began to rain. Jane considered going to the waiting room. A miniature old lady in a red hat with matching luggage sat on a bench by the bus stop sign. *If she isn't going inside, I'm not either.* Jane tried to catch her eye to share this moment of being women who didn't mind a little rain, who didn't mind a lot of things.

Jane explained to Daniel how she used to take pride in her ability to accept whatever came. She liked being the one who helped other people get what they wanted, never forcing anyone to do what she wanted or stepping on toes or hurting anyone's feelings. That's what she thought she was doing when, two weeks after returning from her honeymoon, Jane had made a doctor's appointment she hadn't written on the family calendar and asked for birth control pills. What Seth didn't know wouldn't hurt him, she'd thought.

One night, her brothers and some of Seth's friends (the Vanguard) had come over to hang out (celebrate the successful trial of one of their top twenty-five most important targets). It was a football season Saturday. Someone brought a root beer keg and they'd all camped out in the living room, drunk on adrenaline and too little sleep, to watch Nebraska take on Oklahoma. The living room was directly below Jane and Seth's bedroom where she was studying for her semester practicum exam.

Here, Jane paused to explain that she'd finished her degree at home after her marriage.

She could hear everything her family and their friends said through the air vent. She'd listened with half an ear as she made flashcards. The country music station was playing a retrospective of Patsy Cline, which Jane was enjoying because she knew nothing about country music. These hours she spent studying were the only time she could choose her own music. Otherwise Seth always had something inspirational on like Third Day and Jeremy Camp, or the house was vibrating with one of his beloved ska bands.

At some point, Jane became aware the voices downstairs weren't as loud.

"When do you expect it will be?" asked Phil, always the worrier.

Jane crept out of the semi-circle of rainbow-colored index cards she'd set out on the floor and laid down beside the vent.

"When's the best time to conceive?" asked Seth.

"Just before bed isn't it?"

"Not during?" asked Jamal, joking and uncomfortable.

"I switched the pills two weeks ago," said Seth.

"So she could be pregnant now. What's nine months from today?" asked Aaron.

"June," said Phil.

"They're going to score again!" cried Tommy.

"No trials in June," said Aaron. "We have to make sure Bones isn't distracted by being a new father and all that." He laughed.

Jane had tried to form animal shapes out of the texture of the plaster ceiling. Blotches of red and blue blinked around her vision. She counted how many times they'd had sex that month. Maybe four times, a very slight chance of pregnancy, but still a chance.

Patsy Cline sang with peppy nostalgia as Jane jumped up and ran into the bathroom. She dug through her drawer of hair brushes, rubber bands, and dusty scrunchies until she found her pills in their compact disguise. She'd never seen Seth open that drawer. Certainly, he had no reason to look way in the back unless he was searching for something particular. And he wouldn't know to look for pills.

Unless her mother had told him.

As soon as the thought entered Jane's head she'd known it was true.

Her mother—who barely spoke—had told Seth her secret. She'd stared out the window when Jane tried to express the pressure she was feeling to have kids, and how she hoped her mother would be the one to understand Jane needed to take precautions. She given Jane nothing but her silence, and then she had turned around and given Seth everything.

The pills in her drawer that night looked exactly like her real ones—a cardboard circle with a calendar, each day marked by a little pillow of tin foil. Jane popped out that day's pill. She set it on her tongue and let it dissolve rather than swallowing it with water. Instead of sour medicine, her tongue found the equally displeasing but distinct taste of baking soda.

Jane braced her arms against the counter and gave herself a good long stare down in the mirror. What she saw was not the face of a mother. Try as she might, she wasn't there. Jane kept hearing Seth say, *I switched the pills two weeks ago.* Switched how?

Jane pulled open his bathroom drawer. It had a razor, deodorant— all the usual things. She searched the cabinet beneath the sink. She searched behind the trash can and all the toilet paper rolls. She searched the medicine cabinet, nothing.

Next stop, the bedroom. She'd tripped over the portable stereo and left Patsy singing into the carpet. Her search gained speed. Seth had to have hidden fake birth control pills somewhere. She'd become obsessed with finding them. No drawer was left unopened, no clothes pockets unchecked. If Jane had been as thorough a cleaner as she was a manic searcher that night, her mother would've been proud.

Groans of agony erupted downstairs as Nebraska dropped another pass. Jane prayed to the football gods for the game to go into overtime.

She'd worked up a sweat by then. Her hair stuck to her face and her neck, the back of her nightie to her lower back. She leaned on the bed to catch her breath. That's when it hit her. *The bed.*

She dug her fingers under the lip of the mattress—one, two, three, heave! She shoved it up into the air until its opposite end slid and crashed into Seth's end table. Spread in a pool of silvery foil circles on top of the box spring were, one, two three ... fifteen months' worth of baking soda birth control pills.

Greedily Jane scooped them up, pinched them together and bent them. She ran downstairs with them. Oops, dropped one. It sailed through the air like a flying saucer. Through the entryway she went, in her 'husband's eyes only' nightie, breasts bouncing, nipples ripe enough to cut glass, and fourteen pill packs.

"Look what I found!" Jane flung the packs up into the air, showering the startled men with her discovered treasure.

Seth sprang back as if the packets would burn him. Jamal and Phil looked away in embarrassment at her indecency. Her brothers stared. For a moment, the room was frozen. No one knew what to do, and then Jane started crying.

Aaron recovered first. He stood up and motioned for the others to follow. "We should leave." He didn't even look at her as he walked by. She was Seth's problem now, he'd seemed to say. He couldn't help her. Jane wanted to grab him and make him stay so she wouldn't have to be alone with the man who had betrayed her. But she could also hear Aaron's voice in her head saying she'd committed the first betrayal by getting pills. This was her hole to crawl out of.

"Babies are gifts from God," said Seth. "You can't mess with that, Jane. It isn't right."

She'd looked at him, pleading for him to understand. "But, I can't—"

"None of us can alone. But God helps. And I'll help. We'll do it together." He'd wrapped her in a blanket and patted her like he was putting out a fire.

Over the next month, Seth's attempts to mold her into a model Christian wife had become more forceful. They no longer had casual conversations about the differences in what they believed. Instead, they had arguments. He said a child couldn't be raised in an atmosphere of conflict. He said she needed to see how her desire to challenge what they believed would compromise their parenting. Jane refused to have sex. People at church started coming up to her and recommending marriage counselors.

And then he'd asked her to take a pregnancy test. She agreed but made him promise that if the test was negative he'd give her another year before bringing up the idea of having kids. In turn, Jane promised to stop pursuing her interest in 'secular culture' if the test was positive.

It was positive.

Seth had been overjoyed. The fights stopped. Jane was showered with praise and forgiveness, which had felt good at first. Per their agreement, Jane set about trying to bury the parts of her that didn't fit the rules. She put away her non-classical piano music. She stopped covert trips to art museums. She ignored text messages from her friend Theresa who had been teaching her about wine. She joined a women's Bible study. And then, one weekend, while Seth was on a hunting trip, Jane had skipped her Bible study and rented *SLUT: A Love Story*.

Until then, she'd done what she considered an above average job of stifling her memories of meeting Daniel in New York. She'd thought of herself as on a quest to find the balance she saw embodied in Daniel, a balance between the secular world and the principles of Jane's alternative world. But being pregnant was not about balance or staying in control of buried emotional impulses. Once Jane decided Bible study wasn't happening, she'd driven to Blockbuster like a mad woman in search of the last Starbucks at the end of the world.

But the movie, which mostly exploited Daniel's good looks and chiseled shirtless body, was not the Daniel Jane had been looking for. She returned the movie without finishing it. At the Best Buy across the street from Blockbuster, Jane found the movie soundtracks tucked away on a small shelf by the PC software. She still had Daniel's list. Three years and it hadn't left her purse. She bought titles based solely on Daniel's recommendations. This was what her mother and almost every adult she'd ever known called a 'slippery slope,' an apparently innocuous interest that led into temptation. From there it was only a hop, skip, and a jump into sin and, 'mistakes she'd regret the rest of her life.'

Feasting her ears on Daniel's music, the regret Jane had anticipated for the rest of her life was not being allowed to dream of Daniel, of having a child who would be dependent on her toeing the line for twenty more years and doing it well enough she never realized her mother didn't believe what she should. The worst thing Jane could imagine was causing someone else to doubt because Jane felt the need for a different kind of life.

For the next forty-six hours, Jane had floated through the depths of a symphonic ocean. She'd played movie music while she slept, though she didn't sleep much. The music traveled with her in the car, while she studied, while she shopped for groceries. She hadn't answered the phone because she didn't want to pause during an important theme. She delayed taking a shower until a CD finished. She held one-sided imaginary conversations with Daniel where she told him how she enjoyed this or that track. She reveled in the simple melodies and contrapuntal orchestrations. She forgot to ask herself if what she was doing was right. She did not search for a moral answer to justify her obsession.

When Seth came home from his hunt, he'd found her browning meat for spaghetti sauce and crying into the steam coming up from the pan while she listened to *Titanic*. She had been playing one small section of *An Ocean of Memories* over and over on the little portable speaker she kept in the kitchen. Just past the halfway point of the track, the ethereal orchestra faded away and a naked horn arose from the silence tracing a simple melody filled with old loss, remembering something that could never be regained. She had heard the same melody embedded in the scores of several different Horner albums, each of them calling her to a place she couldn't name because it only existed in her dreams. She dripped tears into her skillet as she listened, wishing she could return to that place.

Seth had jerked her around by the shoulders, terrified that something had happened to the baby. Jane tried to articulate an excuse about hormones making her emotional, but the more she cried the more nervous he had become. Finally, he'd had the sense to turn off the music. In the sudden silence, the cello continued to weave its melody in her head and Jane understood. "I just need to be alone."

Since she had been alone all weekend, Seth had been confused by this request. It didn't occur to him she meant a different kind of alone. After dinner he sat down to watch football. She offered to run out to Dairy Queen to get him dessert. Instead, she drove west out of town. She hadn't stopped until she'd reached the Colorado border.

She hadn't left a note. Jane explained to Daniel that she'd always thought it was kinder for Seth to think what he wanted than have to face the absolute certainty of her abandonment. She couldn't admit that all his hopes for fatherhood—the crib they'd put together in the small bedroom, the stacks of parenting books he'd underlined and dog-eared and flagged with an army of Post-Its—would only ever be hopes.

Jane held it together through most of the story. But when she reached Colorado where she stayed with her aunt and had made the decision to have the abortion, words were impossible. She'd gone so many years pretending none of it had happened. Finally being able to admit it brought a relief she hadn't known possible. She had betrayed everything she knew about being a good woman. Since then, she had lived without any hope of redemption even though she now knew there were other parts of being a woman than the role of wife and mother. Hazy moonlight illuminated Daniel's face. She saw her broken heart mirrored in Daniel's tear-filled eyes. It felt as though they had traveled a lifetime together while sitting on that deck.

He took her hand and held it against his face. He kissed it. By the end of her story their bodies were practically intertwined, the two chairs pressed together with her legs over his lap and his arm around her. Her head on his shoulder. The secrets that had kept them apart had faded to mere specks on a cloudy future horizon.

When he rose and motioned for her to follow him down to Rhea's bedroom on the second floor, Jane knew what would come next. She understood now what Shayla had meant about wishing she'd been with her former boyfriend even after she'd known it would end. This night would be a relic she would carry with her in the long lonely months ahead, something to prove the dream had been real. Something she could pull out and use to confirm she was still worthy of love, however brief, however fated.

CHAPTER 19

Jane woke up alone in Rhea's bed. Daniel had left a note on the side table saying he was down at the beach. Relaxing in the bed, Jane used Alma's phone to check the Amtrak schedule. There were no trains to Canada; it was Sunday. There were fifteen missed calls on Alma's phone. *Alma is way more popular than me,* thought Jane as she logged in to check her messages online.

There was a message from her art dealer date asking if she'd changed her mind about a marriage of convenience. There was a message from Doraceli that sounded a little panicky. She wanted to know if Jane knew why Alma hadn't come to work. Jane replied that she had no idea about Alma; they weren't currently speaking to each other. It sounded a little juvenile, but Jane sent it anyway. The full details were complicated, and Doraceli didn't really deserve to know them anyway.

It was easier not to think about Alma and her plan to tell the FBI about Jane's association with the Vanguard, so Jane chose not to wonder why Alma had not come to work. She did not think about the plan for Tommy to visit Alma and how, perhaps this visit could have precipitated the break-in at Jane's condo. She did not think that maybe, given what she now knew the Vanguard had done to Daniel, she needed to revise her expectations of the level of violence they were capable of committing. None of these very important connections were dots on the horizon of

Jane's consciousness. She thought only that it was not so bad to have to wait one more day before leaving town.

She pulled on Daniel's sweatshirt and went down to the beach. Just as Daniel had predicted, Steve was surfing. Riley and Poppy were out with him. Daniel sat on a log of driftwood nursing a steaming thermos. He moved to one side so there was space for her to sit beside him.

"Morning." He handed her the thermos for a sip. "You may be tempted to think the universe is conspiring to keep you here but actually I bribed Amtrak to cancel the train tonight."

"You're a terrible liar."

"Is it selfish to be glad you're stuck here?"

"If me staying one more day helps with your job, I'm glad, too."

She knew it wasn't the answer he wanted, but he was careful not to let his disappointment show. "We could still go to the police and file a restraining order against your husband. I've got that lawyer's number right here." He waved his phone at her. "Just one call would get it started."

Jane squinted out at the water. "Steve doesn't seem very worried about finding a costar. Do you think that means he's decided?" She watched Poppy glide into a little wave and try to stand up on her board. She managed a steady stance for about three seconds before losing her balance and falling. Even knowing she'd had plenty of practice, Jane worried when the water swallowed her up. Her parents sat out in the channel waiting for the next wave, not paying attention to her. Snatches of what sounded like yelling drifted towards the beach, broken by the breeze.

"He's got a meeting with the producer tomorrow afternoon," said Daniel.

"And the decision will be made at the meeting?"

"Probably."

Poppy rode onto the beach. She rolled off her board, sand sticking to her, laughing. Steve and Riley, having jockeyed for the same wave and knocked each other out of position, waded out of the water onto the beach. Riley came first with Steve sloshing through the foam to catch up to her.

"Would you just stop?" He grabbed her arm and forcibly turned her. "You can't do this without me."

"Fuck off." Riley jerked away. She stormed up the steep steps to Rhea's house. Steve followed, yelling something that got swallowed up in the pockets of air between the rocks. Poppy stood on the beach holding her surfboard. When it was clear neither parent was going to turn around and remember her, she looked to Daniel.

"They're fighting about me."

"It sounds like it's about you but it's really about them." Daniel motioned her over and brushed sand off her arm. "We should do something fun today, huh? Jane needs some fun before she has to go away tomorrow."

"We could go to the water park."

"It will be really crowded today."

"We could go to Pirate's Cove. My friend Mindi is there on Sundays because that's when she's at her dad's house."

"That's a good idea." Daniel turned to Jane who very slightly shook her head to signal that she did not want to spend the day with Poppy. "We'd love to do that with you," he said.

"Can I wear my princess dress?"

"Sure."

"I gotta go get dressed then." She handed Daniel her surfboard and raced up the stairs to the house.

"Daniel, I can't—"

"She's not Leah. She's not going to hurt you or condemn you or anything like what you're afraid of."

"You're determined to break down my walls, aren't you?"

"I know a little about avoidance tactics." He smiled. "But thanks to you, I went to a surfing competition yesterday. I enjoyed it. And I think you're stronger than me."

"I don't know about that."

"Just try it for a few hours. I'll be with you."

"It won't work."

"Just two hours. If you need to, we can hide out alone the rest of the day."

She wanted to love him for pushing her. She'd been waiting for this, a man confident and observant enough to change her in a way she couldn't change herself. *If only . . .* The thought was left unfinished as tears threatened. She hurried up the stairs ahead of him so he wouldn't see.

By the time she'd reached the top of the stairs, Jane had pulled herself together. She waited for Daniel beside the garage instead of going into the house where she might encounter Poppy. Inside the garage, the retro muscle car had its engine back in place. It had moved to the stall closest to the stairs beside Riley's olive-colored SUV and the Maserati. In the stall where the muscle car used to be parked was Jane's Jeep. Steve was in the garage growling to himself like a caged bear.

She moved into the garage and saw he was prying the bent front of the Jeep's hood out from under the grille, his face red from exertion. *Steve Fletcher the mechanic.* She thought the work suited him. It almost redeemed the playboy side of him she hated. How often did *People's* Sexiest Man get down and dirty with car engines to work out his frustration?

He leveraged a tire iron under the hood and shoved down hard to pop it free. When he bent down to pick up another tool, he saw her standing at the door. For a moment she caught a fleeting glimpse of animal ferocity in his face. When it passed, instead of his usual sly charm there was only a nod of acknowledgement, almost acceptance. He pointed to her feet. "There's nails and stuff around."

"I didn't realize you'd had my car towed in."

"You're welcome."

Steve dug his fingers under the hood and shoved it up. His oversized biceps flexed and strained the sleeves of his T-shirt. The bent metal groaned into place. "You had a good time last night," he observed.

"We did."

"Glad one of us is enjoying ourselves."

He looked past her towards the door. Daniel stood a few feet back.

Jane knew it was him without having to turn around. Nobody else walked so carefully they were virtually silent.

"Riley wants to put Poppy in a fucking boarding school. She's already set up the admissions interview—tomorrow afternoon of course, at the same fucking time as the production meeting."

Daniel moved into the garage. "Can't you move it?"

"Nope."

The door from the house opened and Poppy bounded down the stairs in a purple dress covered in glitter and rhinestones. Riley followed her. Steve charged across the garage, nearly knocking Jane over in his rush to intercept Riley before she reached her tank of an SUV. "You can't do this without me."

"Get out of my way."

Poppy's smile vanished. She looked to Daniel. Her eyebrows drew together in a single furrow of worry, a mirror image of Daniel when he was deep in thought. "Ready to go?"

Steve's hand slapped against the side of the SUV. He pinned her up against it, his palms on her shoulders. "I'm her father and I say she's not going to some hotel school where we only see her at Christmas."

"Like you care." Riley shoved her fist into Steve's hip as she ducked under his arm. He tried to grab her. She slashed him across his neck with her nails. Their arms became a jumble of furious movement too fast to know who was doing what. Neither noticed Daniel, Jane, and Poppy walk out to the Prius in the driveway.

"Are they always like that?" asked Jane as Daniel helped Poppy into the back seat and Jane settled into the front passenger seat.

"My mom says Dad's an otter." Poppy leaned into the gap between the seats. Her hand rested just above Jane's shoulder. Jane wanted to touch her, offer comfort in some way but she was also terrified that touching her might break her. "*I* think he's too tall to be an otter."

"That just means he's playful," said Jane.

"And he likes to eat fish." Poppy laughed. It was a very adult laugh, filled with all the sarcasms and innuendos the world had forced upon her. A child in Jane's world would never know such things. She would've been protected.

"Jane and I are going to drive thru to get some breakfast. Have you eaten yet, Poppy?"

"I want chocolate bunny pancakes."

"Those are only at Delco's; we're not going there."

"I don't want anything else."

"You have to eat breakfast."

Poppy flounced back against the seat. "Chocolate bunny pancakes."

Daniel looked to Jane. "Can you do Delco's again?"

Jane sat with her hands clenched in her lap. She nodded. Where they ate breakfast seemed irrelevant.

Daniel covered her hands with his. "Delco's it is."

Poppy insisted they sit at a patio table. The morning smog had burned off and the full force of the sun revealed itself. It was a perfect day.

"I have a surprise for you tomorrow," said Daniel.

Jane had been so distracted by Poppy that she was surprised to look over and see Daniel gazing at her with an open, almost embarrassing affection. "Really?"

"You're very lucky you are stuck here, or you would've missed it."

"You should give her a hint," said Poppy. "Dad always gives me hints when he has a surprise."

"Nope. She just has to wait and see." He reached for her hand under the table.

Jane felt heat rising on her cheeks. She scooted her chair over so she sat closer to him. It still wasn't close enough.

"Once, when I was four, Dad lied and said we were going to Disneyland but instead we went to the zoo and we saw all the baby animals. They were so cute. The baby tigers and the baby zebra. But not the baby penguins—they were ugh, like too fluffy." Poppy dug her fork into her pancakes. "Have you ever been to the zoo, Jane?"

"Not here. I've been to one where I'm from."

"Where are you from?"

"Far away. But we have a very famous zoo there. People come from all over the world to see it."

Poppy looked doubtful. "Does it have pandas? Ms. Watts says our zoo is special because of the pandas. I haven't seen them yet, but Dad promised we'd go before his new movie because they will have to go back to China before he gets back."

There was a pause. Jane realized Poppy was waiting for her to say something.

"I like pandas." Jane caught Daniel's eye. He gave her a discrete thumbs up.

He pushed back from the table. "I'm going to run to the boy's room before we go to the park." He bent down and kissed the top of her head as he passed. "You're fine," he whispered.

Jane heard the frenzy of paparazzi shutters capturing Daniel's display of affection from across the street. She wondered why Daniel didn't seem to be worried people were taking their picture. He'd said he wasn't famous enough for anyone to care what he did, but Jane wasn't convinced. She looked across the street and glared at the paparazzi as though her irritation might shame them into going away.

There were only five of them. They paced the sidewalk, jostling each other for angles, always on the lookout for new celebrity arrivals while also monitoring those already at the restaurant. There was a sixth man standing back from the rest, conspicuous for his lack of movement and lack of a camera. He was taller and had a bulk on him atypical of most southern Californians. He wore a Hawaiian shirt and sunglasses, maybe because he thought that was what people in California wore, maybe as a disguise. Either way it didn't fool her.

Seth.

Jane very carefully continued rotating her gaze among the paparazzi. She allowed it to pass Seth naturally two more times as she reached for her coffee and took a sip. When she set her mug on the table, she allowed the motion to redirect her gaze to her food. She kept eating even though she could no longer taste anything. She smiled at Poppy who had glee-fully eaten both the ears off her chocolate bunny pancake.

Daniel returned to the table visibly preoccupied. As soon as he sat down, he pulled out his phone and began scrolling.

"Daniel?"

"One sec, there's something weird on the news I want to check out."

She saw his hand tremble as he held the phone.

"Daniel." She kept the smile on her face. "We should take a taxi to the park."

"A taxi, that sounds fun."

She reached for her mug only to find it empty. She pretended to drink anyway. "Poppy finish up, we need to leave." She used Alma's phone to order a taxi pickup. As she was finishing, Daniel managed to detach his attention from his phone.

"What are you doing?"

"Have Steve's guys come pick up your car later."

Daniel's hands were shaking now, a full-on earthquake that made the glass tabletop rattle.

"Uncle Daniel, do you need your pills?" asked Poppy.

"If I take my pills I'll have to go to sleep, and I won't be able to play with you."

"What's on the news?" asked Jane.

"Why are we taking a taxi?"

They studied each other across the table, both trying to figure out what the other wouldn't say. Jane thought about texting but somehow putting such a statement into written form made it seem too real. As long as it was just in her mind, as long as she did not look left and see Seth standing behind the paparazzi, there remained the chance her eyes had played tricks on her.

"Poppy, do you need a box?" asked Daniel.

"No, I'm full. I can't eat anymore."

"Run over there and ask the waitress for a box anyway. I want your bunny for later."

Poppy wrinkled her nose. "You don't like chocolate bunnies."

"Poppy, please go ask for a box."

"Fine, okay, I'll do it." Poppy slid out of her chair and under the table where she hopped like a frog and bumped her head on the glass before crawling out and walking inside to find their waitress.

"The FBI have a confidential informant who can identify one of the Vanguard," said Daniel. "Apparently, he was her boyfriend."

Jane wrapped her hands around the metal frame of the table and kept them there to remind herself to be careful what she said. Her new intimacy with Daniel made it easy to forget what remained unspoken between them. "They have a name?"

"Just a face. But these days a face is the end right? There are cameras everywhere. They could have an arrest today. It could be over today." His eyes were lit with a fevered vehemence that frightened her.

"That would be something." Jane pressed her lips together.

"What's this plan with a taxi?"

"My husband is here."

"Where?"

"It doesn't matter where. Your car is too easy to follow."

Daniel nodded. "Okay . . . Do you still want to go to the park?"

"I never wanted to go to the park." She tried on a teasing smile. Poppy was almost back to the table. "But we shouldn't go back to your mom's until we know he's not following us."

The taxi rounded the corner at the end of the block.

"You okay to walk?" she asked.

"I'm fine." As though to prove it, Daniel stood. He was a little unsteady, his movements sloppy, but he managed to shovel Poppy's remaining pancake into the box. Jane took Poppy's hand and walked her to the patio gate just as the taxi pulled up.

"Can I sit by the window?"

"Go for it."

Poppy slid all the way across the back seat. Jane slid into the middle.

Daniel was right behind her. He closed the door a little too hard as he gave the driver directions to the park.

"Poppy, buckle up," said Jane. She reached over and clasped Daniel's hand. Touching him was the only way she could push back her certainty that the end had come for them.

The drive to the park was less than ten minutes, not nearly long enough for Jane to feel safe. As they'd pulled away from Delco's she thought she'd seen a flash of color that could've been Seth's Hawaiian shirt as he sprinted down the sidewalk, probably to a car. She thought it was unlikely that he would've caught up to them no matter how close his car had been. But then, it seemed unlikely that in a city of millions of people he had found her.

Poppy ran across the grass to the playground fashioned to look like a pirate ship. Daniel and Jane followed more slowly. They found a bench where they could keep Poppy in sight but where no one would be able to approach them without being seen.

"What do you want to do?" asked Daniel.

Jane shrugged. It didn't feel like there was anything to be done except leave. "He knows I'm with you now. You're easy to track."

"I'll hire a guard."

"Or you could just drop me off at a hotel."

"I'm not leaving you alone until I put you on that train tomorrow."

"You don't get it. He saw me with Poppy. He probably thinks she's Leah and that you and I have set up a family with his daughter. It's not safe for me to stay with you."

"Maybe it would be good to talk to him. If he knows Leah's not an option maybe he won't want you back."

"He doesn't work like that."

"Jane, this is getting absurd. He can't be as unreasonable as you make him sound. If I was in his shoes I'd want to know." Daniel's leg thumped uncontrollably against the ground. His right hand massaged the base of his neck. "How does such a beautiful day end up being so stressful?"

"Maybe it's me?"

"You *are* in need of a lot of life managing. Almost as much as Steve, which means you're basically helpless." He tried to laugh but his voice caught. He drew a deep breath in and struggled to release it. "It's not you. It's this Vanguard thing. I have to know. But it's maddening not being able to handle knowing."

"You have your Ativan?"

He pulled a prescription bottle out of his pocket.

"You should take one."

"I'll miss half the day."

"I'll still be here. It's better than ending up in that clinic, right?"

"It'll pass. It's just I don't have any water—I keep it in the Prius, but—it'll be fine. I don't really need it."

"Who handles this when it happens?"

"Steve." Daniel looked defeated. "He takes care of the one thing I can't manage: myself."

"This is not a big deal. Take a pill."

Daniel continued to hesitate. The shaking was getting worse. "Daniel." She laid her hand on his hand. It was both a natural gesture and an alien one. Something she had never done and yet had been waiting so long to do.

He nodded. She helped him open the pill bottle. He swallowed one dry and sagged further into defeat. As though to avoid looking at her, he leaned forward and glared at the grass between his legs. Jane pressed up against him and linked her arm through his.

"Uncle Dan, come play!" Poppy waved from the crow's nest of the playground.

Daniel struggled to wave back. He leaned heavily against Jane's shoulder as she texted Steve. "You think the reason we get along is because neither of us manage our lives very well?"

"Speak for yourself," she laughed. "I was doing just fine until this week."

"I'm going to come find you after you leave," murmured Daniel. "We belong together. You see that, right?"

"In a simpler world, maybe."

The pill was taking effect. Jane gently lowered his head onto her lap as he drifted off. She took his phone from his hand and pulled up the browser where the FBI wanted poster was still active. Jane knew what to expect but seeing Tommy's face cut from the family photo taken at her wedding still shocked her. *Did the FBI cut out the rest of the family or had Alma?* Jane wasn't sure it mattered. Her best hope was that she would be able to say goodbye to Daniel and make her train before the FBI came to arrest her.

BREAKING NEWS Bulletin:
FBI Releases image of Vanguard
Terrorist
Sunday 12:16 PST.
Los Angeles, California

FBI Special Investigators Sao and Martens
announced a breakthrough in their search
for the terrorist group known as the
Vanguard. Based on information procured
from a secret informant with ties to the
organization, the below image is believed
to be the terrorist known as Mirt. He is
a Caucasian male approximately six feet
tall, between 25–35 years old with blue
eyes and light brown hair. If you have any
information about a man matching this
description, please call the investigation
hotline 302-666-6478.

CHAPTER 20

Some days, everything Daniel could imagine became real.

Instead of the worn slats of the deck, the raised head of the nail by the railing, the knob of gnarled wood by the leg of his lawn chair, he felt his bare feet on a waxed Firewire V4 cutting turns on a perfect set of Gold Coast waves. He was still a surfer.

He was also a lover. He thought of Jane naked, the curve of her breasts—one a little larger than the other, both of them more than filling his hands—the way the line of her shoulders echoed the shape of her hips, both of them solid and easy to hang on to. She was made of the same stuff of his dream of surfing. This was partly due to the haze of his meds wearing off. But it was also impossible to absorb how quickly his life had been transformed, how everything now felt possible. Surfing and Jane. Getting his career back.

Below him the kitchen screen slapped shut against the frame.

So enters Steven the elder, thought Daniel, in a movie trailer voiceover. *The taller by one point five inches, who made five million dollars on his last movie.* It had been a forgettable summer blockbuster about the end of the world. But he would rather have made twenty thousand doing an indie with a director who'd chosen Steve for his acting ability rather than his A list name. That was what the Hawaii project was about: getting something made that Steve could be proud of, that showcased his talents.

Steve handed Daniel a fresh water bottle. His eyes snagged on Daniel's bare feet—one real foot and one synthetic shell with carved toes fitted around a steel carbon frame—then skipped away. "You'll have to forget about teaching Jane to surf. Surfline updated their forecast for Hawaii. Looks like that swell coming down from Alaska is arriving sooner than expected. And it's gonna be huge."

"Too big?"

"Not for us." He grinned. "It'll hit Oahu a week from Monday. Mom's pissed you'll be out there and she'll be the gimp for once."

"I'm not going out if the waves are more than three feet Hawaiian."

In Daniel's peripheral vision he saw Steve push back his disappointment. Usually he hid behind a glib joke, or toying sarcasm, or a quick one-liner. Instead he came around behind Daniel and bear hugged his chest and the back of the chair against him. "Someday someone's gonna get smart and make a wetsuit with sensors in it like those motion capture suits. I'll be able to go out there and surf and you'll have—I dunno—some kind of visor or something around your head and my suit will transmit everything it feels into your head and it will be just the same as if you were out there."

"That'd be something." Daniel tried not to move so Steve wouldn't back away. He worried about hurting Daniel by being too forceful. Before New York they'd always been at each other, stealing things from pockets, racing, shoving. Rhea used to start phone calls to their father with a list of damages—cracked furniture, holes knocked into walls, complaints from friends' parents. Since New York, they'd learned to be more careful with each other.

Steve rested his chin on Daniel's head. "We'll track down Kelly Slater during the Triple Crown. I bet he could make it happen."

"Bet he could."

They watched the grey lines of smog on the horizon blend with the grey of the ocean, forming the setting of the sun into monochrome bands. The knob of Steve's chin dug into Daniel's skull as Steve rolled his head from side to side, drummed his fingers on Daniel's shoulders.

"You remember last week when I had that really bad attack?"

"I try not to."

"I was watching the press conference with the target and I had a new flashback."

"Anything good?"

"I remember them yelling at me about a girl I shouldn't have messed with. I thought maybe that supports our theory that they meant to grab you instead."

"That's your theory, not mine."

"Do you remember who you were seeing in New York?"

"Nope."

"Humor me."

"I wasn't seeing anyone. There wasn't time. We were behind schedule. Half of it was night shoots."

"There must've been—"

"You're the one who met a girl in New York."

Daniel turned this over in his head and dismissed it. He had only been with Jane a few hours. They hadn't done anything but talk. There had been no reason for anyone to have been watching them. *Unless she had already been married and her husband was spying on her.*

She hadn't been married.

So she said.

Daniel pushed the thoughts away and said, "Do you ever regret not going to the police?"

"Let's not go there, okay?"

"Maybe if I'd have been able to help them catch the—"

"You'd have hurt us more than helped the police."

"I think I should talk to them now."

"Like fuck you should."

"I don't want to live the rest of my life afraid of someone finding out what happened. If this woman can come forward and identify one of them, I should be able to say they targeted me."

"What about me, huh?"

"A Vanguard trial doesn't always ruin someone's career."

"Sure, but no one else has had their little brother attacked in their place. And it wasn't a trial, it was a shit show."

You have no idea.

"The press would destroy me."

Daniel wanted to argue, to say that Steve didn't have a right to say what Daniel could or couldn't do. But Daniel knew that wasn't fair. It was more than a public concern. It was their family. Their parents knowing. Poppy going to school and having her classmates talking about it.

As much as Daniel wanted resolution, he knew it would have to be from a distance. He couldn't imagine a scenario where Steve crossed a line that would make him deserve what would probably be a publicity nightmare. *Unless he tried to sabotage me and Jane.* Something like that, Daniel could shirk all responsibility to the family and expose the secret that would upend their lives.

Far below, the garage door rumbled open. Steve flinched. Daniel felt him shifting gears, preparing for the entrance of other people. "Jane's back."

"Jane's back."

"I think she's warming up to me."

"She's not."

"You can't deny we had a moment yesterday."

There he goes again, rewriting history. The Vanguard attack couldn't be his fault. Just like Jane couldn't be as apathetic to his charms as she appeared.

"We're going to the studio tomorrow morning, but I'll be around if you need me to sit in the production meeting."

"I don't think so."

"Has Rowan found any good guys to replace Garrett?"

"Nope. But I have."

"You're sure you want me?"

"Not really, but Jane seems to have worked a miracle. If it doesn't stick, or she turns out to be less than she appears to be, then I'll know where to find you when you ruin my movie." The teasing sounded like a threat, but it was more than Daniel had hoped for.

"That means a lot, Steve."

"Just to be clear, I'm not saying she's one hundred percent only into you. Women are complicated and you shouldn't feel bad if she gets all hot and bothered sitting next to me at dinner."

"*If* you sit next to her at dinner." Daniel pushed up out of his chair and made as though to run down the stairs. Steve shoved past him, sprinting to make it down to the kitchen first, the way he used to when there was still the chance Daniel would beat him.

CHAPTER 21

Jane hadn't slept well. Rhea's house, a safe and welcoming refuge during the day, had become a shelter for monsters in the night. Every creak and groan became an imagined footstep, an invasion force just moments away from breaking down the door. Her anxiety, fueled by lack of sleep, made it difficult to express the excitement as she and Daniel drove through the gates of the movie studio that owned Steve's *Poseidon* franchise. They drove through what felt like miles of unending rows of warehouses, then parked in a side lot just to the left of the intersection of four buildings. Straight ahead was a one-story pink brick holdover from another era. It had one door and one window, the glass tinted to conceal the interior. To Jane's right was the cavernous open mouth of a sound stage. Behind them was a warehouse.

"Want to guess what we're doing here?" asked Daniel.

"You're signing your contract for Steve's movie?"

He grinned as he led her towards the warehouse. Inside was a labyrinth of desolate dimly-lit hallways with walls that didn't go all the way up to the ceiling where Jane saw a dizzying mix of beams and pipes, bound electrical wires, and tracks for pulleys. Jane stared at their ordered chaos in wonder. "Are we going to watch a movie being made?"

"You'll see."

Jane followed Daniel up a short set of stairs. They came to a stop in front of three unmarked doors. He opened one, a closet. "It's around here somewhere," he muttered, as he opened the door to the far right, obviously bypassing the second door. He went back to the door on the left. "Still a closet, hmmm." Jane rolled her eyes. She stepped forward and opened the door in the middle. She found herself on a balcony looking onto a room below. To her right was a plate window. Behind it, a man and a woman wearing giant earphones bent over a soundboard. They didn't notice her.

An orchestra filled the floor below the balcony. More than a hundred violins, violas, cellos, and basses plus a full brass section were seated in a half circle. The musicians and their instruments were overshadowed by a giant projection screen playing raw footage of a movie Jane didn't recognize. A movie that hadn't been released yet, she realized. The musicians were in the process of recording its soundtrack.

Jane sank to the floor and pressed her face between the bars of the railing. The music picked up tempo. A rising crescendo of urgent circling violins propelled the onscreen action forward as an actress ran through a field. The circling upper strings collided with the lumbering lower strings bowing sharp tones of dissonance, a contrapuntal warning that, even as the hero pursued her goal, her way was not without danger.

Standing on a raised platform in the center of the half-circle of first chair musicians, the conductor cued the trumpets for their upcoming entrance. Jane turned to Daniel, who sat beside her, but with his back against the railing. He barely glanced at the orchestra; he was watching her.

"That's James Horner," he whispered.

Tears burned her eyes. She'd stopped breathing.

This was what it had looked like when music was added to *Titanic*. And before that to *Braveheart*. And before that to *Legends of the Fall*. And before that, after that, so many others. Jane imagined throwing herself over the railing. She would land on her feet and run up to him and interrupt the recording to tell him—tell him what? That her life had turned upside down when she'd met his music. That she'd left her husband in order to experience every day the way his music had made her feel for a few hours one weekend five years ago.

Of course, Jane wasn't actually going to do that. She'd probably say something he'd heard a million times. *Mr. Horner, I'm a huge fan of your work.* It was enough to be there and see the creation with her own eyes. She dug Alma's phone out of her purse and took a picture.

Daniel reached for her hand and laced his fingers through hers. "You look so happy."

"I am." Jane smiled through the tears that slowly blurred her vision and overflowed to roll down her cheeks. "It's a good thing I'm leaving because if we were going to try and make this work, my expectations would be so high after this that you'd never meet them."

He used his thumb to wipe the tears before they dripped off her chin. "I would've liked the chance to try."

He leaned forward and sank his lips into hers. Her hands reached out and clutched the front of his shirt, pulling him closer. She expanded her awareness of every nerve ending her senses could access, pushing them to absorb everything they could of that moment.

Other kisses followed the first kiss as the orchestra transitioned into a section of music that sounded remarkably like the section of the *Titanic* score that brought the sinking of the doomed ocean liner to its tragic finale.

Immanuel Murder Might Mark
Vanguard Turning Point
By Tate Matthews

HAS THE VANGUARD FINALLY KILLED SOMEONE? At 10:45 Monday morning, the investigation of a woman tortured to death in Los Angeles County Saturday night was transferred from the LAPD to the FBI taskforce looking for the Vanguard. Though the woman's name has not been released, it seems likely she was the inside source who leaked the identity of Vanguard soldier, Mirt, to the FBI last week.

Special Investigators Sao and Martens, who have been spearheading the Federal search to find the terrorists for over a decade, have not commented on the case, but the timing is nearly conclusive. The murder coming less than twenty-four hours after the FBI released the picture of Mirt, cannot be a coincidence. Not unlike the mafia, the Vanguard has committed its first murder in order to eliminate a key witness.

Vanguard supporters have always been quick to say the Vanguard are a non-violent organization with a mission to improve the moral fabric of our culture. This mission would be undermined by committing violence. But others claim the Vanguard has only avoided arrest for this long through strategic covert murder.

More on this . . .

- The Vanguard & The FBI: Ten major case breakthroughs since 2000
- TIME Names Vanguard Most Disciplined and Predictable Terrorist Organization

If the FBI finds an evidential link between the murder scene and this man known as Mirt, what does that mean for the majority of Americans who tacitly tolerate the Vanguard as an alternative form of entertainment lampooning celebrities for their extravagant lifestyles?

If this is indeed the case, the implications could have a huge impact on *Libertines'* viewership and perhaps even dampen the unqualified support the Vanguard enjoys in Right Wing circles.

CHAPTER 22

When Daniel and Jane returned from the studio, they discovered Rhea had driven herself to her weekly rummy party at Lynnie's Pub despite the doctor (and Jane) saying she shouldn't drive or drink. Steve was in the garage. From the sound of it, Daniel imagined he was he was doing more damage than repairs to Jane's Jeep. The sound also told Daniel Steve wasn't likely to interrupt them. They could be alone for these last few hours before Daniel drove her to the station. He hadn't explained to his family that she'd be leaving, so it was just as well no one was around to ask questions.

Outside the sky darkened into evening. Daniel delayed turning on the lights. Without light, the hard edges in the front room of Rhea's house were more distinct. The furniture looked like marble withstanding the weathering of centuries, the surfing trophies like sentries to a family dynasty, the three-hundred-pound swordfish his father had caught in Tahiti an imperious symbol of man's physical triumph over the sea. The most recent family photo, taken after a morning surf at Waimea, showed the five of them lined up flexing their left biceps, measuring whose was the largest.

And in the middle of all these archetypes of the only kind of strength his family understood, Jane sat at the piano, a silhouette in the middle of the bay window, as the jagged clifftops turned from grey to brown in the tepid dusk outside. She picked out fractured James Horner melodies. It was the most at peace he'd ever seen her. He liked to think he had given her that peace.

Daniel tended to think of his mother's house as a barnacle defiantly attached to the cliff face, determined to be the last house standing when land became ocean. But Jane's music made the house feel demure. It reminded him of what had attracted him to her in New York, a different kind of strength. One that didn't need to prove itself by showy feats of athleticism or a stubborn bottom line. *If she would just let me help her, we could be together.* Once the Vanguard was arrested he would be able to give her everything; he would be whole again.

While Jane played piano, he checked his phone for news updates. Nothing new had been reported. Daniel skimmed gossip articles about the FBI's possible dead informant. He read an email from his agent saying she'd received a contract for him to sign from Ronan Barrow's production company. There were three all caps texts from Riley telling Daniel to ask Steve if he'd picked Poppy up from school.

Daniel texted Steve. He smiled to himself as the hammering in the garage stopped. A few seconds later Daniel received a text from Steve saying to tell Riley he had not picked up Poppy because of course he'd been at a fucking meeting. The hammering resumed. Daniel texted Riley that Poppy was not with Steve.

Jane had stopped playing. He got up from the couch to show her the texts from his ridiculous family, but stopped short of the piano when he saw she'd become distracted by a pair of headlights far up the road casting ghoulish dancing figures on the cliffs.

"Maybe it's Riley," she said.

The car was a sedan with tinted windows. It pulled into the circular drive at the front of the house.

"They've found me."

Daniel thought he'd misheard. "They?"

She swung off the piano bench and came to him, stood on her toes to reach up and kiss him, a lingering, reluctant kiss. It felt like an ending. "I love you," she said. "It probably won't count later but you have to believe it's true."

Her kiss made him dizzy. He mistook the gravity in her voice for romance.

"This week with you has been the best week of my life."

"Mine too."

Two guys in cheap suits got out of the sedan and walked across the lawn to the front door rather than follow the path.

"Do one last thing for me?"

"Sure," he laughed, "but only if you tell me what's going on. You're all over the place."

"Stall them for a few minutes so I have time to get out."

"What?"

The doorbell was ringing. Jane stepped past him and sprinted down the hallway to the stairs. "Stall them," she called.

Daniel was suddenly thirsty. He heard Jane's footsteps in Rhea's room above his head. The hammering in the garage had stopped. He hoped Steve wasn't on his way up to witness a scene that Daniel sensed was not going to end well. He went to the kitchen for water. Then he walked back to the front of the house, into the entryway, and opened the front door.

"Evening."

The two men held up badges. "I'm Special Investigator Martens."

"Special Deputy Investigator Sao."

"Can I ask what this is about?"

The Vanguard. His toes—the ones he still had and the ones he'd lost—tingled with anticipation that was also a warning. They'd caught the Vanguard. They'd found a recording of his trial that for some reason had never gone live.

"We need to speak to Jane Dalton."

Daniel's thoughts screeched to a stop. He heard the words without absorbing them.

"We believe she's in possession of a cell phone belonging to a woman whose death we're investigating."

The dead informant, Daniel realized. *Can the world be that small?*

"I think you've got the wrong—" Behind him there was a small thud as Jane dropped her duffle bag on the entryway tile.

"What do you mean she's dead?" Jane held out the phone Daniel had assumed was hers. "That's not possible."

"May we come in?" asked Martens even as his partner stepped over the threshold and motioned Daniel aside.

They followed Jane into the living room where she felt her way to the sofa. Daniel joined her. He knew she was upset, but her distress felt distant as he tried to sort through what was happening. For a few seconds the only sound in the house was Jane dry heaving sobs that didn't materialize into tears. Both detectives watched her as though she was the only other person in the room.

They aren't here for me, thought Daniel.

"We'd like to talk about the fight," said Sao.

He listened with limited attention as Jane described an argument she'd had with the dead woman—a woman who had apparently been Jane's best friend—an argument that had culminated with Jane throwing a phone at her friend, which seemed impossible. The listening side of his mind wondered what else he didn't know about Jane, but it was overshadowed by more urgent interest in information. As soon as there was a break in Jane's story, he asked,

"Have you found out anything new about the Vanguard? Did she give you any files? Trial archives?"

"We can't discuss the details of the investigation," said Martens.

They returned to the phone conversation. Sao's voice as he posed pointed questions about why Jane had kept her friend's phone was accusatory. Daniel was aware he should be trying to defend Jane. But she felt so far away.

I could tell them, he thought. *Just roll up my pants and show them. They would talk to me then.*

"Without her phone, the victim couldn't call for help," said Sao.

"Her name is Alma," whispered Jane. "Her name was . . . Alma."

Detective Sao set a folder on the coffee table.

Daniel's pulse leapt in his veins, making him lightheaded. There were answers in that folder. If he could just be patient, hold himself together.

"The morning of her death she emailed our tip line claiming to be dating a member of the terrorist group the Vanguard. You understand, we receive many of these calls from hysterical women—"

"She wasn't hysterical," said Jane.

"The report was elevated when she was discovered dead that evening." Sao dramatically flipped open the folder and there, blown up in eight by twelve was what looked like the still frame from a horror film: a wide shot of a bedroom, black around the corners where the camera flash hadn't reached, green shag carpet, a bleeding woman tied to a chair with a mass of black hair obscuring her face. Jane looked at it, her expression blank. She pushed it aside to look at the next one, the next. She stared at each with an intensity that made Daniel's leg twitch. It felt like Jane knew something she wasn't saying.

Martens pulled a Werther's candy from his pocket and struggled with arthritic fingers to unwrap it. The noise crinkled too loudly in Daniel's ears. He glared at the detective. *She's going to tell us something. Don't distract her.*

"Alma also claimed her coworker just happened to be her boyfriend's sister," said Sao. "This turned out to be the only claim that we could verify. You did very well covering your tracks, but we did eventually find you."

Another folder flipped dramatically open. Daniel stared. The pictures in this new folder were all of Jane. Some were taken when she was a child, most looked like they were from the same time he had met her. Several were pictures of Jane with a man who looked like the FBI's description of the Vanguard soldier Mirt.

Not possible.

"Jane Dalton, formerly Rachel Schaben. Married name Rachel Carter," Sao pronounced the names like a judge pronouncing a sentence.

"You have three brothers, one of whom, Thomas Michael Schaben, seems to match Alma's description."

Daniel tried to look at Jane to confirm how absolutely ludicrous it was to suggest she was related to a member of the Vanguard even as he realized he also hoped it was true. *She knows something.*

Jane continued to study the crime scene pictures as though she hadn't heard. She had focused on a macro shot of the dead woman's neck. The skin had been cut away along the collarbone making a red line like a necklace. The skin had been pulled back.

"Was she branded?" asked Daniel.

"As I said, we can't discuss—"

"Was she branded?" Daniel tried not to look like he was struggling as he demanded Martens answer him. Martens sucked on his candy. He faded in and out of focus as Daniel's nervous system ran wild. The candy clicked against his teeth and then finally stopped. "No. She wasn't branded."

Not like me, thought Daniel. *There aren't any like me.*

Darkness encroached on the edge of his vision. He pushed it back.

"Tell us about Thomas," Sao said to Jane.

"I haven't talked to him in years."

A rush of disappointment so powerful Daniel felt sick. He pushed it back. *Concentrate. Why didn't she say her brother was in the Vanguard when she found out about the brand?*

She doesn't trust me. Thought I'd tell the Feds. They think she's an accomplice.

"How many years?" asked Sao.

"Since college. He used to call me during college. He didn't like that I'd left home because he and I were always together. He didn't get along with our older brothers." Jane was struggling to make eye contact with Sao. She kept looking back at the picture of the woman's neck. A black void threatened to overwhelm Daniel's vision. *She knows something.*

Martens leaned forward, causing Daniel to lean back too quickly.

The room spun. "What's so interesting about this one?" He tapped the picture.

"This kind of cut, along the base of the neck, would be the way you flay the skin off an animal," said Jane.

"Excuse me?" Sao was incredulous.

This isn't the information I need. Daniel wanted to tell her to talk faster, get to the point. Her pain only distantly registered in his perception. It was too complicated to parse out—the best friend, the brother, secrets—*Did she know I'd been attacked?*

The same day we met.

"Tommy's a hunter. It's the only thing that interests him besides baseball. He showed me once how to flay a deer. This was one of the first steps."

I was attacked the same day we met.

"Jane," Martens had significantly softened his voice, "we need to know everything you know about the Vanguard."

Daniel's warning signals intensified. He tried to shake them off. He didn't want it to be true. It didn't seem possible for it to be true. And yet, if she had answers. If she could fill in his missing pieces . . .

What if she hasn't been hiding from a husband?

The room began to tilt and spin like the gyroscope on a crashing airplane. And then all was still. Daniel heard nothing. He saw nothing. The darkness smelled like mildewed cinderblocks. His body ached from being in one position too long. He was so thirsty.

This is the end, he thought. But he did not know why he thought that, or what signals had prompted such a thought. *This is the end.*

He heard a phone ringing and thought, *It must be her brother's phone. He's here with me in New York. He wants to kill me. Why?*

The darkness faded. Slowly, Daniel's vision returned. He was in the living room of his mother's house. There were two mugs of coffee and two glasses of water on the coffee table. The mugs weren't steaming. Both the detectives seemed more relaxed. Jane was a taut statue perched on the edge of the couch beside him.

The ringing phone was in the purse beside Jane's duffle bag in the entryway. He wondered how much time he had lost. How long had the phone had been ringing? She didn't seem to hear the ringing, so Daniel went to get it. He needed an excuse to move, shake out his tense nerves, reorient himself. He hadn't lost time in years. *Steve will think I'm regressing. He won't want me on the movie.* Neither Jane nor the detectives paid attention to him. They didn't seem to have noticed that he'd blanked out. *For how long?*

In the hallway, he leaned against the wall to stabilize himself as he knelt to retrieve the phone. Jane was talking about growing up in a conservative family, the things that were said, and the things left unsaid. "I knew Tommy had tendencies that my mother was trying to control, but it wasn't something out in the open. I left as soon as I could."

"Because of your brother?" asked Sao.

"Because I wanted a fuller understanding of the world."

"How do you think he got involved with the Vanguard?" asked Martens.

Daniel found the phone, an old school flip phone. Steve's name blinked insistently on the greyscale display window.

Why is Steve calling her?

"So you're saying you had no idea your brother was involved with the Vanguard?" asked Sao.

Daniel silenced the phone and carried it with him back into the living room. Jane looked at him with a question in her eyes.

"It's just Steve," he said. "No idea why he'd be calling you instead of me. He and Riley are fighting about Poppy. No one seems to know who was supposed to pick her up from school."

Jane nodded, not appearing particularly interested. But when the phone began to ring again, she snatched it from him and answered it.

"Hello?"

Daniel was close enough to tell the voice on the other end was not Steve. As Jane listened, her hand reached out into air, trying to find the wall to support herself. Daniel offered her his arm.

It's the brother. Daniel strained to hear what was being said. It was a serious voice with a high timbre, speaking deliberately. *Giving instructions.*

"How long have you two known each other?" asked Sao. It was the
first time he had addressed Daniel since entering the house, and now,
as Daniel reluctantly detached his attention from the phonecall, he felt
the full force of the detective's gaze unpeeling his skin, trying to find
Daniel's secrets.

"Eight years."

Jane said, "I understand," and hung up. Daniel watched as she took a
deep breath. She straightened her neck and gave the detectives a sad but
remarkably composed smile. "Detectives, I'm afraid something has come
up that I need to deal with. Do you have any other questions for me?"

"Was that your brother?" asked Sao. His gaze was a hawk's on the
hunt, watching for her to flinch.

"It was Steve." She looked to Daniel with the same remarkably composed expression. "He needs us to go get Poppy."

For a moment, Daniel thought Sao would press further. But Martens
stood and held out business cards, one for Jane, one for Daniel. "Please
be in touch if you think of anything else that might be useful. We know
he asked Alma about you, so it's unlikely he'll leave town without trying
to find you."

"You think he's dangerous to me as well?" asked Jane.

"Yes," said Martens, "you need to stop thinking of him as your little
brother. Call at the first sign of trouble."

"Thank you," said Jane with conviction.

They walked the detectives to the door and remained there watching
until the sedan pulled out of the driveway and disappeared down the
road.

"How are you feeling?" she asked.

Daniel laughed. "How am *I* feeling?"

"I thought maybe all that about the Vanguard was setting you off
again."

"It was." Daniel paused to assess. He was tired. Tomorrow, he would have the aches of an NFL lineman, but the attack had faded. "I think I'm okay right now."

"I need to tell you something."

"That wasn't Steve on the phone?"

She nodded, not showing any surprise that he knew, not showing any surprise that he was so calm. "My husband is holding Poppy at my condo." Her words came slowly, as though she was dragging them through an invisible filter, trying to make them seem less unbelievable. She paused as though waiting for a reaction, then added. "I guess Steve must be there too, since Seth has his phone."

"And your brother?"

"I don't know."

Daniel nodded. He still felt calm. Nothing was shaking. But he was having trouble figuring out what he should say. "Is your husband also in the Vanguard?"

"Yes." The word escaped out of her without air, against her will.

"And they were both in New York the day we met."

Another, even quieter, 'yes.' She had turned away from him and was staring at the wall, braced for what he realized was the inevitable next question. *Did you know?* But he wasn't ready to ask. If she had known, if maybe she had even been a part of what had happened to him—no, he couldn't think about that yet.

"Do you think you could give me a ride to my condo?" she asked softly.

There were other questions he wanted to ask about these men who had destroyed his life. He thought it would be wise to know more before driving to meet them. But the words wouldn't come. There was an ache in his throat, something unresolved, a conclusion his body already understood, but his mind wasn't ready to accept.

"I'll drive you," he said. As they walked towards the garage stairs, he noticed that Jane picked up her duffle bag. She wasn't planning on coming back to the house.

CHAPTER 23

A light mist began to fall as they drove to Jane's condo. It cast a glow on the city the way Ingrid Bergman's skin glowed at the end of *Casablanca,* except the glow Jane saw outside her window was in Technicolor. She saw her hospital lit up in buttery green and silver, a beacon of safety. She would never go there again.

This is the end, thought Jane. *There's no coming back from this.*

"Poppy's fine. As soon as Seth realizes she's not Leah, he'll let her go. He's ... not a bad man."

"And Thomas?" Daniel kept his eyes on the road. Maybe he was already distancing himself from her, replacing his emerging love with warning: she was dangerous.

"Seth can control Tommy," she said with more confidence than she felt.

Between the gaps of the government buildings and a refurbished apartment block, she saw clusters of people walking down the sidewalks heading she didn't know where—restaurants, bars, clubs. Their silhouettes cut across the beams of headlights. She wished she could've had a group of friends who'd meet at this or that place to drink and dance and talk about when they were getting the new iPhone, the chances of the Clippers making the playoffs, if Pop Star X was really a slut, and if Pop Star Z had really smoked weed on stage, or cheated, or had a secret love child. That was the life she'd been building with Alma, except all Alma cared about was sci-fi so there had been no sports and no pop stars, but it had been something.

Now she was dead because of it.

Daniel parked at the condo. "You shouldn't go up there alone."

"It's better for you to be here, ready to drive them away after I get them out."

"We should call the FBI," he said without conviction. "They could help."

"The Vanguard probably has people in the FBI."

"Still, that Sao guy, he seemed pretty determined."

"Yeah, maybe." Jane took a deep breath to calm herself. The sooner she got up there, the sooner this would be over, but she didn't want to leave Daniel. She didn't know how to say goodbye.

"If you're not back in ten minutes, I'm coming up." Something in his jaw tightened, the perfunctory tone of his voice tried to add up to a determination he didn't quite feel. When he'd woken up that morning he'd never imagined he'd come this close to the men who had ruined his life.

I ruined him. He knew that now. It had hung between them the entire drive. If not for Battery Park, his life could've been everything he'd wanted.

"Or I could come with you now."

"Wait fifteen minutes, then call 911," said Jane. "Report the kidnapping. This isn't a Vanguard crime."

She got out of the Prius before he could argue. It was a selfish thing to ask him. If the police got involved and not the FBI, she wouldn't have to bear witness to her knowledge of the Vanguard. As soon as Daniel realized that, he'd think less of her. *If that is even possible.*

Shayla's dog was barking. Inside the echo chamber of the stairs, he sounded miles away. If Jane had a dog it would be barking, scratching at the door getting ready to welcome her. If Jane had a dog, she would know her condo was intruder free, spider free. Instead she stood before her door, slightly out of breath, with her keys in her hand trying to decide if she should knock.

The door was unlocked. She pushed it open. The condo was dark except for a strip of weak light leaking through the gap under her bedroom door. Caution tape rustled around her feet as she stepped inside.

Ambient city glow coming in from the balcony door dimly illuminated the living room. On the couch with his steel toed boots up on the cushions was the spider of all spiders. There was enough light to see the fuzzy profile of his beard and receding hairline with two tentacle arms resting behind his head. She flipped on the light over the breakfast bar and the shadows toying with her imagination scattered to the corners of the room. It was only Seth, very nearly the same as she remembered him—former soldier's body gone a little soft from too much pizza, the lumpy bulk that had once seemed so solid and safe—plus that ridiculous Hawaiian shirt.

"Hello Rachel."

She checked the shadows. Her skin crawled under the gaze of hundreds of invisible eyes; she didn't see Tommy. "You're alone?"

"This is an interesting home you've set up." He rolled off the couch. His momentum carried him halfway across the room towards her. Jane tried not to flinch. "Only one bedroom. No toys."

"I can't afford much."

"But you subscribe to security coverage."

"It's a nice thing to have. I'm thinking of getting a dog."

"I have a cat."

Jane tried to estimate how much time she had before Daniel came and if he would come alone or wait for the police.

"Where's Tommy?"

"With a friend."

The use of the old code her family used when they were among outsiders startled her. *With a friend,* meant Tommy was hiding, probably in the basement of some Vanguard supporter. *Who does he think will overhear him here?* She looked around. Steve and Poppy were most likely in the bedroom. There was no one else.

I'm the outsider.

"Were you with him when he . . ." she couldn't finish the thought.

Seth put his stupid face on, the one that used to trick her into believing he'd misplaced his brain and needed her help. "I'm sorry about your friend. Tommy, he's changed since you left. Angry all the time."

"At me?"

"At everyone. Nothing is enough for him. Just this year—he's been pushing, trying to change how we do things."

"And what about you? Did she deserve to die for betraying the Vanguard?"

Seth's eyes went wide, became all whites with little black dots in the middles as he advanced towards her. She backed up against the wall as he swerved into the entryway and paced the short hallway to the bedroom. He did four circuits, his hands swinging back and forth. "I couldn't save her. By the time I got to the house, she was already gone."

"And North Carolina? And Daniel? Those were all Tommy?" Her words sliced off the end of her tongue like it was a knife. "You are so fucking lucky Daniel didn't go to the police." Jane hadn't quite meant to say 'fuck'—too much time around Steve—it went off like a bomb, the concussions making the too-close hallway walls vibrate as Seth turned on her.

"We branded him because Aaron wouldn't let us brand you! You were willing to expose us just to give him a drink. Ever think how that made us feel, huh?" Seth's hefty bulk backed her up against the wall. She caught a whiff of his deodorant and Irish Spring soap. "He could've recognized you from the park." Seth stuttered in his anger. "You shouldn't have been with him in the first place."

"You would've branded me for that?"

Something fell in Jane's bedroom, a patter of lightweight objects in succession. Seth caught his breath, trying to calm down. Jane considered bolting towards the bedroom door to free Steve. He could probably overpower Seth. They could make a run for the Prius.

I'm done running.

"You needed to be taught a lesson," said Seth softly.

"That only makes sense if you'd told me what you did. But you didn't. It's been a secret all this time. I bet Aaron doesn't even know."

"I regret what happened. It got out of hand. But the motivations were pure. You belonged with us, not him." The confidence in his voice chilled her. *He would do it again,* she thought. *I can't give him that chance.*

She stepped around Seth into the hallway and moved towards the bedroom. She couldn't risk Daniel coming up and meeting Seth. She had to move faster. Seth rushed to intercept her as Jane reached the bedroom door. "Leah's sleeping," he said.

Jane's breath spasmed in her chest. "What did you say?"

Seth responded to what must've been a grotesque mixture of dumfounded contortions on her face by placing a silencing finger across her lips. Taking Jane by the shoulders he gently shifted her to the other side of the hallway so she stood to his right. Since Jane had been sixteen, this had been her place beside him, the place where he said it was easiest to protect her because he was left handed, because any approaching danger would meet his strong hand before it met her. With delicate care he opened the bedroom door.

For a moment, the power of suggestion, combined with the low light of the desk lamp from Goodwill, allowed Jane to see her lost daughter curled up in the middle of the bed, the breeze of her shallow sleeping breaths whispering into the curls of a porcelain doll tucked under her arm. Jane drifted across the room and sat on the edge of the bed. She set her hand on the thin ridge of Leah's ribs and felt the easy cadence of their expanding and contracting, their action governed by a perfect miracle of creation. A little person still intact, somehow resilient to all the confusion and fear Jane had imagined for her. Jane brushed her hair back from her temple and kissed it.

Jane shifted to pull Leah into her arms. Her peripheral vision detected movement. She jumped to her feet ready to lunge for the RAID can in the closet, then she saw Steve's giant feet, his ankles tied together with her favorite dress shirt, thumping against the side of her desk, causing a pile of grocery receipts to fall like a cascade of feathers towards the floor where they joined her already fallen paystubs. He was gagged and blindfolded, a scene eerily reminiscent of how she'd encountered Daniel in that Manhattan basement. His head lolled back and forth. Unintelligible sounds gurgled from his throat.

The spell was broken. It was Poppy in the bed not Leah. Taken from school by a stranger, probably terrified. Steve would never speak to Jane again when he learned it was her fault. Jane was surprised to feel loss at this. They'd just begun to understand each other.

"Where is Leah?" Seth addressed her in a dead monotone. Jane wanted to run at him and ram her body against him, dig her nails in and tear his skin off, scream at him. Instead, she opened her arms and approached in a posture of surrender, slow steady steps, no extraneous movement.

"Leah's gone." Her voice was iron.

"No more games, Rachel. Just the truth."

"I had an abortion." Jane waited in the middle of the room. She'd never spoken this particular truth out loud, not even when she'd told Daniel. She thought the ceiling might come crashing down, thunder and lightning, some cosmic cause and effect, but nothing happened. She'd expected confession to feel different, feel *more*.

"That's not possible," said Seth.

"Isn't it? Maybe I didn't know what you'd done to Daniel but there was plenty of other shit warning me you'd make a godawful parent. And I certainly wasn't prepared to figure it out on my own."

Something in these words must've rung true because Seth stumbled back against the bedroom door. Overgrown toddler sadness filled his eyes with tears.

"You wouldn't accept no for an answer," said Jane. She tried to keep her voice hard, but it was flailing under the pressure. She wanted him to understand, to admit that maybe she'd done the right thing, which of course wasn't going to happen.

"You lied to me," he said.

She felt Seth pulling himself together around this idea of her deceit—the pills she took without telling him, and now an abortion. Jane imagined the sharp stab of knowing slowly becoming the ache that would live in his gut like it did in hers. When he said, "You murdered our daughter," the stab became a spear that pierced her heart. But with it also came relief. Finally, he knew; she was free of her secret.

Seth's eyes shifted to Poppy in the bed. His arms went limp as a fresh surge of tears blinded him. "The girl. She sleeps just like Leah." His head fell forward into his hands. Snot dripped from his nose and bubbled in his beard.

This seemed a safe moment to try and escape. Jane moved to Steve's side and began to feel her way through the knots of her clothes. She couldn't look at Seth. She knew what he was feeling too well. She got Steve's legs free, but his hands were zip tied. She glanced sideways at Seth and asked without expecting an answer, "Where's your knife?"

With grave difficulty, he lifted his head and leveled his gaze at her. "You *are* my wife." He launched across the room and grabbed her arm. Jane wrenched away. He grabbed her again. Her tired body strained with effort as she parried and ducked and finally landed a solid push kick in the side of his calf. Something snapped. Seth gasped as he released her.

Jane dove to the floor. She removed Steve's gag but not the blindfold. If he saw Seth's face he'd be a liability to the Vanguard and they would come after him the way they'd come after Alma.

"Steve? You okay?" She lightly tapped his cheeks.

"You . . ." Steve's lips were swollen and dotted with crusted saliva. "You're . . ."

"What did you dose him with?" she asked Seth.

Seth spoke from the muffled cavern between his chest and thighs. He'd collapsed against the wall. "God will punish you for taking her from me."

For a moment, the words felt as final as though he was a judge reading out a jury's verdict condemning her. She hated that he still had that power over her mind. "Maybe. But that's between Him and me, not you."

Jane spotted Seth's mission bag on the floor by Steve's feet. The knife was probably in it. Just as she reached for it there was a rush of air as Seth slammed into her shoulder. She punched without being able to see and found only air. There was the ceiling. There was the wall. Desk. Seth. She lunged at him. He grabbed her shoulders and held her back. Her arms weren't long enough to reach him, but she could still kick. She turned sideways, throwing him off balance. As he stumbled forward, she delivered a swift kick to his kidney and then, without hesitation, to his groin, a kick even harder than she'd delivered to the bovine guy in the bar.

"You can't fight me, Rachel." Seth gasped.

For a moment Jane thought she heard feet running up the stairwell. She grabbed the knife out of the bag and hurried back to Steve. She was almost through the zip tie when Seth came at her again.

He seized her arm and jerked it upward so hard something snapped in her shoulder. She instinctively stood to alleviate the pressure. "You have to come home." Seth snatched the porcelain doll from Poppy's arms and muscled Jane toward the bedroom door. "You need to repent. No more secrets, we'll start over."

Jane's feet snagged on clothes, and a purse, a waste of money self-help book, dragged them along to slow Seth down as he pulled her towards the door. She was so tired. Her efforts felt useless. As Jane reached out and grasped only empty space, she saw Steve pop the remaining sliver of the zip tie. His movements were imprecise as he massaged his hands then removed the blindfold. Jane gave up her resistance and pushed Seth out the bedroom door before Steve looked their way, squinting as though he couldn't quite trust his eyes to tell him what was going on.

They were almost to the front door. Jane elbowed Seth in his bruised kidney. This only slowed him down for a second. He took both her arms and held her fast. "Why won't you listen to me? You'll never be right in your heart if you don't come home and face this."

"I face it every day and I don't regret it. I'd do it again."

He searched her face for his placid, accepting wife, shook his head at whatever he saw. "There have to be consequences for what you've done." He turned the knob to open the front door. It didn't open. He checked the deadbolt. Tried again. The door didn't budge. He glared at Jane like this was her fault.

Two more tries and he was so frustrated he let go of her arm. He pinched the doll in his armpit so he could use both hands to pull the door.

Jane looked around for a weapon—dirty clothes, clean clothes, purse; nothing useful. She summoned her remaining energy for one last attack. She lined up beside him and delivered a sharp front punch to his jaw to throw him off balance. She waited, counted beats as he stumbled back, his feet doing a blind jig step, until he was facing her. She planted her foot, channeled all her remaining energy up through her heel and drove her right foot into his crotch. The doll fell first. Seth howled, perhaps in pain, perhaps in horror as its face shattered, and then his eyes rolled back, and he crumpled to the ground.

Jane ran to the bedroom for Seth's zip ties. Steve sat on the floor beside the bed with one hand braced on the side and the other on the headboard post trying to pull himself up. When he saw her, he grinned. "You good?"

"Not really."

"Me too."

The crunch of porcelain sounded in the hallway. Jane grabbed a fistful of zip ties and braced herself for another confrontation. But when she returned to the hallway Seth was still laying on the floor, semi-conscious, curled in a ball. It was the door opening against the broken doll making the sound. Daniel was on the other side. "Jane?"

Her heart did a small leap. "I'm here."

Daniel wedged himself through the doorway and stepped over Seth's feet. He wrapped his arms around Jane, holding her so tightly he lifted her off the ground.

"I thought . . ." He stopped, as though the fact that she wasn't hurt negated his worry. He set her down. "Where's Poppy?"

"In the bedroom. Steve's here. They're both fine."

She walked him down the hall. In the bedroom, Steve had managed to pull himself up onto Jane's bed. He laid with his back to them snoring, with Poppy tucked up against his chest. Daniel stared in disbelief. "He's asleep."

Jane returned to the hallway and bound Seth's wrists together. His ankles were too wide for one zip tie so Jane used three in interconnected loops, one of many things Aaron had taught her and Tommy during the survivalist camping weekends they'd taken together. She saw movement in her peripheral vision and looked up to see Daniel standing in the bedroom doorway watching her work. The light wasn't good, but there was enough to see this twist in his face like he was impressed, but also surprised, by her skills.

His gaze shifted past her to Seth on the floor. For a moment, she thought to tell him not to look, that the Vanguard would come after him if they thought he could identify them the way Alma had, but then she realized seeing one of his attackers was more important to him than safety.

"So that's the husband."

"Yeah."

"No sign of your brother?"

"There's no way to find him."

For a moment, she thought Daniel didn't believe her, like she was protecting Tommy, even after what he'd done. *This is why it has to be the end. He'll never trust me now.*

"I guess we should move him so the doorway is clear?" Before she could stop him, Daniel grabbed Seth's shirt and started dragging him into the living room. Jane followed, too tense to help.

Daniel propped Seth up against the couch and stood back to study him. He paid particular attention to Seth's hands, as though measuring them against some imaginary handprint. "He's just a regular guy." Daniel sounded disappointed.

Long moments ticked by filled with Daniel's private thoughts. Jane felt time passing with increasing urgency until finally, she said, "Did you decide to call the police?"

Daniel reluctantly turned away from Seth. "I thought I would come up and see what was going on first. Steve doesn't like publicity. We'll get them down to the car and then call."

Jane nodded. It felt like too much work to tell him that they couldn't report a crime if they'd erased evidence of the victims.

"I'm going to carry Poppy down, then I'll be back okay?" Daniel spoke with an eerie calm. She didn't want to imagine what he was thinking.

She waited until he left then she collected the doll from the entryway. Her face was smashed, but the little porcelain arms and feet attached to the cloth body were still intact, as were the parts of the head where the hair had been glued on. Jane recognized the doll as one of Seth's mother's childhood toys, a gift she'd given them when they'd told her they were having a baby. Jane assumed Seth had brought the doll with him for Leah. Now he knew he'd never give it to her.

She carried the big pieces of the doll's face into the living room. She wadded a kitchen towel into the cavity of the head and gently set the pieces in place, two blue eyes that opened and closed, a little pouty mouth, one and a half rosy cheeks. Jane didn't have the nose.

"She would've liked you," Jane whispered as she propped the doll up against the couch beside Seth. "I'm sorry."

"I'll forgive you if you come home." Seth's voice was only a whisper and his eyes were still closed, but the threat was clear.

She knelt beside him and pressed her hand over his heart. It was the same motion she'd used in New York, trying to calm Daniel without revealing herself, a motion she used to transfer the deepest core of her feelings into another person.

"Don't you dare, for one second, think I'm sorry for you." She lowered her voice and bent close to his face so he would be sure to hear her. "You had no right. No fucking right to manipulate me the way you did."

Someone was behind her. She withdrew too late. Daniel had entered the condo without making a sound. He was observing her from the hallway with mild interest, like a scientist in a lab. "Ready?" he asked, then disappeared around the corner.

"He's no good for you, Rachel," said Seth.

"That was never for you to decide."

"You won't be happy until you repent."

Jane stood, towering over him for the first time in her life. "Don't try to find me again."

"You can't leave me, Rachel. You'll regret it, you hear me?" Seth's voice gained strength as she walked to the hallway and then abruptly died out. When she turned back to look at him one last time, he had fallen a little to his left, leaning into the empty space between him and the doll as though trying to find the missing third of his holy trinity: father, mother, and child.

It took both Jane and Daniel struggling one step at a time to get Steve down to the Prius. With Steve and Poppy buckled into the back seats, Daniel drove away from the condo tower and parked down the street in front of the In N Out. His fingers tapped a silent melody on the steering wheel as the engine ticked. Jane tried to remember to breathe.

Finally, he turned and set Detective Marten's card on the center console. "Your brother needs to be stopped before anyone else dies."

Jane nodded but did not reach for the card or for her phone. Images of the crime scene photos Sao had showed her flickered through her mind, dim impressions of a violence she could not believe was real.

"I need you to prove you're done with them," he said softly.

This wasn't what she'd expected. Behind Daniel's words, she heard the unspoken promise of a future. He hadn't decided to cast her out. She brought her purse up from the floor by her seat and pulled out her burner phone. Her fingers shook as she dialed the number.

Martens answered after only one ring.

"There's a man who might be able to tell you where to find Tommy Schaben." She recited her address and hung up.

Daniel held out his hand. Numbly, she gave him her phone. He got out of the car and dropped it into the trash can by the front door of the building. He leaned into the backseat and pulled a water bottle out of the case by Poppy's feet. Jane glanced back and saw Poppy rub her nose as she shifted in her sleep so her head rested against the door. On the other side of the bench, Steve's long frame was crunched into the small space, his head stuck in the gap between the headrest and the door, his legs slanted sideways and shoved on each side of the water.

What will they remember when they wake up? wondered Jane. Maybe Daniel was willing to accept her, but his family would not.

Daniel started the Prius and pulled out of the lot. Half the water in the bottle Daniel had opened was gone. He tilted it from one side to another as he drove, watching as the water sloshed back and forth. "The drink you brought me that night saved my life."

Jane's chest tightened. It hurt to breathe. "They saw me with you in the park. I didn't—"

Daniel held up his hand. "I've chartered a jet to Oahu. Until your brother is caught, it's not safe here. It will be hard for him to get through an airport without being flagged, so Hawaii seems like a good choice. That's probably not what you want, but I don't think I can put you on a train right now."

Jane thought about pointing out that she was less easy to find alone than she was with him, but the logic of what he was saying didn't matter. His reasons didn't matter. He wanted her with him.

"And after that?" she whispered.

"After that, I'll be busy with the movie, but I could probably still find time to teach you to surf."

Tears burned her eyes. She could hardly articulate the words as she asked, "Is that what you want?"

His jaw moved like he was turning ideas around in his mouth.

"You're the first person in a long time who hasn't looked at me like I'm some fucked-up mess. Unless this whole week has been an act—"

"It hasn't."

"I'm not ready to give that up. That isn't a promise that this is going to work." He paused as he changed lanes on the freeway, checked his mirrors, perhaps stalled to collect his thoughts. "I've lived all this time not knowing why they attacked me. Now I know. Things feel different. It has meaning."

"But if you hadn't met me . . ."

He set the water bottle in the cup holder and positioned both hands on the steering wheel, ten and two. The leather cover squeaked under the force of his grip twisting back and forth. "You're right, our relationship has cost me quite a lot. I'd like to see if we can make it worth it."

"I'm not sure that's possible."

"I'm willing to try if you are." He detached his right hand from the steering wheel and set it on the center console, palm up, fingers open in invitation. After a moment, Jane set her hand in his. He closed his fingers around hers and squeezed so tight, she imagined he would never let her go.

Land Acknowledgement

Jane of Battery Park was written on the ancestral land and traditional territories of the Omaha, Oto, and Pawnee Nations. They are the original custodians of the land on which I have lived and worked while writing this novel.

Personal Acknowledgements

In 2012, I attended the Backspace Writers conference where agent Donald Maass challenged attendees to write what they were scared of—the stories they didn't feel that could be told—because that was where great stories came from. I was young, relatively brazen, and didn't relish the idea of writing about my primary fear of the moment: growing old alone, which didn't seem particularly original or compelling.

Later that summer, I returned to my apartment late at night, turned on my kitchen light and found myself toe to toe with a spider larger than my hand. There is nothing original about arachnophobia either, but in the days and weeks and *months, and years* that followed, the loss of security I felt at home, the encroaching 'what if' of another spider, the cyclical frustration of knowing I was safe, and yet not feeling safe, fueled the early drafts of this novel.

Thank you to Donald Maass and yes, thank you giant spider; I think of you every summer when the CWS starts. You remain one of the greatest terrors of my life. Thank you to Emily Ruth Verona who I met at Backspace and has been a valiant correspondent through this entire process. Thank you to Noah and Amanda Cypher who hosted me on two visits to New York doing work for this book.

Thanks also goes to the students and faculty of the University of Nebraska MFA program who gave feedback on various pieces of this novel. Particular thanks to my mentors Charles Wyatt, Catherine Texier, and Tom Paine. A most special thanks to Kate Gale who championed this book and believed in it enough to publish it.

To Heidi Sell, Genevieve Williams, and Marie Hansen who workshopped more chapters than ended up making the cut on this final draft.

To Holly Richmond and Emily Borgmann who read complete drafts when I thought the novel was finished. (It wasn't). But their feedback was valuable nonetheless.

To Gail Hochman, who remembered my characters and this crazy story six months after reading the manuscript, and gave me the pages of notes that did finally produce this final draft.

To Kristen Anasari, my high school English teacher and the first professional person who took me seriously as a writer.

To James Horner who wrote the soundtrack of my childhood and became my gateway drug to movies, figure skating, opera, dead white symphonic composers, and most importantly, movie scores. He has defined the way I see the world in more ways than I can name and given me some of the greatest unadulterated moments of joy a human can dream of.

Lastly, thank you to the friends and strangers who have shared stories of cultural divide and isolation over the years. To those who started somewhere and came to realize they belonged somewhere else, who had to find their own rules, redefine what they understood as 'right,' who birthed freedom from the ashes of uncertainty and shame.

If you enjoyed this book, please consider supporting me through my Patreon account where you will have access to my writing and research process, receive early announcements for upcoming projects, participate in naming and creating characters, and receive exclusive short stories revealing the Vanguard's side of Jane's story.

ABOUT THE AUTHOR

Born in Kobe, Japan, and raised in the plains, Jaye Viner has spent her life exploring other cultures both near and far. She has two master's degrees from the University of Nebraska and plenty of nonprofessional experience, studying the art of conveying meaning to an audience of readers. Her free time is spent at the salon maintaining her blue hair. She also cooks and worships her cat. Find pictures of both food and queen cat on Instagram. This is her first (published) novel.

Mazo
de la Roche
THE HIDDEN LIFE

Joan Givner

Toronto OXFORD UNIVERSITY PRESS 1989

CANADIAN CATALOGUING IN PUBLICATION DATA

Givner, Joan, 1936-
Mazo de la Roche : the hidden life

Includes bibliographical references and index.
ISBN 0-19-540705-9

1. De la Roche, Mazo, 1879-1961 – Biography.
2. Authors, Canadian (English) – 20th century –
Biography.*   I. Title.

PS8507.E43Z73 1989   C813'.52   C89-093589-0
PR9199.2.D4Z73 1989

Cover drawing: F.H. Varley, *Mazo de la Roche* (private collection).

Oxford University Press, 70 Wynford Drive, Don Mills, Ontario, M3C 1J9

Toronto   Oxford   New York   Delhi   Bombay   Calcutta   Madras   Karachi
Petaling Jaya   Singapore   Hong Kong   Tokyo   Nairobi   Dar es Salaam
Cape Town   Melbourne   Auckland

and associated companies in
Berlin   Ibadan

This book is for
Jane Gallop
and the members of the seminar in
Literary Theory and Feminist Criticism
sponsored by the National Endowment for the Humanities
at the University of Wisconsin, Milwaukee, Summer 1985

'Milwaukee! China, eh? That's a long way.'
Nicholas came to the rescue. 'Milwaukee's not
in China, Mama. It's somewhere in the States.'
'Nonsense! It's in China.'

—*Whiteoaks of Jalna* (London: Macmillan, 1929), p. 182

Contents

Acknowledgements

As the subject of this book did not inspire the confidence of funding agencies, publishers, or literary agents, the support it did receive was doubly valued. The interest of Jane Gallop was important to me in the early stages, especially since it came from outside the context of Canadian literature. Lovat Dickson, racing against time to finish his own writing, after reluctantly granting me an interview, took the trouble to write and express his confidence in the project. Finally, it was Richard Teleky of Oxford University Press who brought the book into being.

I was fortunate in having the support of Esmée Rees, who showed great kindness and patience in answering questions, providing material, and endlessly rehearsing her memories of Mazo de la Roche. I am also grateful to Senator Daniel Lang, who as literary executor has permitted me to quote from both the papers and the published works.

The importance of the writers of earlier books on Mazo de la Roche will be evident from the use I have made of their work. Ronald Hambleton and George Hendrick have shown additional generosity—Ronald Hambleton by placing his research materials at the disposal of scholars in the Thomas Fisher Rare Book Library and George Hendrick by supplying me with materials, information, and advice on request. I cherish the friendship and support of both.

Librarians in many places have made this work possible—Christopher P. Roberts and Kathy Griffin at the Massachusetts Historical Society; Bruce Whiteman at McMaster University Library; Marion Helen Cobb at Queen's University Library; June Gibson at the Archives of Ontario; Audrey Prendergast at the Regina Public Library; Marie Sakon at the Saskatchewan Provincial Library; Marion Powell at the Saskatchewan Legislative Library; George Brandak at the Library of the University of British Columbia; G.E. Mynett at the MacMillan Bloedel Archives; George Luesby at the Newmarket Historical Society; Katherine Martyn and Rachel Grover at the Thomas Fisher Rare Book Library. Marion Lake at the University of Regina Library has borne the brunt of endless ordering of materials through inter-library loan. I am deeply grateful for her kindness and good humour.

Others who have aided the research and made important contributions are Heather Kirk, Peggy Bowyer, secretary to Lord Stockton at Macmillan Publishers in London, Lady Liddell Hart, Reverend Glen Burgomaster, Jennifer Burgomaster, Dorothy Livesay, Ruth McCuaig, and Herbert Orr.

Many friends at the University of Regina have provided moral and other kinds of support. Don Hall has expertly dealt with all the photographs I needed, and colleagues in the department of History have been valuable sources of information: Attila Chanady, Marcia McGovern, and William Brennan; Annabel Robinson, Corinne Gogal, and Diane Secoy-Smith provided expertise in their various fields. Students in my classes in Feminist Approaches to Nineteenth Century Literature and Feminist Approaches to Twentieth Century Literature have provided many insights. In particular I must thank Sherry Klein, a student in both classes, whose reading of *Mary Wakefield* (*Wascana Review* 23:1 [Spring, 1988]) I have used. The President's Fund of the University of Regina made possible my research trips to Toronto, Austin, Texas, and London, England, and helped with the purchase of research materials. My department head, K.G. Probert, has allowed me considerable flexibility in the scheduling of classes so that I have had time to write.

The following read the manuscript and gave useful criticism: Joan Sandomirsky, Sharon Butala, Wayne Schmalz, and, once again, George Hendrick.

Members of my family have helped in various ways. My mother, Elizabeth Short, has ransacked antiquarian stores throughout the south of England and has added many editions to my collection of Mazo de la Roche's works. My daughters have provided me with firsthand experience of the longevity and durability of a childhood play. My husband, David Givner, has for the second time stoically survived the writing of a literary life and accepted the invisible presence of its subject as a member of the household.

Finally, the real heroines of this work are Bette Fiege and Marilyn Bickford, who have overseen the word-processing with complete competence and almost superhuman patience. Truly, this book could not have been written without them.

Preface

In the spring of 1927, when Mazo de la Roche shot overnight to fame and fortune as one of the most successful writers in the world, she was already known in Canada as the author of short stories, plays, and novels. She was virtually unknown in the United States, however, and arrived on the American scene from obscurity. Her spectacular success came after she entered her fourth novel (two had already been published and one rejected) in the competition run by the *Atlantic Monthly* magazine. The prize included, besides the then huge sum of $10,000, publication in serial form in the magazine and in book form by Little, Brown & Co. With such rewards, interest in the competition naturally ran high. The *Atlantic Monthly* offices were deluged with submissions, and the literary community was agog for news of the winner. Subsequent events have become the stuff of legend. When the final selection was made, so the story goes, the unanimous choice was a neatly typed novel with the cryptic title page: Jalna by Mazo de la Roche.[1] The first chapters revealed that Jalna was the ancestral home of an Ontario squirearchy, but the identity of the person behind the exotic, gender-concealing name was less evident.

In early April the *Boston Globe*[2] and the *New York Times*[3] as well as all the Canadian papers[4] broke the news that Mazo de la Roche was a shy, unmarried woman in early middle age who lived quietly with her sister Caroline Clement in a Toronto rooming house. The bare facts, however, rarely explain a person, least of all Mazo de la Roche. The question 'who is she?' never ceased to be asked throughout her life. But even as more 'facts' emerged, there was a sense that the mystery was not so much cleared up as increased, that the 'real' Mazo was never revealed, and that her true identity eluded her fans and her personal friends alike. She remained an enigma and the subject of fascinated scrutiny, especially in Canada.

Perhaps success on such a scale always arouses curiosity, but there were many other factors that fanned it. There was, first of all, her own reticence. She would later list 'privacy' as her hobby,[5] but it was already clear that her dislike for publicity amounted to an obsession. She objected when her publishers put personal information on the dust covers of her novels and forbade them to refer to her familiarly as 'Mazo'.[6] When she granted the rare interview, many of the subjects that the interviewer wished to address were declared out of bounds ahead of time.

When she did give out information, much of it was inaccurate, and biographical notices like the following (which prefaced a 1932 serialization of a novel in *Chatelaine* magazine) raise two questions for every statement of fact:

> It isn't often that the personal stories of famous writers are half as romantic as the novels they write; but to hear about Mazo de la Roche is to listen to a glamorous fairy tale of genius—the kind of genius that has 'an infinite capacity for taking pains'.
>
> For here is a story of a traditional lady of the pen, left without family or fortune, but with a fine old heritage of Canadian courage behind her, and an unquenchable desire to write. It is the tale of a young woman who after years of dogged struggle, suddenly awoke one bright morning to find fame and fortune sitting comfortably on her doorstep.
>
> Miss de la Roche, one of the most noted women writers of the day, hailed on three continents as a master craftsman in literature, winner of the Atlantic Monthly prize of ten thousand dollars and author of half a dozen much discussed novels, is a Canadian of Canadians. On her mother's side of the family are six generations of United Empire Loyalists, and while her father was a native-born Canadian, his people were descendants of an old French Royalist family. Mazo herself was born in Toronto.
>
> When she was still a young girl, her parents died within a year or so of each other, and Mazo de la Roche, an only child, was left alone.[7]

As a biographical record, this is a work of fiction. There were no French Royalists among her father's ancestors. His family was Irish, known as Roche (pronounced 'Roach'), and Mazo was the only one to go by the surname 'de la Roche'. She was born not in Toronto but in Newmarket, Ontario. Her parents died five years apart, her father when she was thirty-six and her mother when she was forty-one. Clearly there was at work here a compulsion to change the record.

But whose compulsion? It turns out that the story of an ancestor guillotined in the French Revolution first appeared in a questionnaire filled out not by Mazo but by Caroline Clement[8]—who was not Mazo's sister, as many thought, but a cousin (Mazo's mother was the niece of Caroline's mother). Unlike Mazo, Caroline did come from United Empire Loyalist stock, and she was orphaned at an early age. There seems, then, to be a conflation of the biographical facts, and it raises some questions about the nature of the relationship between the two women.

It was noted by acquaintances that 'Caroline Clement gave—probably quite unconsciously—the impression that the books were in a sense her work and not Mazo's'.[9] The holograph manuscripts of the novels show most of them to have been written in two hands, Mazo's and Caroline's. There are many questions to be asked about the nature of this symbiotic relationship, which began when Mazo's parents adopted Caroline into their family. 'We came together like two drops of water,' Caroline said.[10] Were they so close that the ego boundaries between them had dissolved and each could claim experiences that belonged to the other? Or did Caroline exert some kind of control over Mazo and her work?

The Jalna series itself raised more questions. As the story unfolded in novel after novel (sixteen in all) the sexual adventures of the Whiteoak family grew more and more turbulent. Brothers seducing each other's wives in the early volumes later gave way to incest, sadism, and demonic possession. Mazo's publishers had problems with her disregard for the incest taboo: half-siblings, for instance, fell in love with each other and decided to live together in defiance of social convention and family disapproval. Jalna fans by this time were legion and so caught up in the lives of her characters that they wrote to Mazo and her publishers protesting the laws and suggesting that they be changed.[11] At the same time her eager public could not help wondering if there was something sinister in her own past (in spite of the impression she gave of having lived a blameless and sheltered life) that accounted for the sexual aberrations of her characters. In such circumstances rumours naturally flourished.

One, not far from the truth, was that she had grown up as plain Maisie or May Roche in a family of little means.[12] Less accurate but very persistent was the rumour that she had been jilted at the altar like Miss Havisham in *Great Expectations*.[13] Later, when in mysterious circumstances she acquired two children, there was much speculation about their origin. Were they really not adopted, as she said, but the illegitimate children of one of the two women? Perhaps not of Mazo, who was so masculine and, after all, in her fifties, but of the younger Caroline? Again, the rumours were fanned by Mazo's fanatical secrecy. She refused to divulge to the children themselves the secret of their origin or even whether they were related to each other. When, after her death, they asked Caroline, she too refused to answer, saying that if Mazo had wanted them to know she would have told them herself.[14]

The predictable nature of the rumours about Mazo de la Roche— jilting at the altar, children born out of wedlock—reflects the limited scripts that could be imagined for women's lives in her time. These allowed for two alternatives: either marriage and motherhood or reluctant spinsterdom. In her book *Last Tales* Isak Dinesen has provided a resonant image for those limited options. Her story 'The Blank Page'[15] tells of a convent in which the nuns weave a fine linen for the bridal sheets of the royal houses of the country. After the wedding night the sheets are returned to the convent. Each one, bearing the blood-stain that testifies to the honour of a royal princess, is duly labelled with her name, framed, and hung on the gallery wall. All the sheets tell the same story, of the exclusive possession of the woman's body and of the legitimacy of her heirs. The princesses have only one means of expression and only one story: the story of the marriage bed and the childbed, written in blood. Yet in the gallery there is one exhibit that exerts a greater fascination than all the rest: an unlabelled frame around a sheet that is blank. Before it the pilgrims stand riveted, wondering what it signifies. A prince's impotence? A princess's dishonour? Refusal? Flight into the arms of another man? Another woman? The variations are endless, for if the story of every traditional marriage is alike for the woman, the story of every blank page is secretive and unlike any other.

The life of Mazo de la Roche is one such story. It was a life for which there was no precedent and no pattern, one that she forged for herself quite outside the established tradition of women's lives. It was one of unparallelled individuality, and, like all such lives, it was shrouded in secrecy and silence. Carolyn Heilbrun has described such lives as 'thwarted . . . lives cut short, lives miraculous in their unapplauded achievement. They are all new stories. Only the female life of prime devotion to male destiny had been told before; for the girl who wanted more there were too few exemplars.'[16]

But how is a lost life to be recovered? The de la Roche papers in the various university libraries are of little help, since they consist mainly of business letters to publishers and reviewers and reveal little of a personal nature. And at Mazo's death Caroline's first act was to destroy her diaries; she claimed to have been acting on Mazo's instructions, and she may well have been.[17] The record, then, is sparse in personally revealing documentation. Not only letters and diaries

4

but witnesses too are lacking, for the children and even those who claimed to be close friends admitted in the end that they were kept at a distance, never received any confidences. This sparcity is balanced, however, by the richness in number and variety of her published works. Before she died Mazo had published, besides the sixteen novels about Jalna, several other novels, numerous short stories, children's books, two books about her own children and one about her pet dog, a history of the seaport of Quebec, and an autobiography. She was an incessant and compulsive writer, and so popular that her publishers were forced to issue works that they thought unsuitable for publication. In fact, almost every line she wrote was published in some form or another.

It is in this prolific outpouring, mixed as it is in quality, that clues to Mazo's inner life are to be found. For even those with strong instincts for privacy and self-protection have powerful counter-instincts to memorialize their lives, to inscribe them in some way and leave permanent traces. Sandra Gilbert and Susan Gubar, in their monumental work *The Madwoman in the Attic*,[18] have shown how nineteenth-century women, locked into literary forms as confined and confining as their roles in life, without legal power, without either psychic or physical space, were impelled by those very deprivations to inscribe their lives in the literary forms they found at their disposal. Mazo de la Roche (who was a young woman of twenty-two when Queen Victoria died) must be included in the ranks of these nineteenth-century writers. Her best works are those that come nearest to tapping the secrets of her inner life—encoding them—and those that express her erotic desire.

Of course, all fiction bears a strong personal imprint, and the use of the work in order to interpret the writer's life is not new; the method of literary psychology was pioneered by Leon Edel in the 1950s. Yet the deciphering of the blank page, as feminist scholars and biographers have been quick to see, requires a special approach. Nancy Miller has suggested placing side by side the 'fictional fiction' and the 'fictions of autobiography' so that the female self can be located in the inter-text between the two. Mindful of the 'kind of biographical "hermeneutics" which reads . . . all women's fiction as autobiography', she sees her proposed method of 'double reading' rather as a dialectical practice 'which would privilege neither autobiography nor the fiction, but take the two writings together in their status as text'.[19] As an exemplary use of this method she cites an essay by Germaine Brée on George Sand, a writer with whom Mazo de la Roche had much in common. The same method can also be applied to Mazo,

5

who in her seventy-eighth year, four years before her death, published her autobiography.

Ringing the Changes[20] is a curious memoir—notable, as might be expected, for its reticence and evasiveness. Most of Mazo's readers and critics were frustrated chiefly by her failure throughout to mention dates, so that all events seem to take place in a chronological limbo. She herself, on the final page of the book, expressed a different reservation:

> Thinking it over, I am convinced that I know little about the writing of an autobiography—that I am without skill in presenting my own life . . . . I realize that I have possibly given too much space to the telling of little things, but these had a way of pushing themselves in. They were important to me.[21]

In the uncovering of the hidden life, the apparently unimportant facts are just as deserving of careful analysis as the glaring omissions, as the following digression shows. Mazo describes an animal that was part of the household when she lived in England:

> Our cook had brought her own little mongrel dog to live with us. She had been paying for his keep with people who were going away. This poor little creature had been so long tied up that he had, to pass the time, acquired the strangest habits. He would rock on his haunches rhythmically for a space, then bend to nibble his left foreleg. He would rock again, then nibble his right foreleg. Both legs had large callouses on them. This little dog, Joey, asked for no affection, would respond to none. All he asked was to be allowed to continue his strange pagan ritual.[22]

A hasty reading might produce impatience or wonder that the writer, already pushed to condense eighty eventful years into three hundred pages, should so recklessly expend space on trivia. A second reading might lead to the conclusion that this image of the mongrel dog, which has stayed so vivid over the years, represents not so much a veering from the main story as a different way of telling it.

A friend remembered that Mazo, watching sea-gulls on a Cornish cliff, suddenly sprang up and cried, 'What a life! To be free like that!'[23] The memory of the cook's dog is a variation on her own heart-felt cry on the Cornish cliff: it is an image of her own desperate sense of being fettered. Moreover, like the dog, she felt herself to be of mixed blood, and she often attributed her own conflicts to the mongrel strain in her heritage. Read in this way the forceful image is not a digression but a vivid illustration of her life, presented with great economy.

A second digression from her autobiography, regarding the pool at her house in Windsor, is equally revealing:

> Now speaking of this pool I must tell of a strange thing I saw there. It was when I was strolling alone. It was in a quiet and lovely spot, between house and orchard, just beyond a pleached alley of old pear trees. I was thinking of what I was about to write but stopped—stunned by what I saw—indeed, *beheld* is a better word. There were forty-nine of the fifty fish, in all their pretty shapes and colours, ranged as an audience, still as death. And there was the fiftieth—largest and most handsome—and astride his neck, the frog which lived on a ferny island in the middle of the pool! The frog clasped his neck in its green arms and the worst was that the captive seemed to like it.
>
> If the faces of goldfish can show consternation, the faces of those forty-nine who witnessed this amorous scene showed it. I felt that only a man could save the horrible situation.
>
> 'Paxton! Paxton!' I called, running like the wind through the pleached alley to the house, where I had seen him at the top of a ladder, doing something to a window.
>
> I tried to explain but I could scarcely speak for excitement. Tolerantly Paxton descended the ladder, and followed me. Sceptically he scanned the pool for signs of distubance. There was none. The frog had disappeared, the goldfish busied themselves as usual about the lily pads. Paxton asked, 'Madam, are you quite sure you saw—what you describe?'[24]

This passage records a ludicrous over-reaction to a simple animal phenomenon. Clearly, when Mazo attributes shock and consternation to the faces of the goldfish witnesses, she is projecting her own emotions. But the meaning of her violent reaction to the sight of two different species linked in an apparently amorous posture is ambiguous. She could have been reacting to the union of two creatures who do not usually mate together—for instance, two members of the same sex. Her cry 'only a man could save the horrible situation' would suggest such an interpretation.

On the other hand, there is also an echo of her own shocked re-action, described elsewhere in the same book, when at a party she saw her beloved Caroline sitting with her hand clasped by a young man. There again she comments, 'The worst was that she seemed to like it.'[25] In fact, her fiction suggests that it was ordinary heterosexual relationships that were strange and foreign to her, beyond her imaginative grasp.

An example of Mazo's failure of the imagination in that area occurs in the scene from *Finch's Fortune* when Renny, the Master of Jalna, having courted and at last won the former wife of his brother Eden, breaks the news on the return from their honeymoon that he intends to go on sharing his bedroom with his thirteen-year-old brother Wakefield, rather than with her. Here is an early version of this scene, later excised from the novel:

> He had broken in on her thoughts by saying in a somewhat constrained voice:
> 'You can sleep with me here, if you like but, in that case, we'll have to put a small bed or something in for Wake. He's always slept in my room, I couldn't think of putting him off by himself with his heart so weak and his nerves often getting rocky in the night. I suppose you won't mind.'
> She had been aghast. A small boy in the room with them. His clothes about. The dressing and undressing. But how and where would they dress and undress? Her cheeks had suddenly flamed. She felt angry with him.
> 'I couldn't possibly do it,' she said, 'Why it would be positively sordid. Is there no one but you who can look after Wakefield at night? Couldn't he sleep in Finch's room? For my part I think he would be far better in a room by himself.'
> He had answered coldly:
> 'He has always slept with me.'
> She had flashed—'Perhaps you would like to have him in bed with us.'
> 'I shouldn't mind it at all.'[26]

Whether the cut was made at the suggestion of an editor, or whether Mazo herself thought better of it, there is no means of knowing, but the final version is only slightly less peculiar:

> He had broken in on her thoughts by saying in a somewhat constrained voice:
> 'I wonder if you would mind very much taking Meggie's room for yourself. It's next door, and it would leave me free to look after Wake. He has always slept with me, you know.'
> She had been startled, even angered by the request. Yet withal a subtle sense of relief had entered into her feelings after the first moment. The idea of a retreat of her own, a harbour for her tastes and her reserves, had not been unpleasant. But to give up the shelter, the provocation of his presence . . . even more, to think that he was suggesting, almost laconically suggesting, the giving up of her presence in his room. After what they had been to each other for three months! After all he had confessed to her of his fevered longings for her when she had been in that house as Eden's wife! Had his longings developed into no desire for sweet companionship?[27]

Thus for those who look beyond the literal surface meaning of her stories, Mazo reveals herself in her writing. She even writes fiction about her fictional strategy. Her story 'Quartet' is a case in point.[28] Here a New England stockbroker visits his childhood love, Alice, who has married an Italian count. The reunion takes place in Naples, in the count's ancestral villa, with the couple's young daughter making up the fourth member of the quartet. Ostensibly it is a familiar story of lost love and marital infidelity, though one critic has seen it as a 'clash of cultures', a New World/Old World conflict.[29] Yet on another level it is about communication, the possibility of sending coded messages and the subversive power of language. Because Alice speaks fluent English and Italian, she can communicate with both her former lover and her husband. They, however, cannot understand each other, since the lover speaks only English and the count is, in his wife's words, 'too stupid and narrow-minded' to learn her language.

The count, a cavalry officer, is frequently unfaithful to his wife, but at the same time he is fiercely possessive, allowing her no freedom to protest, to seek her own erotic pleasure, or to express her desperation. Her lover's presence allows her a rare opportunity to do all three. She speaks out under her husband's nose, confident he will not suspect that he is being verbally cuckolded. His arrogance prevents him from understanding her language, and his egotism makes him think that all utterance merely affirms the value of himself and his possessions. The lover, who *does* understand, is shocked and terrified by Alice's rage. The little girl, who cannot understand the actual words, somehow senses their subversive force and becomes wildly aroused.

The story can be read as a parable of the life and art of Mazo de la Roche. Cramped within patriarchal social and literary conventions, she had no room to live her life freely or to write of it openly. In order to survive, she was forced to adopt strategies of silence and duplicity. One researcher trying to uncover her life commented: '. . . so many red herrings, so much apparent obscuring of the trail. . . . Do you think she was aware of being a very secretive person, or did she merely think of it as well-bred reticence? It seems to have gone beyond the bounds of ordinary inhibition.'[30] Another perceptive observer noticed that 'there was a queer secret look in her eyes that one felt there were all sorts of things she could say really but she'd just like to keep them all to herself.'[31] Yet she did say them—she inscribed her life in her fictions. But she followed Emily Dickinson's advice: 'Tell all the truth, but tell it slant.' In the past decade feminist critics have written extensively about the strategies employed by nineteenth-century women writers who found themselves literally and figuratively confined. Elaine Showalter, for example, has commented:

> Feminist criticism, with its emphasis on the woman writer's inevitable consciousness of her own gender, has allowed us to see meaning in what has previously been empty space. The orthodox plot recedes, and another plot, hitherto submerged in the anonymity of the background, stands out in bold relief like a thumbprint.[32]

The fiction of Mazo de la Roche requires such a reading. When the orthodox plots recede and the submerged plot is brought forward, it is possible to begin to understand her life. Such a method is appropriate both to her current reputation and to this particular moment in the history of literary criticism.

The first biography of Mazo de la Roche was published in 1966. Since she had been dead only five years, her reputation was not then in total eclipse. Yet because Caroline Clement was still living it was not yet possible to write frankly of their personal lives. Instead, Ronald Hambleton, in his pioneering study *Mazo de la Roche of Jalna*, concentrated on setting the ancestral house in order. His work has provided a foundation for the present study, just as I hope my work will help a future biographer.

As each biography prepares the way for the next, so each in turn is a product of its age; to adapt slightly the words of David Bromwich, 'the successful biographies of an age have as much in common as their biographers rather than as little as their [heroines].'[33] The present study is not an exhaustive, definitive study of an established figure: such an undertaking will be possible only when the need to mount strenuous arguments for the merit of the subject has been removed. It is, rather, a provocative defence of a neglected woman writer in a critical climate coloured by feminist criticism. It is, in the Greek sense of the word, an apology for her life.

1

The Advent of Caroline Clement

Mazo prefaces her autobiography with a description of her first meeting with Caroline Clement on a snowy January day that she designates as 'the most important day of my life'.[1] The rhapsodic evocation of this event provides a vivid example of that *jouissance* (pleasure or rapture; literally, play-fulness) which certain French feminist writers have seen as the mark of erotic desire in women's writing.

In creating the scene Mazo uses details that echo the arrival of the Christ child in the gospels—a conceit that is not as inappropriate as it might seem, since in Mazo's personal mythology Caroline does assume the role of saviour. Caroline arrives just after the Christmas season, on a sleigh, heralded by bells and wrapped in swaddling clothes. The unwrapping and showing forth take place with uncles and grandparents standing around like the Magi:

> When I saw there was a child in the bundle, I drew away. In fact, no one noticed me. All were intent on the bundle, from the top of which now hung, like limp petals of a flower, strands of silvery fair hair. Uncle George sat down in my grandfather's arm-chair and began to take layer after layer of shawls from the bundle. He did it with a proud possessive air, as though he was doing a conjuring trick. Everybody stood about, waiting for the climax.
>
> The climax was a small girl, sitting demurely on his knee, her thin little hands folded on her lap, while she stared about her dazed by the sudden change that had lately befallen her.[2]

The catalogue of Caroline's physical attributes appears subsequently throughout Mazo's fiction. These characteristics make up not only her description of Caroline but her stock description of desirable women: silvery hair, blue eyes, flower-like head, the 'pale disc' of the face, the diminutive stature (Caroline grew to no more than five feet), and above all the thin hands, mentioned three times in this prologue.[3] Hands (especially those of artists) had a special significance for Mazo, and she uses them throughout her work both as indications of character and as instruments of creativity and sexuality. It seems likely that she made the successful artist of the Whiteoak family a pianist in part because a pianist's instrument of expression is the hands. And she wished to include a photograph of her own hands in her autobiography. (Her editor vetoed the suggestion.)

After Caroline emerges from her wrappings at this first meeting, she goes at once to Mazo and places her 'thin little hand' in that of the taller girl. Mazo then leads her away from the grown-ups, through the lower rooms of the house to the upper regions and the bedrooms where they can be undisturbed. There they begin to establish their own relationship, within the family home and yet separate, alone together. They begin their relationship with an exchange of gifts. Each offers the other two presents, not tangible objects but abstract, enigmatical gifts, like those exchanged in fairy-tales. Again the analogy is appropriate, for fairy-tales resonate in Mazo's imagination and fiction.[4] They appealed to her because she was troubled by the same sinister subterranean forces that find expression in fairy-tales, and her method of coping with the chaotic elements in her life was always to exorcise them through fantasy. Like the gifts bestowed in fairy-tales, those exchanged by Mazo and Caroline foreshadowed and changed the course of their future lives. Caroline offers her two gifts first, both of which involve birds.

One is the recitation of a long poem, 'The Jackdaw of Rheims', which is not reproduced in the autobiography but was a well-known tale. In the poem a little jackdaw, indulged by a community of clerics in a Gothic cathedral, is attracted by the cardinal's beautiful ring and steals it. A curse subsequently falls upon the bird—he becomes a pariah, his plumage moulting and drooping—but when the ring is restored to its owner he is forgiven and the curse is lifted. In the original version of the poem in *The Ingoldsby Legends* there is a Latin epigraph that translates as follows:

Then the poor Crow was so overcome by the pricking of his conscience, and the curse so tore him to pieces that from then on he began to pine away, he grew thin, avoided all food, nor did he croak any longer: moreover his feathers began to fall out, his wings drooped and he stopped telling all his jokes, and appeared so thin that everyone began to pity him.

> Then the abbot told the priests to absolve the thief again; and as soon
> as he had done this the Crow, to everyone's astonishment, immediately
> became well and recovered his former well-being.[5]

The poem is an oblique foreshadowing of the passage, in a later
chapter, concerning the nervous breakdown Mazo was to suffer in
1903, in which she describes herself as a wounded bird. Like the bird
she does recover, and the agent of her recovery is, as always, Caroline,
the only person who could lift from her the curse of loneliness and
mental collapse.

Caroline's other gift is symbolized by a confrontation, on the landing, with a large stuffed bird that had long been a source of terror to
Mazo: 'Going to bed all by myself, it was a terrifying thing to pass
him. Might he not at any moment swoop from his perch and alight
on one's head? Covering my head with my hands I would fly up the
stairs, my heart pounding against my ribs.'[6] This stuffed bird in her
grandfather's house makes several fictional appearances in her work.[7]
On this first day Mazo tries to scare Caroline by telling her that the
creature comes down from his perch in the night and swoops about
the house. But Caroline, already orphaned and tossed from pillar to
post, knows chimeras and unsubstantial fears when she meets them:
she pooh-poohs them. Moreover, she shows Mazo how to take physical pleasure in the creature's body, urging her to put her hands into
the downy cavities under the wings. Mazo remembers the sensation
thus: 'Oh the downy softness of the space beneath his wings—the
intimate communion with him.'[8] These simple acts explain in coded
form what happened when Caroline stepped into her world. All her
life, Mazo—wracked by internal conflicts and disturbed emotions—
suffered from nightmares. It was Caroline who could keep them at
bay, or soothe her back to sleep.

Like Caroline's gift of the poem, Mazo's first gift also takes a literary
form. She mentions that among her Christmas presents she has a
favourite book, *Through the Looking Glass*. She shares it with Caroline
(who must have reminded her very much of Alice):

> We sat together at a table close to the window to catch the last of the
> daylight and read aloud, page about. I remember how carefully we
> sounded the g in gnat. Our heads—hers fair, mine curly and brown—
> touching. Our legs, in their long black cashmere stockings, dangling.[9]

The scene of the two girls reading 'page about' would be repeated
throughout their lives as each day ended with a shared reading, one
reading aloud to the other. And it would be repeated eventually too

in the writing of the fiction, when they sat writing turn and turn about, Caroline taking dictation when Mazo's hand tired.

But the Alice story itself is also important; in a sense, it underscores the theme of the Prologue itself. The special fascination for Mazo of *Through the Looking Glass* was not merely that it described a young girl entering a fantasy world, but that the nature of that world closely reflected her own experience. The land beyond the mirror shows the real world reversed. People speak in conundrums, saying the opposite of what they mean; when they wish to move forward they must in fact go backwards. Mazo often experienced her own world as a series of such opposites. In her family, tragedies were placed in the realm of the unutterable; the names of dead relatives were not mentioned. Accordingly, she became accustomed to feeling that the unspoken was more powerful than the spoken, the invisible more present than the visible. One of the marked features of the style of the autobiography is that the sentence structure is often inverted. Occasional inverted sentences appear in her fiction, but they are never so extensively used as when she is dealing directly with her own personal experience. She could not, therefore, have selected a text more appropriate than *Through the Looking Glass* for presenting a key to her own strange world.

Mazo, of course, was not alone in appropriating *Through the Looking Glass* as a personal text. For many women writers, as Elaine Showalter has noted, Alice's journey through the looking glass has been an apt analogy for the transition from sanity to disturbed mental states.[10] Mary Cecil called her memoir *Through the Looking Glass*; Antonia White in *Beyond the Glass* describes her character coming to her senses in a mental hospital and watching several women patients playing a weird game of croquet; Virginia Woolf, in her first novel and portrait of herself as an artist, evokes Alice as her fictional counterpart, Rachel Vinrace, enters a state of delirium. In fact, Mazo's first, highly appropriate, choice for the title of her autobiography was 'Scene in a Mirror' (her English publishers decided against it as being too much associated with another of their authors.)[11]

Even before meeting Caroline, Mazo had not been without her own consolations. She was an intelligent, resourceful child, and like Alice she had created her own imaginary world. The sharing of this world was her present to Caroline:

I turned and could just make out the white disc of Caroline's face in the dusk. Should I tell her my secret? There was an expectant tilt to her pale head. Her thin hands were clasped as though in beseeching.

I drew a sigh. 'I have a secret,' I said.

'A secret,' she breathed. 'Oh, I love secrets.'

'I'll tell you,' I said, not able to stop myself, 'if you'll promise never never to tell anyone else.'

'I promise.' And it seemed and was true that she'd die first. 'I will never tell.'

'It was a dream,' I said. 'First it was a dream—then I played it—all by myself. I played it every day. But now you are here, I'll tell you and we'll play it together.'

'What do you call it?' she whispered, as though under the weight of a mystery.

'My play I call it. But now it must be *our* play. We'll play it together— if you think you can.'

'I can play anything—if it's pretend,' she said decidedly. 'I've never tried it but I know I can.'

So then I told her.[12]

Mazo ends the prologue to her story with the promise of sharing the Play and postpones the full disclosure of its nature until a later chapter.

There are many versions of the momentous meeting between the two girls. Lovat Dickson, Mazo's cherished friend and editor, left among his papers a handwritten note dated 23 January 1971 (ten years after Mazo's death and one year before Caroline's):

Caroline has told me this story so many times before: I see them both: Mazo tall for her age—3 years older—plain, seeing in doll-faced C. the little sister she had always dreamed of having—and M's parents openly accepting her too. The two little girls drawing apart from the adults and growing up together, locked together in their own vanities and dreams, and all the time falling in love with each other. C. on M's beautiful dark eyes, and chestnut hair wh. when combed out, came down 'to here'—i.e. midway to her extended arm. M is mute now, no longer about to witness. But one can catch in one's imagination her breathless admiration for such flaxen hair 'down to here'—the ghostly voice comes across the divide—meaning half-way down her arms. A double-sided narcissism.[13]

In some ways the relationship of Mazo and Caroline resembles that of Gertrude Stein and Alice B. Toklas. But there are important differences. Too often the lives of women who chose to live in pairs have been forced into the only pattern in existence for two people living together—that of the heterosexual married couple. In addition, Gertrude Stein was a mature woman when she invited Alice B. Toklas to share her life; she had had other relationships; she already had decided on her life's work; she was sure of her identity. Mazo and

Caroline were together as children, neither one ever had another intimate relationship, and theirs was in place long before Mazo became a writer.

The relationship finds its way into Mazo's fiction in various coded versions. One is the short story 'Dummy Love',[14] which appeared in *Harper's Bazaar* in 1932. Here an artist of sorts (a window-dresser) falls in love with a mannequin. He takes it to his apartment, where he delights in dressing it in exotic costumes on which he spends most of his salary. Always solitary, he never, as a child, joined in the play of other children. Now he worries about his latest form of 'play': 'Throughout his life he had suspected that he was a little queer just because he was so different from those around him. But when it came to making a companion, almost a lover, of a painted dummy, perhaps this was being very queer indeed.'[15]

Sometimes he is a little ashamed of his play: 'he kissed her every evening when he lifted her from the cupboard. He did not kiss her in the mornings, for then he was hurried and rather shamefaced because of his fancies of the night before.'[16] Yet he can justify his pastime because he is practising his art, becoming a better window-dresser. Through his skill he attracts the admiration of a female window-dresser and they become engaged. Marriage is precipitated by the death of her father, from whom she inherits a department store. The artist then fears her jealousy of his private world with the mannequin. But when he invites her into that world and reveals the mannequin in all her splendour, his wife shares his delight: 'She [the mannequin] was not only the glorious centrepiece of their window. She was the adorable emblem of their happiness.'[17]

So Mazo inscribed in her fiction the almost unbelievable happiness she felt when Caroline, besides being a wonderful companion in her beauty, her sweetness, and her loving nature, stepped directly into the fantasy world that had been Mazo's private solace. She might have resented the Play, might have seen it as a rival for Mazo's attention. Instead, she became a joyous partner in that world, so that its boundaries expanded beyond anything Mazo had previously imagined.

Thus the prologue to the autobiography seems to be an artistically contrived re-creation of the girls' first meeting, one that skilfully encapsulates their entire relationship and foreshadows their future life together. Yet Mazo certainly intended to present the episode as literally true, even if retrospectively its mythical dimensions become apparent. Literal truth and poetic truth are not incompatible, and the meeting might reasonably be assumed to have happened exactly as reported. While she does not give exact dates, there is internal evidence by which the date and place can presumably be established:

1. 'I was seven years old.' She was seven in 1886.

2. 'Upstairs I showed her my Christmas presents. . . .' The Christmas tree has just been removed, and so the meeting can be fixed in early January. And since Mazo's birthday was on 15 January, it must have taken place on or around her seventh birthday.

3. ' "I don't live here,' I said, 'I live in Toronto." ' The meeting evidently took place at her Grandfather Lundy's house in Newmarket, Ontario.

Yet these clear facts are contradicted by evidence external to the autobiography:

1. Caroline was probably not yet born in 1886.

2. Caroline's father died on 27 August 1894. After his death she spent time with relatives who 'did not like children' before joining Mazo's family. When she arrived, therefore, Mazo must have been almost sixteen.

3. The Lundy grandparents moved to Parkdale in Toronto in the spring of 1894.

4. It seems unlikely that Mazo would have received the doll she mentions as a Christmas present when she was sixteen. And she remarks elsewhere in the autobiography[18] that she read *Through the Looking Glass* during a period of residence in Galt, Ontario, when she was eleven.

These discrepancies can lead one to conclude that Mazo's account of her meeting with Caroline is pure fabrication—poetic rather than literal truth. All the same, as often happens with Mazo's reconstructions of events, the changes she made in the record are not arbitrary. They have their reasons, and those reasons tell a story of their own.

The change in the date of the meeting is perhaps the easiest to explain. Mazo lied about her age for most of her life, giving the wrong date even on her passport, and in this, as in everything else, Caroline was a willing collaborator: she even had the date 1888 carved on Mazo's gravestone, instead of the accurate 1879. When asked by Ronald Hambleton if she and Mazo were the same age, she replied that they were 'within nine months of each other'.[19]

It was not unusual, of course, for a woman of her time to drop a few years from her age, but Mazo was conspicuously lacking in the usual kind of female vanity. The reason in her case was less connected to her feminine image than to her relationship with Caroline. As they grew older the age difference was barely noticeable, but in childhood it was very significant, and Mazo always took great pains to conceal it. In fact, although Mazo cherished and gave currency to the idea that they were 'raised together as sisters', when they came together Caroline was probably a child of seven and Mazo a young woman in her mid-teens. Caroline was much more likely to have found in Mazo a surrogate parent than a playmate of her own age. A similar relationship—an older adult brother raising an orphaned brother who is still a child—is a recurrent feature in Mazo's fiction, but that was the only place in which she chose to portray the real nature of her early relationship with Caroline.

The placing of the meeting on or around Mazo's seventh birthday provides another footnote to the story of her life, for at that time a tragedy occurred that left an indelible mark on her memory. Both Mazo's grandfather and his oldest son, thirty-year-old Frank Lundy, were employed in Newmarket by a firm that produced wooden products such as roofing shingles and furniture. On the morning of 14 January 1886, the day before her seventh birthday, the son was killed in a particularly gruesome manner:

> In reaching under the main shaft his sleeve was caught by a set screw in an adjoining flunge, drawing his arm and shoulder under the shaft. His head was consequently brought in contact with the circular saw, which was about a foot in diameter, and in an instant was nearly severed from the body in an angle below the left ear and through the neck. . . . Death was instantaneous—he never spoke nor uttered a sound.[20]

The accident not only was the most sensational event to occur in Newmarket for a long time, but it also produced one of the town's largest ceremonial gatherings. The *Newmarket Era*, declaring the funeral to be 'the most largely attended . . . ever in Newmarket on a wet day', devoted a great deal of space to its description. Floral tributes began to arrive at the house as word of the death spread. An engaging and popular young man, Frank Lundy had been a member of the Volunteer Fire Brigade and the ranks of mourners included firemen as well as co-workers, friends, and acquaintances, who flocked in Toronto and from the surrounding towns.

The Methodist church was so crowded that many could not gain admittance and waited outside until the procession re-formed to go to the cemetery to the music of the 'Dead March in Saul' by the town band. Memories of the tragedy lasted long after the funeral. The *Newmarket Era* reprinted its account of the accident a week later for people who wished to send it to friends out of town, and two months later it published a poem called *On the Death of Frank Lundy*, signed merely 'by a friend of the family'. It contained these verses:

> But, hark that wail of anguish,
> Strikes every heart with dread,
> As mute with grief his father
> Bends o'er the loved and dead
> Almost bereft of reason—
> His boy so loved, his pride,
> Like one of old—my son! my son!
> Oh! would thou hadst not died.[21]

Mazo refers to the tragedy in her autobiographical account of her grandparents, and she clearly saw it as one of the important bonds in their relationship with each other. Yet she avoids mentioning the son's name and the nature or date of his death:

Another thing [the grandparents] shared was the agony of grief over the death of their eldest son. Once a year my grandfather visited his grave and brought back a white rose. This he would put into her hand, without a word. The name of the dead son was never spoken in the family. To me, a child, it seemed something sacred and terrible. If by chance it was uttered, a shock struck all. Then a silence followed before talk could be resumed. We children learned to share this shock. None of the loved departed must be mentioned.

It was a black day in springtime when the dead son's clothes were hung out in the breeze to air. I can still picture them now—the suits, the velvet smoking jacket—still rounded by the imprint of his body— or was it the breeze that filled them out? As well as the smoking jacket there was a black velvet smoking cap with a gold tassel which once I secretly tried on, secretly peered at my reflection in the barrel of rain-water and saw the glimmer of the pale face, the dark shine of the eyes, beneath the cap, and shivered at the nearness of death to me who was so small and so alive.[22]

It was further testimony to the vivid impact of this event that many powerful scenes in her fiction are based on it. In *Young Renny* the old grandmother has a ritual airing of her dead husband's clothes every year; there it is her son, Philip, who dons his father's tasselled smoking hat and looks at himself.[23] And three of the most moving chapters in all Mazo's fiction appear in *The Master of Jalna*: her account of the death, lying in state, and burial of the young poet Eden Whiteoak on a cold January day.[24] Although these scenes are based on her memories of her young uncle's death, she seems unable to account for the impact they later had on her and for the source of their power. She wrote to her editor, Edward Weeks:

> Last night Caroline read chapters 18, 19 and 20 of *The Master of Jalna*. Tears ran down my cheeks. Whether it was the hour, the icy blackness outside the windows made me susceptible to the feeling of life's shortness, its tragedy or that it was the writing itself. . . .[25]

There is indirect testimony to the effect of this tragedy on Mazo's childish imagination in the large number of birth-death, birthday-deathday coincidences that stud her fictions. Early in the Jalna saga, the great matriarch Adeline dies on the birthday of young Pheasant Whiteoak, to whom she has just given a ruby ring, and later Pheasant herself gives birth to a son on the birthday of her brother-in-law Finch. One relative's birthday seems to be an auspicious and ominous occasion in the life of another.

The gruesome manner of Frank Lundy's death would not have been lost on Mazo. Her imagination was haunted subsequently by images of grotesque amputation. In one childhood nightmare, for instance, inspired by a horror story heard from a friend, she dreamt of a woman robbed in her grave of a golden arm. A similar image is a telling vehicle for her own horror of psychology: she told Caroline that she would rather send a child to have a limb amputated than to a psychologist or a psychiatrist.[26] Her seventh birthday spent in a house of mourning took on a horrible resonance, symbolizing whatever she felt to be lacking and unlucky in her childhood and in herself. Perhaps the most compelling testimony to the place in her imagination of this gruesome decapitation is her claim that one of her ancestors was guillotined in the French Revolution.[27]

From her grandparents Mazo had a lesson at first hand in dealing with grief. The dead son's name was never mentioned again, nor was the grandfather's ritual yearly visit to the grave, signalled to his wife by the white rose. Mazo learned the lesson well. She learned not only to shroud painful experiences in silence but to manipulate them in various ways. In her autobiography she tried to erase the stain on her birthday by writing over it, palimsestically, the happiest and luckiest event in her life.

And perhaps there was an additional reason for dating Caroline's arrival so specifically. Could it have been that on that fateful day Mazo's sense of horror in the midst of her afflicted family peaked? And did that peak of horror cause her for the first time to take flight into the world of the imagination, just as Alice stepped through the looking glass into her own imaginary world? The coming of Caroline, instead of diminishing the importance of Mazo's inner world, transformed it into something far more adventurous, bigger in scope, even rapturous. Perhaps that is the exact poetic truth in the conflation of the two dates: Mazo's seventh birthday and the arrival of Caroline.

Mazo experienced the world as a chaotic place in which terrible accidents happened. She was unsure of her own position in that world, and in some obscure way felt herself to be dismembered or maimed. Her only recourse in the long, lonely years of her childhood was to take flight into a world of fantasy she could control completely, and that flight became a deep-rooted habit of mind. She learned to cover up the unpleasant circumstances of her life, to obliterate bad memories, to rearrange and reorder experience so that she could bear to face it. This was her strategy for survival. Much later, it became the basis for her art.

2

Life Before Caroline

There is a marked drop in the emotional temperature of her autobiography when Mazo passes from Caroline's arrival to describe the
rest of her family, and a corresponding drop in the literary mode,
from the poetic to the prosaic. As the high-flown lyrical tone is resumed when she returns to Caroline in Chapter 4, the intervening
chapters are in a sense relegated to a parenthetical status. Nevertheless, they are necessary in providing a context for her relationship
with Caroline and for explaining its centrality in her life.

Mazo would not have admitted openly that she had a tormented
childhood. She did not belong to a generation prone to frankness on
such matters, and it would have been unthinkable to her that she
should appraise her parents and grandparents critically. Indeed, when
Lovat Dickson was preparing the jacket blurb for her autobiography
she told him: 'I should be reluctant to give the impression that I had
an unhappy childhood—one to be "*endured*". I was a happy and
cherished child, though my mother's illness overshadowed part of it.
However, I do like "a rather strange childhood".'[1] Yet her account of
the childhood suffering of her fictional representative, Finch Whiteoak, in the midst of a close-knit family, is so detailed and so excru-
ciatingly painful that it is hard not to conclude that her insights owed
much to personal experience. Even her autobiography shows a nov-
elistic flair in evoking childhood misery. She writes of her mother:
'She was so ill that the atmosphere of her condition permeated the
household. When I entered the house after school it descended on
me. Even in classes I was conscious of its oppression.'[2] There is something both vivid and moving in the picture (told without self-pity) of
the child sitting in class, away from home and yet unable to shed its
darksome atmosphere. Mazo was near the truth when she pin-pointed
her mother's illness as a large part of her childhood misery. Yet what

produced that illness, and in how many ways it affected her and undermined her own serenity, she would never fully understand.

Behind the mother, lying a bedridden invalid during Mazo's childhood, looms the figure of the grandfather whom Mazo purports to recall with the warmest affection. The only reservation she ever expressed about him was that he was not much of a provider. Yet her description of him is curiously contradictory. On the one hand, she says he was an indulgent grandfather; on the other, she describes him as a fiercely possessive father, prone to sulking disapproval and bouts of irrational anger that affected his speech and prevented him from pronouncing the name of the object of his wrath.[3]

A letter to the Newmarket paper provides some insight into Daniel Lundy as a stern, fiercely protective parent who could not brook outside interference with his children. It describes an incident that took place in 1884, two years before the death of his oldest son intensified his parental anxieties. This incident concerned his youngest son, eleven-year-old Walter, who was so severely beaten by one of his teachers that there were 'seven distinct marks on the back of his legs, and in one place, about the size of a hand, the blood was oozing through the skin'.[4] Such punishment was not unusual in the school, but Daniel Lundy was the one parent who found it unacceptable. Responding as if to a sexual assault, he brought a case against the schoolmaster before the Bench of Magistrates. The case was dismissed but the irate father persisted in expressing his outrage. His thousand-word letter to the *Newmarket Era* appeared on 4 July. It is significant not only for what it shows about Grandfather Lundy, but also as another event that must have made a profound impression on five-year-old Mazo, who was then living in Newmarket while her father superintended his brother's business. The vein of sadism that critics have often detected in her work may well have owed something to her first-hand observation of the results of her cousin's savage beating and the stir it caused in the family.

In that incident Grandfather Lundy seems to be an appealing character, energetic in protecting his brood and not afraid to speak his mind. On the other hand, the autobiography suggests that he was the stock domineering father of much Victorian fiction and biography. His relationship with Mazo's mother, Alberta, his high-spirited older daughter, is fraught with emotion:

> My mother, his eldest child, seemed to bring out the worst in him. She was highly excitable, highly emotional and her childhood was a time of painful scenes between them. After what he considered a misdeed,

23

he would place her on a sofa beside him and lecture her for an hour. During all this while she would fairly tear herself to pieces with sobbing. Her face would be disfigured by the salt flow of tears. After this the physical chastisement took place. Yet he was still a young man.[5]

Mazo has a very clear memory and understanding of the main targets of her grandfather's hatred: any men who were involved in an intimate way with his women. Yet Mazo reports her mother's dealings with suitors thus:

She was twice engaged before she married my father. I don't know what was my grandfather's attitude towards these suitors. I fancy that he was never given an opportunity to express an opinion. She was so impulsive, so eager for life that she fairly flew to meet it.[6]

Clearly Alberta was not impulsive and eager for life in Mazo's memory, since she was an invalid from the moment her daughter was born. Whether Mazo's grandfather routed the two previous suitors or how Mazo's father succeeded in marrying Alberta we do not know. At any rate, the younger daughter, Mazo's Aunt Eva, was less successful in leaving her father for a husband. She was over thirty before she found a suitor so gentle that even her father approved of him; they were married, but he subsequently died of tuberculosis.[7] The older son married, but he too gravitated back to live in his parents' home; Mazo reports that he 'returned home with a delicate wife and baby'.[8]

When Mazo speaks of her grandfather's kindly nature, she often undercuts her own examples: 'he took whatever I did in good part. It was only my mother who angered him—my mother and Aunt Eva's suitors.'[9] Later she inadvertently contradicts her own remark with an account of the grandfather's reaction when she and Caroline engaged in a boisterously innocent game with some young male friends:

What animals we were I cannot recall, but we were sitting on the floor in these cages when, without warning, Grandpa's tall straight figure appeared in the doorway.

'Put on your jackets,' he said to Caroline and me, ignoring the boys, 'and come home.'

His austere pale face, his stern voice, rendered the boys speechless. Caroline and I snatched up our jackets. She snatched mine, I hers which was much too small for me, and we struggled into them, as we hurried after Grandpa who was already on his way to the street. He did not scold us, as we skulked homeward by his side. His icy silence was enough to make us quail.[10]

Such behaviour in the grandfather was not usually activated by his granddaughter, but rather by his wife's and daughter's doctors and suitors:

> One of her [his wife's] doctors was an object of his aversion. . . . A visit from Dr McKenzie was enough to send Grandpa into a state of frozen disapproval for two days. Once my grandmother was taken suddenly ill and the doctor, making one of his regular calls, went in to see her. While he was there, Grandpa returned, and the sight of the detested doctor, sitting by his wife's bedside, brought on one of Grandpa's worst tempers. He wheeled and left the room but we children heard his wrathful voice later that night.[11]

As a counterpart to his fury with doctors, Mazo records her grandfather's own solicitous care of his women. On one occasion he turned Mazo's mother's bed and bedroom into a veritable bower of greenery with fragrant branches from all the sweet-smelling shrubs he could find. What lover could have been more attentive?

> There were times when his love for my mother was roused and took an almost extravagant turn. I remember how once after she had had a long illness, he was convinced that the scent of pine, balsam and spruce would cure her 'nervous break-down', as it was called. He drove to the woods and returned with mass of greenery, with which he decorated her room. Every space where one of the scented boughs could be hung, the very bed on which she lay, was given its weight. I remember peeping in at her, looking small and rather overpowered by all this— but grateful for his solicitude.[12]

Since Daniel Lundy apparently regarded all approaches to his family by doctors, schoolmasters, and suitors as sexual threats, he must have been highly disturbed by his daughter's pregnancy. Perhaps this explains why the birth was attended not by a Newmarket doctor but by a relative, Dr Patterson of Barrie. It is possible too that some frozen disapproval and blame was directed at the father of the child. The birth was premature, and Mazo describes her infant self as 'a miserable little body . . . a fledgling of three and a half pounds'.[13] She reports the circumstances as follows:

> I was not born where I should have been, in my father's house, but in my grandfather's. My mother was visiting there and made a call at the Rectory where a member of the family was down with scarlet fever. She contracted the disease. She was terribly ill and so not able to go home to have her child. The labour of childbirth, during the ravages of fever, undermined her health which before this had been superb. Never again had she such resistance.[14]

From that time on Alberta Roche was usually incapacitated, unable to carry out the roles of wife and mother. Not strong enough to run a house, she remained bedridden, most of the time in the home of her parents, first in Newmarket and later in Toronto. The passage above, with its reference to the mother's visit, suggests that she had travelled there from some considerable distance. But at that time both families lived and worked in Newmarket. Such misleading remarks are typical of Mazo's habit of covering up the fact that her mother and father often lived apart.

Alberta Roche's illness would seem to be a classic case of the sickness and hysteria suffered by so many nineteenth-century women, repressed and oppressed as they were within the patriarchal structure of their own families. It took the form first of a persistent cough, and later of a disorder of the digestive system so severe that she could not eat normally. In addition, 'Her suffering from nerves was excruciating. I have seen the cords at the back of her neck stand out like taut strings of an instrument on which some wild tune is played, while her dark blue eyes would have a look of strange intensity.'[15] She also suffered from irrational fears: 'One difficulty of her illness was that she now must have the presence of a man always in the house. This masculine presence was, she thought, a protection to her. . . .'[16] She was so ill that if any festivity were taking place in the household, she had to spend the night at the house of a friend. Mazo tells how, when she and Caroline were planning an evening of *tableaux vivants*, 'my mother was to spend the night at a friend's as her nerves could not endure the racket'.[17] She continues:

> Oh, how she would have loved the *tableaux*—the dancing! But more and more often she remained in her bed. Her cough had left her but left her with digestion and nerves so impaired that she was no longer capable of enjoying a normal life. She began to be afraid of being alone.[18]

The only respites in Alberta's long illness seem to have occurred on those occasions when she was called on to act as nurse to other members of the family. When Mazo was ill her mother cared for her, and she nursed her own brother through typhoid fever.[19] When her father was dying, Alberta—as usual, during a commotion in the house— left to stay with a friend; when it was over, she regained her health. Mazo reports that she still had some lingering nervous symptoms: she refused to travel by train and could not endure crowds. But 'she now was able to give my father the companionship his genial nature craved', and 'from this time on she cast off the habits of invalidism and her naturally staunch and spirited nature asserted itself'.[20]

Mazo makes no connection between her grandfather's possessiveness and her mother's illness, or between his death and her recovery. Her 'Grandpa Lundy' was simply 'very near and dear'. If she expresses any reservation, it is because he was a menial factory worker and not materially successful. Years after his death, she wrote to a friend: 'How I wish I could have shared your grandfather! He was so unlike my own. One of them [Daniel Lundy] I remember with love but he never made more than enough to rear his family and leave his widow badly off.'[21] In spite of the protestations of love, and although she was more shielded than her poor mother from the full impact of her grandfather's overpowering attention, Mazo must have suffered indirectly from the atmosphere he created in the house. It is significant that throughout her autobiography Mazo barely mentions her maternal grandmother. In the chapter devoted to 'maternal forebears' she alludes to her in two terse phrases: after her account of the grandfather's rage at the visit of a hated doctor, Mazo writes, 'yet Grandma never complained'.[22] The other reference, sparse compared with the details and examples given to the grandfather, is this: 'Where he was temperamental, she was usually tranquil. Throughout her long and troubled life, she presented a courageous and uncomplaining front.'[23]

Perhaps the self-effacing nature of the grandmother helps to explain one of the inconsistencies in Mazo's accounts of the Lundy home. She often speaks as if she were raised in a house full of men, the implication being that they far outnumbered the women.[24] That may have been the impression in the male-dominated home, but in fact the numbers seem to have been roughly equal. On the male side there was the grandfather, Frank (who died in 1886), George, young Walter, and, from time to time, Mazo's father. On the female side were the grandmother, her daughters Alberta and Eva, George's wife, Mazo, and, later, Caroline.

Mazo recalled Daniel Lundy as a man not only of volatile temper (he once had to be restrained from marching to the house of a girl who had frightened Mazo with a story)[25] but of moral rectitude. For instance, she tells of the time he discovered a book called *The Adventures of Hadji* in the house: he glanced into it, disapproved, and tossed it into the kitchen stove. He did so not to protect his small granddaughter (unbeknownst to him, she had already read it) but because 'it was a very nasty book and I will not have my son tempted to read it'.[26] The autobiography is studded with accounts of Mazo's memories of the disapproval of her elders. When she tried to put on a play, for instance, it was nearly ruined because a friend's mother objected to the red bloomers that were part of her costume. All the same, the grandfather's peremptory act in burning his son's book seems pretty extreme, and it conflicts with Mazo's earlier statement: 'to his sons he was a kind and indulgent father, but my mother, his eldest child, seemed to bring out the worst in him.'[27]

As in the case of of her grandfather, Mazo's description of her mother contains many contradictions that seem to spring from her own ambivalence. Time after time her mother is depicted in a critical or impatient light, tempered at the end by a disclaimer—'she always wanted me to do what I wanted to do!'[28] One such episode took place during a period of residence in Galt (now Cambridge), Ontario, where it was thought that the dry air—the town was situated in the hills— might improve the mother's health. The father is absent on a pro- longed business trip, and the mother is left in Mazo's care, living in a 'residential hotel' in that city. The scenes that Mazo recalls are painful.

She describes how a dog procured by her father and left with them caused a great deal of trouble by his barking: it fell to Mazo, on her mother's orders, to go and beat the dog into silence.[29] Another inci- dent begins with Mazo's mother suggesting that they hire a boat and go out on the river: ' "It will do us both good." ' They set off almost like a pair of lovers, Mazo says: 'I proudly took the oars while . . . my mother held a parasol over her shoulder and trailed her white hand in the water. . . . ' "It will do your cough good," ' I said.' Yet, because of Mazo's negligence, the little excursion ended by making Alberta cough again:

> After a time we drew into the shore and pulled the boat to a safe place. She was a little tired and sat down on a boulder to rest, while I wandered along the shore. When I found myself alone, the strange emotions to which I had been subject of late took possession of me. To be alone— alone! Yet loneliness was what I most feared. On and on I wandered, sometimes picking up a stone to feel its strange smoothness against my cheek. I forgot my mother. I forgot everything but my obsession with the river and its shore. . . . At last I came to a dark little cave and in it I hid myself.
>
> I did not hear my mother's voice calling. I was only conscious of her coming when she appeared in the opening of the cave, looking dis- traught and calling my name, in both relief and anger. She had been so frightened. How could I treat her so? She had imagined all sorts of dreadful things. It was growing dark. It was beginning to rain. . . . It was indeed damp and there was the long rough way back to the boat. She began to cough.[30]

Another incident, vividly remembered, is of Mazo's giving up a skating excursion with Caroline to stay with her mother who 'was having a bad time with her nerves'. The mother understood Mazo's longing to go—'No, no, you must go with the others'—but Mazo saw the fear in her eyes and stayed behind, claiming that she had home-work to do:

As I sat there bent over my book, one hand shading my eyes, my mother said, 'Your hand looks very thin, Mazo. Are you sure you eat enough?'
'Oh, yes, I eat plenty.' My eyes turned from the Latin grammar. I stretched out my hand and examined it. 'It is rather thin,' I agreed, 'but that's because I grow so fast.'
'I suppose it is,' she sighed, then, 'Are you sure, my darling, that you didn't mind not going to the rink?'
'I didn't mind in the least.' And by that time I did not mind. 'I'd rather stay at home with you,' I said.
And never again did I go to the rink or put on my skates.[31]

Whatever the emotion contained in that last line—resignation, re-nunciation, guilt, anger—it is rarely expressed. More often Mazo reports her mother's words and actions dispassionately.

Her account of her parents' reaction to her first short-story effort shows how hurt she was, at the age of nine, when her mother crit-icized her work. Her father, on the other hand, was full of encouragement:

'But, darling,' said my mother, 'do you think a child would ever be so hungry she would eat potato parings?'
'Nancy was,' I said firmly.
'And do you think her mother would quote a text the moment her child was given back to her? It sounds so pompous.'
This was my first experience of criticism and how it hurt!
My father standing by exclaimed, 'I'm dead sure I'd eat potato peel-ings if I were hungry enough and, as for the text—it was the proper thing for the mother to quote. Don't change a word of it. It will probably get the prize.'[32]

When the story was rejected, the father offered practical consolation:

A few weeks later, when I had ceased to think of it, a long envelope was put into my hand. Trembling I opened it and there was my man-uscript returned! With it was enclosed a letter from the editor saying, 'You are very young to have entered the competition but, if the promise shown by this story is fulfilled, you will make a good writer yet.'

'Isn't that splendid!' exclaimed my mother, her pitying eyes on me.

I sat down on a low stool in a corner and covered my face with my hands. Sobs shook me.

Nobody came near me. The family stood about me, realizing that for the moment it was best to leave me to my grief. It was ridiculous, of course, but how well I remember it.

At last my father came to me. He led me to a table and placed two chairs by it. 'Now,' he said, 'I'm going to teach you to play cribbage. It's a good game and you have no idea how comforting a game of cards can be.' He took the pack from the cribbage box and set about dealing it.[33]

Disapproval seems to have been a habit of mind with Mazo's mother. When Mazo asked if she might have a rowing machine and a Bible, she replied that neither one was suitable for a child. When her parents decided that 'it would be good' for Mazo if they read aloud a Shakespearean play and chose *Othello*, it was the mother who brought the performance to an end:

At first the reading went well. They my father read words that made my mother recoil. She cried, 'Oh, you shouldn't read that—not in front of her!' and she cast a solicitous look at me.

'How was I to know what was coming?' he demanded.

'Anyone could see what was coming!'

'Why didn't you stop me then—before I said it?'

'I tried to stop you but I couldn't.'

'Anyhow,' said my father tranquilly, 'she wouldn't understand—not any more than that pug.'

My mother cast doubtful looks on both me and the pug, and we, feeling embarrassed, slunk into the next room.

My mother was always trying to protect my innocence, while my father seemed to think it was its own protection.[34]

It would, of course, be unreasonable to expect a chronically ailing person always to be cheerful; she must often have found a young child trying to her nervous condition. In addition, it was obvious from the beginning that Mazo was not the pretty daughter any mother would wish for. She was a gangling, awkward child with a nervous tremor, and her mother may well have tended to shrink from her. In any event, scenes in which adults rebuff children as they clamour for affection are a frequent part of Mazo's fictional world. Renny Whiteoak, for instance, pushes Finch away as if he is physically disgusting: in one scene Renny says, 'Don't bite your nails. It's a beastly habit,' and Finch, who is feeling particularly close to Renny at that moment, hastily stuffs the incriminating hands into his pockets. A few lines later, Renny tells him: 'Don't sprawl over me that way, snuffling in my face. Have you a cold?'[35]

There were many reasons for Mazo to feel angry with her mother. Alberta was responsible for their dependent position in the grandparents' household, and the fact that mother and daughter were a burden. The ruined health that made her unfit to be a wife and run a house also made her unfit to be a mother like other mothers, to amuse and care for her child, and to protect her from the petty cruelties of her young uncles and aunts. At the same time, Mazo felt obscurely responsible for the mother's state. Later she would attribute this feeling to the fact that her arrival in the world impaired her mother's health. But as a child, her sense of responsibility was inarticulate and disturbing. Torn between anger and guilt, she was deeply troubled.

Furthermore, her mother's weakness seemed inextricably bound up with the fact that she was female. The men in the house had not succumbed to such debilitating illnesses as those suffered by Alberta Roche and Uncle George's unnamed wife. When, in *Finch's Fortune*, Finch learns that his beloved sister Meg, who has been a mother to him (and who incidentally has much in common with Alberta Roche) is ill and in need of surgery, he rushes to the medical dictionary. Mazo describes his panic-stricken reaction to the female condition:

> The more he read, the more bewildered and horror-struck he became. Why, there were a thousand things that might be wrong with Meggie! And each one of them worse than the last. His head pounding, his nerves unstrung, he forgot to listen for Augusta. Women, he thought, why, it was better never to be born at all than be born a woman! How had Meggie lived so long as she had without disaster? How had Grandmother achieved her hundred years? It was a miracle. As he read his heart bled for the mothers of men.[36]

Like Mazo's mother, though for somewhat different reasons, Finch's sister Meg does not eat regular meals; instead, she pampers her fickle appetite with a series of 'little lunches'. Alberta Roche's method of eating was not a matter of choice but the result of a ruined digestive system. Whether the cause was a nervous disorder or, as Mazo suggests, too much medicine, her stomach became incapable of taking hearty meals or a regular diet. Mazo, who was always hungry as a child, saw her mother's weak appetite as a secondary sex characteristic. Later, she would use eating habits as a mark of gender in her fiction: men and stalwart grandmotherly figures beyond the childbearing age eat vigorously, while women have feeble appetites and

eat in a finicky way.[37] Mazo clearly saw many of her mother's weaknesses as characteristic of her gender and drew the obvious conclusion. She was terrified by the idea of being female, prey to all the
miseries that her mother suffered. She felt that if only she were male
she could avoid them and, since men were the 'protectors of weak
women' (a phrase used repeatedly throughout her work) protect her
mother. But she had to face the fact that she was not male. And so—
not a man and yet so firm in her horror and rejection of the female—
she felt somehow stranded between two alternatives, not belonging
to either sex.

Painful enough in itself, that sense of not belonging was aggravated
by other circumstances. One of these was the fact that she had no
home. The words with which she begins her fourth chapter have a
terrible resonance: 'I was not born where I should have been in my
father's house. . . .' Not only was she not born where she should
have been, but she never lived in her father's house, because during
most of her childhood her father had none.

Throughout her autobiography, written so many years afterwards,
Mazo resists the admission that she lived with her grandparents: her
presence in their home is frequently explained as a 'visit'.[38] She knew
well enough that children usually lived with their mothers and fathers
in their own houses. But her father seemed to be under some obscure
kind of banishment, and this made her feel like a pariah. She did not
quite understand how it had come about, but she felt vaguely responsible. Her father was absent most of the time. Her mother lay
in bed, suffering agonies and causing herself and Mazo to be a burden
on the household—which itself, with the stern moral tone inculcated
by the grandfather as well as its atmosphere of sickness, was a place
of deep gloom. She felt trapped in the house and trapped in her girl's
body, a strange creature who belonged nowhere. She felt, in sum,
like a freak.

Years later she wrote a story of another child, not Finch Whiteoak
this time but a little boy called Shaw Manifold. Like Finch, he is
dispossessed. Abandoned by a good father who has died and by a
mother who must leave him while she works, he has no home of his
own. He is cast adrift in the home of a severely repressive grandfather
and a grandmother whose kindly instincts have long ago been snuffed
into silence by her all-powerful husband. The characters of *The Growth
of a Man* were not based on Mazo's own grandparents. But the atmosphere of Shaw Manifold's childhood owed much to her own
painful memories. In her fiction she never stopped trying to come to
terms with that earliest period in her life.

3

The Roches: Protectors of Weak Women

There was a sharp division in the way that Mazo experienced the two sides of her family, and it is reflected in the chapter headings of the autobiography, which place her paternal and maternal forebears in quite separate compartments. Some inherent differences might have been expected between the Anglo-Saxon Lundys and Willsons and the Irish Bryans and Roches. Actually, however, those differences were minimal, since both sides were mainly Protestant families, long-established by Mazo's time in the small Ontario communities where they worked as artisans. One of her Bryan great-uncles even lived for a time in the Lundy house and was a favourite companion of her Lundy grandfather.[1]

The difference lay largely in Mazo's perception of her antecedents. She was close to the Lundys and distant from the Roches: a member of the first household and a visitor in the second. She expressed this difference herself, although she did not realize the full effect of what she was saying:

> My mother's family was much closer to me than my father's, I knew them much more intimately. They seemed closer to me, even though physically and temperamentally I resemble my father's family. My father's father I never saw. Whereas my mother's father, Grandpa Lundy, was very near and dear to me.[2]

The truth was that her ancestral past took its place in the growing series of binary oppositions into which all her experience seemed naturally to fall—between male and female, spoken and not spoken, visible and invisible, present and absent.

Perhaps it was her familiarity with the Lundys that curbed her curiosity about their history. When she sums up her grandfather's background, her information is vague and inaccurate:

He was the descendant of one Sylvester Lundy who had emigrated to New England from Devon in the seventeenth century. In the New World he and his family prospered, but when the American Revolution came, they were staunch Loyalists and were forced to leave property behind and make the long journey to Nova Scotia.[3]

Elsewhere she reports that her grandfather had a favourite brother, Dr John Lundy of Preston, and that, having discovered a Quaker somewhere in their ancestry, the two men 'delighted to multiply him to the calling of each other 'thee' and 'thou' '.[4] In fact, her Lundy ancestors were very likely Quakers two hundred years before. It was not Sylvester Lundy but his son Richard who left Devon in 1676 for the New World. By then the religious persecutions that marked the reign of Charles I were over, but it was no doubt in their wake that Richard followed other Quaker families to Pennsylvania, where he settled in Bucks County and became an elder in the Religious Society of Friends. His descendant Enos Lundy left Pennsylvania in 1805 and emigrated to Canada—not to Nova Scotia, as Mazo says, but to Ontario, where cheap land was available.[5] Though Mazo's memory of her grandfather and his brother addressing each other as 'thee' is partially accurate, the Dr John Lundy she mentions was a cousin rather than a brother.[6]

Of her Grandmother Lundy's family, the Willsons, Mazo discovered a great deal when she was researching her novel *Growth of a Man*, based on the life of her relative H.R. MacMillan, the West Coast lumber magnate. She was fascinated to discover the Willsons' connection with David Willson, the founder of the Children of Peace sect of Sharon, Ontario. When she came to write her autobiography, twenty years later, she directed her typist to copy a whole passage about David Willson from the novel into her chapter on her maternal forebears.[7] It is an odd digression and a disproportionately long account of a somewhat distant connection. Yet, as she did through the autobiography, she included whatever appealed to her imagination—a whimsical technique that often provides some insight into her mind.

The early history of the Lundy family is an interesting account of non-conformity, religious persecution, and emigration. It was less intriguing to her, however, than the mysterious, shady history of her Roche grandfather: '[his] very name had always held a fascination for me—never the warm glowing affection I had felt towards my maternal grandfather, but still a provocative and stimulating influence.'[8] What Mazo chose to believe about her paternal grandfather was that he was of aristocratic French descent, a scholar learned in French, Latin, and Greek who had left behind an impressive library of books in those languages, which she inherited. She ends the chapter on her paternal forebears with this anecdote:

> In my impressionable schooldays the shadow of this grandfather lay across me. The best example I can give of this is that once, when I had come out at the head of my form in French, the teacher of French asked me if I got help at home. As a matter of truth I was given no help at home but, at the sudden question, the shadow of my grandfather fell across me. I was sure he had helped me and I answered yes. For days, for weeks afterward I was troubled by this lie. I felt that I should go to the teacher and explain! I could not bring myself to do it—to try to make her understand that a dead man had helped me with my lessons. I felt there would be something shameful in that.[9]

The story has a fanciful air about it. Yet when the photographs, taken in their mature years, of this grandfather and granddaughter who never met are set side by side, they do show an uncanny physical resemblance. Who knows what temperamental affinity existed between them? In the absence of any other sign of literary achievement on either side of her family, he became her chosen and cherished progenitor.

Since he had died the year after she was born, Mazo's sources of information about her grandfather were family legend and hearsay, and she had little factual information, as shown in a 1914 letter to Ellery Sedgewick, the editor of the *Atlantic Monthly*:

> The other day in a little sketch about myself which I sent you, I made mention of the fact that my grandfather was at one time a professor at The John [*sic*] Hopkins University. Later when I spoke to my father about this, he corrected me, saying that it was not at The John Hopkins but in another of the American Universities that my grandfather taught. He also said that as the period of his residence in The States was short, this item had better be left out.[10]

In truth, Grandfather Roche appears to have been something of a ne'er-do-well. The birthplace listed on his death certificate is Limerick, Ireland.[11] He came to Canada, downplayed his Catholic background, and married into the Protestant Bryan family. After fathering two sons, he deserted the family for reasons never satisfactorily explained—at least to Mazo—and went to live in Baltimore, Maryland. Although he had subsequent periods of residence in Toronto, he did not rejoin his wife. As a result of one brief visit by her to Baltimore, however, she had a third son by him. That John Roche was despised by his wife's family is evident from her father's will, which contained a bequest 'for her sole and separate use and benefit, independent of her present husband John Richmond Roach'.[12]

His profession is unclear, and the college listed as his place of employment in his obituary notice did not exist:

ROCHE: – at Baltimore, Md. on the 24th of July, John Richmond Roche, M.A. formerly Professor of Mathematics, Newton University, age 66 years. Deceased was father of Messrs. Danford and William R. Roche of Newmarket. A large concourse of our citizens were on hand to pay a tribute of respect as the remains were brought to this place for interment.[13]

The one shred of concrete evidence that Mazo had of her grandfather was the following letter, found among her papers and referred to (inaccurately, as usual) in her autobiography:

Willie, My son—

You ought to have answered my letter before this. I was pleased to know that you had taken Grandma on a visit to your place. She is the best of the family; I felt always at home when I saw her—cheerful and generous. If her advice were taken our family would be very differently situated from the way in which we are now.

I have received a magnificent likeness of Danny finely framed; it is quite company for me in my room. I should wish he had sent me a full length likeness. This I will want of you when convenient as I think it will be rather expensive.

I have sent you a fine likeness of a country maiden, carrying a pet deer in her arms; I hope you have received and framed it. Let me know. Such a magnificent, noble, innocent, loving looking woman I should recommend.

In my last letter to Danny I suggested to him the idea of opening Business for himself in a year hence, and that Ma would be a treasure, as where Ma will be there will be Customers; and also unless you were doing exceedingly well that you would return to Toronto and them likewise. There are many advantages and especially, for enterprising men, to be residents in such a city and also that you may be able to do for your families what I had at heart to do for you that you should rank with the best educated men in the kingdom. I fondly hope that you and your brother will not forget that our family should rank with the highest in the land, as they have done, and still do.[14]

This is not the letter of an erudite man. It does appear to be that of a disappointed man who acknowledges that his family is in a sorry state and who, at the same time, has an exaggerated sense of family pride. Clearly he has kept in touch with his sons and presumes to give them advice about their future work. He boldly requests an expensively framed photograph in exchange for a picture his son is expected to have framed at his own expense. An idealized, sentimental picture of female innocence, this gift may have been intended as instruction; perhaps he hoped that his son would avoid the more assertive women who had made his own life unbearable.

But Mazo was not really interested in hard evidence. As far as she was concerned, her grandfather had been a scholar of distinction, and she cherished the thought of the library of scholarly books sent up from Baltimore after his death. Again, her history of this library is full of discrepancies, suggesting that it was probably a small collection of no great value. She tells of twenty-eight packing cases of books being shipped to Toronto and falling into the possession of her grandfather's fourteen-year-old son Francis who, already showing scholarly inclinations, delighted in opening them.[15] Yet this same uncle showed no desire either to keep the books himself or to sell or give them away. They were left to decay in the garage of his older brother for over forty years, until Mazo sorted them out after her uncle's death. She spent days going through the cases—which now numbered thirty, even though she says some had been removed. She sent some to what she vaguely calls 'a Catholic college in Western Canada',[16] and the rest, which she set aside to dispose of to dealers, were stolen. So the great library was dispersed.

Another part of her grandfather's story that Mazo relishes is of the same young son discovering among the packages of books, soon after they came into his possession, a collection of letters from various women in Baltimore. She tells of her uncle's confidence in the tones of a romance:

> What he told me was this: one dark afternoon in November—he had lately passed his fourteenth birthday—he opened for the first time, one of the smallest of the cases. My uncle's deep-set dark eyes looked sombrely into mine. 'What I found,' he said, 'were love letters.'[17]

Thus Mazo could add to the myth of her grandfather's French aristocratic ancestry and scholarly distinction the picture of him as a dashing and romantic lover.

Another colourful member of the Roche family was Mazo's father's older brother, Danford, who impressed her with his adventurous-sounding business trips to Europe and the gifts he brought back from London. He assumed the role of head of the Roche clan, allowing both his grandmother and his mother to live in his ample home until they died. Those two strong women, both long-lived, reinforced Mazo's impression of the Roches as a vigorous and superior race of people.

Whether or not Danford was aided by his father's advice, he did in fact establish a very successful business. Danford Roche and Company, General Store, was the largest credit business in Newmarket; borrowing an idea from the big Eaton store in Toronto, Uncle Danford introduced the credit system to the district.[18] Unlike Grandfather Lundy, who was employed in a factory, her uncle was an employer for whom Mazo's own father worked in the early days of his marriage.[19] It was typical of Danford Roche's ambitious nature that he made a socially advantageous marriage: his wife, Ida, was the daughter of J.J. Pearson, Registrar of North York, Magistrate, Secretary of the Gas Board, and Director of the Cemetery Board.[20]

Perhaps the most concise account of Danford Roche's career is that given in a special edition of the *Newmarket Era* dedicated to 'Progressive Newmarket':

> The general store is one of the largest in this section of the country, if not the very largest. Three floors are devoted to merchandizing. The firm owns the block in which the store is located on the east side of Main Street. A staff of fifteen hands and on busy days twenty are employed.
>
> Mr Roche built the first telephone line north of Toronto—a line between Aurora and Newmarket. At that time the firm had a branch store in Aurora and the line proved useful. He has crossed the Atlantic sixteen times . . . served on the Town Council, is a prominent Freemason and connected with the Presbyterian Church. He is a member of the United Irish League in Toronto and is in full sympathy with the Irish National Movement.[21]

When Mazo was her uncle's guest at 'Limerick House' she felt uncomfortable, intimidated by standards of order and formality that made the atmosphere very different from that of the rough-and-tumble Lundy home: 'I remember being dreadfully homesick there, even during a short visit. The house was too tidy—the meals too regular—the carpets too thick—Auntie Ida's dominance too evident.'[22] Elsewhere Mazo uses the word 'conventional' as a kind of Homeric epithet to describe Aunt Ida and her establishment. It was definitely derogatory.[23] All the same, Mazo was impressed by Danford's family—the 'merchant-prince' himself, his socially prominent wife, and the two older women with their 'pleasant Irish' voices—especially when they were all assembled in the dining room with the portraits of their ancestors on the wall. The memory of her red-haired uncle in his well-appointed house later found expression in her portrait of Renny Whiteoak, the Master of Jalna.

Mazo's father also acquired in his daughter's eyes the glamorous aura of the other members of his family. Compared with her ailing and complaining mother, he represented everything that was energetic, free, generous, and exciting. Though he didn't travel to Europe like Uncle Danford, he was a good talker, and he made his frequent excursions to Montreal and Quebec, as a cigar salesman, seem equally exotic. The Roches' situation was, in fact, similar to that of most families, where the father's absence during the working day enhances his prestige and eases his relationship with the children, while the burden of coping and acting as the disciplinarian lends the mother a repressive air and causes hostile feelings, especially in daughters.

Like his own father before him, Mazo's father was not a 'good provider'. Yet he started life bravely enough as a young husband, first working for his brother and then trying to establish his own grocery store. As Ronald Hambleton reports, he also took an active part in Newmarket life:

> He sat on a coroner's jury, joined the Literary and Debating Society where he spoke in the affirmative on the resolution that 'Certain circumstances may justify a deviation from the truth', joined the Odd Fellows, and began breeding Bedlington terriers, boasting that he could trace the pedigree of one of his dogs back one hundred years.[24]

These activities are quite revealing of Will Roche's character, confirming the interests in literature and public-speaking that his daughter attributes to him, as well as a fondness for stretching the truth. (The subject on which he debated might have provided her epitaph). He apparently had an outgoing and attractive personality, for in June 1884 the paper referred to him as 'a general favourite'.[25]

The first chapter of Mazo's autobiography ends with the remark that she thought an excellent actor was lost in her father.[26] Unfortunately, his dramatic gifts found expression only in histrionic poses and unrealistic ambitions that led to one professional failure after another. Mazo suggests that her father was often away on business. Much of the time he undoubtedly was, but his absences had another reason, as indicated by the annual Toronto street directories. They tell a different story—of frequent job changes and changes of address.[27] In a sense, he was repeating the pattern of his own childhood, being just as absent a parent as his own father was.

Hambleton has suggested that Mazo's father was an ineffective man, often overshadowed both by his more forceful older brother and by his professionally successful younger brother, who became a lawyer.[28] There were indeed many other reasons for him to feel in-effective. In his time the lack of a resident father was a stigma, even though his strong mother coped admirably. Furthermore, her family's hostility to her husband must have been troubling for the children. It is easy to see Will Roche's life-long obsession with the family trees and pedigrees of horses, dogs, and cattle as springing from his own lack of family legitimacy. Later, John Roche's place was taken by Danford, who eventually supported his mother and provided an ex-cellent education for his younger brother—one family picture shows young Francis standing proudly in his academic robes. Yet Will Roche, who had marked literary interests and verbal skills, had little edu-cation; he was forced to go out early to work, probably uncongenial, and to fend for himself.

Then he added to his disadvantages a disastrous marriage. None of the brothers had happy marriages; Mazo suggests that both her uncles were dominated by their wives, and that her Uncle Frank was a reluctant bridegroom who lived the rest of his life cowed and in-hibited by his wife.[29] Both those marriages were childless. Even so, the invalid condition of Alberta Roche made Will's situation the most pitiable of the three. Even his daughter seems to have been aware of his sexual deprivation: 'How often his stalwart frame must have hun-gered for something beyond the sick-room!'[30]

In order, perhaps, to compensate for his failure in so many areas, Will Roche cultivated an aggressive masculinity. Mazo speaks of his impressive stature and bearing, mentions that he built up a collection of guns, and itemizes the books and poems he liked—often works celebrating martial feats and male friendship.[31] His comment to Mazo's mother soon after her birth was 'I'll do almost anything for you, but never ask me to push the pram. I refuse to do that.'[32] Mazo says that he seemed more like a brother than a father, and that he treated her less as a child than as a friend: 'He was my hero, my protector, my gay companion.'[33] Implied in all her comments is that he treated her as a boy. It would not have been unusual for him to have craved a son for his first and, as it turned out, only child. And the exotic name he selected for her, while it did belong to a woman he knew, was certainly not a standard one for females.[34] Mazo reveals that one of his pet names for her was 'Umslopogass', the name of the young Zulu warrior who is the hero's boon companion in a Rider Haggard novel.[35] She, of course, found such a role very acceptable. By evoking patterns of male friendship in fiction for their relationship (Robinson Crusoe was another favourite) he may have affirmed her worth, flattered her by overlooking her female weakness and making her feel free and strong as a young boy.

Their shared love of plays and play-acting and dogs and the outdoor life enhanced their relationship:

> To see a play with my father, to be moved to emotion, either happy or sad, in his company, was to be a pleasure not to be outdone by any in the company of my contemporaries. He and I read books together, drove together, walked together. I contrasted him with the fathers of my friends, who were often stern or fault-finding or repressive. The thought of sternness or punishment in connection with him was unthinkable.[36]

Mazo's father is portrayed as her great support. As we have seen, when she suffered her first rejection slip, her father taught her how to play cribbage as a consolation. In childhood her fondness for games also helped her gain entry to the male side of the family, as described in this account of family weekends:

> Grandpa did not play cards but there would be Uncle Bryan, my father, one of my uncles and myself. Caroline would be sitting with my mother. I don't know how I managed to get on with my studies, yet somehow I did. On Saturdays we would sit in the smoke-filled room (two pipes and a cigar all going), three men and a child playing cards for the greater part of the day. On Sundays, after the morning service. . . . again we played.[37]

To what extent Mazo's descriptions of her father's virtues are grounded in fact is hard to know. In the Galt period, for example, he seems negligent in leaving his ailing wife in the care of a daughter too young for such responsibility, and to that he added the extra burden of a dog neither of them wanted. Yet Mazo betrays no anger that she should have been forced to accept such responsibility.[38] She describes her father's homecoming as triumphant—to her he was a conquering hero laden with wonderful gifts:

> Now the porter brought in my father's travelling bags. We gathered about the table to see our presents unpacked. The things he had brought! From the Coast a Chinese porcelain figure—a table-cover embroidered in a rich design—beaded bags worked by Indians—and, as each article was displayed, he mimicked the strange foreign character from whom he had bought it. We could picture them all. We laughed—almost we cried, in the joy, the relief, of having him with us again.

Nor does she seem to have felt those gifts were small compared with his own finery: 'For himself he had an embroidered Indian hunting jacket of white buckskin given him by a chief and, when he had donned it, my mother and I were lost in admiration.'[39] Mazo is never critical of her father, of his neglect of her mother and herself, of his constant changing of jobs, or of his inability to make money. Even with his tiresome traits, she shows him in a favourable light, badly used by his wife.

Such affection for one parent and side of her family might well have compensated for the hostility Mazo felt for the other. But if the relationship with her father gave her a sense of her own worth, a sense of self, a feeling of security, it was destined only to aggravate her identity confusions. When Mazo thought about her divided nature—and she was too introspective not to—she explained it as the result of a mixed racial heritage. By that she meant not the actual mix of English and Irish, but an imaginary one of English Protestant and French Catholic. It seems clear that she chose those two diametrically opposed strains because they suggested irreconcilable differences. Only an image of such extreme difference could express the conflict Mazo felt within herself. Still, there was a kind of truth in the notion that she was pulled in opposite directions by the maternal and paternal sides of her heritage. Sexual and racial identities are often bound up together in complicated ways, the conflicts in one area reflecting and aggravating those in another. Certainly when Mazo wished to assert the masculine side of her nature, which she often did, she would play up the Roche side of her heritage.

Feminist critics have explored the effects on nineteenth-century women writers of their exclusion from a male-dominated writing tradition.[40] For a woman to attempt the pen was to usurp male authority, to cross gender lines, and to unsex herself. Women were traditionally not the creators of works of art but their subjects, the creators' muses.[41] The cost of crossing those gender lines, in psychological damage and gender confusion, has been well documented.[42] Mazo adds another page to that documentation, for no writer shows more clearly the strategies that were necessary for someone trying to reconcile the contradictory roles of woman and writer. When she wrote, Mazo surrounded herself with the trappings of the male side of her family, taking special pleasure in the chair in which her paternal grandmother had nursed her three sons:

> I sat while writing in a chair which had swayed (for it was cane-seated rocking-chair) beneath the majestic weight of my father's mother. . . . Probably each in turn of her three baby boys had been soothed by its movement; first the lusty, red-haired, pink-cheeked Danford; next the curly-haired Richmond, with his luminous brown eyes; last the pale black-haired François.

As for books of reference, I had only one source. That was Dr John-son's *Dictionary* in two bulky volumes, those sent to my father when he was a boy by his father.[43]

When trousers for women came into fashion, Mazo quickly acquired some and from that time on always wore trousers when she wrote.[44]

For Mazo the wearing of men's clothing and the assumption of a male persona were empowering gestures. Several of the unimportant 'little things' that jostle their way into the autobiography are refer-ences to cross-dressing. One telling incident involves a family crisis in the Lundy household that came about because all the men were away and the presence of a man was essential to Mazo's mother's mental stability. The problem—yet another reference to the all-power-ful and protective qualities of men—was solved by Mazo as she solved so many problems: by play-acting. She could not become a man, but she could pretend to be one. And, once disguised, she could perform a man's function as the protector of weak women:

> Suddenly an inspiration came to me. I would be the instrument to save my mother from fear. She should not be without the sounds of that masculine presence. In Uncle Bryan's bedroom I found a pair of his boots, I put them on and creaked heavily down the stairs, along the passage, past my mother's door, and down the other stairs to the hall below. . . . The deception worked. Thereafter, several times a day, I mounted and descended the stairs, wearing my great-uncle's boots, even, in my girl's voice, forced a deep 'ha!' from my throat as I creaked along the passage.[45]

A more playful instance of cross-dressing took place during the visit of her paternal grandmother, Sarah Roche:

> I persuaded her to dress up in a suit of my father's. Why or how I did this I cannot remember. Probably a perverse mischievous spirit in me wanted to see the undignified transformation and I always had a per-suasive tongue.
>
> Oh, the transformation! With the change of clothes she had become a rather rakish-looking old gentleman-about-town, with a strong re-semblance to her brother, Great-uncle Bryan.
>
> I had never seen my grandmother smile in the way she now smiled at her reflection. She looked positively devil-may-care.
>
> Then my father came in. He gave the seeming old gentleman a look of astonishment, then exclaimed, 'Uncle Bryan!' and held out his hand.
>
> 'It is I,' said my grandmother, in her pleasant Irish voice, and with a shout of laughter he clasped her to his breast.
>
> Such a picture they made the two of them, that my mother and I were helpless from laughter.[46]

Mazo reports these incidents as full of good humour and high spirits, yet her consistent habit of undervaluing the feminine at the expense of the masculine, and of habitually identifying against her own sex, is disturbing. When there was a mutual misunderstanding about gender with the editor of the *Atlantic Monthly*, whom she had addressed as 'Ellen Y. Sedgewick',[47] she apologized and 'confessed' to him that she was 'of the feminine gender'. She wondered if he had addressed his letters to Mr de la Roche because 'my work does not show the customary failings of writers of my sex' and added that she accepted the Mr 'with complaisance'. Similarly, in an anecdote about William Lyon Mackenzie, who escaped to the United States after inciting a riot, she conjoined his flight and his disguise in women's clothes as equal marks of cowardice.[48]

Such attitudes and gender confusions eventually took a disastrous toll on her mental stability. The conflicts did not go away, but built up into an ever-increasing sense of inner turmoil, of which the terrible nightmares she suffered all her life were symptoms. She never managed to shed the feeling that she was unnatural and freakish. But while she was still a child, serious breakdown was kept at bay, for her habit of play-acting provided an ever-available escape hatch.

4

The Fantastic Double Life of the Play

Mazo's disclosure of the elaborate form of play that she shared with Caroline was not only the chief revelation of her autobiography but its *raison d'être*. When her editor, Edward Weeks, made a valiant effort to cut back what he considered the non-essential parts of the original version (fortunately, they have been preserved in the holograph manuscript), he reported to her London publisher that he had met with resistance when he tried to tamper with the story of the Play.[1] Mazo's decision to reveal it broke a forty-year silence and a solemn pact of secrecy with Caroline. And once she had decided to make the gesture, she was determined to tell the story as fully as she wished.

She finally broaches the subject in the fourth chapter of the book. The intervening chapters were necessary, since she could not dispense entirely with her childhood—even though Caroline's absence presented a problem. They were, after all, supposed to have grown up together from the age of seven, a misrepresentation that Mazo plasters over by saying that there were long separations.[2] She adds, contradicting all her own statements of devotion to Caroline, that these separations made little impression:

> I do not even remember Caroline's and my parting. We accepted the fact that I was to go to Galt and she was to remain with other relations, without question. My mind was filled with the excitement of the change. During all the while I lived in Galt I remember writing to her only once.[3]

And she describes that one letter:

> I wrote to her as one of the characters in our Play. He was a young man named Bernard. In this letter I told her of my fine score at cricket and enclosed a picture of myself in cricketing costume, cut from the Illustrated London News—a fine upstanding man. I was eleven![4]

In fact, Mazo was eleven when she moved to Galt, and she had not yet met Caroline. The letter so clearly remembered was written when Mazo was in her late teens and Caroline, now living with the Roche family, had gone off for one of her visits to other relatives. While Mazo mentions in letters that Caroline visited her Clement relatives in in Bradford, Ontario,[5] she avoids all mention of Caroline's closest living relatives, her brother and her mother. Harvey Clement,[6] to whom Caroline was very close, had moved to the United States, where she often visited him. But the women avoid all mention of Caroline's mother, who was alive as late as 1909 and living in Lefroy, Ontario.[7] The fact that Martha Clement was unable to care for her daughter and sent her to relatives at such an early age suggests that she herself was ill and in need of care. If her illness was mental rather than physical, that may explain why both Mazo and Caroline concealed her existence so carefully—even from close friends and family. Of course, this secrecy also enabled Mazo to preserve the myth of Caroline as a solitary orphan, with herself as sole protector and surrogate parent.

The arrival of another girl in the household when Mazo was sixteen might well have dealt a death blow to her already confused sense of self-worth. Such a negative reaction was all the more likely because Caroline was an outstanding success in all the areas in which Mazo so conspicuously failed. She was graceful where Mazo was awkward; pretty where Mazo was plain; blonde and clear-skinned where Mazo was sallow; petite where Mazo was over-grown to the point of causing worry ('my mother's anxiety was for nothing as I grew to a scant five foot eight').[8] In short, Caroline was the daughter that every mother— including Mazo's own—longed for. From the beginning, Mazo dispassionately reports, Alberta Roche and Caroline formed a companionable bond:

> Caroline was not considered strong enough to go to school. . . . During the school week we were separated most of the day, she spending much time with my mother whose health had not improved. The bond between them deepened in those days, so that they became the most congenial of companions. They had the same tastes. They craved beauty to surround them. They loved pretty clothes, elegance in furniture, pictures, ornaments.
>
> What a contrast I was to Caroline who so early learned to appreciate the pleasure of possessing pretty clothes; to whom it came so naturally to learn to sew, to shop, to plan a modest wardrobe, to keep her belongings in perfect order![9]

Happily, the situation was not threatening for Mazo, who though she had no desire to possess feminine qualities, could appreciate them in another. She adored Caroline the moment she saw her, becoming for her the effective 'protector of weak women' that she never succeeded in being for her mother. And Caroline was certainly in need of protection, for her life to that point had been one long train of disasters. Her family had moved from place to place in Canada and the United States as one after another of her father's business ventures failed. Her older sister had died and been buried on a distant prairie.[10] She had lost her father, and her mother had become incapacitated, dependent on the care and charity of her family. The nature of Caroline's early life is recorded in a note by Lovat Dickson:

> Until she was officially adopted by M's parents this C was tossed about between one branch of the family and another—with her brother. Separated once she screamed until she and her brother were reunited, involving several hours screaming and a sleigh drive of several miles.[11]

She was a desperate little waif, her health so undermined by the strain that a weak heart prevented her from going to school.

If Mazo's mother enjoyed Caroline's companionship, however, she was not strong enough to nurture another child. Nor did Mazo's often-absent father care for female companionship; he admired female beauty from a distance, but for day-to-day company preferred men or his boyish, card-playing daughter. In these circumstances Mazo became the chief refuge and support, replacing both Caroline's parents and the brother she loved. Caroline drew strength from her, and in turn gave Mazo strength by making her feel capable of protecting a weaker human being. Quite unpredictably, the relationship turned out to be the happiest event that had happened so far in the lives of these two lonely girls. Mazo, who shared her room and her bed with Caroline, gave solace in the form she knew best, by leading Caroline into the world of the Play. And she found in the younger girl a ready and pliant participant—as Caroline said, while she could not invent anything, she had the ability to follow wherever Mazo might lead.[12]

The style of the autobiography regains its lyrical quality as Mazo recaptures the intense emotion of the Play. She writes of Caroline's initial response: 'She sat there in the wintry twilight, tiny, fragile, receptive as a crystal goblet held beneath a tap.'[13] The simile is typical in describing Mazo's own creative outpouring in images of male sexuality, as a generative flow. Elsewhere she speaks of the play's function as an outlet for the products of her flooded imagination: 'my written stories were mere cups that were inadequate to contain the stream.'[14]

While Mazo traced the development of the Play in a series of passages running throughout her autobiography, its secret and private nature[15] prevented detailed revelations. In her fiction, on the other hand, protected behind the masks of her characters, she suffered from fewer inhibitions. Many of her characters indulge in 'secret play' of their own, and when the autobiographical and fictional accounts are placed side by side, it is possible to understand more clearly the nature of Mazo's Play.

The first and last of Mazo's fictional works depict separate sets of three young children engaging in imaginary plays. In the last, *Morning at Jalna*, the clock is turned back to an earlier era, when the three avuncular figures of the Jalna series were children. Ernest has a private play, which is regarded with respect by his older brother and sister, Nicholas and Augusta:

> They discovered Ernest on the second flight of stairs. He was playing his secret game. This was played with a few discarded chess men, some scraps of paper, and colored stones. He would write directions for the chessmen, move them from one step to another, at the same time making remarks such as—'Live long, O King'—or 'Now is my Solitary Fate' or 'Call the Wolves to their Tea.' Augusta and Nicholas had a respect for this game.[16]

In her first book, *Explorers of the Dawn*, three boys invent pretend games of pirates, which they act out in the privacy of the curtained four-poster bed they share. They have been left in the care of a former governess of their father, the redoubtable Mrs Handsomebody (apparently based on Mazo's mother and on her Aunt Eva). She often punishes them by sending them to bed, but they have learned to transform the punishment into escape:

> We always passed the hours of our confinement on the bed, for the room was very small. . . . But these were not dull times for us. As Elizabethan actors, striding about their bare stage, conjured up brave pictures of gilded halls or leafy forest glades, so we little fellows made a castle stronghold of our bed; or better still, a gallant frigate that sailed beyond the barren walls into unknown seas of adventure, and anchored at last off some rocky island where treasure lay hid among the hills. . . . They were not dull times in that small back room, but gay-colored lawless times, when our fancy was let free. . . .[17]

That description resembles the account of the play invented by Ernest's older brother and sister in *Morning at Jalna*:

They [Augusta and Nicholas] had invented a game, a kind of serial play, in which they had the roles of Elizabethan adventurers, discoverers of new lands, sometimes pirates. Nicholas was known as Sir Francis Drake, sometimes as Sir Walter Raleigh, but Augusta was faithful to the role of Sir Richard Grenville. There being no special character for Ernest to play, he was made to represent all the colored peoples of the strange lands discovered, or even the Spaniards of the Armada. He threw himself into these various parts with the greatest enthusiasm, executing war dances or bartering his lands for a few beads, or being converted to Christianity, as was demanded of him.[18]

As in these fictional versions, in Mazo's early solitary Play all the characters were men—historical figures, explorers, soldiers, noblemen, pirates. Mazo explains why:

The odd thing was that all these characters were males and that only two of them were children, boys of about my own age. Yet, after all, that was scarcely remarkable because at this time I was revelling in volumes of The Boy's Own and Chums, which had belonged to an uncle and which I discovered in the attic. Talbot Baines Reed was my favorite author.[19]

Though she does not acknowledge it directly, it is also possible to see in the Play a strong erotic element. Describing the play's origin, long before Caroline came to the Roche family, she writes: 'First it [the Play] had been a dream, an extraordinarily vivid dream, out of which I had woken with the feeling that I had left something of myself submerged in the dream, and also that I had brought something out of it which would somehow make me different.'[20]

There is in the fiction a hint at the inspiration behind that dream. In *Jalna* Finch Whiteoak has an erotic dream, which is inspired by the arrival at Jalna of his newly wed brother Eden and Eden's wife Alayne:

His mind dwelt on the thought of kissing the mouth of Eden's wife. He was submerged in an abyss of dreaming, his head sunk on his clenched hands. A second self, white and wraithlike, glided from his breast and floated before him in a pale greenish ether. He watched it with detached exaltation in its freedom. It often freed itself from his body at times like these, sometimes disappearing almost instantly, at others floating near him as though beckoning him to follow. Now it moved face downward like one swimming, and another dim shape floated beside it. He pressed his knuckles into his eyes, drawing fiery colors from the lids, trying to see, yet afraid to see, the face of the other figure. But neither of the floating figures had a discernible face. One, he knew, belonged to him because it had emerged from his own body, but the other, fantastically floating, whence came it? Had it risen from the body of the girl in the drawing room below, torn from her by the distraught questing of his own soul? What was she? What was he? Why were they here, all the warm-blooded hungry people, in the house called Jalna?[21]

Finch's erotic dream is solitary. Yet a co-operative and compatible bedfellow can add to the pleasure of the fantasy, as another section of the same book shows. Two of his brothers share a bed because the younger suffers from a weak heart and needs special care. Renny and Wakefield (ages thirty-eight and nine) indulge in a shared play inspired by the same event, the arrival of the newly married brother and his wife:

> Wake, drowsy at last, curled up against Renny's chest and murmured: 'I believe I could go to sleep more quickly if we'd pretend we were somebody else, Renny, please.'
>
> 'Do you? All right. Who shall we be? Living people or people out of the books? You say.'
>
> Wake thought a minute, getting sleepier with each tick of Renny's watch beneath the pillow; then he breathed: 'I think we'll be Eden and Alayne.'
>
> Renny stifled a laugh. 'All right. Which am I?'
>
> Wake considered again, deliciously drowsy, sniffing at the nice odor of tobacco, Windsor soap, and warm flesh that emanated from Renny.
>
> 'I think you'd better be Alayne,' he whispered.
>
> Renny, too, considered this transfiguration. It seemed difficult, but he said resignedly: 'Very well. Fire away.'
>
> There was silence for a space; then Wakefield whispered, twisting a button of Renny's pyjamas: 'You go first, Renny. Say something.'
>
> Renny spoke sweetly: 'Do you love me, Eden?'
>
> Wake chuckled, then answered, seriously: 'Oh heaps. I'll buy you anything you want. What would you like?
>
> 'I'd like a limousine, and an electric toaster, and—a feather boa.'
>
> 'I'll get them all first thing in the morning. Is there anything else you'd like, my girl?'
>
> 'M—yes. I'd like to go to sleep.'
>
> 'Now, see here, you can't,' objected the pseudo-groom. 'Ladies don't pop straight off to sleep like that.'
>
> But apparently this lady did. The only response that Wakefield could elicit was a gentle but persistent snore.
>
> For a moment Wake was deeply hurt, but the steady rise and fall of Renny's chest was soothing. He snuggled closer to him, and soon he too was fast asleep.[22]

Mazo seems to have had from an early age a highly developed erotic sensibility, which sought expression as much as her imaginative faculties did. Possibly her own confusions led her to develop a particularly delicate set of antennae, or perhaps she had become attuned to the sexual vibrations of the household and taken in, without understanding her own knowledge, the lover-like nuances of her grandfather's relationship with her mother. She had, after all, been told of his lengthy chastisements of Alberta, and she had seen his transformation of her sickbed into a green bower.[23]

Mazo also records that she was the accidental observer of a scene that took place between her father and her mother's younger sister, Eva, who one day approached the chair in which Will Roche sat reading and put her arms around him. He firmly detached her arms and went on reading as if nothing had happened. The gesture, which Mazo interpreted as a rebuff, made her feel happily triumphant. As she reports it, and perhaps interpreted it, the scene was relatively harmless.[24] Her readers must wonder, however, if there was some kind of relationship between Will Roche and Eva Lundy, and if he discouraged Eva's advances simply because he suspected that his watchful young daughter might be somewhere about. Certainly one of the marks of the Jalna novels is that the men become the lovers of their brothers' wives. And Mazo's fictions are full of episodes in which a young person either deliberately spies upon or accidentally discovers a pair of lovers.[25] Finch Whiteoak, for example, increases his unpopularity in his family when he discovers and reveals that his brother Eden is the lover of another brother's wife.[26]

That Mazo based the characters in her early Play to some extent on family members and friends is suggested by an episode in which the unscrupulous Aunt Eva tried to get Mazo's father to eavesdrop on the girls. Once the danger had passed, Mazo reports, Caroline turned to her and said coolly 'be Blount again'.[27] The name is very close to Lount, one of Alberta Roche's former suitors. Mazo says that she met Lount when she was seven (that magical age for her, when so much happened). She fell in love with him for 'the charm of his smile, the gaiety of his laugh' (expressions, incidentally, that she has used in describing her father) and he gave her a doll, which she cherished for the rest of her life.[28]

Mazo also knew about the kind of love described in romantic fiction. Her parents were both readers, and their literary tastes divided along gender lines, although both shared an interest in Dickens and Shakespeare. He liked Scott (her mother didn't) and the masculine world of Rider Haggard, while she preferred the Brontës, Jane Austen, and Rhoda Broughton. Mazo sympathized with the tastes of both parents: her mother read novels and poems aloud to her—Mazo cherished the titles of Broughton's novels[29]—and she also liked to sit on the arm of her father's chair as he read and follow along page by page.[30]

The Play, therefore, had already grown considerably even before Caroline came along, moving from single-sex heroic exploits to include romantic and erotic elements. But if Caroline did not, like a latter-day Eve arriving in the Garden of Eden, change the Play overnight from an innocent pastime to a vehicle for erotic impulses, she did add the other dimension required for all the possibilities of the Play to be fully realized. Mazo gives a spare account of Caroline's participation: 'In time I discovered the need of a female character and invented a small girl, a sister to some of the existing 'cast'. She was such a success that I added a woman—and another and another!'[31] The new roles they now played are suggested by an actual drama that Mazo wrote for both of them to act out before an adult audience: 'I wrote the play for Caroline and me. It was called Passage at Arms and a swashbuckling performance it was. My part was that of a dashing cavalier. Caroline was an inn-keeper's daughter and wore a sprig-muslin dress with panniers.'[32]

It is hardly surprising that the Play, rooted as it was in the sexual stirrings of two troubled young girls, should have filled them with guilt and fear of discovery. Mazo conveys a sense of the heady combination of guilt and rapture they felt on one occasion, when they were almost found by Aunt Eva. At the first hint of danger she sprang to her feet, 'as frightened as though I had been caught in something wicked—fearful that our Play might be stopped'. When the danger had passed, she says, 'in the darkness we turned once more to the rapture of our Play'.[33] In her novel *Lark Ascending* she describes a character who has a 'play-acting expression': 'Fay's face wore what Josie called its play-acting expression. It was both rapt and self-conscious. Her eyes were wide-open in a hallucinated fixity. Her dilated nostrils showed her exaltation. Only her self-consciously smiling lips gave her away.'[34] Sometimes the Play assumed such intensity that the two girls were frightened by it:

> During our Play one of these characters met a violent end. We had not been prepared for the devastating effect this would have on us. All the night through we mourned and cried our eyes out. It was only at dawn that we fell into an uneasy sleep.
>
> The next morning my mother remarked on my pallor. 'And you have such blue rings about your eyes,' she said, 'Are you sure you are well?'
>
> 'I'm perfectly well,' I answered, feeling strangely guilty.
>
> Never again did we risk such a bereavement in our Play, and what is more—this particular character was, after a time, raised from the

dead, to live a happy flourishing life as a farmer. As I say, never again would we risk such bereavement—there was quite enough of suffering in our own lives.[35]

The last line sums up very neatly Mazo's craving for the order that was conspicuously lacking in her own disrupted family life, but which could be achieved in the controllable world of the Play.

The word 'orgy' has a number of meanings ranging from 'secret ceremonial rites' through ecstatic dancing and singing, drunken revelry, and loss of control to excessive sexual indulgence. The fiction contains many scenes to suggest that the word in all its meanings applies to Mazo's Play—that it had a tendency to get out of hand and unleash dangerous emotions. An early story, 'The Jilt', depicts a little boy winning the heart of an innocent-looking little girl away from a rival brother. The brother who triumphs does so not through endearments, but by titillating the girl with daring (if childish) obscenity:

The Seraph said in his blandest tone, the one word—
  'Blood!'
Jane gave a tiny, ecstatic shriek.
  'Oh, go on!' she begged, 'say more.'
  'Blood,' repeated The Seraph, firmly, 'Hot blood—told blood—wed blood—thick blood—thin blood—bad blood.' Again Jane squealed in fearful pleasure.
  'Go on,' she urged. 'Worser.'[36]

In *Morning at Jalna* three children are left in the care of a Métis and his black wife on Good Friday. They decide to act out the scene of Christ's crucifixion by constructing a cross on which the younger boy is to be crucified. The married couple play 'the mob' and in so doing work themselves and the children up into a screaming war-dance. Only the intervention of the parents puts an end to the wild scene. The adults are profoundly shocked: 'It's an orgy. Nothing less than an orgy.'[37] The children are severely punished, though both the adults' anger and the children's shame seem exaggerated and are never satisfactorily explained. The disapproval seems to be caused by a sense not that the play was blasphemous but that the emotions displayed were so frenzied, hysterical, out of control. This scene suggests how, in the Play, religious observances may have been absorbed into the erotic content. Mazo mentions in the autobiography that as the result of a spurt of interest in Catholicism, Jesuit priests appeared among the characters.

Another point of interest is Mazo's introduction and use of Métis, Indian, and black characters. Just as in her imagination English/Protestant and French/Catholic pairings were conflated with gender differences, so the non-white races imaged another kind of split within her psyche. Representing the raw, primitive sexual urges that lurk under the civilized surface, this racial imagery is exemplified by parallel scenes in the autobiography and the fiction, both centring upon Shakespeare's *Othello*. In the autobiography, as we have seen, Mazo describes a disastrous reading of the play with her mother and father.[38] In the novel *Return to Jalna*, *Othello* unleashes sexual emotions in its viewers and leads to a kind of 'orgy'. Renny's daughter, Adeline, deceives her parents in order to accompany her cousin and his tutor to see Paul Robeson in the play's title role, and on the way home the tutor is so aroused that he makes advances to her; Renny, however, is lurking in the bushes and manages to rescue his daughter, whom he later punishes by 'taking a stick to her back'.[39]

As the variety of scenes described above suggests, Mazo's and Caroline's Play was not a static form; it was always in flux, responding to their changing needs and evolving and growing as they did, becoming more sophisticated artistically as time went on. One of the first spurts of growth took place when the play was revived after a separation. Caroline had been away on a visit, and when Mazo met her at the station she found her, having been ill, much smaller and thinner, more fragile-looking, than ever. After showing her the new house—probably the grandparents' house on Dunn Street—the two girls walked to the lake. Inhibited, presumably, from expressing their true feelings for each other, they used the Play as the vehicle for their emotions:

> Quietly we savoured the joy of being together once more. We did not put our arms about each other's waists, as most girls would; we did not look into each other's eyes; but, gazing at the lake, we talked and talked, and at last, without effort, took up our parts in the Play again. The characters were few, their doings were wildly imagined, but—oh, the fascination of it![40]

The Play was also an important part of the healing process after what was perhaps the most serious personal crisis in their relationship. Apparently breaking 'some unspoken pact', Caroline had become involved with a young South American neighbour. Mazo is frank in describing her 'hurt anger'—not only that Caroline had responded to the man, but, furthermore, had confided not in Mazo but in her mother. Caroline chose wisely, for Alberta Roche 'was romantic. She would have done anything in her power to help the youthful lovers.' But she was the only one in the family who would support them. The objections were threefold: Caroline was far too young; neither of the young people had means; and 'The South Americans were rigid Catholics. My grandfather was strongly Protestant. He had disliked these foreigners from the start.' The situation was resolved when the South Americans left the country and returned to their home. Caroline was inconsolable, but Mazo was still angry: 'That night she wept after we had gone to bed but I turned my back. . . .'[41]

A few days later, Caroline suffered 'an attack of palpitation of the heart', presumably caused either by the departure of the Roderiguez family or by Mazo's rejection. Mazo was terrified: 'then indeed I felt as though my little world were shaken.' The outcome was two-fold. First, Caroline never again tried to break away from the Roches. She had suffered too much to risk her heart again—either physically or emotionally. The second result was that the Play reached new heights as, like Scheherezade, Mazo struggled to make it the vehicle for saving Caroline, ensuring her well-being, and keeping her bound inextricably to herself:

> As an inspiration came the thought of our Play. In the last summer it had been pushed aside for new pleasures, though never forgotten. Now, I thought, I would bring it out, dress it in brighter yet more subtle colors—make it so interesting that in the pleasure of it we should forget all else.
>
> How well I succeeded! New characters were introduced. All the characters, of both sexes and diverse stations and ages, were divided equally between us and remained so always. They took on a new significance. Their relations with each other became more intense. . . .
>
> Now we learned something new. That was to feel affection for our characters. Certain ones we grew to love, as beings quite separate from ourselves, yet irrevocably bound to us, since no other actor would ever play that part.[42]

Mazo makes it clear that eventually (possibly from this time of crisis) the Play became not merely an occupation that soothed and compensated for other deprivations, but a superior and preferred form of enjoyment:

> Such was the fantastical double life lived by Caroline and me inside the close circle of the family. So entralling did the Play become, so diverse and fascinating the characters to us, that often when we glimpsed our friends coming to see us, we would escape through a side door and go to the lake, where we could uninterrupted pursue our game.[43]

Consequently, when the family moved out of Toronto and went to live in the country (Mazo was thirty-one at the time), it seemed no deprivation at all to be cut off from the society of young people their own age: 'We left our friends, male and female, without misgiving. How could we ever feel isolated or bored when we had our Play?'[44]

Mazo speaks of the Play so frankly, it seems impossible that she ever felt embarrassed about it. Was she never self-conscious about the prolonged life of such entertainment for two adult women? Was not the refusal to give dates in the autobiography an attempt to disguise the fact that the childish game lasted so long? She does make references to the Play on occasions that can be specifically dated. After the success of *Jalna* in 1927, for instance, the two women would return from celebratory parties and go right into the Play. The last reference in the autobiography can be dated to their first year in England, in 1930, when Mazo mentions that her pleasure in seeing the country was somewhat marred by the nightmares she suffered. The reference comes just after she says that friends took her to see a performance of *Romeo and Juliet* at Stratford-upon-Avon. Perhaps the subject matter of Shakespeare's play had some part in her discomfort, the traditional love story reminding her of her own difference and reviving her sense of freakishness; if so, that discomfort was cured by her own Play. A sentence cut out of the final version reads: 'Caroline would wake me up from [the nightmares] and, in the dead of night, we would move into the spell of our "Play" and I would be rescued.'[45]

This passage indicates that the Play lasted until the women were in their fifties—probably throughout their lives. Discovery would have meant shame, or at least ridicule. Did Mazo ever feel guilty about using it to bind Caroline to her in a way of life that had to be shrouded in secrecy? And why, at last, was it so important to her to reveal the Play?

It is tempting to regard this play-acting as absurd, perhaps even as evidence of retarded development. Yet similar male fantasies—as evidenced by the magazines, videos, stage performances, brothels, and massage parlours that cater to them—are accepted as part of ordinary sexual behaviour. To regard Mazo's Play as aberrant is to subscribe to a double standard. It was non-violent, therapeutic, and creative, and Mazo, living in her remote and hermetic world, assumed that the readers of her autobiography would accept it as she did. She clearly placed a high value on the Play—she may even have seen it as the key to her art—and when, in her last years, she felt the need to record her life, the most important part of it had to be included.

Mazo lived in her own inner world more and more as she grew older. That was her real world: the outer one existed only to feed it. All that she achieved—success, travel, fine homes, friendships—meant comparatively little to her. They were valuable only to the extent that they fed her imaginary world, of which she never questioned the superiority. Caroline, on the other hand, while conditioned to the world of the Play, had one foot in the ordinary, everyday world. For her the Play fed the real world—her desire for travel, an adventurous life, beautiful things.

The two women accommodated each other's tastes and tolerated each other's differences. To a certain extent they both managed quite successfully to yoke their imaginary world to the real one. And by the end of their lives, both must have felt satisfaction that they had enjoyed lives as exciting, adventurous, and happy as it was possible to have, though they might not have agreed that of all their experiences the most satisfying was the Play.

5

The Wounded Bird[1]

In view of the assorted conflicts in her life, and particularly her dread of developing feminine traits, some kind of breakdown was predictable as Mazo was forced to make the transition from child to adult, from adolescent to mature woman. She clearly describes her own feelings about being a woman when contemplating the elegant clothes of her mother and a friend:

> I noticed quite suddenly one day, when with them as they shopped, that they were beautiful women. I heard the silken rustle of their skirts, noticed their tiny waists, their long gloves, and how gracefully they held their lovely parasols. Yet I never longed for the day when I should be grown-up and wear such things. I wanted to remain a child secure in the shelter of my home.[2]

She was able to delay growing up because family circumstances kept her in the position of a child in a household where her parents themselves deferred to the authority of the grandfather. Nevertheless, that situation changed when she was twenty-two. After the grandfather's death the family regrouped, with Mazo's father as the head, her recovered and revitalized mother as the 'lady of the house', and her grandmother and young uncle as extras. And just as the grandfather's death invigorated her mother, so it caused Mazo to feel responsible and adult. Her father maintained his long habit of being frequently 'absent on business' and her uncle studied dentistry at the university, leaving Mazo to be the 'protector' of the three women. She drew from that position a sense of power, and there is an exhilaration in the accounts of her plans at this time. There is also a remarkable frankness in her confession of enjoyment when, deliberately putting her grandmother into a position of weakness, she felt her own strength and control grow in proportion:

Every time I came upon Grandma, sitting calm in her rocking chair, I would perch on the arm of it and sit and stroke her forehead. Yet instead of comforting her, it always made her cry. I felt very strong and capable, as though I were no longer a very young girl, almost as though I had the helm of the family ship in my hands and could guide it.[3]

Not only did Mazo feel able to guide the family, but she also began to have career ambitions and wished, like her uncle, to attend university. When this was ruled out, as it was for so many women, she claims to have accepted the limitation of her ambitions: 'I had been ailing and Dr McKenzie, in his dictatorial way, declared that I must not enter the university. I had not the stamina, he said. I accepted this without great disappointment for I did not yearn for hard study and examinations.'[4] All the same, she did not entirely abandon hope, and she had enough yearning for study to compensate by arranging an informal program and attending certain lectures. Even so, she felt herself hampered, symbolically as well as literally, by her petticoat (a word that in childhood she had transformed to the even more cumbersome 'beckittybock'):[5] 'Looking back I can see myself ploughing through deep snow in Queen's Park, my heavy serge skirt encrusted with snow to the knees stopping every so often surreptitiously to straighten out my petticoat, which somehow managed to work itself into a hampering ball between my legs.'[6] She also studied at the Ontario School of Art with the prominent Toronto artist G.A. Reid as her teacher.[7] And she tried to increase the skills in French that she had shown in high school by taking lessons 'from Monsieur Masson in St Joseph Street who went every morning to Mass in the church across the way from his house'.[8] Mazo was obviously straining to develop her varied talents in spite of the restrictions placed upon her by the doctor and her family.

Above all, she was writing stories. When she managed to place the first ones in magazines that paid about $50—a considerable sum in 1902—her feeling of success was increased by the use to which she put her earnings. She bought presents for the women of the household, proudly laying her trophies at their feet. Her first cheque went for a beautiful lamp that her mother had longed for (which, as we have seen, was later broken);[9] the second, for a raincoat and a lovely head of Cleopatra for her mother and the rest for a silver necklace for Caroline.[10] She placed herself with her father as not needing to own such trinkets: 'For some reason my father and I got nothing out of these first earnings. They must be spent headlong, with a bang, on those two.'[11] Disposing of her money in this way gave her the same sense of superiority as did soothing her grandmother's tears. Again she says: 'I felt strong and full of power. I was exhilarated by my success.'[12]

These first stories were set in a small imaginary Quebec community that she named St Loo. Mazo was unfamiliar with French Canada at that time, and as a setting it probably seemed quite foreign and exotic—qualities that many beginning writers favour to heighten the interest of their material. Thinking about it later, however, she commented: 'For some reason I chose to write about French-Canadians, in this my first venture. Why I did this I do not know. I was not a French-Canadian—my connection was with Old France.'[13] Quebec, with its own language and religion within the larger unit of Canada, always seemed to Mazo emblematic of her own separateness. One of her favourite books was William Kirby's 'The Golden Dog', a romantic novel set in Quebec.[14] In addition, she associated her father with French Canada: one of his favourite recitation pieces was a William Henry Drummond poem in supposedly French-Canadian 'broken English',[15] and Mazo remarks that on his trips to Montreal as a salesman, 'he was very much at home among French people. I have heard him say, "When I am with the French I am French. When I am with the English I am British." '[16]

Apart from the French setting and the slightly moralistic tone, these stories have the motifs that appear in her later, more ambitious fictions: the return to the fold (of family, community, church), or the beloved's arms, of various kinds of prodigal sons. In the second story —as in her novel *Finch's Fortune*, which appeared nearly thirty years later—the son inherits and speedily dissipates a fortune. (Perhaps Mazo was already feeling that she had scattered a little too recklessly and generously the large sum she had earned from her first story.)

Mazo's story of the breaking of the valuable lamp and her emphasis on her mother's grief is somewhat puzzling.[17] Was the gift after all a form of appeasement or propitiation for a mother who would have preferred her only daughter to develop some female graces instead of odd career ambitions? For all her sense of power, these early literary efforts must have cost Mazo some heartache for a variety of reasons. In the autobiography she tells of the hard work and worry that went into these early stories—even 'anxious thought for the handwriting itself'.[18] The manuscripts testify to the latter: the first pencil-written versions are laboriously copied out in ink several times. Still, she had beginner's luck, and her first three stories were immediately accepted. Perhaps the most telling details about these early stories are the apostrophe errors—evidence of her lack of education in the most basic skills necessary for a writer. Nor did she know that she should include return postage (luckily, she did not need it).

But there was a more acute kind of anxiety, that of exposing her self and appearing naked before the world. She describes the intensity of her self-revelation:

> My first stories . . . were written in a kind of calculated agony. I had the idea that I must work myself up into a state of excitement before I could write of what was in my mind. I would lie on the sofa in the dim room, my body rigid, my mind hallucinated by the pictures that passed before it. Then I would rise, take up paper and pencil and write. Again I would stretch myself on the sofa. Again I would write. I remember my reflection in the old gilt-framed mirror that hung above the sofa, the glitter in my eyes, the flushed cheeks, as of one in fever.[19]

This detail of writing as she looks into the reversed and inner world in the mirror was repeated some years later when, after her father's death, Mazo sat herself where he sat to write another story: '*Strange* it was to be writing—*stranger* still that it should be a humorous story—in the room where so lately my father had died. *Strange* that I should be sitting in his chair, the tall mirror giving back my reflection instead of his' [emphasis added].[20]

The anxieties of authorship that precipitated her first nervous breakdown in 1903 manifested themselves in a way that was to be repeated several times in the course of her life: the loss, almost-loss, or imagined loss of the manuscript. Twice on later occasions when she was to make journeys she left behind manuscripts of the Jalna novels she was working on, and they were retrieved only at the last moment. The imagined loss of an early story is reported as follows:

> Yet weeks passed—more weeks than the usual time taken to acknowledge receipt of a manuscript—and still no word from the magazine. A *strange* unease took possession of me. There was a tremor in my inmost being. I could not understand it. I went to the post office where I had bought the stamps for the postage. The girl at the wicket remembered me. Yes, she remembered me well and the odd thing was that just after I had left someone had found a ten cent stamp on the floor.
>
> I turned away. Yes, that had been my stamp, I knew. My manuscript was lost. I had no postage on it. . . . *Strange* how the pavements appeared to slant—as though falling away from me. I had a feeling of *strange* excitement, yet I felt weary as never before. When I returned home I found that the floor sloped away from me as the pavement had done, as though into an abyss. I could think of nothing but the lost manuscript [emphasis added].[21]

The letter of acceptance eventually came, but by the time it arrived Mazo was in the throes of a complete collapse, so ill that she no longer cared. The passage (like the description of her effort after the death of her father) uses the word *strange* repetitively. It is tempting to see this habitual losing of manuscripts as symptomatic of a basic conflict between an obsessive need to write and a terrible fear of exposure. Since Mazo felt herself to be disqualified from any of the roles that in her time justified the existence of women, writing had become for her not merely a pastime but her entire *raison d'être*. To write, she said, was 'to do that for which I was made'.[22]

In late February 1903 the old English morality play *Everyman*, was being performed at the Princess Theatre.[23] An unusual contrast to the theatre's usual offerings, it was an interesting performance with no curtain, no orchestra, no footlights, and the players coming and going across a platform on which there was a small setting 'somewhat resembling a cloister'. The effect on Mazo was overwhelming: 'I did not know what was wrong with me and why these new and frightening sensations.'[24] It was apparently not long afterwards that, 'early in Lent', she went to St Michael's Cathedral 'and knelt at each of the stations of the Cross—perhaps hoping for a miracle'. It seems likely that the play, with its religious message, had exacerbated the guilt she was undoubtedly feeling about her 'strange behaviour', her resistance of the female role expected of her and the growing intensity of her love for Caroline. (She had also developed a romantic interest in Catholicism through her reading of the novels of Henry Harland.)[25] Her distaste for the woman in herself and the women in her family culminated when she returned home from the cathedral and announced her sympathy with Catholicism:

> Standing in the doorway of the room I looked in at them as though I were an alien. I told them where I had been and what I had done but I did not tell them why. For I did not myself know. I told them with an air of defiance as though to show that I no longer belonged to them.[26]

This scene is the precursor to a complete breakdown, which she reports in full detail. She was unable to sleep and eat, and so weak that she could not walk downstairs. Her collapsed sense of identity made her fear that she was slipping into oblivion and death, though her young uncle—proceeding with his scientific studies at the university—came into the bedroom she shared with Caroline and scoffed at such an idea:

> 'How are you?' he asked, and I answered in a strangled voice: 'I'm done for—I shall never be well again.' And from my fevered brain I

brought out the fear that haunted me, 'I'm going to die—like Grandpa died.'

He gave a short, angry laugh. He laid his hands on the foot board of the bed and leant over us. 'You couldn't,' he said. 'You couldn't— not even if you tried.'[27]

As for her physician, Dr Mackenzie, Mazo may have exaggerated his callous attitude towards her, but not his ineffectiveness:

He came and stood by the bed and looked down at me, with his jeering smile. 'Well, you've got yourself into a pretty pickle,' he said.

He left me a prescription and dropped in once or twice more to see me. I was to stay in bed, he said, till I had recovered.[28]

But she did not recover for a long time, during which he forgot all about her. It was not for another decade that such illnesses began to be treated. Then, after they had been experienced by men as a result of war trauma and dignified with the label 'shell shock', these hysterical symptoms at last became the subject of serious medical attention.[29] But Mazo's symptoms were very much the same. She suffered from terrible hallucinations, imagining that the roughly plastered walls in the room in which she lay were 'horrible faces that mouthed and grimaced at me'.

Fear had become my companion, my imagination no longer my delightful servant but my cruel master. All that happened was exaggerated. When my pet canary was asphyxiated in his cage from the fumes of a gas heater, all that night I relived his suffering. . . .[30]

Once again, the image of a bird, this time a caged and suffocated pet, becomes the symbol of her own state. Her descriptions approximate those in several 'portraits of artists as young women', in which writers like Charlotte Perkins Gilman, Virginia Woolf, and Katherine Anne Porter based fictions on their early breakdowns.[31]

Once she had suffered her breakdown, Mazo found herself in a vicious circle, because her illness confirmed what she had dreaded most since early childhood: that she was, after all, a weak woman— not a powerful protector of other women but an invalid, dependent and bed-ridden. When the family moved to a house they had taken for the summer, she had to be carried downstairs by her uncle. And of course, in this debilitated state she could not write. She could not even hold a pencil: 'My hand and arm were as though paralysed— as though made of wood. A pain shot through my head. My forehead was wet with sweat. I was helpless to write. I could not force the pencil to move.'[32]

Such collapses of health and identity are usually reflected in erratic sexual behaviour. In women, conditioned from early childhood to understand that the only approved vehicle for female behaviour and self-expression was the physical body, such a means of expressing temporary insanity is predictable. There is, however, very little hint in either Mazo's fiction or her autobiography of what happened between her and Caroline at this time, of how their relationship and the breakdown may have affected each other. In the early stages, Mazo says, Caroline, her bed-fellow, suffered along with her, holding her in her arms during those long wakeful nights.[33] She does not mention the Play, but clearly its curative powers failed in this crisis. Caroline eventually went away on one of her visits and was absent for the later stages of Mazo's illness and recovery.[34]

The extent of Mazo's breakdown can be dated by the gap in the publication of her work. The last of the early stories, 'The Golden Chariot', was published in 1905, winning first prize in the monthly short-story magazine *The Blue Jay*. Mazo did not begin writing again until 1910, although a single story, 'The Regenerate', appeared in April 1907. There are many discrepancies in the accounts of these years. Mazo describes, for instance, being sent by her doctor to stay in a resort hotel by herself. Yet in a later chapter she says that she and Caroline had a schoolgirlish sense of adventure when they left home to travel by themselves a few miles and stay at Aunt Eva's rooming house in Toronto.[35] Moreover, it seems unlikely that any doctor would send a young woman recently recovered from a nervous breakdown to recuperate by herself.

Since Mazo was twenty-eight at the time, to call her a runaway seems slightly absurd. But in fact this is what she seems to be covering up. The alienation that she felt when she went to the Catholic cathedral apparently intensified, and as soon as she had regained the use of her legs she went off by herself. In the autobiography she describes her stay at a hotel at Pointe-au-Baril on Georgian Bay, where most of the patrons were Americans. Run by the Oldfields, the hotel was the Bellevue, built in 1900, and it was probably recommended by Dr MacKenzie, an avid fisherman who frequented the area for many years.[36] Since she was the only Canadian and 'a young girl, alone and fragile',[37] the other guests took a kindly, protective interest in her. But she seems to have had little money and no means of communicating with her family; she says she had to await the arrival of money (from the sale of a story?) before she could pay her bill, leave the island, and go to find them.[38]

When she finally did leave, according to this account, she discovered that the family were no longer in Toronto but somewhere else. She describes—with many explanations about letters gone astray—tracing them to their summer cottage on Lake Simcoe.[39] She stayed overnight in a Toronto hotel (not with Aunt Eva or her grandmother) and then went to the cottage, where there was a happy reunion.[40] The truth of this story seems to be that, after a period of isolation, she did return and become reconciled with her family.

A fictional version of a similar breakdown occurs in *Whiteoaks*, the second volume in the Jalna series. Here Finch Whiteoak is tormented by his family: he is in the last years of high school but doing badly in academic subjects because his real interest is in the arts.[41] Such an interest makes him a pariah in the family, which, even though it includes some men who are artistically inclined, values men of action above artists. It is worth noting that in addition to playing the piano, Finch acts in a play. The family disapproves of both art forms, withholding music lessons and at one point forbidding his playing altogether. Two other incidents, in addition to his neglect of schoolwork, lead to this crisis in his life. First, he has formed a close friendship with Arthur Leigh, a young aesthete. The family finds the friendship 'neurotic' and reacts with outrage to a letter from Arthur that addresses Finch as 'darling'[42] (a form of address used by Mazo and Caroline in the little notes they wrote).[43] Second, they discover that Finch has been burning incense in his room and react with disgust to such a pagan practice. 'He'll be turning Papist next,' says brother Piers.[44]

Finch reacts to his family's persecution by attempting two kinds of flight. He runs away to New York, to the only sympathetic friend he has, the ex-wife of his brother; that flight ends in reconciliation with his family, but their persecution is not over. When they discover that he is the heir to the fortune of his grandmother, the head of the family, they turn on him again. This time his escape takes the form of attempted suicide by drowning.[45]

Although Mazo's expressions of her own life are carefully hidden in her fiction, this novel does shed some light on her breakdown. There are striking parallels between her own experience of collapse and estrangement from her family and Finch Whiteoak's story. Not only has the family insufficient respect for Finch's 'playing', but they are incensed by his flirtation with Catholic rituals. Mazo also makes gender problems very central to Finch's crisis. Inversions of various kinds came easily to her, and Finch's gender difficulties suggest an inverted form of her own. The Whiteoak family disapprove of Finch's artistic endeavours because they believe such occupations are not manly and think he is 'effeminate'.

In the fiction the Whiteoak family gradually become reconciled to Finch, but for reasons that do not reflect particularly well on them. They have a proprietary attitude to family members (shades of Grandfather Lundy), prefer to have them all under one roof, and resent their roaming about the world freely. Since, therefore, they do not wish a public scandal about Finch's inheriting his grandmother's money, they finally accept him as her unlikely heir. It helps that Finch himself is not vindictive, but so eager to be accepted amicably that he allows the family to take advantage of him and drain away his wealth. Finally, they are all preoccupied with their own lives and simply lose interest in persecuting him. When he resumes his playing they pay no attention because he is older, independent, and they have washed their hands of his idiosyncrasies. Finally, the relationship with Arthur Leigh ceases to annoy them because the latter has gone abroad.

The version of the breakdown that appears in the Jalna novel was not to be written for more than twenty years. And Mazo produced very little of anything during the period of her breakdown except for the one story, 'The Regenerate', which she wrote just before leaving Pointe-au-Baril and which sold immediately to H.L. Mencken's *The Smart Set*.[46]

The heroine is Lee Meredith, a young woman from New York who is the quintessential Mazonian female—blonde, blue-eyed, and small. She is escorted on a fishing-trip by Simon Nanabosh, an Indian boy whose wonderful physical appearance fills her with romantic notions regarding not so much the 'noble savage' as the primitive one. Although her notions are really inappropriate to him—he is a missionary-educated man, destined for missionary work—under the influence of her enthusiasm he regresses. Dressing him in feathers, she urges him to become primitive and savage: 'Swell out your chest and cultivate a lust for blood.'[47] Thus encouraged, he cuts the rope that attaches her boat and tries to abduct her. At this point she is thoroughly alarmed, but disaster is averted when various patriarchal figures intervene: the captain of another ship cuts off their flight and returns Lee to her father. Since only Lee knows what Simon had planned, no harm is done. She returns to her father and Simon decides that he had best be a missionary after all.

Like many of Mazo's stories, this one makes little sense except when read in terms of her own complicated psyche, as an expression of her inner world. With its theme of a play that gets out of hand ('Simon and I are playing Indian,' Lee explains when someone is disturbed by their war cries) and brings out the beast in Simon, could it reflect a Play episode with Caroline that got frighteningly out of hand? Does the anti-climactic ending indicate or anticipate a sense in Mazo of danger averted, of dangerously inflamed passions at last brought under control?

Mazo's return to her family is related as the happiest of reconciliations. She tells of finding her mother, her father, and Caroline at a cottage beside Lake Simcoe and of spending an idyllic autumn with them, during which the Play grew to new levels of sophistication. It sounds like a regaining of innocence, a return to prelapsarian happiness, a harmonious solution to a time of disorder and tumult.[48]

On the other hand, this decade during which Mazo moved from thirty to forty should have been a growing time, a period of maturation both for her and for her art. The upheaval would have left her older, with some of her conflicts resolved and with a more experienced view of the world. It might have been a leaping-off point into emotional and artistic growth, in which personal liberation would have coincided with a crucial turning point in history. Artists and writers all over Europe and the eastern United States were, in their various ways, noting the change from one era to another. In 1907 Henry Adams privately printed his autobiography, which, when it was republished in 1918, started a whole decade of discussion on how to write poetry in this new 'Machine Age'. Willa Cather disliked the new ways: she announced that the world broke in two about 1920 (later she said 1922) and that she belonged to the former half.[49] Virginia Woolf hazarded the bold assertion that 'in or about December, 1910, human character changed'.[50] (She picked that date because it marked the opening of the tradition-breaking exhibition in London of the post-impressionist painters.) Gertrude Stein, who had moved to Paris in 1903, published *Tender Buttons* in 1914. James Joyce published *The Dubliners* in 1916, and a year later T.S. Eliot published *Prufrock and Other Observations*.

But Toronto in the second decade of the twentieth century was a small town of 300,000 people; compared with New York, London, and Paris it was a provincial backwater. The literary community was barely aware of the exciting changes taking place elsewhere, and even if it had been, Mazo had moved out of the city and was not yet a member of any literary community. Furthermore, whereas Virginia Woolf and Gertrude Stein had been liberated early by the deaths of their parents, Mazo was drawn back into the Victorian atmosphere of her family home.

Thus her illness and separation from the family were not positive experiences for her growth:

> The effect on me of this illness of the nerves was to make me more dependent on those about me. I had been rather an independent girl— somewhat too sure of myself, I fear, though I don't think anyone would have called me conceited. But now, like a child, I wanted to be told what to do.[51]

That she regressed to childhood is suggested by her correspondence with Ellery Sedgewick of the *Atlantic Monthly*, beginning in 1914. He told her later that when he first wrote to her he had doubts about the length of her skirts—and yet she was then in her mid-thirties. When she was forty-eight she told him that she was a good deal older than he imagined, but very slow in maturing.

As Mazo indicates, during this next decade she regressed; she and Caroline were once again children in the family home, and Mazo regained the sense of cameraderie with her father that she had enjoyed in childhood. However satisfactory this outcome was for the family, Mazo's maturity as a woman and her development as an artist were delayed for at least another ten years.

6

Acton, Ontario

The next three years, like the previous two, were erased from the autobiographical record, but for different reasons. This time it was social embarassment rather than personal disorientation that caused Mazo's reticence. When she returned to the family, Will Roche had undertaken a new venture in Acton, Ontario; now a commuter suburb of Toronto, it was then a small country town. There he acquired and refurbished a residential hotel accommodating local factory workers and itinerant commercial travellers.

In spite of Mazo's suppression of factual information about this phase of her life, there is ample material elsewhere to provide a vivid picture. *The Acton Free Press*, although published only once a week, covered the events of the community very thoroughly. Furthermore, Mazo used the experience acquired during this time as background for two short stories written soon after she left the area, and for two books: *Explorers of the Dawn* and *Delight*. When the newspaper accounts are set beside the fictional ones, the flavour of life in the Acton hotel from 1906 to 1908 is clearly rendered.

The paper reports that in the fall of 1905 Will Roche acquired the oldest hotel in town, a two-storey stone structure that had been built in 1853. While negotiations for the purchase were under way, the building was badly damaged by fire, but Will Roche went ahead, bought the place for $10,000, and embarked on ambitious plans to refurbish it:

> Mr Roach, the new proprietor of the Clark House, has moved to town, and his family are residing in Mr Holmes's house on Main Street. The work of rebuilding the Clark House is progressing, though somewhat slowly. Mr Roach expects the interior work to be completed about the first of December. He has been a commercial traveller for twenty-five years and knows well how a hotel should be conducted and intends

fitting up the premises in a manner to attract the commercial travellers generally. He promises to 'keep hotel' to the satisfaction of all concerned.[1]

He added a wooden third storey immediately and later constructed stables behind the hotel. These no doubt housed, among other items, the Shetland pony and two-wheeled cart in which 'the Misses Roche' (Mazo and Caroline) were often seen driving about town.[2] There were two other hotels in Acton: the Dominion across the street and the Albion, which was subsequently renamed the Station Hotel. In *Delight* (1926) Mazo names the fictional version of the Acton The Duke of York and the rival hotel The British American. The description of The Acton House during its opening week suggests that it was at first far superior to the competition:

The painters were finishing this week the remodeled Clark house, re-named by the new proprietor 'The Acton'. . . . By an artistic use of burlap and embossed metal, the wainscotting and ceilings of the halls, office and bar have been much improved, while the dining room, with its white and gold metal ceiling and burlapped walls in nicely contrast-ing tints of green, makes very attractive quarters. The kitchen has also a metallic ceiling and is treated in white. The stairway to the second floor is turned to the rear and faces the dining room door. The rooms on the second floor including a large sitting room with burlap walls and white silk paper ceiling, with Flemish oak furniture. All the bed-rooms on this floor are furnished with white enameled iron bedsteads and white furniture, with carpets of neat patterns. The servants' quar-ters are on this floor and a back stairway gives them convenient access to dining room and kitchen. The woodwork of the main hall is of Norway pine and brass trimmings. The rooms of the third floor are of good size and airy. The premises throughout are tidy and in a much better sanitary condition than in the old building. It is the intention of Mr W.R. Roach, the new proprietor to erect new brick stables with sheds adjoining in the spring, also an addition to the rear of the hotel to provide three new sample rooms. The front of the building will be adorned with a new porch and balcony and cement platform, with cement steps and railing to the office.[3]

In spite of the elegance of the building that Will Roche created and his ambitious plans for a respectable hotel, life in such places had a definitely seamy side. On 8 July 1909, for instance, bartender John Kelly at the Acton House was fined for being too boisterous in ejecting one of his customers! For all the vigilance of the temperance orga-nizations at the time, drunkenness was rife, and the pages of the paper are full of accounts like the following:

Drunk With a Babe in her Arms
It was a sad spectacle which citizens viewed about seven o'clock on
Saturday evening of a man and woman both reeling drunk coming out
of the Acton House.[4]

That article ended with the question 'Do we need to banish bars from
Acton?'.

There was, however, a side of Acton very different from the hurly-
burly of the hotel bars. There were churches of all denominations and
many of the clergy were colourful characters—grist for the writer's mill.
A level above the clergy and the other professional men was a genuine
aristocracy, the members of which lived in grand homes set in beautiful
gardens. The home of the Beardsmore family, the tannery owners, was
the most impressive. One of the Beardsmores had married the daughter
of Sir William Mackenzie, a Montreal businessman, and Lady MacKenzie
had planned the Acton residence and named it 'Beverly' after the Beardsmore's Toronto establishment.[5] Behind its high walls the Beardsmores
lived a very English life, with nannies, governesses, and pony carts.
The grounds were always at the disposal of the townspeople for the
planning and arranging of community affairs, and one who remembered
a party there was convinced, when she read *Jalna*, that the Whiteoaks
were modelled on the Beardsmores.[6] Caroline Clement once even hinted
that she was engaged to one of the Beardsmores—a tantalizing fragment
of information, so far unconfirmed.[7] The Beardsmores were not the only
aristocratic members of the community: another mansion, 'Fairview'
built in 1855, was described in the local paper as the 'ancestral home'
of the Sidney Smith family.[8]

Of the stories published at this time one dealt with the high life of
Acton and the other with the low. The first, 'The Year's at the Spring'
depicts three motherless boys whose absent father has left them in
the care of his former governess. It is part of a series of stories (although it does not itself appear in the collection) that was published
as *Explorers of the Dawn*, which Mazo considered to be more like a
novel. Here the boys are often bored and confined to their rooms as
punishment, but their days are enlivened by their neighbours—particularly the Bishop, whose pleasant garden they can look into from
their bedroom window, and who often invites them to participate in
the convivial life of his household. In another story in the series,
'Noblesse Oblige', the boys insinuate themselves into the splendid
house and distinguished company of Lord Simon de Lacey (Mazo
seems to have read Frankenstein), the impecunious younger son of
the Duke of Aberfalden.

The setting of the stories was supposedly an English cathedral town. But Christopher Morley, in his foreword—knowing, perhaps, that Mazo had never set foot in England, yet sensing the authenticity of the background—felt compelled to comment:

> The scene of the tale is said to be in England. And yet, to the zealous observer, there will seem to be some flavours that are hardly English. The language of the excellent Mary Ellen, for instance, comes to me with a distinct cisatlantic sound. Nor can I, somehow, visualize a planked back garden in an English Cathedral Town. I am wondering about this, and I conclude that perhaps it is due to the fact that Miss de la Roche lives in Toronto, that delightful city where the virtues of both England and America are said to be subtly and consummately blended.[9]

Mazo did live in Toronto when the book appeared, but when she conceived the stories she lived in Acton, on Main Street, next to the Presbyterian church and its manse; Acton, with its planked pavements and planked back gardens, was the setting of her stories.

The low life of the town also yielded a story and later a novel, both of them considerably more lively than the fictions inspired by the high life. 'Canadian Ida and English Nell' is the story of a Cockney girl who follows her husband to Canada, tracks him down to Acford, finds a job in the Acford House, rescues him from the Canadian wife he has bigamously married, and takes him back to England.[10]

These fictions leave little doubt that Mazo relished the rich flavour of hotel life with its array of idiosyncratic characters, its sounds and smells and crises. In 'Canadian Ida and English Nell' the Acford House is described as having 'a deep stone porch, leading to a low hallway, pleasant with the smell of ale'.[11] The place is also permeated with the smell of local factories, especially the tannery, which the workers who board at the hotel carry back in their clothes. The opening paragraph of *Delight* conveys the sense of anticipation gathering in the air as the evening gets under way:

> The evening meal—supper they called it at The Duke of York—was over; the busy hours between seven and eleven were just commencing. A pleasant stir of preparation was in the air, men sauntered in at the open front door, washed and brushed after their day's work, a look of anticipation and good-fellowship softening their features. Shortly the bus from the evening train would be clattering up to the front door, leaving a half-dozen travellers or possibly a theatrical troupe. It was time they had a show. There had been nothing on in the Town Hall for weeks.[12]

A sharp distinction is made between the various classes of boarders, and Mazo describes in exact detail the arrangement of the dining-room tables, almost medieval in their hierarchical distinctions:

> Breakfast was ready. Already half the boarders were in their places. These were tannery hands, men from the dye works and jam factory, who had to be at their work early. They sat at a long table by themselves, distinct from the commercial table, the table for other transients, and the table for boarders of a higher class. They were boarded at a low rate, had, in consequence, no table napkins or bill-of-fare, wiping their mouths on their handkerchiefs when through eating, and being told what choice there was for them by the waitress.[13]

Many of the incidents described in the pages of *The Acton Free Press* become major elements in *Delight*. The Fireman's Ball, for example, that is a central event in *Delight* was also one of the most important social events in the town—in the Roches' first year at the hotel the supper for the ball was served to over a hundred couples at both the Dominion House and the Acton.[14]

The character of the cook's child in *Delight* immortalizes the small daughter of the landlord of the Dominion, who died during this time. Another incident in which Mazo took an interest was the sudden legacy from England of one Alfred Budd, who worked as porter for the Acton and the Dominion. On 23 January 1908 the paper announced that Budd had inherited a legacy of $1,067 from the estate of his father. Less than a month later a headline announced, 'Alfred Budd Capitalist Dead'. The accompanying story was both tragic and unintentionally comic. Budd had gone to St Clemens with four friends 'ostensibly' to buy horses:

> They put up at the St Clemens hotel, deceased and Nicklin and Warner occupying the same bed. In the morning when Nicklin awoke he found Budd cold and stiff and apparently dead for some time. Since the deceased received his legacy of $1,067 from his father's estate in England, three weeks ago, he has been on a continual spree. Deceased was 40 years of age. He came to Acton eighteen or nineteen years ago. His sudden death is a very natural outcome of his long debauch. He had already gotten rid of over $600 of the money received.[15]

This incident is incorporated into *Delight*, where Edwin Silk, a remittance man, is the admirer of one of the kitchen girls. His death is similar to Alfred Budd's, but in the story the servant, Pearl, inherits what remains of the legacy:

> Silk had died and left her all his fortune. He had driven to the village of Stead on Sunday with three other men, among them Bastien. They

had played poker most of the night. In the morning, one of the men who had slept with Silk found him dead in bed by his side. There was no inquest. Silk had always been a weakling, and the strain of losing three hundred dollars that night had been the last straw to a heart already degenerated.[16]

When Mazo lived there, one of Acton's chief attractions was Fairy Lake, an eighty-acre expanse of water almost enclosing a park. Thickly wooded with cedar, birch, wild cherry, balm of Gilead, and basswood, the shores of the lake were full of wild life, and the lake of speckled trout. Inhabitants of Acton sailed about in boats and punts, enjoying the fishing.[17] Mazo transformed Fairy Lake into the lagoon to which Jimmy Sykes takes the eponymous heroine of the book, Delight Mainprize (Mr and Mrs Henry Mainprize were Mazo's near neighbours) at dawn after they have danced all night at the firemen's ball:

> Before them stretched a level expanse of turf, moist and palely green, on it laying, like a vast ring, the half-mile race track. At one end of the enclosure rose the covered grandstand. On the far side low stables and sheds and, beyond, the wet roofs of houses, showing here and there, a window, gleaming red in the first beams of the sun.
>
> Toward the sunrise the end of the enclosure merged into a dense growth of shrubs, willows, and underbush, now leafless and discovering the glint of water beyond. The wind struck their faces, fresh and moist from the lagoon. Among the bushes a little bird broke into song, fragile as crystal, unpremeditated as the song of the wind. . . .
>
> Across the lagoon stood the dark pine wood, remnant of the ancient forest not yet destroyed. The tapering tree tops rose like delicate minarets against the morning sky.[18]

The scene in which, later, the women of the town dunk and almost drown Delight in the lagoon may have been based on local stories of another era, when a drunken wife-beater was dragged from his house by a group of irate men: he was taken to Fairy Lake and ducked so thoroughly that he nearly drowned, and a doctor had to be rushed to the scene to revive him.

Delight has been singled out for special praise more than any other of Mazo's works. When it first appeared, *The Times Literary Supplement* called it 'a striking book which stands out sharply from among the rather sterile aggregate of Canadian fiction'.[19] It is the only one of her works to be reprinted in the Canadian Library series. Critic George Hendrick chose it 'as perhaps the best of Miss de la Roche'; he saw it as a 'boldly comic novel in the tradition of frontier humor'.[20] And it was one of two favourites of the poet Dorothy Livesay, Mazo's early neighbour and admirer.

Livesay often defended Mazo from critics who felt that the White-oaks were too British or too upper-class: she never tired of pointing out that people like the Whiteoaks settled in Ontario and were the proper stuff of Canadian fiction. All the same, she recorded her own disappointment when, after *Possession* and *Delight*, Mazo turned to the portrayal of Ontario's landed gentry, those who 'became gentle-man farmers, orchardists and horse lovers'. She blamed Mazo's pub-lishers for Mazo's turning her back on 'the way ordinary people really lived, worked, loved and hated', charging that they 'did not want her to write of the down-and-outs, the characters she knew that re-minded her of Dickens, those disinherited . . . those living on the fringes of society'.[21]

There can be little doubt that Mazo had a strong feeling for the 'disinherited' people she portrayed in her early plays, stories, and novels. She understood their lives at first hand, and they appear in her fiction with a freshness often denied the other characters. She had intimate knowledge of kitchens and cooks, and below-stairs at Jalna is a colourful region. But after *Delight* she always portrayed servants with an air of amusement and condescension, carefully dis-sociating herself from them.

She had a particular appreciation of working women and girls, preferring their robust, vigorous bodies and manner to those of their genteel counterparts. (In this she closely resembled Willa Cather writ-ing of the superior charms of the hired girls in *My Antonia*).[22] In her autobiography she remembers and describes systematically all the maids she ever had, each one mentioned by name with a line spec-ifying her particular charms: Ada, 'a voice like velvet'; Susie, 'a com-plexion the loveliest I have ever seen'; Violet, 'the most beautiful girl I have seen'; Berthy Muller, 'a handsome girl, very fair, but she had given her heart to Italy and used a brunette face powder to make herself look dark like an Italian'. Neria Boislier, the governess, 'was a charming young woman. . . half-Scottish, half-French, speaking both languages beautifully. . . . French songs and games she taught the children.' Cissie Bull was 'a fine buxom girl'. . . . 'When she opened the door to visitors, they fairly swooned at sight of so much rural beauty. "What a divine complexion! Wherever did you get her?" ' Bessie had the 'look of the healthy young female trying to be serious.'[23]

She was also fascinated by the fragmented speech of the very young and the socially disadvantaged. Her fondness for rendering baby-talk in her fictions and elsewhere may be cause for groans, but it seems to be part of the same phenomenon—her feeling for those outside society's mainstream who are linguistically hampered, disempowered, rendered incapable of saying what they mean and of being heard with respect.

But if Mazo felt for the socially disadvantaged, ultimately she did not wish to align herself with them. In a way, as we have seen, her family background had prepared her for a split social allegiance. Her father had listed his trade as a 'tinsmith' as late as 1876; on the Lundy side her grandfather and his sons were artisans who worked in local factories; her Aunt Eva, when widowed, ran a profitable rooming house. Yet even though the Lundys had close connections in the professional and landowning classes, Mazo experienced them as belonging to a lower class than the Roches. After Mazo's death, Caroline expressed that sentiment by telling a biographer that 'the Lundys were fine people but she was quite unlike them'.[24] Mazo rejected her Newmarket connections, denying that she had even been born in the town, and she rejected her Acton experience for the same social reason.

Of course, her psyche was shot through with ambivalence—the social issue was just one more strand in a cluster of sexual, national, racial, and religious ambivalences. In later life Mazo's upper-class affectations were often mocked; it has never been very fashionable to shed social and racial liabilities and adopt the camouflage of the mainstream, and, after all, poverty and lack of education are not matters for shame. Yet surely it does not take a great deal of imagination to understand how they might be experienced as shameful by the luckless outsider, and how that shame might be internalized as a general feeling of worthlessness.

Another writer of the same generation made a gesture very similar to Mazo's in breaking from her own class and designating herself an aristocrat. At exactly the same time that Mazo was part of the Acton House, Katherine Anne Porter was living the experience that would inform her most vivid story of her native Texas. In 'Noon Wine' Porter portrayed a class with which she preferred not to identify herself, and when she commented on the story in later years she repudiated all kinship with the characters. Even though she had not changed the names of the cousins on which she based those characters, she wrote: 'Let me give you a glimpse of Mr and Mrs Thompson, not as they were in their lives, for I never knew them. . . . The woman I have called Mrs Thompson—I never knew her name. . . .'[25] She was so successful in suppressing her origins among the plain people and aligning herself with the 'guilt-ridden white-pillar crowd' that at least

one critic praised 'Noon Wine' because its author had shown 'remarkable skill' in making the leap from her own aristocratic milieu
to depict the world of the poor dirt farmer.[26] In fact, most of her fiction
portrays the genteel poverty of the Southern aristocrat. It is not altogether surprising that Porter, marginalized by gender, poverty, and
lack of education, should reject her disadvantaged class.

When Mazo inscribed in her fiction the first-hand knowledge gained
when her father ran the Acton House, she concocted the following
alibi:

> Our cook was a woman who had had picturesque experience and liked
> to tell me of her life as cook in an hotel. I wrote two stories based on
> happenings of which she told me, and sold them to the Metropolitan
> Magazine. These two stories were later the basis of my novel *Delight*.[27]

The story may not be entirely dishonest. Mrs Bye, the cook in *Delight*,
has in common with Alberta Roche an uncertain digestive system and
a tendency to nervous disintegration. If Mazo's mother acted as cook
at the hotel, she may well have been her source for the details of
kitchen life. But clearly Mazo's statement was intended to conceal her
own closeness to her material. That some explanation was necessary
is illustrated by the reaction of William Arthur Deacon when he first
read *Delight*:

> In 1926, when I was reading the second novel, Delight, about two
> English servant girls in a country hotel, Mazo delivered her first pleasant
> corrective shock by describing the blueish tobacco smoke that drifted
> into the hall over the swing-doors of the bar. The observer was coming
> down the stairs. This phenomenon had to be seen to be believed; and
> it was a thing almost extinct in Canada. I rushed to Jean Graham, editor
> of The Canadian Home Journal, and asked: 'Where did Mazo see that?'
> Answer: 'Her uncle kept a hotel in Newmarket.'[28]

Like most of Will Roche's professional endeavours, this one soon
ended. Perhaps he sold the hotel because he sensed that the tide of
opinion was going against the hotels and that the temperance people
would make life impossible one way or another. Perhaps the atmosphere of the place was becoming distasteful to his family, or perhaps
his own congenital restlessness made him wish to change course once
more. The paper reported a change of hands, and W.R. Roche sold
out for more or less what he had paid.[29] Unfortunately, the building
burned to the ground before the next landlord could take over, and
a Canadian literary landmark was lost for ever. For her part, Mazo
appeared to her reading public as having led a completely sheltered

life. To her critics she was a protected woman who had to compensate for a dearth of life experiences with a feverish romantic imagination. Yet she had a breadth and variety of experience quite unusual for a woman of her time and place, and the Acton years were an important part of it.

7

Two Romantic Friendships

As on many previous occasions, Will Roche's disappointment in his latest failure was mitigated by instant enthusiasm for his next enterprise. It was not long after his departure from Acton that he felt sure he had found his niche in life: 'One day he said, "I have missed my vocation. I have tried many things but I know now that I was meant to be a farmer." '[1]

For all their lack of experience and disinclination for acquiring new skills, the farming venture on which the family now embarked was on a fairly grandiose scale. It covered a substantial area of land, beautifully situated beside Lake Ontario and just outside the little town of Bronte, on the stretch of road between Toronto and Hamilton. Besides pedigree stock and the smaller animals, they grew fruit, and they employed a small regular staff, which was supplemented by groups of itinerant workers during the harvest season. The migrant workers, usually groups of native Indians, lived in wooden shacks on the edge of the property.[2]

Neighbours thought the Roches did not take farming seriously, and they watched with some amazement their unorthodox methods and activities. The father was, as usual, often away 'on business', but when he was home he used to lie flat on his back on the water with a book propped open on his stomach, a pastime that earned him the name 'W.R. Book' from the local children. The neighbours thought that the only member of the family with any practical sense was Caroline, and they observed that she worked like a slave for the Roches. They remembered Mazo treating the animals in her care as if they were pets or human members of the household; when they died, she organized funerals, enlisting the help of the local children as pall-bearers.[3]

Ronald Hambleton, in an apt phrase, has described Will Roche's tendency 'to galvanize his family into dances around his latest pose, or latest ambition'.[4] Once again the family was soon infected by his optimism: 'My mother agreed that she was meant to be a farmer's wife. Always he was able to inspire with his own enthusiasms.'[5] And her account of her father's first day on the job bears out her earlier remark that a fine actor was lost in him:

> My father, with his sense of the dramatic, appeared at breakfast, on our first morning there, dressed as he considered appropriately for a farmer. He wore corduroy breeches, leather leggings and an Irish tweed jacket. He looked magnificent. My mother and Caroline and I agreed that he had created the proper atmosphere.[6]

The family did not mock his histrionic gestures. Instead they took their cue from him and threw themselves into the act in the same whimsical spirit, each one selecting an area of speciality that sounded interesting. Will Roche indulged his fascination with pedigree and lineage by going into pedigree stock, his wife chose to rear turkeys, and Caroline 'for some reason known only to herself' decided to raise pigs. Mazo herself picked leghorn hens—'because I had been told they laid many large white eggs'—and eventually had two hundred of them.[7]

While it may seem odd that she she should choose just that area of farm labour traditionally designated as 'women's work', she had always been fascinated by birds. She identified with them and used them as her most basic images. Her novel *Possession* (1923) is set on a farm that is an exact rendering of the Roches', as she explained in a letter to W. A. Deacon at the time of its publication,[8] and the description of a visit by the main character and his brother to the poultry barn contains several of her recurrent motifs. The image of bird wings beating over someone's head, for instance, she used in a letter about this time: 'My life is filled with wind and weather and the beating wings of my own thoughts.'[9] Later she would use it again in the title of her novel *The Thunder of New Wings*. In *Possession* the brothers' visit takes place at Christmas, and the description of their interest in a large white turkey echoes the moment in the opening of Mazo's autobiography when she showed the great white owl to Caroline:

> The turkeys had got into the poultry house and were resting on the highest perch, pecking the heads of the unhappy fowls beneath, so that most of the hens had huddled together in a corner on the floor, while the cocks with ruffled plumage strode up and down before the perches, longing but not daring to attack the intruders. Derek began

to throw the turkeys out over the half-door. With heavy beating of wings they alit in the barnyard and, with scornful dignity, walked unhurriedly to the rail fence where they were supposed to perch.

'Why do they want to be in here?' asked Edmund, cautiously grasping the white hen-turkey.

'Pure cussedness. They know the fowls hate them, and they know we'll throw them out if we catch them, yet they persist.'

'Perhaps they're cold.'

'Not a bit. Feel the depth of that plumage.' He plunged his hand into the downy whiteness of her breast. She drew her head back sharply, uttering a strange hissing noise, and staring into his mouth with her wild black eyes.

'She'd like to peck out one of my teeth. Put your hand on her neck.'

'She's lovely. Like a graceful, pale woman. She's afraid poor thing. I'll send her after the others.' He dropped her lightly over the half-door, and they watched her as she delicately walked into the dusk, trailing her long feet.[10]

It was not, however, until ten years after the farm experiment that the novel was published. In the meantime Mazo's writing was progressing through the slow and fitful publication of short stories. In the first year at the farm she sold the two stories based on her Acton years and then succumbed to another long illness. Not specifying its nature, she wrote, 'I was severely ill for two years. Even now I am not strong.'[11] After the two years had elapsed she returned to the earlier fictional territory, writing another story that dealt with childhood experience and continuing the adventures of the three Curzon boys. She had a stroke of luck in that she placed her second story about them, 'Buried Treasure', in the *Atlantic Monthly*. Not only did she make a substantial sum but, even more significantly for her future career, she made an important ally by starting a friendly correspondence with the editor, Ellery Sedgewick.

On Sedgewick's part the correspondence was undertaken through a misunderstanding, for it was many years before he discovered that the contributor from Bronte was a woman in her mid-thirties. At first, seeing the unusual name, reading the stories about young boys, and getting letters in a childish handwriting, he assumed that Mazo was a teenaged boy. She enlightened him about her sex, but did not, then or later, tell him her age.[12] In subsequent letters she sought advice and poured out her troubles, including the family's desperate financial situation, the failing farm venture, and eventually her father's health. Sedgewick, imagining that he was writing to a gifted teenager burdened with terrible responsibilities beyond her years, was clearly moved by her persistence and courage, and he expressed a wish that they might meet.[13] She refused for two reasons. First, she did not have the money; second, she feared that he might be disappointed and she might return 'the very same Mazo that I went, not quite able to fit myself into any required niche'.[14] Her instincts were correct, for a meeting might have changed the course of her future career. Meanwhile, he continued to give encouragement. To her disappointment, and in spite of some unprofessionally pleading letters on her part, he turned down story after story. But he always gave sound criticism, which Mazo accepted, and she usually sold the stories elsewhere. Finally, four years after his first acceptance, he took another. He had liked 'Explorers of the Dawn' on submission, though he suggested that she might place it more advantageously with *Harper's*, where it would be illustrated; when *Harper's* rejected the story, he took it back.[15]

While Ellery Sedgewick was a distant and revered mentor, Mazo found another distinguished supporter nearer home. Her stories in Canadian magazines attracted the attention of Amelia Beers Garvin (née Warnock), who used the pen-name Katherine Hale. A respected journalist and writer who, as literary editor of the *Mail and Empire*, had established a reputation as a discerning critic, in 1914 she published her first volume of poetry, which was followed by two other volumes and, over the years, prose works as well. In another fifteen years her modest reputation would be far exceeded by Mazo's international fame, but in the early days Mazo looked up to Katherine Hale.

Katherine Hale wrote a colourful article on Mazo, which appeared prominently in February 1914 in the *Toronto Star Weekly*, with the title 'Joan of the Barnyard—A Young Poetess Who Loves Chickens'. She quotes Mazo: 'Did you know that chickens are my principal occupation in life just now? . . . I have hundreds of them to feed, and they must be starving.' The article features a picture of Mazo in traditional dairy-maid pose amid her chickens and it concludes with one of her poems. It also describes her pet animals, whom she calls by name, and quotes her extravagant words on the fascinating aspects of keeping hens:

> If you go in for chicken raising as I do, you live it all with them: the hatching, the care of the tiny tots, then the young scratching about and fighting, the loving and the mating, and the young again, and then of course sometimes the sudden and violent end. And always in entrance and exit they are dramatic. Then too there is such poetry: here are some old boxes scattered about. They seem to spell desolation to you, but

put a few bars across an open end and scatter a little hay on the ground and it becomes a home where there is, I believe, some love and a lot of fighting. Sometimes I make many little homes. . . .[16]

It would have been difficult for Mazo to avoid measuring herself against Katherine Hale. There was only one year's difference in their ages. They had lived in the same Ontario towns, and Mazo noted with interest that Katherine was also of mixed racial heritage—her father of Scotch descent and her mother from the southern United States. Yet Katherine had accomplished so much more than Mazo. She had studied singing in New York and was sought after for recitals; she had published a great deal; she held a job as a professional journalist; and in 1912 she had married John Garvin, a businessman who was also a respected critic and poet. Of course, she had started off with many more advantages than Mazo: a stable home life, education, material wealth, and a well-connected family, and perhaps the knowledge of these advantages tempered Mazo's sense of her own slow progress. She wrote a single paragraph about Katherine in her autobiography, which appeared in the year of the latter's death:

'Katherine Hale' was a member of the Galt family of Warnocks, long friends of my family. When my first short stories were published I looked up to her as a writer of experience. Indeed she was and has been connected with literary life in Toronto for the greater part of her own life, book critic for the Mail, a sensitive poet, and author of a number of books on Canada.[17]

It was true that the paths of the Roches and the Warnocks must have crossed before, perhaps when Mazo lived in the hotel in Galt where Katherine's father was a steel manufacturer. The Warnocks were also relatives of the prominent Massey family in Toronto, and Katherine had stayed with her mother at one of the large Massey homes on Jarvis Street for a time in the early 1900s when the Roches were renting places nearby. It seems unlikely, however, that they were close friends at that time, since the social difference between them was quite wide. But Mazo drew Katherine's attention by her writing, and eventually the whole Warnock family became loyal supporters. In acknowledgement of that support Mazo later dedicated a volume of her plays, *Low Life and Other Plays*, to Katherine's mother, wryly noting the Warnocks' position in society: 'To Mrs James Warnock, who, safe in her pleasant niche in High Life, is ever ready with gentle sympathy for those in Low Life.'[18] The support continued even after Mazo reached the pinnacle of success and had large sums of money to worry about:

then Katherine's brother-in-law, Edward Dimock, became her stock-broker and trusted financial adviser. The friendship, which lasted over forty years, naturally underwent many changes caused by distance, diverging interests, and the different shapes of their careers. Mazo's varying forms of address in her letters to Katherine mark some of these changes. At first, when both women were in their mid-thirties, Mazo writes to 'Dear Katherine Hale', although she signs herself 'lovingly Mazo'. Later she writes to 'Katherine', addressing her fondly as 'dearest' and 'darling', and eventually calls her by a diminutive 'Meme'. Mazo's letters are full of expressions of love, which suggest that she enjoyed with Katherine one of her few intimate female friendships.

At the same time, Mazo's attitude to Katherine Hale was tempered with awe. She had known at first hand few professional women, and none who balanced as effortlessly as Katherine did the roles of artist and wife. Now she had a close friend who shattered the idea of weak women dependent on men for status and protection. It was following Katherine's example that Mazo turned to writing poetry at this time, as her untitled poem at the end of the *Toronto Star* article indicates. The last stanza reads:

> Sleeping grass
> And singing rill!
> O, that kiss
> On Wonder Hill!
> Forget you may,
> Regret you will,
> The flowers that saw
> Remember still.[19]

Soon after they met, Mazo had written to Katherine: 'The way I see you oftenest is at the piano, with your chin upturned, singing. I love to watch you sing, because you sing with your chin and your eyes, and the outside of your throat as well as the inside.'[20] Her appreciation of Katherine's singing posture finds its way into two descriptions of singing women in her fiction: Minnie Ware in *Whiteoaks* and Fay Palmas in *Lark Ascending*. The latter novel was conceived during Mazo's first European trip and set in Sicily, from where she wrote to Katherine in 1929: 'I have that little picture of you with me, and it is one of the first things I set up on my dressing table. There you are, first thing in the morning and last thing at night, smiling out at me!'[21] Later, when Mazo was living in England:

I kissed the little leaf you sent in your letter. It had grown in a place I love and had been touched by one I love.[22]

I am counting the months till I see you, I long for you as I long for Canadian sunshine. Last night we heard Phyllis Neilson-Terry sing a group of Shakespeare's songs over the wireless. It might have been you! . . . Darling, I do remember that night in Russell Hill Road.[23]

Caroline seems never to have felt quite as much warmth for Katherine as Mazo did, and instead formed close friendships with others in Katherine's family. While Mazo wrote frequently to Katherine, Caroline had her own correspondence with Katherine's sister and brother-in-law, Anne and Edward Dimock, and was particularly fond of Katherine's husband.

Nor was Katherine Caroline's only rival for Mazo's attention in this period. There was a male suitor, perhaps the only serious prospect of marriage Mazo ever had: 'As I grew older and young men appeared on the scene, I invariably compared them with [my father] to their disadvantage—till the day when one arrived who could better bear comparison with him.'[24] Pierre Fritz Mansbendel did bear comparison, in part because he shared the French quality that Mazo attributed—without much evidence—to her father's family. A civil engineer in his late thirties who had lived and worked in the United States before coming to Canada, he came from Mulhausen, a part of French-speaking Germany that was returned to France after 1918. As his name suggests, Pierre too was of mixed racial heritage, but Mazo was characteristically selective in describing him: for her he was purely French. His family called him 'Fritz' and 'Fritzi', but to Mazo he was always 'Pierre'.[25]

They met on one of Mazo's visits to Toronto when she happened to be alone; as usual, she was staying with Aunt Eva in the rooming house that the latter, now widowed, had established. Probably Pierre was a paying guest, although the autobiography suggests that he was invited to occupy the top floor of the rooming house only after they had become friends.[26] The two had much in common, reading together, dining out, going to the theatre. Later, when he went out to stay at the farm, Mazo's mother and Caroline had heard so much about Pierre that they were 'prepared to like him'. Mazo's father, however, was less enthusiastic: when the meeting took place, his only comment was a coolly dismissive 'What French eyebrows he has!'[27] His reaction suggests that Will Roche shared some of the patriarchal traits of Grandfather Lundy, disliking his daughter's suitors and not wishing to have his family circle disrupted.

The impression that Pierre made on women was generally one of startling good looks. Years later, Mazo's adopted daughter called her Uncle Pierre the most handsome man she had ever met.[28] 'Am I expected to get used to having that dazzling beauty about the house?'[29] Alberta Roche asked, when he arrrived. Noting that she herself was just as susceptible as her mother to good looks in men, Mazo was genuinely appreciative of Pierre's physical attributes:

> He possessed indeed a sculptured beauty of feature. His hair was thick, jet black and very straight; his head well set on a strong neck; his long, amber-colored eyes beneath clearly-marked brows; his lips full and arrogantly curved, his complexion with no trace of olive but almost fair in its fresh good health. I have never seen more perfect teeth.[30]

Nevertheless, Pierre thought of himself as deformed: as a result of a childhood bout with polio one leg was shorter than the other. In Mazo's eyes this blemish may have added to his fascination, for several of her fictional characters suffer from similar afflictions.

Recalling Mazo's reaction to Caroline's handsome foreign 'beau' several years earlier, one may wonder how Caroline felt, faced with a similar liaison. But in the autobiography Mazo takes up the subject of Caroline's reaction as if for the first time: 'While writing this I have asked Caroline to tell me what were her feelings toward Pierre at that time. She thought a moment and then answered: 'I felt both antagonism and fear. . . . I don't know why it was, but that was what I felt.' '[31] At the time, apparently, Caroline's approval was not sought, nor her disapproval expressed. There was no offended turning of Caroline's back on Mazo, as the latter had done to her.

Perhaps Caroline was aware that Mazo and Pierre were not carrying on any kind of courtship or amorous relationship, and knew that—whatever the rest of the family thought—they would never be more than friends. Mazo's grandmother, however, said that she had never seen a man more in love.[32] Perhaps she misinterpreted Pierre's European gallantry; perhaps she simply cast a romantic aura over the friendship, as relatives often tend to do.

Everything indicates that Pierre treated Mazo as her father did, with a male camaraderie, as someone to be cherished for her masculine traits. In fact, Pierre seems to have had little appreciation for the kind of female qualities that Caroline, for instance, manifested. Mazo describes his condescension:

> Pierre's attitude toward her was one of complete lack of understanding. Because she was small and blonde and pretty he thought of her as frivolous—ignoring her cool, critical quality. Once, when she picked

up a book of essays he had been reading, he took it from her with a curt, 'But, my dear, you would not yet understand this'—and deeply offended her.[33]

Mazo, for her part, was not inclined to assume the role of desirable and alluring female. When she mentions sex, she makes it clear that she was not interested sexually in the young men she knew; furthermore, she had an aversion to being touched:

> As I remember, we and our friends talked not at all of sex or marriage as a reality, though we were enthralled by it in romantic fiction and the theatre. The reason for this, I think, was that the times were hard. There was little money in the hands of young men. . . . As for us growing girls, sex was scarcely a reality. Indeed we felt something ugly in the word. We were captivated by the romance in stories like *The Prisoner of Zenda* and Richard Harding Davis' *Princess Aline*.[34]

> When I had been smoking a surreptious cigarette with him [a young man named Gordon], at night on the verandah, and he had put his arm about me, I had swiftly withdrawn. I was like a highly strung filly that will not endure a hand laid on her.[35]

> There were incipient affairs of the heart, though the memory of Roderigo made Caroline supercilious toward these provincial youths, and I retained my dislike of being touched. An attempt at hand-holding, a hand stealing toward my waist was enough to make me fiercely withdraw. I loved to attract but to hold bored me. Also there was something almost boyish in me. I looked on sex as rather silly. There was so much that was more interesting.[36]

Apparently the aversion to physical contact applied only to men: Mazo wrote to Katherine Hale, 'Darling, my arms are about you! Can you feel them!' and 'A great hefty hug and a kiss from your Mazo.'[37]

But there were other aspects of male friendship besides the physical part that Mazo disliked. She was unwilling to subordinate her own interests to Pierre's: 'I wanted him to give me freedom to be myself without hindrance. He craved freedom to be moody or gay as he chose, without regard for me.'[38] When Pierre developed a passion for kite-flying, she was frankly bored and made no attempt to hide it: 'It was not in me to be the sort of female who knows no boredom, no fatigue, so long as she can trail after the man she fancies.'[39] And after one of his visits to the farm she was restive at the interruption in her writing schedule: 'When Pierre's visit was over I returned to the story with a tranquillity I could not find when he was in the house with me.'[40]

Clearly Mazo was a lukewarm partner in this relationship. Yet even if Pierre was no more interested in physical intimacy, as he approached forty he was seeking the stability of a permanent home, and the companionship and convenience of a wife who would look after him. He surprised the family one night on a visit to the fruit farm by declaring: 'There are those who say, and it is often said in my country, that a man should marry for convenience—for a housekeeper rather than for love.'[41]

He surprised them even more when, some time later, they became aware of the significance of that remark. During the time he had spent in Aunt Eva's house, he had been the object of not only her solicitous attentions, but also her matrimonial hopes. After all, he was strikingly handsome, youthful, and engaged in a well-paying profession. She had shown him the advantages of having a good housekeeper when she nursed him through tonsillitis, and although at first Pierre had paid her 'no more than a polite consideration' she had shown her superiority over her niece as a companion by sharing his enthusiasm for kite-flying. 'It was amusing', says Mazo, 'to see this trig little middle-aged woman doggedly pursuing the movements of the kite.'[42] She also makes Aunt Eva twenty years older than Pierre, although the real difference was only nine years.[43] When the pair announced their intention to marry, the gamut of emotions in the Roche family can easily be guessed at. Caroline must have been relieved, Alberta and Will Roche astonished, and Mazo—even if she did not want to marry—more than a little hurt. She must also have had a sense of déjà vu, remembering from her childhood the strange scene of Aunt Eva's advances towards Will Roche.

A marriage between Mazo and Pierre was clearly unthinkable. Judging by the Jalna novels, she had very little understanding of heterosexual relationships or of sexual habits between married couples. And even if Pierre had imagined an unconsummated marriage (as his declaration about the purpose of marriage may suggest) she could never have assumed the role of 'wife'. Yet she long cherished the illusion of Pierre as a kind of lost love, and he became part of the legend that surrounded her life.

Even though Pierre and Eva moved to New York City, they kept in close touch with Mazo, who visited them both before and after her successful career took her there; in later years they would often be on hand at the dock when she sailed for Europe. She describes her relationship with Pierre in the early days of his marriage as being tinged with embarrassment. If Aunt Eva surprised them in private conversation they started guiltily, just as Mazo and Caroline had done as children when Aunt Eva came into the room. Mazo reports that Pierre soon felt trapped in the marriage and he began to look at her reproachfully, as if she were responsible for his predicament.[44] Her words are borne out by other members of the family: a cousin's wife described Pierre as 'a prince' and Aunt Eva as 'a very difficult woman to live with because she was used to being spoilt by everyone'.[45] Nevertheless, the friendship beween Mazo and Pierre grew and mellowed over the years. After Aunt Eva's death, he made annual visits to stay with Mazo in Toronto; when he died he left her a gift of $1,000 and Caroline one of $500.[46]

The longevity of Mazo's friendships both with Pierre and with Katherine Hale testifies to the intensity and unusual nature of her relationships. In both cases there were erotic overtones. Her appreciation of Katherine's beauty of appearance and manner suggests a physical attraction. And her description of her feelings when meeting Pierre at the train certainly echoes the standard romantic evocations of sexual excitement: 'When I heard the train's whistle, my heart beat with painful excitement. When I went toward him on the platform and saw his face alight with pleasure, my legs trembled beneath me and he exclaimed at my pallor.'[47] Both Katherine and Pierre were muse figures in the sense that they inspired certain fictional works and served as models for characters in them—although the equation between actual people and characters in her work is not direct. (Her use of Finch Whiteoak as her personal representative was the exception rather than the rule). It was as if her family and friends formed a resident company of actors who, more or less type-cast by Mazo, played a series of versions of themselves; sometimes aspects of the players were joined with aspects of their creator to form a character. And because the characters were linked to her family and friends, her attitude towards them varied. Some are lovingly, even passionately drawn, and some bear the brunt of her hostility.

With Katherine and Pierre Mazo entered into relationships that also involved others. In the friendship with Katherine, Caroline played an uneasy extra partner, as did Katherine's businessman husband, John Garvin; in the relationship with Pierre she was displaced by Aunt Eva. These triangles were projected into the fiction. In *Whiteoaks* the songstress Minnie Ware lures the poet Eden Whiteoak away from his estranged wife, Alayne; in *Lark Ascending* Fay Palmas leaves her staid admirer Purley Bond for an exotic Sicilian count; and in *Whiteoak Heritage* a very young Eden Whiteoak falls into the snares of an experienced older seductress, the widow Amy Stroud. Pierre contributes something also to the lame orphan boy in *The Boy in the House*, and a great deal to Piers Whiteoak, the handsome farmer who returns from the Second World War and a prisoner-of-war camp missing a leg.

All the same, in spite of her sensuous enjoyment of her two friends, Mazo could not avoid a sense of her own oddness, of existing in a kind of no-man's-land. Just as she felt herself caught between the gender polarities of man and woman, not wanting either extreme, so she felt caught between the rigid and mutually exclusive alternatives for sexual relationships. What she felt for Katherine and Pierre was not mere friendship—it was far more erotic than that. But her eroticism did not imply a need for physical consummation.

In an earlier era Mazo might have found more acceptance of such friendships.[48] But she lived in a time when all human relationships—even those between women—were being anatomized. Richard von Krafft-Ebing, Sigmund Freud, and Havelock Ellis had done their work, and while she would not have read it herself, the general climate of opinion was coloured and changed by their theories. She knew that in the eyes of the world, she would be considered a freak.

In an unpublished poem written about this time, Mazo expressed her sense of not-belonging by projecting it onto that misfit of the barnyard, the guinea fowl. She describes the creature as 'shamed' by its lack of sex appeal to the other birds and by its exclusion from the joys of mating. Only in dream does the guinea fowl find fulfilment:

The Guinea Fowl
Shut in the yard with forty hens,
And four cocks, flushed and game,
It glides in angry, graceful darts,
Forgetting not its shame,

In all the gobbling, greedy flock,
That scratches, squawks and pecks,
Not one a fallen feather cares
What is the guinea's sex.

It is but there to guard the flock,
From swooping hawk or crow
By warning wild it earns its keep,
Nor mating joys can know.

The pullet preens her milk-white breast,
Sweet glow her amber eyes,
The cockerel his wattles shakes
And his young ardour tries

But pouting breast and glowing eyes
And wattles red as fire,
Provoke no stir in Guinea's blood
Awake no fond desire.

With lacy plummage drooping low.
With tragic, painted face,
In and about the scurrying flock
It runs its fruitless race.

Yet dreaming on the perch at night,
Where two plump hens make room,
Who knows what other painted face
May beckon through the gloom?[49]

8

Emerging from the Parental Shadow

While Mazo may have been rationalizing when she said in her autobiography that she could not make a commitment to Pierre because her family needed her,[1] she was not exaggerating the crisis at home. The idyllic situation of the early months on the fruit farm, when the Roches coasted along on the work of the previous occupants, was short-lived. Soon the problems of unreliable help, crop failures, accidents, and illnesses among the animals began to take their toll. In addition, a series of family deaths had occurred; there were many visits to the family plots in the Newmarket cemetery where both the Roches and the Lundys were buried. The first to go, in 1911, was Mazo's 86-year-old grandmother, Sarah Roche.[2] (It may have been a legacy from her that allowed Will Roche eventually to purchase the farm.) In a way, her death was the least painful since she had never been a part of Mazo's immediate family. The death of Louise Lundy, on the other hand, was painful, because she had been such a fixture in Mazo's early years.[3] Next, George Lundy, Alberta's oldest brother, died prematurely, at the age of fifty-two, in 1914.[4] Her trip to Buffalo for his funeral may have been the basis of 'Freedom',[5] a story in which the Curzon boys have a wonderful holiday from Mrs Handsomebody's strict regime and see a different aspect of her when she reappears; she is softened by grief and treats them tenderly, 'crying about a little *wee* boy . . . she used to cuddle long ago.'

The next blow was the most severe of Mazo's life. Late in 1914 she discovered that her father had only a few months to live. Ten years later she told Katherine Hale:

As for my darling father—Dr Carven, when he examined him in August, said it would be a miracle if he lived till Christmas. And he lived till the next July. I cannot let myself think of it. He and I were like one person in some ways. I loved him too much. I remember going to the shore and throwing myself on the stones. I remember how the noise of the waves drowned my screams.[6]

Deaths were always likely to upset the delicate balance of Mazo's psyche and make her feel either strengthened or dangerously weakened. Her father's death gave her a frightening sense that her world was disintegrating, because it reversed her deep-rooted sense of male strength and female fragility. Her shock at this reversal is recorded in the autobiography by her juxtaposition of two scenes. In the first she describes herself (rather like Jane Eyre, watching unobserved as the blind and feeble Rochester emerges from his house) coming upon her father leaning on his wife's arm:

> I stood at the edge of the bluff watching them as they moved slowly toward the house. But—was that really my father? That gaunt man whose coat hung loosely on his broad shoulders—whose dark eyes looked so large and hollow? . . . And that was he—leaning on the arm of my frail mother![7]

Mazo follows this scene with one of herself lying, as she had told Katherine Hale, on the stones beside the lake, screaming in anguish:

> I stumbled down the side of the bluff to the stony shore. . . . There were the tumbling green waves, casting themselves with thunder on the stones. It was the time of the equinox. Their roar was my fastness. I heard someone giving terrible cries—hoarse cries, as though torn from the breast. Surely it could not be I who uttered them. . . .[8]

In her fictional variations on this scene her characters often cry, 'I am nothing'. Mazo does not specify the cause of her father's death, speaking of it vaguely as a decline. He was only sixty-two, and it seems likely that any physical ailment must have been aggravated by his disappointment in yet another failed career—especially if that included the loss of his mother's legacy. Mazo states unequivocally that they were now 'ruined'. The farm and all their assets were sold (an event recorded in the farm sale in *Possession*) and they rented half of a small furnished house while they waited for Will Roche to die. Six months before the death, she wrote plaintively to Ellery Sedgewick that they had moved to the farm four years ago, she had sold two stories the same year and had then been severely ill for two years. 'Even now I am not strong':

> The farming turned out to be a failure and m, father, who still continued his town business has been obliged to expend all his income to repair

our losses here, and in fertilizer for this picturesque waste of sand [?] to which we are tied.

Last August he contracted a serious illness, from which he has not yet recovered, and which has made it necessary for him to resign his position. So you can understand how precarious our position is, with our rent going behind and our resources failing. . . . I only tell it that you may . . . better understand what my writing means to me—a hope for the future of my parents and my adopted sister, a refuge from worries, and a perpetual springing life within me that will not be quenched.[9]

It may seem surprising that Mazo, with her newly recovered and precarious equanimity, should have coped with the dual loss of her home and her father as well as she did. In order to do so she drew upon three time-honoured means. The first, as she had learned early from her maternal grandparents, was silence:

My uncle insisted that hope should not be taken from us. All through the winter that followed we lived in hope—otherwise we could not have borne it. Or did we only pretend we hoped? Certainly, everything we saw was evidence against hope. We were ruined financially and knew it, but never acknowledged it even to each other. . . .[10]

We waited for what was going to happen in that house of which we occupied half. . . . Never did we acknowledge what we waited for— only lived from day to day.[11]

Next, Mazo was able to give her father a gift that cheered his last months much as Caroline's arrival had brightened her own life years before. He asked for a dog, and she found a small female Scottie (of champion stock) that he could train, care for, and play with. In fact, she uses the same words and phrases to describe the two arrivals. Like Caroline, Bunty is said to have arrived at Christmas when the snow was whirling. She came on a sleigh and was carried into the midst of the waiting family where the uncovering and the showing forth took place. And Mazo describes the little dog as manifesting the same characteristics Caroline did on her arrival—curiosity, timidity, roguish interest, and, above all, courage. Even the phrase 'What appalling changes for a tiny being' echoes her comment on Caroline's arrival.[12]

The third means of survival during the death watch was the predictable one: retreat into the seductive and controllable world of the Play:

Isolated so, and thrusting from our minds the shadows that deepened about us, we would throw ourselves into our Play with an almost impassioned eagerness. From my fertile brain a new situation or plot would emerge and we would so sink ourselves in it that our characters took on a most vivid reality. In their imagined suffering we relieved our own. In their pleasure we took deep breaths of reflected pleasure. Three characters in particular became our favorites and so identified with us, regardless of sex, that we indeed became them. A slight change in the manner of speaking was enough to identify them. Like a fresh wind they came to us.[13]

Thus tragedy brought about a new phase in the growth of the Play.

When Will Roche finally died, the person most affected besides the thirty-six-year-old Mazo was her father's elder brother, Danford Roche; he and Mazo clung together and wept. Ever-practical Caroline took care of the arrangements for the funeral; as Mazo says, she 'attended to the things that had to be done'. She describes her mother's reaction as restrained: 'not a tear fell from my mother's eyes'; as at the death of her own father, Alberta Roche once again 'bore her heartbreak'.[14] Possibly the deaths of these two men who had so complicated her life were not unmitigated disasters. Mazo noted that her mother showed remarkable control during the main tragedies of her life. All the same, Mazo's perception that her father was mourned more by his brother than by his wife must have reinforced her sense of the strength of brotherly love compared with the weaker marital bond.

The mother, once again demonstrating the family's love of play-acting, threw herself whole-heartedly into the role of widow, and devised an attractive costume:

She was a striking figure in her mourning black, for she was beautifully proportioned, erect, and had clear-cut aquiline features, fair skin and dark blue eyes. She had had a small hat, with a short but wide widow's veil, made for her, and this was most becoming. Her hair, that just showed beneath the brim, was a light, rather gingerish brown. Her hands and feet were beautiful.[15]

Another of the Alberta's gestures was more enigmatic. All her life she had suffered from her husband's love of dogs. Yet one of her first acts after her husband's death, in spite of the cost, inconvenience, and the fact that they already had one, was to insist on purchasing a dog of her own. Once Mazo and Caroline had been persuaded, she selected an ugly puppy with a 'horrified yellow eye', and appeared 'elated, flushed, her eyes shining'.[16] Was this choice of a dog remarkable for its lack of caste, the quintessentially ugly mongrel, an act of defiance—a celebration of freedom from her husband's taste for expensive dogs with long pedigrees?

With the two dogs the women then established themselves in a rented house on Huron Street in Toronto. Mazo describes them as 'three fragile women, with almost invisible means of support'[17]—a very uncharacteristic form of self-description for her, and perhaps a justification of the steps she and Caroline were now forced to take in earning a living.

Although Mazo would never have admitted as much, her father's death was a liberating event for all three women. He had never been a dependable provider, but as long as he was the nominal head of the household, it had not been possible for the women to step in and provide a stable income. Once they were bereaved, they were free to do what was necessary, and while they were not lavish, life was easier.

Mazo's mother in her sixties was not prepared to change her way of life: because she expected to live in a comfortable house, one was rented. Because she also expected to spend the summer by a lake, they would rent a city house and let it go during the summer, to avoid paying rent on two places. Apart from looking after the house, one of Alberta Roche's main occupations during these war years was the knitting of socks for the soldiers.[18] (Mazo regarded this work with some scepticism, as her mother insisted on knitting only white socks, an impractical colour for use in the trenches.)

Mazo continued to work at her writing, the only kind of work that was congenial for her. As she had already sold stories for considerable sums, it might seem that she was continuing as before, but in fact there was a significant difference. Whereas in the past she had often spent her earnings on luxury items, she now used them for living expenses. And since the household depended on her earnings, her status changed in a subtle but important way. She was set, as she approached forty, on the road to becoming a professional writer.

Still, Mazo's earnings were variable, and it fell to Caroline to provide the family's main income. She found a job as a filing clerk in the legislative building and quickly moved up through the ranks to the responsible position of Chief Statistician. She once described her contribution to the family this way:

> I supplied the bread and butter and the roof after her father died. Everything had to go and we were in very straightened circumstances; and her mother wasn't used to privations of any kind or even economies of any kind, and we had to change our mode of living drastically. I had a small sum of money which I had inherited from my grandfather, but I felt like the man of the family then, I felt Mazo must go on with her writing.[19]

It is hard not to conclude that the others took advantage of her. She was now in her early thirties, a beautiful and clever woman who might reasonably have expected more from life than the burden of working to provide for Mazo and Alberta Roche. Mazo, looking back, seems to acknowledge a certain selfishness: 'I took it for granted that she should be the principal pillar of our little household.'[20] During the summers Mazo and her mother took a cottage at Lake Simcoe, leaving Caroline in a rooming house (their own house was rented to provide funds for the cottage) to come out on weekends and join them for her two-week summer vacation. The situation suggests that the family felt she owed them something, and that she agreed.

On the other hand, Caroline seemed to slip naturally into the role of provider and to relish being the mainstay of the family. She had even less education than Mazo, since her heart problems had prevented regular attendance at school. Relegated to the domestic arena, she had been quite happy to develop traditionally female skills. Already, on the farm, she had learned the satisfaction of being the practical, capable one on whom everyone else depended: it gave her status in the family and made her indispensable. It was she who coped with the practical arrangements of Will Roche's funeral, and now she stepped in to provide for the two other women. Mazo describes her at this time:

> The position in the Civil Service to which she had looked forward was not for a time forthcoming. In the meanwhile she secured one job after another, always bettering herself. She had a talent for appearing to know more than she did, and there was something in her face that inspired confidence. Before a year had passed she was firmly established in a post in the Parliament buildings.[21]

Evidently Caroline maximized her talents by bluffing a little: when responsibility was thrust on her she accepted it eagerly and quickly mastered the necessary skills. And along the way she acquired secretarial skills useful to Mazo's writing. Thus the two women embarked on the careers they would pursue in the future: Mazo as professional writer and Caroline as the writer's helpmate, companion, and secretary.

In 1920 this period of growth, change, and freedom culminated in a final liberating event: the death of Alberta Roche. All three women had succumbed to the plague of influenza that swept across the North American continent at the end of the First World War. Mazo and Caroline survived, but Alberta did not. Her death was sudden, and she was buried beside her husband in an unmarked grave in the Newmarket cemetery. Mazo often spoke later of her parents' deaths, within five years of each other, as the great tragedies of her life. No doubt her mother's death reactivated all the sorrow of her father's, for Caroline was frightened enough to write a letter—introducing herself as Mazo's sister—to Ellery Sedgewick and ask for his help:

> Not only the health but the mind of my sister has suffered by this shock and she feels that she no longer has the incentive or even the power to write. It seems to me that a word of encouragement from you might be of great value to her in these tragic days. Her gifts are too precious to be thrown aside.[22]

Sedgewick, with his usual patience and courtesy, wrote a short letter of encouragement,[23] and Mazo did recover. Her mother's death was not a blow of the same gravity as her father's, and, though ever the dutiful daughter in her remarks about her mother, the regrets quickly gave way to accounts of new-found happiness. Her first Christmas alone with Caroline turned out to be a wonderful time of parties and play-acting, for they were invited to be house-guests of the Garvins 'in their delightful house in Russell Hill Road'.[24] Now at last Mazo could live exactly as she liked, working, making friends, going about as she wished—without having to placate her mother, worry about leaving her alone, and face returning from every outing to that presence whose mental and physical suffering had been a terrifying fixture of her life.

In the previous decade she produced a mere dozen or so short stories. Ten of these were collected in the volume *Explorers of the Dawn*, which was published in 1922 by Macmillan in Canada, Knopf in the US, and Cassell and Company in England. Yet the small output of short stories is a misleading gauge of what she accomplished, for the events of this time provided a wealth of material on which she would draw for the rest of her life. 'A writer's childhood is his capital,' said Graham Greene. For many writers that is true, but for Mazo it was her fourth decade, when she was gradually shedding her parental influence, that provided that capital.

When the Roche family had been forced to leave the farm and move into more modest accommodations, the new place offered a rich setting for fiction:

> This was a strange house to which we moved, part of it old and weather-beaten, covered by vines and climbing roses. The remainder, a much later addition, was always called 'the new wing' by the owners, though it was more than fifty years old. It was like a separate house, for it had its own front door and porch, its own hall and drawing-room, sparsely furnished with some good pieces brought from England by the naval officer who had built the house. His two daughters lived in the old part. A portrait of this officer hung in our livingroom and there was a gilt-framed mirror and a marble-topped table.[25]

During the months of the death watch Mazo apparently brooded on the 'strange' arrangement of the two families living side by side under one roof. On one side was the family unit of which she was a part, and on the other two elderly sisters whom she described as 'strange, sensitive, neurotic creatures'.[26] The arrangement provided an image for Mazo's own past, when she and Caroline had created their own private space while living under the same roof as their family. The 'divided house' became a recurring and important fixture in her personal iconography, and appeared in numerous subsequent fictions. It is used most extensively in the novella *The Boy in the House* (not published until 1952), where the description of the house is so vivid as to suggest that an early draft was written while she lived there. Indeed, she sent an early version to Ellery Sedgewick in 1924, with the explanation that 'Teddy' was a real boy, 'a pathetic little fellow'.[27]

Yet in spite of the sparcity of publications there are many signs that towards the end of her thirties Mazo was growing as an artist. The short stories were becoming more mature as she moved from using extraneous material to tapping her own inner emotions. The subject matter is really more suitable for children's literature. But nearing the end of the period she struggled to express her own deep and barely articulated inner conflicts.

One story in particular, 'The Cobbler and the Cobbler's Wife', presents so complete a condensation of Mazo's main themes that it provides a key to all her future works. The first story she submitted for publication after her mother's death, it was rejected by Ellery Sedgewick in December 1930 because, although it was readable, 'a common sense judgement would hold it too imaginative for *The Atlantic*'.[28] A summary of the various elements will show how complex the story is for a fiction of twenty-five pages:

1. The three boys, David, John and Alexander Curzon, go to a dark, woolly-haired cobbler who breeds canaries—and who Mrs Handsomebody says is 'half-gypsy'—to have some shoes repaired. When Mrs Handsomebody feels that they have been overcharged, she gets the cobbler (Mr Martindale) to repair her own 'prunella gaiter'.

2. Inserted in the above is a story told to the boys while they wait for the shoe repair, a tale with a Prometheus motif about a young student who is brewing a potion that will benefit all mankind. As he does so he unwittingly asphyxiates a nest of birds. The entire bird population masses together—darkening the sky, turning day to night—descends, and tears him apart.

3. The cobbler asks the boys to take care of a large caged bird called Coppertoes. He does so because his wife—who has been mad since the gypsies stole her daughter at birth—is suffering from a delusion that Coppertoes will come out of his cage, swoop about the house at night, peck food, and make a nest in her hair. When the boys take the bird home, it attacks and tears apart the cage of stuffed birds. Mrs Handsomebody imagines that one of the stuffed birds has come to life. Gasping 'Come to life after all these years', she falls unconscious.

4. The fourth episode is the most interesting and bizarre of all. Late at night the three boys see the cobbler hurrying off to a pond where his wife has gone to drown herself. He is joined in his rescue operation by the three boys and a lamplighter. By a wild coincidence, the cobbler's long-lost daughter, now eighteen, heads for the same pool, at the same time, to drown herself. She does not know who she is (she doesn't even have a name) and cries, 'I am nothing'. The daughter has to enter the pool in a gingerly way to avoid stepping on the mother. The men rescue the girl and the mother is drowned. The cobbler recognizes his daughter by a cleft in her ear where she was pecked at birth by a jealous bird. They are reunited and live happily after, no one giving much thought or regret to the drowned mother. After celebrating the reunion of the cobbler and his daughter, the boys return to Mrs Handsomebody, who seems somewhat mellowed after her shock with the stuffed birds.

Clearly many 'little things' identifiable from the autobiography have pushed their way into this story, including the ubiquitous owl from the landing of the Lundy house. In the cobbler's unsuccessful effort to rescue his drowning wife, the struggle 'shattered the reflection of the moon like pale amber glass'. The detail is reminiscent of Mazo's gift to her mother of 'an ornate lamp, the base of wrought iron, the bowl of bronze, the shade of beautiful amber glass, like a full moon'[29]— the same shade that was broken and caused Alberta such grief. Finally, the asphyxiation of the birds recalls Mazo's breakdown during which 'all that happened was exaggerated. When my pet canary was asphyxiated in his cage from the fumes of a gas heater, all that night I relived his suffering.'[30]

Among the motifs that Mazo struggled to express in this story are the following:

1. The Prometheus figure who is able to bring light and life to mankind is doomed to be tormented for doing so. And the tormentors are in the form of birds.

2. There is a daughter marked (or maimed) at birth by a jealous fate (again in the form of a bird). Lost among alien people, she is driven to despair and self-annihilation by not knowing her own identity.

3. Finally she is restored to her father, her rightful heritage, and her sense of identity simultaneously with the death of her mother. This curious episode recalls Virginia Woolf's statement that before a woman can write she must kill the angel in the house; as Phyllis Rose has pointed out, it was Virginia Woolf's mother who was the personification in her life of the angel in the house.[31]

'The Cobbler and the Cobbler's Wife' is a powerful manifestation of the feelings that Mazo could express only indirectly at the death of her mother. It is not surprising that she should have drawn on fairy-tale elements: the capacity of fairy-tales to yoke together overt and covert meanings, to use broad supernatural effects to suggest buried emotions, was naturally appealing to her. (Mazo also related to writers who managed to use such effects in their work—Isak Dinesen's *Seven Gothic Tales*, for instance, was a favourite with both Mazo and Caroline.)

The problem was that Mazo's experiences and gender confusion were so unconventional that a very innovative form was necessary to express them. She was not alone among women writers in needing a new form of expression; many of her contemporaries found their own. Gertrude Stein was engaging in daring literary experiments, as were Virginia Woolf, Djuna Barnes, and others. But Mazo, writing in a provincial backwater, was not aware of the possibilities that were opening up for such expression. She wavered uneasily between the dominant form of realism (clearly the form that was least able to serve her) and her memories of fairy-tales. Perhaps she never really found the form best suited to the expression of her psyche.

Mazo must have known that 'The Cobbler and the Cobbler's Wife' was not successful, for she was unable to place it in any journal. Yet it is in some ways her most complex and interesting story. It is certainly the one most revealing of her art and her life in 1920.

9

Delight

If ever in her life Mazo de la Roche came close to being happy, it was when, after the death of her mother, she was free for the first time to live alone with Caroline. Mazo herself would have been horrified by the suggestion that that death was a liberating event, but the two women had enjoyed neither a happy childhood nor a carefree adolescence, and even as adults they had been subject both to the approval of an older generation and to the need to protect the mental stability of Alberta Roche. Later, financial success and fame would bring their own responsibilities and problems. But for a few years in the early 1920s Mazo could do exactly as she liked.

The new life did not begin immediately after Alberta Roche's death, for both Mazo and Caroline went to visit relatives. Mazo's holiday with Pierre and Eva in New York was not pleasant, partly because of the oppressive heat and partly because of her discomfort in Pierre's company since the marriage. She escaped as often as she could and walked with Bunty, who was now completely blind, around the streets of the neighbourhood. She could hardly wait for the visit to end. When she finally got back to Toronto, the reunion with Caroline was ecstatic:

> We (Bunty and I) left New York at a time of torrid heat but in Toronto a cool breeze was blowing. Caroline met me at the Union Station. As the train drew in it was easy to distinguish her in the crowd on the platform, slim and straight in her black and white dress, a wing of bright hair against her little black hat. How pale her face was and how blue her eyes!
>
> After the sorrow, after the separation, it was an almost unbearable happiness to be together again.[1]

Already the two women had adopted each other as sisters,[2] the nearest they could come to formalizing their relationship and ritualizing their life-long commitment to each other. From this time forth, there was never any question of suitors or other close relationships for either woman.

Immediately after their reunion, they went north for a summer holiday, sub-letting their Toronto home in order to pay the rent on a flat with a pleasant verandah above a launch-house in Muskoka. The launch-house was beside a sheltered bay, surrounded by dense woods, and they had a row boat and a canoe at their disposal, both of which they used, even though neither could swim. At night they sat on the verandah, looking out over the lake and listening to the loon. They took the flat for two summers in a row, and although the second was spoilt by terrific heat—there was no refrigerator, and Mazo remembered dripping butter from a spoon onto pieces of bread—their joyous mood was not dispelled:

> In spite of all this discomfort we often were gay. Our laughter would mingle with the laughter of the loon, as we dipped our oars into the dark water and saw the great red moon rise out of the wood. Even then there was no lapping of the lake on the shore—just a breathless tropic stillness.[3]

Her accounts are full of her sense of returning vigour: 'it was a time of return to physical vitality'; 'my health wonderfully improved'.[4] The greatest joy of this time was that it brought a great surge of creative energy. No longer were short stories squeezed out painfully at infrequent intervals: plays and full-length novels began to pour forth.

Even as the new work was getting under way, Mazo had the satisfaction of seeing the short stories of the previous decade appear as the collection *Explorers of the Dawn*. A curious book about three children, it seemed poised mid-way between children's literature and adult fiction. Christopher Morley, in his Foreword, tried to place it in a context:

> There will be some readers, I think, who will look through it as through an open window, into a land of clear gusty winds and March sunshine and volleying church bells on Sunday mornings, into a land of terrible contradictions, a land whose émigrés look back to it tenderly, yet without too poignant regret—the Almost Forgotten Land of childhood.[5]

Mazo wrote the dedication to her mother: 'But a short while ago, A. de la R. laughed with me over the adventures of these little fellows. To the memory of that happy laughter I dedicate the book.'

It is fairly safe to conclude that Alberta Roche would not have found Mazo's subsequent works so amusing. Their basis in the family's life, their frank sexuality, and their language would certainly have offended her sense of propriety. The first of these novels was *Possession*, 'conceived' during the first idyllic summer in Muskoka[6] and finished the fall after the second, when Mazo stayed on alone to complete the work. She needed to be alone—away even from Caroline—for such a task.

Her feelings about the book are expressed in a letter to William Arthur Deacon, who had recently taken over as literary editor of *Saturday Night* and whose opinions already carried some weight:

> I see . . . that you will review my novel *Possession*. Someway, before you read it, I want to tell you that I lived on just such a farm as Grimstone for years, so that I know the life whereof I write. I have tried with all the power that is in me to depict the life on this farm, in that warm belt of Western Ontario, where on a fine day the spray of Niagara is visible. I have tried to reproduce something of the mingling of the old and the new world beneath the roof of Grimstone, and to give the feeling of the sensuous fullness of the summer there.
>
> Some of the happiest, and by far the most tragic years of my life were spent there, so that I have a sort of passionate sensitiveness about the book that you may understand. I gave two years to the writing of it and wish I could have given more.[7]

But the novel was more than Mazo suggested. She had not abandoned the probing of her own inner conflicts that had crept into the later *Explorers of the Dawn* stories. In *Possession*, however, she tried to keep within the confines of realism, eschewing Gothic, fairy-tale, and surreal effects. The novel is indeed a celebration of the fruit farm, but it is at the same time an inscription of Mazo's own conflict between the powerful illicit sexuality that she presents as natural and the cool, passionless, 'civilized' affection condoned by society. Her main character, Derek Vale, is torn between two women—the pale Anglo-Saxon Grace and the exotic Indian Fawnie. Grace's reserve leaves him open to seduction by Fawnie, and so it is with her that he links his life: without marrying her, he becomes the father of her child. This unorthodox liaison makes Derek a social outcast and turns his orderly home into a place of anarchy and disorder. (Did Mazo in some way feel that the disintegration of the farm was related to her sexuality?) Yet Derek is almost powerless to resist the pull of the primitive forces, 'possessed' as he is.

The novel has many flaws. The story is full of digressions; Buckskin, the son of Derek and Fawnie, appears to be the result of a kiss; and the chapter titles are often unintentionally amusing (the one dealing with the death of the child is *Buckskin Strikes His Tent*). Oddly enough, however, the critics of this novel focussed less on the fairly obvious weaknesses than on irrelevant matters. Although it was well-received in England, Michael Sadleir wondered if 'the exotic foreign elements' were not making him respond to it more eagerly than was quite justified.[8] Canadian critics, setting a pattern that was to dog Mazo for the rest of her life, focussed on whether or not the novel was 'truly Canadian'. On the whole, it was considered to have passed the test with flying colours, though Raymond Knister did point out that the farm, with its lake-side setting and manorial house, was not typical.[9] (It is unfortunate that there were no literary critics on hand when Will Roche bought the farm to point out that it was more romantic than functional.)

Possession was finished the year that *Explorers of the Dawn* appeared and was published the next year, giving Mazo a well-justified sense of growing productivity and providing her entrée into the literary circles of Toronto. There were a number of very active literary clubs, including the Men's and Women's Press Clubs, the Writers' Club, the Canadian Authors' Association, and the Heliconian Club. At a meeting of the Heliconian Club someone said to her, 'the man who is most interested in your writing is Hugh Eayrs and he is here today'.[10]

Hugh Eayrs was an Englishman who had come to Canada at the age of eighteen and, when he was only twenty-six, had been appointed president of Macmillan of Canada. The exuberant personality that had gained him that position also quickly endeared him to Mazo; he became her close friend as well as editor and mentor. One of his first acts after they met was to persuade her to defect from Knopf to Macmillan, and he drafted a series of letters that finally brought about her release. She always felt guilty about this transaction, thinking that she had used Knopf shabbily.

When she was not working on her own fiction, Mazo took other writing jobs to help with the household expenses. She reviewed books for Eaton's department store, and in the summer of 1922 undertook to write a travel brochure about Nova Scotia.[11] One of the fringe benefits of the latter was an all-expenses-paid trip to various places in Nova Scotia. Her doctor had recommended a rest and sea air as a cure for exhaustion, and, as with all trips and changes of scene, there was the added incentive that it might provide material for a new work of fiction.

Mazo's next novel, *The Thunder of New Wings*, was a logical thematic sequel to *Possession*, dealing with the inheritance of an ancestral home after the death of the father, and the problem of harmonizing within one family conflicting and various racial strains. These strains are represented by three geographical locations—Devon, Quebec, and, as a result of the holiday Mazo had spent there alone, Nova Scotia. She was enchanted with the place and appropriated it as part of the imagery on which she projected her own inner world, seeing the Celtic influence in the province as appropriate to the male side of her heritage.

In this novel, as in 'The Cobbler and the Cobbler's Wife', fairy-tale elements abound: a wicked stepmother, a changeling son, and an arrangement of three sisters. It ends in a series of wildly improbable and coincidental circumstances including a shipwreck in which all the superfluous characters are drowned. Although in a novel with a basis in realism such effects seem absurd, a reading of Isak Dinesen's *Seven Gothic Tales* may suggest the kind of form towards which Mazo was striving.

Hugh Eayrs concluded that the novel failed because Mazo had moved from describing places she knew well (like the fruit-farm) to places she knew not at all (Devon) or only superficially (Nova Scotia). Mazo concurred:

> I saw where I had gone terribly wrong. I had been so struck by that place in Nova Scotia, the strangeness of it to me, an Ontarian, that I had crammed all sorts of irrelevant 'guidebookish' descriptions into the story, which was quite able to stand on its own legs. Rereading it I thought—What a film it would make![12]

Even before Eayrs told her that the novel was an unworthy successor to *Possession*, Mazo was filled with foreboding. She was to meet with him over tea in her apartment, and before his arrival she had received an unexpected visit from an aunt:

> When she left, the first thing I did was to knock over the teapot, shattering it into fragments. The tea lay in an amber pool on the floor. I was aghast. It was a bad omen. All the Celtic superstition, the dark side of my nature, reared itself.[13]

Her disappointment over Eayrs's rejection of the work might have been devastating, but she took it surprisingly well. When he suggested that she rewrite the novel, she decided she 'had had enough of it. I flung the manuscript into a drawer and tried to forget it. I took long walks.'[14]

She did not, however, set the book aside without trying to persuade her English publisher to accept it. She had already met Daniel Macmillan and his wife during a visit they made to Canada, and in later decades they were to become her closest friends, although it was only after forty years that they addressed each other by first names. Yet their relations were very cordial from the start, and Mrs Macmillan regularly sent English magazines to Mazo. Accordingly, after Eayrs rejected *Thunder of New Wings*, Mazo—who was never above trying to play off one publisher against the other—wrote to Macmillan:

> The American Macmillans have rejected it, and also Mr Knopf. While this has worried me very much from a material point of view, it has not destroyed my faith in the book. I shall be much more deeply concerned if you do not like it.
>
> Both the American houses seem to resent the fact that it is not a second *Possession*. It was quite a different side of me which wrote this book. Perhaps you will tell me to suppress that side in future!
>
> But surely there is something splendid about Captain Haight and old Teg. Something rather lovely about Vicky, and Theo, and young Ayrton!
>
> To me it seems a more English than American novel. As a small instance, I think Americans would not appreciate the old ladies and their canary in the train.[15]

Unfortunately, Macmillan, who had liked and published *Possession*, did not care for her latest work any more than the other publishers.

Nothing testifies so strongly to Mazo's equilibrium and general well-being at this time as her balanced acceptance of the failure of her second novel. In fact, she had more than long walks to rouse her spirits, for Caroline, during Mazo's month-long absence in Nova Scotia, had had an idea described in the autobiography as 'stupendous'.[16]

Caroline's own holiday time came while Mazo was away, so she had taken Bunty to a guest-house near the (then) little village of Clarkson. There she discovered that some of the land nearby was being sold 'at a price within reach of people of moderate means', and decided to buy one of the lots: 'Caroline's nimble mind caught at the idea of small house in the woods where we could spend our summers. Eagerly I caught the fever (what a place for writing!)':

> Before Trail Cottage was completed friends would motor us out to see it. With a grand gesture we would welcome them to its windowless magnificence. It smelt of the clean new pine wood. Trees crowded all about. From the virgin soil sprang trilliums, bloodroot, columbines, rare fringed gentian, trailing arbutus, and where there was no flower or fern, the wintergreen spread its glossy carpet, showed its scarlet

berries. Oh, but the air was sweet with scent of flowers and unspoilt countryside!

The finished cottage was perfect:

> Our little roof never leaked, our two verandahs, one front and one back, behaved just as verandahs should. Our casements opened and shut with never a squeak of protest. We had no plumbing problems, for a well was dug, a spring discovered, and a pump installed, convenient to the kitchen. . . . A drink of pure spring water out of a tin dipper—what a pleasure! Its coolness touches the lips; it is balm to the tongue; bliss to the palate; a blessing to throat; a benefit to the stomach. . . .
>
> Oh, I pity millionaires who never have had the experience of building a *little* house![17]

Mazo's trip to Nova Scotia was her last extended separation from Caroline; as long as they lived, they were never again apart for more than a day or two. Much later, Mazo was to write: 'surely there is to each of us one human being loved above all others, one house, one horse, one dog.'[18] In the years ahead they would occupy many splendid homes—a farmhouse in Devon, a Gothic Rectory, a mansion in the Malvern hills, a huge house in Windsor—but none afforded them as much pleasure as the cottage in the woods at Clarkson. More space in the autobiography is devoted to it than to any other of their homes. Its charms were entirely of the rustic kind. Water had to be drawn from a spring several steps from the back door, and although there was a small lavatory, it lacked a bath tub. Yet, however slender their means, the two were so untrained in domestic skills that they rarely attempted their own housekeeping: even in the woods they had a gardener and 'a willing little woman' who did the washing and cleaning. Caroline walked each day to the station to commute to Queen's Park, and Mazo was in charge of the evening meal—a pretty rudimentary affair.

It was the perfect combination of solitude and company so hard for a writer to achieve without loneliness. She had the day to herself and yet the return of Caroline to look forward to in the evening. The work she did at this time reflected her happiness. *Delight* may not have been her best work (though some would always claim it was) but few would dispute that it was her most exuberant, that it radiated her delight, that word she associated with Trail Cottage and which is synonymous with 'joy': 'It was a delight to settle down in Trail Cottage, with the woodland fluttering in new green leaves, the flowers of May drawing strength from the virgin soil—a delight to walk to the farmhouse for milk, to gather watercress from the stream, to drink tea beneath the graceful white birches.'[19]

All the outside pressures had been removed from the relationship—the constraints of family and society; the threat of suitors who might take Caroline away; the claims on Caroline's affections from close members of her own family. Now Mazo could at last relax and rejoice in the possession of her love. And Caroline could be accepted as Muse. Mazo expressed her feelings in a poem she wrote at the time:

> *To C.*
> How kind the moon is to the night
> As you are kind to me,
> Making its cloistered darkness bright,
> Making its darkness fair to see.
>
> The gentle moon with silver clothes
> That mounted [?] in darkness drear,
> As you give your sweet radiance
> To make me smile when you are near.
>
> In silence dreams the lonely night,
> Until the moon ere long
> Awakes a bird to voice delight,
> As in my heart you wake a song.[20]

Her joy found its fullest expression in the novel she dedicated to Caroline (who until 1930 used the original spelling of her name):

> To my dear Carolyn
> The Story of Delight
> is Lovingly Inscribed
> Christmas 1925

For the setting of *Delight* Mazo went back in time before *Possession*, to the years in Acton when she had been preoccupied with the running of the hotel. In those days she had felt less secure about Caroline, seeing her become the object of masculine admiration. Now that Caroline was safe, Mazo could look back over twenty years and depict those early anxieties with gaiety.

The theme of the novel is linked to that of *Possession* in its portrayal of the conflict between sexual vitality and numerous interdictions placed on it by the civilized world. The novel depicts a series of lovers whose union is opposed by society for various reasons: the lovers are married to other people, belong to different social classes or to feuding families, and, in one instance, are too closely related for a healthy marriage. The one obstacle never mentioned is that the lovers belong to the same sex.

One married pair, Charley and Mrs Bye, have a daughter with a cleft palate, a deformity that causes speculation that the Byes are more closely related than is proper for husband and wife. (In a later novel Mazo mentions children whose speech deformities are the result of 'in-breeding'.) In *Delight* she carefully reproduces Queenie Bye's speech, spelling out phonetically the songs she sings as she marches around the kitchen:

> I 'ad a poh eye
> I 'ad a poh eye
> [I had a sore eye]

and

> We aw mar'h toge'her
> We aw mar'h toge'her
> We aw mar'h toge'her
> Nih'ly in a waow[21]

Queenie Bye's speech can be seen as a resonant image for Mazo, who was prevented from speaking out clearly and openly by the socially unacceptable nature of her relationship with Caroline. The whole novel is a celebration of her desire for Caroline, and yet she could only express that desire in an indirect or broken way. Like Queenie Bye, Mazo was tongue-tied.

Another mismatched couple are May Masters and her cockney husband who, May finds, has entered into a second marriage: she poses as his cousin until she can lure him away from his second wife and back to England. The servant Pearl and the remittance man Edwin Silk are also kept apart, in this case by the difference in their social classes. When he dies, Pearl inherits his small fortune and becomes a middle-class woman, ever-faithful to his memory.

The main story, however, focusses upon the beautiful Delight Main-prize, who has many suitors all conspiring to keep her from her true love Jimmy Sykes, until the lovers, having overcome all obstacles, are happily reunited. One critic has summed up the theme in the phrase 'sex conquer[s] all'.[22] Yet that does not seem quite the appropriate description for a novel in which so little actual sexual activity takes place and, when it does, is of such a covert kind. For instance, at Delight's request two of her suitors try to pierce her ears. One is too gentle to effect the penetration properly and gives up, horrified by the sight of blood, while the other takes a sadistic pleasure in the job.

The novel is full of such displaced sexual references, the most striking of which is Delight's attachment to a teapot she has inherited from her grandmother. She strokes what is described as its round belly and sleeps with the spout pointed towards her lips. She prays that the teapot will not be broken, and her prayer is answered.

> Oh, but she was grateful to Him! Her whole body quivered with love and gratitude. She could not bear to part with the pot tonight. She would lay it on the other pillow, next to the wall where it could not roll off. It would be company, a bedfellow, almost. She placed it snugly on the pillow, smiled at it tenderly, blew out the light and got in beside it.
> It really was company in this lonely place. She laid one warm hand on its shiny fluted belly. Its spout curved toward her parted lips.
> She thought:
> 'I am so happy I cannot sleep.'
> And, in a moment, she slept.[23]

The really striking feature of this novel is its frank celebration of Delight's sexual charms. Customers are drawn in large numbers to the hotel by the prospect of seeing Delight move to and fro with heavy trays 'from which the flowing lines of her arms merged exquisitely into her breast and waist'. Delight's first appearance in the novel is described as follows:

> He looked from the point he had reached at the top of the stairs down at the figure coming slowly up, weighted by a canvas-covered basket. Her hair shielded her face, but he saw the curve of a splendid young breast under a thin black blouse, and a rounded throat that gleamed like satin.
> With a sigh she pulled her drooping hat, disarranging the hair about her ears. It was a shining, pale gold, springing from the roots with strong vitality, waving closely over her head, and clinging in little curls about her temples and nape. But her skin was not blond. Rather the exquisite, golden brown of some rare brunettes, with a warm glow on the cheeks, as when firelight touches the surface of a lovely brazen urn. Her eyes were an intense, dark brown, sleepy now, under thick lashes that seemed to cling together wilfully as though to veil the emotion reflected in their depths. Here was mystery, thought Kirke. And her mouth, he thought, was the very throne of sweetness, as it curved with parted lips, pink as pigeon's feet. His shrewd eyes observed the lovely line that swept from her round chin to her breast, her perfect shoulders, her strong neck, her hands coarsened by work.[24]

The privacy of her bedroom allows Delight to display herself to even greater effect:

She had been sitting on the side of the bed pulling off her stockings, and now she flung herself back on her pillow, opening her mouth in a wide yawn and stretching her arms above her head. Her chemise, drawn upward, disclosed her strong, white thighs, glistening in the lamplight. She rocked her body from side to side in an abandon of relaxation. . . .

The red sunlight stained the warm whiteness of her body to the blush of an apple blossom. Her breasts, gently rising and falling, lay like sleeping flowers between her rounded arms. A tangle of yellow curls hung over her drowsy dark eyes.[25]

None of these descriptions seems particularly shocking in our time, of course, but in 1926, when the book was published, some critics found it crude. The Canadian reviews in particular were unfavourable, and Mazo felt from this time on that she was better appreciated elsewhere. The *Canadian Forum* reviewer wrote: 'Treated as an idyll, the story could have been charming; as a tragedy it might have been terrific; but Miss de la Roche has tried to fuse the materials for both in a spirit of high comedy, and it can't be done.'[26] That review lay alongside one of *Mrs Dalloway*, Virginia Woolf's lyrical portrayal of a woman who was moved to sexual ecstasy only by a girlhood friend, Sally Seaton. That book was declared to be 'brilliant and extremely ineffective and irritating.'

Mazo found her first experience with unfavourable reviews very unsettling: given the personal nature of the novel's subject, she could not help taking them as critical not only of her work but of herself. Yet once again her resilience asserted itself, and she went directly on to another novel. Nothing could stop her momentum. The subject matter of Mazo's next novel had been in her mind some time earlier, but she had set it aside to write *Delight*:

Jalna came into my head a long time ago, but it was vague, and while I was just beginning to think about it, *Delight* came suddenly and quite clearly into my mind, and I started to work on it.

All the time I was writing *Delight*, bits of *Jalna* would keep sticking up their heads and pushing their way into the other story. I had quite a time to make them wait.

So many of the Canadian novels came from the roaring west, or from romantic Quebec, and it amused me to write one all about a humble corner in Ontario.[27]

When Mazo first began to wrestle with the material that eventually became *Jalna*, she intended to write a play about a brother and sister living in their ancestral home in the midst of a large family of uncles, step-brothers, and loyal retainers. When the play became a novel the original brother and sister were named Renny and Meggie Whiteoak. 'From the very first the characters created themselves. They leaped from my imagination and from memories of my own family.'[28]

One other important element in the creation of *Jalna* Mazo did not mention. A few years earlier, when she was searching for some congenial means of supplementing the income she earned from her writing, she had worked as a book reviewer for Eaton's department store. It was probably during this period that she read *The Forsyte Saga*, the first trilogy of which was published in Canada in 1922. Critics over the years often compared the Jalna and Forsyte series, but Mazo always denied that she had read more than the first book, *A Man of Property*. Nevertheless, when *Jalna* first appeared, she listed Galsworthy among her favourite authors (along with Tolstoy, Thomas Hardy, and Sheila Kay-Smith).[29]

The similarities between the early books in the Jalna series and *The Forsyte Saga* make it hard to deny that she took her original inspiration from Galsworthy, transporting, transplanting, and transforming his English social comedy to her own purposes. Her affinity for his work is not hard to understand. The Forsyte clan remains close-knit in a changing world; in spite of internecine rivalries and feuds, the generations, mutually supportive and respectful, come together to celebrate family occasions in the mansions that change hands but never pass out of the family. Such permanence, such family solidarity and substance, free from the dread of imminent dispersal, was Mazo's most cherished dream.

And there was one part of the Forsyte story that struck an even more responsive chord in Mazo. Galsworthy's biographers have revealed the incident that most marked him and his fiction: a love affair with his cousin's wife. This domestic tangle resulted eventually in the woman's divorcing her husband and marrying Galsworthy, a situation that recurs in his fiction as cousins fall in love, marry, or are prohibited from marriage by the problems inherited from an earlier generation.

A comparison of *A Man of Property* and *Jalna* reveals many close parallels—from the genealogy at the beginning, with its pattern of repeating idiosyncratic family names, to the plot structure and even chapter headings. One of the closest parallels is between the two heroines, Irene Heron of *The Forsyte Saga* and Alayne Archer of *Jalna*—both beautiful, cultured, well-educated women, the daughters of professors, impecunious but more sophisticated than the Forsyte and

Whiteoak families into which they marry. Each leaves one member of the family to marry another and continue the family line, and each is distinguished by the coldness of her temperament.

Striking as the similarities are, however, the difference between the two sagas are even more interesting. Some changes were determined by the practical necessities of transplanting the family chronicle from English to Canadian soil and some by Mazo's own personal experiences. The social texture of the Forsytes' life in London was foreign to Canada. Mazo might have placed her family in Toronto, but she chose instead the country life she had come to love on the farm. The changing seasons, the revolving crops, the business of raising animals provided her background and her texture.

She made her family more earthy, more outdoorsy, more uncouth, and at the same time more vital than the fastidious Forsytes. There are no elegant drawing rooms or stylish dinner parties at Jalna. Family meetings are boisterous affairs with everyone eating mightily of abundant meals, clamouring for more gravy and dumplings and washing it all down with endless cups of tea. Quarrels break out and swiftly become brawls in which even the old people lash out with fists and walking sticks. The Whiteoaks come to dinner smelling of the stables and worse. There are no well-staffed day nurseries, and the babies are brought to the table with everyone else; clearly, Mazo also liked to have everyone under one roof. Finally, instead of a patriarchal figure like old Jolyon or old Swithin Forsyte, the dominant figure in Mazo's series is matriarchal Adeline Whiteoak, the most irrepressible, greedy, noisy, and vital member of the whole clan. She outlives by many years her husband, who beside her seems a weak figure, and she continues to dominate family life long after she is dead.

Mazo wanted to name the Whiteoaks' ancestral home for an Indian military station, and Caroline brought from one of her fellow-workers at the legislature a list of such stations. From it Mazo selected the name Jalna, because it was short and looked attractive on the page. She wrote of her setting:

> Jalna was inspired by the traditions of that part of Southern Ontario on the fringe of which we had built Trail Cottage. The descendants of the retired military and naval officers who had settled there stoutly clung to British traditions. No house in particular was pictured; no family portrayed.[30]

In fact, the lot on which Trail Cottage was built had originally been part of a larger estate that had on it a house named for the Indian station of Benares. While there is something of Benares in the description of Jalna, however, so there is also something of many other houses, estates, families, and locations.

Although Canadian critics have often rejected the Whiteoaks family as hopelessly atypical, Mazo had known many such families and observed them carefully. Many readers have their own candidates for the house and the family. If one thought the Whiteoaks were based on the Beardsmore family of Acton, the novelist Timothy Findley, who worked on the screenplay of the Jalna series produced for the CBC in 1972, remains convinced that Jalna was based on the Sibbalds' home at Sibbald's Point on the south side of Lake Simcoe[31]—the spot Caroline chose for Mazo's and her own final resting place. In addition, Mazo had lived near the two large houses belonging to the prominent Massey family on Jarvis Street in Toronto, and if neither of them adds anything to Jalna, surely the sight of the Massey carriages setting off on Sunday mornings had something to do with the Whiteoaks' horse-drawn processions to church. Finally, as a guest at Limerick House, her Uncle Danford's ample home in Newmarket, Mazo had probably seen at the dining-room table both her paternal grandmother and her great grandmother sitting under portraits of their Irish ancestors, with her red-haired uncle Danford presiding over the whole strong-willed group—a typical Whiteoak scene.

Whatever the specific elements of her inspiration may have been, certainly they were clear in Mazo's mind: 'That summer I lived with the Whiteoaks, completely absorbed by them. In fancy I opened the door of Jalna, passed inside, listened to what was going on.'[32] At the top of the first page she wrote *Jalna*, and then, in her curiously steady way, she worked through the novel chapter by chapter from beginning to end with very little revision. In the evening, as each one was finished, Caroline would read it aloud, and together the two women would discuss the direction of future chapters. It would be a long time—if ever—before Mazo was again as happy as she was during those productive years at Trail Cottage.

10

The Year of Wonder

When the full glare of national and international attention fell on Mazo, she and Caroline were living on the third floor at 86 Yorkville Avenue, then a quiet residential street, now a fashionable area of boutiques and outdoor cafés. The house still stands, next door to a hairdressing salon, though it goes unnoticed as a literary landmark. The women occupied a light airy room, crammed with family heirlooms and heavy furniture, in which they could entertain small groups of friends. As the modest place became a part of the story surrounding the spectacular success, they became a little self-conscious about it. Offended when William Arthur Deacon called it a 'bed-sitting room', Caroline carefully explained that it was an apartment.[1] Edward Weeks, describing his first meeting with Mazo, tactfully called it a 'studio-apartment'.[2] It was the first really satisfactory place they had found for the winter months. After deciding that the upkeep of a rented house was impractical, they had been plagued by under-heated rooms, but this one was warm, with a large fireplace and a chimney that 'drew well;' it was also close to the Parliament buildings where Caroline worked, and there was a small garden for Bunty.

The ambience of a rooming house interested Mazo, in whom there was a strong voyeuristic streak. Moreover, living with Caroline as a small, self-contained unit within a larger group was a familiar experience, and a means by which she had often gathered story material. In one interview she gave her formula for the writer's life:

> Teas, bridges and clubs are interesting, but they are not what I call real life. I am not in any sense a club woman. Let your would-be authoress immerse herself in real life. Let her keep a boarding house, go out as domestic, engage herself to a millionaire or a tinker.[3]

116

Mrs Gertrude Pringle's house was no exception. One occupant was a businessman on whom Mazo spied through his transom when she came downstairs each morning to take Bunty to the garden. (She said it made her feel 'serene' to see him kneeling in prayer.) Another was a Miss Turner who did hand-weaving on a large loom and loved cats. Listening to the sounds coming from her room, Mazo eventually wrote a story about her—'Electric Storm'—which she considered one of her best.

Gertrude Pringle herself was to become an indispensable ally in the months ahead, acting as social secretary and guardian of Mazo's privacy—roles for which she was well-suited. She had had ten years' experience writing an information column in leading Canadian magazines and a daily newspaper, and five years later published a definitive work on Canadian rules of etiquette: *Etiquette in Canada: The Blue Book of Canadian Social Usage*, the justification for which she gave as follows:

> Another reason why a book on etiquette as practised in Canada is so much more needed is to combat the influence of motion pictures with their bizarre way of representing social life. . . . The rules that people of good breeding observe in their social contacts go by the board in motion pictures, under the exigencies of the camera.[4]

The social scene to which Mrs Pringle catered is indicated by the chapter headings in the book, which included such subjects as *Bringing Out A Daughter*, *Home Training for Daughters*, and *Addressing Titled and Other Important Personages*.

Something of the relationship that existed between Mrs Pringle and her lodgers is indicated by the articles she wrote about Mazo. She was under the impression that the two women came from a very distinguished background and were, if not 'titled personages', at least of aristocratic European ancestry. Mazo's uncertainty about the occupation of her paternal grandfather was put aside and the story of his university position in the United States revived; his wife was described as the 'daughter of a great Irish beauty of her day'; Mazo's furniture was said to have come from the 'old home' in Ireland; and the souvenirs that Will Roche had brought back from his trips to the west coast became 'rare pieces of Chinese porcelain'. In addition, Mrs Pringle related an extraordinary story:

> That there was once another Mazo de la Roche came to light recently. In a Toronto home hangs a portrait in oils, representing a charming woman in quaint old time costume. It must be at least 200 years old.

On the back is inscribed in old script, Mazo de la Roche, Lady. This painting was brought to Canada about seventy years ago and came from Stoodleigh Court in Devonshire, and most probably represents an ancestress of our Canadian Mazo who had married into an English family.[5]

Clearly adapting her life-story to meet the desired social standards, Mazo apparently never told Mrs Pringle that her family came from Newmarket and had once run a hotel in Acton. This elaborate game of pretend must have had its dangers, since Toronto was a small place in 1927 and there was a very good chance that Mrs Pringle would find out the truth.

As an active member of the city's literary community—as well as a journalist, she was a member of the executive committee of the Toronto branch of the Canadian Authors' Association—Gertrude Pringle was naturally interested in Mazo's writing. She read *Delight* with enjoyment—although she was predictably shocked by Mazo's use of the word 'belly' for the teapot.

She was to publish a second article on her distinguished lodger at the height of the latter's fame, in which she described, from her own observations, Mazo's working habits:

Few novelists spend less time in the actual writing of their books. For an hour and a half each morning, or at most two hours, Miss de la Roche, pencil in hand and drawing board on knee, puts down her story word for word as she has thought it out. There is no hesitation; everything is clear-cut, clear and vivid in her mind. When evening comes, she reads aloud what she has written to Miss Carolyn Clement, her adopted sister and cousin, chum and dearest friend with whom she lives. The two girls then discuss the story and as a result a few minor changes may be made, a paragraph or two rewritten or one adjective substituted for another. But while she spends little time in writing, she does devote much time to thinking out a story, living in a world of her own creation whose characters at times are more real to her than those among whom she moves.[6]

The first winter that Mazo spent with Mrs Pringle, covering as it did the period from the completion of *Jalna* to the winning of the *Atlantic Monthly* prize, was a tense one. There are conflicting accounts of events, particularly of the circumstances in which Mazo came to enter the competition. According to Edward Weeks, it was Hugh Eayrs's idea: 'Hugh was her publisher and literary adviser. She trusted him absolutely, and it was he who counselled her to submit the book in the *Atlantic* contest when the American branch of Macmillan failed to show the enthusiasm which he felt the novel deserved.'[7] In her autobiography, however, Mazo claims the impulsive decision to enter the competition as her own:

> In time *Jalna* was finished and the typed manuscript sent to Macmillans of New York. Hugh Eayrs had already expressed great hopes for it. The New York house agreed and were to publish it in a few months. Preparations were on the way. Then, in a chance copy of the *Atlantic Monthly* I came upon the notice of a competition. . . . Then brightly came the thought that as my chances of winning were slight it would do no harm to anyone and would be satisfaction to me just to send *Jalna*. . . . I could not resist the temptation.[8]

Yet her letter to Ellery Sedgewick in February 1927 tells a slightly different story:

> Would it be possible for you to give me an idea as to when the results of the Atlantic Competition will be made known?
>
> I have entered my new novel JALNA in it, and, as I suppose my chance of winning the prize is remote, I should like to make arrangements for its publication next Fall by another firm, in case it is returned by you.
>
> I have been with Macmillans, and I know they will be interested in the new book. However, I do not wish to close a contract with any publisher until I am sure JALNA has not been chosen by your judges.[9]

Two years earlier she had submitted her play *Low Life* to two competitions (one held by the Montreal Branch of the Canadian Authors' Association and one by the Imperial Order of the Daughters of the Empire). When she won both, she returned the prize money at once to the IODE, but she reports in her autobiography that she could not return the money because she had already spent it. Ronald Hambleton, who got to the truth of the matter, concluded that she reported her own behaviour as discreditable because 'she loved to be thought naughty and incorrigible'.[10] But possibly these two instances in which she confesses to shady dealings of which she was not, in fact, guilty reflect rather her own uneasy feelings of guilt and shame in sending out her work for publication.

The official story was that Mazo was a complete unknown when she won the prize. In 1938 Hugh Eayrs wrote in the *Canadian Bookman* that 'the editor of the *Atlantic Monthly* had no idea whatever whether she was a man or a woman, whether a practised writer or an unknown one. Submission of manuscripts was under pen-names and the judges had awarded the prize to Mazo de la Roche and that was that.'[11] Edward Weeks, a member of the editorial board, told how the *Atlantic Monthly*, which had expected about 500 manuscripts, found itself deluged with 1117, so that readers had to be recruited from all sides. The editors' wives were enlisted as well as a librarian from the Boston Public Library. It was this woman who passed the first verdict—one that was subsequently echoed by some very distinguished critics: 'This is the story of a large love-making family in Canada, dominated by the old grandmother. The brothers have unseemly affairs with their sisters-in-law, and there is quite a lot about the stable, including the odour. Not recommended.'[12] Then Weeks himself, noting that the manuscript was professionally typed and intrigued by its enigmatic title page, read it and found it compelling. He passed it along to other readers. Over the next two months the field was narrowed first to twelve and then to six before, finally, *Jalna* was proclaimed the unanimous choice. The librarian was paid for 'her unimaginative thoroughness, but discouraged from further endeavor'.[13] The one fact that was deliberately concealed at this time was that Mazo had for seventeen years been a protegée of the editor of the *Atlantic*.

In the two years before the announcement of the competition, Mazo's letters to Ellery Sedgewick had diminished and become sparse in personal information. With more friends and mentors at home, she was no longer dependent on his encouragement. But when she heard about the competition she wrote at once to ask him about it, enclosing a copy of her recently published plays as well as all the English reviews of *Delight*. She also told him that, for all her recent successes, she still had not freed herself from the 'hampering bonds of comparative poverty'.[14] He replied at once, urging her to enter the competition, and remained her staunch ally throughout. Athough he liked *Jalna* very much on its own merits, there seems little doubt that it was above all his longstanding sympathy for the struggling author that influenced the outcome of the competition. Alfred McIntyre of Little, Brown (which had a co-publishing arrangement with the *Atlantic Monthly*) thought the prize should go to a novel called *Matts* but nevertheless agreed that *Jalna* should be published; he suggested offering the same contract that was being proposed to another competitor, Mary Ellen Chase, for *An Upland Romance*.

After Mazo's death, when Edward Weeks came to Toronto to speak on the occasion of the Thomas Fisher Rare Book Library's acquisition of her papers, he mentioned for the first time that 'it was in the nature of a homecoming when she turned to us again with *Jalna*'.[15] Yet when *Jalna* was serialized in the *Atlantic* the contributors notes studiously avoided the fact that Mazo had previously published there.

The suspense that preceded the announcement of the prize was greatly increased because of Sedgewick's determination to inform

Mazo of her success himself. Since he was ill, there was a considerable delay between the first hints of the outcome and the final word that she had won. He had had his secretary call with the message 'Happy news awaits you',[16] and by the time they knew what the happy news was they were almost ill from suspense. Mazo's response was so ingenuous that Sedgewick must have been convinced all over again of her youth and unworldliness:

> I have spoken to you of my sister. As a matter of fact she is my sister by adoption, my cousin in reality. A frail little thing—my one, my dearest possession, who has cherished me—agonized over me—only too much—more than I deserve. Just now she said to me: 'I cannot think of the prize at all—even the glory of it—because of the beauty and the sweetness of his letter!' She meant your letter.
>
> Your name has been so often on our lips these past weeks. It fell from them with the awful glibness of the name of the Almighty, and with as little hope of comprehending the plans of the divine mind.[17]

Since the publishers wished the maximum amount of publicity in return for their $10,000, Mazo and Caroline had to keep the news secret until the announcement to the press could be fully orchestrated.

The story broke in Canada on 12 April 1927. Gertrude Pringle reported what happened:

> As soon as the news became known, Miss de la Roche's telephone began to ring, likewise her doorbell, and the two kept up an unceasing and exciting duet all day long. Came an endless procession of messenger boys bearing telegrams of congratulation, florists' boxes with every kind of flowers, reporters to interview and friends to felicitate her. The next day she had lost her voice. But that was only a temporary fly in her ointment of joy.[18]

The news of Mazo's success was greeted with an outburst of nationalistic pride and the universal cry that Canadian literature had at last come of age. That pronouncement has been heard several times since, but in 1927 it was less familiar. The fact that another Canadian writer, Martha Ostenso, had won a larger prize some years before was forgotten—partly because she had been born in Norway and had had to claim American citizenship in order to be eligible for the prize.

The extent to which Mazo's triumph was hailed as a Canadian success deserves some emphasis, because for the last part of her life she was hounded by criticism that her work was not 'truly Canadian'. Ten years later Hugh Eayrs would make the following statement, somewhat wearily, on her behalf:

121

Here let me answer once more, as I am never tired of doing on the platform and in print, the wild accusation thrown at Miss de la Roche that her work is not Canadian. What is a Canadian novel?. . . . I am sick and tired of this sort of nonsense. I am ashamed that it should be confined to my own country, Canada, for it is most certainly never heard elsewhere in the English-speaking world or without.[19]

When the acclamations of 1927 are reviewed, the 'wild accusations' appear as a backlash to the early emphasis on the very Canadianness of her work. The Prime Minister of Canada, for instance, the Right Honourable Mackenzie King, wrote her a pompous and somewhat incoherent letter, the intent of which seems to have been to praise her for setting her novel on Canadian soil:

I know, of course, as everyone must know, that in quite recent years, Canadian writers have won mention abroad. I need not cite instances; yours for the moment will suffice. But what impresses me is the fact that when a Canadian author sets the scene of a novel in Canada, the charge of misrepresentation—a grievous thing at its best—is almost nil. This is of all the more importance, then, when, as will be the case with your novel Jalna, the first great mass of readers will be citizens of a country other than our own. . . .[20]

A number of civic celebrations were staged in Toronto in the weeks immediately after the announcement, the most impressive of them a gala banquet held at the Queen's Hotel by the Toronto Branch of the Canadian Authors Association. The chairman was the President of the local branch, Sir Charles G.D. Roberts, and Bliss Carman was in the audience. Mazo was presented with a floral bouquet and a tea-service, and in his toast Roberts thanked her for having 'proved beyond a doubt that there actually is something called Canadian literature'.[21]

She was the heroine of the hour. In the same week that the Toronto Council of Women gave a huge banquet for her at Casa Loma—a Gothic fantasy of a castle owned by the city—her play 'Come True' was presented at the Hart House theatre as part of an all-Canadian week of plays. Maclean's Magazine announced that she had won a prize for her short story 'Good Friday'. When the Arts and Letters Club planned a dinner in her honour, its secretary wrote to invite Ellery Sedgewick. Stressing the importance of the occasion, he said that the dinner was looked upon as a most significant event in the intellectual life of the city; in addition, it was the first time that the club had ever held a function of this kind in honour of a lady.[22]

Sedgewick was not very eager to attend, but thought that the magazine should be represented 'in view of the importance of some of the guests'.[23] In the event, Edward Weeks was given the assignment of going to Toronto to present Mazo with her $10,000 cheque at the dinner.

In June, when the first instalment of *Jalna* appeared in the *Atlantic Monthly*, the lead story was Hemingway's 'Fifty Grand'. The contributors column introduced her to the world as follows:

> Mazo de la Roche, the author of the *Atlantic* prize novel, lives with her sister in Toronto, where for a dozen years she has been writing—first short stories, then novels and plays. As her name indicates, she is of French descent. One of her royalist ancestors was guillotined in the Revolution. 'Since then,' she says, 'we have been notable only for our improvidence.'[24]

When the second contributors notice referred to Trail Cottage as a 'bungalow in the Ontario forest', Mazo wrote to Weeks to protest the description.[25]

As it happened, the two women did not spend very long at Trail Cottage that summer. Instead they travelled with Mrs Eayrs and her maid to the seaside resort of Rockport, Massachusetts, where they rented a house furnished in true New England style with authentic Colonial pieces, a spinning wheel, old blue china, 'rag' carpets, and an attic with a steep sloping roof, remote from any sound but the movement of the tides. Being by the sea was a new experience; they learned to swim and picnicked on the beach each day. And Mazo, never happy to be away from her writing, began a new novel in the attic,[26] for already her publishers were thinking of a sequel to *Jalna*. In fact, being in Massachusetts allowed Mazo to forge close personal friendships with her publishers. At last she met her staunch supporter Ellery Sedgewick, who had a summer place near Rockport, and in Boston she was the guest of honour at dinner parties given by Edward Weeks and Alfred McIntyre, the president of Little, Brown.

From Boston Mazo and Caroline proceeded to New York, appearing before Aunt Eva and Pierre in their new trappings as celebrities. Aunt Eva had been amazed and delighted to discover Mazo's success when she opened the *New York Times* one morning. Mazo and Caroline had numerous invitations and provided an exciting diversion for their relatives, who by Mazo's account lived an dull, isolated life 'in that great city'.[27] Next they returned for an all too brief stay at Trail Cottage before going back for the winter to Mrs Pringle's, and even then the celebrations continued. In November Mazo wrote to Weeks of the distractions that had prevented her from making progress on the new novel:

> In London—a luncheon, a Press Club tea, and a dinner of two hundred guests, at which last I spoke. All this in one day! Oh God! Oh London, Ont.! . . . In Ottawa—a really magnificent luncheon at the Chateau Laurier, given by the Canadian Club, a tea by the Press Club, and a small dinner by the wife of a Cabinet Minister. Four hundred and twenty at the luncheon. It is a great strain to speak to so many people, and what with travelling at night, and seeing faces, faces, faces, I am tired.[28]

It had indeed been a heady, exciting year. Mazo had won acclamation, sudden wealth, a lucrative market for future work, a new circle of admiring friends, and fame in another country while becoming a prophet with honour in her own. She had succeeded beyond her wildest dreams, and should have been ecstatically happy.

Less than a year after she received the prize, however, Mazo had a complete breakdown—almost as serious as the collapse she had suffered twenty-four years earlier and with many of the same symptoms, including 'crawling, insidious pains [moving] with dreadful regularity over my temples, down the back of my neck'.[29] In the early part of 1928 she was so ill that she could not even write a postcard. The prescribed rest did nothing, and the recommended nightcap of Scotch and water only aggravated her condition. She was sent for a series of electric shock treatments, and after each she was worse than before. She summed up her condition thus: 'I felt myself to be almost an outcast from the normal world.'[30]

11

Recovery

In order to understand Mazo's breakdown, it is necessary to review from a different perspective the events of the *annus mirabilis* that began with the announcement of the *Atlantic Monthly* prize. When the two women retreated to the guest-house in Niagara Falls, worn out by the suspense and sworn to secrecy before the official announcement, Mazo was so ill that she could not finish a meal without having to return to her bedroom to cough. She could not even fill out the questionnaire sent by the magazine's publicity department.[1]

The anxiety with which she approached the publication of her work had been a constant in her life from the moment she started to write. It was now twenty-four years since the imagined loss of an early story had precipitated a complete breakdown. Yet the emotional turmoil as she waited for the contest decision—torn between fear of rejection and the fear of being exposed to public scrutiny—still threatened her mental and physical health. She knew well that if she were successful the barrage of publicity this time would be on a vast scale. Her suspense was therefore far greater than the ordinary kind, and when it was resolved she dreaded what she accurately called 'the ordeal of publicity ahead'. Even the arrival of the questionnaire may have aggravated her illness, the questions reminding her of her inadequacy as a writer facing the literary world.

Biographers are sometimes accused of acting like sleuths tracking down guilty criminals. Mazo's answers to the questionnaire show another side of that coin, revealing a writer acting like a guilty criminal with much to hide. In fact, women writers of Mazo's generation did have a great deal to hide—inadequate education, lack of the experience appropriate to a writer, unorthodox domestic and family arrangements, and the sense that they were dubious heirs to a divided family heritage. Because of Mazo's illness it fell to Caroline to complete the questionnaire, and she concocted an image through a mixture of fabrication, half-truth, and whimsy. In the autobiography Mazo explained: 'When a questionnaire came from Little, Brown for use in publicity I felt too ill to answer the questions. Caroline filled in the form as best she could, with only a few mistakes.'[2]

In addition to changing the place of birth she withheld Mazo's age, which was never disclosed even to close friends: she was generally assumed to be at least ten years younger than she was, and at this time was variously referred to as 'a young woman' and 'woman well over thirty'[3]—both misleading descriptions of a woman approaching fifty. (Gertrude Pringle wrote, 'There is something of a gallant boy in her bearing.')[4] Her educational background changed from public to private. And while Mazo might have been expected to mention her scholar-grandfather as the possible source of her literary talent, instead she invoked the spectre of her decapitated maternal uncle, transforming him into an ancestor guillotined in the French Revolution. Together with the somewhat frivolous details that conclude the questionnaire, that response evokes an image that was perhaps the only one she could present. Between the alternatives of 'man of letters' and 'authoress' she could choose only the latter. Rather than claiming to be intelligent, well-informed, and professional about her 'career', she presented herself as improvident, whimsical, charming and modest. If she had any inclination to appear masterful, intelligent, and worldly, she could manifest those traits only in the secret world of the Play. Accordingly, the questionnaire was filled out as follows:

Birthplace: Toronto

Date: uncertain

School: Education mostly private, with an erratic dash or two into the University of Toronto.

Any Ancestral Notables: In the French Revolution one of them was guillotined. Since then we have been notable only for our improvidence.

Peculiarities: I have seen only one moving picture play, and never want to see another. I refuse to tell the name of the play.

Tastes: Mingling with good-natured city crowds, hobnobing [*sic*] with simple country folk, driving a horse, keeping dogs, the theater.

Distastes: Telephones, department stores, lifts, comic supplements, noisy patriotism, speeches, lectures, helpful information of any kind.

Superstitions: A prey to all of them! Mirrors—ladders—salt—the new moon—the portents of spiders seen at certain hours, that is:

matin—chagrin
midi—souci
soir—espoir

Ultimate ambition: To escape the Canadian winter.

Favorite sports: sailing and canoeing

Career advised to adopt: Studied art for a time with the object of becoming an illustrator but even while I was bent over a drawing board my brain was full of fancies, and I soon turned to writing.[5]

In the *Atlantic Monthly* offices the questionnaire was received with some surprise, since it seemed to contradict dramatically the impression of waif-like deprivation that Mazo had been conveying for the last thirteen years. One memo exchanged by the editors conveys their reaction:

The humorous bits are delightful and can be used to advantage but to send a 12 year old snap shot! I'm wondering if the single visit to the movies also took place 12 years ago!!! Also I think we've been worrying unduly about her poverty—these facts do not corroborate our surmises![6]

It was suggested that the photograph problem be solved by having an artist do a charcoal sketch to take its place.

The questionnaire was only the first of a series of attempts to probe into Mazo's personal life. For the next month she was bombarded with reporters' requests for interviews. Even routine questions were difficult to answer. When asked about her hobbies, for instance, she was always embarrassed because, in fact, she had none; as she told one interviewer, 'I'm like a kangaroo, who can't do anything but jump so he goes right on jumping.'[7] She did not even read as much as most writers did. One interviewer who visited Trail Cottage, astonished by the lack of reading material there, was even more astonished to learn that Mazo did not read magazines and had never seen a movie.[8] Usually she fielded such questions by casting around in her past: she told the same reporter she was an avid gardener, and that her aim was to have a good asparagus bed.[9] In the *Atlantic* questionnaire, remembering her holiday in Muskoka several years earlier, she listed boating and canoeing. On the whole it was easier to falsify, yet to do so took its own kind of toll in making her feel once more like a fraud. And the events arranged to celebrate her triumph often underscored her anomalous position. 'PUBLIC MEN AND FELLOW CRAFTSMEN PRAISE PRIZE-WINNING AUTHORESS' proclaimed the headline above *The Globe's* description of the city of Toronto's banquet in her honour.[10] She was given a floral bouquet and a silver tea service—both suitable trophies for an 'authoress'. The women of the city held separate fêtes for Mazo, and these were written up in the section of the paper entitled 'WHAT WOMEN ARE DOING', a regular column with a look-what-the-girls-are-getting-into-now theme. At the Casa Loma banquet for 280 women, the stress was on the modesty and charm of the guest of honour. The 'winsome Canadian authoress' was praised for being 'clothed' with 'a sweet humility of soul', and 'there was little that was sound, solemn or serious in her gay remarks'.[11]

When Edward Weeks came to present her cheque at the banquet of the Arts and Letters Club, he teased her on a subject that became a standing joke between them and one that he habitually mentioned in subsequent accounts of her first meeting:

> Before I left Boston on my initial visit I had inquired of our head proof-reader whether there were any points about 'Jalna' she wished me to discuss with the author. Our proofreader was a woman, and very nice about the decencies of life . . . she said . . . 'I wish you would ask her how such a large family—a family whose sons bring their wives home—could live in a house with so few bedrooms. I don't think she has bothered to work it out. . . .' I had fun in weaving this inquiry into my speech, and as I turned toward the guest of honor to make my point, I saw that she was blushing . . . .[12]

When she returned the galley proofs, Mazo sent along a note explaining the bedroom arrangements and ending, 'This, I think you will agree, is very snug.' Years later, when she had grown more assertive in her relations with her publishers, she took Weeks to task for his endless revival of the old story:

> I see you still cherish that letter of mine about the bedrooms at Jalna and I have a suggestion to make. It is that when my time comes and you erect a tombstone to me you will have graven on it these words:

> I THINK
> YOU WILL AGREE
> WITH ME
> THAT THIS IS VERY SNUG[13]

In fact, Edward Weeks had a tendency to combine an impeccably chivalrous attitude to women with a subtle (and probably unconscious) disparagement. When the floods of manuscripts arrived for the competition, he says, the editors' wives enlisted in the reading process were called 'the harem';[14] the librarian who dismissed the *Jalna* manuscript was paid for her unimaginative thoroughness and discouraged from further effort; when a rival publishing house sent out a female scout to lure Mazo away from Little, Brown, Weeks expressed a desire to spank the scout, who was henceforth known between them as 'the spankable woman'.[15] Often his put-downs were subtle compliments to the women present, invitations to them to identify against women and see themselves as somehow a cut above the rest. As women have done through the ages, Mazo and Caroline readily went along, enjoying such amusements as a song-and-dance routine in which he parodied (to the tune of 'Sing Something Simple') a Boston debutante. As Weeks described it:

> I was quite a dancer in those days and among other trifles I had devised a parody of a Boston debutante which I danced with a broomstick as my partner. So, after one dinner party, Mazo draped me in Caroline's mulberry bed-spread with an evil looking turban made up of one of her green scarves, and I put on an act.[16]

Of course, his last wish was to offend or harm, and the women were not consciously hurt. Yet the fact was that the new circle of editors and publishers with whom Mazo at this time formed friend- ships, and who were to become her closest friends, did not regard her as their equal. They formed relationships among themselves based, in part, on their paternalistic attitudes towards her. Weeks, for in- stance, from his first visit to Toronto developed a close friendship with Hugh Eayrs. The two became golfing partners and had the habit of referring to Mazo and Caroline as 'the girls'. Later, Lovat Dickson remembered that Hugh Eayrs privately made fun to him of Mazo's snobbisms, while in public he kept up a flirtatious relationship with her.[17]

Mazo must have been acutely aware of her exclusion from the masculine world of which she was now a part. Twenty years her junior, Weeks already had a distinguished record both academic and military. He had attended Cornell and Harvard and done graduate work at Cambridge; he served with the French Army in World War I and later with the US army, and for his services received the Croix de Guerre and the Volunteer Medal. He was justifiably proud of his background, wearing his Harvard tie to his first meeting with Mazo and later explaining his restrained response to one of her novels by the fact that he was a Harvard man and not inclined to be effusive.[18]

All this is not to suggest that Edward Weeks was deliberately as- sertive of his masculine superiority. He was simply a man trafficking in the conversational currency of his time—the man-to-man approach to fellow publishers, the male cameraderie, and the unconscious con- descension to women. At the same time, Mazo's equally unconscious acceptance of his denigration, and her connivance in it, did not lessen its disastrous consequences for her delicately balanced psyche, its corrosive effect on her sense of identity.

It is little wonder that after each social occasion Mazo needed the soothing therapy of the Play:

> In these pressing and breathless days was our Play forgotten? Were our People cast aside? Never. Returning to our flat after a reception— my throat almost too tired for speech—we would turn to the pleasure, the relaxation, of our make-believe world, so much more satisfying than the material world. . . . Our last words before sleep overtook us would be, not a bit of amusing gossip we had heard that day, not speculation on what our future might be, but words spoken from the mouths of actors in our Play.[19]

She told one interviewer: 'I wish I had a hole, like a fox, and could crawl into it and hide.'[20] And in a letter to George A. Reid, just over a month after the prize was announced, she wrote how delicious it was to be relaxing at Trail Cottage and hearing the song of the birds instead of the telephone.[21] If she had stayed there in seclusion, the collapse that happened at the end of the next six months might possibly have been averted.

Not all the pressures of the time were related to Mazo's difficulty in adjusting to her new status as noted author and famous person. There were other shocks. In June her father's youngest brother, the last of the Roches, died after suffering what Mazo describes as 'an overpowering breakdown'—the result, apparently, of the 'terrible years of strain with his morbid and exacting wife'.[22] Once again she had to make the gloomy pilgrimage to the Newmarket cemetery. Did she feel any sense of embarrassment at the contrast between the clearly engraved name 'Roche' on all the tombstones and her own now famous version of the name? Did she wonder if any of those attending the funeral or reading about it made the connection between her beheaded uncle Frank and the guillotined French ancestor? If she did feel uneasy, it must have been a familiar sensation at this time. When, six months later, on Christmas Eve, her dog Bunty—the last connection with her father—died, these two events must have represented the passing of a part of her life.

But there was another factor in Mazo's breakdown, and it sprang from the activity that was at the very core of her being. In Rockport, in the rented holiday house, she had begun a sequel to *Jalna*: 'It was in the attic, the window overlooking the harbour, that I wrote the first chapters of *Whiteoaks*, a sequel to *Jalna*. I sat in my attic revelling in the fish smell left by the receding tide and renewed my intimacy with the Whiteoaks.'[23]

The task was begun easily enough—the first half of the book was almost completed when she left Rockport—but after that she began to have serious difficulties. After the numerous distractions in Boston, New York, Toronto, and Ottawa, she got back to work only in November. But even when the frenetic social round was over and she and was again living relatively quietly at 86 Yorkville, her writing did not proceed smoothly. The reason was inherent in the subject matter of the novel itself.

She wrote of her characters' tendency to take over her work. In *Jalna* it had been Adeline Whiteoak: 'The grandmother . . . refused to remain a minor character but arrogantly, supported on either side by a son, marched to the center of the stage.'[24] Now, in the sequel, another character moved into the spotlight and remained there: Finch Whiteoak, the character with whom Mazo was most identified. Through Finch she began to tell the story of her own early life, including her first breakdown, her estrangement from her family, and her flight from them. Given that in her previous novels she had been working gradually backwards, from the fruit farm to the Acton years, in a way it was natural that she should now go back to that period of her life. Yet there was a difference in that that phase was far more painful than the others.

In living through and writing about that time Mazo reopened the old wounds and reactivated buried conflicts. It is not clear whether she turned to examine that earlier breakdown because she sensed another approaching or whether the exploration of the early breakdown produced the second; perhaps both happened at once. The situation was rather like Sylvia Plath's when, having written about her early suicide and breakdown in *The Bell Jar*, she then moved into a repetition of the earlier pattern. This kind of literary activity is bold and dangerous. At the fifteenth chapter in her book Mazo became completely blocked.

Her autobiographical account of the writing details her anxiety. When she left Rockport she forgot the manuscript that had so absorbed her in the previous weeks: 'We went to Boston. But in the excitement I forgot my manuscript, left in the attic. Weeks later it was sent to me to Canada. I had not missed it!'[25] This loss, a repetition of the incident that had heralded in her first breakdown, was to be repeated again with her next novel, *Finch's Fortune*. An image in her autobiography conveys better than any prosaic description the fear she felt at the prospect of exposing her world to public scrutiny. When she returned to Trail College, she visited Bunty's grave:

> Grass had covered Bunty's grave and close beside it a meadow lark had built her nest, there on the ground, her eggs exposed to the mercy of any who discovered them. Every morning I went to see if they were safe. One morning the nest was empty. Snake or squirrel or other vandal had taken them.[26]

When she finally recovered it was spring. She described the experience this way:

> Only a writer who has suffered an attack of nerves, such as I had passed through, can quite understand the effort of beginning, the tremendous eagerness to put down the first words, the fear of defeat, of breakdown.
>
> I knew what I wanted to write. The words were at my hand. But could I write them?
>
> One line I wrote. Then a strange rigidity struck my nerves. The pencil would not move. I could not budge it. Helpless I stared at the paper. One line! One line of ten words! And I could not—not to save my life—write another.
>
> It might have been expected that I should have been depressed. Not so. I had written—after those long months—I had written! And though it was just one line, it was a beginning. I could scarcely bear to wait till tomorrow when I might write again. All the rest of the day my spirit sang. I walked on air, counting the tardy hours.
>
> The following day I wrote another line. The day after that I wrote six lines. The next day, half a page. In a week I had written a page. I was in full swing.[27]

What gave Mazo the strength to overcome her fears and drag herself back to health? The starting point came when a nurse at the clinic to which she was going for shock treatments advised her to stop them:

> One morning at the hospital the nurse said to me, 'I am sure these treatments are bad for you. Do you find yourself in more pain all the time?
>
> I said I did.
>
> 'Then,' she said earnestly, 'don't come any more. I'm sure I'm right. But please do not tell them I said so.'[28]

In addition, Caroline left the civil service. *Jalna* had removed the need for her income, and now she could devote herself to looking after Mazo—she read to her, massaged her neck and temples, and nursed her back to health. The final step was the recognition of both women that the public life must end, and that only in privacy and anonymity could Mazo keep her health and continue her work:

> If *Jalna* had given us independence, just as certainly it had, for the time being, stolen our privacy. Above all things we longed to relax, to be unknown. We chose a small guest-house in the Niagara Peninsula. . . . What a refuge it seemed—with breakfast in bed and the dozen other guests neither speaking to us nor we to them.[29]

When they returned to Trail Cottage Mazo's recovery was under way. In order to help her work and to ensure her privacy, she had brought a roadside fruit stand from the Niagara area, which she set up as a writing room. Caroline named it 'The Folly', and it makes its appearance in Mazo's fiction as 'Fiddler's Hut'. Its chief purpose must have been to provide a writing room away from Caroline now that she was home during the days. In any event, it soon proved impractical: retaining the heat, it was stifling, and was given to the gardener John Bird for his tools. The result was that instead of leaving Mazo to work undisturbed, Caroline soon incorporated herself into the writing process:

> Caroline said to me, 'You are getting along so slowly in writing this book, I am wondering if it would be possible for you to dictate a little of it every morning to me. Even if it were only half a page, it would be something to help you till your nerves are quite well again.' . . .
> Caroline was the only one to whom I could have dictated. Not only did this working together help me to accomplish much more but it gave me confidence in myself. No longer did I think, 'How much shall I be able to write today? Shall I suffer for it?' No—I wrote what I could, then hastened to where Caroline was waiting, eager to put on paper what was in my mind. I should perhaps write two pages, while she could write three or four. And so the novel *Whiteoaks* moved towards its finish.[30]

From the end of the fifteenth chapter on, the holograph manuscript is written in two hands, as are most of the subsequent novels. Thus the situation of the Play, in which Caroline was the eager follower, the willing partner and muse, had been extended to the creative process. Mazo not only felt more confident but was stimulated by Caroline's supportive presence, just as she had been long ago when Caroline entered so readily into her private world.

This stimulus was exactly what Mazo needed in order to finish the book that was nearest to the bone, that tapped the deepest part of herself. The work that came out of this struggle was the strongest novel in the Jalna series, arguably the best she ever wrote. Finch is clearly the focal character, and his struggle to emerge as a man provides a rich psychological drama to which the other events—the return and flight of Eden, the love story of Renny and Alayne, the death and funeral of the grandmother—are closely linked.

When the editors saw *Whiteoaks* they were jubilant. Edward Weeks wrote to Mazo that he was confident that her powers were increasing. His appreciation was quite genuine, for he wrote separately to Hugh Eayrs saying that he thought it superior to *Jalna* and praising the 'firm and sensitive way in which . . . she has brought out the characters of Finch and Renny. These men have grown mightily in the two years that separates the books, and it seems to me more than any thing else, they give evidence of Mazo's increasing powers.'[31] For his part, Eayrs called it a 'stunning performance', much superior to *Jalna*, and opined that it placed Mazo 'amongst the masters of the modern novel'.[32] As if to confirm their judgement, it took only two weeks for the book to leap to second place on the National Bestseller List in the United States. For Mazo the triumph was more than literary: it was a personal triumph too. She had gone back to that desperate earlier time, worked through it, relived it, had almost gone under a second time, and had come out on solid ground. She certainly had reasons for rejoicing. There was not the surprise, not the public celebration that *Jalna* had caused, but a profound sense of joy and deliverance.

The two women stayed late at Trail Cottage that year, contentedly enjoying the fall, the solitude, and each other's company. But inevitably the season turned cold and it was necessary to move back to the city for the winter. This time they did not return to Gertrude Pringle's house, perhaps finding the intimacy that had developed there intrusive. Instead, they moved to a nearby rooming house (Mazo called it a 'pension') at 192 Bloor Street West.[33]

Mazo has left a vivid picture of Mrs Billings's house in the story 'Peter—A Rock'. Young Ffolkes is the only man and the only young person among seventeen elderly women guests. Their conversation is mainly about church and hospital, and accordingly they take an almost overpowering interest in the affairs of the unusual person in their midst. When he entertains friends who give 'vent to loud masculine guffaws' they smile indulgently. When they read that he plans a late evening, they feel a vicarious satisfaction:

> The front door was locked early at Mrs Dowling's and it was a rule of the house that any of the guests who stayed out late should lay a slip of paper on the table in the hall informing the parlormaid of the fact so that she might stay up to let him in. Young Ffolkes had often a

sneaking sort of feeling when, night after night, he laid his slip of paper bearing the words, 'Mr Ffolkes will be out late,' on the hall table. Each one of the ladies read this slip, not with disapproval, as he imagined, but with a certain exhilaration. It was almost as though she were out with him herself.[34]

Young Ffolkes is the darling of the house, as Mazo and Caroline must have been, conspicuous among the other guests for their relative youth, their active social life, and Mazo's fame. They went out a great deal to parties and theatres; they entertained friends in their room and in the dining room; they even joined a dancing club. The experience must have given them a sensation of being young and daring that they had rarely known during their actual youth.

It was a wonderfully lighthearted time, as they were no longer awed by their new wealth and yet still sufficiently unspoiled to find it exhilarating. They could contemplate changes and plan activities without having to consider money: 'It was pleasant to buy clothes without worry over their cost.' Even more pleasurable was another prospect: 'We felt that a chapter in our lives was closed. A new world was opening up. We thought we should like to take a trip right round it.'[35] At first they decided on a round-the-world cruise, but that plan was modified at the suggestion of Professor Pelham Edgar, and they set off instead for Europe.

12

Passage to Europe

Taking a sightseeing trip abroad is something that anyone recently possessed of a fortune might be expected to do. But Mazo and Caroline were not ordinary people, and they embarked on their first long journey in a different spirit from most tourists. In fact, they thought of this less as their first journey than as a revisiting of familiar places, since long before they had the means to travel, their imaginations had conjured up very adequate substitutes.

Looking back at their destination, one might wonder at the choice of Mussolini's Italy. But of course it was not Mussolini's Italy to them—perhaps not even modern Italy at all. None of their letters of the time indicate the slightest interest in the political situation. Rather, it was the fantasy world of their youth:

> An observer might have called us little stay-at-homes who knew nothing of travel, but how wrong a conception of our life! For we travelled when we willed, in the freedom of our Play. Well we knew the rugged shore of a certain island off the west coast of Scotland. We explored sandy beach and wooded hill of England. After reading Henry Harland's novels of Italy, that became our favorite country. . . .[1]

It was, then, to the Italy of fiction that they headed. Lovat Dickson described the next period of their life as 'living the dream',[2] a phrase that suggests some of the hazards inherent in trying to match reality to fantasy. In the first place, there were practical problems. All who knew Mazo described her nervousness about the practical details of ordinary life—such as getting places on time, or finding a cab with a safe driver. They record Caroline's strenuous efforts to prevent her from being ruffled. Yet travelling, even in the most luxurious and protected circumstances, always involves upheaval. Mazo kept a little flask of brandy in her purse for times of stress and soothed her nerves by taking frequent sips.[3] She must have needed many before the *Vulcania*, an Italian liner on its maiden voyage, set sail from New York carrying her on her first trip to Europe. Even so, she did not avoid a bronchial cough—the infallible sign of stress for Mazo.

The stress was particularly intense at this time because her Boston publishers seized the excuse of her departure to create a great burst of publicity. They arranged an elaborate luncheon on board the ship just before it left New York. Edward Weeks described the event with great satisfaction to Hugh Eayrs:

> We were fortunate enough to get on her trail early in the morning, and so had her in the guest of honor's seat when our sixty-five guests showed up. Among them were—Dr Canby, Amy Loveman, Donald Adams of *The Times*, Irita Van Doren, Miss Seaman and Mr Brett, . . . the Literary Guild and BOMC crowd, and all of the important book buyers in the city. The luncheon was given in the main salon of the S.S. Vulcania, that magnificent new Italian liner. . . . At Mazo's table were Mazo and Caroline, Wallis Howe of our N.Y. office, Frederick Melcher, Miss Ulrick of Coward-McCann, and myself. During lunch Seward Collins artist from the Bookman made several sketches of Mazo, who was quite unaware of the fact. . . . When the tumult had subsided, the two girls, the Howes, Mr and Mrs Ross and my wife retired to her mother's house where they took things easy with some tea and Scotch at the elbow.[4]

Mazo herself wrote a proud account of the event to Katherine Hale:

> After the luncheon a photographer from the New York Times took pictures of me on deck. After that half a dozen of us went for tea in a quite magnificent house on West 53rd Street. Our hostess was Lady Thornton's lovely sister, Mrs Edward Weeks. . . . After that we had dinner in a restaurant where there was no lack of cocktails (which I detest) then we motored to Hoboken (under the river) to Christopher Morley's theater. We reached our boat at half past eleven, shortly before she sailed.[5]

It was in her autobiography, thirty years later, that Mazo recorded her true feelings as she looked back on the gala event: all the activities coming just after her recovery from flu were exhausting and made her seasick for the first two days of the voyage. The event revived some of the trauma that had surrounded her early success, and she wrote that she was left feeling so drained that she was almost suicidal:

> I still have the photograph, in which, wearing a great bunch of violets, I look dreadfully like a movie star. That night, casting myself on my berth completely exhausted, I burst into tears. I thought I knew what

movie stars felt when they took an overdose of sleeping tablets and ended all publicity.[6]

All the same, life on board ship was very much to her taste, and she soon regained her enthusiasm for living out the dream. She was to sail across the Atlantic many times in future years, but this first crossing was the most thrilling. In addition to being suspended in her own private world with Caroline, she was surrounded by a throng of characters from many different countries that she could observe and draw on for her fiction.

Yet the sudden change from one culture to another was unsettling. For one with Mazo's precarious sense of identity, the removal from familiar surroundings to foreign soil was jarring. 'Culture shock' is perhaps too mild a phrase to cover all the ramifications. During this period she wavered between moments of euphoria and an insidious sense of dislocation and unreality. Perhaps it was no coincidence that their holiday was marred by one health complication after another. As well as the persistent bronchial cough, Mazo suffered from two bouts of flu, and later, in the bright Mediterranean glare of the sun, from eye problems. When they arrived in Sicily her cough immediately disappeared, but then it was Caroline's turn to be ill: she came down with a severe attack of flu that required daily visits from the doctor and worried Mazo greatly. Only after Caroline had got over the flu and both of them recovered from a serious case of sunburn were they finally able to settle down and enjoy themselves.[7]

Of course, Mazo's enjoyment was not of the orthodox kind. She said herself that no one could have seen less of the place, since she did not explore with a guide-book, inspect sites of historical interest, or absorb local color.[8] Paradoxically, however, though she saw less than most tourists, she profited enormously from the little she did see. Unusual surroundings excited her imagination, fed her inner world, and provided story material. By all accounts she spent much of her time lying in a pool of sunlight on the bedroom floor and dictating stories, which Caroline typed out on a borrowed typewriter.[9] The three stories she produced on the spot were quickly and profitably placed and paid all the (considerable) expenses of the trip.

The place that caused this burst of creativity was Taormina, a town with many layers of history. Founded in AD 358 by Andromachus, it was made into a Roman military colony because of its important strategic position high above the island's beaches; just outside the town are the ruins of a Greco-Roman amphitheatre. From the nineteenth century on it became a favoured resort of Britons, who left a legacy of splendid villas set in expansive and colourful English gardens.

Mazo divided her time between two establishments with a flavour that was more British than Italian. She stayed at the Hotel Villa San Pancrazio, run by the widow of an English doctor, and her social life revolved around the Casa Campobella, owned by a former big-game hunter from Montreal, Percival Campbell, and his English companion, Miles Wood. They lived an affluent high-Bohemian life, acting as patrons for local artists and making their antique-filled villa a centre for social and artistic events. Miles Wood, who was a playwright and actor as well as an artist, staged plays in the villa's roof-topped theatre. As an established playwright Mazo had a natural entrée into their salon and was soon pressed into service to write plays for future performances.[10]

The atmosphere of Taormina was so much to her taste that she planned to return every year for the rest of her life. The conflicting cultures of the place provided a new set of images for the basic psychic conflicts that fuelled her work, and her interesting new friends were to appear in her fiction. She saw in Campbell and Wood's relationship a parallel to her own and Caroline's, and their easy way of life suggested possibilities for herself.

The three stories that Mazo wrote in Taormina show a preoccupation with comparing, in durability and vitality, unorthodox relationships with those condoned by society and formalized by marriage. The mixed racial strains of the characters in all these stories provide images for gender and sexual orientation, the 'other countries' that the characters inhabit being sexual as well as geographical. 'The Broken Fan'[11] takes place on a liner in mid-ocean, a setting that suspends the characters in a no-man's land between countries. The main characters are a rich woman (evidently widowed) of mixed race and a lover about twenty years her junior who is financially dependent on her. The two have only surnames—Mrs Friedland and Wolfe—and the story concerns her tormented jealousy over him. She knows that the ties that bind them are as insubstantial as the tissue-paper streamers tossed over them at a ball. Moreover, he is attracted to a Jewish girl who is close to his own age and the only single person in a group of married couples. For Mazo the story is unusually devoid of plot; it has no climax and no dénouement. Like all the stories she wrote at this time, it shows a sophisticated use of symbolism and some grasp of modern short-story techniques. It ends with a powerful symbol of the tormented woman: her broken fan becomes a wounded bird, its spokes snapped to pieces like broken limbs, and its colour is green—for jealousy.

The two other stories[12] depict women caught between two lovers— one staid and Anglo-Saxon, the other Mediterranean and dangerously sexual. In both cases a relative of the woman makes the trio of characters into a quartet. A fourth story, 'Guy and Gaetano',[13] belongs in setting and theme to the same group, although it was written two years later, on her return visit, and never published. Its effect is that of a story such as 'The Jewellry' by Guy de Maupassant, with a surprise discovery, after her death, of a woman's secret and separate love life. Yet like many of Mazo's apparently hackneyed fictions, it is far more than a pale imitation. A newly bereaved son discovers that, just before her death, his mother had arranged a liaison with a lover. She had appeared to be a blameless Italian matron, spending her time entertaining at tea in a tower room (where, incidentally, there are no books—because 'like most women of her race, she had cared much for talk and little for reading'). A headless statue of the Virgin Mary early in the story alerts the reader to the possibility of flawed womanhood, but the revelation of his mother's double life comes as a shock to her son. He takes her place at the assignation, gives her English-speaking lover his come-uppance, and determines both to protect his father from the knowledge of his wife's duplicity and to take her place in his affections. (There are overtones of incest, as the son closely resembles his mother, and the three have always looked like siblings). The love affair with the idealized, ethereal, non-sexual woman must be preserved at all costs.

All these stories are highly complex fictions in which the subversive subtexts, full of covert meanings, are completely at odds with the bland surfaces. The most ambitious work inspired by Mazo's glimpse of Italy, however, is her novel *Lark Ascending*, which was published three years later. An expanded version of the quartet theme, like the stories it owes its inspiration both to the transition from Canada to Italy and to the vibrations set up in Mazo by her relationship with Caroline, which had recently undergone a transformation.

Any relationship is destabilized—for better or worse—when one partner suddenly gains a fortune. In the case of Mazo and Caroline, not only their way of life but the balance of power between them had changed drastically. Until 1928 Caroline's civil-service job had been the chief source of income. Her sense of self-sacrifice is evident in a light-hearted poem she produced for a party game in the twenties:

Little Miss Muffet
Sat on a tuffet
(A government job by-the-way)
And mused on her author so gay.
'If I could compell'er
To write a bestseller
I'd chuck this old tuffet away.[14]

In addition to serving as the bread-winner, Caroline had been responsible for making both Trail Cottage and their winter apartments habitable and attractive. She also did all the shopping, listened tirelessly to 'works in progress', and typed the manuscripts. In other words, the smooth running of their daily life devolved entirely upon her, and Mazo's complete dependence gave Caroline a measure of power.

But in a stroke, in the spring of 1927, everything had changed. Mazo became the sole provider on a much more successful scale than Caroline had ever been. And while Mazo was both vague about the value of money and quick to talk about her pliable nature, she kept complete control of the purse-strings. There were no shared bank accounts or houses purchased in joint names: when Mazo died, Caroline expressed gratitude that she was bequeathed the house and the means to maintain it.

It was probably no accident that at the same time as the financial ascendency in the relationship was reversed, Caroline made herself indispensable to the creative process. She helped Mazo through her acute writer's block by sitting with her as she worked and taking dictation. The preserved manuscripts of the next fifteen years, written turn and turn about, show what a demanding process this must have been. And since she was such an important part of the creative process, Caroline exercised a certain control over the finished product, as the following incident makes clear.

When *Whiteoaks* was under way, *Cosmopolitan* magazine had paid two thousand dollars for the option on the serialization, but when the book was finished the editors insisted on a different ending. Mazo records that she wavered ('as always I longed to be told what to do'), but Caroline's response was unequivocal:

Caroline looked me firmly in the eyes. 'You are not to attempt it,' she said. 'It would ruin the story. It would be madness.'

'But it would change the ending only for the magazine,' I insisted, wishing really to rouse her. 'It would not affect the book.'

'It will affect you,' she declared. 'I won't see you ruin your health.'

'But twenty-five thousand dollars. . . .'

'What is twenty-five thousand dollars?' she demanded scornfully in a rags-to-riches tone. 'I won't let you do it.'[15]

Mazo was persuaded and the book was serialized with its original ending—though less profitably—in the *Atlantic Monthly*.

And just as Caroline's participation in the creative process had grown, so her influence extended gradually to many other areas. It was she who, in the next years, was responsible for acquiring the grand houses and gardens, for hiring and supervising the servants, and generally for raising their standard of living to a very high level indeed. In spite of these duties, it was a long time before she agreed to relinquish any of the secretarial and bookkeeping tasks, and this she did only when ill-health and failing eye-sight forced her to. A few years later, in an unusually frank handwritten note to Hugh Eayrs during one of Caroline's absences, Mazo complained of her tenacity:

> Yet always I write, write, and always struggle vainly to catch up with my correspondence. Always I look forward to the time when my man- uscript and business papers will be in order but that time will never come while Caroline is my secretary. She has too much on her mind. It is really one person's work to run this house. She loves the garden which takes a lot of her time, she loves the house, she clings to every- thing connected with my work. So—there we are.[16]

Another factor in the shifting nature of their union may have been that as Mazo grew older, her dependence on Caroline diminished. Most of the friends who observed them shared Lovat Dickson's opin- ion: 'She and Caroline were deeply attached, but I don't think they were lesbian lovers as Gertrude Stein and Alice B. Toklas were, or Radclyffe Hall and Una Trowbridge were. But they were "man and wife" in a peculiar way.'[17]

There was no outward sign of tension; Mazo and Caroline appeared to move in complete harmony into a new and different phase of their life together. Only in Mazo's fiction do signs begin to appear of a preoccupation with the power balance of relationships. It was around this time that she had her fictional representative Finch Whiteoak (in *Finch's Fortune*, written 1929-30) fall into the clutches of and later marry a cousin who is so possessive that her obsession drives him literally mad.

In *Lark Ascending* Mazo explores the symbiotic relationship between an artist and his muse. Though the story never reaches the night- marish Gothic depths of madness, the word 'possession' in various forms is used repeatedly throughout the novel. The title recalls Shake-speare's early sonnet in which his relationship with the young man who is the 'onlie begetter' of the poems is still formal and placid:

> Haply I think on thee, and then my state,
> Like to the lark at break of day arising
> From sullen earth sings hymns at Heaven's gate;
> For they sweet love remembr'd such wealth brings
> That then I scorn to change my state with kings.

Those lines well express Mazo's often-repeated acknowledgements of Caroline's part in her life and her work. Indeed, the rising-lark motif, which Mazo eventually took as her own emblem, is engraved on her tombstone above her family motto.

In the novel one of the four main characters, Diego Palmas, a young painter of mixed race, is loved by a cousin, Josie Froward, who, having been taken in by the family, 'worked like a dog' for them. Although Diego does not return Josie's love, he is dependent on her help in his painting:

> He had the ability to create and she knew she did not have it. But she had the power to interpret what he created. She could take his formless, ill-judged creations and build them up, coax them into a kind of se-renity, so that they satisfied the senses, not tormented them. Josie loved paintings as Diego did not.
>
> She had conquered her shyness sufficiently to come secretly with Diego to Mr Selby for lessons. She had got up at dawn, she had worked into the night, in order to find time for this secret expression of her being. All she did she kept hidden in her attic room where no one went but herself. But it was over the pictures which she and Diego had painted together that she exulted. He got all the credit for these. No one knew that she had put a brush to them. These were the pictures that puzzled Mr Selby. Under his eye Diego showed only a chaotic, primitive promise. Away from him Diego painted things that made him stare.[18]

The possibility that Caroline herself ever had any literary talents or aspirations is rarely mentioned. Yet in a letter to Raymond Knister (probably written in 1924) Mazo enclosed two poems by Caroline, who she thought had 'an interesting talent'.[19] She wrote that Caroline was too shy to send them around herself, but would be tremendously encouraged if Knister thought they were good enough for his *Midland* magazine. Apart from the informal private verses she wrote to ac-company her birthday and Christmas gifts for Mazo, however, noth-ing did come of Caroline's talent for verse.

The other members of the quartet in *Lark Ascending* are Diego's mother, Fay Palmas, and her long-time admirer, a stalwart though somewhat dull druggist called Purley Bond. Liberated by her widowhood from toiling in the family's bakery business, Fay gains possession of a small fortune, leads the other characters to Italy, marries an Italian count, and becomes the chatelaine of his ancient villa. By virtue of her beauty and talent as a singer she soon establishes a salon and becomes a celebrated member of international society. Yet when her husband, impecunious himself, soon gambles away her fortune, Josie and Purley have to help her turn her salon into a money-making venture.

Fay, like Josie, owes a great deal to Mazo's study of Caroline. Purley Bond had looked forward to the joy of guiding Fay to new experiences:

> He had pictured these excursions with himself as leader, always at Fay's side, listening to her excited laughter, her naive comments on it all. He had thought they would be drawn closer in the foreign lands.[20]

But Fay proves to be much more adept than he in adapting to their new experiences and surroundings, and she shows 'a primitive determination not to allow conventions to deprive her of this romantic escape from the tameness of ordinary relations:'[21] 'She felt power to change the circumstances that surrounded her, to create a new life—after all those years of being hedged in, helpless to free herself from the forces that had trapped her.'[22]

Mazo's usual method (Finch Whiteoak is something of an exception) was to separate the various strands of her own nature and parcel them out among different characters. There is something of her in Diego, in Purley Bond, and even in Fay Palmas, just as there is something of Caroline in Josie Froward and Fay. But she also drew on her repertory company of family and friends, and the basic quartet of *Lark Ascending* owes much to Katherine Hale and John Garvin. While Mazo travelled, Katherine (who had visited and written of many of the same places) was much in her mind. She set up Katherine's portrait beside her bed wherever she was and wrote to her of *Lark Ascending*: 'I thought you would love that book. In it a certain part of me spoke to a certain part of you—those parts of us which laugh together.'[23]

The relationship between Caroline, Mazo, Katherine Hale, and John Garvin had over the past fifteen years undergone the same kind of upheavals as Mazo's relationship with Caroline. In the beginning Mazo had revered Katherine as an established writer and a woman of position and wealth. After the death of Alberta Roche, Mazo and

Caroline, living on slender means, had been happy to spend Christmas with the Garvins in their luxurious house on Russell Hill Road. But over the years, as Mazo's literary and financial fortunes had risen, Katherine's had declined. Although Garvin's business concerns had occasionally gone up, the direction was mainly down, and twice Katherine had experienced the painful process of having her homes full of elegant furniture and family heirlooms sold from under her. Finally, she and Garvin had separated, although they remained friends and saw each other daily as long as he lived. But Katherine was most often in the company of a younger admirer whom Mazo despised (her opinion was no doubt tinged by her anti-Semitism) as a social climber.[24]

Fortunately, Katherine Hale had many social connections, and her rich friends always supported her money-making endeavours. Chief among these were literary recitals given in pleasant surroundings at which tea and refreshments were served and a fee tactfully requested. (Katherine had trained as a singer, but as pneumonia and time had impaired her voice she no longer sang except to groups of intimate friends.)[25]

The details of Katherine's life suggest that she contributed much both to Mazo's imagination and to *Lark Ascending*. Her young admirer believed that John Garvin and Caroline loved each other and, while his judgement was probably naïve and romantic, it does suggest something of the manner in which the four friends functioned together, with the rapport of the two artists, Katherine and Mazo, balanced by the warm friendship between their partners.

Whatever the inspiration, Mazo's resolution to *Lark Ascending* is almost too neat. Mother and son, Fay and Diego, temperamentally attuned to Sicily, remain there happily, both their duplicitous foreign lovers and their dependable Anglo-Saxon ones having conveniently paired off together. The foreign lovers drift away and Josie and Purley return purposefully to New England and a conventional marriage.

In the last chapter of the novel Mazo makes an unusual (for her) fictional gesture in the form of a self-referential epilogue. She introduces two women 'of nearly fifty' who have been saving up for years and are now making their first visit to 'the very Throne of Romance,' just two years after the events of the story.[26] They meet romance in the person of Fay Palmas and are excited to come face to face with a genuine countess who owns an ancient villa. They are saddened to learn that like many members of old families, she has had to go into the antique business in order to maintain the ancestral home. When Fay says that she once went to New England, and that she speaks

English just a little, she seems to believe her own fictions: there is no indication whether her deception is intentional. In any case, the conclusion is clear that between their unadventurous life and Fay's, even if it is based on make-believe, hers is preferable. Who would not choose to live in 'the very Throne of Romance'?

For Mazo and Caroline, it was not so much that they wished to abandon the throne of romance as that they felt it could also exist elsewhere. At the end of their holiday in Sicily they were eager to move on. They sailed from Naples to England and, for all their intentions to return, their love affair with Taormina turned out to be no more than a brief interlude.

At two years.

At eleven years.

*At Lake Simcoe in the early
1920s with her dog, Bunty.*

Caroline in London, 1937.

Mazo and Caroline in the early 1930s. (Courtesy of Esmée Rees.)

Esmée and René with their nanny in St James's Park, London, in the mid-1930s. (Courtesy of Esmée Rees.)

Benares, the house near Trail Cottage that is generally thought to be the model for Jalna. (Courtesy of Esmée Rees.)

Vale House in Windsor. (Courtesy of Esmée Rees.)

Mazo in the garden at Windrush Hill, 1944.

Mazo and Caroline at a Toronto reception in the late 1950s. (Courtesy of Esmée Rees.)

The graves of Mazo, Caroline, and René in the churchyard at Sibbald's Point, overlooking Lake Simcoe. (Courtesy of Heather Kirk.)

13

England, Act One: Being 'Country People'[1]

The side of her nature that Sicily stirred was not one that Mazo was comfortable in having exposed, even to herself. She wrote to Arnold Palmer, the English critic who became her friend: 'I am a queer fish and perhaps Sicily has made me queerer. . . . Yet, more or less I have always been so. Perhaps that is what it is to be of mixed race'.[2] To Edward Weeks she said more prosaically that the air of Sicily was 'too exciting' and that she could not relax there. The more temperate climate of England suited her better, she claimed. In fact, however, the attraction was not so much the weather as the English social climate.

Full of excitement when she arrived in London, she recorded her feelings in a letter to Anne Dimock: 'Then the train, Trafalgar Square, the lions, the Houses of Parliament, Buckingham Palace, bang, bang, bang, one after another like so many explosions.'[3] Finch Whiteoak, in Mazo's next novel, experiences similar sensations:

> There they were, crowded into a taxi, making their way through the traffic of the London streets—Finch on one of the drop-seats, almost dislocating his neck in the effort to see out of both windows at once. It was too unreal, seeing the places he had heard of so familiarly all his life. Westminster Bridge, the Houses of Parliament, Trafalgar Square, the lions, Buckingham Palace! They thundered at him like a series of explosions. It was too much. It was overwhelming.[4]

Mazo's admiration for all that England represented is fascinating. Having internalized all the pain that her situation in life caused her, outwardly she identified with all that diminished her—both as a woman and as a member of a British colony. She relished the hierarchical structure of English society and all its manifestations of male supremacy and imperialism. When she lived in London, as she often did in her eight-and-a-half years of residence in England, she headed directly for Westminster, loving to live in the shadow of the Houses of Parliament and Buckingham Palace. And nothing was more symptomatic of her attitude than her reverence for the royal family.

She made a habit of journeying from wherever she was living (often a four-hour train journey each way) to attend whatever royal function was taking place in London. Her publishers and other connections managed to get her vantage points along the route or in Westminster Abbey so that she felt like a member of the extended family as she attended royal funerals and weddings. In 1934, for instance, she rushed off to see the marriage of the Duke of Kent to Marina, the youngest daughter of Prince Nicholas of Greece and Denmark and Helen Vladimirovna, Grand Duchess of Russia, writing that she and Caroline were given splendid seats and that it was all quite unforgettable: 'Nowhere in the world can pageantry be staged as it can in Old England.'[5]

It was, therefore, highly gratifying for Mazo to learn through the secretary to Queen Mary that Her Majesty had read each of the Jalna books, expressed great delight in them, and asked if she could have a signed copy of *The Master of Jalna*. Honoured to fulfil the request, Mazo had a handsome tooled-leather volume bound for the presentation. She was less pleased when, seizing the opportunity for some favourable publicity, Edward Weeks wrote a tribute to Mazo in the *Atlantic Monthly*,[6] accompanied by pictures of 'The Queen's Book'. Incensed that Macmillan of Canada seemed to be getting the credit for the specially bound copy, she wrote to Weeks demanding a correction in the next issue:

> What the hell do you mean by giving the Macmillan Co. of Canada credit for the book? I have been so furious about that I have refrained from writing. The Macmillan Co. had absolutely nothing to do with it beyond suggesting the name of the man who did the work. I interviewed him, chose the design and paid $40 for the book. What annoys me is that to the readers of the Atlantic the incident should be presented as a commercial one whereas it was a purely personal one between her Majesty and myself.
>
> I should like to write you a note to publish in The Contributors' Column correcting that statement. At what date should you have it for your next number?[7]

He managed to soothe her, as he did so expertly in many similar matters, and the royal family continued to be among her most loyal fans. In later years the papers proclaimed that when someone offered George VI a copy of one of her books he said that he had already read it and (as the headlines went) 'THE QUEEN HAS TOO'.[8] Later, Elizabeth II became a fan and was said to owe her interest in her future dominion to her early reading of the Jalna books.[9]

That the royal family should have been Jalna fans is entirely plausible. The similarities between the Whiteoak and Windsor clans is so marked that the same pen might have invented both. Both are self-sufficient in their family solidarity, impervious to current fashion, and so full of personal rectitude and family pride that even personal weaknesses are flaunted as badges. They share fairly simple tastes in their daily lives, and both invite the term 'soap opera' for the complications in their private lives. They are overwhelmingly horsey, dog-ridden, philistine, and anti-intellectual. Their ideal men tend to the tough military mould, each generation producing almost to order a series of sons and a single daughter. Finally, each generation produces at least one maverick to depart from the family mould and cause alarm for his non-conformity to the family ideal and his 'weakness' for the performing arts. Very telling is the strict patriarchal order of both houses and the gender polarities that mark the expected behaviour of their members, and the strong privileging of the masculine over the feminine. If the women become athletic, energetic, and strong, they are accepted. If the men turn out to be artistic and intellectual, there is consternation.

The similarity between the two houses was not entirely coincidental, since Mazo had long studied the royal family. There is a little of Queen Victoria in the matriarch Adeline Whiteoak, and a little of Queen Alexandra in Augusta Whiteoak, who wears Queen Alexandra fringes. Mazo had a special affection for the young Prince of Wales and was very disapproving of Wallis Simpson during the abdication scandal of 1936. Eden Whiteoak was based partly on Edward, and his entanglement with the experienced and previously married Amy Stroud was in part inspired by her feelings about the abdication.

But the royal family was by no means the only thing that attracted Mazo to England. She loved the country's history, the countryside, and the unfamiliar birds and flowers, as well as the new words for the hills and valleys and waterways of an unfamiliar landscape; unexpected surprises like a military parade and a fox hunt delighted her. Even the bland English cuisine suited her rather plain taste in food: with her fondness for cakes in particular and dessert in general, she loved sampling tipsy pudding, gooseberry tart, and scones with Devon cream and strawberry jam.

Caroline's joy at being in England was slightly different. Always more worldly than Mazo, and something of a snob, she was pleased with the entry they suddenly gained into elevated social circles. She loved being invited to grand homes run by well-trained staffs—'four servants to wait on six of us'—and wrote detailed accounts to the Dimocks:

> Aren't London dinner parties delightful things? We were asked to several and two very nice ones were given for Mazo. One by a member of her publishing house here—Mr Daniel Macmillan, the other by a charming elderly woman with whom we got acquainted on shipboard coming from Naples two years ago. The first was a party of more or less young literary and artistic people—and in a very modern London house in Belgravia. The second a party of old or elderly people—and in an old Adams house in Portland Place. My dear Anne—such a contrast—and we enjoyed them equally! Such perfectly charming and interesting elderly people it is delightful to meet. They seem more Georgian or Elizabethan than Victorian. And that beautiful house. One dinner which we both enjoyed very much was a small one given by Violet Hunt—divorced wife of Ford Madox Heuffer the writer.[10]

Mazo had for many years thought of her spiritual home not merely as England, but more specifically as the southwest from whence, centuries earlier, the Lundys had sailed for the New World. Spotting in the paper soon after she arrived an advertisement for a place to rent in Devon on the edge of Dartmoor, she decided to move there. A satisfactory arrangement was worked out with the owners for a two-month occupancy of the place, modestly named 'The Cottage.'[11] A small stone house in a lovely garden, it came equipped with a maid and a dog. Mazo liked the owners, Captain and Mrs Dyke-Acland, as much as she did the house and she saw a striking physical resemblance between them and her mother.[12] Through them she made friends in the neighbourhood, most of whom, she noted proudly, were military people with distinguished records. Like Finch Whiteoak, who on arriving in England 'pictured himself as a leaf blown back across the sea', she felt that she had come home. She wrote to Weeks:

> somewhere-in-Devon
> which is almost the same as somewhere-in-heaven
>
> My dear Ted,
> Do you know Devon? Its greenness, its roundness, its deep red soil, its lanes, between hedges overrunning with roses. Its girls with blazing cheeks and sing-song voices.[13]

This time Mazo did not, as she had done in Sicily, immediately transform her new experience into fiction. There was always a part of her that rejected immediate and present surroundings and made her carve out her own world and her own space. Now, for all her love of Devon, she shut it out of her fictional life. Instead, she looked back to the divided house in which she had lived during the last months of her father's life. The result was *Portrait of a Dog*, an auto-biographical novel in the form of an extended apostrophe to Bunty, beginning in December 1915 and telling the story of the dog's life. Her conclusion of the work coincided with the end of her two months at The Cottage.

Her American publishers were not overjoyed at the prospect of a dog story, as she reported in a letter to W.A. Deacon:

> I don't think you need worry about my 'writing new stuff with money in view'. My imagination simply won't stand forcing. Also there is something in my disposition which rebels at authority—even the authority of my public. To illustrate this let me tell you that I spent the summer and early autumn writing something that I am quite sure my American publishers looked on as a waste of my time. Indeed one of the heads of the company wrote imploring me—'not to go down any by-paths.'[14]

Nevertheless, she persisted, and the combined forces of dog-lovers everywhere and of Mazo's ever-increasing popularity produced brisk sales. In March 1931 Ellery Sedgewick wrote to say that he knew the book was charming but had not thought other people would respond in such numbers to its charm. It was, he said, remarkable how intelligent people were![15]

Not ready to leave Devon when the lease expired, Mazo and Caroline found another place in Winkleigh, a five-hundred-year-old (the precise age varied from account to account) farmhouse called Seckington in spacious grounds that included fields and an orchard. Mazo described their decision to take it:

> What a wonderful place to live, said Caroline, almost at the edge of the moor, and always we have loved the country. We really are country people, you know, she said fixing me with a look from her clear blue eyes, and if we took this house, it would solve the problem of what to do with all the bed-linen and so forth that we bought for The Cottage. . . . I had never before heard of taking a house just for the protection of a dozen sheets, but when Caroline says a thing it always sounds so reasonable. I, on the contrary, may make a profoundly sensible remark but I make it in such a manner that people only laugh.[16]

Since the house would not be available for occupancy until the end of October, they decided to embark once again on a round of visits to places they had always wanted to see, beginning with Cornwall and then going to the Cotswolds, Oxford, London, and back to Devon. Wherever possible they avoided hotels and tried to rent small houses in which they could maintain their privacy. The following letter from Bude, Cornwall, to Edward Weeks well illustrates Mazo's mood at this time. She was happy to be seeing England, but her mind was already incubating a third volume in the Jalna series:

> What dreadful things holiday resorts are! We came here for a week on our way to Scotland and we had not been here for a day before we were wondering why we had come and still more why we were going to Scotland. These days the desire to write is on me and hotels are no place for that. On the spur of the moment, we went to a house agent and took the last furnished house on his list. Here we shall stay enjoying the peace and picnicking on these glorious Cornish cliffs. For September we have a cottage on the Cotswolds. We look forward to London in October.
>
> Thoughts of another sequel are often with me but I have made no beginning. . . . If I do not write any more about them it will not be because they are not continuing their life in my mind. In fact, vigorous incidents come into it, work their will, pass away and are forgotten. But certain happenings have solidified and will perhaps insist on being written down.[17]

The prolonged holiday was not entirely peaceful, for in the Cotswolds Mazo began again to suffer the severe head pains that had afflicted her in the past. Once more she was in her fictional world and, through the character of Finch Whiteoak, re-entering that tormented period of her own early life, probing sensitive areas and suffering the consequences. Although Caroline in her letters spoke only of colds and more routine illnesses, Mazo wrote to Katherine Hale that she had had to have electrical treatments. With Caroline's help, however, when they returned to Seckington she was able to start work immediately on the new novel.

The return to Devon was like a homecoming. A modest staff of three—a maid, a cook and a gardener—had gone ahead and prepared the place for them. Caroline described their return:

> I do love London. But oh, the getting back to Seckington! How I wish you could see it and know how lovely it can look. It is such a big sprawling inviting place and its approach through a 1/4 mile avenue of beeches, meeting overhead, make me feel as though in a mysterious green tunnel that might lead *anywhere*. And how it shone for our return. Our cook and the maid had been here for a week and everything was in perfect order. Fires on every hearth, flowers in every room—brasses

and silver shining. And such a dinner. Roast young duck, tipsy pudding—and for tea cook's marvellous home-made bread![18]

Here they both worked very hard, Mazo at her book and Caroline
doing several jobs at the same time, each of which might have exhausted a less energetic person. Besides acting as amanuensis in the
writing of the stories, keeping Mazo company, and listening tirelessly
to her ideas, she typed the manuscript of *Portrait of a Dog* and made
a condensed version of it for publication in *Good Housekeeping*.[19] She
also acted as chatelaine and supervised the house, the garden, and
the staff. 'Housekeeping', she wrote the Dimocks, 'is so much more
complicated here than at home.' She also found time for a new hobby
that had begun in Sicily when she admired the contents of Percival
Campbell's villa: antique-collecting, that favourite pastime of the nou-
veau riche. In her letters she spoke as if her present way of life was
quite natural to her, and if there was an air of play-acting about it, it
was still a very convincing act.

Once they were settled in Seckington the new novel, *Finch's Fortune*,
proceeded very well. It fell into two parts as Mazo yoked together
her recent experiences in coming to England and her memories of the
past. She has Finch suffer the torments of disappointed love, and yet
shows his movement from outcast to accepted member of his family
and society. In the early stages of the book she wrote Weeks confidently about her progress:

> I believe I have done it again! Caroline has been reading aloud the first
> half of the new book and we are thrilled by the way it goes. Finch
> develops. He feels the pain of passion for a woman—his cousin, Sarah
> Court. All the other characters go on living, pressing inevitably forward,
> sometimes I almost feel without my volition. I can't help thinking that
> the movement of the book is as strong and free and (how shall I put
> it?) half-mad as ever.[20]

It is an awkward book in many ways. Mazo had a tendency to
include travelogue materials in her work, and, like *The Thunder of New
Wings*, *Finch's Fortune* is crammed with 'guidebookish' descriptions
of her recent experiences. She inserted accounts of her arrival in
London, her time in Devon—including the story of a shepherd who
was once found dead on the doorstep of Seckington—her delight at
seeing the hunt when she was having lunch at the Lygon Arms in
Broadway, and her memories of Bude, Cornwall.

Another problem with the novel was Mazo's lack of first-hand experience in ordinary heterosexual relationships. Perhaps she had no
second-hand experience, of the kind that family life usually provides,

either; she grew up knowing that her parents did not sleep together. To Mazo, sharing the same bed and engaging in erotic play seems to have been imaginable only between siblings. Accordingly, some of the scenes are quite bizarre. One of them, Renny's return to Jalna after his marriage, when he resumes sleeping with his little brother, has already been discussed. But the main plot of *Finch's Fortune* revolves around Finch's love for his cousin, Sarah Court, who reciprocates his love but marries his best friend, Arthur Leigh. Sarah's explanation, that she married Arthur because she was unsure of Finch's love,[21] is totally unconvincing. If Finch, Mazo's fictional representative, is seen as a woman, however, the whole relationship is much more plausible: Sarah might well have accepted an eligible male suitor in order to reject a socially unacceptable relationship (in which marriage was out of the question) with a passionate female lover.

The novel ends with Finch's return from England as a man of the world, someone who has come of age. Yet his brothers are not impressed, especially as there is no visible sign of his experiences: he dresses as badly as ever, remains gauche and awkward, and has failed to bring the expected presents. All the same, family is family. The book ends with reconciliation: Pheasant's new baby is born on his birthday, and Eden dedicates his volume of poetry to 'Brother Finch'. Though Finch's love relationship may be unresolved and tormenting, his sibling relationships are harmonious; as a lover Finch has failed, but as a brother he is triumphant, loved by all.

After finishing the novel Mazo fell prey to depression once again. This was not the severe mental and emotional disturbance that often attended her fictional probings of her past, but a restlessness and gloom that she attributed in part to the English climate: 'Always a lover of the sun, I now sometimes suffered from depression. I asked myself why we had not remained in Italy. Yet in fair weather I was content.'[22] It may be significant that it is at this point in the autobiography that the story appears of the little mongrel dog, who from being so long tied up had developed his own private ritual of rocking and nibbling his foreleg—a compelling image of a restricted life.[23]

She decided to return to Canada for a visit of a few months, now seeing her own country as a symbol of space and freedom: 'Something in me cried out for Canada, the hot sunshine, the light thin air, the high-up blue sky, the voices of old friends.[24] Though Caroline was reluctant—she claimed she was not really Canadian at heart, even though she was a sixth-generation native—they packed up, closed Seckington, and set out. Once back in Canada they embarked on a kind of odyssey revisiting territory that had been important to them in the past, including the Niagara Peninsula, Toronto, Trail Cottage, and Ojibway Island at Pointe-au-Baril on Georgian Bay.

Meanwhile, Mazo's publishers were reading the manuscript of *Finch's Fortune* with mixed feelings. Alfred McIntyre wrote:

> I like it very much as a whole, although I don't think it winds up as well as it might. It seems to me the situation between Renny and Alayne is left quite unsettled, and I should have liked to see F encounter his cousin once in the book after she comes to Canada as Mrs Leigh. If there is any general feeling that the last part of the book needs improving, there is time to have it done, provided Miss de la Roche can see it our way.[25]

Edward Weeks too wanted to talk Mazo into making changes. He had some difficulty getting in touch with her during her travels, but finally managed to arrange a visit in Toronto. It seems to have been a pleasant re-establishment of their friendship, but few of the recommended changes were made.

When the women decided at the end of 1930 to return to Europe, they were not sorry to leave Canada. They had visited old friends and familiar places, as they had planned, but they had been neither hailed as celebrities nor treated with the deference they had expected. Their disappointment in their own country was one that they would continue to feel for a long time.

Retracing their steps of two years earlier, they visited Pierre and Eva in New York, where once again Mazo's anxiety about her work on the eve of its publication manifested itself: she left the manuscript of *Finch's Fortune* in her hotel. Fortunately, the loss was discovered before the ship sailed, and a breakneck dash by taxi restored the manuscript to her just in time.[26]

The crossing was even rougher than before, and the two women were ill most of the time. Once in Europe they made a slow journey back to England, meandering overland through Rome, Florence, and Paris. According to the autobiography, Caroline became uncharacteristically whining in Paris, complaining of their rootless existence and longing to have her own roof over her head and a houseful of dogs.[27] On this unhappy note they left for London, where they rented a house for six weeks before going back to Seckington.

14

England, Act Two: Becoming a Family[1]

For Mazo's readers one of the most tantalizing parts of her own story was her adoption, in 1931, of two small children. Not only was it totally unorthodox for two middle-aged women (Mazo was fifty-two) to adopt children, but both the motivation and the means by which the transaction took place appeared inexplicable. As usual, Mazo's own extreme secrecy added to the mystery: she refused ever to explain the circumstances of the adoption either to her close friends or to the children themselves. Edward Weeks said in a letter that he had heard a rumour about the children and complained that 'nobody tells me anything'.[2] Mazo's own letters at the time to Katherine Hale and John Garvin show that they were kept very much in the dark.

In August she wrote to Garvin:

> I have a big new responsibility now as I suppose Memé has told you, in two adopted children. I am sure you will think them lovely little things when you see them. They are so good and already show unusual intelligence. She in a very feminine way—he entirely masculine. I must send you a snap of them with me.[3]

And in 1933 she wrote to Katherine:

> It is just four years ago since we met the children's parents in Italy. The mother died just after we reached Canada and soon after the baby's birth—the father had gone six months before. While I was home I had it in mind to take them but was not sure that it could be arranged. Next April it will be two years since they came to us. Esmée was then two years and five months old and Baby nine months.[4]

After Mazo's death, Caroline elaborated on this story in an interview with Ronald Hambleton,[5] explaining that the parents were an English couple they had met in Italy. The husband, a 'very promising artist', had been in delicate health, and some time after the news came of his death, the wife's mother had written from London to tell them she too had died. When they went to meet the grandmother, she said she might manage the little girl but she could not manage both children, especially since the boy was only a baby.

Caroline was not always frank in her conversations with Hambleton, however, and the story itself sounds implausible. It does not seem likely, for instance, that a fairly young grandmother—'in her fifties'—who had just suffered such a loss would so easily relinquish her daughter's children. When Hambleton questioned René on the subject, it was obvious that he knew nothing and had not presumed to probe:

> About Esmée—We're not blood relatives but there was a connection there somewhere. We do not know who we are. When we were young she told us we were adopted, and nothing further. No, the only one who can give you any information on that would be Miss Clement; and I asked her once and she said: this was after Mother's death and she said, 'Your mother never wanted you to know; if she had she would have told you'; and that is where the subject ended.
>
> I believe actually she had met some people in Sicily . . . a painter as a matter of fact and he had T.B., and I believe that the wife was going to have a child and I believe that when Mother returned to England the father had died of T.B. and the wife had died in childbirth. However, that's just literally a fable—I haven't any fact on this. This would be about 1931. Harold Macmillan did the entire legal action.[6]

In later years one of the persistent rumours about the adoption was that Harold Macmillan, in his powerful political position, had brought in an act of Parliament to make it possible. But he did not enter politics until ten years after the children were born, and the correspondence shows that it was his brother Daniel to whom Mazo turned for help. Soon after the initial Jalna success she had asked his advice about adoption procedures, but had finally balked at the idea of taking in children of unknown parentage. When, a few years later, she heard of two children available for adoption from a background she found acceptable, she wrote to Macmillan asking him to recommend someone to handle the legal part of the process.[7] The papers were processed at the General Registry Office at Titchfield in Hampshire,[8] but no information available to the general public indicates the country of origin of the children; they might have been Canadian, American, or British. The only possible clue is that less than a year before Mazo left England for the trip to Canada from which she would return via New York, her New York agent had been devastated by the death, in a car crash, of a close friend who might possibly have been the children's father. Certainly the story 'Baby Girl', written about this time, suggests that Mazo had first-hand knowledge of a rough Atlantic crossing with a small child. If she did adopt the children in New York, that might in part explain her forgetting the manuscript of *Finch's Fortune*.[9] At any rate, it is abundantly clear that secrecy was a way of life with Mazo. She was secretive even about inconsequential matters, and that she should be so in this case is not necessarily an indication of anything sinister.

As for motivation, it was no doubt very similar to anyone else's; the desire to care for and bring up children is not special to hetero-sexual couples. Mazo's novel *Possession*, published when she was forty-four, reverberates with longing for a child. And she boasted to the children's first nurse that she had managed to 'get' them without 'going to the trouble of having them'.[10] Practically, she could not have acquired the children earlier, since she would neither have been able to afford their support nor have been allowed to adopt them. As it was, she could offer the children every educational and material advantage and could be perceived to do so.

Nor was adoption a novel idea for her. After all, the 'most important day of [her] life' had been the one when her 'adopted' cousin came into her life. Seeing Caroline as an orphan, she romanticized the idea of a poor child arriving on the doorstep in swaddling clothes. And since she and Caroline had chosen adoption as their means of formalizing their own relationship, it was natural than when she reached the peak of her professional success, Mazo should crown that success by acquiring a family.

Many fictional adoptions followed the arrival of Mazo's own children. Renny Whiteoak adopts the daughter of his brother Eden by Eden's mistress Minnie Ware;[11] Maurice Vaughan finds on his doorstep, in swaddling clothes, the daughter of his casual liaison with a gypsy;[12] in the short story 'Auntimay' a woman, after becoming rich, adopts the child of her impoverished niece.[13] No doubt Mazo wished to found a small dynasty that would perpetuate her family line. The special characteristic of her dynasty was that it combined the traits not only of her actual family but also of her fictional family, the two having by this time merged in her imagination. When the children came to her they had their own names. For the little girl, originally named Patricia or Patty, Mazo chose Esmée—a variation of her own name, with its two syllables and unusual middle 'z' sound. The baby, Michael, she renamed Michael Richmond René. The Richmond was her father's middle name and René—the name by which he was known—a variation on that of the Master of Jalna, Renny Whiteoak. As might have been expected, Mazo claimed the primary role of mother (known to the children as 'Mummie') while Caroline was relegated to the subsidiary role of aunt:

> It was a tremendous responsibility yet I shouldered it without undue consideration. Our little family of two suddenly had become four. Infant innocence was now mine to protect, to nourish beneath a maternal wing. As for Caroline, there never was a more generous and loving aunt.[14]

The children were an additional asset for Mazo in her work. Having always drawn on her family experiences, she may, consciously or unconsciously, have felt that by extending her family she would infuse new life into her writing. It certainly happened that simultaneously with the arrival of the children a whole new younger generation invigorated the Whiteoak chronicles. Besides the adoptions mentioned above, the Master of Jalna and his wife became parents,[15] as did various other brothers. And just as Mazo had spelled herself off from earlier stints with the Whiteoaks by writing the life of her pet dog, so in the next years she wrote two thinly disguised biographical accounts of her children's early years, in which she changed their names to Gillian and Diggory.

From the point of view of the women themselves, the biggest obstacle to assuming the responsibility of children may have been the time involved. Neither one had any experience with child care, and even Caroline had little experience with routine domestic tasks. It is hard to imagine them feeding, bathing, and changing children, and Mazo in particular guarded her working time against any kind of disturbance. But their exposure to upper-class English family life had shown them that the joys of parenthood did not depend on the day-to-day business of child-raising: in the families they admired, children were cared for by servants and spent a hallowed hour a day visiting their parents. The arrangement must have appealed to Mazo and Caroline because their own childhood joys had come not from the adults in their families, but from their own private relationship with each other.

When they first took in Esmée and René, it was clear that Seckington, with its primitive plumbing and heating, was not a suitable home. They therefore placed the children in the care of the widowed daughter of a local clergyman, a woman already experienced in caring both for her own children and for those of Anglo-Indian families who sent them to England for a season. The woman took them into her home and brought them to Seckington for daily visits with their new parents.[16]

Soon they found another place, the Old Rectory at Hawkchurch, with ample room for a day nursery, a night nursery, and the servants' quarters necessary for the extra maids and nanny. The children's quarters were distant from Mazo's and Caroline's rooms so that they would not be disturbed by the noise. From the moment they acquired the children, neither woman took on the job of feeding or changing them. Even on picnics, a nurse or nanny usually accompanied the party, though Mazo did enjoy taking the children to church or on uncomplicated outings that involved no messy feeding or cleaning up.[17]

The general attitude among close friends at the time was that the children were fortunate in finding such a comfortable home. Ellery Sedgewick, on receiving a family photograph some years later, wrote:

> The picture of your children told the story of Christmas better than the printed word. One could really see the sheen of the grass in the soft English air, and no two children ever looked happier. What extraordinary little autobiographies they will have to tell sometime, starting from Nowhere and coming out on the Highroad of Happiness. . . . I will warrant these children are the best of all your works.[18]

And after Mazo's death, when René told an interviewer how happy his childhood had been, Caroline was eager to confirm that assessment:

> Oh they were. . . well they should have been; they really had a happy home if ever children had. Mazo seemed to know just exactly how to amuse children and what would amuse them; when she couldn't be with them, they had pets and they had a perfectly charming governess, a French girl, until René was eight and got out of hand, and needed to go to school.[19]

Mazo and Caroline never knew the extent to which René's later life would be unhappy, nor how much Esmée would regret the lack of an ordinary family life. It would be, in any case, useless to connect childhood deprivations with later problems, or to measure the children's early lives against those of supposedly ideal families. The motives for adoption are rarely simple or selfless, but a complicated mixture of obscure personal needs and whims of the moment. If Mazo and Caroline suffered a failure of the imagination in contemplating their future with the children, it was no greater than that of most natural parents unprepared for the vicissitudes of any child-parent relationship.

While progress has been made in recent years in accepting the possibility of various methods of raising children, there is still a tendency to see homosexual or same-sex couples as somehow injurious to 'normal' development. Certainly Edward Weeks felt that René must inevitably suffer from the lack of a strong male role model. He therefore took it upon himself to provide gifts that would inculcate a healthy masculinity: in the early days he sent cowboys suits; later, fishing equipment and subscriptions to sports magazines.[20]

It must be noted, however, that the harm, if any, suffered by Mazo's children was that suffered by most traditional families—namely, an insistent and excessive stress on gender, sexual stereotypes, and gender polarization. The insistence with which Mazo stressed gender in raising her children is well illustrated in the books she wrote about their early years. Clearly, the importance she attached to their being manly and feminine respectively was related to her own sense of failure to really belong to either sex. Like any natural parent, what she most wished for her children was that they should succeed where she had failed. And, as in any typical family, it was from this anxiety that the difficulties sprang both in her children's lives and in her relationship with them.

When Edward Weeks became the father first of a daughter and then of a son, she told him: 'You will find him very different from Sara. It is perfectly amazing how soon the diversity of sex makes its appearance.'[21] The 'diversity of sex' in Mazo's children was rooted as much in the eyes and expectations of the parents as in biological differences, as shown in her early fictional account of the children, *Beside a Norman Tower*: 'They are dressed alike in fawn-colored woollen suits and caps, but a glance is enough to show that the one sitting in the chair is a girl and that the one who occupies the perambulator will one day be a man.'[22] Mazo reads into all the children's experiences her own unconscious fixations about gender. This is her account of their reaction to a group of workmen who come to the house:

> Gillian and Diggory delight in the presence of the workmen. They trot after them as they stride past, swinging pots of paint. They stand, with upturned faces, gazing at them mounted high on long ladders. Gillian singles out Chad's handsome son Peter.
> 'Peter Chad,' she observes, with an air of complacence, 'belongs to me.
> But to Diggory something profound has happened. He has discovered a strange bond between himself and these men. He realizes that one day he too will climb ladders, swing a hammer, stride in heavy boots that crunch the gravel. Among all 'mens' he realizes that a fellowship exists. Though Gillian is bigger and stronger than he, she will never be a man. When the men notice him he gives them a look of grateful understanding.[23]

Mazo reports with pride Diggory's sense of being a man. When he is saying his prayers and Nannie prompts him to ask God to bless him and make him a good boy, 'He opens his eyes wide. "But, Nannie," he murmurs reproachfully, "Chad an' me are *Mens*." '[24]

At two years old Diggory insists on taking off all his clothes, standing in his pram stark naked, and declaring that he is a man:

> 'Mens,' murmured Diggory, 'Me and Chad mens.'
> He gets up to his feet and stands swaying at the foot of the pram. He looks up at the great sky, at the bright weathercock facing west, at the starlings hovering about the chimney. There is nothing he cannot do. He can jump. He can fly. He can sit on the church tower like the weathercock, if he so wills. He is free as air.[25]

When that paragraph is compared with Mazo's heartfelt cry on seeing seagulls wheeling about the cliffs—'What a life! To be free like that'—it is easy to see the extent to which she equates freedom with masculinity.

Letters to friends hammer away at the same theme—delight when René manifests manly characteristics and Esmée feminine ones. Esmée was a pretty child with long blonde hair and an Alice-in-Wonderland look that must have reminded Mazo of Caroline. Mazo stresses always her beauty and her daintiness: 'my tiny Esmée'; 'Esmée waved a tiny hand'. In fact, she was inordinately proud of the appearance of both children: 'Of the forty children who had been present at the Children's Party on board, mine were the most beautiful.'[26] Given such gender obsession, difficulties were inevitable. The children did not, of course, fit into the expected roles: Esmée's athletic skills appeared early and have continued all her life, while René was less outgoing. When she was eight Mazo wrote to Hugh Eayrs that Esmée could turn somersaults as well as any boy of ten. Already the seeds were being sown for a sense of inadequacy in René that was to increase disastrously over the years.

Whatever damage the children may have suffered, however, it was not yet apparent; for the most part the children's early years seemed idyllic. As René told Ronald Hambleton:

> It couldn't have been a happier upbringing. I think there was more laughter at our dining room table than at any other across Canada.[27]

The four began life together as a family when they left Seckington and moved into a Gothic rectory next to the church in Hawkchurch, overlooking the valley of the river Axe. This was in the heart of the region from which the Lundy family had emigrated to the New World in the seventeenth century, and the location bolstered Mazo's sense

of having re-established her own family. The house was a stone building with mullioned and arched windows like those of a cathedral.
There were attics for the servants, two nurseries and—always an
important feature of the houses Mazo chose—spacious and romantic
gardens. The plans for the rebuilding of the place had been drawn
up in 1859 by John Hicks, the Dorchester architect to whom Thomas
Hardy was articled in his youth.

Here Mazo began a new phase of her life as the head of a family—
and a very affluent life it was. Yet in her work habits and simple daily
routine Mazo preserved the plain, almost ascetic life that had always
been necessary to her. She worked in the morning, took a walk with
Caroline before lunch, rested in the afternoon, had tea, spent an hour
with the children, had dinner, and spent the rest of the evening
reading aloud to Caroline or listening while Caroline read either from
her own work or from other novels. Although Mazo did not spend
a great deal of time in the children's company, she was a wonderfully
entertaining parent when she chose. Her *Explorers of the Dawn* short
stories show that her own childlike qualities made her responsive and
interested in children and able to relate to them easily on their own
level. There was dancing and romping—more than once Mazo was
embarrassed as a guest was unexpectedly ushered into the room while
she was being a bear or other ferocious beast—as were quieter pastimes, including story-telling and play-acting. In 1936 she wrote to
Weeks: 'at the children's bedtime I must make up stories for them
and I'm really doing them rather a lovely serial.'[28] Among the games
Mazo invented was the Knock family, in which the children were
Augustus and Matilda Knock and Mazo was the parent who would
punish them not for what they had done wrong but for what they
had done well—another example of her fondness for through-the-
looking-glass inversions, or whatever reversed the natural order of
things. As in many things, Caroline's attitude was the predictable
grown-up, disapproving one. She refused to participate in the Knock
game: 'I thought it was enough to turn their morals upside down.'[29]

Stimulated by her new life and romantic surroundings, Mazo wrote
in rapid succession *Lark Ascending*, her Sicilian novel; *Beside a Norman
Tower*, her account of the children; and *The Master of Jalna*, the fourth
novel in the Jalna series. Of course, her publishers—at least those in
North America—did not respond with equal enthusiasm to each of
these novels. When Mazo described *Lark Ascending*, Weeks and Eayrs
exchanged worried letters over her use of American characters without any grasp of their historical background or any real familiarity
with American 'types'. Weeks wrote anxiously to Eayrs: 'I hope like

the Dickens that Mazo's American characters will be of such individualistic cast that they can be accepted without too much questioning. I confess I do feel somewhat apprehensive on this score, but there is nothing to be gained by passing this on to her.'[30] Eayrs was considerably more sanguine, since he had recognized from the beginning that Mazo's characters had little to do with national characteristics but were rather her own unique creations. He reassured Weeks: 'I don't really think she knows much about Americans, or perhaps I had better say about the American type. She is pretty likely, don't you think, to choose rather singular and un-typical folk as her characters.'[31]

One matter Weeks felt compelled to broach to Mazo herself—the Indian ancestry of her heroine, Fay Palmas:

> The reference to Indian heritage is legitimate here but it ought not to be presented as of so recent occurence. Inter-marriage between the Indians and the colonists ceased at an early date,—for one reason because the Indians were either exterminated or driven out of reach.[32]

She promised to dilute some of Fay's Indian blood: 'I turned Fay's ancestor into a missionary who married the Indian girl in the wilds of Canada, which will perhaps be more convincing to American readers.'[33] When the book finally appeared, the publishers were pleasantly surprised: for Mazo's loyal body of readers, she could do no wrong. Yet there were always problems in publishing her works, simply because she wrote so much and because publishers in three countries were involved in anything she did. Another source of annoyance, and a justifiable one, at this time was Mazo's New York agent, Francis Jones; seeing how well her work was selling, he thought this an ideal time to bring out her second novel, written ten years earlier. This was *The Thunder of New Wings*, which Hugh Eayrs had correctly deemed an inadequate successor to *Possession*. Weeks was horrified when Jones, praising it as almost Dickensian in quality, tried to urge its publication. Taking great care not to upset Mazo, Weeks turned down the publication, which could only have harmed her reputation, and in order to protect the copyright produced a limited run of the novel in cheap paperback, reproducing Caroline's original typescript.[34] Its existence was tactfully kept from Mazo.

Apart from these minor problems, however, everything was going well. But perhaps Mazo was not accustomed to such serenity, such smooth contentedness, for suddenly she decided that she wished to return to Canada. The rented house must be relinquished, the furniture sold or stored, the servants let go, and the family transported across the Atlantic. Caroline was perfectly at home in England, as always, and never wanted to leave, but Mazo yearned for Canada, feeling that her creative energy needed some Canadian air and, above all, sunshine in order to sustain itself. Perhaps, too, she felt in some ways exiled, as if she did not really belong in England. Accordingly, Caroline set about the the practical work of closing the house and packing up all their possessions.

During the last stages of this process the family moved to a pleasant hotel in Lyme Regis. Mazo's account contains a vivid description of the last days and of the servants' and Caroline's grief at their parting. It is hard to avoid the feeling that Mazo almost relished the pain she was causing at this time to both Caroline and their devoted chauffeur, Charles Chant:

> Caroline, in spite of heart-ache, took time to fill the house with flowers. . . . There were still things to be done at the Rectory. Every morning Chant would motor Caroline there and in the late afternoon bring her back, carrying flowers and a heavy heart. Chant would creak up the back stairs of the hotel to the bathroom where the nurse was bathing the children. She would sit with the baby, pink from his bath, wrapped in a towel; the nurse proudly possessive, Chant tenderly worshipping.[35]

Mazo herself seems to have shared at least some of Caroline's regret:

> Only when Thomas Cook's men, five in two vans, appeared at the door could we believe in our departure from the loved spot. But the men began to carry out the furniture and place it in the van. As I watched I thought of how often I had seen this miserable business— this tearing up of roots.[36]

Back in Canada they managed to find another beautiful place to rent, near Trail Cottage. Belonging to a Colonel Pont-Armour, Springfield Farm was surrounded by forty acres of woods and orchards; across the valley, Mazo wrote to Edward Weeks, she could see the Whiteoaks church ('not that the scene of the books is drawn entirely from this part. Some of it comes from near Niagara').[37] They brought their car from England and got a local man to act as chauffeur.

But in spite of the ideal setting, things did not go well. They suffered from the extreme heat, and the children became ill as they never were in England: 'We have felt quite discouraged and that all things were against our coming at this time. Yet we have built so much on this summer—on our return to Canada.'[38] Hugh Eayrs put a different interpretation on their disillusionment. He felt that, after their literary success and elevation into high society, they had expected to return to some kind of acknowledgement in their own country. They did not, he felt, take well to being received casually:

> Confidentially, and very much so, they are rather fed up at Canada. I think they expected a much warmer welcome and a great deal of shouting about their returning, and they have not improved the situation themselves by being rather high hat as Canadians see it, since their stay in England. . . . Relations are a little strained simply because of this extraordinary Queen Victoria attitude, and you know Ted, there *is* more than one novelist extant. I am as fond of the girls as ever but I think it is a great mistake for them, in their own interests, to high hat everybody in the immediate vicinity.[39]

In April the family moved from the outskirts to the heart of Toronto and began to adjust to life in Canada. Eayrs reported their new sense of well-being in a letter to Weeks:

> She is a good deal happier and more contented now that she is back from England, though she is shortly going over for good, than she was when she was last down here. She has moved now and is with Mrs Billings and feeling quite cheery; she has taken up four or five engagements and found them not too bad after all, and is, as I say, at the moment quite all right in every way.[40]

For the winter they rented a house on Castle Frank Road, where family life had a pleasant informality that it had lacked in England:

> The room I had chosen for the nursery was too cold for children so they lived in and out of our rooms, which pleased them very well. Nanny was adaptable. . . . She had endured the torrid heat of the past summer without complaint. Now with stolid composure she faced the bitter cold. The children enjoyed the snow. With their toboggan they gambolled in the snowdrifts on the lawn. I taught them to make a snowman. Caroline taught them Christmas carols. For playmates they had Hugh Eayrs' fine little sons.[41]

Thus Mazo returned to her roots and tried to reconcile herself to the lukewarm reception of her work and herself. But she was always restless, and another move was imminent. The family stayed in Canada for less than a year before returning to England, first for a short visit and then for what was to be their longest period of residence there.

15

England, Act Three: Theatre Mad

Sailing back to England in the summer of 1934, the family had no pre-arranged accommodations and no clear idea of where they wished to settle. As a consequence, they spent the next six months drifting from hotel to rented house and back to hotel. They moved so often that it became Esmée's favourite game to shift mountains of toys from one part of the room to another in imitation of the constant upheavals.[1] Finally, however, they found a home at Colwall in the Cotswolds, where they lived for over two years, the longest period they spent under one roof during their whole time in England.

The Winnings was large, austere, cold, inconvenient, hard to heat, and manageable only with a staff of several servants. But there were seven acres of beautiful grounds, some cultivated and some designated as 'wilderness', and the upper stories afforded wonderful views over the Malvern Hills, the black mountains of Wales, and the rolling countryside of Herefordshire and Worcestershire. Practical concerns counted for little against dreams of enchanted gardens and mysterious woodlands waiting to yield their secrets to explorers. Alone in her study on the top floor, Mazo could look up from writing about Piers Whiteoak and see where Langland had set his Vision of Piers Ploughman.[2]

The house had belonged to an engineer who had built (in honour of Queen Victoria's Golden Jubilee) the Jubilee Drive that spanned the Malvern Hills. He was also responsible for the landscaping: hills and valleys and hundreds of exotic and rare trees from all parts of the world—Douglas pines, Scotch firs, fig trees, magnolias, rhododendrons, weeping willows, and weeping beeches brought from Holland. There was a lily pool with a fountain, a dark woodland 'wilderness', an underground tunnel built to provide work for the unemployed, fruit orchards, and a stone quarry, the sides of which were transformed into a rock garden full of alpine plants, with a small pool in the centre.

Mazo tells of discovering The Winnings 'in the thick yellow sunlight of St Martin's summer' when the atmosphere was heavy and dream-like.[3] She went through in a daze, hardly noticing the house, mes-merized by the beauty of its surroundings. She took it on sight and realized what she had undertaken only when she saw the army of painters, plumbers, plasterers, and paperhangers struggling to make it habitable. There was no electricity, only gas, and their elaborate crystal chandelier, which had been in storage since they left the Rec-tory, was reassembled for practical use in the dining room.

Her book about the children's life here, a companion-piece to *Beside a Norman Tower*, is much more humorous and successful than the earlier work. She called it *The Very House*, by a substitution charac-teristic of her fictional method, taking the name of the house they had occupied temporarily before moving into The Winnings. Of the two names The Winnings is perhaps the more poetic, a corruption of The Wynnowings (from a time when grain was brought to be winnowed). Yet *The Very House*, with its connotations of authenticity and truthfulness, has a resonance all its own.

By contrast, there is something unauthentic and pretentious in Mazo's descriptions of her life-style and the disproportionate number of servants—cook, parlourmaid, daily, nurse, gardener, and handy-man chauffeur—she hired to maintain it. A brief four years earlier Caroline had exclaimed to the Dimocks about a London dinner party at which four servants waited on six people, but now she took such service for granted.[4]

Yet the play-acting, if silly, was harmless. No one, least of all those employed, was exploited. Under the affectations—the dressing for dinner, the day and night nurseries, the parlourmaid's lighting of the chandelier—was a zany, robust family life completely at odds with the formal trappings. Much of the spontaneous life of the house, with its two impractical mistresses, derived from the antics of their unruly dogs. Tradespeople quickly learned to defend themselves as best they could from the dogs, who would tear down on them from the house: the butcher feared for his trousers, while the baker brought an extra basket as a decoy—even so, he often had to be 'rescued' by the cook.

Parlourmaids and nannies, trained in schools of rigid protocol by 'the gentry', evidently found the foreign family refreshing. Moreover, there is abundant testimony to the women's kindness to those who worked for them, a kindness that continued long after their employ-ment ended. They sent gifts of money to former servants in England for the rest of their lives, never forgetting them, and the custom has been carried on by Esmée. When a gardener who occupied a lodge on the grounds of one house was being threatened with eviction by a subsequent tenant, Mazo wrote numerous letters to her publisher about the situation. Eventually, Harold Macmillan himself, by then in politics and burdened with heavy responsibilities, was prevailed upon to intervene on the man's behalf and look after his future.[5] And there was genuine sorrow among the servants whenever Mazo folded tents and moved to another location.

Sometimes Mazo's accounts suggest that the servants' devotion sprang from their feeling that their kindly employers needed their protection, as when carol-singers besieged the house one Christmas. Word travelled quickly around the village pubs that choruses were appreciated at The Winnings and lavishly rewarded. Soon groups of singers in all degrees of insobriety were serenading the house long after the inhabitants had retired for the night. It fell to the children's nurse to cope with the situation:

'Who is there?' she demanded.
'Genuine unemployed,' came the husky answer. 'May us sing carols to you.'
'It's a queer time to ask, when you've been shouting them for the past ten minutes,' she answered angrily. 'How dare you wake people up at this hour? How dare you come pounding at people's doors? You ought to be ashamed of yourselves! No one wants to hear you sing. Go away!' She glared into the keyhole through which she was speaking.[6]

The group rolled off down the road at first lugubrious, then resentful, and finally breaking into a rowdy chorus of 'Little Brown Jug'.

When they left the Cotswolds two years later, Mazo writes, there was 'general mourning'. That was expected from the servants, but she was surprised that the community should have felt sad to see them depart. She concluded: 'we thought we had made no impression on that cold and restrained community. But I believe they thought that in losing us they were losing something odd, even bizarre, of which in time (say thirty years) they might become fond.'[7]

In *The Very House* Mazo's love of performances of every kind is abundantly clear. She relishes not only the amateur performances of her children in their Sunday schools, dancing classes, and day schools, but the pageants presented at village fêtes as well as professional circuses, ballets, and plays. One of the attractions of Colwall was its convenience for Stratford-upon-Avon and the Malvern Festival. They often motored to Stratford, having picnic lunches on the way there and picnic teas on the return journey. At the Malvern Festival she saw George Bernard Shaw sleep through a performance of one of his own plays and was shocked by his rudeness to his hostess at a tea party.

When favourite guests were expected, the children would urge Mazo to write a play for the occasion:

'We could do a play,' says Gillian.
 'What sort of play?'
 'The sort we often do with you. Just some pretend play.'[8]

The result is a play about Kind Alfred and the cakes, written, like Mazo's own childhood efforts, for a cast of two, with the children's nurse doubling as costume-mistress and prompter while Karen (Caroline) takes charge of properties.

Throughout *The Very House*, as throughout her life, the passion for plays in all forms is the strong thread of continuity. As we have seen, memorable performances punctuate her autobiography—going to the Toronto theatre with her father and weeping copious tears over Sidney Carton's renunciation speech; witnessing the embarrassed collapse of her parent's rendering of *Othello* to her; seeing *Everyman* at the start of her mental collapse; winning two competitions simultaneously for the same play; having her plays performed at the Hart House theatre; seeing Christopher Morley's revival of a melodrama in Hoboken the night before she first sailed to Europe; participating in the roof-top theatricals at the Villa Campobella in Taormina; and, finally, seeing for the first time the great productions during the London theatre season. From the time she arrived in England she had made a habit of renting houses in London at regular intervals for a month or so of concentrated theatre-going. What could be more natural than Mazo's dream of seeing her Whiteoaks presented on the stage?

There had been intermittent suggestions that the Jalna novels should be dramatized, and she had already been approached by someone who was interested in dramatizing *Lark Ascending*.[9] But finally, in the spring of 1933, she resolved to make her own dramatization of *Whiteoaks*. In the early stages she was encouraged by two of her friends with theatrical experience. One was the actor Raymond Massey, whom she had met in England and would have liked to produce the play. He felt that he had too many other commitments to undertake the job, but he gave her good advice about how to proceed.[10] The other friend was St John Ervine, a leading playwright of the time. Mazo had been a staunch admirer of his work since she had first seen it performed in Toronto, and she had expressed her admiration by incorporating a production of his *John Ferguson* into her second novel (Finch joins an amateur theatrical group and plays the part of Cloutie John).[11] Apart from their dramatic interests, Mazo had a natural affinity for the crusty, conservative Ervine, whose attitude to women she documents thus: 'St John Ervine desires to worship Woman on a pedestal but when she gets down off the pedestal and puts on slacks, shorts, blue jeans or any other masculine nether garment, he fairly hates her and enjoys telling her so.'[12] He, in turn, told Mazo he wished she would not let her women characters 'bounce' around in 'bloody trousers', and often adopted a scolding tone—which she seemed to enjoy.[13] She referred to him as one of her closest friends, and yet it is an indication of the nature of her friendships that, after Mazo's death, Mrs Ervine told an interviewer they did not know her 'at all well', and that they never kept her letters.[14] Mazo, however, did keep some of Ervine's letters, many of which contained advice on literary and dramatic matters: 'If you do not work, work, work your thoughts, as the Chorus in Henry V bids the audience do, and turn this MS into one of the finest plays of our time, I shall never forgive you. The stuff's there.'[15]

Mazo's enthusiasm for writing a play had been fanned during a two-month visit to London in February and March of 1933, when she saw many of the current successful productions. Then, returning to Canada shortly afterwards, she began her own dramatization. During a brief illness of Mazo's in the fall in Toronto, Caroline reported to Edward Weeks: '. . . let me whisper. She has been working on a dramatization of Jalna while in bed. She is theater mad.'[16]

Her enthusiasm ran so high that when she heard that the actress and producer Nancy Price, whom Raymond Massey had recommended, was interested, she could hardly wait to get back to England and talk to her. In spite of misgivings about leaving the children so far away in the charge of servants, there was no question of being separated from Caroline, and the two women sailed to England just after Christmas, 1934. In London they settled in the Goring Hotel in Belgravia and made themselves available for consultations about the play. These did not go entirely smoothly, since Nancy Price, who was to play Adeline, found Mazo's original attempts at dramatization to be quite impossible.

Mazo might well have been expected to be a superb dramatist. After all, she had won prizes for two early plays, and her skill in creating great dramatic scenes is one of her chief virtues as a novelist. Her previous plays, however, had been one-act efforts, and her first attempt at dramatizing the Whiteoaks consisted of a long series of short scenes; Nancy Price said that when she first saw Mazo's script, it had been taken straight from the books as a kind of pageant in five acts requiring twelve scene changes.[17] Accounts of how much Mazo's original script contributed to the final version have varied over the years; Caroline later said that Mazo did most of it and that Price did very little.[18] The latter, on the other hand, said that she did most of it.[19] What seems most likely is that Mazo did a great deal of writing and rewriting following Price's directions. She found the rewriting burdensome and complained about it in letters, but she respected Price's competence, and so badly wanted to see the play performed that she complied with instructions, even though she complained: 'After two and half years of waiting for a production of my play Nancy Price suggested I should write a new last act. I decided to put the play out of my mind, to forget about it.'[20] Price declared afterwards that she and Mazo did not like each other, but that Mazo depended on her because she made money.[21] As for Mazo, it was in the early fifties, when a dramatization of *Mary Wakefield* was being done, that she fully realized Price's worth. She told Lovat Dickson that she was 'a bit of a devil' but that she had a good knowledge of the theatre.[22]

One delay followed another. Mazo records her feelings about the play's slow progress in her autobiography:

> Plays were disappointing. The trouble with my plays is that they offer no important part to tempt a female star, with the exception of Whiteoaks and in it the star must take the part of a centenarian. St John Ervine had said to me, 'You must cut out that business of the false teeth. No actress will ever consent to it. . . .'[23]

> The manuscript of *Whiteoaks*—the play—was in the hands of Nancy Price but she was unable she said, to interest a manager in it. Again and again I wondered if ever it would be produced and reached the point where I did not care much.[24]

But at last the play did become a reality, and Mazo's excitement, which had waned over the long wait, now revived again. She was involved in all the final decisions and in particular in the choosing of the cast.

Opening night at the Little Theatre in the Adelphi on Monday, 13 April 1936, was one of the most exciting occasions of Mazo's life. Telegrams and flowers flowed in during the day from friends in Canada and the United States and Mazo wore orchids sent by Hugh Eayrs. The suspense was dreadful: 'What awful things first nights are! And the days preceding them. Never shall I forget the despair, the excitement and the exhilaration of the past weeks. The publishing of a novel is a rest cure compared to it. Publishers are angels as compared to producers.'[25] All the same, everything went well. Lovat Dickson, at Mazo's side, said the opening was like 'a very successful children's party'.[26] There were many curtain calls, followed by cries for Mazo to make a short speech. Afterwards she gave a party at the house in Stafford Place for sixty people, including the cast and all the friends who were in town for the occasion. Finally getting to bed at three, she was up early the next morning eagerly reading the reviews. Seven were good—especially those by Ivor Brown in *The Observer*, Charles Morgan in *The Times*, and Littlewood in *The Post*—and one, by James Agate in the *Sunday Times*, was, according to Mazo, 'horrid'. St John Ervine gave his verdict in a letter: 'You fill me with envy because you put into each person's mouth exactly the speech which fits it. I ought to add that your sense of atmosphere is as strong as Chekov's—indeed, the play greatly reminds me of his work.'[27]

In spite of the first-night excitement the play had a somewhat slow start. When, after two months at the Little Theatre, it was transferred to the Playhouse under Charing Cross Bridge, for some reason its luck changed, and it ran for almost three years. George Bernard Shaw wrote to Nancy Price that there had been nothing like it since Sir Henry Irving captured London in Erickman-Chatrian's *The Bells*. Possibly the display of Shaw's accolade in lights had something to do with the attention it subsequently received. After the London run it went to New York, where it opened at the Hudson Theater on 24 March 1938. Later in the year it went to Toronto and then toured various parts of Canada, playing to an almost empty house in such places as the Capitol Theater, Regina, for one night with Ethel Barrymore as Adeline.[28]

Most of the crucial experiences in Mazo's life found their way into her fiction sooner or later, and the London theatre was no exception. In *Wakefield's Course*, a rambling catch-all of a book that she wrote four years later, Wakefield, the youngest Whiteoak, has become an actor. He and a young actress, Molly Griffith, with whom he has fallen in love are to appear on the London stage in a play by an unknown playwright. There are vivid descriptions of the tense days leading up the first performance, including the last rehearsal with the playwright Trimble constantly being ordered to write extra lines and scenes. The first night itself is a tense occasion, but, despite some hitches, it goes off very successfully. Cries of 'author, author' bring Trimble to the stage:

> With still more reluctance he made his way down the aisle and on to
> the stage. An expectant silence fell. Mr Trimble, in rather crumpled
> evening clothes, made a really brilliant speech but spoke so low that
> only the members of the orchestra heard it. He was once again ap-
> plauded and the orchestra began to play the National Anthem.[29]

After the performance there is a celebration party at the house behind
Buckingham Palace where Wakefield is living with Finch and his wife.
The next morning the papers are brought in and the reviews looked
at, the good ones read aloud several times. After the excitement of
the first night, audiences fall off and the play seems doomed, but
unaccountably, 'by one of those mysteries of the theater which no
one can solve', its fortunes change.[30] It is transferred to another theatre, and after a successful run there it goes to New York.

When Mazo's own play went to New York the reviews for the most
part combined self-congratulatory ignorance of the Jalna novels with
assertions that they were pale imitations of *The Forsyte Saga*, all couched
in the smart-alecky tone that Mazo was often prey to. *Theater Arts
Monthly*, in one of the milder reviews, found the acting to be 'distinctly
ham of the most blatant variety', and thought that Stephen Haggard's
portrayal of Finch had musicianship and effeminacy lying too close
together to be attractive.[31] Joseph Wood Krutch, in a review entitled
The Forsyte Boys in Canada, admitted that he had never read any of
the Jalna novels but said that the play was enough to convince him
of the author's literary genealogy: 'John Galsworthy begot Hugh Walpole, and Hugh Walpole thereupon begot Miss de la Roche.' He
concluded that the most ardent admirers of the Galsworthy-Walpole
manner were persons of rather sluggish imagination.[32] *Time* also damned
the Jalna novels as 'second-rate Forsyte Saga' and said of the play:

> Whiteoaks does nothing in three acts it could not do better in one. Its
> sharpish characterizations never make up for its dragging plot. Actress
> Barrymore, looking like a cross between her brother Lionel and the
> wolf dressed up as Red Riding Hood's grandmother, carries the whole
> play on her bent, centenarian back. Her expert performance gains in
> effect from the audience's kindly feeling that anything a 101-year-old
> woman says is remarkably witty.[33]

It is small wonder that in self-defence Mazo often asserted she had
read nothing of *The Forsyte Saga* after the first book, or that her anti-
American sentiments grew strong over the next few years.

When *Whiteoaks* went to New York, Mazo and Caroline sailed over
to be present at some of the performances, although they missed the
opening night. Mazo's delight in her play never waned. She attended

rehearsals, stood in line among the crowds waiting for tickets, and especially loved knowing that the royal family enjoyed it. (Queen Mary came several times, and once was particularly eager to see Adeline's parrot who, despite Nancy Price's nervousness and his own phobia about gloves, refrained from snapping at the royal hand that was extended to touch him.) Perhaps Mazo's description of Finch is a true picture of herself as member of the audience:

> Finch watched enthralled. There had been a time when he had had a success in amateur theatricals, had even thought of becoming an actor. All that came back to him now. He threw himself into the scene, now in the person of one of the players, now another. It was a moving play. . . . Wake and Molly did it so well that Finch laughed out loud. Fortunately the audience did the same. Finch was in despair with himself. 'Shall I never grow up?' he thought. Yet he again forgot his self-restraint and, at the fall of the curtain, applauded loudly.[34]

She befriended a number of the cast members, entertaining them at her home and taking an interest in their lives. They in turn observed her carefully, and the interviews they gave after her death have provided some of the most insightful comments of any from those who knew her.

Unlike the people who saw her in the light of her works, the cast members were both perceptive and objective, and the theatrical images they often used were well suited to explaining her character:

> I thought of her as a detached insular kind of person. I mean to say you never knew her. [Nancy Price][35]

> There was a queer secret look in her eyes that one felt there were all sorts of things she could say really but she'd just like to keep them all to herself.
>
> I don't know what she felt about drama. I think she was frightened of it. She was frightened to let go. She was frightened to be her real self. That isn't like an actress, I know, but there are a great many actresses who are frightened to let themselves go in real life and can let themselves go when they are safely behind the footlights and on the stage, and it is quite possible that Mazo might have been a wonderful actress and on the stage, shielded by the lights, shielded by a dark house, shielded by all the things that help actors, she might have been a wonderful actress. [Irene Henshall][36]

> She was very birdlike, very pointed features, a nervous thin bird, anyway jerky, very jerky . . . thin hands always moving and her head went up and down like a jackdaw's head.

I liked her very much. She appealed to me like a child. I always thought the world terrified her. We felt she needed to be protected. We felt she couldn't cope in some way. Things frightened her like would she be able to get a taxi back to her hotel. Little everyday things seemed to sort of make her nervous.

She had some sort of fear that dreadful things would happen—things go wrong with her life—which were entirely in her own imagination because she was perfectly sensible but you couldn't call her competent because of this quality of being scared.

I think she found parties and things like that really rather a nightmare. I think she didn't find it easy to meet people, and always liked to have other people there so that she was never brought face to face with somebody alone that might make demands on her that she might not be able to meet. She liked to meet people with either her cousin or other friends so the conversation would stay very general. She was highly oversensitive. She had this over-heated imagination. She couldn't get over our casual rather bold way of living. I do honestly think that she was only happy locked away in her dreams and her writing and this complete world that she created.

I think illness or any tremendous emotion alarmed her genuinely— she withdrew from life. The hurly burly was not for her at all. I think Mazo's actual technique and craftsmanship were not up to her emotional understanding. She would have been taken more seriously if her style had been more sophisticated—whether this has anything to do with education. . . . She had a sort of Latin emotional sensitivity. I don't remember her as being witty at all. . . . She undoubtedly understood very profound things but she remained I always felt a lady novelist—too reticent. Liked her enormously. [Mrs Stephen Haggard, later Mrs Richard Elmhirst][37]

One never knew the real Mazo, and she acted what she wanted you to think she was. I sometimes think that Mazo might have been a wonderful actress because one never knew the real Mazo. I got a flash. . . she was just acting the part of Mazo, and I wondered if I would have liked to know the real Mazo. I just don't know. [Irene Henshall][38]

Amid all the distractions connected with the play, Mazo had continued to write novels. But the process was by no means simple or mechanical. In particular, there was a great change in her relationship with her publishers. Before leaving Canada she had started a fifth volume in the Whiteoaks series; provisionally called 'Cousin Malahide', it featured the arrival of a distant member of the clan from Ireland. Continuing with it when she moved to England, she had sent some of the early chapters to Boston.

Perhaps because her life was in such upheaval, the story was not well structured. Mazo did little revision, and the coherence of her novels depended on the intensity of her imagination. There were no plans or outlines pinned over her desk to ensure an orderly progress. (In fact, there was no desk: she wrote in pencil, sitting in an armchair or rocker with a drawing-board on her lap.) But the method was not infallible, and some works were less tightly constructed, more loosely episodic than others. *Cousin Malahide* was one of these. When her Boston publishers received the early chapters they blithely pointed out its flaws:

> We all realized from the first, of course, that it was audacious, even risky to turn the clock back in Jalna . . . new danger has manifested itself in the first ninety pages of the new script. Renny, Maurice and Meg *are* in their immaturity somewhat more watered [*sic*] than we like to think, but what is worse, is to remark in the new characters which you have introduced a tendency to be quaint and bizarre beyond the reader's credulity. Cousin Malahide with his simper and his highly artificial ejaculations, Philip with his annoying lisp, the wooden Mary and the almost absurd fainting fit of Maurice's father.[39]

It was the last time they criticized Mazo's work so boldly.

Her response was unequivocal: if they didn't like her work, she would take it elsewhere.[40] They knew how easy it would be for her to move, because she had told them of scouts from rival publishing houses who dogged her steps even when she was on holiday. They learned that their inexperienced and hitherto gentle and grateful author had formidable powers of resistance. The publishers capitulated instantly, and it fell to Edward Weeks to write the soothing letters, stressing that the early chapters she had sent had not provided a fair sample. They now realized that the book was a splendid work and could not be better.[41]

Always less concerned with monitoring in detail the literary content of her work, Macmillan of England nevertheless did intervene in the matter of the title. Mazo's North American publishers, aware that the volumes with the best sales were those with 'Whiteoaks' and 'Jalna' in the title, wanted a similar title for the new work. Daniel Macmillan was less insistent, however, or less confident in the talismanic quality of the two words, and decided on *Young Renny*.[42] Rather than being grateful for the more rigorous scrutiny applied to her work by her American publishers, Mazo felt Daniel Macmillan was more appreciative. Henceforth she sent the first manuscript of all her books to him. A year after *Young Renny*, and just when the play was beginning its successful London run, *Whiteoaks Harvest* appeared. It was to be four years before the next—one of the longest intervals between Jalna books in their thirty-four year history.

Inevitably interest in the play subsided. Its run ended in 1939, the war intervened, and soon England's theatres were closed. But Mazo never stopped yearning for the theatre. She wrote other plays, sent them around, longed for Nancy Price's expertise. Only in 1955 did she finally give up the idea of writing for the theatre. At last Lovat Dickson, who had done numerous errands, contacting possible producers and theatre people, told her: 'How happy I am to see that you are done with the theater. . . . I believe that novelists handicap themselves dreadfully when they start to write plays. . . .' [43]

16

Transition

When Mazo and Caroline left The Winnings they broke the pattern of returning for extended visits to Canada. This time they rooted themselves firmly in British soil. Moving to Windsor, just a short distance from the Castle and Eton College, they acquired a huge Elizabethan mansion with part of its earliest structure still intact. For the first time since Trail Cottage, Mazo bought rather than rented a house. She apparently saw the purchase as something of a defection from her native land, for she warned her Toronto publisher not to let the news get out as she did not wish to upset her relatives there.[1]

Ronald Hambleton described Mazo's ownership of Vale House as 'the summit of her climb upward. . . as a woman of property'.[2] Another friend said the house rivalled Windsor Castle in its splendour.[3] Since it was torn down after the war to make way for a housing estate, only Mazo's description remains:

> My study in Vale House was a restful and beautiful room. Though its windows did not give on to noble hills and distant mountains, through their small leaded panes I could see the cherry tree, the well-ordered garden. Its walls were hung with tapestries and there was a musician's gallery served by a short flight of stairs, with an air of medieval romance. . . . Beyond a hallway, past my study, was the schoolroom, to which the children had been promoted from nursery days. It was an immense room with beamed ceiling and windows of old greenish bottle glass. Out of it opened a conservatory which was always full of flowering plants and, again beyond, a huge ballroom where we kept odds and ends and where Stephen Haggard intended, some time later, to produce plays.[4]

There were lawns, greenhouses, and twenty acres of land let out to a farmer with a herd of Jersey cows that gave the place a pleasantly rural aspect. They had an orchard, a gazebo, a lily pond, a sunken garden, and even a nightingale to sing in the evenings.

A major attraction, of course, was the proximity of Windsor Castle and Eton. Almost everyone they met had something to do with one place or the other, and René was immediately entered for Eton. The royal family, long regarded as distant relatives by Mazo, were now close neighbours, and she could participate in their ceremonial occasions. Caroline wrote to friends:

> We had splendid seats for the unveiling of the Memorial at Windsor . . . we were in the window of a small confectioner just above the Memorial and could look, without effort, directly into the faces of the King and Queen, Queen Mary, the two Royal Dukes and their wives. It was a brilliant and interesting spectacle and we are looking forward to another on the 12th of June when they make their Royal Entry into Windsor in the state carriages. We have a splendid window for that occasion. We also hope to see the state drive to Ascot.[5]

The two women often had their chauffeur drive them to Ascot, where they walked while the children and dogs romped on the grass; and for the big occasions they found a spot in Windsor Great Park from which to watch the royal processions go by. Although they were given good seats for George VI's coronation, they passed it up because they were required to be there at seven in the morning.

Moving was always a time of exhilaration. Describing the process to the Dimocks, Caroline said it took four days from the time the movers came to the Winnings until they had placed the last of the things in Vale House:

> The weather was suddenly summer—April 2nd—and the 4th my birthday. The children were still in Colwall with Nanny and Mazo and I spent the day in the sun on their terrace—as happy and content as two humans can be—with the house in wildest confusion and the garden lying in ordered peace and sweetness. I shall not soon forget that birthday![6]

It was exactly ten years since the success of *Jalna* had turned the course of Mazo's life, but neither the excitement nor the creative energy had waned. After each minor setback there was some new success, some new experience. Her writing had flourished, her circle of friends had increased, and the travels and domestic arrangements had continued to provide new satisfactions. In the last years there had been the children, the theatrical success, and the final settling in England, at the very heart of everything she most admired about the British social system.

It was somehow typical of Mazo's deep-rooted ambivalence that at the same time as she settled permanently in England ('scarcely had we been a fortnight in Vale House')[7] she immersed herself in the most Canadian of her books. She was now living her own version of the English dream, in which a person of lowly birth not only rises to a position of wealth and power but—much more difficult to achieve— like Eliza Doolittle, passes herself off in the most elevated circles as a born aristocrat. When, in her autobiography, Mazo lists her friends at this time, she sounds more like Caroline than herself: Clare Stuart-Worley, 'grand-daughter of Sir John Millais'; Sir John Hanbury-Williams, 'who lived in the Henry III tower of Windsor Castle'; Mrs Montgomery, 'who had been born there because her father, Sir Henry Ponsonby, had been secretary to Queen Victoria'; and Mrs Graham Smith, 'sister of Lady Asquith', who was so crippled with arthritis that when she came to lunch 'her chauffeur carried her into the house'.[8]

Nevertheless, the Canadian dream that was to be the subject of her next book was closer to the familiar American success story, telling of a man's battle to overcome poverty, humble birth, and ill health to triumph as one of the richest and most powerful men in his country. The story she chose was a true one, and the man was her collateral cousin, Harvey Reginald MacMillan. Six years younger than Mazo, he shared with both her and Caroline a maternal great-grandfather, Hiram Robinson Willson. He had grown up in the Newmarket area and, like Mazo, had been raised in the home of his grandparents. Because his father had died when he was two, his mother had supported him by working as a housekeeper for $4 a month, and at seventeen he had enrolled in the Ontario Agricultural College at Guelph simply because that was the cheapest education he could get. There he supported himself with a job at the school's experimental forestry plot, and thus started, almost by accident, his lifelong preoccupation with forestry and forest products. After graduating, he put himself through Yale and earned a Master of Forestry there. Then one summer he was assigned to Waterton National Park. For an expedition into the mountains he took on a guide whose inexperience matched his own, with the result that the packhorses were lost and the two young men found themselves stranded on the mountain without supplies for a whole night. Huddling together for warmth, they found themselves in the morning almost buried under a heavy fall of snow. Not surprisingly, MacMillan became ill with a persistent cold, and when he eventually went to a doctor in Ottawa he discovered that he had an advanced case of tuberculosis, the result of exposure in the mountains and of years of overwork. He spent the next two and a half years in a sanatorium in Quebec fighting for his life and not expected to recover. But thanks to his own determination and the care of his devoted mother, he survived to build up a great lumber empire in British Columbia and become the foremost industrialist and philanthropist in that province.[9]

This was the story that Mazo now determined to tell. It was a new departure, and one that seemed unaccountable to her publishers; when the manuscript arrived, Weeks was puzzled: 'We have here a biographical novel. A story which, as I suspect, Mazo has written as a tribute to the memory of the parents of her adopted children, both of whom died of tuberculosis.'[10]

But the choice of subject matter was a natural one for Mazo. She had always longed for signs of distinction in her ancestors and family, and in H.R. MacMillan she had no need to invent or exaggerate: the heroic facts spoke for themselves. Furthermore, her cousin's story closely paralleled her own. Not knowing a great deal about his early childhood, she read into it a story of desolation and unhappiness similar to her own: like her, he had been 'abandoned' by his parents and thrust on the not-very-tender mercies of his grandparents and other relatives. She saw in his long physical breakdown a parallel to her own mental troubles and in his triumphant emergence a parallel to her own subsequent success. One of the readers for her Boston publisher noted, in an otherwise negative assessment of the book, that 'some of the slants on the main character are good, though I find them reminiscent of young Finch'.[11] His comment was accurate: both Finch Whiteoak and H.R. MacMillan served her constant need to recreate and come to terms with her own past. For Ronald Hambleton, the reading of this book was revelatory:

> It was not until I came to *Growth of a Man*, a novel not in the Jalna series, that the suspicion first hit me that behind the façade of Mazo de la Roche lay a biographical labyrinth, for I saw in that book whole passages that were later transferred to her so-called autobiography word for word, names of people only being altered. The conclusion was inescapable; she had either written part of her unknown life story into *Growth of a Man*, or her autobiography had in it chunks of pure fiction.[12]

Indeed she did write some of her own experiences into this book, and to them she added some of Caroline's. The latter's accounts of childhood visits to her uncle Dr Clement, of Bradford, became the model for the hero's visits to Dr Clemency in *Growth of a Man*.[13]

But there was an even more compelling motivation behind the book than Mazo's own desire to write again the story of her tormented childhood. Ever since she had adopted the two children, their lives had fuelled both her imagination and her writing. Her mind moved around their lives, fantasizing, embroidering, predicting their future. For Esmée the obvious ending was a dynastic marriage of some kind, but for René the script was more problematic. Now Mazo came to see her cousin Reggie MacMillan as a suitable and manly role model. When she wrote her version of his life she was imagining a heroic scenario, a Canadian success story to which her son might aspire. Strong-willed Esmée refused to accept anyone else's plans for her, but René, the weaker and more malleable character of the two, accepted Mazo's script completely. Edward Weeks came to realize the connection between René and the novel, for he wrote:

> *Growth of a Man* is I believe the strongest and best of her diversions, a story which in some respects her step-son René has fulfilled in his career for as you may know he is a man at home in the woods, a friend of the Indians, and a lover of nature.[14]

René was only six when *Growth of a Man* was written. Thirteen years later, writing to MacMillan for advice about her son's career, Mazo told him that René was keen about forestry and had 'never wavered from this since he was a child'.[15] To her inquiries about launching her son in a forestry career, MacMillan had written that René could do nothing better than to enter the University of Toronto Forestry School.[16] In spite of this advice, René went to British Columbia, MacMillan's province, to seek out his eminent relative, who was, Mazo wrote, 'by way of being a hero to him'.[17] MacMillan wrote to Mazo courteously apologizing that the demands on his time had made him unavailable when René called on him at his office, and promising that his wife would be inviting the boy over some evening.[18] Mazo's efforts in this matter were typical of her habit of trying to promote René's career through her own male contacts. On one occasion, when Lovat Dickson tried to arrange a luncheon with Maurice Macmillan for the children, she wrote to ask that René go alone, without Esmée: 'I so much want him to meet men of your sort in a "man's world". If she were there he would be overshadowed.'[19] René did later enroll in the forestry school of the University of British Columbia, but he soon dropped out. A loner and a misfit, he was happiest outdoors, but even with the strenuous efforts of Mazo and her friends, he had difficulty in establishing a successful career.

When Mazo began to write *Growth of a Man* she was already on friendly terms with her cousin and may have conceived the project during his 1935 visit to The Winnings. She told him immediately that she intended to write his life story and that she counted on his co-operation. Although he went along with her wishes, he did express some self-consciousness and doubt:

> I have also felt somewhat diffident about getting myself into a book (even by an outstanding Canadian author), which, when it began to appear in my neighborhood might give me cause for embarrassment and incline me to hide from the public eye. One is not accustomed to having oneself uncovered and feels, no matter how one goes about it, the result can only be something like an expressionless figure in a stained-glass window.[20]

When the novel finally appeared, he wrote her that some people reading the reviews, had already recognized him in the hero, Shaw Manifold.[21] His wife did not conceal her dislike of the work from Mazo, and much later MacMillan himself told an interviewer that he had never read it. Nevertheless, the cousins were to maintain friendly relations; in the next decade Mazo and Caroline would be their house-guests both in Vancouver and at their summer home at Qualicum Beach on Vancouver Island. Ten years after the book appeared, when Mazo was asked by a reporter from *Time* about the connection between her hero and her cousin, she flatly denied that any existed. This time it was consideration for MacMillan rather than her own secretiveness that lay behind the deception:

> A representative of Time called me up and asked me if I had ever written a book about you. As you had not given me permission to disclose that you were the subject of GROWTH OF A MAN and as I have a strong feeling that Edna does not like the book, I denied that I had ever written a book about you. . . . To tell the truth, I should have liked to say that GROWTH OF A MAN was at least suggested by your early life. . . .[22]

When she began writing she plied him by mail with lists of questions. Above all, she wanted factual information: about the length of his stay in the sanatorium, about the doctors and other patients. She was very specific in her instructions, telling him that statistics and dry facts did not mean much to her, and yet no tiny detail was irrelevant, because some 'small spark' might 'set my imagination aflame'.[23] Apparently self-conscious about using live models and actual experiences in her fiction, she also advised him to destroy the letters containing her requests for information. It was typical of her self-centred, demanding nature that she expected someone so busy to take the time to write a detailed autobiography. She also expected him to visit her: 'After I get past a certain point I must see a certain man in order to get certain information before I can go any further. And this man lives in Vancouver. I hope he will come to England this year because I simply can't go out there.'[24] When his visit did not materialize, she complained: 'I hoped that when you came to London you would take me to one of the great shipping offices so that I might see something of its workings. But this was impossible, so the book ends before Shaw enters the lumber business.'[25]

Not only did he fail to come to England, but suddenly he stopped responding to her questions. Later, explaining that illness had intervened, he resumed the correspondence with full accounts of his early life and the cause of his illness. It was almost too late, for by that time the book was nearly finished. Nevertheless, Mazo was forgiving:

> Of course I have forgiven you! But there was a time when I felt that I never could! It has all been very strange but I am somewhat of a believer in destiny and the book which I believe to be a fine one, has had to seek its own way, without the help from you I had hoped for. The result is a quite different novel from the one I proposed to write. When I had not you to guide me there was nothing to do but to set my imagination free and let it work its will with Shaw Manifold. Whatever he is or is not, he is certainly not a 'figure in a stained glass window' as you seemed to fear.[26]

She added several paragraphs after receiving his letter, but the book was, after all, fiction, and the lack of factual information had given her scope to invent the life of Shaw Manifold. Many of the characters she added are among the most colourful in the book. And although she said that his failure to come to England was responsible for her ending the story early in his career, that was, in fact, the period she was most interested in: 'To write of your later life and brilliant successes would be too stupendous a task for me and rather out of my line, as I know nothing of business.'[27]

Yet, for all the merits of its parts—the minor characters, the wonderful descriptions of the land—the book as a whole was flat. Although Mazo had taken some liberties, she could not manipulate her main character as freely as if he were a fictional creation. And there were too many fundamental ways in which H.R. MacMillan differed from Mazo. In spite of his painful childhood and his bout with TB, he was not a social or sexual misfit: he had a conventional education, made a conventional marriage to his childhood sweetheart, was a conventional family man. Such a life was too foreign to Mazo. Finch Whiteoak, by contrast, had shared her neuroses. In him, as an artist, they seemed quite acceptable; nor did they disqualify him from artistic success, any more than they did Mazo. This, after all, is the triumph of artistic success, that the misfit can gain acceptance in a roundabout way. Mazo tried to solve the problem of her hero's conforming by giving him an alter ego, a minor character who appears at key points throughout Shaw Manifold's life. This is Joe Potts, who meets Shaw in childhood, robs his grandfather, elopes with a neighbour's daughter, and whom Shaw later discovers in a trapper's cabin. There, under a new name, Jack Searle, he is dividing his attentions between his wife and a 'half-breed girl'. One of the last scenes in the novel is a meeting on a ship between Shaw and a deck steward who turns out to be Searle. But the two characters, Shaw and Potts/Searle, cannot be merged into a really memorable fictional creation.

In her autobiography Mazo writes of her disappointment that *Growth of a Man* had fewer and less enthusiastic readers than the Whiteoaks books; yet 'Alfred McIntyre, my Boston publisher, liked it best of my novels'.[28] That statement shows either her self-delusion or his tact, for McIntyre, to whom the novel was dedicated, was in fact dismayed; he published it reluctantly and only out of fear of losing the next Whiteoak book to another publisher. When he saw the lukewarm reaction the book received, he sent a memo to Weeks telling him that at the publishers' conference he would personally deal with the importance of 'this book in the future of Miss de la Roche as a publishing property':

> I suggest that you tell Mr Walcott something of the history of our publishing relations with this author. If he knew much about them he would never say 'I expect we shall have to publish it,' or 'with a great deal of working over this could be made into something of a book.' Whatever the Atlantic editorial staff may think of this novel, I anticipate that it will be published without much of any working over unless the author is to be allowed to go to another publisher. Look up your letter to Miss de la Roche dated Aug. 27th 1934, and a cable that came to your office from her as a result. I am sorry in a way that I saw Mr Walcott's report which came along with the ms. and I think it would be just as well to lock it up.[29]

Her English publishers were much less critical—and much less determined to keep her writing nothing but Jalna novels. Daniel Macmillan expressed his admiration of *Growth of a Man* and even suggested that she bring out a collection of short stories, the prospect of which filled the Boston people with horror. McIntyre wrote in wearied tones: 'she wants a collection of animal stories brought out next spring, and I guess we'll have to do it'.[30] (The collection appeared as *The Sacred*

Bullock and Other Stories.) Her best stories are those in which she inscribes her own feelings of isolation, frustrated love and tormented devotion, such as 'Peter—A Rock' which depicts a canine version of Finch Whiteoak. Here a devoted master is forced when he takes a trip to leave behind his dog. The dog is left with an affectionate family who has no understanding of the dog's frenzied reaction when it hears a recording of its owner's voice on the dictaphone. Finally, numbed by too much of this torture the dog becomes almost cata-tonic—a rock (une roche).

Of a later manuscript, *The Two Saplings*, another Boston reader made a comment that applies equally well to *Growth of a Man*: 'This manu-script demonstrates again that only when she is writing about Jalna does Mazo exert her full nature and that skill in characterization which has kept the Whiteoaks alive so happily and so long.'[31] Indeed, it was only through the Whiteoak family that Mazo could express fully her own vision, with all its quirks. Nor did she need much prodding from fans and publishers to resume the Whiteoak saga; after each excursion into new territory, she swung back thankfully to Jalna. Following *Growth of a Man* she began an account of Jalna after the 1914-18 war, when Renny and Maurice Vaughan return to Canada from Europe. Perhaps related to her own return from biographical fiction to Jalna was her sudden impulsive decision to pull up roots once more and go back to Toronto. She had lived in Vale House for just under two years.

There were many reasons to leave Windsor in late 1938 and early 1939. War was expected at any time; gas masks were being issued. When friends advised them to leave for the country, since Windsor was so near to London, they tried to find a house in Devon, but many others had the same idea. There was nothing available. Also, in No-vember of 1938 Mazo had been in hospital for a month following surgery to remove a large cyst from her throat. Feeling that her re-covery had been too slow, she said she needed a climate that suited her better. Since she complained about the physical climate every-where she went, however, it may be that she was expressing a more general kind of discomfort: a sense that the social and emotional climate had once again become oppressive, that she had been dis-appointed yet again in her hope that somewhere she might fit in. Mazo really was too different both in her past experiences and in her present way of life to be accepted by those she listed as her 'friends'. Perhaps, too, she felt that this phase of her life—as the chatelaine of an Elizabethan mansion with a son destined for Eton—was already, like another act in the on-going play of her life, beginning to stale.

All the same, Mazo's migrations were more often not explicable by external circumstances. In this instance, her next novel probably played a large part in the decision. As she wrote to Weeks:

> We shall sell the house if we can—if not, let it and send the furniture to Canada. A heartbreak, as we thought we were settled in for life. But Windsor does not agree with me. I have a deep longing for the Canadian scene and feel that, if I am to go on writing books about Jalna, my brain must have some Canadian air now and again.[32]

Nevertheless, the family did not proceed directly to Canada. Instead, they sailed from Liverpool to Boston, where they established themselves, with the cook, maid, and dogs, in a house on Chestnut Street across from Edward Weeks. One of the reasons she gave for this destination was that no long rail journey was required on arrival. Yet, like most of Mazo's decisions, this one was was influenced in part by an earlier pattern. She wanted to find some spot for the summer similar to Rockport, where ten years earlier, after the success of *Jalna*, she had begun the second book in the series. As soon as they were settled in Boston, Caroline began looking, and she finally found a house on a lake near Center Harbour in New Hampshire, surrounded by almost a hundred acres of field and woodland. There they proceeded with a retinue that included a cook and a Harvard student who replaced the children's governess. And there Mazo finished her next book, the seventh in the Jalna series.

When Edward Weeks wrote the obligatory letter of congratulation (this time with complete sincerity), he marvelled at what she had accomplished amid the upheaval of moving, transporting her entourage from one continent to another and living in rented houses.[33] But dramatic changes of scene were always stimulating to her imagination. It was partly the exhilaration of moving and partly the relief of returning to her true literary territory that caused this resurgence of her creative talent. The novel that finally appeared with the lacklustre title of *Whiteoak Heritage* rivalled *Whiteoaks* in its richness and vitality.

Beginning with Renny's return to Jalna after the First World War, the action revolves around one of Mazo's favourite devices: a divided house, the inhabitants of which involve the men of Jalna in a variety of erotic entanglements. On one side of the thin partition that divides the house is Mrs Stroud; experienced, previously married, and approaching middle age, she owes something to Mrs Wallis Simpson and her recent creation of havoc in the royal family. Mrs Stroud's home is described as full of charm and 'feminine order', and her door-knocker fittingly depicts a Medusa head.[34] In contrast, the 'gypsy-like disorder' of the household on the other side gives free rein to the 'strange imaginative by-ways' of Mazo's erotic fantasies.[35] The inhabitants of this side pass themselves off as a brother and his widowed sister and her child, but in fact they are husband, wife, and child. Yet there is nothing feminine about this 'wife': she is a horse-trainer, aptly described by another character as 'that jockey that goes about cursing and swearing in men's clothes'.

Although the word 'affair' is tossed about frequently in this novel, it is often in a stilted fashion, as if Mazo had picked up the current vocabulary without really understanding its application. Various characters embark on affairs and semi-affairs with each other, but it is the relationship between Renny Whiteoak and the woman in men's clothing whom he calls 'Kit' that galvanizes Mazo's imagination. The erotic scenes between them are among the most powerful she ever wrote. With this central plot in place, and with the freedom to develop passionate love scenes between what were virtually two men, Mazo's teeming imagination went on to fill the rest of the book with wonderful insights into the minds of lonely children, accounts of animals and horse-training, and the adventures of a whole cast of lively servants. Any of these subjects made tiresome reading when a whole book was devoted to it, but together, subsumed into a larger novel, they provide a wonderful density of texture.

The book was welcomed not only by Mazo's publishers and fans on three continents but even by critics. Writing in the *Peterborough Examiner*, Robertson Davies, a self-proclaimed admirer of the Whiteoak novels, thought Adeline and Renny the most vivid characters in a book which 'fills in a few gaps which the previous books have left in our knowledge of this odd tribe'.[36]

Davies—who knew a good story when he saw one—never joined the chorus of jeerers at Mazo de la Roche. He called her 'that rare creature in the literary world, a born story-teller. She made literally millions of readers eager to know what would happen next to the Whiteoak family . . . she created a world and peopled it, and invited the reader to lose himself inside her world for the duration of each novel.'[37]

These two Canadian writers had a great deal in common. Although they both laid claim to Celtic rather than Anglo-Saxon temperaments, both shared many of the basically conservative Anglo-Saxon values. Both had a passion for the theatre that fed their story-telling skills and their ability to create spectacular dramatic effects in their fiction. Mazo never lived to enjoy Robertson Davies at the height of his powers and take pleasure in the stature of her admirer. But on her

death he wrote, again in the *Examiner*, one of the most fitting tributes—fitting in that it was not the fulsome praise of a sceptic turned
sentimental by death, but the final word of one who always assessed
her work fairly: 'The creation of the Jalna books is the most protracted
single feat of literary invention in the brief history of Canada's
literature.'[38]

17

Return to Canada

Mazo regarded her life after 1940 as a downhill run. How could it not seem anti-climactic after the glorious preceding decade? Her auto-biography ends with the return to Canada; the subsequent sixteen years are summed up in a sentence: 'and there for years I lived and wrote quite a number of books.'[1] Edward Weeks objected to that conclusion, but she refused to expand: 'who wants to read again of those war years?'[2]

Mazo tended to blame the drabness of the next period of her life on the war and its after-effects. In the early forties, she says, she was 'inwardly shaken by blasts of news, waiting for which we sat tense by the radio'.[3] In fact, though, she lived largely in an inner world of her own, distanced from political and external events, and as might be expected, her letters during the war show her concerns to be largely personal; world events appear to have been relegated to the periphery of her consciousness.

In the early days, for example, the outbreak of war was eclipsed for Mazo by her grief over the premature death of Hugh Eayrs, on whom she had depended as a friend and mentor for twenty years. He had known her before she was famous, helped to orchestrate her success, rejoiced in her triumphs, and defended her from criticism and other annoyances. When she had travelled from Boston to To-ronto six months earlier, he had accompanied her, offering his own, more comfortable accommodations on the train even though he was ill. His death left her desolate.[4] She wrote to Weeks at the time of the fall of France: 'I need all your friendship in these days. I have lost my best friend and my country is at war. My home in England, my loved friends there, our Empire are all at stake.'[5]

It was little consolation at the time, as she did not fully realize what was happening, but already Lovat Dickson—'dear Rache'—was stepping into the gap left by Hugh Eayrs. She suggested to Daniel Macmillan that Dickson should be sent to Canada to fill Hugh's position with Macmillan in Toronto.[6] In London, however, he was required to fill the place left by Harold Macmillan's move from publishing to politics. In spite of the distance and the war, letters flew back and forth between Mazo and Dickson, and after a time she asked him to replace Hugh as the guardian of her children: 'There is no one with whom I would entrust the guidance of these two precious beings with more confidence than with you. You give out a warmth that few have it in them to give.'[7] Early in her relationship with him Mazo had spotted that generosity and begun to take advantage of it. Nothing shows her self-centredness during the war years better than the stream of requests she sent to her publishers in London, and in particular to Dickson. While Daniel Macmillan was asked to send the special kind of 'Royal Sovereign' lead pencils that she could not find in Canada,[8] Dickson was asked to send all the clippings and books he could find on the Grand National steeplechase, in preparation for the horse-training episodes in subsequent novels.[9] In both cases the request was conscientiously filled and Mazo was deeply gratified.[10] By far the most complicated chore, however, was imposed by Caroline: that of arranging to have all her books, as they came out, specially bound in leather by a Malvern craftsman, for her to give to Mazo at Christmas.

During the period when these requests were being made, the Macmillan company was having difficulty functioning at all. The process of evacuation was in full swing, and many unbombed businesses were preparing to move out of London. Macmillan decided to stay in its offices in St Martin's Street and make a part of the basement habitable for the staff, much depleted by those who had departed for the armed forces.[11] Mazo must have known of these difficulties, but she made little mention of them. Typically, it was the death of the Duke of Kent that caused her the most anguish: 'What terrible things happen between the writing of letters to friends! The last is the death of the Duke of Kent. It came here as a great shock where he was much liked. I have seen him a number of times and admired him.'[12]

For Mazo, the greatest deprivation of the war was that she could not return to England as she had planned to do after a year's visit to Canada. Her letters are studded with cries of 'homesickness' for England, as undoubtedly they would have been for Canada if she had been confined to England—for her homesickness was really for a place that never existed. Nearly every letter from this period contains a variation on the cry:

In these sad days the sight of an English stamp gives me a feeling of nostalgia. Not that I am unhappy here but my heart is truly in England.

I wish I were in London today—raids and all!

As for us, we are often lonely here. Our twelve [*sic*] years in England spoilt us for the New World. In fact, we were spoilt for it long before we left it—nor were even born for it!

We are always making plans and never knowing if we can carry them out. One thing is certain—I cannot spent the rest of my days in Canada![13]

Inevitably, just as she had blamed the English weather when she began to feel ill at ease there, Mazo blamed the Canadian climate. She told Alfred McIntyre: 'The extremes of this climate don't agree with us so well as the climate of England.'[14] Actually, both the house and the standard of living she maintained from 1940 to 1945 were very similar to those she had enjoyed in England. While she was still in the Boston area, her uncle Walter, her mother's younger brother, had managed to find her an ample and elegant house on the outskirts of Toronto, on the road to Newmarket. Its setting was rural enough to remind her of the Gloucestershire countryside, and she renamed it 'Windrush Hill' after a valley in the Cotswolds. An architect had added an extra wing so that she could have her usual roomy 'study', and she had established a poultry yard reminiscent of the one at the fruit farm thirty years before. As servants were still available and gas was not yet severely rationed, she kept a car and a chauffeur who drove the children to school and back each day. René was enrolled in the preparatory department of Upper Canada College, sometimes described as 'the Eton of Canada', while Esmée attended Havergal College, a daughter school of Cheltenham Ladies College. But her upper-class English lifestyle, even with the added comforts that were no longer possible in England, failed to console her.

By the time Mazo moved house again, gas was rationed, help was scarce, and houses were hard to find. She gave up the car and chauffeur, sent the children to board at schools outside Toronto, used taxis for her own transportation, and chose a house on Russell Hill Road, with a garden too small to require a full-time gardener. It must have seemed sadly humdrum, but Mazo always claimed that her surroundings were secondary to her writing; as she said of her splendid study in Vale House, 'it does not, in truth, very much matter to me where I write, provided I have paper, pencil and quiet'.[15]

Now, at the invitation of Doubleday (her own publishers gave her a special dispensation), Mazo undertook a history of the seaport of Quebec. Exhilarated at the prospect of venturing into a new genre, she described the project as a cuckoo's egg deposited in 'the austere nest of the historians'.[16] Caroline brought piles of books from local libraries, and at meal times Mazo curdled the stomachs of her children with stories of barbarism and torture.[17] And as usual there was a personal reason for her enthusiasm for this subject, for she saw Quebec as a part of her personal history. When she was a child her father had brought back wonderful stories of his visits there, which had so fired her imagination that she chose the place as the setting for her first stories. In addition, the historical perspective allowed her to insert in her account a capsule history of the Marquis de la Roche (no relation), who came from France in 1584, and a reference to her great-grandparents, who came from Ireland in the first part of the nineteenth century.[18]

Moreover, just as the animal subjects in some of her stories provided images for herself, so Quebec—'this towering Rock'—[19] was an emblem. When Ronald Hambleton suggested in an interview that her personality and her background were mirrored on the surface of everything she wrote, she scoffed at the idea. To her jeering remark 'I should like you to show me myself mirrored on my study of the seaport of Quebec',[20] Hambleton responded that that was the exception. All the same, her description of the city is imbued with details applicable to herself. Writing of the city's isolation, uniqueness, steadfastness, she stresses the duality of its two cultures, two languages: although a meeting-place of French and English, it is alienated because it speaks a language that mainstream Canada chooses not to learn. She also comments on the appropriateness of Joan of Arc—a figure with whom she identified for many reasons—as the subject of an important statue:[21] Joan was disowned and victimized by both the English and the French, because although the English burned her, it was the French who tried and sold her to the English in the first place.

Writing in itself, however, was only part of the whole process of her work, and in these years the other part started to sour. Suddenly both her publishers and the public seemed less enthusiastic. In 1943 she wrote to Weeks:

> I feel that I cannot face a future in which I shall write each book in distrust of my power to please you and send it to Boston with foreboding. . . . I cannot face a future of scrapping every alternative book and drastically revising and putting a lot of hard work into the rewriting of one you *may* agree to publish.[22]

The Atlantic Monthly Press did now receive almost every other book with grave misgivings. They welcomed *Whiteoak Heritage*, *Wakefield's Course*, and *Return to Jalna*, but between those books came a collection of animal stories (*The Sacred Bullock and Other Stories*), a very inferior Jalna novel (*The Building of Jalna*), and another book so bad that it was one of a handful they refused to publish it at all. In a sense, the situation was little different from before, when the Jalna books had been interspersed with *Portrait of a Dog*, the two books about the children, and the two non-Jalna novels. Then, success with every second book had seemed a good batting average for the American publishers, while for some reason the English publishers took in their stride everything that came along.

Perhaps the difference now was that the weak books were getting weaker while the Jalna novels rarely matched the strengths of earlier efforts. In addition, the series had gone on so long that the books were no longer considered in the category of serious literature; as the publishers had feared when she went beyond the original trilogy, they had even become something of a joke. Sometimes the humour at Mazo's expense was merely mischievous, but at the other extreme there were malicious reviews fuelled by professional jealousy and outright misogyny. Irreverent critics had a field day with headlines: 'Another Log on the Whiteoak Pile', 'Jalna . . . . 11th Stanza', 'And On and On', 'Under the Spreading Whiteoak Tree', 'The Whelping of Jalna', and so on.[23]

References to the Whiteoaks in other literary works abounded. She had good reason to write the following complaint to her Boston publisher:

> My secretary has drawn my attention to the name of a character in a book by Ellery Queen published by you. Pg. 83 of the pocket edition of *The Murderer is a Fox*. There is a reference to a servant girl called 'Maizie Le Roche'. I am surprised that an author would do such a thing to another author. I think you would be annoyed, as I am, if a book were published in which there was such a parody of your name, for instance a garbage collector named 'Alfrid McEntyre'.[24]

Tactfully, McIntyre wrote back to say that he doubted Ellery Queen read much outside detective fiction, and that he was sure the name was mere coincidence. He promised, all the same, that in future editions the offending name would be changed to Mamie de Pinna.[25] Another reference came in Nancy Mitford's light-hearted novel *The Blessing*, when a somewhat naïve Englishwoman is introduced into French society after the war:

They put Grace on a high-backed needlework chair facing the window, sat round her in a semi-circle, and plied her with weak port wine, biscuits and questions. They passed from Mr Charles Morgan, about whom she knew lamentably little, to Miss Mazo de la Roche, about whom she knew less. They gave her to understand that one of the most serious deprivations caused by the war had been that of Les Whiteoaks of Jalna.[26]

Mitford's intention was probably as satirical as Queen's, but Mazo liked the reference to her great popularity in France. She returned the compliment by inserting the following conversation in *Variable Winds at Jalna*:

He [Finch] came to Bell's side, and taking the picture of a woman that Bell had cut from a magazine he asked, 'Who is she?'
'Nancy Mitford.'
'Never heard of her, but I like her looks. What does she do?'
'Writes books I dote on,' answered Bell.
'She's rather beautiful and rather wicked, I should guess,' said Finch, holding the picture at arm's length to view it.
Hearing this talk of a woman, Renny at once joined them.
'It's Nancy Mitford,' said Finch. 'She writes books that Humphrey dotes on.'
'I know about her,' said Renny, with an approving look at the pictured face. 'Alayne admires her too.'[27]

For all the jokes, sales were still brisk enough that Mazo's publishers dreaded her leaving them for their competitors. Edward Weeks dealt with the problems one book at a time, though sometimes the demands on his diplomatic skills were considerable. Fortunately, although *Wakefield's Course* had a thoroughly absurd ending it was balanced by some very strong sections with Mazo at her Gothic best, and the book was published as it stood. *The Two Saplings*, on the other hand, was so awful that even Daniel Macmillan disliked it and insisted that the ending be changed.

There is little to be said for this short novel, which compares the English and American cultures at the outbreak of the war. An English and an American boy are exchanged at birth in a London clinic. By the wildest of coincidences, the mistake becomes evident when the two families meet by chance on a channel steamer and the physical resemblances between the true sons and the true parents are unmistakable. After the mistake has been verified by the nurse who made it (and still lives conveniently near the hospital), the two families agree on an exchange whereby each of the boys will live for a year with his true parents—without knowing that this is the case. The

English boy is unhappy in the United States and the American boy rather less so in England.

While the book does feature Mazo's perennial theme of identifying the true heir, it is little more than a travelogue describing the places she had known over the last few years—from the nursing home in which she had her throat operation and her house in the Cotswolds to a 'crammers' school in Malvern, Eton College, the house in Boston, and finally the New Hampshire farmhouse in which she spent the summer. For the most part it is a disaster. The episodes set in England show her snobbish, sycophantic love of British society; those set in the United States, an equally mindless anti-Americanism. When Weeks pointed out that the American family speak a crude parody of American speech, Mazo responded that Caroline had taken the American slang from a story she had read in *The Saturday Evening Post* and from a novel by John Marquand.[28] Weeks said she had done well to look to those sources, but had overlooked the fact that slang varies on various levels of American society, just as it does in England: an American family of the status she had in mind would not use expletives like 'Gosh, Gee and Golly' as much as she thought, 'even though such usage does give the English readers pleasure'.[29]

The original ending (reminiscent of *The Thunder of New Wings*) had the English boy shipwrecked and drowned on an American holiday, an incident that Daniel Macmillan thought would be too depressing at a time when so many English children were being evacuated to safety in North America.[30] Mazo, in an unusually accommodating mood, agreed to change it, and the book was published in England. But even when she softened the portrait of the American mother—who had made an unpleasant contrast with the English one—the Atlantic Monthly Press refused to published it. Mazo thought they were annoyed at being reminded that the United States had come into the war relatively late. As she told Lovat Dickson, 'at this time, you see, they consider themselves more important than the other Allies and they want nothing to remind them of their former days'.[31] Her indignation grew when their reaction to her next book, even though it was in the Jalna series, was again cold.

It was Edward Weeks who, as early as 1933, had suggested at a conference that she 'turn the Jalna clock back' to an earlier time. Then he had thought that she might tell the story of Adeline and Philip's arrival in Canada and the building of the house.[32] She had taken his advice and turned back the clock, but not so far as he had suggested. Now she did write *The Building of Jalna*, but the result was as unsuccessful as her first attempt at *Young Renny* had been. When the press let her know that the book was not one of her best, she wrote back angrily, blaming the falling sales of her books on the fact that less money was being spent on advertising them. And again she used the perennial threat of looking for a new publisher. She felt sure that Alfred McIntyre would be sorry to lose her as a friend, but 'as a publisher I imagine that he would scarcely be conscious of my departure':

> You have been my publishers for sixteen years and it would go sorely against the grain for me to leave you. But the point does not rest with *The Building of Jalna* alone. I feel that I cannot face a future in which I shall write each book in distrust of my power to please you and send it to Boston with foreboding. . . . I cannot face a future of scrapping every alternative book and drastically revising and putting a lot of hard work into the rewriting of one you *may* agree to publish.[33]

Matters were patched up, as usual, by Weeks. He flew to Toronto, and by the time he left she had been talked into both revising *The Building of Jalna* and remaining with the publishing house. He even managed to persuade her that the decline in sales was due more to the fact that the Whiteoaks, having become an institution, were prey to the ups and downs attending any such series.[34]

While Mazo was often virulently anti-American and pro-Canadian in her letters, she had always resented the Canadian attitude to her work. In earlier days she had been conscious of hostile reviews, charges that she was not truly Canadian, and had grown accustomed to the situation. But in recent years her resentment had focussed—not without foundation—on a single grudge: that she had been deliberately passed over and snubbed in the matter of the most prestigious Canadian literary honour, the Governor General's Award.

The fact was that Mazo had written a number of novels eminently qualified as contenders. But the awards were instituted only in 1937, when she had already written *Possession*, *Delight*, and the strongest of the Jalna books. In 1938, when *Growth of a Man* was a possible contender, it was narrowly beaten out by Gwethalyn Graham's *Swiss Sonata*; in 1941 *Wakefield's Course* lost to Alan Sullivan's *Three Came to Ville Marie*; and in 1944 *The Building of Jalna* was no competition for Gwethalyn Graham's *Earth and High Heaven*. Year after year she was mortified when the awards were announced and she learned that many of her acquaintances, friends, and near contemporaries had won for the second time: Gwethalyn Graham, Laura Salverson, Hugh McLennan, and a young friend from her Trail Cottage days, Dorothy Livesay. Naturally she became soured and disparaging of this coveted award, saying that it had been won by 'so many mediocre books' and by 'so many who afterward simply faded from view.' Though she was honoured in other ways, earning a silver medal from the University of Alberta—which she travelled to Banff to accept—and an honorary degree from the University of Toronto, these tributes did not erase the disappointment caused by her failure to win the Governor General's Award.

This disappointment accounts in part for her obsession with a far more prestigious award: the Nobel Prize. In 1938 and then more aggressively in the late 1940s and early 1950s, she mounted her own personal campaign of badgering and nagging her publishers, particularly Edward Weeks. It was perhaps no coincidence that she first became interested in the Nobel when the Governor General's Award was inaugurated, and she was tactlessly, mistakenly, tipped off that she was likely to win for *The Growth of Man*. Soon afterwards she approached Daniel Macmillan:

> Do you know that I have a secret ambition! I am now going to divulge it to you. Several of my Scandinavian readers have written suggesting that I might well win the Nobel Prize for fiction. I should like very much to do this. Is it awarded for the merits of one particular book or for the sum of the author's work? Does the publisher submit his author's work? And would you think it fantastic to submit mine?[35]

> Thank you for going to so much trouble for me regarding the Nobel Prize. I had known little or nothing of its scope. The thought of being a possible candidate would never have entered my head had it not been for letters from readers in Norway and Sweden. The names of most of the winners of the Prize for Literature are almost overpowering in their distinction but I don't feel at all humble before the names of Sigrid Undset, Sinclair Lewis or John Galsworthy.[36]

Nothing came of Mazo's efforts at this time, however, and thoughts of the Nobel remained quiescent for another decade. Then, disappointed by the reception of her more recent novels, she again approached Edward Weeks:

> I wonder if you have done anything about this [nomination] for me. Ever since Lovat Dickson told me that you had in mind to do this the thought has been like a flame to me—sometimes sinking but never dying—sometimes in a blaze of hope. It would mean a tremendous lot to me. You can guess the reasons. They require no guessing, but there is another one of which I will tell you one day.[37]

There is, of course, no record of what Weeks had said to Dickson. He may have suggested casually that, because of her great popularity in Europe, she had an outside chance of winning the Nobel. At any rate, Mazo later consoled herself with his reported comment that if she had been an American she would have won. However Weeks himself may have felt about the subject, he certainly lived to regret that she ever got wind of it, because she nagged him endlessly.

At first she urged him to approach Vincent Massey, even sending Massey's address so that Weeks could contact him before he returned to Canada in 1951.[38] Massey, however, was not eager to make the nomination, and told Weeks that it would be better if it came not from an individual but from the Royal Society of Canada.[39] Furious, Mazo wrote to Weeks claiming that Massey's entire career had been a series of adroit and opportunist moves: when he had nominated Louis St Laurent for the Nobel Prize, for instance, he was returning a favour St Laurent had done for him in Quebec.[40] In her autobiography she administered another slap-down, declaring of Jarvis Street that 'pillars of the Methodist Church, such as the Masseys, lived there'.[41] Deciding to look elsewhere for the nomination, she turned to Mr Gladstone Murray (former Director General of Broadcasting) and Judge Hope. When the University of Toronto gave her the honorary degree, she cherished it in part as a stepping-stone towards the Nobel, and told Weeks that when he came to Toronto he should meet certain people of influence there.[42]

Weeks admitted that they had taken the wrong direction. Somewhat wearily he suggested alternate routes: St John Ervine, or some member of the Académie Française who was known to be a Whiteoak admirer. Slyly, he added that Lovat Dickson could probably help in scouting the matter.[43] Nothing did happen, of course, but it was a long time before Mazo gave up hoping for what she coyly referred to as 'the mysterious honor' that Weeks had in mind for her.

If anyone had predicted in 1939 that Mazo would not return to England for ten years, she would not have believed it. Yet even when the war was over and travel was again possible, her return was delayed—first by the uncertainty of obtaining reservations of the kind she wanted, and later by Caroline's illness. She wrote to Dickson that she would return in 1948 or pine away and die for sight of England.[44] Finally, a year later, she and Caroline went first to Ireland and then on to England, where Dickson made all the arrangements for car rentals, chauffeured Daimlers, and hotels.

As usual, it was Mazo's literary projects that dictated the itinerary. She was already thinking of a future Jalna book in which Adeline, the daughter of Renny and Alayne, and the physical reincarnation of her grandmother, old Adeline, would become involved in a protracted and difficult relationship with an Irishman. To this end Mazo for the first time went to Ireland, the location of many vivid scenes in earlier books. She had a 'delightful' voyage across the Atlantic and then a 'delightful' ninety-mile drive from Cobh to Bantry in County Cork, where she spent the next three weeks at Ardnagashell House, a hotel run by a retired British colonel.[45] The surroundings suited her so well that she seriously considered settling down to live in Ireland. In England she visited Devon and the countryside she had loved; at the Moor Head Hotel in Hindhead she was delighted to be accommodated in a chalet in the grounds, where René and Esmée joined her, while Lovat Dickson and his family stayed in the main part of the hotel. In London her reunion with Betty and Daniel Macmillan was especially warm after their long separation, and the occasion was marked by the fact that, after twenty-six years of formality, the four friends now began to use each other's first names.

Another pleasant aspect of this homecoming pilgrimage was that it coincided with the publication of the eleventh book in the Jalna series—one that had been favorably received even by the Bostonions. Alfred McIntyre's admiration of *Mary Wakefield* was such that he suggested Mazo consider returning again to an earlier time for a book set in the period between *The Building of Jalna* and this latest work.[46] Critical consensus would later place it among the four weakest in the series. Yet Mazo's failures show a great variety in their flaws, and this was an interesting failure, one that provides insights into her own psyche of the kind that animated her most powerful novels.

It is the story of the courtship and marriage of Philip Whiteoak and his second wife, Mary Wakefield, who becomes the mother of Piers, Eden, Finch, and Wakefield. English by birth, she comes out to Jalna during a prolonged absence of Adeline, having been hired in London as a governess for Meg and Renny by a bungling Uncle Ernest, who was captivated by her good looks. Barely qualified for the work, she instead wins the heart of Philip who, in spite of his mother's initial antagonism and his own faint-heartedness (he is a very weak man), marries her.[47]

As critics were quick to note, the book is very much influenced by *Jane Eyre*; there is even a running-away episode similar to Jane's flight from Thornfield Hall after the discovery that Rochester is already married. Critic George Hendrick wrote: 'Mary is a pale imitation (and imitation she definitely is) of Jane, but the imitation is without artistic merit of any kind. Miss de la Roche's novel will certainly never be discussed for its literary merits.'[48] Yet to label the book an imitation is misleading, for Mazo did not so much copy *Jane Eyre* as rewrite and reshape it according to her own desires. Her characters are not feeble versions of the original triangle of the governess, Rochester, and his mad wife (whom feminist critics have seen as an alter ego of Jane Eyre herself). Mazo has rewritten the triangle so that the man is a weak, shadowy character, and the action revolves around the relationship between the two women. Although her original title, 'Philip and Mary', gave way to *Mary Wakefield*, a more appropriate title would have been *Adeline and Mary*: charting the conflict and reconciliation between the two women, the book suggests erotic overtones in their relationship that are only barely suppressed. Even in the final wedding scene, Philip is eclipsed by the two women:

> Adeline took [Mary] in her arms and held her close. 'Goodbye, my dear,' she said, 'and I hope you will be very, very happy.'
> Their breasts together, they stood embraced, their eyes mysterious. Strangely, in that moment, Mary remembered the scene [an angry confrontation between the two] in her bedroom, her triumph over Adeline that had brought her so many tears. 'I had the best of her,' she thought, 'but never shall again.'
> 'Thank you, dear Mrs Whiteoak,' she murmured.[49]

Between Philip and Mary, by contrast, there is little physical contact, and even their conversation after the wedding is stilted:

> In the carriage, he took her hand, held it a moment in silence, then said:
> 'I'm the happiest man on earth.'
> 'Oh,' she said, 'I hope we shall have long lives and be consciously happy every day of them.'
> 'Of course we shall. . . . You've had enough of unhappiness, my sweet. And I will see to it that you have no more.'[50]

Nice sentiments, but hardly as emotionally charged as the moment when the two women cling to one another with breasts pressed together and eyes mysterious, thinking of earlier encounters in the bedroom.

The critics, reading and writing from heterosexual assumptions, all failed to see the story for what it was, a highly unusual and subversive one about relationships between women. Almost unanimously they read it as a straight *amor vincit omnia* story and then often condemned it on those terms. The Windsor *Daily Star*, for example, found 'it is frankly a love story with a plot that is as old as English fiction'.[51] Nevertheless, the Literary Guild chose *Mary Wakefield* as its Guild selection and expected to sell 500,000 copies. That would push sales of her novels, then being translated into a dozen languages, near the two-million mark.

18

Last Years

There can be little doubt that the chief disappointment of Mazo's last years was the knowledge that her children would not live out her hopes for them. Since so many of the extravagant dreams she had built for herself and Caroline had come true, it must have been doubly disappointing that she could not control the destinies of the next generation. Of the two, René was the more troubled; yet whatever he did, he remained the favourite he had always been. When he was very young a fortune-teller predicted a premature death, and Mazo and Caroline always feared the prophecy would come true.[1] Although he outlived both of them, he was to die at the age of fifty-four after a long bout with cancer.

Esmée, the stronger character and by her own account a determined survivor, had early wrested control of her own life from Mazo. If she was the happier, however, she was also the one who became most estranged from her mother. Ellery Sedgewick's early assumption that the children had been set down on the Highroad of Happiness was clearly false.[2] Yet so too would be the conclusion that they were victims, deprived of ordinary family lives. Somewhere between those two extremes lies the truth of most family relationships. The relationship between Mazo and her children followed a familiar pattern: an idyllic childhood followed by a troubled adolescence in which conflicts simmered towards eventual explosion. Typically, the situation came to a head when the children were making career decisions and marital choices. Later the pattern was one of resigned acceptance, with quarrels patched up and disappointments accepted.[3]

Still, the family did have its peculiarities. A complicating factor was the extreme age difference: the parents were in their sixties as the children approached adolescence. This, together with Mazo's own Victorian upbringing, aggravated the generation-gap problems. Then there was the hermetic relationship with Caroline, a tie so strong that it excluded other people from intimacy and relegated them to the periphery of her life.

Added to these difficulties was the most damaging element of all: the projection onto her own children of the gender polarities that had tormented Mazo herself. Accordingly, the chief asset of an all-female household—escape from the crippling strictures of patriarchy—was lost. Having internalized patriarchal values herself, Mazo instilled them in the children. In fact, the titles of the books she wrote about the children—*Beside a Norman Tower* and *The Very House*, the first a Gothic rectory and the second a nineteenth-century house built by an engineer in the service of Queen Victoria—are particularly apt in evoking their archaic upbringing.

Childhood ended abruptly for Esmée and René with the return to Canada in 1939. Although they had attended schools only sporadically in England—Esmée day schools and René, having got 'out of hand',[4] a small boarding school in Malvern—after 1939 their lives were spent exclusively in schools and summer camps. Then approaching adolescence, they had outgrown nannies and governesses. Yet neither Mazo nor Caroline had the time or inclination for close supervision. Subsequently, their only times together were brief periods at the end of summer and the Christmas holidays, when they contributed to Mazo's idea of family festivity.

She chose their schools carefully, transferring them from Havergal and Upper Canada College respectively to smaller schools where she thought they would be happier. She also spent generously on their education, although she did once wonder in a letter to Lovat Dickson if she was getting value for her money:

> I wonder if these expensive schools are worth all we put into them. Some of our nicest friends here simply cannot afford them and send their children to the collegiates. On the other hand, some rather strange people are sending their children to the private schools. But certainly in this country the background of a good school does not matter as much as in England.[5]

She never planned for them to be educated exclusively in Canada, and though her motives were not entirely snobbish, they were certainly not academic. She told Dickson that she would hate 'to think of their having all their education in Canada'. Canada seemed swamped by American values, and its materialism frightened her.[6] The fact was that Mazo was very old-fashioned, and the English schools appealed to her because they belonged to an earlier era.

Dickson went to considerable trouble to get the children into English schools. He even managed to find a place for René at Rugby with his own son, which was kept open for two years,[7] and he talked to Sir Kenneth Barnes, the head of Royal Academy of Dramatic Art in London, about a suitable school in which Esmée could study ballet (though Mazo doubted her talent).[8] But because it was not convenient for Mazo to take them over, the plans fell through.

Eventually reconciling herself to the children's being educated in Canada, Mazo saw some merits in the local schools. Her taste for the rugged country and outdoor life made her appreciate the activities available. To Dickson she praised North American summer camps, where the children took long canoe trips, had bonfires and singing at night, and took part in concerts and plays.[9] She also reported with enthusiasm that when René was at Lakefield he shot rabbits, fried them in his hut, and ate them for tea while boys in the school diningroom were eating cold sausage: 'A boy really has a good time in this country,' she said.[10]

It became clear to Mazo very early that René was not a well-adjusted child, and she poured out her anxieties to both Dickson and Weeks. Her letters on the subject tended to follow a pattern: worrying that he was neither a scholar nor a good mixer, and yet reassuring herself and others that he was sensitive, affectionate, and 'mature'. Often she compared him with Esmée, who was so obviously a good mixer, 'sociable and pleasure-loving'.[11] The following assessments of her children's characters are typical:

> He has an interesting, sensitive and adult mind in some ways but is very careless in his studies. He goes to meet exams in happy confidence and, when he comes out badly, is surprised but not too deeply troubled. He is trying his junior matric this summer and she the senior. She is practical and unimaginative, with a great love of life and a good time. He is much the more demonstrative and indeed the more affectionate but she has a kindly sweet nature.[12]

> You ask about the children. Esmée flourishes, bored with school at times but always throwing herself into the life of it, fashioned from her inmost fibre for a good time—awfully pretty. But how different René! I often wish you were near him. I am sure you could do a lot for him. He is rather unhappy at school—does not get on well with his work! The truth is he has rather a lonely spirit. He is not a good mixer, though when he is at home, he enjoys our friends and they are always delighted with him. He is no student but has a mature mind and sometimes writes so well that I often feel that creative writing will be his future. But one can never tell.[13]

Esmée articulated her grievances about her parents and home life, with the result that her own adjustment was easier, though at the same time their relationship became more difficult. Resenting the small amount of time Mazo and Caroline spent with her and René, she said that she was never a part of their lives. Even as a child, she recalled being annoyed on outings when the two women would whisper and laugh with each other at things kept secret from the children. She felt that they were totally selfish.[14] Judging from Esmée's correspondance with Mazo when she was in school and summer camp, she must have received few letters or visits, and from time to time Mazo apparently urged her not to bother coming home—because there was flu in Toronto, because the snow was melting, because there was nothing to do.[15]

One of Esmée's particularly unhappy memories is of Mazo's promises to speak at school functions. She did speak once at a Havergal graduation ceremony but on other occasions pleaded illness at the last minute and cancelled. Since extensive preparations had been made for the visit and excitement was running high, Esmée was mortified. She was all the more angry when she returned home to find Mazo quite well, chatting and laughing with Caroline.[16] Later, Esmée felt the fact of her adoption and unusual home situation to be a stigma. To what extent René shared these feelings it is impossible to say, for he articulated his grievances less clearly than Esmée did. But Mazo wrote to Weeks during his high-school days that he had developed a 'pensive' mood that made her uneasy.[17]

Paradoxically, many of the problems the children faced concerned money. While very large amounts were lavished on their care in schools, on holidays and nannies, money for day-to-day expenditures was not forthcoming. Again, the situation is perhaps fairly common, since money gives parents a control that they are often reluctant to relinquish. In Esmée's life financial matters were complicated by the fact that Mazo had little idea of the value of money. Living in a state described by several of her friends as a 'cocoon', she was isolated from the marketplace. (Caroline did all the shopping, even buying Mazo's clothes or having them sent to the house on approval). Esmée has recalled sitting on the staircase with René outside the room in which Mazo and Caroline were sitting and tossing a coin to decide which one would enter to get money for a movie. Many other mortifying memories involved clothes. Instead of buying clothes for Esmée or thinking about what young people of her age were wearing, Caroline would have a dressmaker make over clothing discarded by Mazo and herself. Inevitably, Esmée would be turned out, to her horror, in the costume of an earlier era; one of her most painful memories is of attending a high-school formal in a dress that made her resemble a Kate Greenaway character.

Yet Mazo was capable of great generosity when it came to giving presents. In *The Very House* she records René's extreme delight on being given an elaborate toy car for his fifth birthday:

> Everyone . . . stood in wonder as he climbed into the car and pedalled it along the drive. A boy! Almost a man! The owner driver of a car!
>
> He seemed to know by instinct how to steer it, how to back and turn in the smallest possible space. He never sounded the hooter needlessly but only when there was a crossing of paths. Yet, when at last he was persuaded to let Gillian have a turn, she was in a quiver of nerves.
>
> 'Save me! Save me!' she screamed as the car sped down the steep drive towards the lily pond.
>
> She all but overthrew it when she tried to back and turn. With an ecstatic smile she constantly sounded the horn. Truly she had no way with mechanical things. She was a girl! A woman! 'With all the virtues of the sex!' cried Mummie embracing her.[18]

The gesture was repeated when René reached twenty-one and Mazo surprised him with a very expensive foreign sports car. He went to the show-room, chose one for himself, and was so excited that he threw up his lunch.[19] A footnote to this vignette of family life is that Esmée, far from being a mechanical bungler, was and is immensely practical, a good driver who takes special pleasure in owning a good car.

Comparing the happy early days, with them, the magic hours in Mazo's study, the later lack of interest, the banishment to schools and camps, Esmée concluded that she and René were taken in as 'toys' when they were very young and, like toys, discarded when they were less malleable, when they needed sympathetic understanding, patience, and time. There is considerable truth in her conclusion; if not 'toys' to Mazo, they were certainly 'material'. And this they never ceased to be, even—or perhaps especially—when things went awry.

Like many writers, Mazo admitted to a shameless curiosity about other people, amounting almost to voyeurism. According to her autobiography, Caroline often had to warn her in restaurants and other public places not to stare so.[20] Both her autobiography and her fiction are filled with accounts of spying and watching other people in extreme situations.[21] Finch spies on people, sometimes deliberately and sometimes by an unexpected accident. Through a knot in the floorboard he and George Fennel, in George's bedroom, watch a pair of backward lovers in the kitchen below.[22] And it is Finch's stumbling upon Eden and Pheasant together that prevents their elopement, causing a whole train of crises in the first Jalna book.[23]

Mazo's 'spying' on her own children took various forms. When they were very young it was the duty of their nannies and nurses to report to her at the end of the day the amusing things they had said.[24] It was not, apparently, through her own close observation that she filled her accounts of their lives with such rich detail. Later, when the children went to school, she had an insatiable curiosity for stories of their life there: René described her as 'pumping' him for anecdotes. (Like young Adeline Whiteoak, she found the boys' school far more interesting than the girls'[25] and took a special interest in the ritualistic canings, descriptions of which she includes in a number of works.)

When the children grew older, Mazo's spying activities may have been motivated by the desire not only to seek out material, but also to monitor their friendships, especially Esmée's. She tended to disapprove of Esmée's friends more than she did René's, finding them in her own phrase 'strange', outside the social pale. She also had a bad habit of getting to Esmée's mail and opening it before she did. But Esmée did not accept such prying without retaliation. Once, when she returned from camp to find a letter in the garbage from a friend whom Mazo considered unsuitable, she fished it out, pieced it together, and left it where Mazo could find it.[26]

When Esmée and René emerged from their years of boarding school and summer camps they were both unsettled and unprepared to find their way in the world. Esmée went back to Switzerland for a time, returned home, found a job in a bank. René was not happy as a student even after the two women had paid a visit to Vancouver and found an apartment for him, which Caroline furnished with second-hand furniture.[27] In the early months of 1953 they were shocked to hear that he was to be married, had left his forestry course, and was looking for a job in order to support his wife and the baby already on the way.[28] Mazo and Caroline did not attend the wedding, but were given a detailed account of the occasion by Ethel Wilson.

In the early fifties Mazo's neighbour Enid Graham, a doctor's wife and active hostess, had brought Mrs Wilson, who was in Toronto while her husband attended a medical convention, to tea at Mazo's house. Ethel Wilson had thoroughly enjoyed the occasion and wrote that she was grateful to Enid Graham for the gift of knowing Mazo.[29] The friendship between the two writers progressed steadily, mainly in letters that were addressed first to 'Dear Miss de la Roche' and eventually to 'Darling Mazo.' There were also regular meetings when

Mazo was in British Columbia or when Mrs Wilson accompanied her husband to future conventions in Toronto. She expressed gratitude for being 'admitted to intimacy' with Mazo and had a warm admiration for her work, and for the way she had accomplished it 'no creative writing classes, no studying at the University of Iowa etc. etc. Simply, you could write, and you did.'[30] The friendship was clearly not based on literary admiration, for it was only in 1955 that Mazo requested from their mutual publisher a copy of *The Swamp Angel* because 'I am ashamed to say I have read nothing of hers'.[31] There was also a sticky moment when in 1955 Mazo heard that Ethel Wilson had said in a television interview that Canada had not produced one novelist of note. Yet it is an indication of her warm feeling that instead of expressing her annoyance, she simply wrote 'Surely you were very unfair to yourself.'[32]

Describing René's wedding, Mrs Wilson gave graphic details of the bride's dress, the reading of Mazo's wire, and of René's speech. Familiar with the bride, Kim, and her family, she wrote reassuringly that Kim was the kind of girl to make a dear and good wife: she would 'not think of herself, but René's well-being will, I am sure, come first always.'[33]

Later, when Mazo met Kim, she told Edward Weeks she found in her the daughterly, affectionate nature she had missed in Esmée, and that she would not have wished anything otherwise.[34] In fact, René could do no wrong in Mazo's eyes, and she did everything in her power (or, rather, Lovat Dickson's) to find jobs for him.[35] Eventually he found his most satisfying work with the Indian Affairs Department. Years before, when Dickson had brought Grey Owl to Mazo's house, the old man had spent the entire visit in René's room:[36] perhaps he gave René the inspiration that Mazo had hoped he would find in her cousin H.R. MacMillan.

Several months after the wedding of René and Kim, Esmée herself married a former school acquaintance of René's—a neighbour in Forest Hill Village who was not welcome in Mazo's house. By Esmée's account the main objection to the marriage was that his parents were divorced. The wedding followed years of friction between mother and daughter, and Esmée had not expected to be given a formal wedding. That a reception was provided she put down to some 'romantic impulse' on the part of Caroline, who must have intervened with Mazo. The latter wrote in jaundiced tones to Weeks that some of the sixty wedding guests who came to the house were their own special friends 'but the majority [were] from the other camp and most of them quite strange to us'. For months afterwards there was little contact between Esmée and the two women.[37]

Not surprisingly, Mazo expressed cool dislike of Esmée's engagement ring, the groom himself, and his family, and relations between them were strained for some time. She became ill from the time of the wedding and told Weeks: 'I believe that not a little of my ill-health during the past two years is due to the strain and disappointment she has caused me. It is far too painful but I have a feeling that you do not understand.'[38] As her letters to Weeks at this time contain a number of similar reproaches for his lack of sympathy, it is hard not to conclude that he was more sympathetic to Esmée than he cared to admit to Mazo.

No doubt part of the reason for these tensions was that Esmée, like many of those supposedly close to Mazo, had little insight into her relationship with Caroline. She had been surprised to learn how much Caroline knew about the trial of the English writer Radclyffe Hall, because she assumed that her aunt was too 'straight-laced' to know of such matters. And when her husband and others offered the opinion that Mazo and Caroline were a lesbian couple, she disagreed. Thus Esmée had no way of knowing that when Mazo balked at the wedding ceremony and expressed dislike of the groom and the ring, her hostility was only in part personal. The wedding ceremony was for her a symbol of everything from which she was excluded, a vivid reminder that her powerful, enduring love was of a kind that could not be ceremonially acknowledged.

The Jalna books are full of gala occasions such as birthdays, home-comings, family reunions, and funerals, but there are very few weddings. The important marriages—those between Pheasant and Piers, Eden and Alayne, Renny and Alayne and Finch and Sarah—all take place off-stage and without ceremony. When weddings do take place, in *Mary Wakefield* and *Centenary at Jalna*, the focus is not on the bride and groom but, respectively, on the bride and her mother-in-law and the bride and her father. And even then, the author appears to be more interested in the exchange of wedding presents.

Although Mazo was especially hurt that she received no word from the young couple when she was ill and no offer of help from them when she moved to her last house on Ava Crescent,[39] eventually communications were re-established and family Christmasses celebrated together as usual. Mazo and Caroline visited the small apartment in which Esmée started her married life, and they grew to like her husband. Finally, Mazo wrote to Weeks that they had come to accept the fact that Esmée was 'the kind of person who hurts you unconsciously'.[40] The relationship with René and his wife was much more successful. Mazo was delighted to be a grandmother, found christenings much more to her taste than weddings, and was happy that René's son bore such 'family' names as Pierre and Richmond (although he later reverted to the more ordinary 'Michael').

Now, perhaps stimulated by the arrival of grandchildren, she turned to children's books. These presented as much difficulty for her American publishers as had the collections of short stories and the earlier books about her dog and her own children. The first, *The Song of Lambert*, is the story of twin lambs: the male of the pair has an unusual talent for singing, whish is despised by the lamb community but much appreciated by his devoted sister.[41] (Even in a children's book Mazo left the imprint of her early life.) Her long-experienced reader in Boston said cautiously that with really good illustrations and the de la Roche name, it might make a modest sale and be worth publishing in order to keep her happy;[42] falling into the whimsical tone of the book itself, Weeks suggested that they let the little lamb graze in his pasture until after their next meeting.[43] No doubt he hoped to stave off publication, but the bargaining that took place during his next visit to Toronto resulted in a promise of publication, and he requested the plates from Macmillan—the English, as usual, had been content to publish anything with her name on it—so that an American edition could be arranged.

The next book, the story of a pair of pigeons, was declared by the Boston reader to be everything he considered worst in children's books: it was coy, unoriginal, and sentimental, and the title, *Bill and Coo*, was embarrassing:

> Since I do not have a full understanding of all the problems that might beset the Press if the ms. were to be rejected, I shall refrain from a definite recommendation. However, I feel quite certain that none of the better children's book editors would leap at Bill and Coo.[44]

John Gray at Macmillan in Toronto worried over what librarians with enlightened ideas about children's literature might make of it.[45] But it was published, with this blurb on the jacket: 'In language of great simplicity and with a story-teller's art Mazo de la Roche tells of the little seraph whose coming spreads beauty where harshness and envy had been before'.[46]

Bill and Coo was evidently one way of adapting to the situation of René's marriage. Mazo's more sinister feelings about the children were expressed, according to custom, in the next two Jalna books. Roma, the natural daughter of Eden and his mistress Minnie Ware, who had come into the Whiteoak saga after the children were first adopted, had always had traits reminiscent of Esmée. Now, in *Variable Winds at Jalna*, Roma's character was fleshed out. A cold, opportunistic young woman, materialistic and scheming, she finally seduces away from her cousin Adeline Whiteoak the man who has come from Ireland to marry her. She has no sense of loyalty either to her cousin or to the solidarity of the Whiteoak family, to which she does not really feel she belongs and in which she has no pride: 'Roma is damned proud of being the daughter of a poet. She knows the titles of all Uncle Eden's poems, but has she ever read one of them? I doubt it';[47] 'There's nothing very jolly or generous about Roma . . .'; 'She's the most self-sufficient being I have ever known . . .'. Thus Mazo builds up her fictional portrait with its basis in the character (as she perceived it) of Esmée and with the addition of some negative traits she had associated with women ever since her experience with Aunt Eva, who had shown a tendency to take over other women's lovers.

René, in an interview, said that his sister was a character throughout one book and did not realize it.[48] His thoughts about the next book would have been even more interesting, for *Centenary at Jalna* contains a portrait of Finch and his son. Although Mazo focusses more on Finch as a father than she does on Dennis, his son, this is one of the most disturbing of all her fictions, and in it the Gothic vein reaches new heights.

The portrait of Finch as a father is one of total negligence. He is so engrossed in his artistic work and in his second wife that he cannot bear the sight of his son by Sarah Court. The pathetic, lonely little boy so yearns for affection that he constantly invents stories about his father and their plans to travel together. Mazo knew such yearning well. As she said of herself in 1910: 'My father (more like brother than father) would say to me: "Before long I shall be able to afford a splendid trip for us. We'll see England, France, Ireland together." Always together—together always.'[49]

Under the pressure of paternal neglect and inherited maternal genes, however, Dennis develops into a monster. His love of his father reaches beyond filial devotion to the kind of demonic possessiveness his mother had shown. He depicts himself as a suffering Christ, at one point daubing himself with blood from mosquito bites, extending his arms, and crying, 'I'm crucified.'[50] He tries to drown his baby cousin and brings about the death of his father's second wife, for whom he has developed a fanatical hatred: when she goes into labour and asks him to call the doctor, he delays and, finally, when it is too late to save her, calls a veterinarian.

The climax of this curious book is a wedding—an arranged dynastic match between cousins descended from the original founders of Jalna, whom they vividly resemble and whose names they bear. The second Adeline and Philip are the children of Renny and Piers, the stalwart half-brothers whose makeup is not marred by the weak artistic genes introduced into the family by Mary Whiteoak. The children, therefore, are strong-willed, vigorous, and masculine: she is a talented horse-woman and he a military man, a younger brother destined to be the next Master of Jalna. Renny, the reigning master, is delighted by the match: 'The day had come when Renny led his only daughter up the aisle to give her in marriage to the bridegroom of his choice.'[51] They are to live in Renny's house, and on the return from the church she insists that her father ride in the car with her and the groom. Afterwards her father tells her: 'Now you will stand in the receiving line and behave yourself properly. No more tantrums or I'll take a stick to your back.'[52]

Adeline does not (yet) love her husband, and the marriage is sure to be stormy, but the continuity of the Whiteoak family line is ensured. There will be another generation of horsey, military men, the odd horsey woman, no doubt a few unfortunate throw-backs with artistic temperaments—poets, actors and so on—but these can be tolerated as the expected aberrations in any family. Adeline and Philip are dead. Long live Adeline and Philip.

The American and British publishing houses, when they received this manuscript, split along lines that must have seemed only too familiar. Lovat Dickson genuinely liked the book, appreciating the power of Mazo's Gothic creations and finding Dennis a remarkable study in child psychology.[53] Edward Weeks, predictably, thought the many coincidences and implausibilities too much but limited his requests for corrections to three of the most egregious excesses: Adeline's docile acceptance of the arranged marriage, Finch's carelessness in leaving his wife alone when she was on the point of giving birth, and a sailing scene with a sudden storm and narrowly averted disaster.[54]

Letters and telegrams flew back and forth. Dickson said he did not think there could be any logic in the actions of a little boy impelled by love and jealousy.[55] Mazo said that she drew her characters from her observation of Canadian youngsters like René and Esmée's husband when they were younger, and that maybe Canadians were different from Americans.[56] All the same, when Weeks insisted, she made some changes, adding paragraphs here and there to make Finch's absence from his wife's side more reasonable (a servant was supposed to be there) and Adeline's acceptance of the marriage less docile (fits of weeping, temper and other signs of resistance).[57] Concessions were made, friendly relations maintained, and in a long-established pattern the book was published, with Mazo objecting only—as she often did— to the jacket design.[58]

When she had finished work on the book Mazo was ready once again for a trip to England. Hearing of her prospective visit, coinciding as it would with the publication of the fifteenth book in the series and the thirty-fifth year of her association with Macmillan, the company decided to stage a gala celebration in its offices, then in St Martin's Street behind the National Gallery. When Maurice Macmillan wrote to sound her out—it was well known that she shied away from such occasions—he said he had in mind a cocktail party, and that he wanted to transform the offices into a replica of Jalna, perhaps of the centenary banquet in the book.[59] Mazo agreed. Perhaps her decision was influenced by her recent disappointment in being excluded from the celebrations when the *Atlantic Monthly* had celebrated its centenerary in 1957. She was offended enough to write to Weeks: 'The Atlantic Centenary has received considerable notice here—I confess that I am more than a little hurt by the way I and my long connection with the Atlantic were ignored. Caroline was hurt for my sake but too proud to speak of it. I am not.'[60]

The Macmillan party more than made up for the *Atlantic*'s snub, for she was treated like visiting royalty throughout her visit. Although a professional public-relations firm was hired to cope with the party and, particularly, the press,[61] Lovat Dickson moved behind the scenes to ensure that Mazo had every comfort.[62] Writing for reservations at her London hotel, he told the manager that 'one of our most distinguished authors' required accommodations,[63] and he reminded Maurice Macmillan to call her in case she felt nervous about the party and sad because her friend of thirty years, Betty Macmillan, was no longer living to greet her. Before she sailed from Liverpool, both he and Macmillan sent bouquets to her cabin.[64]

The trip was to be Mazo's last. It was fitting that she made it happily and in the grand style of a travelling celebrity. Photographers and press men crowded into her cabin before she sailed—she found them 'very nice'—and the ship's bookstore carried most of her books in the Pan edition, many of which she was asked to sign.[65] When the ship docked in Montreal, an official of the Cunard Company came to welcome her, and a young man was provided to help her through customs.[66]

For all the acclaim, however, Mazo was already being regarded less as a great writer than as a great monument, remarkable for having endured so long. She wrote Daniel Macmillan that she had been surprised by the frequency of the word 'elderly' in the newspaper coverage of her visit, because she had never thought of herself as old.[67] Years later, when Dickson recalled the party at the publishing house, he remembered it this way:

> Macmillan fitted up the office, old oak Victorian Gothic, broad carpeted corridors hung with pictures of famous Victorian authors—transferred into a cabin in the wilderness, bear skins nailed to the wall, snowshoes, guns, imitation snow. A press conference in the chairman's room, assembled London Press are there. They are all young and suddenly and cruelly they burst the fantasy, their questions teasing at first and then bitter and envious at the prosperity of the aged keeping up this parody. This is typical of socialist England at that time. The ladies are heartbroken and leave the party early on the excuse of fatigue. They hurry back to Canada.[68]

The year 1958 ended with a happy celebration of Christmas with twelve people sitting down to Christmas dinner at Ava Crescent— her children and grandchildren, Uncle Walter and Aunt Jessie, and two bachelor friends who were always on hand for festive occasions.[69] Like many who have grown up in straitened circumstances, Mazo took a childlike joy in Christmas festivities and gifts. When, soon after the children had arrived, one or two friends had sent gifts to them rather than to Mazo and Caroline she had been filled with alarm. She quickly warned all her friends not to adopt this habit, as the children had quite enough gifts and she and Caroline adored getting them.[70] Her attitude towards presents was demanding and shamelessly greedy.

Edward Weeks had not needed to be warned about diverting gifts to the children, but had always sent a fine Christmas package that included everyone in the family. Once in the early days when the package included jig-saw puzzles for the children, Mazo pounced on them before they ever reached the nursery;[71] she even built several episodes of *The Master of Jalna* around the Whiteoaks' sudden obsession with jig-saw puzzles. If by chance he sent gifts that had been duplicated, Mazo did not hesitate to return them with a request for an exchange. Weeks, long-suffering, would comply with the apology that he should have realized that Esmée had a watch, a camera, or whatever.[72] No doubt his patience was helped by the fact that he did not shop or pay for the gifts himself; Mazo would have been surprised to see his notes requesting quick reimbursement in cash from the press's purchasing department to help with his own shopping.[73]

In later years she had often anticipated Weeks's Christmas present by requesting items that she liked and could not find in Canada, such as certain brands of tea. Nevertheless, her gratitude and relish for what she received always sounded genuine. In 1958 she wrote: 'Never was your Christmas box more welcomed! Usually it arrives some days before Christmas but this year we watched for it in vain. It arrived on Boxing Day.'[74]

19

The End of a Saga

The publication of *Centenary at Jalna* had a final quality to it. The chief event of the book—the celebration of the hundredth birthday of the house of Jalna—had been replicated by the Macmillan festivities in London. As Mazo was approaching her eightieth birthday, it would have been appropriate for the series to have ended there. Unfortunately, this was not to be. Although after three volumes her publishers had sagely agreed that they had had enough of a good thing,[1] they had lived to learn that the sturdy Whiteoak clan would end only when she did. They had predicted the ridicule that an attenuated series would invite and, when it came, they had consoled themselves with the material gains she brought them. They had even encouraged her by thinking up new directions for the Whiteoaks. Weeks's idea for 'turning back the clock at Jalna' had produced the weakest novel to date. But even that book was not the disaster that the last one was to prove.

In fact, the new book too was inspired by Weeks: this time he suggested that she infuse new life into the series by bringing in the American Civil War. The idea owed its origin to *Gone With the Wind*, one of the few novels that, twenty years earlier, had challenged Mazo's regular position at the top of the best-seller lists. There was a certain irony in the situation, in that Margaret Mitchell herself may have been influenced by *Jalna*. If she read the serialized version in late 1927 and 1928, when she was working on her novel, she must have been struck by the resemblance between Mazo's Irish family and her own O'Haras.[2]

We do know that in 1928 Mitchell changed the name of her heroine's home from Fontenoy Hall to Tara, a name with the simple effectiveness of Jalna. She also renamed her main character, originally Pansy, and was said to have spent hours searching for the right name[3]—

though she needed only to look into *Jalna*, where Miss Pink blushes and turns into 'Miss Scarlett'.[4] As for her title, that too appears almost word for word in *Whiteoaks*: in one of that novel's most emotional scenes, Renny finds himself face to face with Alayne, whom he loves and thinks he has lost. When she asks him if the time since they last met seems long or short to him, he replies simply, 'Gone like the wind'.[5]

There is no record of Mazo's having read *Gone With the Wind*, and it was thirty years later that she began her own Civil War novel. Weeks sent her Mary Boykin Chestnut's *A Diary from Dixie*, which she loved and treated as a reliable historical source book—she wrote him gratefully that she had never before heard of Jefferson Davis; she had heard of John Brown and Stonewall Jackson, but did not know whether they were North or South. 'Now', she concluded, 'I know everything.'[6] She did not, of course, and the result was a book so flawed that it caused consternation even among her British publishers. Lovat Dickson chided Weeks:

> In our minds [we] did not bless you for suggesting the subject, as I think you did! The chief trouble with the book is that Mazo has tacked the Jalna story on to the historical background of the Civil War, of which she knows nothing, and which I think had very little effect on Canada.[7]

In addition, Mazo's rendering of Southern speech, particularly of the slaves, was hopeless.[8]

Jointly and separately Mazo's editors wrestled with the problems. When Dickson visited Toronto in early October 1959 and spent a day with Mazo going over the proofs, he reported to Weeks that she was 'most helpful and cooperative',[9] although she insisted on keeping a very implausible last chapter. Dickson remembered the visit as a pleasant one, with Mazo's life going on as usual—cocktails in the library, dinner in the dining-room with a place set at the table for the cat (a dish of scraps on a placemat), and an hour afterwards around an enormous log fire in the large drawing room.[10] A week later Mazo was stricken with her final illness.

According to René's wife, she had had Parkinson's disease for years and was now suffering from hardening of the arteries and rheumatoid arthritis as well. There were quick changes in her state, and in the worst times she was unconscious for hours. For Caroline the situation was beyond words. She wrote to Weeks but could not bring herself to describe in words Mazo's condition and the doctor's prognosis:

> If I were talking to you I could tell you what the doctors have told René but I simply cannot put it in black and white in a letter. Naturally, Mazo knows nothing of the verdict. . . . I have watched that bright and lively spirit being quenched bit by bit and will it ever recover I ask myself a thousand times.[11]

Although Mazo did not leave her bed again except to be wheeled into the sunshine for brief periods, Caroline continued to hope for improvement—and to report to Weeks that it had taken place. A visitor describing the household at this time fell as observers so often did, automatically, into theatrical terms:

> The last time I saw Mazo the dear lady was exceedingly unwell and she was lying in her magnificent bed, you know she looked like a queen. The whole mise-en-scène, the whole house, the situation as far as the servants were concerned, all suggested a kind of regal decline.[12]

Somehow, amid all this turmoil, her last book was ushered into print. It is by no means unusual to see artists going on long after their powers have diminished, goaded by their agents, by financial necessity and often, like Mazo, by some inner imperative. Whether it is Katherine Hepburn appearing in a television drama or Margot Fonteyn dancing to recorded music in provincial towns, the spectacle is brave and touching. Such was Mazo's last book—ridiculous in its scope, full of historical absurdities and unlikely coincidences, and yet with flashes of the old skill—original new characters, familiar ones re-imagined, all pulled together into great dramatic scenes. When it reached Mazo, in one of the stable periods about a year before her death, she was pleased with it and liked the cover design.[13] Weeks wrote that this book had a special meaning for all who knew her, and understood, as her readers could not, how valiantly she had carried it through.[14] He managed to speak to some of the reviewers and indicate the circumstances surrounding the book's production, so that it might be described in the context of her entire career. The result in *Newsweek* was as follows:

> Full of the old hustle-bustle narrative energy that Jalna fans expect, the book gives no hint that a truly grave danger to the Whiteoak clan exists in real life. At 75, Mazo de la Roche—the slender aquiline lady whose serial saga has entrapped readers in fifteen languages lies bedridden with a complication of illnesses which has left her too weak to write. In the Toronto home where she lives with a cousin-companion, Miss de la Roche was carried downstairs one day recently and established on a chaise-longue to speak with her old friend, Edward Weeks. . . .

Merely to carry on a conversation was a taxing effort for her, Weeks said and there was no discussion of future books.[15]

Mazo died quietly in the early hours of the morning on 12 July 1961, with all the family at her bedside. The extent to which Caroline was devastated could only be guessed at, for she went immediately into her own room and closed the door.[16] Later she sent a telegram to Lovat Dickson: 'MAZO LEFT US LAST NIGHT PLEASE TELL THE OTHERS'.[17] René took a strong drink and Esmée, practical as always, assisted the nurse with the laying out.

When Mazo died, the most fitting place for her remains would have been the pleasant cemetery in Newmarket where, on grassy slopes under trees, generations of Roches and Lundys were buried side by side, surrounded by other graves marked with the names that appear in the Jalna novels—Adelines and Philips, Whiteoaks, Wakefields, and Binns. She would have been near the house, still standing on Prospect Street, where she was born and grew up, and close to the large place that had once been Limerick House, the home of her uncle Danford Roche. Her funeral might even have taken place in the church that three-quarters of a century earlier had overflowed with mourners for her young uncle.

But Mazo's connection was always more to imaginary characters than to real people, and perhaps she did not wish her distinguished mourners to note the discrepancy between her own French name and that of her Roche forebears. The funeral took place at the Anglican Cathedral of St James. She had stipulated in her will[18] that she should be buried there if she died in Canada and near Axminster if she died in England—but Caroline, alledgedly following a later verbal request, chose the cemetery at Sibbald's Point on Lake Simcoe, fifteen miles from Newmarket.[19] Dating from the late 1700s, it is a pioneer cemetery that resembles the graveyard of an old English country church, although its lakeside setting is special to Canada.

Once again Mazo, wishing to belong, had positioned herself in such a way that she only reinforced her status as an outsider—a fact that was brought home when the family tried to place a window in the church to her memory. The congregation was split over whether to allow such a memorial for one who had never been a member of the church. When the deciding vote in favour was cast by a local bookseller, the window was created and placed in the church porch.[20] Depicting St Francis with many birds and animals, it reads: 'HE PRAY-ETH BEST WHO LOVETH BEST ALL THINGS BOTH GREAT AND SMALL. In abiding memory of Mazo de la Roche 1888-1961.'

Caroline had the same birthdate, erroneous by nine years, carved on the gravestone—a monument to a self-created image. Though the Celtic cross resembles the Roche grave in the Newmarket cemetery, it bears the spurious family motto 'DIEU EST MA ROCHE' surrounding a medallion that features a lark ascending. Caroline added a motto of her own: 'DEATH INTERRUPTS ALL THAT IS MORTAL'.

A historic marker has been erected in the same cemetery at the grave of Stephen Leacock, but none to celebrate the memory of Mazo de la Roche. Instead, the city of Newmarket claimed her by establishing a marker there. In a way, the disposal of her remains exemplifies the convoluted and irrational path that Mazo travelled throughout her life in her self-defeating search to find her own people and place in the world. In fact, the only secure place she ever found was the private space that she created with Caroline.

For most of Mazo's readers around the world, news of her death came in the papers. The accounts of her life once more repeated the misinformation—largely the result of her own evasions and inventions—that had always surrounded her. Her age was given variously as 71 (the *Toronto Daily Star*), 73 (the *Telegram*), and, correctly, 82 (*Time*). William French in the *Globe and Mail* cautiously said that she was 'reported variously as 73, 76, and 82'. He also invoked the story most likely to infuriate her fellow-countrymen:

> Miss de la Roche's spiritual home was England, a country she loved. After the success of her first book . . . she quietly packed up amid the acclaim and moved to England, where she remained for 12 years. The reserve of the English and the country's quiet charm suited her personality.[21]

A headline in the *Telegram* reported, with some accuracy, 'AUTHORESS LEFT 30-YEAR RIDDLE', but the riddle turned out merely to be whether Benares was or was not the original model for Jalna. (On the whole, the article suggests that it was, on the grounds that when the play *Whiteoaks* was produced in Toronto, Mazo sent the set designer out there to make sketches.)[22]

Her relationship with Caroline, that life-long partnership of love and devotion, was passed over in silence, although one or two articles wrongly noted that she had died 'in the home of' her cousin.[23] In contrast, since it was hard to imagine a woman's life not centred upon a man, much was made of the young Frenchman she had once nearly married. Hinting at romantic love and heartbreak, the artist's gesture of abnegation for the demands of her art, she was quoted as saying that she 'wanted him to give me my freedom without hindrance'.[24]

William Arthur Deacon approached the romantic question from a literary angle:

> Her love for Renny was that of a woman for a man. Renny had red hair and loved horses. He had a will of iron and was, in all ways, as masculine as humans are made. He occupies more space than any other character. I believe that only the artist in Mazo prevented her from writing about Renny all the time.[25]

Far-fetched as that may seem, Mazo herself had once told Lovat Dickson that 'There was a man like Renny. He loved me. But he married someone else. There were good reasons. I understood why.'[26]

Obituaries are not the place for author-bashing, and only one or two, like the following, contained the virulent hostility that had marked the reviews of Mazo's books:

> Gentlefolk at Little Whiffle-Under-Flay curled up happily with crumpets and the latest novel about Jalna, the Whiteoaks clan's Southern Ontario rural domain. Imperial army subalterns devoured dog-eared copies from the mess library. Even Canadians in the backwoods and main streets retreated pleasurably from reality in the stories Miss de la Roche gave them as their pioneer roots.
>
> Mazo de la Roche's death yesterday at the age of 82 will be regretted by her admirers, not as an inconsolable loss to Canadian literature, but because there will be no more Jalna.[27]

Unlike the reviews of her books, which had become increasingly dismissive, the obituaries stressed her vast popularity outside her native land and merely hinted at her limitations. Robert Fulford, for example, wrote that

> Canadians went to them looking for a realistic account of Canadian life, and found instead a fairy-tale countryside populated by implausibly old-world characters. Europeans, on the other hand, took them for what they were—romantic novels of escape, beyond real artistic or realistic criticism.[28]

W.A. Deacon, as he said in his obituary tribute, had known Mazo for forty years. Their acquaintanceship predated *Possession* when she had written humbly and naïvely to explain her book to a prospective reviewer. Over the years, as the relationship changed, he had written to her more respectfully, as a journalist to a writer of international stature. They passed to first-name intimacy, but that intimacy did not bring trust or warmth. Even while she was writing cordially to him, she was storming to Hugh Eayrs about Deacon's spite and ill-feeling and the 'little chorus of hate from Toronto and Hamilton' that he led.[29]

Nor was her suspicion of him lessened by his involvement in the Governor General's Awards. Now at her death he had the last word, and he expressed his feelings about her safe in the knowledge that she would never read them. Even though he knew that she disliked the story and had corrected him both in conversations and letters, he could not resist describing the location of their first meeting as a bedsitter in Gertrude Pringle's house. And he summed up her work as follows:

> She lived in the most momentous period of history and ignored it all—
> its politics and science, the Great Depression and two world wars. . . .
> They teach nothing, offer only the pleasure of seeing character in
> action—escapism if you like. Readers there will long be, among
> folk everywhere, who read just for pleasure.[30]

The most gracious tribute to Mazo, both as an artist and as a person, was Robertson Davies'. Of the artist he wrote:

> Miss de la Roche was not a stylist or a philosopher; she was that rare
> creature in the literary world, a born story-teller. . . . The creation of
> the Jalna books is the most protracted single feat of literary invention
> in the brief history of Canada's literature.

Of the person:

> It would not be suitable to end this brief comment on her life without
> some mention of her kindness and understanding towards young peo-
> ple, to whom she gave advice, affection, and money without stint. Nor
> was she a person who was interested only in backing winners. Not
> only was Mazo de la Roche a novelist of unusual gifts, she was also a
> woman of uncommon breadth and vigour of spirit.[31]

One other who praised her unreservedly was Edward Weeks. Long before, when Hugh Eayrs had died, she had written to him, 'See that you outlive me, Ted.'[32] He did. He came up from Boston to her funeral and he returned a last time in 1963, when the University of Toronto's Library of Rare Books and Special Collections celebrated the acquisition of the one-millionth item for its Special Collections. This material consisted of Mazo's books—first editions in English and translations into foreign languages—a large collection of fan letters, some personal correspondence, and, most important, unpublished materials and the holograph manuscripts, written in pencil on her drawing board, of much of her fiction. The collection was rich, and it was appropriately placed in the university she had briefly attended, which had given her an honorary degree, and in a library located in the area of the city she knew best—near the College of Art, the Parliament buildings where Caroline had worked, near so many of the houses and apartments she had lived in, and only a stone's throw from Mrs Pringle's house, where she had received the news of her first big success.

Weeks had been asked to add his own collection of Mazo's letters and other materials to the University of Toronto's archive.[33] These constituted the one other extensive collection of her materials—correspondance personal and literary, as well as many readers' reports on her manuscripts—and would have made the library the chief repository of information for students of Mazo de la Roche. Unfortunately, Weeks declined, explaining that it was a tradition for Atlantic Monthly editors to keep their papers.[34] Later they were sold, along with his other papers, to the Harry Ransome Humanities Research Center at the University of Texas in Austin. (It is, of course, entirely reasonable that the integrity of one person's collection should be maintained.) Consequently, the second most important collection of Mazo's papers must be sought in Texas, alongside many of the great collections of twentieth-century British authors. Mazo might have been mildly astonished at seeing her papers in Texas, but she would not have objected to the company. By chance, then, even the disposal of her literary remains reflects Mazo's fundamental ambivalence about her own country.

Nevertheless, Weeks had a fine sense of occasion. His speech was a fitting tribute to Mazo, although she would not have appreciated his resurrecting once more the old story about the 'snug' bedroom situation at Jalna.[35] He also told the oft-repeated story of his first visit to Toronto, describing Mazo as she then was in the little room crowded with family furniture. And he ended his speech by emphasizing her love for Canada and the Canadian land, a subject too rarely stressed in reviews and discussions of her work. As illustrations he chose three descriptions of seasonal changes at Jalna, among them the following:

> It was a day of thick yellow autumn sunshine. A circular bed of nasturtiums around two old cedar trees burned like a slow fire. The lawn still had a film of heavy dew drawn across it, and a procession of bronze turkeys, led by the red-faced old cock, left a dark trail where their feet had brushed it.[36]

He commented that Mazo's love for Canada was bred in her mind and her bone, and that such descriptive passages—'prose painting in the style of the great Dutch masters'—attest to this love.

225

The European appreciation of Mazo de la Roche is often attributed to a fondness for a social texture that is false. A possibility rarely mentioned is that Europeans, with their relatively tame surroundings, have responded strongly to the Canadian landscape that Mazo described. Perhaps one reason Canadians have been less enthusiastic is that they have taken for granted what she so lovingly rendered.

20

Caroline Alone

When Caroline closed the door on her grief, the gesture was typical of a long habit of self-protection and concealment. Even more hidden and irretrievable than Mazo's, her life remains the stubborn mystery at the centre of Mazo's story. She rarely spoke for herself in print, and in the autobiography she is described entirely by Mazo. Few of the letters she wrote to friends have survived, and most of them are on inconsequential matters—endless thank-you notes for floral offerings and invitations from those who knew Mazo's annoyance when Caroline was excluded—but Caroline must have known that the flowers, like the invitations, were really Mazo's; that she was honoured only because Mazo valued her. Yet she apparently never resented that subordinate status, and she was generally agreed to be that rare person who can play second fiddle gracefully.[1] Like many a wife, she took sincere pride in her partner and vicarious pleasure in her successes, and was angered only when she felt that Mazo was slighted.

Mazo put Caroline in her fiction in various guises. Her physical features and alliterating name appear in Alayne Archer, Renny's wife, while her orphaned condition and disinherited state resemble those of the 'illegitimate' Pheasant Vaughan, who becomes a Whiteoak by marriage. Then there are the two wives of Finch Whiteoak—first his cousin Sarah Court, whose powerful sexuality and possessiveness (she even tries to control Jalna itself) literally drive him mad; second, the chronically ailing woman he marries after Sarah dies, for whom he is tender and protective. These characters hint not only at the various aspects of Caroline, but at Mazo's shifting feelings for her. Of all these characters Mazo names a model for only one, explaining in her autobiography that Sarah Court was based on a woman she saw in an Oxford restaurant.[2]

Those who knew Caroline habitually called her 'sweet'[3]—an adjective often applied indiscriminately to people of her diminutive stature and fair colouring. Certainly she appeared gentle and charming. In her thank-you letters she adopts the mannerisms of a certain kind of Englishwoman, girlish and gushing and reminiscent of the gay young things of the twenties. She has a tendency to refer to herself as 'one', to her readers as 'my dears', and to overuse expressions like 'utterly', 'too utterly', 'horrid', and 'ghastly'.[4] Marguerite Dickson remembered her at a London dinner party, raising her hand like a little girl for permission to leave the room while Mazo smiled in fond amusement.[5] Dorothy Livesay recalled her even in the Trail Cottage days as affected, speaking 'limitation English' and boasting of kinship with Mark Twain.[6]

Contradicting the veneer of sweetness, however, are a few episodes in the autobiography that portray her as forceful and disapproving: when she met hostile critics she cut them dead;[7] she refused to take part in the Knock game, telling Mazo it would corrupt the children's morals.[8] Esmée remembers that, visiting Caroline in later years, she went out with friends for a late evening and returned to find herself locked out of the house.[9] Caroline often comes across, in short, as bossy. The same impression is conveyed in the querulous, censorious tone of a recorded interview, as well as in some of the letters—notably one, allegedly unsuspected by Mazo, to Edward Weeks:

Various happenings proceeding her illness had been depressing her spirits. The highly sensitive artistic temperament [sic] is, I suppose, more vulnerable than is well. Though I must say that Mazo is usually evenly balanced. But she did feel—and I too, for that matter that you and Mrs Cloud showed much less enthusiasm for *Renny's Daughter* than is usually the case when you have read a new Whiteoak. Then there was the elimination of the chapter at the school which she very much disliked cutting out and which her English publishers particularly liked. There was the matter of the blurb on the jacket of Mr McLennan's book which Little Brown published this spring. In case you had not seen it I will quote the sentence Mazo strongly objected to. '*Barometer Rising* is recognized today as virtually the first of what is now a contemporary literature in Canada.'

Strange words indeed on the jacket of a book by a new author brought out by Mazo's publishers of more than 20 years. She wrote to Mr Thornhill, drawing his attention to this but he did not even go to the trouble of answering her letter. . . . Never before have I heard her exclaim 'I will never write another book!' Her writing has always been such a joy to her.[10]

Although Mazo claimed to value Caroline's critical ability, the novels show no sign of benefitting from the judgement of anyone but Weeks. The manuscripts were never greatly changed from their first writing, and Caroline seems to have raised no objections to the gaucheries that worried the professional editors. After Mazo's death she asked Lovat Dickson for advice about a maudlin poem—on the death of a cocker spaniel—sent to her by a fan of Mazo's who wished to get it published. Dickson told her frankly that it was really dreadful poetry and only touched her heart because she was kind and gentle.[11]

Years before, W.A. Deacon had by a naïve question called forth from Mazo the following outburst, in which she equated Carolin's presence with life itself: 'You suppose Caroline is still with me! Still with me! Do I breathe? Do I live? Have I not made away with myself? Yes, she is still with me!'[12] Now Caroline poured forth her grief to Weeks and, above all, to Dickson, whom she regarded as a kind of younger brother:

> My dear dear Rache,
>
> I feel numb and empty of all emotion save that of pity—if that is an emotion. Pity—a searing pity—for my darling Mazo who so loved and so clung to life . . . pity for the whole human race—born to be loved and give their love only to be torn apart from the loved one. Forgive me if to you my very dear and understanding friend, I make this cry from the depths of my suffering heart. I will not do it again.
>
> Mazo's last illness was so brief and the end so sudden and unexpected that the blow was stunning. In your letter you spoke of how beautiful she looked on your last visit. She was beautiful . . . in *every way*.
>
> [The children] are doing everything in their power to lighten my burden even when their own grief was hard to bear. Poor dears, they have lost the best friend they will ever know.[13]
>
> There must be thousands and thousands of these mss. and all by hand and in pencil. All the work of her dear, tireless hands and brain.[14]

Speaking of her life after Mazo, Caroline often, like many bereaved, wavers between courage and self-pity. She says she is grateful that Mazo left her the house and the means to keep it up, but adds that she does have some means of her own. She loves the house for its memories, both happy and sad. She speaks of her devoted servants and of the children, who visit when they can. René comes for lunch most days when he lives in Toronto; he looks after her business affairs, plays cribbage, reads to her, and is 'more than a companion'. Esmée comes in less frequently because her husband now works in Montreal and she can get away only for a few days at a time.[15] Both the children take her for holidays—René to New England, Esmée to nearby lake resorts and once to the Bahamas. When Dickson mentions going to England, she says she cannot face the memories that would ambush her there.[16] Only now and again does she complain, mainly about her health and about being alone. When the children and their families are all out of town she has to spend Thanksgiving alone, dining on sweetbreads instead of turkey and pumpkin pie. She ends her letter: 'I have just been called to my lonely lunch—a meal for which I do not much care—and so will say goodbye.'[17]

She takes an interest in current affairs, again reacting most often with disapproval. She is infuriated by the rising tide of Canadian nationalism in the 1960s, and fears for the Queen's safety on her 1967 visit to Canada. She writes to Dickson:

> And now this awful business of the flag and the disgraceful behaviour at the time of the Queen's visit. I, among many, am deeply humiliated. If—and when—you come to my front door you will see a large, defiant and very handsome ensign floating above your head and there it is going to stay, come what may in the way of maple leaves. Did you ever hear of so sorry an idea?[18]

A number of decisions on literary matters still remained to be made, and Caroline approached them with a good deal of uncertainty, seemingly unsure about what Mazo would have wished. The first of these decisions concerned a planned biography of Mazo by Ronald Hambleton, who over the years had been a staunch admirer. A freelance writer and journalist, Hambleton had written the script for a 1957 television dramatization of *Whiteoaks*, had interviewed Mazo for CBC radio, had done an excellent job of collecting and arranging for interviews with friends, family, and former employees of Mazo, and had prepared a CBC documentary about her. It seemed a logical next step that he should attempt the biography.[19]

Mazo's opinion of Hambleton had changed during their association. At first, she had been hostile and suspicious, as she was of any interviewer, calling him 'the friendly icicle' and telling Weeks that he made her feel 'prickly' all over and dried up her talk.[20] But two months later, when the interview was broadcast, she wrote Ethel Wilson that Hambleton was 'very very good as an interviewer and, as you say—quite different from the usual. On my part I like him better and better'.[21] When he approached Caroline on the subject of biography, he made a good initial impression. It was only after she consulted with Weeks and Dickson that she began to have grave doubts. From their letters it is clear that Mazo's publishers objected not so much to

Hambleton as biographer as to any biography at all. The people most sympathetic to his endeavour at the beginning were John Gray, the president of Macmillan of Canada, who thought him 'a serious man of letters'[22] and Caroline Clement. Caroline, however, was generally confused, torn between favouring a memorial book to Mazo and fearing what it would entail. She then begged Dickson to do the book, which she apparently imagined as similar to Mazo's own autobiography.[23]

Genuinely puzzled over why Hambleton should wish to write a book with such limited prospects for financial success, Dickson declined the undertaking because he was at a stage in his life when he could not undertake projects without financial remuneration. Nevertheless, his comments on the ideal biography provide a rare frank appraisal of her life and work:

> What there is to do is a memoir, by someone who knew her, an affectionate, slightly teasing study of by no means an uncommon phenomena, the writer with a gift for flowing narrative who luckily stakes out a locale which is romantic and unfamiliar, and peoples it with characters who represent the virtues and the vices, much as in the early miracle plays. An affectionate portrait would please her readers; the teasing note they would hardly notice, and it would disarm the critics. That's Dr Dickson's prescription, and at all costs the patient must not be burdened with anything serious![24]

Dickson said he was prepared to see Hambleton and help him but would not allow him to use his words in a context 'that may be awfully wrong, and which might involve me in the booting the critics will give him if my premonitions should prove correct'.[25]

Weeks said that the book would add much to an understanding of Mazo, but that he preferred to let her own work speak for itself.[26] In dealing with Hambleton he used his practised diplomatic skills. He did not, of course, offer a contract, but encouraged him to submit the book when it was finished. Although he agreed to be interviewed in Boston, he gave Hambleton only general literary information about Mazo's work (which could easily have been acquired elsewhere), and vouchsafed no personal information.[27]

Hambleton set to work, therefore, without knowing whether permission to publish much of the book's contents would be given or witheld, and not knowing who would publish it. As he makes clear in his own 1977 memoirs, he had no illusions about Mazo:

> I had interviewed the woman, and I had heard her tell me these fibs with a straight face. But then, why should she not? She had come to

believe that she was 'born and raised on a fruit and stock farm in the rich agricultural country near Oakville. . . .' The familiar phrases, as e.e. cummings could have said, 'come out like a ribbon lie flat on the brush. . . .'[28]

He well understood that it would have been 'quixotic' for her American publishers to put their imprint on a book that contradicted not only their publicity but her own autobiography.

The process of gathering information from Mazo's family and friends was a story in itself, for a life like Mazo's is a web of obfuscation that entangles all who are connected with it. Weeks must have known that in the much-vaunted relationship between editor and writer of which he often spoke there was much that was manipulative and not entirely honest. Réne had problems of his own to hide, apart from his mother's falsification of her ancestral record. And Caroline's position was even more convoluted. Hambleton has given some indication of these difficulties in his own book:

> It was important at all times to preserve the grudging entrée I had into the de la Roche household, where René de la Roche, the adopted son, so resented my invasion of his mother's privacy he could scarcely bring himself to be civil to me. Caroline Clement, the adopted sister and cousin, who had always appeared to me to enjoy the de la Roche fame quite frankly and openly, was ambivalent: on the one hand, she loved to be in the limelight, to be known as the casket in which reposed all the de la Roche secrets; but on the other, she was so conditioned to privacy that she was able to replay word for word whole phrases and even paragraphs that I had heard Mazo de la Roche use.[29]

Even more bizarre is Hambleton's account of his attempts to interview the respected journalist J.B. (Hamish) McGeachy, columnist for the *Financial Post*, Hambleton's colleague on a panel show, and friend (of sorts) to Mazo and Caroline:

> Among his friends and admirers were Mazo de la Roche and her cousin Caroline Clement, so naturally while I was gathering material for a documentary on de la Roche some time after her death, I taped an interview with McGeachy, who happened to be awash even though it was not yet ten in the morning. He would not put off the interview, however, but went on to record nearly a full hour of material, most of it either scurrilous, scatological or obscene, in which he held these two women up to ridicule. His speculations on their sex life were especially imaginative. Later, his wife telephoned to ask me to destroy the tapes, but the call was unnecessary: I had already done so.[30]

232

However imaginative McGeachy's misogynist fantasies might have been, they were pure invention, for when Hambleton recorded McGeachy in a more sober mood, his observations evoked the spectre of Mazo, like Miss Havisham, humiliated by desertion at the altar. McGeachy's active imagination had heterosexual limits.[31]

In the end Weeks rejected the book. In a tart letter to Hambleton he said that although he had done a 'careful and decent' job, he had spent a disproportionate amount of time delving into the subject's past and failed to capture the personality of Mazo herself:

> The biographical passages seldom succeed in catching her nervous copperwire animation. You do occasionally allude to her mischievous sense of humour and the streak of cruelty in her writing, but her supreme confidence in herself, her capacity for friendship which went so deep with a friend like St John Ervine, her dependence upon Hugh Eayrs and the give and take which she enjoyed with me, are not revealed as fully as they might be.[32]

Hambleton did not let the criticism go unanswered, pointing out that Weeks had witheld all personal information or opinions about Mazo and that Mrs Ervine had denied that Mazo was a close friend of her husband. And he described the aims of his book:

> What I set out to do was to write about a century of Whiteoaks, about a century of immigration, about a century of familial relationships, and about a good writer who was in her own way a prophet and a social critic. About the craft of writing, about the literary climate of the last half century, and at the same time to put her into context, rescuing her from that limbo where many of her well-wishers would try to keep her.[33]

Another friend of Mazo's who was in touch with Hambleton at this time was Dorothy Livesay. Having been a near neighbour at Trail Cottage, she had become something of an authority on those early years and was preparing her own reminiscences of Mazo. Livesay too was aware that Mazo concealed much of her past: she wrote to Hambleton saying that she knew Mazo quite well but suspected much mystery, and that Caroline would tell her nothing and avoided all questions.[34] Quite generously, because his own book was not yet published, Hambleton responded to her pleas for assistance, sending information about Mazo's ancestry and providing dates of certain events and other pieces of his research so that she could add factual material to her own memories.[35]

Livesay subsequently wrote valuable accounts of Mazo's life at Trail Cottage. But she tended to forget the generous help that she had received from Hambleton and charged him with carelessness and inaccuracies, sometimes publicly and sometimes privately, advising the next biographer not to believe any of his research because he had lied about her distant Livesay cousins.[36]

Hambleton's own story goes a long way towards explaining the emphasis in his own life of Mazo. His experience as a British-born immigrant who came to Canada in childhood and returned to England as a young adult, 'a wild colonial boy', because he 'hungered for a society of a kind not available in Vancouver,'[37] may account for his preoccupation with the immigration patterns of Mazo's ancestors. While all future biographies will depend on what he so assiduously gathered—as he says, 'another five years or so, and much of this historical material could have disappeared'[38]—there are some distortions. He sees Mazo's anti-Americanism, for example, exclusively as the legacy of her British ancestors. Even more unfortunately, he summed up her life in a well-turned phrase that soon developed a life of its own and gained wide currency as her epitaph: 'her chief significance is as the last mourner for the dying British influence in Canada'.[39]

When Hambleton's book finally appeared in 1966, Caroline's response was a mixture of confusion and anger. She asked Hambleton why he had written that Mazo was born in Newmarket, said that there were many papers to show that de la Roche was a family name, and expressed the opinion that Mazo's autobiography 'sufficiently covered the ground'. She said that nothing of the real Mazo de la Roche or her family emerged from his work, despite its detail, and she advised him somewhat rudely to confine his writing to either fiction or criticism in future.[40] She must have felt that, as executor, she had betrayed everything that Mazo held dear. But that painful experience was not to be last, for she was soon afterwards caught up in negotiations for the television rights to the Jalna series. Although, as she wrote to Weeks, she would rather not give permission, she knew that a series would mean a great deal of money for René and Esmée, and that it would stimulate sale of the books.[41] Offers came in from England, Australia, and the United States. She was, as usual, getting a great deal of advice, this time from Lovat Dickson, René, Esmée and Senator Daniel Lang. Lang felt strongly that the contract should go to a Canadian company. Caroline apparently did not agree but did not know how much weight her own opinion carried, for she wrote secretly to Weeks: 'Could you find out for me, if, as literary executor, could I give the word to go ahead to the BBC in spite of any opposition from any other source? Please don't mention this to anyone.'[42]

Eventually, however, the contract went to a Canadian company. Hopes for success ran very high. The *Toronto Daily Star*'s Patrick Scott said that the CBC might 'well be embarking on the most important mission ever undertaken by Canadian television'. Blaik Kirby of the *Globe and Mail* said, 'Jalna may well mean the end of the Canadian inferiority complex' and the Producer-Director, John Trent says, 'this is the first chance we have of changing our own image'.[43] Not everyone, of course, agreed with those aspirations, and Mazo's old nemesis, *Saturday Night*, published an editorial that included the following paragraph:

> Mazo de la Roche was, of course, the most colonial of all Canadian authors, a writer who apparently saw nothing wrong with Ontario except the fact that it wasn't in England. This detail she corrected by writing book after book in which a collection of related redardates talked, acted, thought, ate and dressed English-style, on the western outskirts of Toronto. Her work spread across the civilized world, a beacon of light for Anglophiles everywhere in an era when the sun was just beginning to set on the Empire.[44]

An excellent cast was lined up, headed by Kate Reid who was to play both the first and second Adelines, and Timothy Findley was engaged as one of the scriptwriters.

Throughout the negotiations Caroline was wooed with gifts of flowers, books, and recordings of music she liked, but one fact was hidden from her until the last minute: the plan for the series included extending the story beyond what Mazo had written, adding new characters and events. When the pilot episode was about to be broadcast and it was no longer possible to keep from Caroline what had been done, a tactful member of the company was delegated to break the news. She reported that Caroline was silent for a long moment and then asked if anything could be done to stop it. When she learned that it was too late, she asked members of the family to stay away from the official showing.[45] As it turned out, the series was by general consensus declared to be a failure, and quietly put to rest.

By the time it was shown, however, Caroline's health had deteriorated so much that she required constant nursing care and depended on others for such tasks as writing letters.[46] Yet she maintained contact with friends with surprising persistence; for instance, when she had not heard from Weeks for some time, she dictated a letter to his secretary requesting news. She was much concerned for his well-being when he was widowed, apparently imagining that his life, like hers after Mazo's death, would be over:

You will have to live on memories. Indeed, my heart aches for you and if I were not such a poor crippled creature I should go to you. I might be able to give you a little comfort. As it is, I go nowhere and do nothing, my heart had [sic] been troublesome and makes me very tired.[47]

In fact, Weeks went on writing and editing for many years, married again, and continued to speak with Caroline by telephone and send flowers until her death in the summer of 1972.[48]

Caroline had survived for eleven years alone, provided for by Mazo, sustained by memories, her life still revolving around Mazo and her works. Since the children's lives had taken them outside Toronto, she died alone, although Esmée had visited the day before. Apart from some small legacies to her brother's children, her modest personal estate was divided equally between René and Esmée.[49]

Only a handful of family mourners attended her funeral. She was buried beside Mazo, as the latter had requested in her will: beside Mazo's large, ornate cross stands Caroline's smaller one, completely plain except for the words 'HAND IN HAND WE KEPT THE FAITH'. A casual observer might take the reference to be of Christian significance. But the faith she shared with Mazo was a private one, to which there were only two adherents. Their life-long devotion to each other could be acknowledged only by that oblique reference.

The gravestone erected for René when he died twelve years later is overshadowed by the women's large crosses. But it flaunts the de la Roche name, repeats the family medallion and motto of Mazo's stone, and acknowledges his third wife: 'BELOVED HUSBAND OF BIANCA MARIA'.

It is one of the ironies of the Whiteoak saga that the personal fortune of Adeline Whiteoak, the matriarch of the dynasty, is finally bestowed on the unlikely Finch. The disposition of Mazo's personal fortune had its own ironies. She had placed her estate in trust so that Caroline would be provided for as long as she lived, but wished that after Caroline's death everything would go to René. It was only at the urging of her legal adviser that she had been prevailed upon to leave anything to Esmée; because, as she explained, René's needs were greater,[50] Esmée would receive only one-quarter. As a consequence, the major part of Mazo's fortune—including the future income from sales of her books—was inherited by Bianca Maria, whom René had married five years before his death and who had never met either Mazo or Caroline. 'Mazo's room'—the ornate bed in which she died, the books bound in leather over the years by the craftsman in Malvern, the Varley portrait done in the nineteen-twenties, the gold medal she was awarded in the early fifties—is preserved in Bianca de la Roche's house, and the house is in Newmarket.[51]

Epilogue

Any writer with an output as prolific as that of Mazo de la Roche is bound to be uneven. But if less than a quarter of her work is allowed to be first-rate—*Delight*, the first Jalna novels, a dozen short stories—that is still enough to constitute a solid literary reputation. And outside this core there are numerous lesser works worthy of attention, including *Possession, Lark Ascending, Ringing the Changes*, the supposedly weak *Mary Wakefield*—for the unsuccessful works of truly original writers are often more interesting than the best work of dull ones.

Yet there has been an obstinate tendency to judge Mazo by those books or passages that stand up least well to scrutiny—the products of ill-judgement or extreme old age. And hand in hand with the critical disdain has gone the personal denigration, expertly anatomized in Mary Ellman's *Thinking About Women*,[1] that often accrues to women writers. Many of the reviews of Mazo's work provide classic examples—with a Canadian twist—of what Ellman terms 'phallic criticism'. The following appeared in the *Ottawa Citizen* in 1960:

> Not being a dyed-in-the-wool Mazo de la Roche fan, I cannot consciously say I know much about the Jalna saga. But I admire her technique as a novelist much as I could admire the brains of a space scientist. Perhaps my distaste for this pinched-face genius comes from having met her once.
>
> The heroine is not Mrs Whiteoak, the Irish-born wife of the English husband, Peter [*sic*] Whiteoak, but her daughter Gussie. It is conjured that the precocious Augusta, with her bossiness over her brothers which could made the kid a lady dragon when she grows up, is really in embryo, the formidable grandmother of the later Jalna books. This I cannot prove. I just throw it in on a venture.
>
> I suppose my personal distaste for the Whiteoaks and their pen puppeteer is that Mazo de la Roche is such an Anglo-phile she has to send

the Jalna children to England to school. Upper Canada College is not good enough for them. Always tender references to England, never a kind word for Ottawa or Montreal or the Maritimes. The authoress makes the Whiteoaks some kind of tourists who farm temporarily in Ontario, but really belong to an English manor.

You begin to wonder if Mazo de la Roche knows the words of O Canada.[2]

It is instructive to examine the component parts of this review. First, the critic establishes his credentials by proclaiming his ignorance of the writer's work. He then bolsters the superiority of judgement thus proven by showing only a slight familiarity with the work under review: he misquotes the name of the main character, gives an array of incorrect facts, and produces one false hypothesis. Next, the review presents an excellent example of phallic criticism in merging the attack on the book with an attack on the writer's physical charms or lack of them: abandoning all pretense of objectivity, he smugly admits that he is put off by the writer's homely face. Such jibes have been directed at women writers from George Eliot to Virginia Woolf. Last, there is the questioning of the writer's patriotism and Canadian identity. Imagine having to repatriate Dante and Joyce because they lived elsewhere and criticized their native lands! Again, the reviewer bases his attack on prejudice, rumour, and general hostility, for all his facts are inaccurate. Canadian schools were good enough for the Jalna children: three generations of them attended, as did Mazo and her children, Ontario schools and the University of Toronto. (She was interested enough in the schools to enshrine, in Chapter 10 of *Renny's Daughter*, her fond observations of Upper Canada College, Lakefield, Havergal College, and Ovenden; considered irrelevant by her American publisher, it was struck out of one edition, but it remains in most).

Mazo did something extraordinary for a woman of her generation: she seized power in what had hitherto been a masculine bailiwick. Not only did she amass a fortune, but she did it through her mastery of the language, thus confirming Humpty Dumpty's statement to Alice that whoever learns to control words 'can master the whole lot of them'. Venturing beyond the female writer's traditional fictional territory of books for ladies and children, she came to tower over her male colleagues. And as an American publicist pointed out in 1927, 'she is the first Canadian author to crash through with something big . . . for years'.[3] By her achievement Mazo won the independence to live—more or less—as a law unto herself. Naturally she suffered for such *hubris*: her punishment was to be held up to ridicule, a grotesque target for anyone to mock.

Even her so-called friends were full of secret malevolence for her success, as the truly shocking story of Ronald Hambleton's interview with Hamish McGeachy shows. A decade after her death, Kildare Dobbs in a newspaper article recalled Mazo's kindness to him as to many others. A guest at her 'ye-olde-Tudor Forest Hill mansion' many Christmas Eves, he mocked her pride in her friendship with the British prime minister. As for her work, which he had read at the age of sixteen, when he preferred Evelyn Waugh and Aldous Huxley, 'it was impossible to take Jalna seriously'. The headline to Dobbs's article proclaimed 'OUR CRITIC ENJOYS JALNA BOOKS THE WAY HE ENJOYS A COMIC STRIP'.[4]

Under the pressure of such scorn, to enjoy Mazo became a risky business. Many of her readers were forced to be closet admirers, afraid to invite shame from those of 'superior' tastes. One Canadian writer recalls her experience as a Jalna fan:

> One of my high school friends and I were fans and read everything in the Sussex Public Library. My mother didn't disapprove. She read them all along with me. When I got to university, I discovered that they were supposed to be trash, and became rather ashamed of my taste. I suppose her chief influence on me would be that she was a woman and a Canadian who made a great success.[5]

Of course, Mazo also had loyal supporters to treat the insults with the contempt they deserved, among them Hugh Eayrs as long as he lived, and Dorothy Livesay, who never tired of defending the heroine of her younger days. Unfortunately, their efforts were largely wasted, for Mazo's detractors were inaccessible to reasonable argument. Rooted in nebulous prejudice, their attacks were difficult to refute. The charge of Mazo's un-Canadianness, for example, was often a metonymic cover for something else. When reviewers objected that 'she is not one of us', the 'us' was as much a matter of gender as of national identity.

But even as the scurrilous *Ottawa Citizen* review was being written, the topography of Canadian literature was changing; women writers were moving from the periphery into the mainstream, and soon the pre-eminence of women in Canadian literature was to be an indisputable fact. That same year Margaret Atwood and Margaret Laurence published their first books, quickly followed by Jane Rule, Alice Munro, and numerous others. The first Harlequin Romance had been written, and that Canadian institution (founded in Canada and representing a much larger proportion of the book market in Canada than elsewhere) is as significant a manifestation of the centrality of women in

Canadian fiction as is the achievement of the great writers. The stream of literary excellence has many tributaries; it is fed by the needs of readers as much as by the efforts of writers. Nancy Armstrong's *Desire and Domestic Fiction: A Political History of the Novel*,[6] which explores the rise of women's writing in eighteenth- and nineteenth-century England by examining conduct books and treatises written for women, illustrates the point. No burst of literary activity can be explained simply by examining the major figures in isolation.

Both Margaret Atwood and Margaret Laurence have harked back to the nineteenth-century writers Susanna Moodie and Catharine Parr Traill, listening to them as voices to be reckoned with. By doing so they have gestured towards a female line of descent that branched out from English roots, established itself in Canadian soil, and was unified by one preoccupation—the quest for a woman's story.

Susanna Moodie and Catharine Parr Traill were members of an English literary family similar to the Brontës, with whom they were roughly contemporary. Like the Brontës, the Stricklands drew strength in childhood from their own hermetic world, though the lives of the five sisters later diverged dramatically. Three of them remained, unmarried, in England, where they worked collaboratively as writers. Casting about for heroines, they began by writing the lives of the British queens. Carolyn Heilbrun has recently explained the the choice of queens as comfortable subjects for women writers:

> When biographers come to write the life of a woman . . . they have had to struggle with the inevitable conflict between the destiny of being unambiguously a woman and the woman subject's palpable desire, or fate, to be something else. Except when writing about queens, biographers of women have not, therefore, been at ease with their subjects.[7]

Agnes Strickland had the temerity to write a life of Queen Victoria during the monarch's lifetime. The Queen was furious and wrote 'not allowed' all over the margins. But the Stricklands were undeterred by what was not allowed. Even though they were not permitted access to the public-records office that contained the material for their work, they managed, and Agnes in collaboration with Elizabeth (who balked at having her name appear on the books) wrote a multi-volume series called *Queens of England*. After Agnes's death, in a pioneering effort of her own, sister Jane Margaret wrote *A Life of Agnes Strickland*.[8]

The exigencies of life in Canada, far from the complex social texture of city and court, meant that Moodie and Traill struggled alone to define themselves as women and as writers. Margaret Atwood understood that Moodie had much to say that could not be openly expressed:

What kept bringing me back to the subject—and to Susanna Moodie's own work—were the hints, the gaps between what was said and what hovered, just unsaid, between the lines, and the conflict between what Mrs Moodie felt she ought to think and feel and what she actually did think and feel.[9]

Atwood's intuition of what Susanna Moodie was not 'allowed' to say recalled Willa Cather's words on the same subject: 'It is the inexplicable presence of the thing not named, of the overtone divined by the ear but not heard by it, the verbal mood, the emotional aura of the fact or the thing or the deed, that gives high quality to the novel or the drama. . . .'[10] It took roughly a century for the tentative beginnings made by the Strickland sisters to reach their fruition in Atwood and Laurence.[11] Yet there is an even greater gap between what was expressed obliquely by Moodie and Traill and the fully conscious and sophisticated explorations of the female self in the works of the later writers.

Mazo de la Roche's life bridges the temporal gap. When she was a young girl, Moodie and Traill were still living in Ontario; at the end of her life, Atwood and Laurence, not far from where she lived, were beginning to write. Mazo's life bridges the two centuries in another sense too. Although she was only in her early twenties when the nineteenth century ended, Mazo was not easily pulled into the new century: she had lived too long in the homes first of her grandparents, then of her parents. Moreover, she lived in Toronto rather than New York, London, or Paris, as did such contemporaries as Willa Cather and the modernists—Virginia Woolf, Gertrude Stein, Djuna Barnes.

More importantly, Mazo's work forms the transition between the Atwood-Laurence generation and their nineteenth-century foremothers. She went far beyond Moodie and Traill in attempting the ambitious fictional form of the novel. Yet there were still many things that could not be named, many places in which she felt not allowed to go. She was still, like Susanna Moodie, forced to inscribe her own female desire obliquely, working in and around the limitations of the novel form at her disposal. The reading public expected a traditional heterosexual plot and she provided it. Yet, as Willa Cather knew, the unspoken meanings exerted a power of their own, and many readers felt that powerful undertow.

Mazo drew her strength and her inspiration from her hermetic relationship with her beloved Caroline. Paradoxically, the same relationship cut her off from the institution she most yearned for—the family. In life as in fiction, the plot was exclusively heterosexual. There was no role in the traditional family for an adult woman who was neither a wife nor a mother. Unmarried women were like the aunts in Dylan Thomas's Christmas idyl, 'not wanted in the kitchen or anywhere else for that matter'.

All her life, Mazo strained towards creating a family. She tried to become a mother by adopting two children, and for a time that endeavour was successful. Much more successful was the family she created in her fiction. At Jalna everyone stayed more or less under one roof, and everyone had an appointed role. Even Meg Whiteoak, who resisted marriage for a long time, finally succumbed, married twice and had a child.

Yet Mazo could not identify with her women characters or even in her imagination play their roles as wives and mothers. Her fictional representative was something of a misfit, but he was a man—Finch Whiteoak. Sometimes she could identify with his brother Renny and sometimes with his grandmother, the centegenarian Adeline—toothless, genderless, and freed by old age from the restrictions of her sex. The possibility of a resolution to Mazo's conflicts of sexual identity— the desire to be a member of a family and the desire for autonomy— were never resolved, hence the never-ending serial form of her novels. Those conflicts have not been resolved even by the generation of Canadian writers that flourished after her death, but at least the problems of gender have been articulated clearly and treated openly.

When the life and works of Mazo de la Roche are taken together in their status as text and set against, say, Margaret Atwood's works— from *The Journals of Susanna Moodie* through *The Edible Woman* (with its satirical reference to *Alice in Wonderland*) to *The Handmaid's Tale*, the possibilities for intertextual readings are many and illuminating. Mordecai Richler recently declared Mazo de la Roche to be 'dispensable'.[12] Yet it may be the final irony of her life that while she never shed her status as outsider and non-belonger, that very status has at last made her an indispensable part of Canadian literary history.

Notes

Unless otherwise specified, all manuscript sources cited in the text are held by the Mazo de la Roche Collection, Thomas Fisher Rare Book Library, University of Toronto. Other locations are abbreviated as follows:

HRHRC Harry Ransome Humanities Research Centre, University of Texas, Austin, Texas
MHS Massachusetts Historical Society, Boston, Mass.
MUL McMaster University Library, Hamilton, Ont.
NAC National Archives of Canada, Ottawa
QUA Queen's University Archives, Kingston, Ont. (Lorne and Edith Pierce Collection of Canadian Manuscripts)

PREFACE

[1] Edward Weeks, *In Friendly Candor* (London: Hutchison, 1960), p. 85.
[2] *Boston Globe*, 11 April 1927.
[3] *New York Times*, 11 April 1927.
[4] *The Globe* (Toronto), 12 April 1927; *Toronto Star*, 11 April 1927.
[5] *Time*, 17 Jan. 1949, p. 22.
[6] Edward Weeks Papers, HRHRC, Mazo de la Roche to Weeks, 2 Feb. 1935.
[7] *Chatelaine*, June 1932, p. 4.
[8] Weeks Papers, Questionnaire, 31 March 1927.
[9] Ronald Hambleton, *The Secret of Jalna* (Toronto: Paperjacks, 1972), p. 97.
[10] Caroline Clement interviewed by Ronald Hambleton, 19 Feb. 1964.
[11] Letters in the Mazo de la Roche Papers.
[12] Agnes and Grace Fairburn interviewed by Hambleton; Dorothy Livesay, Foreword to Douglas Daymond, ed., *Selected Stories of Mazo de la Roche* (Ottawa: University of Ottawa Press, 1979), p. 12.
[13] J.P. (Hamish) McGeachy interviewed by Hambleton.
[14] Clement interviewed by Hambleton, 19 Feb. 1964.

[15]See Susan Gubar, '"The Blank Page" and the Issues of Female Creativity', in Elaine Showalter, ed., *The New Feminist Criticism: Essays on Women, Literature and Theory* (New York: Pantheon, 1985), pp. 292-313.

[16]Carolyn Heilbrun, 'Discovering the Lost Lives of Women', *New York Times Book Review*, 24 June 1984, p. 1.26.

[17]Hambleton, *Secret of Jalna*, p. 160.

[18]Sandra M. Gilbert and Susan Gubar, *The Madwoman in the Attic* (Newhaven: Yale University Press, 1979), p. 76.

[19]Nancy Miller, 'Women's Autobiography in France: For a Dialectics of Identification', in Sally McConnell-Ginet, Ruth Borker, and Nelly Furman, eds, *Women and Language in Literature and Society* (New York: Praeger, 1980), pp. 258-73.

[20]Mazo de la Roche, *Ringing the Changes: An Autobiography* (Toronto: Macmillan, 1959).

[21]*Ibid.*, p. 304.

[22]*Ibid.*, p. 219.

[23]Ronald Hambleton, *Mazo de la Roche of Jalna* (Toronto: General, 1966), p. 39.

[24]*Ringing*, p. 277.

[25]*Ibid.*, p. 83.

[26]Holograph manuscript of *Finch's Fortune*.

[27]Mazo de la Roche, *Finch's Fortune* (Macmillan: Toronto, 1931), p. 28.

[28]Mazo de la Roche, 'Quartet', *Harper's Bazaar*, June 1930, pp. 34-8. Reprinted in Daymond, ed., *Selected Stories of Mazo de la Roche*.

[29]Daymond, Introduction to *Selected Stories of Mazo de la Roche*, p. 19.

[30]Marjorie Whitelaw to Hambleton, 6 July 1964.

[31]Nancy Price interviewed by Marjorie Whitelaw.

[32]Elaine Showalter, 'Review Essay', *Signs* 1, no. 2 (Winter 1975), p. 435.

[33]David Bromwich, 'The Uses of Biography', *Yale Review* 73, no. 2 (1984), p. 167.

1: THE ADVENT OF CAROLINE CLEMENT

[1]Mazo de la Roche, *Ringing the Changes: An Autobiography* (Toronto: Macmillan, 1959), p. xi.

[2]*Ibid.*, p. xii.

[3]*Ibid.*, pp. xii, xvi; c.f. 'The Crossroad', unpublished early short story, and Mazo de la Roche, *Jalna* (Toronto: Macmillan, 1927) pp. 86, 105.

[4]Heather Kirk, 'The Fairy-Tale Elements in the Early Work of Mazo de la Roche', *Wascana Review* 22, no. 1 (Spring 1987), pp. 3-17.

[5]*The Ingoldsby Legends, or, Mirth and Marvels* (London and New York: Frederick Warne, 1891).

[6]*Ringing*, p. xiii.

[7]Mazo de la Roche, *Explorers of the Dawn* (Toronto: Macmillan, 1922), p. 226; *Possession* (Toronto: Macmillan, 1923), p. 93; *Finch's Fortune* (London: Macmillan, 1931), p. 39.

[8]*Ringing*, p. xiv.

[9]*Ibid.*, p. xv.

[10]Elaine Showalter, *The Female Malady* (New York: Viking Penguin, 1987), p. 211.

[11]Macmillan Publishers, London, H. Lovat Dickson to Mazo de la Roche, 17 Feb. 1956.

[12]*Ringing*, p. xvi.

[13]H. Lovat Dickson Papers, NAC, MG30, D 237, undated note.

[14]Mazo de la Roche, 'Dummy Love', *Harper's Bazaar*, April 1932, pp. 14-95.

[15]*Ibid.*, p. 15.

[16]*Ibid.*

[17]*Ibid.* p. 95.

[18]*Ringing*, p. 54.

[19]Caroline Clement interviewed by Ronald Hambleton, 19 Feb. 1964.

[20]'Fearful Accident', *Newmarket Era*, 15 Jan. 1886.

[21]'On the Death of Frank Lundy by a friend of the family', *Newmarket Era*, 12 March 1886.

[22]*Ringing*, p. 6.

[23]Mazo de la Roche, *Young Renny* (Toronto: Macmillan, 1935), p. 176.

[24]Mazo de la Roche, *The Master of Jalna* (Toronto: Macmillan, 1933), p. 210.

[25]Edward Weeks Papers, HRHRC, de la Roche to Weeks, 12 Dec. 1932.

[26]Clement interviewed by Hambleton.

[27]Weeks Papers, Questionnaire, 31 March 1927.

2: LIFE BEFORE CAROLINE

[1]Mazo de la Roche to H. Lovat Dickson, 14 Oct. 1956, quoted in Ronald Hambleton, *Mazo de la Roche of Jalna* (Toronto: General, 1966), pp. 94-5.

[2]Mazo de la Roche, *Ringing the Changes: An Autobiography* (Toronto: Macmillan, 1959), pp. 77-8.

[3]*Ibid.*, p. 5.

[4]D.A. Lundy, 'To the editor of the Newmarket Era', *Newmarket Era*, 11 July 1884.

[5]*Ringing*, p. 3.

[6]*Ibid.*, p. 11.

[7]Obituary of James Smith, *Newmarket Era*, 1 March 1906.

[8]Holograph manuscript of *Ringing*.

[9]*Ringing*, p. 5.

[10]*Ibid.*, p. 71.

[11]*Ibid.*, p. 3.

[12]*Ibid.*

[13]*Ibid.*, p. 29.

[14]*Ibid.*

[15]*Ibid.*, p. 77.

[16]*Ibid.*, p. 78.

[17]*Ibid.*, p. 75.

[18]*Ibid.*, p. 76.
[19]*Ibid.*, p. 95.
[20]*Ibid.*, pp. 90, 95.
[21]Mazo de la Roche to Arnold Palmer, 9 Jan. 1930. This letter is quoted in its entirety in Hambleton, *Mazo de la Roche*, pp. 27-9.
[22]*Ringing*, p. 3.
[23]*Ibid.*, pp. 5-6.
[24]de la Roche to Palmer, 9 Jan. 1930.
[25]*Ringing*, p. 33.
[26]*Ibid.*, p. 43.
[27]*Ibid.*, p. 3.
[28]*Ibid.*, p. 55.
[29]*Ibid.*, p. 59.
[30]*Ibid.*, p. 61.
[31]*Ibid.*, p. 81.
[32]*Ibid.*, p. 41.
[33]*Ibid.*, p. 41-2.
[34]*Ibid.*, p. 55.
[35]Mazo de la Roche, *Whiteoaks of Jalna* (London: Macmillan, 1929), p. 91.
[36]Mazo de la Roche, *Finch's Fortune* (London: Macmillan, 1931), p. 222.
[37]Mazo de la Roche, *Jalna* (London: Macmillan, 1927), pp. 153, 241.
[38]*Ringing*, pp. xiii, 29, 32.

3: THE ROCHES: PROTECTORS OF WEAK WOMEN

[1]Mazo de la Roche, *Ringing the Changes: An Autobiography* (Toronto: Macmillan, 1959), p. 79.
[2]*Ibid.*, p. 2.
[3]*Ibid.*
[4]*Ibid.*, p. 4.
[5]William Clinton Armstrong, *The Lundy Family and their Descendants* (New Brunswick, N.J.: J. Heidingsfield, Printer, 1902), pp. 149, 150.
[6]*Ibid.*, p. 153.
[7]Holograph ms. of *Ringing*.
[8]*Ringing*, p. 180.
[9]*Ibid.*, p. 27-8.
[10]Atlantic Monthly Papers, MHS, Mazo de la Roche to Ellery Sedgewick, 3 Sept. 1914.
[11]de la Roche Papers.
[12]Ronald Hambleton, *Mazo de la Roche of Jalna* (Toronto: General, 1966), p. 85.
[13]*Ibid.*, p. 80.
[14]de la Roche Papers; *Ringing*, p. 17.
[15]*Ringing*, p. 26.
[16]*Ibid.*, p. 180.
[17]*Ibid.*, p. 26.
[18]*Newmarket Era*, 16 March 1906.
[19]*Ibid.*, 6 June 1884, 15 Aug. 1886.

[20]Hambleton, *Mazo de la Roche*, p. 91.

[21]*Newmarket Era*, 16 March 1906.

[22]*Ringing*, p. 98.

[23]*Ibid.*, pp. 98.

[24]Hambleton, *Mazo de la Roche*, p. 94.

[25]*Newmarket Era*, 6 June 1884.

[26]*Ringing*, p. 12. The holograph ms. continues: '. . . a fine actor or at any rate a speaker was lost in him. Did my thoughts turn backward to him when I wrote of Renny Whiteoak. Possibly. I do not know.'

[27]Listings from the Toronto City Directories made by Ronald Hambleton.

[28]Hambleton, *Mazo de la Roche*, p. 96.

[29]*Ringing*, p. 191.

[30]*Ibid.*, p. 91.

[31]*Ibid.*, pp. 53, 55.

[32]*Ibid.*, p. 31.

[33]*Ibid*, p. 53.

[34]Obituary in the *Oshawa Reformer*, 11 May 1927: 'On Monday May 9th at her residence, 283 Simcoe Street North, Oshawa, Mazo Thwaite, beloved wife of Robert Williams.'

[35]*Ringing*, p. 53.

[36]*Ibid.*, p. 55.

[37]*Ibid.*, p. 79.

[38]*Ibid.*, p. 59.

[39]*Ibid.*, p. 62.

[40]Sandra M. Gilbert and Susan Gubar, *The Madwoman in the Attic* (Newhaven: Yale University Press, 1979).

[41]Susan Gubar, '"The Blank Page" and the Issues of Female Creativity', in Elaine Showalter, ed., *The New Feminist Criticism* (New York: Pantheon, 1985), pp. 292-313.

[42]Elaine Showalter, *The Female Malady* (New York: Viking Penguin, 1985).

[43]*Ringing*, p. 175.

[44]Caroline Clement interviewed by Ronald Hambleton, 19 Feb. 1964.

[45]*Ringing*, p. 80.

[46]*Ibid.*, p. 100.

[47]Atlantic Monthly Papers, MHS, de la Roche to Sedgewick, 28 Aug. 1914; *Ringing*, p. 136.

[48]*Ringing*, p. 166.

4: THE FANTASTIC DOUBLE LIFE OF THE PLAY

[1]Edward Weeks Papers, HRHRC, Weeks to Daniel Macmillan, 7 Sept. 1956.

[2]Mazo de la Roche, *Ringing the Changes: An Autobiography* (Toronto: Macmillan, 1959), p. 45.

[3]*Ibid.*, p. 46.

[4]*Ibid.* In the holograph ms. is added the line 'I do not think Caroline answered the letter'.

[5]Macmillan Papers, MUL, **Mazo de la Roche to Hugh Eayrs**, 20 Oct. 1938.

[6]In the genealogy of Hiram R. Willson and Caroline P. McLeod (pamphlet, loaned by the family), under MARTHA WILLSON (p. 17) are listed as family 'I Mary Elizabeth Clement died at age eleven; II Harvey Clement B. March 1869, D. 31 December 1919; III Caroline Louise Clement: B. 4 April 1879.' The source for Caroline's birthdate may have been *Ringing the Changes*.

[7]The same pamphlet contains the following extract from the *Aurora Banner*: 'On Thursday, February 11, 1909, there was a memorable gathering at the home of Mr and Mrs Wellington Willson on the 1st Concession of Whitchurch. The occasion was the celebration of their diamond wedding. . . . At the gathering were Harvey of Buffalo, a steam boat engineer, and his wife. . . . Others present were three sisters of Mr Wilson: Mrs Lundy of Toronto, Mrs Clement of Lefroy and Mrs Rogerson of Lefroy, with her husband.'

[8]*Ringing*, p. 69.

[9]*Ibid.*, p. 68.

[10]*Ibid.*, p. 10.

[11]H. Lovat Dickson Papers, PAC, notes.

[12]Caroline Clement interviewed by Ronald Hambleton, 19 Feb. 1964.

[13]*Ringing*, p. 38.

[14]*Ibid.*, p. 116.

[15]*Ibid.*, p. 38.

[16]Mazo de la Roche, *Morning at Jalna* (Toronto: Macmillan, 1960), p. 214.

[17]Mazo de la Roche, *Explorers of the Dawn* (Toronto: Macmillan, 1922), p. 25.

[18]*Morning at Jalna*, p. 120.

[19]*Ringing*, p. 38.

[20]*Ibid.*, p. 38.

[21]Mazo de la Roche, *Jalna* (Toronto: Macmillan, 1927), p. 164.

[22]*Ibid.*, p. 161.

[23]*Ringing*, p. 3.

[24]Holograph ms. of *Ringing*, p. 94.

[25]*Whiteoaks of Jalna*, p. 101.

[26]*Jalna*, p. 310.

[27]*Ringing*, p. 40.

[28]*Ibid.*, p. 11.

[29]*Ibid.*, p. 52.

[30]*Ibid.*, p. 53.

[31]*Ibid.*, p. 39.

[32]*Ibid.*, p. 74.

[33]*Ibid.*, p. 40.

[34]Mazo de la Roche, *Lark Ascending* (Boston: Little, Brown, 1932), p. 284.

[35]*Ringing*, p. 85.

[36]*Explorers of the Dawn*, p. 73.

[37]*Morning at Jalna*, p. 203.

[38]*Ringing*, p. 55.

[39]Mazo de la Roche, *Return to Jalna* (London: Macmillan, 1952), p. 253.

[40]*Ringing*, p. 67.

[41]*Ibid.*, pp. 83-4.
[42]*Ibid.*, p. 85.
[43]*Ibid.*, p. 86.
[44]*Ibid.*, p. 122.
[45]Holograph ms. of *Ringing.*

5: THE WOUNDED BIRD

[1]In the holograph ms. of *Ringing the Changes* the title for Chapter VII, which deals with the breakdown, was changed from 'The Wounded Bird' to 'Clipped Wings'.
[2]Mazo de la Roche, *Ringing the Changes: An Autobiography* (Toronto: Macmillan, 1959), p. 44.
[3]*Ibid.*, p. 89.
[4]*Ibid.*, p. 93-4.
[5]From the holograph version of the autobiography the following paragraph is deleted: 'Here are a few examples of the words I invented, though whether playfully or in a kind of egotism I do not know:—

For petticoat	— beckittybock
For bonnet	— marta
For jacket	— couchet
For socks	— gilly gaws
For a ten-acre-field	— a pennicofee'

[6]*Ringing*, p. 101.
[7]*Ibid.*, p. 94; Ronald Hambleton, *Mazo de la Roche of Jalna* (Toronto: General, 1966), p. 107.
[8]*Ringing*, p. 101.
[9]*Ibid.*, p. 97.
[10]*Ibid.*, p. 101.
[11]*Ibid.*
[12]*Ibid.*
[13]*Ibid.*, p. 95.
[14]In *Whiteoak Heritage* (Toronto: Macmillan, 1940) Amy Stroud remembers reading *The Golden Dog* during a visit to Quebec (p. 113). In *Finch's Fortune* (Toronto: Macmillan 1931) Eden Whiteoak is working on a long poem entitled *New France* (p. 151). His major work is entitled *The Golden Sturgeon.*
[15]*Ringing*, p. 54.
[16]*Ibid.*, p. 46.
[17]*Ibid.*, p. 97.
[18]*Ibid.*, p. 102.
[19]*Ibid.*, p. 96.
[20]*Ibid.*, p. 146.
[21]*Ibid.*, p. 102.
[22]*Ibid.*, p. 107.
[23]The performance of *Everyman* was reported in *The Globe*, 26 Feb. 1903.

[24]*Ringing*, p. 102.

[25]The novels of Henry Harland, which influenced Mazo's interest in Catholicism, were published in the early part of the century: *The Cardinal's Snuff Box* in 1900; *The Lady Paramount* in 1902; *My Friend Prospero* in 1904; and *The Royal End* in 1909.

[26]*Ringing*, p. 102.

[27]*Ibid.*, p. 104.

[28]*Ibid.*, p. 103.

[29]Sandra M. Gilbert and Susan Gubar, 'Soldier's Heart: Literary Men, Literary Women, and the Great War', *Signs* 8 (1983), pp. 422-50.

[30]*Ringing*, p. 105.

[31]Charlotte Perkins Gilman, "The Yellow Wallpaper" in Ann J. Lane, ed., *The Charlotte Perkins Gilman Reader* (New York: Pantheon Books, 1980), pp. 3-21; Virginia Woolf, *The Voyage Out* (London: Hogarth Press, 1915); Katherine Anne Porter, 'Pale Horse, Pale Rider', in *The Collected Stories of Katherine Anne Porter* (New York: Harcourt, Brace, 1965), pp. 269-317.

[32]*Ringing*, p. 107.

[33]*Ibid.*, p. 104.

[34]*Ibid.*, p. 105.

[35]*Ibid.*, p. 123.

[36]*Ibid.*, p. 108.

[37]Ruth H. McCuaig to author, 6 Oct. 1988.

[38]*Ringing*, pp. 108, 113.

[39]*Ibid.*, p. 114.

[40]*Ibid.*

[41]Mazo de la Roche, *Whiteoaks of Jalna* (London: Macmillan, 1929), p. 39.

[42]*Ibid.*, p. 122. The letter reads:

Dearest Finch,

After you were gone last night, I was very much disturbed. You were preoccupied—not like your old self with me. Cannot you tell me what is wrong? It would be a terrible thing to me if the clarity of our relationship were clouded. Write to me, darling Finch.

Arthur

[43]Esmée Rees interviewed by author, 15 Feb. 1988.

[44]*Whiteoaks*, p. 299.

[45]*Ibid.*, p. 305.

[46]*Ringing*, p. 114. The story 'The Regenerate' is reprinted in Burt Rascoe and Groff Conklin, eds, *The Smart Set Anthology* (New York: Reynal and Hitchcock, 1934), pp. 660-74. The acknowledgement is for 'The Regenerate' (April 1907).

[47]C.f. 'The Jilt' in *Explorers of the Dawn* (Toronto: Macmillan, 1922), p. 73.

[48]*Ringing*, pp. 115, 116.

[49]Elizabeth Shepley Sergeant, *Willa Cather: A Memoir* (Lincoln: University of Nebraska Press, 1953), p. 159.

[50]Virginia Woolf, 'Mr Bennett and Mrs Brown', reprinted in *Collected Essays* vol. 1, ed. Leonard Woolf (London: Chatto & Windus, 1966) pp. 319-37.

[51]*Ringing*, p. 107.

6: ACTON, ONTARIO

[1]*Acton Free Press*, 26 Oct. 1905.

[2]*Acton's Early Days*, published by the Acton Free Press in 1939, reprinted from the columns 'The Old Man of the Big Clock Tower' as they appeared in the *Acton Free Press*. The following paragraph appears on p. 51:

'It will be recalled by many that A. Roach [*sic*], the second last hotel landlord in the building, was the father of the since famous Mazo de la Roche. The family will be remembered by many. They did not reside in the hotel, but in the house now occupied by Mr and Mrs John Dunn, on Main Street, and it does not require older residents to recall the Misses Roche driving about town with the Shetland pony and two-wheeled cart.'

[3]*Free Press*, 1 Feb. 1906.

[4]*Ibid.*, 8 April 1909.

[5]*Acton's Early Days*, p. 271.

[6]Jean MacKenzie to Ronald Hambleton, 29 Dec. 1966.

[7]Esmée Rees interviewed by author, 9 Nov. 1986.

[8]*Acton's Early Days*, p. 81.

[9]Christopher Morley, Foreword to Mazo de la Roche, *Explorers of the Dawn* (Toronto: Macmillan, 1931), p. 12.

[10]'Canadian Ida and English Nell', in Douglas Daymond, ed., *Selected Stories of Mazo de la Roche* (Ottawa: University of Ottawa Press, 1979), pp. 57-74.

[11]*Ibid.*, p. 58.

[12]Mazo de la Roche, *Delight* (Toronto: McClelland & Stewart [New Canadian Library], 1961), p. 11.

[13]*Ibid.*, p. 25.

[14]*Free Press*, 13 Dec. 1906.

[15]*Ibid.*, 13 Feb. 1908.

[16]*Delight*, p. 149.

[17]*Acton's Early Days*.

[18]*Delight*, p. 62.

[19]*Times Literary Supplement*, 26 Aug. 1926.

[20]George Hendrick, *Mazo de la Roche* (New York: Twayne, 1970), p. 51.

[21]Dorothy Livesay, Forward to *Selected Stories*, p. 13.

[22]Willa Cather, *My Antonia* (Boston: Houghton Mifflin, 1918), p. 198.

[23]*Ringing*, pp. 216, 209, 268, 283, 275, 228, 267.

[24]Caroline Clement to Ronald Hambleton, undated.

[25]Katherine Anne Porter, *The Collected Essays and Occasional Writings of Katherine Anne Porter* (New York: Delacorte Press, 1970), p. 478.

[26]See Joan Givner, *Katherine Anne Porter: A Life* (New York: Simon and Schuster, 1982), p. 76.

[27]*Ringing*, p. 121.

[28]W. A. Deacon, 'Memories of Mazo de la Roche', *Globe and Mail*, 22 July 1961.

[29]*Free Press*, 22 Oct. 1908.

7: TWO ROMANTIC FRIENDSHIPS

[1]Mazo de la Roche, *Ringing the Changes: An Autobiography* (Toronto: Macmillan, 1959), p. 116.
[2]*Ibid.*, pp. 116-21.
[3]Ronald Hambleton, *Mazo de la Roche of Jalna* (Toronto: General, 1966), pp. 102-3.
[4]Ronald Hambleton, *The Secret of Jalna* (Toronto: Paperjacks, 1972), p. 70.
[5]*Ringing*, p. 116.
[6]*Ibid.*, p. 118.
[7]*Ibid.*
[8]Mazo de la Roche to W. A. Deacon, 16 March 1923.
[9]Katherine Hale Papers, Pierce Collection, QUA, de la Roche to Katherine Hale, 22 Jan. [1914].
[10]Mazo de la Roche, *Possession* (Toronto: Macmillan, 1923).
[11]Atlantic Monthly Papers, MHS, de la Roche to Ellery Sedgewick, 14 Feb. 1915.
[12]*Ibid.*, de la Roche to Sedgewick, 28 Aug. 1914.
[13]*Ibid.*, Sedgewick to de la Roche, 5 Feb. 1915.
[14]*Ibid.*, de la Roche to Sedgewick, 14 Feb. 1915.
[15]*Ibid.*, Sedgewick to de la Roche, 25 Feb. 1915; 31 Dec. 1918; 1 July 1919.
[16]Katherine Hale, 'Joan of the Barnyard', *Toronto Star Weekly*, 7 Feb. 1914.
[17]*Ringing*, p. 160.
[18]Mazo de la Roche, *Low Life and Other Plays* (Boston: Little, Brown, 1929).
[19]In Hale, 'Joan of the Barnyard'.
[20]Hale Papers, de la Roche to Hale, 22 Jan. 1914.
[21]*Ibid.*, de la Roche to Hale, 5 April 1929; 18 Nov. 1929; 12 Oct. 1932.
[22]*Ibid.*, de la Roche to Hale, 6 April 1929.
[23]*Ibid.*, de la Roche to Hale, 12 Oct. 1932.
[24]*Ringing*, p. 53.
[25]Cecile Lundy interviewed by author, 3 Nov. 1987.
[26]*Ringing*, p. 127.
[27]*Ibid.*, p. 125.
[28]Esmée Rees interviewed by author, 9 Nov. 1986.
[29]*Ringing*, p. 125.
[30]*Ibid.*
[31]*Ibid.*
[32]*Ibid*, p. 123.
[33]*Ibid.*, p. 125.
[34]*Ibid.*, p. 73.
[35]*Ibid.*, p. 83.
[36]*Ibid*, p. 93.
[37]Hale Papers, de la Roche to Hale, 20 May 1930.

[38]*Ringing*, p. 124.

[39]*Ibid.*, p. 126.

[40]*Ibid.*

[41]*Ibid.*, p. 135.

[42]*Ibid.*, p. 126.

[43]*Ibid.*, p. 135; c.f. de la Roche Papers, death certificate of Eva Mansbendel.

[44]*Ringing*, p. 155.

[45]Cecile Lundy interviewed by author, 3 Nov. 1987.

[46]de la Roche Papers, will of Fritz Pierre Mansbendel.

[47]*Ringing*, p. 124.

[48]Carroll Smith-Rosenberg, *Disorderly Conduct: Visions of Gender in Victorian America* (New York: Oxford University Press, 1985).

[49]de la Roche Papers.

8: EMERGING FROM THE PARENTAL SHADOW

[1]Mazo de la Roche, *Ringing the Changes: An Autobiography* (Toronto: Macmillan, 1959), p. 135.

[2]*Ibid.*, p. 129.

[3]*Ibid.*, p. 132.

[4]The death certificate indicates that George Lundy was 52 when he died in Buffalo on 30 Jan. 1914.

[5]Mazo de la Roche, *Explorers of the Dawn*, pp. 127-59.

[6]Katherine Hale Papers, Pierce Collection, QUA, Mazo de la Roche to Hale, 20 May 1931.

[7]*Ringing*, p. 137.

[8]*Ibid.*

[9]Atlantic Monthly Papers, MHS, Mazo de la Roche to Ellery Sedgewick, 14 Feb. 1915.

[10]*Ringing*, pp. 136-7.

[11]*Ibid.*, p. 144.

[12]*Ibid.*, p. 140.

[13]*Ibid.*, p. 143.

[14]*Ibid.*, p. 144.

[15]*Ibid.*, p. 148.

[16]*Ibid.*, pp. 62-3, 147.

[17]*Ibid.*, p. 148.

[18]*Ibid.*, p. 150.

[19]Ronald Hambleton, *The Secret of Jalna* (Toronto: Paperjacks, 1972), p. 70.

[20]*Ringing*, p. 148.

[21]*Ibid.*

[22]Atlantic Papers, Caroline Clement to Sedgewick, 19 April 1920.

[23]*Ibid.*, Sedgewick to de la Roche, 25 April 1920.

[24]*Ringing*, p. 160.

[25]*Ibid.*, p. 142.

[26]*Ibid.*, p. 144.

[27]Atlantic Papers, de la Roche to Sedgewick, 14 June 1924.

[28]*Ibid.*, Sedgewick to de la Roche, 30 Dec. 1920.

[29]*Ringing*, p. 97.

[30]*Ibid.*, p. 105.

[31]Phyllis Rose, *Woman of Letters: A Life of Virginia Woolf* (New York: Oxford University Press, 1978).

9: DELIGHT

[1]Mazo de la Roche, *Ringing the Changes: An Autobiography* (Toronto: Macmillan, 1959), p. 156.

[2]Although Ronald Hambleton dates the adoption from 1920, Mazo referred to Caroline as her 'adopted sister' in a February 1915 letter to Ellery Sedgewick.

[3]*Ringing*, p. 161.

[4]*Ibid.*, 157.

[5]Christopher Morley, Foreword to Mazo de la Roche, *Explorers of the Dawn* (Toronto: Macmillan, 1922), p. 13.

[6]*Ringing*, p. 157.

[7]Mazo de la Roche to W. A. Deacon, 16 March 1923.

[8]Michael Sadleir, ' "Possession" by Mazo de la Roche', *Canadian Bookman*, May 1923, p. 129.

[9]Raymond Knister, 'Book of the Week', *Border Cities Star*, 14 April 1923, p. 2.

[10]*Ringing*, p. 158.

[11]*Ibid.*, p. 164.

[12]*Ibid.*, p. 166-7.

[13]*Ibid.*, p. 167.

[14]*Ibid.*

[15]Macmillan Publishers, London, de la Roche to Daniel Macmillan, 30 July 1924.

[16]*Ringing*, p. 165.

[17]*Ibid.*, pp. 168, 169-70.

[18]*Ibid.*, p. 203.

[19]*Ibid.*, p. 191.

[20]de la Roche Papers.

[21]Mazo de la Roche, *Delight* (Toronto: McClelland and Stewart, 1961), pp. 45, 30.

[22]George Hendrick, *Mazo de la Roche* (New York: Twayne, 1970), p. 55.

[23]*Delight*, p. 128.

[24]*Ibid.*, p. 14.

[25]*Ibid.*, pp. 20, 25.

[26]Desmond Pacey 'Introduction' to *Delight*, p. viii.

[27]Muriel Brewster, 'Writer Wants to Hide from the Limelight', *Toronto Star Weekly*, 16 April 1927.

[28]*Ringing*, p. 181.

[29]'Prize Novel Entirely Imaginary and Purposeless, Says Authoress', *The Globe* (Toronto), 12 April 1927, p. 1.

[30]*Ringing*, p. 181.
[31]Timothy Findley interviewed by author, 6 Jan. 1988.
[32]*Ringing*, p. 182.

10: THE YEAR OF WONDER

[1]Caroline Clement interviewed by Ronald Hambleton, 19 Feb. 1964.
[2]Edward Weeks, 'My Memories of Mazo', *Varsity Graduate* (University of Toronto) Spring, 1963, pp. 46-92.
[3]Norma Phillips Muir, 'She Has Never Seen a Movie', *Toronto Star Weekly*, 31 July 1926.
[4]Gertrude Pringle, *Etiquette in Canada: The Blue Book of Canadian Social Usage* (Toronto: McClelland and Stewart, 1932), p. viii.
[5]Gertrude Pringle, 'World Fame to Canadian Author', *Canadian Magazine*, May 1927, p. 32.
[6]*Ibid.* p. 31.
[7]Weeks, 'Memories of Mazo'.
[8]Mazo de la Roche, *Ringing the Changes: An Autobiography* (Toronto: Macmillan, 1959), p. 185.
[9]Atlantic Monthly Papers, MHS, Mazo de la Roche to Ellery Sedgewick, 21 Feb. 1927.
[10]Ronald Hambleton, *Mazo de la Roche* of Jalna (Toronto: General, 1966), pp. 10-11.
[11]Hugh Eayrs, 'Mazo de la Roche', *Canadian Bookman* 20 (Oct./Nov. 1938), pp. 17-22.
[12]Edward Weeks, In *Friendly Candor* (London: Hutchison, 1960), p. 85.
[13]*Ibid.*, p. 86.
[14]Atlantic Papers, Sedgewick to de la Roche, 11 Sept. 1925.
[15]Weeks, *In Friendly Candor*, p. 85.
[16]Atlantic Papers, de la Roche to Sedgewick, 28 March 1927.
[17]*Ibid.*
[18]Pringle, 'World Fame to Canadian Author', p. 32.
[19]Eayrs, 'Mazo de la Roche'.
[20]Mackenzie King to Mazo de la Roche, 29 April 1927.
[21]'Public Men and Fellow-Craftsmen Praise Prize-Winning Authoress', *The Globe* (Toronto), 9 May 1927.
[22]Atlantic Papers, E.J. Hathaway to Sedgewick, 14 April 1927.
[23]*Ibid.*, 'Memorandum for Mr Sedgewick', unsigned, 18 April 1927.
[24]'Contributors Column', *Atlantic Monthly*, June 1927.
[25]Edward Weeks Papers, HRHRC, de la Roche to Publicity Department, *Atlantic Monthly*, 1 June 1927.
[26]*Ringing*, p. 191.
[27]*Ibid.*, p. 193.
[28]Weeks Papers, de la Roche to Weeks, 29 Nov. 1927.
[29]*Ringing*, p. 195-6.

[30]*Ibid.*, p. 196.

11: RECOVERY

[1]Mazo de la Roche, *Ringing the Changes: An Autobiography* (Toronto: Macmillan, 1959), p. 188.

[2]*Ibid.*, p. 188.

[3]Dorothy Foster Gilman, 'Mazo de la Roche and Her Prize-Winning Jalna', *Boston Evening Transcript*, 15 Oct. 1927. Gertrude Pringle, 'Miss Mazo de la Roche: Canadian Novelist and Coming Playwright', *Saturday Night*, 29 Jan. 1927, p. 21.

[4]Gertrude Pringle, 'World Fame to Canadian Author', *Canadian Magazine*, May 1927, p. 21.

[5]Edward Weeks Papers, HRHRC, Questionnaire, 31 March 1927.

[6]*Ibid.*, unsigned memo, [CFS] 7 April 1927.

[7]Muriel Brewster, 'Writer Wants to Hide from the Limelight', *Toronto Star Weekly*, 16 April, 1927, p. 7.

[8]Norma Phillips Muir, 'She Has Never Seen a Movie', *Toronto Star Weekly*, 31 July 1926.

[9]*Ibid.*

[10]'Public Men and Fellow-Craftsmen Praise Prize-Winning Authoress', *The Globe* (Toronto), 9 May 1927, p. 1.

[11]'Local Women Honor Author of "Jalna"', *The Globe*, n.d., p. 16.

[12]Edward Weeks, *In Friendly Candor* (London: Hutchison, 1960), pp. 88-9.

[13]Edward Weeks Papers, HRHRC, Mazo de la Roche to Edward Weeks, 22 April 1952.

[14]Weeks, *In Friendly Candor*, p. 85.

[15]Weeks Papers, Weeks to de la Roche, 12 Sept. 1928; de la Roche to Weeks, 1 Nov. 1928.

[16]Edward Weeks, 'My Memories of Mazo', *Varsity Graduate* (University of Toronto) Spring 1963, p. 49.

[17]H. Lovat Dickson Papers, NAC, MG30, D 237 undated note: 'The fun H.S.E. [Hugh Eayrs] privately made to me about Mazo and her snobbisms. Plainly he had to keep up a flirtations attitude which neither of them took seriously, but which Mazo would have resented if it had been withdrawn.'

[18]Weeks Papers, Weeks to de la Roche, 14 Nov. 1957.

[19]*Ringing*, p. 190.

[20]Brewster, 'Writer Wants to Hide', p. 7.

[21]G.A. Reid Papers, Art Gallery of Ontario Library, de la Roche to Reid, 24 May 1927.

[22]*Ringing*, p. 191.

[23]*Ibid.*

[24]*Ibid.*, p. 181.

[25]*Ibid.*, p. 192.

[26]*Ibid.*, p. 198.

[27]*Ibid.*, p. 199-200.
[28]*Ibid.*, p. 196-7.
[29]*Ibid.*, p. 197.
[30]*Ibid.*, p. 201.
[31]Weeks Papers, Weeks to Hugh Eayrs, 26 Jan. 1929.
[32]*Ibid.*, Eayrs to Weeks, 14 Jan. 1929.
[33]*Ringing*, p. 206.
[34]Mazo de la Roche, *The Sacred Bullock and Other Stories* (Boston: Little, Brown, 1939), p. 192.
[35]*Ringing*, p. 202.

12: PASSAGE TO EUROPE

[1]Mazo de la Roche, *Ringing the Changes: An Autobiography* (Toronto: Macmillan, 1959), p. 92.
[2]H. Lovat Dickson Papers, NAC, MG30, D 237, Notes for a documentary drama on the life of Mazo de la Roche, Act III 1929-1940, 'Living the Dream'.
[3]Katherine Hale Papers, Pierce Collection, QUA, Mazo de la Roche to Katherine Hale, 19 June 1930.
[4]Edward Weeks Papers, HRHRC, Weeks to Hugh Eayrs, 11 Jan. 1929.
[5]Hale Papers, de la Roche to Hale, 27 Jan. 1929.
[6]*Ringing*, p. 207.
[7]Hale Papers, de la Roche to Hale, 5 April 1929.
[8]*Ibid.*
[9]*Ringing*, p. 207.
[10]Hale Papers, de la Roche to Hale, 5 April 1929.
[11]Mazo de la Roche, *A Boy in the House and Other Stories* (Boston: Little, Brown, 1952), pp. 80-91.
[12]Mazo de la Roche, 'She Went Abroad', *The Bystander*, April 1930, pp. 25-9; Mazo de la Roche, 'Quartet', in Douglas Daymond, ed., *Selected Stories of Mazo de la Roche* (Ottawa: University of Ottawa Press, 1979), pp. 125-33.
[13]'Guy and Gaetano', unpublished story.
[14]Edward Weeks Papers, HRHRC, de la Roche to Weeks, 13 Sept. 1951.
[15]*Ringing*, p. 202.
[16]Macmillan Papers, MUL, de la Roche to Hugh Eayrs, 30 March 1936.
[17]H. Lovat Dickson Papers, NAC, MG30, D 237, notes for a documentary drama.
[18]Mazo de la Roche, *Lark Ascending* (Boston: Little, Brown and Co., 1932), p. 17.
[19]Raymond Knister Papers, Pierce Collection, QUA, de la Roche to Knister, 3 Jan. [1924?].
[20]*Lark Ascending*, p. 106.
[21]*Ibid.*, p. 92.
[22]*Ibid.*, p. 105. .
[23]Hale Papers, de la Roche to Hale, 10 Dec. 1932.

[24]Herbert Orr interviewed by author, 11 Feb. 1988; Esmée Rees interviewed by author, 15 Feb. 1988.

[25]Laddie Dennis interviewed by author, 14 Feb. 1988; Herbert Orr interviewed by author, 14 Feb. 1988.

[26]*Lark Ascending*, p. 298.

13: ENGLAND, ACT ONE

[1]Mazo de la Roche, *Ringing the Changes: An Autobiography* (Toronto: Macmillan, 1959), p. 211

[2]Mazo de la Roche to Arnold Palmer, 4 May 1929.

[3]de la Roche to Anne Dimock, 15 June 1929.

[4]Mazo de la Roche, *Finch's Fortune* (London: Macmillan, 1931), p. 110.

[5]de la Roche to Dimock, 3 Dec. 1934.

[6]*Atlantic Monthly*, March 1934.

[7]Edward Weeks Papers, HRHRC, de la Roche to Weeks, 15 March 1934.

[8]'Make-Believe Canada', *Time*, 21 July 1961, p. 8.

[9]Margaret Saville, 'The Royal Edinburghs', *The Herald* (Montreal), 11 Sept. 1951.

[10]Caroline Clement to Anne Dimock, 12 June 1930.

[11]*Ringing*, p. 209.

[12]Katherine Hale and John Garvin Papers, Pierce Collection, QUA, de la Roche to Garvin, 2 May 1932.

[13]Weeks Papers, de la Roche to Weeks, undated note, 1929.

[14]de la Roche to W.A. Deacon, 12 March 1930.

[15]Atlantic Monthly Papers, MHS, Ellery Sedgewick to de la Roche, 6 March 1931.

[16]*Ringing*, p. 211.

[17]Weeks Papers, de la Roche to Weeks, 31 July 1929.

[18]Pierce Collection, QUA, Clement to Dimock, 12 June 1930.

[19]Mazo de la Roche, 'My Scottie: The Portrait of a Well-Loved Dog', *Good Housekeeping* 91, (Oct. 1930), pp. 30-119.

[20]Weeks Papers, de la Roche to Weeks, 24 June 1930.

[21]*Finch's Fortune*, p. 196.

[22]*Ringing*, p. 219.

[23]*Ibid*.

[24]*Ibid.*, p. 220.

[25]Atlantic Papers, Alfred McIntyre to Sedgewick, 6 Oct. 1930.

[26]*Ringing*, p. 221.

[27]*Ringing*, p. 223.

14: ENGLAND, ACT TWO

[1]Mazo de la Roche, *Ringing the Changes: An Autobiography* (Toronto: Macmillan, 1959), p. 224.

[2]Edward Weeks Papers, HRHRC, Weeks to Mazo de la Roche, 16 Sept. 1931.

[3]Katherine Hale and John Garvin Papers, Pierce Collection, QUA, de la Roche to Garvin, 3 Aug. 1931.

[4]*Ibid.*, de la Roche to Hale, 16 Jan. 1933.

[5]Caroline Clement interviewed by Ronald Hambleton, 19 Feb. 1964.

[6]René de la Roche interviewed by Ronald Hambleton, 1964.

[7]Macmillan Publishers, London, Mazo de la Roche to Daniel Macmillan, 26 Feb. 1932. The letter reads:

'It is almost three years since you kindly gave a reference for me in regard to my adopting a child. However, I changed my mind about taking a child of whose antecedents I knew nothing. It really seemed too great a risk.

Now I am very glad that I did nothing in that way as within a year two friends of mine died, leaving two lovely little children and with no relations who could provide for them.'

[8]H. Lovat Dickson Papers, NAC, MG30, D 237.

[9]*Ringing*, p. 221; Mazo de la Roche, 'The Baby Girl', *London Mercury*, Oct. 1932, pp. 498-507.

[10]Nanny Bowerman interviewed by Marjorie Whitelaw.

[11]Mazo de la Roche, *Whiteoak Harvest* (London: Macmillan, 1936).

[12]Mazo de la Roche, *Young Renny* (London: Macmillan, 1935).

[13]Mazo de la Roche, *A Boy in the House and Other Stories* (Boston: Little Brown, 1952).

[14]*Ringing*, p. 224. Mazo's use of the 'maternal wing' image here is interesting in view of Ellen Moer's comment in *Literary Women* (Garden City, N.Y.: Doubleday Anchor, 1977) that 'One bird metaphor . . . —that of the nesting-bird for motherhood—which so naturally occurs to male writers, seems striking by its absence from women's literature, or by the bitterness with which it is used to imply rejection of the maternal role' (p. 375).

[15]Mazo de la Roche, *The Master of Jalna* (London: Macmillan, 1933).

[16]The Revd Peter Nixson, Vicar of the Church of All Saints, Winkleigh, Devon to author, 18 Feb. 1987.

[17]Esmée Rees interviewed by author, 11 Oct. 1985.

[18]Atlantic Monthly Papers, MHS, Ellery Sedgewick to de la Roche, 28 Dec. 1936.

[19]Clement interviewed by Hambleton, 19 Feb. 1964.

[20]Weeks Papers, de la Roche to Weeks, 27 Feb. 1937.

[21]*Ibid.*, de la Roche to Weeks, 24 April 1935.

[22]Mazo de la Roche, *Beside a Norman Tower* (London: Macmillan, 1934), p. 2.

[23]*Ibid.*, pp. 74-5.

[24]*Ibid.*, p. 76.

[25]*Ibid.*, p. 80.

[26]*Ringing*, p. 248.

[27]René de la Roche interviewed by Hambleton, 1964.

[28]Weeks Papers, de la Roche to Weeks, 20 Jan. 1936.

[29]*Ringing*, p. 258; Clement interviewed by Hambleton, 19 Feb. 1964.

[30]Weeks Papers, Weeks to Hugh Eayrs, 16 Oct. 1931.

[31]*Ibid.*, Eayrs to Weeks, 19 Oct. 1931.

[32]*Ibid.*, Weeks to Eayrs, 9 April 1932.

[33]*Ibid.*, de la Roche to Weeks, 2 May 1931.

[34]*Ibid.*, Weeks, undated note on *The Thunder of New Wings*.

[35]*Ringing*, pp. 237-8.

[36]*Ibid.*, p. 237.

[37]Weeks Papers, de la Roche to Weeks, 24 July 1933.

[38]*Ibid.*

[39]*Ibid.*, Eayrs to Weeks, 5 Sept. 1933.

[40]*Ibid.*, Eayrs to Weeks, 24 April 1934.

[41]Ringing, pp. 241-2.

15: ENGLAND, ACT THREE

[1]Mazo de la Roche, *The Very House* (Toronto: Macmillan, 1937), p. 83.

[2]Mazo de la Roche, 'The Winnings: Our Home in the Cotswolds', *Arts and Decoration*, Jan. 1937, pp. 23-7; reprinted in Ronald Hambleton, *The Secret of Jalna* (Toronto: Paperjacks, 1972), p. 116.

[3]'The Winnings'.

[4]Pierce Collection, QUA, Caroline Clement to Anne Dimock, 20 Nov. 1929.

[5]Macmillan Publishers, London, Mazo de la Roche to Harold Macmillan, 16 Jan. 1946; Harold Macmillan to Messers Lovegrove and Durrant, 11 Jan. 1946.

[6]*The Very House*, p. 169.

[7]Mazo de la Roche, *Ringing the Changes: An Autobiography* (Toronto: Macmillan, 1959), p. 274.

[8]*The Very House*, p. 129.

[9]Macmillan, London, de la Roche to Daniel Macmillan, 14 Nov. 1932.

[10]Ronald Hambleton, *Mazo de la Roche of Jalna* (Toronto: General, 1966), p. 140.

[11]Mazo de la Roche, *Whiteoaks of Jalna* (London: Macmillan, 1929).

[12]*Ringing*, p. 233.

[13]St John Ervine to Mazo de la Roche, 16 June 1936; 2 Feb. 1937; 2 March 1942; 12 March 1955.

[14]Ronald Hambleton to Edward Weeks, 18 Dec. 1965; Hambleton, *Mazo de la Roche*, p. 29.

[15]Ervine to de la Roche, 28 Nov. 1932.

[16]Edward Weeks Papers, HRHRC, Caroline Clement to Weeks, 24 Nov. 1933.

[17]Nancy Price interviewed by Marjorie Whitelaw.

[18]Caroline Clement interviewed by Ronald Hambleton, 19 Feb. 1964.

[19]Price interviewed by Whitelaw.

[20]*Ringing*, p. 266.

[21]Hambleton, *Mazo de la Roche*, p. 146.

[22]Macmillan, London, de la Roche to H. Lovat Dickson, 7 Sept. 1951.

[23]*Ringing*, pp. 262.

[24]*Ibid.*, p. 265.

[25]Weeks Papers, de la Roche to Weeks, 4 May 1936.

[26]H. Lovat Dickson interviewed by Ronald Hambleton.

[27]Ervine to de la Roche.

[28]Max Bortnick interviewed by author, 23 Aug. 1988. For a different account see *Ringing*, p. 286.

[29]Mazo de la Roche, *Wakefield's Course* (London: Macmillan, 1941), p. 168.

[30]*Ibid.*, p. 196.

[31]'Broadway in Review', *Theater Arts Monthly*, undated clipping, pp. 330-3.

[32]Joseph Wood Krutch, 'The Forsyte Boys in Canada', *The Nation*, 2 April 1938, pp. 394, 395.

[33]'Whiteoaks', *Time*, 4 April 1938, p. 21.

[34]*Wakefield's Course*, p. 166.

[35]Price interviewed by Whitelaw.

[36]Irene Henshall interviewed by Whitelaw.

[37]Mrs Richard Elmhirst interviewed by Whitelaw.

[38]Henshall interviewed by Whitelaw.

[39]Weeks Papers, Weeks to de la Roche, 27 Aug. 1934.

[40]*Ibid.*, de la Roche to Alfred McIntyre, 18 Sept. 1934.

[41]*Ibid.*, Weeks to de la Roche, 10 Nov. 1934.

[42]Macmillan, London, de la Roche to Daniel Macmillan, 19 Nov. 1934.

[43]*Ibid.*, Dickson to de la Roche, 11 Nov. 1955.

16: TRANSITION

[1]Macmillan Papers, MUL, Mazo de la Roche to Hugh Eayrs, 19 Jan. 1937.

[2]Ronald Hambleton, *The Secret of Jalna* (Toronto: Paperjacks, 1972), p. 125.

[3]Cynthia McGeachy interviewed by Ronald Hambleton.

[4]Mazo de la Roche, *Ringing the Changes: An Autobiography* (Toronto: Macmillan, 1959), p. 279.

[5]Caroline Clement to Edward and Anne Dimock, 1 May 1937.

[6]*Ibid.*

[7]*Ringing*, p. 279.

[8]*Ibid.*, p. 277-8.

[9]Donald MacKay, *Empire of Wood: The MacMillan Bloedel Story* (Vancouver/ Toronto, Seattle: University of Washington Press, 1982), pp. 27-43.

[10]Edward Weeks Papers, HRHRC, note, 10 Feb. 1938.

[11]*Ibid.*, John Walcott to Weeks, 1 Feb. 1938.

[12]Ronald Hambleton, *How I Earned $250,000 as a Free Lance Writer* (Toronto: Bartholomew Green, 1977), p. 163.

[13]Macmillan Papers, de la Roche to Eayrs, 20 Oct. 1938.

[14]Atlantic Monthly Papers, MHS, Weeks to Douglas Daymond, 2 March 1972.

[15]MacMillan Bloedel Archives, de la Roche to H.R. MacMillan, 25 July 1951.

[16]*Ibid.*, MacMillan to de la Roche, 11 Jan. 1945.

[17]*Ibid.*, de la Roche to MacMillan, undated.

[18]*Ibid.*, MacMillan to de la Roche, 23 Oct. 1951.

[19]Macmillan Publishers, London, de la Roche to H. Lovat Dickson, undated, 1949.

[20]MacMillan Bloedel Archives, MacMillan to de la Roche, 11 Nov. 1937.

[21]MacMillan to de la Roche, 2 Nov. 1938.

[22]MacMillan Bloedel Archives, de la Roche to MacMillan, 22 Feb. 1949.

[23]*Ibid.*, de la Roche to MacMillan, 14 June 1937.

[24]Weeks Papers, de la Roche to Weeks, 15 May 1937.

[25]MacMillan Bloedel Archives, de la Roche to MacMillan, 28 Jan. 1937.

[26]*Ibid.*, de la Roche to MacMillan, 28 Dec. 1937.

[27]*Ibid.*, de la Roche to MacMillan, 26 May 1937.

[28]*Ringing*, p. 279.

[29]Weeks Papers, HRHRC, Alfred McIntyre to Weeks, 4 Feb. 1938.

[30]*Ibid.*, McIntyre to Weeks, 28 June 1938.

[31]*Ibid.*, C.R. Everitt, note, 14 Aug. 1941.

[32]*Ibid.*, de la Roche to Weeks, 5 Jan. 1939.

[33]Weeks to de la Roche, 2 Oct. 1939.

[34]Mazo de la Roche, *Whiteoak Heritage* (London: Macmillan, 1940), p. 213.

[35]George Hendrick, *Mazo de la Roche* (New York: Twayne, 1970), p. 62.

[36]Robertson Davies, *The Well-Tempered Critic*, ed. Judith Skelton Grant (Toronto: McClelland and Stewart, 1981), p. 141 (reprinted from the *Peterborough Examiner*, 30 Nov. 1940).

[37]*Ibid.*, p. 226 (reprinted from the *Peterborough Examiner*, 13 July 1961).

[38]*Ibid.*

17: RETURN TO CANADA

[1]Mazo de la Roche, *Ringing the Changes: An Autobiography* (Toronto: Macmillan, 1959), pp. 303-4.

[2]Macmillan Publishers, London, Mazo de la Roche to H. Lovat Dickson, 28 Jan. 1956.

[3]*Ringing*, p. 304.

[4]Macmillan, London, de la Roche to Dickson, 21 Oct. 1940.

[5]Edward Weeks Papers, HRHRC, de la Roche to Weeks, 21 June 1940.

[6]Macmillan, London, de la Roche to Daniel Macmillan, 19 May 1940.

[7]*Ibid.*, de la Roche to Dickson, 7 Nov. 1946.

[8]*Ibid.*, de la Roche to Macmillan, 4 Dec. 1939.

[9]*Ibid.*, de la Roche to Dickson, 25 May 1939.

[10]*Ibid.*, de la Roche to Macmillan, 27 July 1939.

[11]Charles Morgan, *The House of Macmillan 1843-1943* (London: Macmillan, 1943), pp. 236-7.

[12]Macmillan, London, de la Roche to Dickson, 29 Aug. 1942.

[13]*Ibid.*, de la Roche to MacMillan, 19 Nov. 1939; to Dickson, 21 Oct. 1940, 8 Jan. 1942, and 26 Nov. 1944.

[14]Weeks Papers, de la Roche to Alfred McIntyre, 21 Oct. 1944.

[15]Ringing, p. 280.

[16]Mazo de la Roche, *Quebec: Historic Seaport* (New York: Doubleday, 1944), p. viii.

[17]René de la Roche interviewed by Ronald Hambleton.

[18]*Quebec: Historic Seaport*, pp. 21-2; p. 182.

[19]*Ibid.*, p. 1.

[20]Mazo de la Roche interviewed by Hambleton, Jan. 1955.

[21]*Quebec: Historic Seaport*, p. 198.

[22]Weeks Papers, de la Roche to Weeks, 7 April 1943.

[23]*Saskatoon Star Phoenix*, 28 Nov. 1953; *Vancouver Sun*, 17 Feb. 1949; *Vancouver News Herald*, 13 Feb. 1947; *Manchester Guardian*, undated clipping, 1958; *Time*, Nov. 1953, p. 88.

[24]de la Roche to McIntyre, 1 Nov. 1948.

[25]Weeks Papers, McIntyre to de la Roche, 4 Nov. 1948, 18 Nov. 1948.

[26]Nancy Mitford, *The Blessing* (London: Penguin Books, 1957), p. 66.

[27]Mazo de la Roche, *Variable Winds at Jalna* (London: Pan 1958), p. 154.

[28]Weeks Papers, de la Roche to Weeks, 17 June 1942.

[29]Weeks to de la Roche, 8 July 1942.

[30]Weeks Papers, de la Roche to Weeks, 10 April 1942.

[31]Macmillan, London, de la Roche to H. Lovat Dickson, 20 May 1942.

[32]Weeks Papers, Weeks to de la Roche, 3 April 1933.

[33]*Ibid.*, de la Roche to Weeks, 7 April 1943.

[34]Weeks to de la Roche, 13 April 1943.

[35]Macmillan, London, de la Roche to Macmillan, 3 Oct. 1938.

[36]*Ibid.*, de la Roche to Macmillan, 19 Oct. 1938.

[37]Weeks Papers, de la Roche to Weeks, 27 Feb. 1951.

[38]*Ibid.*, de la Roche to Weeks, 17 April 1951.

[39]*Ibid.*, Vincent Massey to Weeks, 6 April 1951.

[40]Weeks Papers, de la Roche to Weeks, undated letter from The Carolina Inn, Summerville, South Carolina [March 1952].

[41]*Ringing*, p. 90.

[42]Weeks Papers, de la Roche to Weeks, 31 May 1954.

[43]*Ibid.*, Weeks to de la Roche, 7 April 1952.

[44]Macmillan, London, de la Roche to Dickson, 22 April 1947.

[45]Weeks Papers, de la Roche to Weeks, 13 May 1949.

[46]*Ibid.*, Alfred McIntyre, Reader's Report, 7 June 1948.

[47]Mazo de la Roche, *Mary Wakefield* (Toronto: Macmillan, 1949).

[48]George Hendrick, *Mazo de la Roche* (New York: Twayne, 1970), p. 75.

[49]*Mary Wakefield*, p. 292.

[50]*Ibid.*, p. 291.

[51]*Daily Star* (Windsor), 15 Jan. 1948.

18: LAST YEARS

[1]Esmée Rees interviewed by author, 5 Feb. 1986.

[2]Atlantic Monthly Papers, MHS, Ellery Sedgewick to Mazo de la Roche, 28 Dec. 1936.

[3]Edward Weeks Papers, HRHRC, de la Roche to Weeks, 19 Nov. 1953.

[4]Caroline Clement interviewed by Ronald Hambleton, 19 Feb. 1964.

[5]Macmillan Publishers, London, de la Roche to H. Lovat Dickson, 8 Jan. 1960.

[6]*Ibid.*, de la Roche to Dickson, 13 Aug. 1944.

[7]*Ibid.*, de la Roche to Dickson, 28 May 1945.

[8]*Ibid.*, de la Roche to Dickson, 3 June 1946.

[9]*Ibid.*, de la Roche to Dickson, 13 Aug. 1944.

[10]*Ibid.*, de la Roche to Dickson, 26 Nov. 1944.

[11]*Ibid.*, de la Roche to Dickson, 7 Nov. 1946.

[12]*Ibid.*, de la Roche to Dickson, 22 April 1947.

[13]Weeks Papers, de la Roche to Weeks, 28 Nov. 1946.

[14]Rees interviewed by author, 11 Oct. 1985.

[15]Rees to de la Roche, 18 Feb. 1942.

[16]Rees interviewed by author, 11 Oct. 1985.

[17]Weeks Papers, de la Roche to Weeks, 31 July 1948.

[18]Mazo de la Roche, *The Very House* (Toronto: Macmillan, 1937), p. 125.

[19]Macmillan, London, de la Roche to Dickson, 20 May 1951.

[20]Mazo de la Roche, *Ringing the Changes: An Autobiography* (Toronto: Macmillan, 1959), p. 217.

[21]*Ibid.*, p. 40.

[22]Mazo de la Roche, *Whiteoaks of Jalna* (London: Macmillan, 1929), pp. 101-2.

[23]Mazo de la Roche, *Jalna* (Toronto: Macmillan, 1927), p. 310.

[24]Nanny Bowerman interviewed by Marjorie Whitelaw.

[25]Mazo de la Roche, *Renny's Daughter* (London: Macmillan, 1951), p. 113.

[26]Rees interviewed by author, 11 Oct. 1985.

[27]Weeks Papers, de la Roche to Weeks, 12 July 1952.

[28]*Ibid.*, de la Roche to Weeks, 3 Feb. 1953.

[29]Ethel Wilson to de la Roche, 14 April [1952?].

[30]Wilson to de la Roche, 22 Feb. [1952?].

[31]Ethel Wilson Papers, University of British Columbia Library, de la Roche to Wilson, 15 Nov. 1955.

[32]*Ibid.*, de la Roche to Wilson, 16 Aug. 1955.

[33]Wilson to de la Roche, 21 Feb. 1953.

[34]Weeks Papers, de la Roche to Weeks, 5 March 1953.

[35]Macmillan, London, Dickson to C.P. Snow, 22 Sept. 1954; Dickson, undated memorandum to Daniel Macmillan.

[36]Dickson interviewed by author, 5 Feb. 1986.

[37]Weeks Papers, de la Roche to Weeks, 8 June 1953.

[38]*Ibid.*

[39]*Ibid.*

[40]*Ibid.*, de la Roche to Weeks, 19 Nov. 1953.

[41]Mazo de la Roche, *The Song of Lambert* (Toronto: Macmillan, 1955).

[42]Weeks Papers, Jeannette Cloud to Weeks, undated note.

[43]*Ibid.*, Weeks to de la Roche, 1 April 1955.

[44]*Ibid.*, E. McLeod to Weeks, 9 Dec. 1957.

[45]Macmillan, London, John Gray to Dickson, 20 April 1955.

[46]Mazo de la Roche, *Bill and Coo* (Toronto: Macmillan, 1958).

[47]Mazo de la Roche, *Variable Winds at Jalna* (Toronto: Macmillan, 1954), pp. 40, 104, 189, 225.

[48]René de la Roche interviewed by Ronald Hambleton.

[49]*Ringing*, p. 116.

[50]Mazo de la Roche, *Centenary at Jalna* (New York: Fawcett Crest, 1958), p. 60.

[51]*Ibid.*, p. 283

[52]*Ibid.*, p. 285.

[53]Weeks Papers, Dickson to Weeks, 21 Nov. 1957.

[54]*Ibid.*, Weeks to de la Roche, 14 Nov. 1957.

[55]*Ibid.*, Dickson to Weeks, 21 Nov. 1957.

[56]*Ibid.*, de la Roche to Weeks, 25 Nov. 1957.

[57]*Ibid.*, Weeks to de la Roche, 2 Dec. 1957.

[58]*Ibid.*, Weeks to de la Roche, 5 Dec. 1957.

[59]Macmillan, London, Maurice Macmillan to de la Roche, 12 March 1958.

[60]Weeks Papers, de la Roche to Weeks, undated.

[61]Macmillan, London, William Buchan to Rowland Clark, 13 May 1958.

[62]*Ibid.*, detailed arrangements for television and press conference.

[63]*Ibid.*, Dickson to The Manager, The Stafford Hotel, 20 Feb. 1958.

[64]*Ibid.*, Dickson to Maurice Macmillan, undated note [1958].

[65]*Ibid.*, de la Roche to Maurice Macmillan, 28 July 1958.

[66]*Ibid.*, de la Roche to Dickson, 30 July 1958.

[67]*Ibid.*, de la Roche to Daniel Macmillan, 10 Aug. 1958.

[68]H. Lovat Dickson Papers, NAC, MG30, D 237, Notes for a documentary drama.

[69]Weeks Papers, de la Roche to Weeks, 30 Dec. 1958.

[70]Katherine Hale Papers, Pierce Collection, QUA, de la Roche to Katherine Hale, 31 Dec. 1936.

[71]Weeks Papers, de la Roche to Weeks, 20 Jan. 1936.

[72]Weeks to de la Roche, 4 Feb. 1937.

[73]Atlantic Monthly Papers, MHS, Weeks to Mr Goodearl, 14 Dec. 1970.

[74]Weeks Papers, de la Roche to Weeks, 30 Dec. 1958.

19: THE END OF A SAGA

[1]Edward Weeks Papers, HRHRC, Weeks to Hugh Eayrs, 28 Jan. 1931.

[2]Sally Townsend, 'Young Adeline, Mistress of Jalna, is Twin Sister to Scarlett O'Hara', *Globe and Mail*, 25 Nov. 1945.

[3]Anne Edwards, *Road to Tara* (New Haven and New York: Ticknor and Fields, 1983), p. 141.

[4]Mazo de la Roche, *Jalna* (Toronto: Macmillan, 1927), p. 277.

[5]Mazo de la Roche, *Whiteoaks of Jalna* (Toronto: Macmillan, 1929), p. 171.

[6]Weeks Papers, de la Roche to Weeks, 8 Feb. 1957.

[7]*Ibid.*, H. Lovat Dickson to Weeks, 19 June 1959.

[8]*Ibid.*, Weeks to de la Roche, 24 Sept. 1958.

[9]*Ibid.*, Dickson to Weeks, 8 Feb. 1960.

[10]H. Lovat Dickson Papers, NAC, MG30, D 237, notes.

[11]Weeks Papers, Caroline Clement to Weeks, undated [after Christmas 1959].

[12]Hamish McGeachy interviewed by Ronald Hambleton.

[13]Macmillan Publishers, London, Clement to Dickson, 14 July 1960.

[14]Weeks Papers, Weeks to de la Roche, 10 Aug. 1960.

[15]'Whiteoak Saga', *Newsweek*, 19 Sept. 1960, p. 124.

[16]Esmée Rees interviewed by author, 14 Aug. 1988.

[17]Macmillan, London, Clement to Dickson, 12 July 1961.

[18]de la Roche Papers.

[19]Ronald Hambleton, *The Secret of Jalna* (Toronto: Paperjacks, 1972), p. 159.

[20]*Ibid.*, p. 160.

[21]William French, 'Creator of Jalna Series, Most Successful Canadian Writer, Mazo de la Roche, Dies at Home', *Globe and Mail*, 13 July 1961, p. 10.

[22]'Authoress Left 30-Year Riddle', *Telegram* (Toronto), 13 July 1961.

[23]'Author of Jalna Dies, Aged 73', *Telegram*, 12 July 1961.

[24]'Make-Believe Canada', *Time*, 21 July 1961.

[25]William A. Deacon, 'Memories of Mazo de la Roche', *Globe and Mail*, 22 July 1961.

[26]Dickson Papers, undated.

[27]'Jalna's End', unidentified newspaper clipping, 11 July 1961.

[28]Robert Fulford, 'Mazo de la Roche', *Toronto Daily Star*, 13 July 1961.

[29]Macmillan Papers, MUL, de la Roche to Eayrs, 13 Feb. 1937. On 4 Nov. 1936 she wrote to Eayrs: 'Deacon's review in the M and E is spiteful mis-statement that I am going to the States but not to Canada I find very annoying. I think there is much ill-feeling behind it.'

[30]Deacon, 'Memories of Mazo de la Roche'.

[31]Robertson Davies, *The Well-Tempered Critic*, ed. Judith Skelton Grant (Toronto: McClelland and Stewart, 1981), p. 226 (reprinted from the *Peterborough Examiner*, 13 July 1961).

[32]Weeks Papers, de la Roche to Weeks, 23 May 1940.

[33]*Ibid.*, John Gray to Weeks, 18 Oct. 1961. Gray to Weeks, 1 Nov. 1961.

[34]*Ibid.*, Weeks to Gray, 23 Oct. 1961.

[35]*Ibid.*, de la Roche to Weeks, 22 April 1952.

[36]Edward Weeks, 'My Memories of Mazo', *Varsity Graduate* (University of Toronto), Spring 1963; quoted from *Jalna* (London: Macmillan, 1927), p. 129.

20: CAROLINE ALONE

[1]Mrs Stephen Haggard (now Mrs Richard Elmhirst) interviewed by Marjorie Whitelaw.

[2]Mazo de la Roche, *Ringing the Changes: An Autobiography* (Toronto: Macmillan, 1959), p. 217.

[3]Cecile Lundy interviewed by author, 3 Nov. 1987.

[4]Edward Weeks Papers, HRHRC, Caroline Clement to Weeks, undated [Spring 1933].

[5]Marguerite Dickson interviewed by author, 5 Feb. 1986.

[6]Dorothy Livesay, 'Remembering Mazo', Foreword to Douglas Daymond, ed., *Selected Stories of Mazo de la Roche* (Ottawa: University of Ottawa Press, 1970).

[7]Ronald Hambleton, *The Secret of Jalna* (Toronto: Paperjacks, 1972), p. 98.

[8]Ronald Hambleton, *Mazo de la Roche of Jalna* (Toronto: General, 1966), p. 137.

[9]Esmée Rees interviewed by author, 5 Feb. 1986.

[10]Weeks Papers, Clement to Weeks, 7 Nov. 1951.

[11]Macmillan Publishers, London, H. Lovat Dickson to Clement, 2 May 1961.

[12]de la Roche to W.A. Deacon, 12 March 1930.

[13]Macmillan, London, Clement to Dickson, 2 Aug. 1961.

[14]*Ibid.*, Clement to Dickson, 30 Oct. 1961.

[15]H. Lovat Dickson Papers, NAC, MG30, D 237, Clement to Dickson, 11 Feb. 1964.

[16]Macmillan, London, Clement to Dickson, 26 Jan. 1964.

[17]Dickson Papers, Clement to Dickson, Thanksgiving Day [1964].

[18]*Ibid.*, Clement to Dickson, 3 Nov. 1964.

[19]Ronald Hambleton, *How I Earned $250,000 as a Free Lance Writer* (Toronto: Bartholomew Green, 1977), p. 163.

[20]Weeks Papers, de la Roche to Weeks, 21 Feb. 1955.

[21]Ethel Wilson Papers, University of British Columbia Library, de la Roche to Wilson, 7 April 1955.

[22]Dickson Papers, A.D. Maclean to Dickson, 31 Aug. 1964.

[23]*Ibid.*, Clement to Dickson, 9 Aug. 1964.

[24]*Ibid.*, Dickson to Maclean, 12 Sept. 1964.

[25]*Ibid.*, Dickson to Maclean, 1 Sept. 1964.

[26]*Ibid.*, Weeks to Maclean, 15 Sept. 1964.

[27]Ronald Hambleton to Weeks, 18 Dec. 1965.

[28]Hambleton, *How I Earned $250,000*, pp. 162, 163, 164.

[29]*Ibid.*, p. 162.

[30]*Ibid.*, p. 121.

[31]Hamish McGeachy interviewed by Ronald Hambleton.

[32]Weeks to Hambleton, 24 Aug. 1965.

[33]Hambleton to Weeks, 18 Dec. 1965.

[34]Dorothy Livesay to Hambleton, 5 April 1966.

[35]Hambleton to Livesay, April 1966.

[36]Livesay to author, undated [Nov. 1986].

[37]Hambleton, *How I Earned $250,000*, pp. 28, 29.

[38]*Ibid.*, p. 163.

[39]Hambleton, *Mazo de la Roche of Jalna*, p. 217.

[40]Clement to Hambleton, undated note.

[41]Atlantic Monthly Papers. MHS, Clement to Weeks, 28 Sept. 1970.

[42]*Ibid.*, Clement to Weeks, 24 Jan. 1970.

[43]'Now the Jalna Saga', *Time*, 26 July 1971, p. 10.

[44]'Lessons from Jalna', *Saturday Night*, April 1972.

[45]Hambleton, *Secret of Jalna*, p. 172.

[46]Esmée Rees interviewed by author, 14 Aug. 1988.

[47]Atlantic Papers, Clement to Weeks, 2 Aug. 1970.

[48]*Ibid.*, letters.

[49]Rees interviewed by author, 14 Aug. 1988.

[50]Rees interviewed by author, 5 Feb. 1986.

[51]Rees interviewed by author, 2 Aug. 1988.

EPILOGUE

[1]Mary Ellman, *Thinking About Women* (New York: Harcourt Brace Jovanovich, 1968), p. 27.

[2]Austin F. Cross, 'Morning at Jalna', *Ottawa Citizen*, 3 Sept. 1960.

[3]Atlantic Monthly Papers, MHS, F.M. Clouter to Lloyd G. Stratton, 2 April 1927.

[4]Kildare Dobbs, 'Our critic enjoys Jalna books the way he enjoys a comic strip', *Toronto Star*, 15 Jan. 1972, p. 61.

[5]Elizabeth Brewster to author, 6 Sept. 1986.

[6]Nancy Armstrong, *Desire and Domestic Fiction: A Political History of the Novel* (New York: Oxford University Press, 1987).

[7]Carolyn Heilbrun, *Writing a Woman's Life* (New York: W.W. Norton, 1988), p. 21.

[8]Winifred I. Haward, 'Agnes Strickland: The Suffolk Authoress of The Lives of the Queens of England', *East Anglia Magazine* 13 (1954-55), p. 232.

[9]Margaret Atwood, 'Introduction' to Susanna Moodie, *Roughing It in the Bush* (London: Virago Press, 1986).

[10]Willa Cather, *Not Under Forty* (New York: Alfred A. Knopf, 1936), p. 50.

[11]Coral Anne Howells, *Private and Fictional Words: Canadian Women Novelists of the 1970s and 1980s* (London and New York: Methuen, 1987); Ann Edwards Boutelle, 'Margaret Atwood, Margaret Lawrence, and Their Nineteenth-Century Forerunners', in Alice Kessler-Harris and William McBrien, eds, *Faith of a (Woman) Writer* (Westport, Connecticut: Greenwood Press, 1988).

[12]Joel Yanofsky, 'Mordecai Then and Now', *Books in Canada*, Aug.-Sept. 1988, p. 3.

Index